Woman's
Estate

Woman's Estate

Merle Jones

PIATKUS

DISCLAIMER

The Petrograd Communiqué scandal, the event which triggered the action of *Woman's Estate*, was inspired by the celebrated Zinoviev Letter incident of the mid-1920s. Beyond this connection, however, there is no link with the real personalities who participated in the historical event. All the characters and incidents portrayed in *Woman's Estate* are fictitious and any resemblance to persons living or dead is coincidental.

Copyright © 1988 by Merle Jones

This edition first published in
Great Britain in 1988 by
Judy Piatkus (Publishers) Ltd of
5 Windmill Street, London W1
by arrangement with
Sphere Books Ltd, London W8

British Library Cataloguing in Publication Data

Jones, Merle
    Woman's estate
    I. Title
    823'914 [F]
    ISBN 0-86188-741-7

Printed and bound in Great Britain by
Billing & Sons Ltd, Worcester

TO
ALLAN COHEN
and
VIVIAN MORRIS
who threw lifebelts

CHAPTER ONE

London, 1927

'Come along, Diana. Roland has been waiting patiently while you loiter over that interminable fitting. It wouldn't do you any harm to make him feel he's a little more important than your dressmaker!'

'But he's not! Lakie is far more precious to me than that little bore – she makes me pretty!'

The icy calm of her mother's expression told Diana she had overstepped the mark, although Lady Sarah's next words were restrained enough.

'Mrs Kerslake cannot enjoy being referred to as "Lakie" by a child. Please go to my sitting room and wait until I come to you. Go now – the fitting is over.'

Her voice had not risen but her tone killed the rebellion that bubbled momentarily in her daughter. Diana shrugged out of the dove-coloured silk and hastily put on her woollen frock. She started to speak as Lady Sarah turned away, but thought better of it and left the room. As the door closed behind Diana, Lady Sarah swept up the slip of a half-made dress and crumpled it with a sudden, savage gesture. When she spoke again her tone was still calm but her erratic movements betrayed her barely-controlled fury.

I'd hate to have her as my mother, thought Louise Kerslake, watching her warily.

'Mrs Kerslake.' Lady Sarah managed a frosty smile. 'I think the prospect of a grown-up frock has made my daughter a child again. It would clearly be a waste of time to dress her as an adult while she has no idea of the appropriate behaviour.

'Please send me an account for the finished gown with

the bill for your other work and leave the garment with me now. There will be no need to make time for further fittings. Now, I'm sure that you have plenty of other work to keep you busy. Forget about my daughter for the present.'

Still holding the dress, she made a dismissive gesture and turned away from the dressmaker. Outraged though she was, Louise sensed that few people ever dared to challenge Sarah Hartley's authority and knew she was unlikely to be one of them. She was spending two weeks at Clarges Street, producing a winter wardrobe for the two Hartley girls, a few afternoon frocks for Lady Sarah and the ballgown for Diana Hartley's Coming Out dance next season. Future commissions depended too heavily on her success at this one for her to provoke her client now. She left to get on with her work.

As soon as Mrs Kerslake had departed, Lady Sarah turned and followed her out on to the long landing, but continued along it to her sitting room. Diana was hunched on a Bergère chair, a mutinous expression on her face. The girl's mother opened the top drawer of a small commode and removed a pair of silver sewing shears. Then she joined her daughter and took the chair on the other side of the Adam fireplace. Diana watched, apprehension turning swiftly to voluble protest as she realised what her mother was doing. As though it were the most natural thing in the world, Lady Sarah began slicing through the fragile silk of the unfinished evening gown with the razor-sharp scissors.

In a dreamy voice, she said: 'Naughty children have their toys taken away; rude children should be beaten. Since I am forbidden to beat you I shall show you the consequences of rudeness. Your party frock, Miss Hartley!'

She brandished a handful of silk tatters at the horror-stricken girl, who shouted in her outrage. 'Mama – how could you? Why? That was Louise Kerslake's best work. She's already spent weeks on it and it cost a fortune! How can I ever replace it?'

'Simple, my dear. You can not. If your behaviour has improved sufficiently by the time you are Out, you will wear something I have chosen for you – possibly one of those pretty white outfits you already have. I always thought that grey was unsuitable for a debutante, anyway! Regarding the "why" of the matter, I should have thought that was painfully obvious' – Diana was sobbing by now, but Lady Sarah did not even pause – 'Not only did you talk familiarly with a tradeswoman, but you insulted Roland in her presence. If you choose to behave like a shop girl you must expect to be treated like one. Your father was quite wrong to say you could choose one of your frocks for the Season. You have no idea of what is suitable. Now I shall make the choice – and I suggest that you refrain from going to him about this matter or you really will suffer for it!

'Come along, Diana. Go back to your room and clean up your face. You look like a snivelling street urchin. Roland is still downstairs, I imagine – though heaven knows why he is so patient – and I have no intention of letting you neglect him further.'

She rose, dismissing her daughter much as she had dismissed Louise Kerslake a short while before. After a false start at further protest, a demoralised Diana broke into fresh sobs and hurried past her mother into the corridor. Only then did Sarah Hartley permit herself a wintry smile as she shut the door behind the child.

Louise Kerslake stood on the stairs, two floors up, listening to Diana's misery. It was increasingly difficult to refrain from telling Sarah Hartley to stop punishing her daughter simply for being alive. Still, thought Louise, Miss Diana isn't cold or hungry and she's unusually fortunate to be a child still at almost seventeen. She turned and continued her ascent to the sewing room. Louise had been raised in conditions which Diana would have found inconceivable, and had survived. I'd better keep my sympathy for those who need it most, she reflected. This one will be all right if that bitch doesn't break her spirit. If she's that miserable, she'll accept Roland Lenton's proposal as soon as he offers it and escape from her mother for good. In Louise's world there was no such thing as absolute freedom, and the comfortable prison of a loveless marriage was an appealing alternative to domination by a half-crazy mother.

Alexander Hartley sat at the handsome mahogany desk in his palatial room at the Foreign Office. In moments of tranquillity he sometimes reflected that if one had to work for a humble crust, these were eminently suitable surroundings in which to do so. Such a shame the money wasn't better! At the moment, money was very firmly on his mind. A matter he had thought satisfactorily dead and buried years before looked ominously likely to surface again and cause him considerable embarrassment – possibly something more serious than embarrassment, too. A frown creased his faultless patrician features. God damn these bloody jumped-up guttersnipe Socialists – sticking their noses into matters which were rightly not their concern; attempting to tell gentlemen how to conduct international affairs! When he considered what he stood to lose, his face twisted into an expression of savagery. Disgraced, and all because those oiks refused to see when they were beaten! He rose, went to a wall cupboard from which he took a hat and umbrella, then prepared to leave. As he crossed his outer office, the middle-aged secretary looked up, unsurprised at his early departure.

'I'm at an urgent meeting and cannot be reached before tomorrow, should anyone require me, Miss Philimore,' he told her.

'Yes sir. Oh – Mr Hartley, don't forget that you're seeing the Foreign Secretary at ten o'clock in the morning.'

'Thank you, Miss Philimore. I had not forgotten.'

Walking down Whitehall, Hartley wondered whether his appointment this afternoon would serve any useful purpose. Somehow he doubted it, but one must try. He entered Westminster underground station and took a train to South Kensington. Minutes later he was seated in an establishment not known for its patronage by senior Foreign Office officials.

La Mignonne was not French, as its name suggested, but an exotic East European café run by a muscular Polish woman of uncertain years. It specialised in heavy red velvet, heavy red wines and even heavier desserts. Alexander Hartley was interested in none of them. The woman who joined him would have drawn attention anywhere but here the *habitués* made it a matter of principle not to scrutinise their fellow customers – not openly, at least. Ninotchka Chaliapin was tall and statuesque, with clouds of black hair worn unfashionably long and huge, luminous dark eyes. Her clothes were the height of Parisian chic and no one would ever have mistaken her for an English rose. She moved sinuously to the secluded table Hartley had chosen at the rear of the restaurant, collapsed gracefully on to the red-and-gilt chair and ordered tea and cake from the waitress. Only then did she indicate that she recognised Alexander Hartley's existence.

'My dearest Alexei – such a bother for you to come all the way here to see me when you are very busy. Was it worth the journey, my darling?' His light-hearted response required an almost visible effort. 'As always, Ninotchka. You look divine and it cheers me to see you!'

He smiled at her with modest expectancy, but said no more. In a little while her composure slipped somewhat.

'Well, Alexei – aren't you going to say anything?'

'I was waiting for you to do so, my love. I assumed you'd have some news for me.'

'News?'

'Financial news, dear girl. We have some unfinished business, remember?'

'But Alexander – that was over centuries ago! I had quite forgotten . . .'

This time his composure slipped. 'Oh, for Christ's sake stop leading me round the mulberry bush! If it's going to be assassination, at least let's make it a quick death! Is anyone going to step in or not?'

'Step in, Alexei? I do not understand. Who could help?'

'Someone with plenty of money, of course. Someone who owes me a very big favour. I didn't think I'd need to ask for it, but it seems I shall need to after all. Now, will they pay up?'

'Pay up for what, my Alexei? – You talk in riddles!'

'Ninotchka – you know I cannot tell you more specifically in a public place and if only you would co-operate we could discuss the matter without needing to refer to it too bluntly. If you persist in this evasive nonsense it will only delay things a little longer. We shall still have to sort them out and, believe me, the more difficult it becomes, the more difficult I shall become!'

Her pliant manner evaporated. The great sleepy eyes blazed at him momentarily. He felt scorched. Her voice was penetrating but too low to be heard beyond their secluded corner.

'Really, Mr Hartley – do you think they will rescue you now? They would find it far more useful if the world were able to go on believing the Petrograd Communiqué might just be genuine. The last thing they want is for you to walk away obviously healthy, wealthy and no longer in need of a job at the Foreign Office!'

'Ninotchka – why have Florian and Irons put the screws on? Why this legal action? I was totally unprepared for it and you know I never got any currency profits.'

She gave him a pitying smile, her face soft and languid once more.

'You seem to forget that Florian and Irons are a perfectly respectable merchant bank. Why should it make any difference to them whether or not you made any profit on a currency transaction? Their proper concern is to recover business debts which are owed to them. I believe you and I together still owe them well over £40,000.'

'But come off it, Ninotchka – my understanding was that they, er, were rather more than just a merchant bank. You all made it seem that they had more ... political motives than mere money. When the currency thing failed to come off I was philosophical about it because I thought that I simply hadn't managed to make a bit on the side while serving my country, as I'd hoped to do. It never occurred to me that they'd act as a "real" bank and start dunning me for the debt. It could ruin me. I know £900 a year is a good salary, but not when one lives as well as I have to. I thought they were just going to write off the currency thing, as well as finding a way of helping me with my other debts.'

'Alexei, these people we both know. They try not to leave anything to chance. They were thrown out of very warm comfortable nests by a big angry bear not much more than ten years ago. They no longer risk being in the power of anyone, least of all a very, well, accessible man like you. You chose to place yourself in a vulnerable position and I fear they have exploited it to the hilt.'

'Then I and my family are ruined?'

'Your family, yes, but not you – well at least, not according to my standards. You might not be too pleased at the outcome, of course.'

'What on earth is that supposed to mean?'

'It means that you will not starve or freeze to death. In fact, you'll be quite comfortable – certainly up to the standard you could expect if you had inherited a little money from a kinsman. But the Foreign Office will bid you farewell and you will be stripped of your public position. You see, it has to be clear that you were not acting for what you stood to gain from outside interests. In the eyes of the world you must be ruined.'

Hartley could no longer avoid acknowledging that he, too, had been tricked. He was as much a victim as the politicians whose careers he had so lightly destroyed. His face had taken on a greyish tinge but his voice was steady as he asked her the next question.

'What am I to do now?'

'Why, nothing! You are an innocent man caught up in a web of intrigue and accusation. You are bewildered by it all. You will respond as any senior Civil Servant would to the action which your Government sets in motion. You will say all the right things; make all the appropriate denials. In due course they will find you guilty of gross misconduct and dismiss you from the Service. As an English gentleman you cannot possibly stay in this country to face public humiliation day after day, so you will pack up and go off to the Continent – somewhere close to Nice or Cannes, perhaps. Pounds go a long way there, even in these impoverished days!'

'But I shan't have any pounds, Ninotchka. I haven't a penny of my own, remember, beyond what I earn at the Foreign Office.'

'Ah, that's where my friends will step in. A modest but fully adequate sterling allowance will be paid into Crédit Lyonnais for you at regular intervals and you should be able to live comfortably.'

'But my daughters – how will they survive? Diana is about to be presented at Court!'

'Well, my dear, that will hardly be a problem now, will it? I cannot see Their Majesties being very happy about such an introduction! Girls have always had the means of survival in their power. Do you think I got through 1917 by rushing to hide behind the Tzarina's skirts?'

He gave up. Deep in her eyes he read the bitter resentment of the dispossessed against the rest of the world and realised that this woman, so long beloved, was content to see him go to the wall and was positively happy that his daughters would suffer. Hartley rose and turned to go, tossing a half-crown on the table as he did so.

'Here, my dearest, permit me to give you tea – it's the least I can do in the circumstances!'

He stalked out into the street and turned away from the underground station to head for Mayfair on foot. Ninotchka looked speculatively after him, a reflective smile playing about her lips.

He was walking moodily along Clarges Street, wondering whether he could face going home yet, when he saw her come slamming out through the front door of Number Six and rush ahead of him, unconscious of his presence. Instantly all his indecision vanished. Something was wrong with Diana and he must help. Hartley speeded up and drew level with Diana, as he did so leaning forward and gently taking her by the shoulder.

'Slow down, favoured daughter! Why so agitated?' The

note of jauntiness in his voice surprised him with its apparent genuineness.

'Oh, Papa, thank heaven it's you! I don't know what I should have done!' She crumpled tearfully into his arms.

Hartley glanced around. There were few passers-by in the street at the moment and, fortunately, no one they knew. His manner changed subtly.

'Come along, Diana. Mustn't look idiotic in the street, eh? How about some tea while we sort it out?' Dear God, he thought, if I drink much more of the stuff this afternoon I'll turn into a bloody samovar. She was calming down already. His mere presence always improved her behaviour.

'I think it's a Brown's day, don't you? The Ritz is a bit public when one feels a little . . . *distrait*.'

'Mandarin, I do love you! If you were here all the time there wouldn't be any trouble!' Diana was a child again, her beautiful face suffused with pleasure at the prospect of a small unexpected treat.

She took his arm and strutted proudly along beside him, conscious of the distinguished figure he cut. They turned back along Clarges Street, into Piccadilly and eastward to Albemarle Street, where one of the world's great family hotels awaited their pleasure. Brown's was unashamedly English and conservative, a haven of large leather sofas, larger open fires and satisfyingly self-indulgent afternoon teas. Hartley sighed as Diana waded into the exquisite selection of tiny sandwiches, toasted muffins and squashy cream cakes. Why was it that at her age, however big the problem might be, it never put one off one's food, he wondered. He sat back and stirred his cup of China tea and waited for her to finish. Eventually she had eaten her fill and was embarking on her third cup of tea.

'Now, Diana, perhaps you would care to tell me what made my elder daughter go tearing off down the street like a lost urchin this afternoon.' His tone was deliberately light-hearted to avoid upsetting her again. Nevertheless he wanted her to understand that such behaviour could not normally be tolerated.

Her face clouded momentarily, then cleared.

'Somehow it doesn't seem important, now that you're here,' she said. 'I had a really frightful row with the Duchess and I couldn't bear to be in the house with her for another minute. Honestly, Papa, I don't know how I can go home and face her again.'

'My darling, it would help if you tried to stop using that awful nickname. You know that was just our little joke when you were much younger. Your mother's nothing if not sensitive, and if she ever realised that we referred to her in such a manner, neither of us could expect any quarter! But that's beside the point. You must have done something to provoke the old thing – she's usually content to leave you alone these days unless you actually stand in her way, isn't she?'

Diana looked forlorn. 'It just shows how little time you've spent with us recently. I wish it were still like that, but it's not. Ever since you took a hand in my Coming Out and allowed me to have a say in matters she's been utterly horrid to me. It's as if it should be her presentation at Court and I were cheating her of it.'

Out of the mouths of babes and sucklings! thought Hartley. Still, one couldn't admit to a seventeen-year-old that one's wife – her mother – was unbalanced enough to begrudge her daughter's Coming Out because she herself had thrown it all away and eloped. He was startled back from his reverie by Diana's next words.

'. . . and if I didn't have you, even when you're not at home very much, I don't think I could bear it any longer.'

It's now or never, old man, he told himself. It'll hurt the child anyway, but you can't reassure her and then disappear. 'You know, my darling, it's quite likely that I shan't always be there,' he told her.

To his distress, she misunderstood completely. 'Oh, Papa, I know it's fashionable for men of your age to go on about "I might not be here for ever, old girl" – intimations of mortality biting deep again! – but this is serious, not a matter for mixing up with daydreams. This is happening to me now!'

He tried again. 'I'm talking about now, my dearest girl. Sometimes things work out crookedly for Mandarins, too, you know, and when they do . . .'

She was full of consternation, her immediate woes forgotten in the awful thought that her father might have problems.

'What's happened? Are we in trouble over money or something?'

Hartley winced. That one was close to the bone! Still, let's steer right away from that side of things for the moment. He glanced around to make sure that they were well away from the few other people in the large room, then spoke in a low, portentous voice.

'Sometimes one is called on to do things that are not quite in the normal line of duty, for the greater good, Diana,' he told her, gazing into her eyes with desperate sincerity. 'I have been drawn into that sort of net. I was asked to do something of vast importance – something vital to the interests of this country. When I was asked to do it, they told me that there was a great deal of risk involved: risk to my good name and fortune, not to my life, but nevertheless of the greatest magnitude. What it amounted to was that if we succeeded totally, my reward would be knowledge of our achievement for England, nothing more. If we failed, such harm would have been done to the interests of this country as could not be put right for a generation. There was also a third possibility, that the mission would succeed but not so completely that we would escape undetected. In this case, some of us – particularly myself – would be completely disgraced and dismissed from the Service.

'The prospects were made crystal clear and we were not compelled to participate. It was all strictly voluntary. I decided that I owed my country this much, and agreed to go ahead. I need hardly tell you that my efforts were successful, but only partially so. England will live to fight another day. Alexander Hartley, I fear, will not – at least, not as His Majesty's Assistant Secretary at the Foreign Office!'

He settled back in his chair, reflecting that it was better to give the child this version of events. It would be hard enough for her to handle in any case, but at least this way she would regard him as her secret hero, no matter what the world said about him. And the world was about to say plenty.

Diana looked stricken. 'But Papa, they can't do this to you – not for acting out of patriotism! They must make it all right for you. It's not fair – no one can destroy your whole life when you've been working for the sake of your country!'

Only slightly behind outrage came curiosity. 'What will they say you did, Mandarin?'

He knew she was still with him – she had gone back to using his family pet name once more. He sought an acceptable way of presenting current events as they affected Alexander Hartley.

'There's a case going through the courts in which a merchant bank is suing a client for failing to settle up after some currency transactions. The Opposition is demanding that the Government holds a full-scale enquiry regarding the likely involvement of very senior Foreign Office officials – notably myself. The story is that I deliberately created a colossal international political scandal a couple of years ago, in order to weaken the pound on the currency markets and make a fortune by trading on my advance knowledge of the scandal.'

'And did you?' There was death in her look.

'Yes and no . . . Don't draw any wrong conclusions, my darling, I'm on the side of the angels, I promise! Yes, I did create the scandal. No, I was not planning to make my fortune from it. I was persuaded that it was in the interests of my country to do it. I still believe that. But I knew from the beginning that if there were any accusations that someone inside the Foreign Office was responsible, there was no question of the Government admitting liability for it. It would be made known that I had acted alone, for purely personal gain, and they would throw me to the wolves. They have. It was vital at the time that the Labour

Party should lose the forthcoming General Election. Believe me, we had the most damning evidence that key Labour politicians were ready to hand England over lock, stock and barrel to the Russians. The trouble was that it was not the sort of evidence one could place before the public. Therefore we forged secret documents which purported to have been exchanged between the Soviet authorities and senior Labour Party men and then made sure that the press got hold of them.

'Unfortunately, your old father is not the stuff of which great forgers are made and although we achieved the objective of losing the Election for Labour, many influential people were suspicious about the authenticity of the documents. As time passed, pressure mounted for a public enquiry and even my most powerful friends were unable to protect me. Their next step had to be to discredit me as an individual, so that the enquiry would find strong reasons to believe I had acted alone for personal gain and for no other purpose. It is not difficult for men as powerful as these to . . . adjust history. They had laid the false trail from the beginning, anyway, just in case things went wrong. By the time the clamour was growing for an enquiry, they were able to light the fuse and now the court case is in progress which will prove that I have been deeply involved in currency speculation. I am as good as ruined.'

'Papa – the Duchess will kill you!'

His heart spilled over with love for Diana and at this point he almost broke down. He had just destroyed her world and her first thought was for him. He smiled thinly.

'I think no one would dispute the probability of that.'

'Never mind, Mandarin. We can pack up and go right away; abroad, obviously. I'm sure no one would care about this silly story in Australia or Canada. We could start again there.'

'Dearest Diana, I'm afraid that you are in a world of fantasy. Do you really think your mother will let me inside the house when she knows about all this? I shall be more of an outcast from my family than from the rest of society.'

'Well, then, the three of us – you, me and Lettie – will

go off and do it. I'm old enough to run things for you. After all in some countries women are mothers and heads of households at seventeen!'

'And in this country women are still legally infants at seventeen. Diana, Sarah will have you and Lettie locked away from me so quickly once all is public that you won't have time to blow me a goodbye kiss, and there's nothing you can do about it.'

The full significance of what he had told her was only beginning to dawn on Diana. 'You mean that *she* will control us and you won't be able to come anywhere near us, or protect me from her or . . . or anything?'

'Precisely, child. I fear you will have to grit your teeth and put up with her for the next four years until you are twenty-one, or find an eligible young man and marry him very quickly. Otherwise it is extremely unlikely that you will see me again until you are legally, as well as physically grown up.'

She did not cry, or reproach him in any way. She simply sat very still, dwarfed by the big armchair, and digested the terrible import of what he was saying. Her next remark surprised him with its astuteness. Her head was a lot older than seventeen, even if her emotions were not.

'But there won't be any eligible young men, will there, Mandarin? In their eyes I shall be the daughter of a scoundrel and none of them will want my skeletons in their cupboards. It's going to be a choice of running off with the grocer's boy or waiting until I'm twenty-one.' She tried a little smile at her own joke. It failed, miserably.

'Oh, I don't think it will be that gloomy. Perhaps it will be better not to Come Out – in fact I'm not sure how happy the Palace would be at the prospect of your presentation at Court – but there will be lots of nice young men from respectable families who'd marry you tomorrow, scandal or no scandal.'

Her eyes blazed momentarily.

'You make me sound like a prize heifer with a slight flaw in her pedigree – not quite up to Smithfield but good enough for breeding stock down on the farm! I was

14

supposed to be destined for a brilliant marriage, remember? All those tales of honeymoons in Venice and cruising the Aegean in my princely husband's yacht – the stories you told me to make the Duchess easier to bear – I took them seriously, Papa. Do you really think that I'll be happy now to go off and live in Croydon with a dentist?'

Hartley flinched. There was no question about whose daughter she was! All his own snobbery and elitism throbbed through her words and for once he wished he had instilled less rigid values in her. Diana might be devastated, but she was handling the situation better than he was at the moment. She rose, cold and dignified.

'I think we'd better go back to Clarges Street. We appear to have said everything there is to be said at the moment, except Goodbye.'

'Please, Diana, tell me one thing,' said Hartley. 'Do you accept that I am no criminal – that I did what I did for the sake of England?'

'Oh yes, Papa, I believe you,' she answered wearily. 'I just wish you'd loved me more than England.'

She turned and walked out of Brown's.

CHAPTER TWO

It was a long, distressing winter, a winter after which nothing could ever be quite the same. The drab months witnessed Alexander Hartley's public disgrace and ruin. Only days after his teatime conversation with Diana, the case of Florian and Irons vs Mrs Nina Grant was yielding sensational material for the London and national press.

Mrs Grant's maid gave particularly rivetting testimony about a Mr Hartley who had paid regular visits to her mistress's Brighton and London homes and who had frequently stayed for days at a time (no reference was made to Mr Grant's whereabouts). The lovely Mrs Grant – a refugee from the recent Bolshevik Revolution in Russia – then entered the witness box herself. Smiling at the judge, she explained in an appealingly throaty accent that as a destitute exile she had married an Englishman a few years ago, only to discover that he was a rogue who abandoned her. Mr Hartley, one of her husband's few decent friends, had been kind and helped her as an investment adviser – no, she had no idea why an important Englishman should be so good to her for no obvious reason, but he seemed to grow very fond of her. She had followed his advice, having no experience of the Stock Market or of currency speculation to guide her in independent dealing. Her only funds had been the proceeds of the sale of her mother's jewellery – the sole remnants of the family fortune which she had kept intact on her escape from Russia with the retreating Whites.

By the time a judgment was handed down, every male reader of the popular press regarded Alexander Hartley as a bounder who had taken advantage of a young woman deprived by history of parental protection. The women were rather more cynical about Ninotchka's role as innocent dupe, but they disapproved thoroughly of Alexander, too. The Government, which had turned a blind eye to the whole matter until now, was forced to take action. Late in October, 1927, they appointed a Special Board of Enquiry under a trio of senior Treasury men to investigate 'certain statements made in course of the case Florian & Irons vs Grant affecting Civil Servants'.

The press were excluded from this one. All they could do was to hang around outside the building where the enquiry was being held, noting the names and presumed roles in the scandal of the witnesses who arrived and departed at regular intervals. Over four days, the witnesses spoke blandly of their respected senior colleague. Money troubles? Well, one had heard some rumours, but then since the War many sound men were living in reduced circumstances. Hartley had always displayed an exemplary attitude to king and country which was, after all, what mattered most. It began to appear that the Establishment had closed ranks to protect its own. Well, well, thought Hartley, perhaps Ninotchka should have realised the power of the English upper classs under pressure!

She had. Annie Hutton, Ninotchka's maid in her days as Mrs Grant, was brought forward once more, as the penultimate witness. Hartley listened impassively to her evidence. No other was really needed. He knew at last that what all the others had said was nothing before this.

Hutton was well-scrubbed, ingenuous and apparently utterly sincere. 'I started working as a housemaid for Mrs Grant in a furnished house at Margate in the spring of 1924,' she told the Enquiry. 'We was there for about two months, then we moved to Brighton because she said a toff what knew her husband was going to help her improve herself.'

'Did you ever meet this benefactor?' asked the Chairman.

'Yes Sir, often. He came down to Brighton almost every week-end and then we moved up to Town and he was about the place all the time.'

'Is he present today?'

'Oh, yes, Sir. That's him over there' – pointing at Hartley – 'Couldn't never forget a face like that, could I? They was ever so happy at first but when she moved up to London they both started getting a bit testy. He'd come to the house she rented in Earl's Court every morning around 10 o'clock and she'd leave orders no one was to interrupt her. One day he was dead crotchety with me and that wasn't at all like him. After he'd gone she apologised for him and said they'd lost a lot of money through speculating in francs; that Mr Hartley would have to leave the Foreign Office and get another job. She said she'd have to get work too, but didn't seem to think people would have anything much for a Russian refugee with no training.

'This must have been the beginning of October and she was telephoning a lot to Florian and Irons. She kept on saying she was expecting certain funds and if only they'd wait a bit longer everything would be all right. Mr Hartley was practically living there at the time and they was going out to lunch and tea every day as though they had all the money in the world. Then Mr Hartley's picture was in the newspapers and Mrs Grant telephoned the bank again to say it was all right; that 60,000 francs would be coming to them soon. Then a young chap come in with Mr Hartley – one of his junior colleagues, he said. They all had a glass of champagne and Mrs Grant laughed and said wasn't Mr Hartley clever to do it all when the Prime Minister's back was turned.

'She said that now the Prime Minister was going to be thrown out Mr Hartley and the young man would be made. Then of course they had the General Election and on the Monday they announced that Labour had got turfed out. Mr Hartley come back the following night and this Russian gentleman I hadn't seen before was there. Mr Hartley stayed that night but the Russian left about nine and when they showed him out I heard Mrs Grant say "Come on, we're equal partners in this!"'

The final witness was the chairman of the committee of enquiry which the Labour Party had set up following the Petrograd Communiqué publicity in the press three years before. David Pritchard, MP, squirmed visibly as the chairman of the present enquiry asked: 'Is it not true that you considered the evidence reiterated today by the last witness almost three years ago when your own Party investigated the matter after losing the General Election?'

'We did.'

'And what action did you take?'

'I sent for Mr Hartley and said, "Now look here, Hartley, this is the kind of thing that's going about. It's only fair that you should know about it and I am taking the straightforward course of showing it to you right away." He thanked me for it and his answer was, "There is not only not a vestige of truth in it, it is not only absurd and ridiculous, but the fact is that Mrs Grant's husband was a college chum of mine and I merely visited the house."

'I accepted his rebuttal unreservedly, and told him so.'

'Was any further action deemed necessary?'

'Good heavens, Sir Miles, the man was a gentleman and a senior Civil Servant. Are you suggesting I should have questioned his word of honour?'

The witnesses were discharged, the enquiry closed and the panel retired to consider the evidence. Two weeks later a statement was issued to the papers: 'Presumably, the idea must have been to bring about conditions likely to produce a marked effect upon the course of foreign exchanges, so that an astute speculator, knowing in advance what that effect would probably be, would be enabled by extensive and timely sales or purchases to reap the benefit of his act.'

The language of the summary might be deliberately confusing, but the results of the act so vaguely described could not be misunderstood.

'We find it difficult to see any circumstances of extenuation. Mr Hartley was an official of wide experience, an Assistant Under-Secretary of State; yet he encouraged, instead of checking, speculative transactions on the part of those junior to himself, and even shared transactions with them. The extent and duration of his speculations were such as to involve him in serious financial embarrassment.

'We cannot doubt that he was conscious of the impropriety of what he was doing, and we do not regard it as any sufficient excuse that he did not at any time make use of official information for his private ends.'

The Foreign Secretary dismissed Hartley from the Civil Service the following day. Discharged from his post, pilloried in the popular press, he finally slipped quietly from the country, and from Diana's life, late in November. Not that she saw him for some time before that. Confined to the nursery floor for the first time in years, she and Lettie peeped round-eyed over the banisters throughout his last meeting with their mother in Clarges Street. They were in the library, talking in low monotones for an interminable time. Then Alexander Hartley's voice rose, pleading, agitated beyond anything his children had heard before.

'At least, Sarah, promise me that they'll get a little tenderness and understanding. They're young and vulnerable and they should have mother and father to support them over the next few years. If I cannot be with them, at least try to be less unbending yourself.'

Both girls awaited a tirade from Lady Sarah. Although so young, either could have told Hartley that their mother was immune to such pleas and that only great good fortune would save him from a monumental tongue-lashing. It never came. They were unable to catch their mother's response because it was astonishingly low and well-modulated. What they did grasp was the tone of satisfaction in every word she uttered.

'I don't need to overhear what she's saying,' whispered Diana. 'I know, as surely as if I were in the room with them. She's gloating – over him and us. She's got us just where she wants us and the fact that he is escaping, however horrid it is for him, will make things worse for you and me.'

Lettie stared at her, abashed. 'Does that mean you won't be Coming Out, Diana?' she asked, tremulously.

'I wish it did,' rejoined her sister. 'The last thing I want after all this is to go through the Season with all those horrible fat old dowagers sneering at me and whispering about the Mandarin's sins to their cronies. I'd prefer to go abroad for a year – anything rather than endure that torment – so guess what the Duchess will make me do!'

Lettie remained silent. Diana's assessment of the situation tallied so exactly with what both girls knew of their mother's character that words were superfluous. Without question, Diana would be forced to do whatever was most repugnant to her. The encounter which seemed to be drawing to a close downstairs was their father's last desperate effort to win some concession for them. They knew he might as well have saved what remained of his dignity, even though they appreciated his concern for them. At that moment the library doors burst open and Hartley stormed out. His face was ashen, the hands which pushed the big brass door handles trembling. Heading for the staircase, he turned to speak to the woman behind him.

'My only consolation, dearest Duchess, is that we'll meet in the deepest pit of hell. I might even get a chance to stoke the fire under you! I've never met such an evil woman in my life!'

From inside the library they heard Lady Sarah's voice: 'From you, that's almost a compliment. You must have known so many evil women, at least I have the satisfaction of knowing I am a nonpareil!'

As she finished speaking, she emerged from the library. She was smiling in triumph, her victory complete. Now she was savouring every moment of her enemy's eclipse.

'When you are wallowing in some whore's arms in some whore's town in some third-rate country, just remember that thanks to you, your children are totally under my control. By the time I have finished with them, they'll wish you had never been born, dearest Alexander!'

He stopped, obviously pole-axed by the venomous intensity with which she spoke.

'But they're your children, too, Sarah. How can you think of them in such a manner, even for a moment?' His outrage was genuine.

'They have not been my children since the day you

started poisoning their minds against me,' she told him, at last beginning to sound provoked. 'Every time I attempted to discipline them or show them the proper way to behave, you were there like some depraved tempter, waving a pretty present and telling them that your way was better. Well, now they know it isn't! And as they have been taught so brutally, I shall take advantage of circumstances to attempt to undo some of the damage you have done to their characters. They won't laugh in future when they call me the Duchess!'

Knowing about the nickname can't have improved her temper, thought Diana, detachedly. That hasn't done us any good! Her attention started drifting from the squalid scene below. She knew the inevitable ending as if it were some old play she had seen before. She had known this would happen the moment her father told her of the scandal over tea at Brown's. Now it only remained to cut off the loose ends of her girlhood and begin the unpleasant business of adult life.

Finally the altercation between her parents petered out. Both were so rigidly trained in the behaviour of a class which was constantly overheard by servants that their own conventions forced them back to at least a superficial civility. The newspapers might know that Alexander Hartley was a criminal and a scoundrel, but the servants were to be given no opportunity of fomenting further gossip from the snippets they picked up within these walls. Acknowledging defeat, Hartley turned back towards the staircase, hurried down it and slipped out of the front door, closing it quietly behind him.

Is that the last time I shall see him? Diana wondered. No – I must never doubt him, whatever anyone says. I have his word that he has behaved honourably. One day I shall be with him again . . . Nevertheless she was confused about exactly what her father was supposed to have done. Diana did not doubt his version, but the story imparted over the tea table had been vague and full of hints at international intrigue which she was too young to understand. She had read the papers avidly from then on, saving every crumb of information. But it all seemed to go back to a scandal that had become so familiar a couple of years ago that everyone except she remembered it. What *was* he supposed to have done?

She got the official answer a couple of months later when the Conservative Government finally bowed to Labour demands for parliamentary time to debate what had become known as the Francs Case. Immediately after the Christmas recess, *The Times* carried a report of parliamentary proceedings and a summary of the scandal. From that she learned that in 1924, immediately after the Labour Government had called a General Election, various national newspapers had published what was alleged to be the text of a secret letter written by the Soviet Communist Praesidium at a secret meeting in Leningrad (still resolutely referred to as Petrograd by the anti-Bolshevik press). Addressed to the leaders of the key British trade unions, it incited them to arm the working classes and make them ready to overthrow their capitalist masters. The text was full of holes; no original was ever produced; the versions which appeared in the papers were not official releases. Nevertheless the impact on a middle class already running scared after the recent political upheavals abroad was enough to topple Labour from power and return the Conservatives to their ruling position.

The defeated Labour Party protested that they were victims of betrayal by the Civil Service – supposedly politically impartial, but known to favour the old order from which all senior members were recruited – in conspiracy with the Conservative Party. All requests for an enquiry were refused and the matter would have been dropped for good had not an obscure bank sued someone on the fringe of the scandal for non-settlement of an account. The affair was finally consigned to history with an official declaration that any conspiracy had been financial, not political; intended for personal gain, not control of a country. In short, Alexander Hartley was blamed for it all.

Unfortunately for Diana, none of what she read gave a

clue whether her father had told her the truth. Was he a patriot trying to save England from what he saw as the Red Menace, or merely a scoundrel who had seen in political malpractice a way of paying his debts and making his young mistress rich? She believed him, but inside her a voice started asking for proof and could never again be silenced without an authoritative answer.

With her father gone – Diana had no idea where – she had no reason for wishing to stay in London. When her mother told them that they were going to stay with her family in the country, Diana acquiesced silently. Her surrender angered the older woman far more than any rebellion could have. Lady Sarah needed Diana's resistance to spice the meat of her revenge. Seeking conflict, she felt cheated by this submissiveness and hoped for a return of the spirited girl who had fled sobbing from her boudoir after seeing her ball dress destroyed. She was doomed to disappointment.

The Digby-Lentons had now become fully reconciled with their elder daughter. As a lovely seventeen-year-old, Sarah had been aimed for higher things than Alexander Hartley. Her father was an earl, but a poor one. A Regency ancestor had disposed of the family's millions and much of its land across various card tables and his heirs had been forced to marry well or live frugally ever since. Impeccable ancestry and dazzling beauty had assured Lady Sarah of a brilliant marriage, but sexual passion intervened. She met Alexander Hartley at the second ball of the 1909 Season and lost her heart immediately. Until then she had been as keen as her parents to make a good marriage and enjoy luxury for the rest of her life. Alexander ended all that. He came from an excellent family, but where her forebears had gambled away some of their patrimony, his had dispensed with all of it, including the estates. What the Regency buck had left intact, the Victorian spendthrift had finished off. The family seat in Gloucestershire had been auctioned off to satisfy creditors a week after Alexander was christened at the parish church. He received a first-rate education and his family connections ensured that he was invited to all the best houses, but from the beginning it was universally understood that he would never own anything he had not earned for himself.

The temporary madness of romantic love convinced Sarah that none of this mattered. Alexander was aware that a rich marriage was as vital to him as it was to her, but was beguiled by her cool beauty into thinking that he could make both their fortunes unaided. They ran away together within three weeks to a handfast marriage at Gretna Green. Their families, both deploring the situation, reluctantly accepted the inevitable. Even if the Digby-Lentons could have arranged an annulment, no one with the required wealth and connections would want to marry Sarah now. The young pair were welcomed back into London Society and fêted for a while, but Sarah's family never gave them more than a formal blessing. Alexander was not invited to Stanhope, their Leicestershire mansion, and they never mentioned him if they could avoid doing so.

The years had dealt kindly with Lady Sarah's looks but not with her temperament. Within a year of her marriage she recognised that she had made a fatal mistake. Passion did not last and neither she nor Alexander appeared to possess a talent for creating love to replace it. He took refuge in a wild social life, she in growing introspection about what her life might have been if she had never met him. It turned her into a shrill, unbalanced martinet and, as she saw genuine love bloom for the first time in Hartley, for his daughter, not for her, the bitterness spread to engulf the baby. Hartley was an exceptionally able man and rose rapidly through the ranks at the Foreign Office. By his mid-thirties, he had reached a position which very few achieved before the age of fifty in those days. When the infant Soviet Union was finally recognised by the Western powers, he was one of the most senior diplomats involved in Britain's negotiations with the new Government. His salary was handsome and he had made a few reasonably successful investments on the recommendation of some merchant banker friends. But his total income could not begin to keep up with his womanising and Lady Sarah's penchant for the best of everything. He slipped inexorably into the sort of debt which can be cleared only by a great inheritance or a great crime.

The Hartleys lived in some style at a small Mayfair mansion grudgingly donated as a belated wedding present by the Digby-Lentons. Apart from the family town house, it was their one remaining Mayfair property, but even their disapproval of the marriage did not make it possible for them to bear the loss of face implicit in a Digby-Lenton girl having to set up home in Bloomsbury or Bayswater. The Hartleys owned the property outright, but Alexander's income had to cover its upkeep, wages and food for a full domestic staff and a nanny and later a governess for the girls ('School? Girls from our family never go to school!' Sarah had exclaimed when he suggested it.) Then there was the entertaining, the furniture, the beautiful clothes . . . the list was endless and very, very expensive.

When Hartley's apparent villainy – his forging of the Petrograd Communiqué – was exposed to the public gaze, it was reasonable to suggest that he had misused his position of power to speculate on the currency market. His advance knowledge of the damage that an international crisis would do to sterling put him in an excellent position to buy francs cheaply and sell them at a large profit when the pound fell. As he was inventing the crisis by forging documents to discredit the Labour Party, he knew exactly when the run on sterling was likely to occur. Once a public enquiry had been instituted, the state of his personal financial affairs alone ensured a swift end to Hartley's Civil Service career.

The passage of time altered the circumstances of the Digby-Lentons. James, Sarah's brother and heir to the earldom, had married a fabulously rich heiress whose father fancied having a title in the family. They had been wealthy for long enough for the rough edges to have worn off their behaviour and superficially, at least, Hermione was as aristocratic as any woman born into the Digby-Lenton clan. Within a decade the estates blossomed into fresh prosperity and when the catastrophe of the Petrograd scandal struck

Lady Sarah, she was instantly welcomed back into the fold – minus her black sheep of a husband, of course. Lady Sarah's father grumbled lengthily about the scandal but on balance he was not dissatisfied by the way things had worked out. His elder daughter resembled him strongly and had always been his favourite. He was pleased to have the benefit of his daughter-in-law's money, but she was quiet and biddable and he found her rather boring. Sarah had spirit, still looked heart-warmingly beautiful and had two delightful children. For years Hartley had been the main sticking-point and now he was gone. The Digby-Lentons were an old family. They had weathered other scandals in the past without permanent damage and this one would be the same.

The Earl of Ingleton knew what havoc an unsuitable marriage could cause and having seen Sarah slip into one, he was determined that neither of his granddaughters would go the same way. He agreed to finance Diana's and, later, Lettie's Seasons, but only on condition that their mother made sure there was no possibility of an ill-chosen match. Soon after the little family arrived at Stanhope in mid-December, the Earl shut himself in his study with Lady Sarah to plan a campaign for marrying off Diana.

'We shall have to forget about anything too grand,' he said. 'The Petrograd incident is too fresh in everyone's minds. Lettie should be all right when the time comes. We can rustle up a good financial settlement with the help of James's little milch cow and a pretty girl like Lettie with a few more years for memories to get dulled will sail into marriage with a nice comfortable peer in the shires. With Diana we'll be damn' lucky to get one of our sort to marry the gel at all, and I'm damned if I'll see a granddaughter of mine married to some tradesman!'

Sarah shuddered exaggeratedly. 'It might come to that, Papa. There's no real money to soften the blow and no one who could afford to keep her is likely to want her, with her reputation. A successful academic or lawyer might be the only realistic candidate.'

'Not as long as I have any say in it!' snapped the old

man. 'How does she feel about Maud's boy? Bit struck on 'er, I hear?'

Lady Sarah shrugged. 'Absolutely besotted. He follows her like a pet poodle and she treats him abominably. Oh – she likes him well enough, after all they've known each other since they were children, but she's too sure of him ever to notice him as a suitor. Anyway, unless things have changed, he's no great prospect!'

'Don't draw hasty conclusions, my dear,' her father told her. 'I got a letter this morning telling me that young Jeremy Lenton has been drowned in Canada. His Uncle Ralph may still be fighting fit, but when he finally shuffles off that means Roland gets the title – and Granby.'

He sat back and watched his daughter's expression speculatively. 'D'you think the gel can land 'im?'

'If she doesn't, I'll know the reason why!' said Lady Sarah crisply.

Granby was one of the largest and most beautiful estates in Devon, if somewhat run down. It comprised thousands of acres of good agricultural land, a handful of villages and a huge Victorian mansion. Ironically the recently-deceased Jeremy had once been widely tipped as a future husband for Sarah, before she lost her head over Alexander. Perhaps he would never have gone to his death in Canada if . . . with a short-tempered snort she set aside the fantasy and got back to the realistic prospects.

'Don't try too hard, Sarah,' said the Earl. 'I know you've endured a great deal, but you might push Diana too far and find that she'll do anything rather than what we want, just to spite you.'

The old boy is making sense, Sarah told herself. I hate the child so much that if I cannot control it I shall end up with her round my neck until the end of my days, because I'll make her unmarriageable. Perhaps I'd better try gentler tactics. It never occurred to her that Diana was planning to leave her mother the moment she could legally do so. Women like Lady Sarah found it impossible to believe that anyone would ever voluntarily abandon them. In her mind, she had abandoned her husband and people left her only when she cast them aside. Therefore it would be necessary to 'place' Diana if she were ever to be rid of the girl.

'What is Roland doing during the holidays?' asked the Earl.

'Oh, joining his uncle at Granby and having one of those vast Victorian Christmases with all the Lenton-Everett cousins that his Uncle Ralph relishes so,' Sarah told him.

'But he hasn't dropped you after the scandal?'

'Good heavens, no! He was at Clarges Street within hours of the news breaking to mop up Diana's tears!' said Lady Sarah scornfully.

The Earl was secretly exasperated. Really, he thought. Sarah can be so blinded by resentment at times that she fails completely to recognise an opportunity!

'What did the gel say to him?'

'Nothing. She refused to see him.'

'Good thinking. Nothing she could usefully have said at the time and the longer she leaves it the more concerned about her the boy will be.'

'It was nothing of the sort, Papa. She despises Roland and it will be a minor miracle if I persuade her to be civil to him, let alone embark on a courtship.'

'She needn't embark on a courtship, silly girl. She can simply permit herself to be courted Now, enough of this conversation for the moment. I want a glass of champagne before dinner!'

CHAPTER THREE

Diana stood dolefully at a tall first-floor drawing room window in the Clarges Street house. London was sparkling with spring but she felt as if the winter were still gripping her. Part of this was real grief for her lost father, part self-pity caused by six months of uninterrupted baiting by her mother. In the street below, smart men and women were hurrying to and from expensive places, the pleasant weather reflected in cheerful expressions and a general air of well-being. Diana longed to catch it, but it eluded her. She turned away from the window and headed downstairs. In the hall she heard her mother finishing a telephone conversation, her smooth voice made deliberately attractive to whoever was at the other end of the line.

'Well, all right, I'll come over for an hour or so, as it's such a lovely afternoon. But I must get back here shortly after five. See you in a few minutes.'

Suddenly Diana was unable to bear the thought of another barbed conversation with her mother, even a momentary exchange which this surely would be. Almost in self-defence, she seized the hall telephone and asked to be connected with Roland Lenton's number. Since the Digby-Lenton planning session on her future, she had been guarded like a nun, but Roland was encouraged to see her, alone or in company, and to take her out as often as he wished. She had fallen into the habit of using the arrangement as an escape hatch. Roland was aware that she did it but was a sensitive young man, genuinely fond of her and sympathetic about the way she was treated. As a result she enjoyed more freedom than her mother realised, if only to get away alone from time to time to heal her spiritual wounds.

Now she suggested that they meet for tea, nervously watching her mother approach as she waited for his answer. Roland was about to leave for a business appointment which could not be postponed. He expressed regrets and listened, understanding, while Diana plunged on as though he was agreeing.

'Right, then, about twenty minutes, Roland.' Lady Sarah, smiling frostily, passed her with a tiny wave and left the house. As the front door closed, Diana heaved a huge sigh of relief and dropped the pretence.

'Thank you Roland, you are a brick. I'll do the same for you one day! It's the Duchess being tyrannical again. I just want to get out for a while.'

'Of course, dear girl. Take care of yourself. I only wish I could be with you. Perhaps we could meet this evening . . .'

But having achieved her purpose, Diana was already losing interest in Roland. 'Oh, yes − perhaps. Try me a little later, if I'm in. Otherwise we can always *really* have tea together some time.' She hung up before he could suggest some other firm appointment, turned and skipped out of the house, pausing only to check that her mother was out of sight.

For years Diana had turned to food for comfort when the stresses of her young life were too harsh for her. Encouraged by a nanny who was always on hand with a sweet biscuit or a cup of cocoa, she progressed to thickly buttered toast and rich fruit cake as she grew older and the crises more frequent. Only her intense nervous energy kept her slender, for she ate like a navvy. Now she needed the relief that only love or a vast intake of carbohydrates could provide and it was deliciously close to hand. She headed for Brown's, humming a popular song under her breath. Twenty minutes later, Diana was surrounded by the biggest tea she had ever ordered. Her favourite waiter was on duty and with his connivance she was exploring the delights of the hotel chef patissier's repertoire.

'The *petits salambos à l'orange* are quite spectacular, mademoiselle,' the waiter told her with the relish of a fellow glutton. 'And then, perhaps, a slice of either the St Honoré or the Paris-Brest or maybe both?' They grinned at each other conspiratorially.

He went off to get her a large pot of tea. She always drank Assam with sweet, creamy concoctions, because she enjoyed the strong contrast provided by the astringent brew. She was just pouring a cup when the waiter returned, this time bearing aloft a small tray on which was a confection unlike anything she had seen before. He placed it reverently on the table before her.

'Pierre, what on earth *is* it? Can I afford it?' She giggled with some embarrassment, her upper-class English reticence suddenly reasserting itself among all this over-indulgence to whisper that she was making an exhibition of herself.

'It's a Knickerbocker Glory, ma'am, and you don't have to afford it – I'd be delighted if you'd accept it from me.'

The speaker, who joined her as the waiter departed, was American, but not the sort of American she had heard caricatured as loud-mouthed and boastful. The accent was restrained, the tone quiet. It sounded almost like a cross between what she would normally identify as American and standard English. Attempting a look of cool detachment, Diana prepared to deliver a snub. Then she looked at him and her impulse changed. He was tall, slender but well-muscled, with dark brown hair and remarkably penetrating light-grey eyes thrown into sharp contrast by his most striking feature – a deep bronze suntan, completely alien in London at this time of year. Taking her entranced silence as an invitation to stay, he made himself comfortable.

'Hi – I'm Ben Lassiter and that's a Knickerbocker Glory, as I just said.'

Grateful for any excuse to break out of her enchantment, Diana said inanely 'But one wears knickerbockers for shooting!'

He laughed. 'Not this kind, ma'am. The Knickerbockers were among the founding fathers of New York so it follows that a Knickerbocker Glory is a dessert fit for the *crème de la crème* of New York Society. Personally I doubt that. Some of them wouldn't reach further than half way up the glass!'

Hardly surprising, Diana thought, tearing her attention from the beautiful young man for long enough to look carefully at the huge ice-cream sundae before her. It stood at least fourteen inches high and appeared to comprise layers of exotic fruits, syrups and candies of endless shades, topped by a vast cloud of ice-cream and whipped cream and scattered with tiny sweetmeats. She turned back to Lassiter, obviously expecting an explanation for his beneficence.

'You seemed to be having such a wonderful time,' he said, gesturing at the cakes and tea. 'I couldn't resist supplying a little crowning glory. Please don't be cross. I was so burning to talk to you that it seemed like a pretty good excuse!'

Diana chuckled at his honesty. Her friendliness, completely against the code of behaviour she had been taught since birth, was intensified by the knowledge that it would have reduced her mother to speechless fury.

'Well, Ben Lassiter, there must be more to you than a cream ice. What brings you to this bastion of the English establishment?'

'A holiday and a strong desire to enjoy the best available. I've been told that Brown's is one of the best-kept secrets of the English rich.'

'Or in my case the English poor.'

'I've just left a business venture in the States and I wanted a little relaxation somewhere completely different,' he went on. 'This is it. I was trying to convince myself that tea was a habit I'd acquire eventually when this vision appeared and I just had to tempt it off its pedestal with a Knickerbocker Glory.'

'Nonsense – I'm just a good excuse for you to stop drinking tea!' she scolded him, but her smile made her intentions clear.

Diana found herself unaccountably content to sit and listen to his odd, clipped speech and look at the young man's arrestingly handsome face. Years later, she realised that her father must have looked just like Ben Lassiter at the same age. At the moment, though, such thoughts did not occur to her.

'What can you be doing that qualifies as a "business venture"?' she asked. 'It sounds frightfully grand.'

He started to be dismissive but then a boyish sense of mischief swept him up and he told her.

'You look like the sort of girl who'd appreciate a good joke. Well, how d'you like this for a laugh? All I really want to do is go to the West Coast and get into the movie business – not as an actor, something behind the scenes. It's the only place to be in the States right now. But my family are "The" Lassiters and Wall Street was the only place my father would consider for my future. I wound up studying law at Harvard, probably the most boring subject on God's sweet earth, so I took to playing a little poker to improve the shining hour. There was rather a nasty little scandal. The son of another of our first families decided I won too often and started making very loud noises about me cheating. I don't – ever.' His face darkened at the memory.

'Anyway, when I got to know what he'd been saying I strolled over to his room and . . . rearranged him a little. The college authorities didn't really approve and his Daddy was just about to give them a new gym, so I was invited to depart for fresh fields and poker games new.'

'Oh, Ben, that's awful! Were you given no chance of defending your reputation?'

He was surprised and pleased that Diana immediately championed his interests, without knowing that her own background gave her ample cause to demand a hearing for the prematurely condemned.

'Don't worry, kid, there's a happy ending! The little jerk never asked for a cent of his money back and, believe me, I'd cleaned him out! I slipped it in the old sock and went to see Poppa. Poppa was not amused and started saying some painful things about my commencing labour at the family treadmill the following Monday. I declined gracefully, he said no again to my movie ambitions and threatened to disinherit me. We agreed there and then to part company. He was, of course, convinced that as soon as I wore out my silk underpants I'd come crawling back. He knew naught of Junior Moneybags' legacy!'

Diana was enthralled. He was the first daring young rebel she had ever met.

'So what did you do then, go to Hollywood?'

Lassiter laughed.

'I've got plenty of chutzpah, but even I knew that my nest egg wouldn't last long enough for me to learn how to survive there. No, that was strictly if Pa was paying, and he wasn't.

'It had to be fast and very profitable and so it had to be speculation. In America in 1924 there was just one place to speculate apart from Wall Street – Florida.'

He went on to describe his adventures that summer and they sounded as if they had come straight out of an account of an able young fellow pursuing the American Dream.

When Ben had arrived at Palm Beach the notorious Mizner brothers were carving their names in dollar bills all over the coast. He simply kept his eyes and ears open and mapped out the Mizners' planned line of expansion. As they had not yet moved out of Palm Beach city limits, this was not as incredible as it might later have appeared. The inevitable point when boom became bonanza had not been reached and the conservative locals were watching with their hands still firmly on their billfolds. Ben was one of the first waves of outsiders to arrive and he cashed in on it. Junior's thousand dollars bought an incredible five hundred acres, much of it ocean frontage, in the sleepy coastal area of Miami. When the Mizners arrived a month later, Ben immediately sold out a hundred of the less desirable acres at $500 an acre, leaving him with $50,000 and the best part of the land intact. Thereafter he was able to sell out in stages as the market rose.

'But I thought that everyone lost their money when the Florida boom went bad,' said Diana, who had read avidly of the financial disaster which had overtaken the speculators when the market went cold.

'Amateurs, my dear, amateurs,' said Ben with mock hauteur. 'You simply had to be there at the right time and use your head to get away with a lot of dough. There were various ways of doing it. At least one guy, a Chicago newspaperman by the name of Ben Hecht, used it as a springboard to a Hollywood career, just as I intended at first. He worked as a freelance publicist for local real estate companies at crazy fees and he never invested a cent – just saved it. When he pulled out he had enough to stay afloat on the Coast while he sold his first few scripts. He's never looked back. I never got round to Hollywood, but I made so much with the little-by-little approach that I stopped caring too much. Once I had my fifty thou' safe, whatever happened I was infinitely better off than when I arrived. Then I took a look at the people who were moving in there.

'The Mizners had this standard deal where they set the price so high that even fairly rich investors couldn't afford to shell out the whole amount in one go. They divided it into three instalments, but they didn't check out their purchasers too carefully and an awful lot of them couldn't come across with the big bucks. And then the boom started to run out of steam and those who could afford it didn't fancy Florida any longer. So there were Addison and Wilson, holding a hell of a lot of sixty per cent shares of valueless lots when they'd spent more than the thirty per cent advance building the client's house on the site. The result was financial suicide.'

'Well, what did you do that was so clever?'

'I sold a lot cheaper than they did – no house deal, just the plot of land – and I took a hundred per cent in one swallow, no instalment plan for me. I only released controlled amounts of land each time, so I didn't depress the market and I always held on to plenty of land for the next price rise. When the market topped off, I dumped all the lots I had left and I still got a good price. One last thing. From the start I made it a rule never to re-invest in Florida. I put the cash into Government bonds or overseas operations. When I eventually got out I was worth four million dollars.'

He sat back, obviously satisfied with the impression his words had made. She stared at him, round-eyed with wonder.

'Well, lady, does my four million buy me some information?'

'Of course. What do you want to know?'

'Your name, stupid! Last time I called a lady ma'am for any length of time, she was about a hundred years old!'

'My name is Diana Hartley, I'm seventeen, I live just around the corner and you have impressed me more than anyone I ever met!'

'Hey, Diana, that's quite a return on my investment!'

They giggled together, each as comfortable in the other's company as if they had been friends for life.

'What was it like, Ben? It must have been fairyland.'

'Hell, no! More like an eastern bazaar. Addison was the architect – at least that's what he called himself. If he was, then I'm a Supreme Court Judge! He had no formal architectural training at all, although he could draw a little. And he had this fixation on Spanish colonial and Moorish building styles. The customers loved all the trimmings and squiggles so much they often didn't notice that Addison had forgotten such unimportant little items as staircases and doors. My favourite story about the standard of Addison's designs comes from a rich thug down there named Harry Thaw. Harry married a showgirl who had been – uh – interfered with by another of the Florida architects, Stanford White. Thaw was so incensed when he heard what Stanford had done to his girl that he shot the guy. When he eventually got released from custody he took one look at what Mizner had done to Florida in the meantime and yelled out "My God! I shot the wrong architect!"'

Ben went on with such outrageous stories until Diana forgot there was an outside world. Suddenly she was aware that the teatime clientele had left and they were alone in the big sitting room. She looked up at the clock and panicked.

'Oh, no! It's over an hour after I should be home! My mother will kill me!'

She jumped from her chair and rushed towards the door, without a backward glance. Lassiter dashed after her, surprised by her sudden change of mood but determined not to lose her.

'Hey, hold on! Surely she can't be bad enough to throw you into a Cinderella impression at the chime of a clock?'

'She is, she is! Please don't hold me up – you don't understand how awful it is. I could be locked up for weeks after this!'

Realising she was on the edge of hysterics, Ben stood aside, but then followed as she hurried out of the hotel's Dover Street entrance. He kept pace with her as she cut around the back of Berkeley Square, down Lansdowne Road, heading for Clarges Street by the shortest route.

'Please don't follow me, Ben. I shall be in enough trouble as it is. If she sees me with a man that will make it quite impossible!'

'Promise me you'll come back to Brown's as soon as you can and I'll leave you for the present – but I'll expect an explanation,' he told her.

'Anything as long as you go now.' She was in an agony of anxiety. 'Be there each day for tea and I'll come the first day I can, promise. Now, please leave me alone!'

He finally acceded to her request. Perplexed, he stood watching her hurry along Curzon Street, turning into Clarges Street practically at a run.

The house was silent when Diana got in. She stood in the hall, her heart fluttering wildly, unsure whether she was waiting for her mother to descend in wrath or gauging her chances of making the staircase undetected. Her indecision was shattered by a completely unexpected voice.

'Ah, there you are, my dear! Your mother didn't tell me you were likely to be so long.'

Diana almost fainted with relief, although bewilderment was close behind. Instead of Lady Sarah, red in tooth and claw, she was faced by the mild-mannered, beautifully-dressed figure of her Aunt Hermione.

'Oh – uh – I think perhaps she expected me earlier. Where is Mama?'

Her aunt's face assumed the expression adults adopt to indicate a solemnity they do not really feel.

'Her sister – your Aunt Alice. She's been ill for some time, as you know, but she's suddenly taken a turn for the worse. She's been asking for your mother and Sarah finally decided she could not delay any longer. She's gone to Perth on the overnight train and she doesn't expect to return for some weeks.'

Her relief was so great that Diana was almost afraid to contemplate the full meaning of what Hermione said. She stood stammering in the hall. Hermione misinterpreted the girl's indecisiveness.

'I know, Diana, you'll be worried about the Season. I remember how much it meant to me. Your mother was most concerned that everything should continue according to plan.'

I bet she was, thought Diana. How she must have hated going to Aunt Alice and leaving me here unsupervised. I'm lucky she didn't postpone my Coming Out by a year and take me off to that benighted glen with her! Hermione was speaking again.

'. . . and she felt it would be too disruptive to move both of you up to Brook Street with all the tradesmen calling here and so forth, so I volunteered to come here as a sort of living-in chaperone until she comes back. I do hope you don't mind.'

'Mind? Oh, Aunt, it's absolutely super of you!' It was not hard for Diana to make an inordinate fuss of Hermione's selflessness. Ninety per cent of her reaction was genuine anyway.

She knew exactly why her mother had rejected the prospect of sending the girls to live at the family mansion in Brook Street, even when distraught about her favourite sister. Society would think she was unable to maintain a separate establishment any longer and that she had fled London, leaving her children in the care of rich relatives, to dodge her creditors. Sarah's pride would never have permitted such speculation. Dear Aunt Alice, please recover slowly, Diana prayed silently. Hermione came forward and put an arm around Diana. She was a gentle, loving soul, with strong views about the way Sarah treated Diana. Although the family would never be aware of it, she was determined to see the girl enjoyed a better summer than she could previously have hoped.

'I know it's all a little sudden, my dear, but I'm sure we shall get along splendidly. If you like, the three of us can dine together when I have no engagements and you're not off junketing. It seems silly to preserve a nursery atmosphere and sentence poor Lettie to solitary meals when we're an all-female house, doesn't it?'

Oh, I'm going to like you, Diana silently sang as she hurried upstairs. It all seemed much too good to be true and she was afraid to consider the possibilities for further acquaintance with Ben Lassiter. Such a golden opportunity really was a miracle and she felt almost superstitious – as though, if she contemplated it now, it might all be snatched away from her. Life had not taught Diana much about people like Hermione Lenton. Her world had always been inhabited by egotists like her father or dominated by the increasingly irrational behaviour of her mother. So when Hermione made it clear next morning that, unless Diana particularly wished for her company during the daytime, she was free to do as she wished within reason, the girl immediately assumed that her aunt was acting from laziness rather than kindness. No one had made decisions before which were based solely on Diana's pleasure and comfort, so the mistake was understandable.

In fact Hermione Digby-Lenton, Lady Stanmore, was rather more sensitive than Diana imagined and considerably more intelligent than her in-laws had ever suspected. For years she had watched helplessly while her sister-in-law terrorised Diana and Lettie, aware that silent sympathy was all she could give them. Now she was finally in a position to befriend Diana and show the girl that she could expect better treatment from some adults than she had received so far.

None of this intruded on Diana's self-preoccupation at the moment. She was aware only that suddenly she was free of her mother. As she left the Clarges Street house at four o'clock she tried to tell herself she was not heading for Brown's. Of course you can't go back and see him – at least not on the first day after such a frightful scene, the strategist inside her said. You shouldn't go back at all; he's a stranger; probably completely unsuitable; he tells you far too much intimate detail about his financial affairs; and in any case, you should make yourself harder to get than that. Going back less than twenty-four hours after such an exit will convince him you're neurotic, or easy, or both! Nevertheless her feet took her inexorably back towards Brown's, as if they knew better than her brain what would make her happy.

As it happened, Diana did not have to face the humiliation of seeking out Lassiter. She had taken the quieter Berkeley Square route rather than going along Piccadilly, just in case someone noticed her and told the family. As she turned up Hay Hill, she heard a triumphant shout of recognition and looked round to see Ben hurrying towards her.

'Cinderella, I've found you!' It was obvious that he had been out looking for her. They headed for Brown's as if by tacit agreement.

'I knew that if I hung around here long enough, I'd run into you,' he told her. 'I was quite prepared to go on looking for the next three months if necessary.'

'Only three months? So much for masculine tenacity!' said Diana.

'Oh, don't get me wrong. After that I was thinking in terms of knocking on doors or hiring a private eye.'

Flattered in spite of herself, Diana smiled at him. She got such pleasure from his company that any counterfeit modesty seemed churlish.

The waiter in Brown's welcomed them as though they were newly-weds on honeymoon. Diana was intoxicated by the welter of new impressions that were crowding in on her.

Inevitably, Ben Lassiter benefited from her new domestic circumstances. Incapable of distinguishing between new infatuation and new freedon, she was already lumping both together and calling them love. Lassiter was surprised to find this delectable young Society woman as approachable as an ordinary schoolgirl but assumed that, as in his own set, the emancipation of the 1920s was permeating even the most reactionary sector of society. He had no real idea how unusual her life had been or that she behaved as she did because no one had shown her how normal girls of her station were expected to conduct themselves in public. Part of Lassiter eagerly took advantage of the situation without questioning it because she was extremely attractive and unexpectedly available. His better nature was genuinely entranced with the girl and he was ready to fall in love with her.

Thanks to Hermione, Diana spent as little time as possible in Clarges Street, apart from making sure she was present for dinner whenever her aunt was dining in. Unused to the company of girls of her own age, she had always treated Lettie like a friend as well as a sister and the younger girl knew much of what was going on. But there were limits even to what she told Lettie. Diana started censoring her confidences after the first evening she spent with Ben. For months afterwards she shivered at the thought of what her mother would have done to her had she ever found out about that night.

The following morning Hermione told the girls that she was dining with friends that evening. 'I believe that you are joining the Lentons in South Molton Street for the evening and Lettie is visiting Cousin Julia,' she said to Diana.

'Yes – it's years since I met Great Uncle Ralph and Roland keeps insisting that I should know him better – I can't think why.'

Hermione looked wise and adult. Diana felt a twinge of contempt. Of course I understand why he wants me on friendly terms with the old boy, she thought impatiently. But if any of you think I'm marrying Roland just to fit conveniently into the drawer you've made for me, you can think again! At present, love meant Ben Lassiter. Diana had used Roland's name a lot lately to convince her aunt that she was occupying her time suitably. In fact she had seen very little of him that spring. Each time her mother sent her a stern, stilted note from the Highlands, Diana guiltily contacted Roland and spent a couple of hours with him, her superstitious nature half convinced that her omniscient mother would somehow sense the estrangement if she did not make these occasional efforts. She was as egotistical in her way as her father and it never occurred to her that Hermione was only partially deceived by her behaviour and Roland not at all. Hermione felt that after so much restriction Diana deserved to spread her wings a little. Roland loved her so much that he was willing to do almost anything to please her. If this included pretending to be an unobservant ninny, he endured it in the hope that eventually she would decide to spend her life with him. At the moment, nothing was further from Diana's thoughts.

So far her meetings with the glamorous American had been confined to mornings and afternoons. Even when they were Out, girls of Diana's age and from an old-fashioned background did not go unchaperoned in mixed company. In her pre-Season state, they normally did not appear in public at all in the evening. A place at the family dinner table when guests were invited was as far as they were permitted to go. Visits to the theatre were allowed in more progressive households, but again, in fully chaperoned groups.

Ben had just acquired a motor car — a beautiful supercharged open Bentley in deep racing green. He was inordinately proud of it and had invited Diana to accompany him on a country picnic. They planned it carefully so that she could leave home mid-morning, enjoy most of the day out and still be back in time to go to dinner as though nothing had happened. Then Fate dealt her another surprise hand. Diana was dressing for her motor outing when Roland telephoned to say that Sir Ralph was suffering from a dental abscess and the last thing he could face was a dinner party that evening. It never occurred to the old man to let Roland act as host and allow the event to go ahead without him. He instructed his nephew to put everyone off. It was a few minutes before Diana realised that Aunt Hermione was at the hairdresser's and that she would be gone by the time the older woman returned. There was consequently no need to tell her that the evening's engagement was cancelled. She could dine with Ben!

As usual, they met outside Brown's. Diana got into the shiny new car, sparking with anticipation. Ben had never seen her in such a state of high excitement. Involuntarily he leaned across and briefly touched her cheek.

'Why so excited, Lady D? It's just an ordinary run-of-the-mill picnic!'

She laughed at the absurdity of the remark. 'Ben – you're sitting in one of the most expensive cars ever made. Knowing you, the boot is crammed with Veuve Clicquot and *foie gras* and cashmere travel rugs and silky cushions – and you call it an ordinary run-of-the-mill picnic!'

His laugh echoed hers, but then he became grave again.

'No, beautiful girl, there's something different about you today, something almost abandoned. What on earth has happened?'

'School's out!' she cried, unable to contain herself any longer. 'Aunt H thinks I'm dining at Roland's, but she's out and he's cancelled. I'm free until all hours!'

He was surprisingly self-contained about her revelation. The big car slid silently away from the kerb and he was soon edging it expertly westward through the mid-morning traffic. Her excitement was abruptly damped by his reserved response.

'What's wrong? I thought you'd be thrilled to have all day instead of rushing me back to the nursery at the end of the afternoon, but you don't seem particularly pleased. I'm beginning to wonder whether you're planning to see someone else this evening.'

'For such a bright kid you're quite a goose at times,' he told her, exasperated. 'You've had such a god-awful upbringing, sheltered in all the wrong ways, that when you get a taste of freedom you go crazy! Don't you realise the

44

risk you're running? How d'you get back into the house after your midnight revels, for instance?'

'Oh, that's easy. Whoever stays up for Aunt Hermione – her maid, usually – will let me in. That's what would happen if I'd been at Great Uncle Ralph's. Their chauffeur would bring me back and leave me at the front door.'

'And what do you tell your aunt tomorrow when you're asked how things were at Great Uncle Ralph's and what Lady Posh had to say to Lord Tosh?'

Diana winced at his deliberate vulgarity, but beneath her indignation she began to realise he was right.

'I ... I'd pretend it went ahead as planned until just beforehand,' she faltered, 'and then say Roland took me to dinner to make up for it all having been cancelled at the last minute!'

She ended on a brighter note, liking the sound of her proposed deception.

'You don't think Master Roland will be somewhat reluctant to cover for you dating another guy?'

'Why not? He always backs me when I want to avoid Mama's snooping.'

'Diana, even you must see this is different. I happen to think Lenton sounds like a thoroughly decent chap who only lets you get away with murder because he adores you and knows your mother treats you badly. But there's no way any man will stand by and provide the alibi for his girl to go off with another fellow!'

'I am *not* Roland Lenton's girl!' Diana injected extra anger into her response because now she knew Ben was right but she could not bear to admit it.

'You may think that; I may think that; but does he? Anyhow, it's not simply that. Your reputation has enough dents already through no fault of your own. You shouldn't be risking it further and that's my main concern. If you were caught out dating a clean-cut all-American boy at three in the afternoon, nobody would do more than raise their eyebrows and bawl you out a little, except perhaps your dreadful mother. If you were surprised listening to sweet nothings across a candle-lit table after telling your folks you were at a family affair, you'd be done in for good.

'I'm also thinking about myself. In case you haven't noticed, I'm male, young and vigorous, I'm crazy about you and I find it pretty tough keeping my hands off you at high noon in Bond Street. So suddenly you take it into your head that we should have a little more soft lights and seclusion! I'm left with a choice of which way I hurt you. Either I wreck your future or I reject you and give your pride an awful knock. On top of that, if I do try to be strong and resist temptation, I'll kick myself for it later, because believe me, I want you the worst way!'

Feeling very adult, Diana gently pressed his arm. 'You're so sweet, Ben. But really, can't we simply look forward to a proper civilised day together instead of just grabbing a few hours? That's all I was planning.'

His look was pitying. 'Sure, kid – sure as I'm riding this bicycle!'

'Don't be cynical. I don't have to be compromised simply because I've been out for the day. Goodness, some debutantes were behaving quite outrageously fifteen or twenty years ago and there's been a war and all sorts of changes since then!'

'Those girls tended to be daughters of dukes or multimillionaires or both, and when you're that well established it's quite easy to be a grand *bohème*. They'd write you off as a grande cocotte instead, baby.'

She was growing even more indignant because a small voice deep inside her said he was right and that he was behaving admirably in an effort to protect her from her own impulses. Diana wanted her own way and was prepared to make a scene if she didn't get it.

'All right, Stainless Stephen! If you're such a white knight, maybe I shouldn't be out unchaperoned with you at all. You'd better drive me back to Clarges Street and I'll spend the day with Lettie.'

'I'm not letting you behave like a spoiled child and ruin the day for us both,' he told her firmly. 'You're going to have to learn to fend for yourself and be grown up very soon. Let's regard today as a practice run. We'll behave like sane, sober citizens, have a whale of a time and decide this afternoon what the evening will bring. Is that a deal?'

Realising that the alternative was a ruined day and possibly a permanent rupture with Ben, Diana fought to control her temper and agreed to a truce. He was resolutely funny, pleasant and light-hearted and soon the stormy scene was all but forgotten as she expanded in the warmth of his company. The grime of Shepherd's Bush gave way to the village-like air of Chiswick and eventually the western suburbs petered out into an almost rural landscape. Ben wanted to explore the Thames valley. He had a romantic picture of secluded waters reflecting ancient weeping willows and graceful white mansions glimpsed across watermeadows from the far bank of the river. And they found his Thames, just as he had pictured it. They picnicked on the grass at Runnymede, Diana authoritatively telling him a wildly inaccurate version of King John and Magna Carta, which he corrected with ill-concealed merriment.

'Where did you get your education, you little savage?' he asked finally with a grin.

She was indignant. 'The Mandarin was a first-class teacher and when the time came he got us a governess. Mind you, they didn't seem to stay very long and some of them weren't all that bright – but I was properly educated!'

'Whatever you say,' he told her soothingly, privately speculating on what Alexander Hartley had considered essential qualifications in his daughters' governesses. He suspected that long legs, big blue eyes and a responsive temperament had been more important than familiarity with Magna Carta. He changed the subject.

'See? You weren't quite right about the contents of the trunk. The champagne is Bollinger and the car rugs are camel hair. There's *foie gras*, though!'

She watched appreciatively as he unpacked the hamper. It also contained cold truffled chicken, eggs in aspic and a basket of out-of-season nectarines from heaven knew where.

'So much more civilised than bootleg gin,' said Ben, raising a champagne flute to his lips.

Diana agreed, still delighted at the sheer novelty of champagne. She couldn't bring herself to tell Ben that apart from the odd clandestine sip provided by her father, she had never really tasted it. When she fell silent immediately after this burst of enthusiasm, he thought she was reflecting on their earlier disagreement; but she was remembering past grief.

'Strange,' she told him, 'I really had forgotten it, but Mama tried to kill me here once.'

'Oh, come on, Diana, not even you can get away with *that* much melodrama!'

'No, honestly, it's true. If you knew her, it wouldn't be so hard to believe. It was when the Mandarin still spent a lot of time with us, a couple of years after the War ended. I must have been about ten years old. We'd driven up here for a picnic. Papa was teasing me and making a fuss about how pretty I looked in the new frock he'd brought me from Paris. Suddenly Mama started making horrid remarks about how she'd only got a lace blouse. It got very heated and I wandered off to the edge of the water to try and shut out the quarrel. I don't know what they said to each other then, but the next thing I knew Mama was beside me, furious, dragging at my arm and shrieking "It's you – it's all your fault, you brat! I'll settle it, I've had enough of this!" Then she got me to the very edge of the bank and threw me in.'

'She *what?*'

'Honestly, Ben. I know it's hard to believe, but it's true. Papa dived in and pulled me out, then we drove back to town as fast as we could with me wrapped in a car rug. I can still remember thinking that Grandpapa would be angry because we'd borrowed his Daimler and I was dripping all over it. I suppose it was all so awful that I pushed it right out of my mind and it never came back to me until we were here today.'

'Well what happened to her? Didn't your father or grand-father do something to prevent her from repeating the performance? You can get through a lot of daughters pretty damn' quick that way!'

'I don't know what happened after we got home, only that we never went on another picnic.'

He was stunned by her almost casual revelation of such a traumatic incident and failed to provide any comforting chatter. She did not seem to need it, anyway. After gazing moodily at the water for a while, she uttered a rather brittle giggle, said 'More champagne, M'sieur, *s'il vous plait!*' and returned to talking of less eventful family excursions. Ben decided to follow her lead and made no further reference to the matter.

After lunch, light-headed with champagne and spring sunshine, they drove on along quiet roads shaded by huge old trees just sprouting their first tender green of the year. Late in the afternoon they were in Bray, just upriver from Maidenhead. Diana had become pensive again as they strolled hand-in-hand through the little village.

'I always thought my father was a Vicar of Bray reborn,' she said with a sigh. 'I wish I'd been right. It's so much easier to survive if you're a born opportunist.'

Ben was unfamiliar with the legendary cleric. Diana sang him the old song about the canny churchman who modified his religious principles with each change of monarch and as a result survived three reigns unscathed. Lassiter stood silent for a moment after her clear young voice had died away.

'Don't make him too much of a hero, Diana,' he said eventually. 'You could get hurt even worse if you do.'

She gazed steadily back at him and said, 'I must have faith in him, Ben. No one else does. He's completely abandoned – I don't even know where, but I hold on to the feeling that if I go on trusting him, one day he'll get what he deserves.'

'Maybe he already has.'

'Leave it, Ben! I can't discuss it objectively, I'm too close. Just leave it.'

He shrugged and they turned away from the pretty old church. He must make her talk it out some time, but clearly now was not right. Lassiter turned his thoughts to happier prospects.

Conscious that the exchange in Bray had shaken her, Ben was a little unsteady himself after her revelations at Runnymede. Earlier, when they made peace after their argument, he had resolved to take her home immediately when they got back to London.

He knew her day would be spoiled if it finished with sour words about the Vicar of Bray ousting the brighter memories of their trip. Oh well, my boy, he thought, let's see how good your powers of self control can be under extreme provocation.

A little before six o'clock, the powerful car was nosing back into London. Diana was still cheerful but clearly apprehensive about his plans for the rest of the evening. She had resigned herself to being home early, her instinctive intelligence finally winning the argument with her impetuous nature and convincing her that willfulness would have all the unfortunate effects Ben had predicted. But her happiness had evaporated at Bray when she considered her father's plight. She had realised with a shock that not only political opponents and the gutter press but also reasonable people like Lassiter might think that Alexander Hartley was a rogue. As a result she knew it would be hard to maintain her good intentions about being reasonable when Ben inevitably suggested she go straight home. She couldn't believe her good fortune when he swept past the Clarges Street junction and carried on along Piccadilly, also passing the end of Albemarle Street where Brown's was located.

'Where are we going? I thought . . .'

'Don't do that – it tends to have disastrous consequences. Just sit in the nice automobile and see where the man will take you!' He turned into Jermyn Street, the home of expensive men's shops and exclusive bachelor apartments. Her puzzlement grew.

'Isn't it a little late in the day to visit your shirtmaker?' she asked, trying to keep the growing excitement out of her voice.

'You wanted to know where I was going this evening,

Miss Curiosity, now's your chance to find out!' He stopped the car outside an unobtrusive front door between an antique shop and a tailoring establishment, got out and came round to Diana's side.

'Would Milady care to inspect the premises?' He bowed like a stage butler and opened the car door, ushering her towards the building.

Inside the front door was a long narrow passage which broadened into a solidly masculine vestibule.

'Welcome to Marlborough Chambers, apartments for discerning gentlemen,' he said in a dreadful parody of a 'genteel' English accent. 'A chap must have his *pied à terre* in town and I got mine yesterday.'

He led the way to a small lift at the rear of the vestibule and they went up four floors. In front of the door which faced them opposite the lift, he stopped for a moment.

'Before we go in, I must tell you not to expect the usual sort of place,' he said. 'It's pretty special. I think you'll love it as much as I do but it's not exactly high fashion.'

He unlocked the front door, let her in and switched on the lights. She gasped. The small apartment was a perfect period piece, a little bit of history preserved into the modern age. It was fully furnished and the decoration and fittings were clearly originals from the turn of the century.

'Like it?' asked Ben. 'I've been crazy about the Arts and Crafts Movement since I first heard about it in college. I remember looking at pictures of a Charles Rennie Mackintosh chair and wishing the whole thing had never gone out of style. They've destroyed so much of it in England since the War in the interests of what they call modernity that I couldn't believe this when I saw it.'

'It's absolutely divine – but how has it survived? Even the rugs and tiles look original!'

'The owner was a dear old boy who had come here as a flaming youth in 1903 when it was built. As far as he was concerned, good design came to an end with Art Nouveau and he was determined to stay with it. So he maintained it all perfectly and never changed a thing. I think I might just spend the next twenty-five years here!'

'When do you move in?'

'I was thinking of the week-end – not that it matters. It's mine now and all I have to do is pack up my traps at Brown's, leave a forwarding address and check out. I was beginning to get a little concerned about the risk you run every time you meet me in the lounge over there. This will be far more secluded – if you can trust me!'

'Oh, it's too good to be true, like a storybook hide-away. I think I might spend the next twenty-five years here, too!'

Their eyes locked, the meaning of the day and the implications of what they had both said over the past few minutes hovering between them. Lassiter knew he was lost and realised he had ceased to care the moment the front door closed behind them.

'Come see the living room,' he said abruptly. 'Maybe it'll change your mind.'

At the front of the apartment, little yellow-shaded Tiffany style lamps gave a sunny glow to the drawing room. It continued the charming doll's house theme of the rest of the place, with mellow wood-panelled walls and a tiled fireplace with small individual upholstered oak settles built in on either side.

Delighted, Diana flung herself down on one.

'All we need is a crackling fire, a toasting fork and a pile of muffins to make the illusion complete!' she cried. 'It's absolutely magical and I never want to go out there into the big bad world again!'

Rising, she came back across the room and hugged him. 'You're so clever to have found it!'

His arms locked tightly around her slim waist and he crushed her body close, kissing her for the first time with real passion. Diana staggered slightly against him and moaned gently as he drew away, pulling his face back down to hers and seeking his lips again with eager, if inexpert, passion of her own.

'I promised myself I wouldn't do this, for both our sakes,' he said, his voice roughened by excitement. He held her away from him and gave her a slight shake to re-assert some sort of reality between them. She swayed dreamily again, an inviting smile curving her full lips.

'Oh, hell, Diana, help me! I can't be the white knight for both of us!'

'Who wants a white knight? Let's sin and enjoy it . . .'

'Sometimes I think you haven't the vaguest idea what sin is!'

Gently he pressed her down on to the soft, faded woollen hearth rug, then sat down beside her, exercising more self-control than he had ever thought he possessed.

'Beautiful girl, forgive me if I've got it wrong, but I can't help feeling that inside that woman's body is a very young, inexperienced little kid. What you're looking to do is a pretty grown-up thing and once you start, there's no stopping – it's for keeps. Now you talk as if you know what you're doing, but somehow I just don't believe you. This is the last chance you get to yell stop. Are you gonna take it?'

Her big green eyes were swimming with tears, he never knew whether from sadness or ecstacy, for her mood was unreadable. She reached out and drew a soft finger down his cheek, mutely adoring him for a moment.

'I don't know what it will be like, Ben. I suppose I don't even really know what it is. But I feel as if I belong with you. I couldn't bear it if you just patted me on the head now and took me home.

'I want all these stupid things off' – she flipped at her clothes – 'and I want to feel my bare skin pressed tight against yours all over. And then I just want to see what happens between us.'

He made one final last ditch effort to dissuade her. 'It might bring your world crashing down around you . . .'

'I don't care if it brings everyone else's world crashing down around me. I want you like that and I want you now. Please, please, just teach me to grow up with love!'

Gently, he reached out for her hand and raised her to her feet, leading her through to the bedroom.

Ben lit one of the little yellow-shaded lamps. He left the curtains undrawn on the London twilight, for they were above the level of the buildings opposite and no one could see into the room. He turned back the white cover of the double bed, already made up for his moving in, and gestured to her to lie down.

With infinite patience, he undressed her, peeling away the fine silk stockings from her long, coltishly slim legs. Diana was wearing a lightweight frock with buttons down the front. He unfastened them and slipped her arms from the brief sleeves. She wriggled out of the skirt. Underneath it she wore only a fine voile camisole and loose matching knickers. He eased them down over the curve of her hips, delighting in her flat belly and the dusting of red-gold pubic hair which shimmered in the subdued lamplight. Her breasts were surprisingly large, and became taut as her arms stretched up to pull him down beside her. Instead of responding, he simply kissed the tips of her outstretched fingers before bending to take up her clothes and fold them carefully over an oak chest. Then he undressed himself.

Diana lay watching him, wide-eyed and devoid of shyness. She gasped when he turned towards her and she saw the extent of his erection. He smiled reassuringly and slid into the bed beside her, taking her hand and putting it firmly on him.

'It's OK baby,' he said with a soft laugh. 'Feel – it's not as rock-hard as it looks. Nothing to put you off there.'

This time her intake of breath was pure pleasure as her fingers started moving appreciatively over him. He groaned in a mixture of excitement and anguish. 'I hope you're feeling in the mood, old thing, because I'm getting there pretty fast!'

He turned towards her with harsher passion, his firm hands seeking out the soft, moist places of her body. All thoughts of restraint fled from both of them and as she had not known enough of what she was encouraging to feel nervous, she had no fears to subdue. Lassiter was that rare type of male who only fully enjoyed sexuality when his lover was as aroused as himself, so he made sure that her excitement kept pace with his. His teeth closed around her tiny pink nipples in playful pretence of biting them, until they grew hard with excitement, then he shifted his mouth slowly, deliberately down her body, intruding occasionally through the silky red-gold hair, stirring her into unbearable desire to scale the great wave of their joint passion. Finally, when she thought she would faint if the tension mounted further, he drew back from her for a moment and deftly slipped one of the pillows beneath her. Then, very gently and with infinite slowness, he slid inside her, murmuring pet names and covering her face and throat with tiny kisses. As he started gently to move back and forth inside her, he realised that his own passion was too strong to contain any longer and pressed forward, hard into her, moaning convulsively.

Diana let out a wracking cry and arched her back up towards him, her hands locking into his shoulders like small vices. At his huge climactic thrust, she slid into an ecstatic orgasm too and fell away from him, sobbing in the most unalloyed pleasure she had ever experienced. They were both too overcome by the unexpected intensity of the final moments to say or do anything for a while. They simply lay, locked together, lips against one another's sweating bodies. Finally Diana broke the silence.

'D'you mean to tell me they've been giving me mint humbugs all these years when I could have been having that?'

Lassiter exploded into laughter.

'You goddamned little philistine! I've been lying here recovering and wondering whether you'd ever get over having your maidenhead snatched and you feed me a line like that! You'll come to a bad end, Lady D!'

'If that's how you come to it, the sooner the better, I say,' she responded.

Then the laughter receded and she kissed him gently, suddenly very solemn.

'Thank you for making it so beautiful for me. Whatever happens now, I'll always have that.'

It was as though someone else, not himself, said 'The only thing that's going to happen is that you and I are getting married, sharpish. I'm not letting a piece of tail like you run round loose any longer than I have to. Someone else might spot your possibilities!' Having said it, however, he realised that the prospect of a lifetime spent in this girl's company was thoroughly alluring.

Her reaction surprised him.

'Let's talk about that when we've cooled down a little, my handsome lover. I think now we'd better think about me getting dressed and going home, then I might manage to escape again some night.'

Now she was being sensible and he was reluctant to let her go. He was quite happy to cuddle close to her and make good use of every minute up to about midnight before trying to smuggle her back into Clarges Street. He was forced to admit that she was right, however, and after lying in each other's arms for a few minutes they started to dress ready to leave.

'April is no time to take a bath in England in unheated water without any towels around,' said Ben. 'I'm afraid, therefore, you'll have to go home in your present seductive state and slip into some warm bubbles there. I'm only too happy to keep your scent on me for a little longer.'

Diana walked back into the sitting room and strolled around as if memorising the furniture and pictures. 'I'll always think of this little room as a sort of magic home,' she said, 'wherever I end up eventually.'

'My dear girl, you'll end up here as Mrs Lassiter until it suits us to go back. Stateside,' he said heartily. But he experienced a slight frisson nevertheless at her tone. It was almost as though she had some foreknowledge that this place and its owner were nothing more than staging posts in her life and that soon she would have moved on, out of reach of both.

He shook off the absurd fancy. 'Come on, my lovely Diana – I'll take you home.'

He quenched the golden lights on the happiest evening of his twenty five years.

Hermione knew that her niece was in love for the first time. To anyone who took more than a passing interest in

Diana, it was obvious that she was blossoming. Not that she had much chance to do so within the stringent financial controls that Sarah had imposed in her determination to maintain her own opulent appearance. Hermione was about to change all that. They met at breakfast – unusually. Diana and Lettie normally ate theirs in the nursery and Hermione had a tray in her room. Now Hermione suppressed a smile as she noted the large meal with which the girl was clearly fortifying herself for what she must see as the wrath to come. Hermione herself took little from the well-laden sideboard. Her body was inclined towards the generous curves of an earlier fashion era and the boyish look of the 1920s required strict self-control. Sitting down, she smiled encouragingly at Diana. Her niece promptly returned to attacking a plate of devilled kidneys.

'If you have no plans for the next few mornings, I thought we might start sorting out your wardrobe for the Season,' said Hermione.

Diana immediately lost interest in her plate and set down her knife and fork with exaggerated care.

'Am . . . am I really going to have new frocks and things, then?' Her tone was hopeful but hesitant.

'Oh, I think frocks, stockings, underthings, hats and the full rig, including a grown-up hairstyle and some cosmetics, don't you?'

She was rewarded by a glimpse of the leaping exhilaration that seized Diana. With an effort, Hermione went on behaving as if all this were expected and as though she were only acting as Sarah's proxy.

'I remembered your mother having mentioned that Louise Kerslake had started on some clothes for you when the . . . difficulties . . . occurred last autumn, so I took the liberty of making a new appointment with her. She should arrive in about an hour.'

Diana could no longer conceal her joy. She swept to her feet and rushed around the large table to embrace Hermione. 'Oh, Aunt, how did you guess she was my favourite dressmaker? Lakie is the best there is!'

Hermione pretended a coolness she did not feel, but gave

the girl a quick hug just the same. 'I rather think a certain Mademoiselle Chanel would take issue with you there, but Mrs Kerslake is certainly talented enough to make you an excellent everyday wardrobe. Then I thought that for your dance, we might do something really special. I wonder whether you're grown up enough yet for a dress by Patou?'

Diana's face was a picture.

'Patou! But Aunt H, that's impossible. We could never run to it, could we?'

'Well, perhaps just this once, as a special present. It's not every day that I get a chance to chaperone a beautiful young woman and I seem destined to have sons, not daughters of my own. So let's say it's a consolation prize to myself for the daughter I'm not going to dress for her Season, shall we?

'I want to do you justice, my dear. I think one of Patou's younger styles might do very well. Have you any thoughts on colour?'

'Anything as long as it's not white!' rejoined Diana promptly. Hermione had a fleeting vision of what Sarah must have had in mind for the girl.

'Unless you're superstitious, I think that lovely new green they call eau-de-Nil would look wonderful with your hair and eyes. Of course, we shall ask Mrs Kerslake for some evening frocks, too. I believe they are her forte.'

A spark of malice kindled in Diana's eyes. 'There was one thing she never had a chance to finish for me. I think Mama – uh – discarded it. If Lakie could do it again?'

'Certainly, Diana. Unless, of course, it was put aside because it was unsuitable.'

Hermione had a reasonable idea that the gown had been withheld as punishment or because it made her niece look too fetching. Probably both. Well, she could justly plead ignorance of any such nonsense if Sarah attacked her later for undermining a mother's authority. At such times Hermione found it useful to take refuge behind an expression of well-meaning stupidity. She had a strong suspicion that Diana had been punished more than enough.

Nevertheless, she had to explain the ground rules to Diana before the girl misunderstood her new freedom and overdid it. Hermione had no trouble in distinguishing between sympathy and sentimentality. It was time to ensure that Diana was aware of the difference, too.

'Diana, I have no wish to upset you by referring too much to the past, but we must discuss one or two things. If we talk about them now, with any luck we shan't have to do so again.'

Her niece's bubbly mood evaporated. 'Very well, Aunt, but I didn't realise I'd done anything wrong.'

'Of course you haven't! It's just that I think we've treated you as a child for too long and tried not to burden you with the need to consider your position as a young adult. You've had a decidedly odd life until now and unless someone talks to you about it, you'll have no idea how to conduct yourself, or what reasonable people might expect of you.'

The girl nodded, still apprehensive but willing to listen.

'To say the least, your Mama has not been kind to you and Lettie. Perhaps it was because she was so unhappy herself; whatever the reason, I intend to see you have a much better time from now on. But I don't want you thinking that you are a deprived orphan because your Mama treated you badly and others appear to victimise you for your father's disgrace. Emotionally, your parents gave you a bad start, without meaning to. They also gave you a Mayfair mansion, servants and a private education. You spend months every year down at Stanhope where you have your own pony, ride to hounds and regularly do dozens of things which less fortunate people never even try. That's given you a huge start on all but the most privileged people you'll meet.

'Life is about to improve immensely for you, but I have to make sure that you don't turn into a spoiled brat. As a result you might think sometimes that I'm harsh. Believe me, my dear, I have nothing but your happiness at heart. I shall never try to trap you or make you look silly, but I shall also try not to let you get away with anything – and with your spirit, you'll try! Now, let's start as we mean to go on, as friends.'

She observed with pleasure that her niece was beginning to relax and was looking at her with a new regard which bordered on worship. They were close enough in age to be sisters. Although she had two sons and had been married thirteen years, Hermione was not much over thirty. The age gap was made even narrower by the fact that Coming Out in 1913 had thrown her into a social system which had already relaxed beyond recognition since Queen Victoria's death and was about to change still further under the pressure of the Great War. Hermione's attitudes were far more akin to those of the Flapper era than to those of the long Edwardian afternoon. Like Diana, she had known the giddy heights of a secret romance. Hermione had been a dutiful daughter of much-loved parents, though, and had recognised that the penniless young painter who so stirred her passion would have made an impossible husband.

After a magical springtime of longing and fulfilment, she had put him aside and accepted the proposal of James Digby-Lenton, Viscount Stanmore, thereby crowning her father's ambition for noble grandchildren. Her rewards had been complete security, comfort, social prestige – and almost total lack of any profound human affection until this new closeness to Diana had begun to develop. Hermione needed Diana almost as much as the girl needed her. Her present success in communicating with Diana carried her away somewhat and she shelved her original intention to talk through more of the girl's potential social and emotional problems. Time enough for all that later on – at least they were starting off on a friendly footing. Now she could turn to a more enjoyable aspect of the relationship – spending money on her niece.

On balance, Hermione had probably done much better than most heiresses of her generation who were carried off for their fortunes by impoverished aristocrats. With exceptions like Lady Sarah, the Digby-Lentons were a reasonably civilised family and she was not treated as either a hostage or a downtrodden parvenue, as some of her female acquaintances were. She remained in full control of a considerable private fortune, as only her father's money had gone to buy her membership of the Digby-Lenton tribe. Her mother had left her a controlling interest in a Staffordshire pottery producing fine china, as well as a small, exclusive glass works with a highly profitable bottling plant subsidiary. The Digby-Lentons had no access to these funds and she accounted for them to no one. This was the store which augmented the main subsidy for Diana which came from what was originally her money too but was now the Lenton family fortune.

One way or another, Diana was likely to match the most well-endowed debutante of her Season. Hermione looked forward to every moment. The fact that her haughty sister-in-law would forbid it all if she could as vulgar show, gave the whole escapade added savour.

They spent a blissful hour planning their campaign for the weeks leading up to the first official event of the London Season – the May private view of the Royal Academy Summer Exhibition. By the time Diana excused herself to prepare for Louise Kerslake's arrival, they had agreed on exactly what was needed and where and when to get it. The entire operation revolved around a three-day trip to Paris for final fittings of the Patou ball gown. Mrs Kerslake was to be sent to the French capital with a muslin toile as a guide to her young client's measurements and a choice of design. It would require intensive persuasion by Hermione to make Patou accept someone else's toile, but Hermione spent a great deal of money at the couture house and if her request was refused they could always make an extra trip to Paris to have the fittings done on the spot.

I hope they agree to what I want, she mused. That dressmaker deserves a little boost – she's very talented and turning out a whole Coming Out wardrobe like this could be exactly what her business needs. A Paris trip on her own will be a nice treat for her, too. She rang for a servant and left instructions that Mrs Kerslake should call to see her in the morning room after the fitting was over.

CHAPTER FOUR

Louise Kerslake knew where she wanted to go. She was less sure that she would ever get there. Certainly the heights seemed far away from the top of the Number Fourteen bus in which she was travelling from her Fulham home to Mayfair. Still, she reflected, she had already come quite a distance. Her name was not Louise Kerslake; it was Blodwen Louise Williams. As long as she could remember, she had been determined to lose the Blodwen. It was bad enough in the South Wales mining valleys where she had grown up and they all called her Blod, but downright impossible in London where it made people burst out laughing and treat her as some kind of peasant simpleton.

Her mother had liked the name Louise – 'Nice royal sound to it, that' she used to say – and now Louise had used it for so long that little Blodwen could have been another person. There had been no question of choice about Blodwen's future. The youngest of nine children of an unemployed collier, she was destined for domestic service. And as there were very few people employing servants in the Rhymney Valley in 1913, that meant moving away from home at an early age. It was no great loss. All she remembered of her childhood was deprivation, dirt and quarrels. Soon after her thirteenth birthday she was scrubbed, de-loused and dressed in her one good frock to be sent for inspection at a big house in Cardiff. Her mother suddenly turned tearful about the whole thing, an attitude Blodwen found odd until she saw the handful of sympathy money passed over to the 'gallant little Welshwoman' who was apparently parting with her youngest chick only to give the child a good start in life.

Once Mrs Williams had departed, however, things were

a little different. Mrs Kerslake, Blodwen's new employer, was a woman who saved her sympathetic face for the outside world and became something of a tyrant in the privacy of her own home. Blodwen had been engaged as a nursery maid for the Kerslake children. After the initial interview she seldom saw Mrs Kerslake at first. Nanny became her ruler and negotiations with the domain outside the nursery were conducted through her. There were four Kerslake children, a baby girl six months old, a boy of two, and two older girls aged five and four. Blodwen swiftly found herself thrust into a fourteen-hour day of washing, scrubbing, cleaning and mending – all skills she acquired instantaneously as none of them had been much practised at her home. She was an intelligent girl, though, and both experience and instinct told her that self-improvement lay in silent obedience coupled with keen observation of what went on around her.

Cardiff was at its raffish zenith, the riches of the booming coal industry pouring into the pockets of the coal barons who had built their mansions along Park Place. As she drifted into exhausted slumber each Saturday night, Blodwen renewed her silent vow not to attempt escape into the arms of one of the brawling colliers who occasionally racketed along the street outside after the pubs had closed. She had seen that life and wanted none of it. Opportunity came from an unexpected quarter. Not wanting to visit her family during her monthly day off, she spent the time improving her skill at the one chore which gave her any pleasure – sewing. She became particularly keen on achieving handiwork fine enough to restore to their original pristine condition some of the worn fancy blouses passed on by her employer. After about six months, Mrs Kerslake suddenly had the girl's skill forcibly drawn to her attention when the baby had an unexpected tantrum in her arms and tore away the lace jabot on the front of a particularly expensive new afternoon frock. White with fury, she thrust the screaming bundle back into Blodwen's arms – it was Nanny's day off – and began roundly abusing the girl for allowing little Enid to get out of control. The nursery maid suppressed her own temper and calmly offered to repair the garment.

Mrs Kerslake paused momentarily in her ranting. 'A little Valleys guttersnip like you, repair this? You'd probably only make it even worse. For God's sake get out and take the baby with you!'

When she had calmed down, Jean Kerslake's innate stinginess asserted itself. The gown had cost a fortune – heaven knew what Albert would say when he saw the James Howell's department store account that month – and this was the first time she had worn it. The girl was unlikely to damage it further and if all else failed she could always send it for professional repair. In the meantime, she had worked out a way of having it mended for nothing. She sent for Blodwen again after changing into another frock. The damaged garment was folded neatly on a chair beside her.

'You think you can make this look as good as new?' she asked.

'I know I can, Madam.'

'Hmm, very sure of yourself, aren't you? Well, we shall see. I'm going to give you a chance to show how good you are, but I'm not prepared to risk the loss of the gown if you really botch it, so in that case I shall send it to be repaired properly and stop the money from your wages.'

She waited for a moment, half expecting a protest that the condition was unfair, but none came. Probably too stupid to realise I'm stealing a march on her, thought Jean. Blodwen was well aware of the injustice of the proposal, but she was confident enough of her ability to regard the possible loss of wages as remote. In a surprisingly short time she had finished. It was a good job – so good that Jean Kerslake suspected the girl had substituted a different garment. When she inspected the work closely, she realised that the effect had been achieved by removing yards of lace from around the tear and appliqueing it back over the finished repair, with the tiniest stitches Jean had ever seen. Blodwen's days in the nursery were numbered.

The girl's tone was impassive and even Jean Kerslake's

malicious spirit was at a loss to detect any insolence: 'Is it to your satisfaction, Madam?'

'Quite adequate, thank you, Blodwen. I think we can find more for you to practise on. You may go back to the nursery now.'

Blodwen's life did not become much easier, because her employer was a discontented, excessively demanding woman. But at least now she was doing something she enjoyed. She was not paid more. Instead Mrs Kerslake financed training five mornings a week in the best dressmaking establishment in South Wales. Even though Blodwen had to make up for the concessions by working long into the night on sewing jobs for Jean Kerslake, she was thankful to be in private service and not a full-time dressmaking apprentice. The girls at Madame Antoinette's started work at 8 am and never finished in less than 12 hours. During the Season it was far worse, as the floods of orders came for ball gowns, and the workrooms went on operating until 3 am, with the same eight o'clock start in prospect however late they stopped. To make matters worse, many of the apprentices lived in and their families paid for the privilege of having them trained. Madame Antoinette was a product of the greatest French couture house – Worth – and had fetched up in South Wales as the result of a somewhat ill-advised marriage. After her husband's death she had turned her dressmaking skills to enormous profit, instinctively trading on a mixture of real talent and training and the snobbery of the local nouveaux riches who wanted Paris fashions at Cardiff prices.

Her establishment was run like a miniature couture house, even down to using French terms to describe staff functions. The apprentice was an *arpette*, indentured from the age of fourteen to nineteen, when she became a *deuxième main qualifiée* – a qualified second-class seamstress. Above her in the pecking order was the *première main qualifiée*, the first-class seamstress. They worked together under the instructions of the fitter and the *vendeuse* to produce clothes to the client's order. At the top of the tree was the *couturière*, as Madame Antoinette liked to call herself. In fact she had been a fitter for Worth, but knew her trade inside out and had the flair and originality to claim a star role. Madame Antoinette eyed Blodwen neutrally when Jean Kerslake took the girl along to start her training. Mrs Kerslake made a minimal introduction, told Blodwen brusquely to be back at Park Place by 1.30 each day after lunching with the apprentices, then left. A speculative silence followed.

'You want to do this thing?' asked Madame Antoinette.

Blodwen was surprised. 'I didn't realise I had a choice, Madame.'

'We all 'ave a choice, child. You do not 'ave to stay with 'er if you do not want it.'

'Don't they have coalmining areas in France, then, Madame?'

Madame Antoinette laughed. 'You are right, girl, of course you 'ave no choice. Well, I make no secret of the fact that you are 'ere because Mrs Kerslake 'as promised to increase 'er regular orders and to pay me very well for training you. I am not a charity for miners' daughters. Are you any good?'

'I think so, but I only know from looking at what other people do. I brought some of the little things I've been doing to show you.'

She took out a few small pieces of work from her dingy bag. Madame Antoinette made a moue of surprise.

'You did these without 'elp from a seamstress?'

'Didn't know what a seamstress was until Mrs Kerslake mentioned you, Madame Antoinette.'

'My child, I think perhaps you 'ave a prosperous future if you are sensible. Come – I 'ave a lot to teach you.'

In the months that followed, Blodwen learned far more than the tricks of couture. She modelled herself consciously on Madame Antoinette and on Gabrielle, Madame's younger sister who was head *vendeuse*. She started noticing that when all the women in the room were fussily covered in frills and lace, a severe shape in plain silk dominated every other outfit. She noticed that cut was everything and that an outfit with no trimmings at all was better than a lot of cheap clutter. On the practical side she learned to produce supple, invisible seams, to cut fabric so that it fell in soft curves and to apply trims so that only an expert could detect the fastening. She was thankful for her near-perfect eyesight, because the ensuing two years of additional sewing by lamplight late at night would have half blinded her otherwise. The first of those two years was given over to her training under Madame Antoinette. The woman was professional to the fingertips and recognised the best talent when she saw it. After some six months, she stopped Blodwen as the girl was departing for Park Place at the end of a morning session.

'Blodwen, you know you are a first-rate seamstress without my needing to tell you. You 'ave learned more in a few months with me than many of my girls learn in five years as apprentices. If you wish to join me as a *première main qualifiée* at the end of your year's training, I will be 'appy to take you. It will make much difference to the way you live, I think.'

'Madame Antoinette, that's wonderful! But would I be up to it? Some of the top hands take ten years to reach that!'

'They are merely dressmakers. You will be a *couturière!*'

Blodwen went off to her little maidservant's bedroom, overjoyed at the offer. After a little thought she decided that it was less simple than Madame imagined. She did not like Jean Kerslake and had few illusions about why the woman was paying to have her trained. Nevertheless she felt a sense of obligation and wished to discharge it before joining Madame Antoinette. She tried to explain her feelings at their next meeting. Madame listened impassively, then said: 'You do not feel that you 'ave repaid 'er already with the works of art she is wearing on 'er back that you created for pennies?'

'Of course I know that, Madame, but she would never accept it and Cardiff isn't such a big place that I can afford an enemy like her. If I stay a year or eighteen months after my training and then come to you, not even she can say I'm ungrateful or anything.'

'I think you are mistaken, child. That woman will always

make trouble for those she cannot manipulate and you may as well get it over with in six months from now as in eighteen months or two years. Still – I only want to 'ave you 'ere. I shall not go away and I would prefer it later than not at all. You do as you think best. Just don't go to another *couturière*!'

They seldom discussed the matter again, apart from an occasional reassurance from Madame that she had meant the offer seriously. As the months passed, Blodwen became completely indispensable to Mrs Kerslake. The War was upon them and there were all sorts of shortages. Jean Kerslake was able to attend fund-raising meetings mounted to buy comforts for 'Our Boys' as the best-dressed woman in the room and still tell everyone that her wardrobe cost her next to nothing.

By 1916, Blodwen was unrecognisable as the scrawny waif who had arrived in Park Place three years before. She had grown much taller and had developed a beautiful body – too slender for current tastes, but a perfect model for the quietly elegant clothes she was creating for herself under the guidance of magazines like *Gazette du Bon Ton*. She had also trained herself to speak a clear, unaccented English, totally different from her original rough Valleys Anglo-Welsh. Jean Kerslake followed the frilly school of fashion, so she dismissed Blodwen as a drab little domestic and thought no more of the matter. Her brother-in-law Charles developed a different view. Charles was a subaltern with the South Wales Borderers, all swagger stick and immaculately-cut uniform, and fond of telling his cronies he knew a tasty little pullet when he saw one. He was home on leave from his safe posting with the general staff well behind the lines on the Western Front. Jean Kerslake welcomed his presence as a house guest. Her brother-in-law's uniform silenced those who were suggesting that at only thirty-three, her husband Albert should be a soldier, not a profiteering civilian. And Charlie was quite a social asset, with his accounts of the latest Paris fashions and slightly risqué tales of high life in the French capital.

Blodwen never stood a chance. A more experienced woman would have dismissed Charlie Kerslake as a third-rate masher. To Blodwen he was the handsome sophisticated hero of her fantasies. She was completely innocent of sexual knowledge and Charlie promptly set about filling in the blanks that followed the fade-outs in Blodwen's Elinor Glyn novels. Later, in France, he told his friends that he was glad to get back into action for a rest from so many women. His sister-in-law's friends turned out to require more in the way of entertainment than stories from Paris, and some of them were quite attractive pieces if only one could get them to keep their mouths shut for five minutes at a time. As for the little seamstress ... those collier chappies didn't know a good thing when they had it!

Their involvement started because Charlie was at a loose end one day when Jean Kerslake had gone off for an afternoon's charity work and gossip. The war had scattered such male friends as he normally saw in the area so now, at an hour when women were keeping female company, he had nothing to occupy him and no companionship. That was when he remembered the little seamstress. Blodwen had returned from Maison Antoinette preoccupied with a complex dressmaking project and mentally she was a thousand miles from Park Place. She sat in the sewing room, surrounded by clouds of cream silk organza which she was attempting to fashion into a tiered ball gown. Jean Kerslake had light-heartedly chosen the most elaborate drawing in her fashion magazine for copying, with no thought of the fact that the original had been created by a Paris master with a whole couture house at his disposal. Now Blodwen was attempting to reproduce it in a tiny sewing room with her own hands, a Singer sewing machine and Madame Antoinette's advice. It was no mean task.

'I say, talk about trailing clouds of glory!'

She glanced up, startled. Charles Kerslake had just stuck his head around the door and was surveying her, surrounded by her mountain of fragile silk. Blodwen blushed furiously and looked away.

'Oh – it's you, sir! I didn't think anyone was at home.

I'm just trying to sort out this new gown for Mrs Kers-lake . . .'

'On a day like this? No day for work, especially for a pretty little thing like you. Come on – out to play!'

In fact it was her afternoon off. Blodwen had simply been more interested in the problems of the new gown than in going out for a few hours. Now, with the prospect of such glamorous company, her priorities were changing quickly. She made a token protest, but her heart was not in it.

'Really, sir, I don't think Mrs Kerslake would approve . . .'

'Nonsense, my dear! Jean just went off out telling me to treat the place as if it were my own. Now if it *were*, then I'd go straight out with the prettiest girl in the house, whoever she was. And that girl is you, Miss Williams, Ma'am!'

The fact that he remembered her surname completely disarmed her. Then he really noticed me, she thought, wonderingly. In her novels, the shy, pretty heroine was frequently sought out by the handsome, eligible hero in the most unpromising circumstances. The encounter invariably led to a fairytale marriage and the achievement of the heroine's heart's desire. The everyday Blodwen knew that life was not like this. She knew that her suitors were likely to be dockers, miners or shopkeepers and she wanted none of them, preferring to support herself. But if a romantic hero forced his way into her life, she had no intention of turning him away. In Blodwen's simplistic world, there were plenty of villains, but her lack of experience left her without many wicked characteristics to ascribe to them. It never occurred to her that Charles Kerslake wanted bed-ding rather than wedding. Of course, it never occurred to Charlie that a servant girl would think his intentions went anywhere beyond a dirty week-end by the sea. Men like Charlie did not marry girls like Blodwen. Blodwen's only defence was to refuse his advances and to do that she had to know them for what they were.

An hour later they were in Roath Park, strolling between well-manicured flower beds towards the ornamental lake.

Charles hired a rowing boat and they set out across the sparkling water. Blodwen looked enchanting. Her glossy dark brown hair was piled into neat curls and topped by a simple broad-brimmed hat in a fine cream straw, with two ox-eye daisies threaded into the hatband. Her frock was a triumph of studied artlessness. The soft muslin was pin-tucked from shoulder to waist, where it was caught in by a broad, deeply pleated cummerbund. The skirt, cut in three layers to give the fabric body, fell in soft gathers to ankle level and was hand-embroidered with tiny sprigs of flowers. Long, diaphanous sleeves and a Puritan collar completed the picture of a highly sophisticated little girl. Charlie was unable to believe his good fortune. He had made his conquest just by being Charlie. He was tall – over six feet – and well-muscled, in an age when working-class men tended to be small and puny because of bad nutrition. His golden hair was immaculately cut and brushed across the forehead from a side parting. A luxuriant moustache added strength to his somewhat petulant mouth. His teeth were even and very clean. What Blodwen saw before her was everything in appearance that prosperity could buy. It was light years away from the rickets, dirt, toothlessness and general ill-health of the slums and she wanted it. All Charlie wanted was an engaging day out, a quick flirtation and a few hours in a double bed with this delightful little creature. He would have been back on the Western Front within hours had he known the thoughts which were flitting through her head. He had also bargained without his sister-in-law's tyrannical domestic regime: When he suggested another outing tomorrow, Blodwen was horrified.

'But I only get a half day every two weeks!' she told him, incredulous at his assumption that she was available for social pursuits at the drop of a hat.

'You mean you have to hang around the house all the time apart from that? I don't believe it!'

'But it's true – though I'd hardly call it hanging around; I'm working almost every moment. I do get a day off, but that's just once a month. It's due the week after next . . .' she hesitated, then blurted 'I could always get another day

71

if I said I wanted to go home for the week-end. I often don't take my day off so Mrs Kerslake would probably let me!'

Afterwards she was to wonder again and again what had persuaded her to say such a thing. If she was going away from the Kerslake house overnight, where was she to stay? Maybe there had always been a little trollop in there fighting to get out, she once reflected, years later. At the time she certainly had no full realisation that a bedroom with Charlie was the obvious destination. Their first afternoon ended idyllically over strawberries and cream in the little park tea room. She forbore to tell him that she had never tasted them before. That was when she decided she was going to marry him. Charlie's plans were rather different. For the rest of that week he divided his time between flirting with his sister-in-law's friends in the drawing room and with Blodwen in the sewing room. He had never been interested in a servant before – probably because his mother had taken care to staff her house with plain middle-aged women – and he had never paused to think how little freedom they had. Now it was in his interest to see that Blodwen got such freedom, for the moment, anyway. By the week-end he had persuaded her to tell Jean she wanted the following week-end off.

It happened to suit Mrs Kerslake to say yes; she and her husband had been invited to a country house party by a woman from whom she had been angling for an invitation for months. As a result she was not even very interested in Charles's casual announcement that he was off to see some chums in Gloucestershire from Friday until early the following week. As the days passed, Blodwen felt as if a great bubble of excitement were expanding inside her, ready to explode into perfection by the week-end. She still worked at Madame Antoinette's three mornings a week to keep her technique abreast of the latest fashion. For once her work fell short of its usual high standard. Handing back a clumsily-sewn seam to be re-done, Madame stopped moment-arily and said: 'It is unlike you, *ma petite*. You show signs of going mad over some man. Is that it?'

Blodwen wondered many times whether things would have been different if she had told Madame, but the fatalist in her was convinced that she was set headlong on her chosen course and it would have taken more than a French *couturière* to stop her. As it happened she denied Madame the opportunity.

'Why, er, no Madame. Mrs Kerslake is working me very hard on her summer frocks and I'm getting rather tired. I'll try to be better tomorrow.'

Madame Antoinette continued to gaze at her for a moment, then, apparently dismissing the entire matter from her mind, said, 'Really?' and turned away. Blodwen was silently thankful when Friday came and she tucked into the last meal of the week – for ever, as it turned out – around the big kitchen table in the seamstresses' quarters. She practically skipped back to Park Place, to discover that Mr and Mrs Kerslake had already gone off for their house party and that Charlie was waiting eagerly for her.

'Come on, old girl, we can make an early start. Think of it, Friday, Saturday and Sunday with no one to answer to. What a time we'll have!'

Blodwen pushed away the thought that he had not once mentioned marriage. He would in good time. He was too excited now. She rushed upstairs and finished off the packing she had virtually completed the previous night. Only an evening dress and the flimsiest of chiffon *peignoirs* were left out, hanging as long as possible to preserve the delicate fabrics from creases. She packed them away and turned to leave the little room. As she did so, Charles moved in through the door. He was so big and the room so small that his aggressive maleness seemed to swamp it.

'Carry your bag, lady?' he asked in exaggerated imitation cockney.

He stood very close, looking down into her bright hazel eyes, and the laughter ebbed from his face, replaced by passion. Suddenly his arms were around her and he was pressing her back against the wall, his big powerful body straining against hers. She felt an answering excitement in herself but the mean little room prevented her from letting go of her control. She fought him off and stood back, panting, as he stared at her, his eyes suddenly flat and intense like an animal's.

'What's wrong? D'you think we're going on a church picnic?'

'No, Charlie, but . . . not here. Please not here . . .'

He glanced about him, apparently disorientated for a moment.

'Oh, no, quite. Get Jean in a bit of a lather if the other servants told her, hey? Never mind, save it for later.'

Her misgivings were beginning to harden, but Blodwen was committed now and she kept telling herself she was being silly. Good humour restored, Charles Keslake picked up her bag and carried it downstairs. A cab delivered them at Cardiff General Station and within a short time they were trundling off in a first-class carriage – another first for Blodwen – towards the Severn Tunnel and Bristol.

'What's so special about Bristol, Charlie?'

'Damn, good music hall, that's all. We'll stay at Weston-Super-Mare tomorrow night, though. Too many familiar faces in the city.'

Again she felt a frisson of apprehension. Her sensible, down-to-earth self was fighting the love-struck girl with little success, but Charlie was not exactly being tactful in his attitude to their relationship. She subdued her sense of self-preservation by making herself a promise to confront him about his plans that evening at dinner. Before they got off the train at Bristol, he took a jeweller's box from his coat pocket. Her heart somersaulted, but she was doomed to bitter disappointment.

'Better put this on for form's sake, me dear. You're Mrs Laker for the time being, all right?'

'But Charlie, I don't . . .'

'Hotels and all that. Frightfully bad form to check into the same suite as single people. They might even feel they don't want to let us in.'

His patience waned as she hesitated. 'Come on, come on – surely you didn't think we'd be popping into the nearest

74

registry office outside the station to tie the knot before finding somewhere to stay?'

Of course, she rationalised. It will be all right tonight. By tomorrow he'll arrange it all legally and no one will ever know ... Believe that and you'll believe anything, you dunce! said her more realistic voice, but she stifled it. Charlie was now firmly set on course. He was going to bathe, change, dine, see a music hall performance and bed a new girl. However tempted he might be to jumble the running order, he would stick to it. When he saw Blodwen in her evening gown, he almost changed his mind, but consoled himself that she would be even better for the wait.

'My God, you'd pass for a lady before Jean did any time!' he exclaimed as she emerged into the drawing room of their suite, clad in a glorious confection of spangled midnight blue.

'Perhaps I am ...' she said.

'Don't get carried away, Blodwen. You'll only get hurt.'

Again she brushed aside the inevitable conclusion. He is in love with me – he *is*.

They left the hotel suite and went downstairs to dinner. Blodwen's looks, clothes and bearing made her seem years older than sixteen and it was perfectly believable that she was a young bride away on a trip with her husband. The years at Park Place had taught her which knives and forks to use and how to hold them.

Charlie was wearing his uniform – 'I've made arrangements for some good old-fashioned food and I don't want to risk someone suggesting I'm a column-dodging profiteer. The uniform puts a stop to that' – he had told her. The meal that followed left Blodwen speechless. Charlie might be an imitation soldier and an insensitive idiot when it came to emotional perception, but his stint in France had taught him a lot about good food and drink. The meal which followed was beyond anything the girl had ever imagined. It started with a small, perfect golden melon for each of them, liberally laced with champagne. The flavour of the fruit alone was intoxicating. Next came *consommé*

Messaline — a strong clear chicken soup garnished with cocks' kidneys, tiny strips of pimiento and rice.

Filet de sole orientale followed. 'This is wonderful,' said Blodwen. 'I know it's sole, but what's the rest of it?'

'Lobster chopped into a curried cream and egg sauce. Supposed to get the old passions going. Does it?'

She blushed and looked down at her plate. It was certainly making her inhibitions fade. They had barely started, it seemed. As successive courses appeared, Blodwen was thankful that each was served in small quantities. It was a delightful way to eat, but obviously fiendishly expensive. *Côtelette de volaille Maréchale* came next. This was a small piece of chicken breast, egged and crumbed then fried in butter, garnished with sliced truffle and buttered asparagus tips. As an alternative she was offered *noisette d'agneau Rachel*, a lamb cutlet set on an artichoke heart and garnished with bone marrow.

Charlie ate that while she dealt with the chicken. To her amazement, there was more: boned quails cooked in a casserole with wine and peeled grapes, then a *foie gras parfait* — a sort of *fois gras* gâteau. The pudding was a triumph — *pêches Adrienne*, a combination of ripe peaches, wild strawberry ice cream and meringues, coated with curacao mousse and topped wtih crystallised rose petals and spun sugar. As Charlie explained the ingredients, Blodwen was seized by a desire to giggle hysterically at the thought that a week ago she had tasted strawberries and cream for the first time. They drank champagne throughout the meal but much as she loved it, she had the sense to drink very sparingly. She noticed that Charlie did not over-indulge either, although she was not experienced enough to realise why. After two glorious hours of self-indulgence, they moved on to the Hippodrome for the last house of the night's music hall.

A pretty little redhead called Maidie Scott was twinkling away as they took their seats:

> 'For you don't know Nellie like I do,
> Said the naughty little bird on Nellie's hat!'

The audience loved her, and she was a very attractive artist, her voice full of inoffensive ribaldry. Maidie sang a run of popular hit songs, including 'Champagne Charlie', which delighted Blodwen as being particularly appropriate. Her act was followed by knockabout clowns, a superb juggler and a team of acrobats. But Charlie, a seasoned music hall veteran, had come for the top of the bill – Marie Lloyd.

'Welsh name, but as cockney as Bow Bells and really magnificent,' he said. 'She can say more with a wiggle of one eyebrow that that little Scott girl could with the whole of her body!'

Blodwen, taken with Maidie, was sceptical until she saw the queen of music hall. Marie Lloyd romped through her act, singing each of the songs she had made into family favourites as if for the first time. She closed the show with an immortal which always held a place in Blodwen's heart long after she had forgotten what Charlie Kerslake looked like – 'The Boy I Love is Up in the Gallery'. Blodwen sat, moved to tears in spite of herself, as the buxom middle-aged star raised her arms and her voice, embraced her people, the gallery audience, and told them she loved them in a way that only she could. Even Charlie brushed the back of his hand across his eyes as the star finished, to tumultuous applause. Charlie was, in spite of his many failings, a natural seducer. He had a knack of serving up exactly the things his victims found attractive and of holding himself in check until they were most vulnerable. Unfortunately, having possessed them he had little sense of the proper behaviour. In fact he was a cad.

Blodwen left the music hall with him on a cloud of euphoria. She had dined like a queen, been entertained by the best in the land, and was staying in the most luxurious hotel she had ever seen. She was ripe for the plucking. Back in their suite, champagne was waiting in an ice bucket. Subdued lamps gave the bedroom a romantic glow. She sipped a flute of wine then drifted into the bathroom and changed into the gorgeous *peignoir* which she had made for herself.

She rejoined Charlie. He rose, gazing at her with undisguised pleasure. 'Good God, you really are beautiful! Who ever said brown hair was dull?'

Her hair spread down her back in a glowing, flowing curtain, which could have been designed to make men fantasise about wrapping themselves in it. Charlie moved forward and bent to kiss her, a long leisurely caress, deepening to excitement as the feel and smell of her took him over. Ask Blodwen's own sexuality began to colour her judgment, she reached vainly for the shreds of her earlier resolve. As him, ask him now, her fading childish self whispered. As he drew her into the bedroom, she made a last attempt.

'Charlie – you haven't said anything yet about when we get married . . .'

He stopped in his tracks. 'When we *what*?'

'Get married, Charlie. We are going to, aren't we?'

To her mortification, he roared with laughter. 'Married? You and me? Look, Blodwen, you're a beautiful girl. You make me want to do all sorts of things to you for a very long time, but marriage is not one of them. Now come on, into bed. I want to undress and get to know you better.'

He patted her backside and pushed her gently towards the big bed. For some reason the gesture maddened her enough to make her persist. 'Well I want to get to know you better too – but only if we're getting married!'

He was becoming exasperated. 'Blodwen, I didn't want to spell this out but you're making me. You're a lovely girl but you're my sister-in-law's dressmaker, for God's sake! I'd be a laughing stock if we were married.

'You can't have thought that's what I had in mind . . . it must have been clear that I was looking for a bit of fun and I thought you were, too.'

Charlie began to take his clothes off.

'You can stop doing that, Charlie Kerslake, and go and do it in the other room. I may be only a servant but I'm also only sixteen years old. Of course I didn't know what you had in your mind. I still don't, apart from you wanting to mess about with me, but I know that decent women don't unless they're married and that it's serious enough for me to lose my job damned quick when your bloody precious sister-in-law realises where I am.

'D'you think the other servants'll keep quiet for five minutes after she comes back about seeing us drive off in a cab together? I may be ignorant, but it's marriage or nothing. Now are you getting out into that sitting room or am I?'

She was too angry to realise that his face had once more taken on the flat, unfeeling expression she had seen in her room back in Cardiff. As he stepped towards her she realised that she no longer had any say in what was happening.

'Are you trying to tell me what to do, you little bitch?' The quiet tone was at variance with what he was saying. She began to back away. He followed her, step for step.

'Charlie, please. You can't force me – I don't even understand what it is you want to do. Please let me be!'

He laughed – again with minimal expression. 'Don't worry, you'll learn soon enough. And by Christ you'll like it, or I'll know the reason why!'

He lunged forward towards her as she turned to evade him. The ribbon on her negligée untied and pulled aside to reveal an equally silky nightgown beneath. Charlie seized a handful of fine silk and pulled. The tiny stitches parted and the gown fell away, revealing Blodwen's smooth, slender body. Her hands jerked upward involuntarily to cover her nakedness.

'Don't do that, little girl – it's a waste of time,' he said, with a chuckle that made her shiver. Then he reached forward and pinioned her arms without any difficulty. She gasped with fright at his strength.

'Let me go! Let me go or I'll scream so loud that everyone in the hotel will come!'

He laughed again. 'You're my wife, remember? Men can do what they like with their wives. Reasonable chastisement and all that . . . If you were just a whore someone might do something. What a shame!'

Holding her easily with one arm, he stripped the torn

gown away with the other. 'Oh, I'm going to enjoy this. There's nothing like a bit of resistance!'

He dragged her across the room and threw her on to the bed, holding her again with one arm while he loosened and removed his trousers. She was lying, panic-sticken, sideways on the bed. As he kicked away his trousers and underpants, she gave a little cry of fear.

Charlie laughed mirthlessly. 'What's the matter? Never seen anything like that before?'

Staring at his huge erection, she shook her head. 'Wait till you see what I can do with it. You'll be clamouring for more!'

He threw himself down on her, pinning her against the soft eiderdown. She struggled hard but his weight and excitement were too much for her. Charlie twisted her face towards his and clamped his mouth over her soft lips. His tongue forced its way between her teeth and he loosened his grip on her arms to fondle her breasts. It did not help her to escape because the weight of his big body kept her prisoner. Her wriggling only seemed to excite him even more. As his hands worked over her, she began to feel excitement mingling with her terror and resentment. Her nipples hardened like little arrowheads beneath his questing fingers and she felt waves of moist heat spreading outwards between her thighs. Blodwen began to relax and his hands slid inside her. She uttered a little moan of pleasure and relaxed completely.

'Like that, do you? Better than the coal boys used to do to you?'

His brutality snapped her back to reality. 'Get off me, you swine! Let me be!'

He drew back and fetched her a ringing open-handed slap across the face. 'Behave, you little tart. I'm having you any way I like and the sooner you decide to lie back and enjoy it the better!'

Charlie bent over her once more, biting at her soft body, thrusting his hands and lips all over her until she had no idea what was happening to her. Vaguely she began to realise that whatever he was doing was exciting her enough to make her resistance totally ineffectual. He was still half dressed and drew back from her momentarily to remove the rest of his cothes. She lay panting like a winded animal, staring up at him.

'Got you going, have I? Wait till you see what this can do!' He gestured at his hugely erect penis and began pressing it against her belly. 'God, that feels good! You should take this up for a living, you sexy little bitch. Wait till I get it into you – then you'll really go crazy.'

Later she reproached herself for the fact that she did just that. Through all his insults and sexual incitement, he was gradually keying her up to a point of excruciating expectation. Her whole body was shrieking for him and she felt her hands sliding down on to his penis as if they were commanded by his will, not hers. Surprisingly it felt warm, firm and exciting, not the hideous weapon that it appeared. She began to guide it towards her, moaning gently.

'That's a good girl. Can't get enough already, can you? We'll be at it all night at this rate!'

He knelt over her, spreading her legs, and started to enter her. She gave a little cry of pain. It only heightened his pleasure and he pushed himself into her with some force. At first the pain of his entry drove off her passion, but the tension quickly returned and suddenly her world seemed to collapse on itself. A huge spasm shook her and she heard her own voice calling out as if it belonged to someone else. She felt a similar wave sweep through Charlie's body. He slumped against her, but she was too spent to notice his weight or to care about it.

Charlie was an energetic and reasonably talented lover. Blodwen, having discovered the pleasures of sex, was enthusiastic. The night passed quickly and passionately and they slept late into the morning. They ate a huge breakfast with the relish of healthy young animals, then checked out of the hotel and moved on to Weston-Super-Mare. By now Blodwen was resolutely refusing to contemplate what might happen beyond tomorrow and concentrating on the moment's excitement. She relished her stroll along the sunny seafront in her elegant summer frock. When they returned to the hotel to change for dinner, he undressed her, carried her giggling to the large bath and climbed in with her. There they drank champagne together and eventually tottered down to the restaurant, slightly tipsy and just a little damp. By the time they had finished a dinner which was princely without competing with that of the night before, Blodwen was half-way to believing that this would go on for ever because they were getting on so well. They returned to their love-making in the soft summer night and she drifted off to sleep on a pillow of romantic clichés. Sunday passed in much the same way.

She realised she had made a fatal mistake when she woke up alone on the Monday morning. On the dressing table were six five-pound notes and a few lines scrawled on a used envelope:

> *Forgot to tell you I'm due to rejoin the regiment today. Didn't want to disturb you so I've paid the bill and left you a little spending money. Hope there's no trouble from Jean! See you soon,*
>
> Champagne Charlie

Champagne Charlie – more like Cider Apple Charlie, she thought, furious at having been caught out so easily. But she came from a tough background with little time for regrets, and knew better than to moon over the loss of a great love. Rage was all that remained. When her anger subsided somewhat, though, it was replaced by anxiety and mounting fear. Going off with Charles for the week-end, she had innocently assumed it was the preliminary to the marriage of her dreams. He had soon rooted out that idea, but nevertheless, in departing from Park Place she had thought never to return as a servant. Now she was fairly sure she would never be permitted to return at all, as servant or anything else.

She was not completely without resources. Always unsure of Jean Kerslake's moods, she had persuaded Madame Antoinette to provide her with a glowing testimonial on completion of her initial dressmaking training period, and she still treasured it. In fact Madame had repeated her offer of a top hand's job a couple of weeks ago. Had it not been for Charlie's presence in Park Place, Blodwen would have accepted immediately. Even if she chose not to go back to Madame Antoinette now, with the reference and the ability to demonstrate her talent, she need never be without work. But how on earth did she get started? The wide world was completely unknown to her. Until now, someone had always told her what to do and where to go. From today she was on her own. At that point, exhilaration began to replace the fear. After all, £30 was more than a year's wages! She was sixteen years old, pretty and talented and had just acquired a large chunk of worldly wisdom.

Years later, when she knew how lucky she had been not to become pregnant that week-end, she was apt to wince at just how naive the young Blodwen still was. But at least ignorance had spared her a month of terrified waiting before setting out on an untrammelled future. Taking her time to bathe and dress, she contemplated her next move. South Wales was the only destination in her mind initially, but she reflected that it might not be the best place to work with Jean Kerslake anywhere nearby. She had seen middle-class matrons accomplish the summary dismissal of skilled hands at Madame Antoinette's. Madame did not like to take such action, but when it was the employee or the customer, the employee had to go. Blodwen could not afford to risk that fate.

She checked out of the hotel without having reached any firm decision, travelled into Bristol and strolled leisurely around the shops but lacked the confidence to have lunch alone in public. As she entered the mock-Gothic splendours of Bristol Temple Meads railway station towards the end of the morning, it occurred to Blodwen that she had been looking for her future in the wrong direction. If she turned east instead of west, the blissful anonymity of London beckoned her, offering work, advancement and a completely new life. Starting as she meant to continue, the unemployed seamstress bought herself a first-class single ticket to Paddington and shook the dust of Wales from her feet for ever.

She was to learn that nothing is ever as clear-cut as one sees it at sixteen. The wartime mass exodus from the service industries to munitions had robbed the great department stores of much of their work force. Blodwen sat in a refreshment room at Paddington Station with an evening newspaper open at the employment columns and sighed with relief as she saw the number of vacancies which existed. She marked four with a blue pencil, then left to find somewhere to stay. 'Somewhere' was a drab but respectable establishment which proclaimed itself as offering comfortable accommodation for single women. The interminable rules against admission of male visitors convinced her that the hotel was utterly safe and the charges were modest. The decor made her want to weep but she consoled herself that she would find a permanent, more cheerful home as soon as she had a job.

Blodwen's first job enquiry produced an offer of employment at a wage which would have made her feel rich in Cardiff. Here in London she realised she would need every penny if she was to do anything beyond barely surviving. The floor manager in the evening gown department of an exclusive store interviewed her. He looked approvingly at her immaculate clothes and smart hairstyle. She had taken the precaution of adding four years to her age to raise her earning potential.

'Your experience appears somewhat limited, Miss Williams,' said the manager. 'One job hardly qualifies you as a senior *vendeuse*.'

She smiled with a confidence she was far from feeling.

'If you put my coat and skirt on sale here, what price would you ask?' she said, with apparently perfect self-assurance.

He was taken aback, but became interested and offered an assessment. 'I'd place it in Tailored Costumes, and if I could obtain the gabardine to make it with the war on, I would say it would cost about six guineas. Are you suggesting that you got a bargain and therefore that you know how to select and sell garments?'

'Hardly. Plenty of women could do that. No – I made the costume myself for less than two guineas.' Sitting back to enjoy his amazement, she refrained from telling him it had actually cost her nothing because Madame had given her the material from a cancelled consignment.

'You made that, and you're applying for a post as saleswoman rather than setting up as a tailoress?' he was puzzled.

'No mystery, Mr Travers. I wanted to come to London. I could have had a little business in South Wales but I want to live in the big city. I used all my savings to come here and look for a job, so I haven't got anything left to start my own business.'

He had already read her reference and heard the tale she had concocted about being a sort of family retainer to the Kerslakes. Her latest story convinced him that she was offering too good an opportunity to miss.

'Very well, Miss Williams, we'll give you a start. It's most unusual for someone as young as you to hold a position of such responsibility, but we shall see how you manage.'

Damned liar, thought Blodwen during her first week. Although she was the only new member of staff at senior *vendeuse* level, the store was taking on very young and inexperienced sales assistants and grateful to get anyone in face of the competition presented by factory work. Still, Blodwen was earning more and enjoying a higher status than she would ever have thought possible.

With her earnings and the back-up of the remainder of Charlie's £30 she was able to find herself comfortable rented rooms and equip them for sewing as well as living. Hammersmith was hardly glamorous, but she was able to paint and paper her rooms in cheerful colours and soon made a bright little nest for herself. Her name was becoming a nuisance. Colleagues at the store smiled patronisingly when told what the initial B signified and she heard at least one of them refer to her sneeringly as Blod from the Valleys. She toyed with the thought of a change for some time but baulked at dealing with the inevitable mockery from her business associates. A new romantic involvement solved her dilemma.

One Saturday afternoon she had used the opportunity of early closing at the store to visit a textile exhibition at the Victoria and Albert Museum in South Kensington. Afterwards, in the busy tea room, she was politely but firmly picked up by a strikingly handsome army officer who asked to share her table. For the first time, she introduced herself as Louise. Williams seemed too commonplace a surname and on the spur of the moment, she borrowed Charlie's, the first distinguished name that came to mind. The name was hers for life.

Harold Gill was a gentle Warwickshire farmer torn away from his wife in the Midlands and transplanted to the blood and mud of Flanders as were so many of his generation, with an officer's rank which these days seemed to be a death sentence. He was not interested in the frenetic pursuit of champagne and chorus girls which some of his fellow officers chose as an antidote to panic. Instead he was attempting to see as many beautiful and rare objects as possible to keep the horrors of the Front at bay for at least a little while.

'Whatever possessed you to talk to me like that when we met?' he asked her later.

She laughed. 'Probably the uniform. We're all told how wonderful our fighting men are and what a rough time they're having that it makes you feel like a traitor if you snub a soldier.'

She knew him a lot longer before she was able to admit that girls of her class were so schooled to obey their social superiors that the mere sight of an officer's uniform had been enough to ensure her respectful attention. Louise was now seventeen years old. Unable to dissemble with Harold, she admitted that she was years younger than her employers thought. That was when he confessed that he was a married man. They were dining together at the Piccadilly Hotel, a solidly comfortable establishment that made the battlefields seem as remote as the stars. Harold was gazing at her in open admiration.

'Would I be intruding on private grief if I asked how such a lovely girl had remained unmarried? Have you lost a sweetheart at the Front?'

Louise laughed. 'Give me a chance to grow up! I was seventeen last week.'

He was aghast. 'But you seem so mature, so adult. My God, what am I doing? You're only a child!'

She was concerned at his obvious distress, and puzzled too.

'Harold, I came out with you because I wanted to. We're in a respectable public place, dining together. What's so awful about that?'

'If I'd told you at the beginning, you wouldn't be dining with me. I – I'm married.'

'Is that all? D'you think it likely that a man with your looks would be running around unattached?'

''Then you don't mind?' He was obviously not altogether pleased.

'Of course I mind, but I like your company and even at seventeen I've done enough living of my own to know you have to take every chance you get. It's no good waiting for a perfect man or you never live at all!'

He sighed. 'You know, Dorothea, my wife, is twenty-six and she hasn't the insight or experience to understand that.'

Neither would I if you were my husband and I heard you were out taking what chance had to offer in the Piccadilly Hotel with a pretty girl, thought Louise. Aloud, she said: 'Some women have to grow up far earlier than others. I've been looking after myself for a very long time.'

'I'd like to change that for you, Louise.'

She smiled at him with genuine tenderness. 'It's a kind thought, but think before you talk. You are a soldier and you're in one of the most dangerous places on the whole Front. How can I possibly ask you to add me to your list of worries? And if you do get through that unhurt, you'll be coming back to Dorothea when it all ends. It would be silly of me to expect anything from you. Your life is already mapped out for you. I'm just a little bit on the side.'

'Don't say that – not ever! You insult me and you insult yourself even more! I've never done what I did today before. I always thought the men who did that sort of thing led shallow, empty lives. But somehow I simply couldn't pass your table without speaking to you. There was something about you that I couldn't bear to lose, and I'm never going to let you go now that I've found you.'

She stifled an urge to weep. This man had known her only a few hours and he was talking as though she were the great love of his life! Louise attempted to be sensible. Her experience with Charles Kerslake was enough to convince her that she was no good judge of men. But instinct told her that this man was different and that he meant what he said, however unlikely it might seem. She decided that an honest reaction was the best one.

'I don't know quite how we go on from here. We met this afternoon and now we're talking to each other as if it was the night of our wedding. Perhaps it would be better if we finished our dinner and then you found a cab for me and we said goodbye.'

'Perhaps it would. Or perhaps this is the one time you really should take a chance. All I can promise is that I shall try with all my might to see you don't suffer because of me.'

He turned and picked up the large menu. 'Now, let's let such serious matters take care of themselves for a while and enjoy a good dinner. Time enough for you to tell me what happens to us in future after our lovely evening!'

It said much for their compatibility and pleasure in each other's company that they were able to pass the time very pleasantly without the inevitable consequences intruding. Louise had never been treated as an equal by a gentleman and now she felt infinitely flattered that it was happening. Charles had behaved as though she was a sort of superior tart – a good companion but in a sense a commodity to be bought, enjoyed and set aside. Harold made it clear that he found her desirable, but he was also interested in what interested her. He wanted to know about her mind as well as her body. He was fascinated by the idea of a young woman being completely alone and surviving without support from family or husband.

'But don't you ever miss having someone to rely on, someone to turn to when you have troubles?'

For the first time she felt impatient with him. 'Of course I do, but who ever volunteered to take care of someone like me? My father was always drunk or too idle to care; my mother just wanted to sell me off to the highest bidder who had a respectable use for me; my employer wanted to get as much out of me as possible for as little money as she had to part with. Which of them d'you think would have looked after me when I was in trouble?

'I was a good girl' – she laughed at the irony of the expression – 'I never knew what bad girls did. But that didn't save me. Your womenfolk would say I was "ruined" by a man, but in fact the man was one of them, one of the respectable folk who should know better. If they ever found out what happened to me I'm sure they'll have said that he was being young and high-spirited, where I was nothing but a scheming little minx who led him on. He was six or seven years older than me but they always manage to behave as if a sixteen-year-old girl should be more grown up than a twenty-two-year-old man – if the girl is a servant, that is. If she's from a good family then it's different. Then they call the man a cad!'

Louise was flushed with anger at the injustice of it all. She had never spoken to anyone of her treatment at Charlie's hands and had not realised until now how ill-used she felt. The Valleys Welsh accent, carefully ironed out of her normal speech, popped out and her soft voice reverted to its natural delicious sing-song. Although he was moved by what she was saying, Harold was totally captivated by the girl's look and sound. He could now see that she was as young as she had told him – little more than a child who had been forced to take on the trappings of adulthood. Impulsively, he broke the promise he had made to himself not to try and influence her. He leaned across the table and covered her small, work-hardened hands with his big one.

'I think it's time someone protected you and showed you that some gentlemen don't behave like the villain in a bad romance.'

She sat very still, looking down at his hand on hers, then up into his eyes.

'Just one thing, Harold. If you think you're ever going to have to lie to me, get up now and let's say goodbye. I may be young but I'm old enough to know I don't want liars around me. If we are staying together you must tell me the truth – always.'

'I promise, Louise. You may not always want the truth, though.'

'I'd rather live with unwanted truth than with nice lies.'

He called for the bill and went home to Hammersmith with her.

CHAPTER FIVE

Since 1914 the war had been little more than background to Louise's growing up. Charles Kerslake was the only serving soldier she had known and he had made it clear that his contacts assured him of a safe job well clear of the Flanders mincing machine. She had seen the stark headlines in the newspapers and read the strident propaganda of the recruitment posters, but somehow it all seemed remoter than one of her romantic novels, living as she did in an area where many men remained in the mines rather than enlisting as soldiers. Suddenly the conflict was of consuming interest. Harold Gill gave her any number of reasons to care what was happening on the Western Front.

He was on a two-week furlough after a series of long and bloody engagements. He had travelled back to Warwickshire expecting to recover in peace from the hell he had left but his wife was unequal to the strain of prolonged absences interspersed with short visits home. He had problems, too. Flanders was his world now and his wife seemed to be wrapped in unreality. He was spiritually incapable of touching her any more and her physical proximity became harder to bear by the minute. The atmosphere at the farm was so bad that after two days he had a blazing row with her and caught the first train to London, uncertain of what he would do with the rest of his leave. He had just finished an attempt to recapture some peace among the art treasures of the museum when he encountered Louise. Now he sank gratefully into the easy chair before the fire in her Hammersmith apartment.

'This feels more like home than the farm!'

She was apologetic. 'It must seem terribly plain after what you're used to.'

'Believe me, my dear, I've never been more content!'

Louise, at a loss to know how one entertained a man in the privacy of home, bustled into the kitchen and made tea. When she returned with it, he laughed.

'What's the matter? Have I done something wrong?' She was defensive.

'No, no – quite the reverse! I can't really imagine a professional seductress taking a man home after dinner for a cup of tea, that's all!'

She began to react angrily at the implication that she might have been a professional seductress, but good sense prevailed when she reminded herself that 'nice' girls most certainly didn't entertain married men alone, particularly so late at night. Louise returned his smile and sat down opposite him.

'I suppose I don't fit in to any normal picture of what girls are like,' she said, 'because I don't really know myself. There was never anybody to tell me.'

Harold remembered her forlorn little speech about no one looking after her and understood. She had to feel her way in each relationship, learning by luck or error. The sooner he started fending for her, the better. He talked to her about trivial subjects, content to absorb the quiet atmosphere of the little flat as he did so.

She watched him cautiously, her encounter with Charlie very much in mind, wondering when Harold would leap at her and start tearing off her clothes. He, in turn, began wondering after a while how he could decently embark on a sexual encounter with a girl he had treated as a friend since the moment they met. The longer they talked, the less likely it seemed, and he was seriously considering saying goodnight when she solved the problem for him. Putting down her cup, she moved across to him and held out her hand.

'Don't you think we've said enough for now?'

He rose, slipped his arm around her waist, and went with her into the warm little bedroom. Charlie Kerslake had changed from a boisterous schoolboy to a beast of prey when the prospect of sex had been raised. Louise waited apprehensively for a similar transformation in Harold. It did not occur. Closing the bedroom door behind them, he turned to embrace her, tilting her chin with his fingers so that his first kiss softly enclosed her lips. The gentleness of his approach disarmed her. She swayed against him with a sigh and he moved across to the bed with her dreamily following.

'Oh, dear, Harold – how do they make this bit romantic? I'll have to take off my corset!'

'I could always take it off for you, I might even enjoy it!'

Like two children at a new game, they unhooked and unthreaded her complicated underclothes. As his fingers touched the silky fabric and silkier skin his excitement grew and communicated itself to her. Still fully dressed, he finally stood back and looked at her, naked in the lamplight, as if she were a particularly exciting work of art.

'You're perfect,' he murmured, 'absolutely perfect! I could look at you for ever!'

After a few moments of stillness, she slipped into the big brass bed and waited for him to undress. As he did so, he talked to her, matter-of-factly, as if they had always been together.

'I've never really looked at a woman in the flesh like that. Dorothea always undresses in another room and puts on huge nightgowns,' he told her. 'It's odd, because she enjoys making love. Just gets nervous at the idea of being seen without clothes, as though they were her armour or something.'

Louise wondered how his wife could feel uncomfortable or awkward with Harold. Of all men, he seemed the one most likely to put any woman at her ease. Then she set aside the speculation. She could hardly expect ever to understand the viewpoint of the one woman who would be her arch-rival if she ever learned of Louise's existence. All women need a Harold Gill after a Charles Kerslake. Louise's good fortune was to find one. He was no Don Juan and she was as much a guide to him in their loving as he was to her. But their night of touching, exploring and gentle laughter interspersed with passion tied her to him more permanently than any moments of satisfied lust with Charlie could have done.

The remainder of his leave passed in pure euphoria. The next day was Sunday, so she was able to be with him. They went for a walk beside the Thames in the crisp spring sunshine and sat on a terrace beside Hammersmith Bridge for steak and kidney pudding and porter at lunchtime.

Their passion was mounting again by then and they hurried back to the flat, breathless and laughing, to make love throughout the afternoon. Hunger coaxed them out once more that evening. 'Only the Savoy will do,' Harold announced grandly. 'Let's treat it as a wedding breakfast!'

By the end of the evening they were forced to consider the following few days. Louise had not worked at the store long enough to be entitled to holidays before the summer, but already they were both conscious that they had only ten days left before Harold returned to France. Louise went in on the Monday and spent most of her time glancing furtively at the clock. The time dragged and she was conscious every moment that Harold was alone somewhere. When she finally got away and travelled home on the Piccadilly Line in the evening crush, she entered an unrecognisable flat. The living room had been turned into a cave of flowers, with every conceivable species of spring blossom crowding together in a splendour of scented freshness. To complete the picture, a bowl of perfect fruit on the table begged to be consumed. Louise found Harold in the kitchen, where a bottle of champagne was cooling in the sink and he was just finishing putting out a mind-boggling range of Harrod's delicacies on her cheap chain store plates.

'Harold, that's the first time anyone ever got me a present! And it's all so wonderful – you are a love!'

'Present? Nonsense – just a bunch of flowers and a bite of supper. Here's the present!'

He handed over a chunky jeweller's case. She opened it, to discover a plain gold wedding ring and a lovely diamond and emerald engagement ring. Speechless, she looked up at him.

'You know it has to be a pretence, but in my mind I mean it,' he said. 'It doesn't feel like just a few days since we met and now I never want to be without you again. Please wear them for me. They are the real thing, if that matters.'

Silently, Louise put the rings on the third finger of her left hand, then moved across to kiss him. He drew her down on to his knee.

'Even with all my shopping activity, I've missed you dreadfully today,' he said. 'I have a proposal which I hope you'll agree to. You are a highly-skilled dressmaker. Now is the time to leave your job and set up alone. Advertise in the newspapers; don't expect to make a living wage at first. Eventually you'll be very successful. I'll see that you don't starve while you're becoming established.'

'But I earn twenty five shillings a week – you can't make that up for me and find the money for me to advertise!' Louise was horrified at the mere idea.

'Darling, I don't know whether the fact that I'm a farmer misled you, but it's quite a big farm,' said Harold. 'My father was Sir George Gill, the biscuit king. When he died my elder brother Jeffrey got the biscuit business and I got the estate – all ten thousand acres of it. I assure you I can afford to get you started!'

She never went back to her job. Next day she wrote a letter saying that owing to a change in family circumstances, she was unable to continue working at the store. Harold posted the letter and then bore her off for a week of pure pleasure before letting her start to think about the new business venture. He was careful about ensuring her material well-being if anything happened to him. Before returning to France, he contacted his stockbroker, took advice about a range of safe stocks and had a small portfolio set up in her name. It guaranteed her an income of at least £100 a year and they were both aware that if he were killed next week she had a measure of security.

Then, suddenly, he was a uniformed stranger preparing to leave for Victoria Station en route for France and Louise began to understand what war meant to those who waited at home. She had been out getting a few small things for him to take away with him, but something made her change her plans and return early to Hammersmith. She arrived to find his kit bag beside the front door, obviously ready for departure. Louise dashed inside, calling his name. She found him in the bedroom, where he had clearly just left a letter for her. Harold faced her, resignation, embarrassment and relief mixing almost comically on his face.

'I . . . I thought it would be less painful for you if I just went before you got back,' he said. 'But I wanted to see you again so badly that I hung around a bit —' he brightened '— and you came back!'

Louise chided him gently for trying to disappear so unobtrusively, but she knew he had been thinking of her and could not be harsh with him.

Eventually she went with him to the station and waved until his train had disappeared from view.

Louise kept his letters close enough to read periodically until she was a very old woman. Then she parcelled them up and lodged them with her solicitor, along with her will and instructions that they should be cremated with her.

BEF

April 30, 1917

Dearest Lou

The sun shines, the air is warm and bright and the skylarks sing and toss about the sky. And beneath them is the landscape of the moon as seen by Hieronymus Bosch. Incidentally the larks are here only because there are few Frenchmen in this sector. All over France it is 'le sport' to shoot the little birds, but here we are all English or German and either we are terrible shots or we are so sick of killing that we leave the birds to sing in peace. They are so normal that it makes the landscape even more insane than it would seem otherwise.

We are recommended to use a strange device to minimise the risk of injury if we are attacked by night. We dig a little ditch inside our tents and within the ditch we set up our camp beds. As a result we lie at ground level but clear of the ground. It is supposed to give our frail bodies a chance of surviving the shock of a hit. I leave you to decide how likely that is!

I did not expect more than the odd quick trip to Paris before the end of summer, but I must have pleased someone, somewhere Up There, because it looks as though I shall get to London for a few days in late May. Don't rely on it, my dear, but perhaps we shall go boating on the Serpentine after all!

The medics have been looking into the exact nature of lousiness. You learn ten minutes after arrival that the louse is no respecter of persons – he jumps alike on rich and poor man! It seems that the average level is twenty lice per man, but some poor devils harbour as many as three hundred. Clean shirts are re-infested within two days. It throws a pretty grim light on our normal conditions to think that we regard a shirt as still being clean after two days!

Enough of this squalor! I'm thinking a lot about you and our future, reading a great deal and concentrating on looking up at those skylarks. Remember your heart is my prisoner!

My love, for ever. Hal

He wrote vivid, articulate letters, full of tantalising details which mystified her. Who was Hieronymus Bosch? She found out and her exploration of the Flemish master's work told her more about what Harold was seeing on the battlefield than chapters of purple prose. Louise became increasingly conscious of the depth of his education and the lack of her own. In the lengthening summer evenings, as she stitched away at the frocks which were beginning to be ordered at last, she started to teach herself about the world about her and about the past, all with a view to sharing experience and interests with Harold when the slaughter was over. Somehow she was able to keep her fears for his safety in a separate pocket. They woke her in the middle of the night, drenched with sweat at the thought of him lying smashed in a mud-filled trench somewhere. He will survive, he will! she told herself. I must be able to give him back just a little of what he's giving me! In the morning, she pushed the black monsters away and determinedly went on sewing, learning and exploring London.

Wheels were turning that were unstoppable. The French had attacked to end the war on April 16. The Nivelle assault failed and the French army mutinied, but among the British leadership only General Haig knew. And he kept that deadly secret to himself when he pressed for a massive new attack on the Ypres Salient, an attack that could hope to succeed only with equally strong French back-up. On May 13 Haig took control from General Plumer, a realist with no illusions about what could be achieved. On June 2 Marshal Petain told Haig that the French could not provide the backing he needed. On June 7 Haig began his attack.

BEF
June 9, 1917
Dearest Lou
One day the historians will say that Messines was fought in just one day. It's a lie. The sappers had been mining under the Wytschaete Ridge for months in advance. Heavy artillery in huge concentrations had been brought up behind the lines, and tanks were assigned to go in over enemy lines once they'd been breached. The preliminary bombardment went on for seven days and nights and that was almost as wearing on us as it was on the Germans. They were locked in their tunnels and trenches though and not even food could be got in to them.

Just before the battle it became quieter. At one point our forward batteries were silent for a while and all you could hear was the hiss of the German gas shells and somewhere a cockerel crowing to welcome the bloodiest day yet. Dawn was the signal for our guns to open fire and suddenly the whole sky was a sheet of red as flame went up from about twenty mines — great towers of shattered earth and smoke, all illumined by that flame, like some infernal firework display. The blast was so severe that many of us were thrown on the ground. There were dead Germans everywhere. The New Zealanders were through Messines in little more than an hour and we went in through Battle Wood just south of Zillebeke. The generals are filled with delight but oh, Louise, the death, both Germans and Allies! One cannot talk of victory after seeing what I saw — the first line of our advance blotted out, dead and wounded piled on each other's backs; the second wave coming up behind and clustering like so many sheep until they were knocked over in their tracks and just lay there, flailing about and trying to rise again . . . and we were the victors . . .

Afterwards, we listened to the tramp, tramp, tramp of our infantry going through . . . drooped shoulders, eyes bulging, faces unshaven, the snappy step replaced by a stagger. I was watching them with a sapper, who turned to me and said 'They keep tramping into the jaws of death. More crosses are erected and RIP is their only epitaph. It's more than the poor bastards could hope for in life, sir!'

I don't know how we all endure, but somehow we do. Remember I blithely thought I'd get a spot of leave late in May and it never came off? Well this time, it will. Seems they don't know quite what to do with us old hands for the moment. The pressure is on the New Army at present and we've been pulled back beyond the ruin of Vlamertinghe Church on the 'safe' side of Ypres.

Really I shouldn't write in tones of such despair — it's as though I'm reaching out to taint you with the foulness of these terrible trenches. But I have to tell you what it is like because someone back at home must know. We cannot go on letting our women and children believe that Flanders is like some grand contest between medieval knights. It's not like that at all. There is nobility, but not the nobility of Englishman against German. It's the nobility of Man against Death. Nothing else counts. Pray for me, my love. I have nothing to pray to any more.

Your loving Hal.

99

He came home for a week at the end of June, a dazzlingly sunny week when Louise felt more like a nurse than a lover. Throughout the first two nights he woke at intervals, weeping, alternately shivering and sweating. Soon, though, the quiet, the cleanliness and her love worked their magic. On the third day they were strolling in Kensington Gardens, watching the children sailing their model boats on the Round Pond.

'If I thought one of those little boys would have to grow up to see what I've seen this year, I'd sooner he died now,' said Harold. 'Still, I suppose the hope that none of them will have to fight is the only reason most of us go on with it.'

He was silent for the rest of their walk, but gradually Louise saw the pain and horror begin to recede and by the evening, when they attended an open-air concert, he seemed almost the man Louise had met in April. Harold stopped referring to the war and eventually she felt she had to ask him whether he was trying to shield her from its horrors.

'No – once I'm with you, I don't seem to need to talk about it. It's when we're apart and I can only write to you that I have to describe it. Otherwise I prefer just to enjoy your beauty and wholeness and pretend the rest happens to another Harold Gill. If I did anything else I think I'd go mad.'

Their parting the following Sunday afternoon was tranquil. Both of them were certain that this was not their last time together and they seemed to have made a silent agreement to act on that certainty. On July 31 he was among the thousands who were flung into the mud-bath of the Third Battle of Ypres. He went physically unscathed through Pilckem, Langemarck and the Menin Road. Louise sent him cheerful, loving letters in response to the stark descriptions of nightmare. She refrained from telling him that she was pregnant.

By the end of October the newspapers seemed to be saying just one word – Passchendaele. Harold was in the thick of the fighting. Early in the month she received letters that talked of mud so deep that mules and men drowned in it. Then there was unbroken silence. Louise learned to pray. Day and night she willed him to be alive and whole, but still no word came.

BEF
November 15, 1917

Dearest Lou
You must be insane with worry. Well cheer up – I appear to have got myself a blighty wound! One minute we were struggling up to our armpits through a great lake of mud beneath that benighted ridge. The next there was a mighty roar and I found myself clear of the mud – and of my boots! – and flying through the air. I landed in a very odd position upside down in a shell hole and there I stayed. My leg had snapped neatly across the shin as I landed, but otherwise no harm done. I'm now safely behind the lines in a hospital that's as clean as your lovely little flat, but not nearly as comfortable. They'll let me come back to England for convalescence and extended leave in a week or so. May I come to you?

I've thought this over very carefully and I haven't come to this decision lightly. Dorothea has become a stranger to me. I have had so little time with you and I don't know when this wretched war will end. They tell me my leg will not be ready for action again until the New Year and that means we can spend Christmas together. Dorothea was so upset by my presence on my last trip home that it will be no problem to convince her that it's best for me to stay away now. She'll pretend it's for my sake, but really it's her inability to live with the thought of war. Please say you'll have me! They're shipping me off to a convalescent home near Windsor for two weeks. Come and see me as Mrs Gill and I'm sure they'll give you custody quick as a flash.

Your battered but faithful Hal.

Louise wept with gratitude at his deliverance, then sent off a letter which simply said

Dear Hal
Come home as quickly as you can

Your loving wife Lou.

'It was too clean a break, Lou. Unless I'm very lucky, the Huns are going to get another shot or two at me yet!'

Harold's tone was jovial but Louise knew him well enough now to realise he was trying to tell her what he feared without alarming her too much. She forced a smile.

'You'll never be back there before it all stops, darling! The whole country is turning against the war. It can't possibly go on for more than a couple of months and surely they won't be sending back men who are just getting over wounds.'

'I wish I shared your optimism. I never told you how lucky I was to be sent back here to convalesce. It was just that the break was a bit dirtier than I let on at the time. If it had been completely straightforward, they would have kept me at a field hospital in France. But even after a blighty wound, I've known of men declared fit on Monday in London, rejoin their regiments in Flanders on Wednesday and get blown to bits on Thursday. Some factory girl in Germany could be putting the finishing touches on a bullet with my name on it right at this moment.'

Louise shuddered at the thought and pulled the soft fat eiderdown higher over them. They were in the Hammersmith flat, still warm from lovemaking, but the thought of what awaited him outside chilled her to the heart. She had not thought a month ago that she would resent his speedy recovery, but she did. With every day his strength increased, so did her fears for his safety. She had even caught herself wishing that he had lost the leg, because then they could never have sent him back. As it was, he was due for a medical in the second week of January and they both knew that his time in London after that could be counted in days rather than weeks. They had managed to make a good Christmas, tucked into the little flat with its flower-strewn wallpaper the colour of spring sunshine. Cheerful fires crackled in the grate and for the first time Louise took pleasure in cooking competently. Their fragrant leg of pork, crowned with perfect crackling and followed by too much plum pudding and brandy sauce gave them an illusion, at least, of permanence, well-being and safety.

But by New Year's Eve there was an undercurrent of fear at the approach of the unthinkable. Louise's pregnancy was now obvious and seemed to emphasise their precarious situation. They laughed, drank champagne together and made love enthusiastically, but each was play-acting for the sake of the other. Ypres was very close. On January 10 Harold went for his medical. There was a dusting of dirty snow on the pavement where Louise awaited him. He emerged, trying to look jaunty.

'His Majesty's Forces will be pleased to receive their knight errant on January 15.' He smiled as he said it but his lips looked stiff with terror. From then until his departure, they clung to each other for reassurance, but none was to be had. On January 15, Louise waved him off from Victoria, something she had hoped never to do again. On the 16, she collapsed in the street and six hours later prematurely gave birth to a stillborn son in Hammersmith Hospital. Learning that there was no one at home to look after her, the obstetrician ordered that she remain in the ward until she was strong enough to manage alone. For a week Louise stared at the wall and answered monosyllabically when spoken to. Then she forced herself back to life's awful reality and wrote to Harold – a light, loving letter which made no mention of her loss. On the ninth day she discharged herself, in spite of the consultant's opposition. She refused to let letters mount up unanswered back at the flat.

There were no letters. She tried not to panic. He had been silent this long before. Probably there was a big push on and he was delirious with weariness in the trenches . . .

. . . Or dead in No Man's Land. No, God no! I've lost enough, not him, too! Louise's mind refused to accept the terrible possibility. She filled a hot water bottle and climbed wearily into the big brass bed where they had made love so often. Where they had made their lost son. Where they had said their last goodbye? The letter from Harold, when it arrived, was the last thing she wanted. He had written it immediately before returning to France and had deposited it with his solicitor.

Darling Lou

There is nothing I can write to comfort you. I can't even comfort myself. I don't want to die. I want to hold our newborn child. I want to acknowledge it as mine, and you as my wife. I'm just twenty-eight and I have so much to look forward to, but between me and our future lies that nightmare landscape, those guns and the certainty of death.

I wish I felt that I would be an exception, but we were both aware that Christmas was my last chance, weren't we? You made it precious beyond hope, Lou. You made my life worth dying for, but I wish I didn't have to die.

I have made provision of a kind for you; hopelessly inadequate when you look at my paper worth, but I know my people well enough to realise that if the family ever found out about you, they would move heaven and earth to see you received nothing from the estate. Were it not for this, you would inherit equally with Dorothea, for there is enough to keep both of you.

All I could come up with in the short term is my liquid assets, and with everything tied up in the land they are precious little. On the advice of the stockbroker and my lawyer, I have set aside enough capital for you to live while you have our child and for about a year after that. There's also enough to buy a modest house, either in Hammersmith or in the country if you prefer. Should you decide on the country, there will be sufficient income from the remaining funds which I have invested to enable you to live comfortably without working. In London it will be another matter; but then there is so much opportunity for talent such as yours that as long as you can rely on the basic

*security I've managed to provide, you will prosper, I am
sure.*

*All this talk of money, Lou, makes it seem as though I
do not care, but it's because I care so much that I must write
like this. Now I must say the most painful thing of all. You
have to let me go. As I write this letter you are still well
short of your eighteenth birthday. You cannot spend the rest
of your days with the memory of a dead man who was gone
before you had a chance to finish growing up. You gave my
life a joy and a glow I could never have known without you.
Now it's time for you to lock me away in your heart and
when another man comes into your life, as one surely will,
say goodbye to me and go to him. Our child will always be a
piece of me for you to cherish.*

*Goodnight, my Louise. My thoughts and love are with you
tonight and every night as long as I live. But I fear that will
be all too short a time.*

Your Hal.

Louise wondered how to end her life too. The papers from
the solicitor were scattered around Harold's last lines,
stained with her tears: an agreement to be signed taking
possession of the income and capital; a covering letter
asking whether she wished the firm to represent her interests in the future. Without Hal – and without even his
child for comfort – none of it seemed to matter. But her
character had been formed in a savage environment where
life ended unpredictably, without ceremony or justice.
Louise had learned early that it was self-neglect rather than
grief that killed people and she was too spirited to neglect
herself for long. In the end unlooked-for help cured her.
After reading the letter three times through endless tears,
she began to feel drowsy. Her head drooped; she slid down
in the farmhouse chair once beloved by Harold and
oblivion pulled her gently away from her tragedy. She
woke, cold and cramped, beside the dead fire. Only the
sunny flower sprays on the wallpaper held the February
night at bay. Louise shivered and moved to the bedroom,
taking the crumpled papers with her. For the next week

she stirred from the bedroom only to get tea, bread and honey. When the bread ran out she switched to biscuits, hardly caring what she ate or how infrequently.

A neighbour called eventually – a woman widowed early in the war who recognised the signs in someone else. Louise gratefully accepted the offer of shopping but refused company as politely as possible. She felt that she would never be ready to mix socially with humanity again, but even that changed. The war widow, Mrs Crawford, took charge half-way through the second week. When she knocked with a bag of shopping, she took one look at Louise's now skinny form and shadowed eyes and firmly pushed past her into the unheated inner hallway.

'I know it's none of my business, love, but you're obviously not up to looking after yourself at present and nobody else seems to be around.'

Louise began a weak protest, but it tailed off in face of the cheerful, stubborn little face which confronted her.

'Oh, look, you haven't even lit your fire. It's like the Arctic in here!'

'I – I stayed in bed. Wasn't really up to doing much.'

'No, silly girl. You should still be in the hospital. Never mind, you'll be all right with a bit of spoiling.'

Louise smiled – almost, it seemed, for the first time since Harold went back to Flanders. 'No one ever spoiled me except him.'

'I know, love, I was an orphan when I met my Ronnie. In service, I was, with a rotten couple who chivvied me from pillar to post. When he come and talked to me as though I really counted for something, I thought he was talking to someone else for a minute. Even when we'd been married ten years it still surprised me sometimes, but it was lovely while it lasted!'

Mrs Crawford dumped her shopping bag, took out a large cotton pinafore, put it on and set to work. An hour later there were fires in the living room and bedroom, clean sheets on the bed and Louise was propped up against a mound of pillows giving her attention to a tray of boiled eggs, fresh bread and butter and piping hot tea. To her own considerable surprise, she finished it all and asked for more bread and butter. Her neighbour stayed and chattered, not about trivia but about the mechanics of grief, the compensatory joys of having been loved and what the world outside was doing during Louise's withdrawal. They became real friends and as the grim days of February softened into March, Louise accepted that she would live again without Harold and the baby. When she felt able to face it, she went with Edna Crawford to see the solicitor. He told her about the circumstances of Harold's death – a burst of machine gun fire in a charge – and gave her details of where her lover had been buried.

'Go there when it's all over,' Edna told her. 'My Ronnie copped his on the Somme. I'm going there when the silly buggers have had their fill of killing. Just going to say goodbye; satisfy myself they done right by him. Then I can start again.'

'Just like that, Edna? You'll be able to close a door on that life and go on to something else as if it had never happened?'

'Don't be bloody daft – it's only because of that life that I'll be able to start again. How could a little ex-skivvy get going running a shop and cheeking all the reps if she hadn't had Ronnie to show her how? He'll never go from me and neither will your Harold go from you. He turned you into a lady, girl, and don't you forget it! You owe it to him to use what he taught you and be better for it. Otherwise he really will have gone in vain!'

Edna Crawford ran a grocery business a couple of doors from Louise's flat. In peacetime Ronnie had been the boss, talking to the tradesmen and buying the supplies, and Edna had served the customers and set up the deliveries. They had made a good team – enjoyed themselves too much to care a lot when children failed to come along. But part of that teamwork had involved Ronnie teaching Edna his side of the business and once she had coped with losing him, she found she could run the shop herself as competently as once they had done together. She was training up a local lad to work for her, so that she had time for herself when she wanted it. Now she was concentrating on putting together a new life. She absorbed Louise into it all without a ripple; and Louise, in time, recovered.

Some of Edna's customers were the local professionals – lawyers, doctors and mid-level civil servants. They ate well and their wives liked to dress well. When Louise had recovered sufficiently to begin getting bored, the shopkeeper started recommending her to make clothes for them. The business began to flourish modestly and eventually Louise broke into the outer fringes of Society, when the well-connected wife of a local doctor passed on her name to a Belgravia cousin. It was the first major move towards achievement of her amibition to become a *couturière*. The spring was followed by a glorious summer. Everyone was weary of the war. There had simply been too many deaths. The world had changed beyond recognition but as long as the now impoverished giants wrestled in the Flanders mud, the survivors were unable to fashion a new order to replace the old.

When it all eventually ended in November, there was a momentary air of anticlimax. Louise and Edna were among the thousands of wives and sweethearts who jostled for permission to visit the battlefields and honour their dead. They were firmly told to wait by a War Office which was too aware of the impossibility of letting civilians see the Armageddon that still remained to be tidied up on the Western Front. It was 1921 before they finally got to the places where their menfolk's remains had been laid to rest. They travelled together to Boulogne, then parted as Edna moved south through France to the Somme and Louise journeyed eastward into Belgium.

They had buried him at La Plus Douve Farm Cemetery – a Front Line burial ground from 1915 to the early summer of 1918. The thousands of dignified white tombstones mingled the dead of Canada, New Zealand and Australia with those of the United Kingdom. Louise stood before the little plot of ground, at peace. There was nothing of Harold here. He was with her, or perhaps in the Warwickshire countryside. But it was fitting that this small stone bookmark should remind history of another good man who had died for humanity's vanity. Louise was leaving the cemetery, passing rank on rank of the endless white stones, when she noticed a singularly familiar name. She stopped, stunned by the macabre coincidence of what she was seeing. Before her, upon a stone identical to Harold's but in a different regimental section, was inscribed the name of Charles Kerslake, the seducer whose name she had taken on impulse when she met Harold. She turned away. Poor Charlie, she thought. So much for your powerful friends and your safe posting! It got you no further in the end than the honest men who took their turn without string-pulling. You all fed the same worms.

She met up with Edna again in Boulogne. They had discussed the possibility of a rendezvous in Paris but both felt that a pleasure trip would make an inappropriate end to such a grim pilgrimage. Many other mourning family groups were heading back to England. There was an air of unreality about the journey, as though the pilgrims found difficulty in reconciling their pictures of mud and carnage with the neat, almost suburban quality of the graveyards they had seen that week.

'I doubt we could have endured it if we'd seen it as it was when they were there,' Louise said aloud.

Edna smiled with infinite sadness. 'You got that, too, did you? It was just like that down on the Somme. All unreal, somehow, as if the battle had never been near there. But then we saw some of them little tatty bits of woodlands that they've left for a memorial, and that's when I cried. My Ron died in a wood. Never did like the countryside . . .' Tears filled her eyes and she turned away.

By the time they had settled in again back in London, Louise realised she was through the worst of her grieving. She was still very young and her situation was far from unique in the aftermath of the war. In fact she was among the lucky ones, with a home of her own and a trade which was still in demand. She bought a house near Hammersmith Grove and started building for a good future, earning a steady living with basic commissions from private clients and shops, but always keeping her sights fixed on the possibility of creating expensive clothes for fashionable people who would develop her reputation and turn her into a Society dressmaker.

The work piled up and time passed swiftly. She had little time for leisure and when she did it was either a trip to the theatre or concert hall with Edna, who harboured a totally unexpected love of Mozart, or solitary visits to museums. Louise loved London and thrived on its bustle. Her months as an apparently widowed businesswoman slipped imperceptibly into years. If she ever yearned for masculine companionship, the memory of her perfect compatibility with Harold quickly dispelled the inclination.

She had lost touch with her South Wales family years ago – with all of them, that is, except her cousin May. May had done better than the other Williamses. She had married a shopkeeper and had become a pillar of chapel and school board. She had once made contact when an outing brought her to Cardiff and it happened to be the young Blodwen's day off. They had gone out together and finding plenty to talk about, had stayed in touch ever since. May was the only one who knew about the change of identity to Louise Kerslake, the love affair with Harold and the miscarriage. In 1927, when she was beginning to prosper, Louise received a plea for help from May. Her seventeen-year-old daughter Evangeline was in terrible trouble and May's husband George was about to disown the girl. Evangeline had, it seemed, been pursuing other forms of education when sent to Cardiff for her weekly music lessons. She was more than slightly pregnant, refused to discuss the identity of the baby's father, and kept insisting that marriage was out of the question. The village was unaware of the scandal brewing behind the Owens' respectable lace curtains but it was only a matter of time. If Louise could not do something to help Evangeline, the girl would be destitute, for George Owen saw to it that his wife did not have enough spare housekeeping money to finance a prodigal daughter. Louise offered to take Evangeline without a second thought, expected baby and all. She had a very strong awareness that there but for the grace of God and petty cash went she.

CHAPTER SIX

The baby was born at a small London nursing home and brought back to Hammersmith. 'If you're going to try and make me have her adopted, I'm leaving!' said Evangeline as Louise put her to bed in her little white-furnished room.

'I was about to do just that. At sixteen you have to be free to grow up and you can't do that saddled with a growing child of your own. How would you live?'

'I don't know but I'll find some way. I'm not giving her up, I'm not!' She attempted to glower threateningly and looked about as convincing as a cross kitten. Louise grinned at her.

'I'm being unkind, Evangeline, and I apologise. I was proposing to adopt her myself. I think I've done just about all my growing up.'

'Oh, you are a smasher! But how can you do it just like that? Won't everyone around here know all about it when she gets old enough to go to school?'

'Evie, love, if you think any daughter of mine would be caught dead in a Hammersmith council school you can think again! But in any case, you're forgetting that this is London, not Fochrhiw. We simply move a couple of miles and no one is any the wiser. They'll all accept that I'm a widow and you're my young cousin looking after the baby.'

And that was what duly happened. Within two months Louise had disposed of the Hammersmith house and they had moved to a new house and workshop in Filmer Road, Fulham. The baby was registered as Imogen Kerslake and the life of Fulham went on completely unruffled by the arrival of the unorthodox little family. Since then, Louise had made every effort to teach Evangeline to be a top-class dressmaker, but they were both aware that she would never be more than a competent seamstress. She was, however, a marvellous organiser and made everything run on oiled wheels in both business and home. Nevertheless Louise was getting worried about her. Evangeline was an intelligent, spirited girl and would not be content for ever to hang around a back street dressmaking establishment being diplomatic to middle-aged women. Eventually, she might take over management of the business from Louise, but she needed an interlude elsewhere, a chance to inhabit a wider world. Louise had considered having the girl trained as a secretary, but found the idea generated more potential problems than it solved. Evangeline needed to acquire a metropolitan gloss if management at the high-class end of the dressmaking business was to be her target. It would be hard to find if she had to spend years in some undistinguished typing pool. There was also the matter of letting her loose in an environment where she would be in day-to-day, unsupervised contact with men. Louise did not trust Evie to stay out of the trouble which had brought her to London in the first place.

This consideration was very much on Louise's mind as she travelled to her appointment with Diana Hartley on a bright spring morning in 1928. How could she put her young cousin in the way of a little experience which would teach her without harming her? It turned out that Diana's aunt had the answer. Louise scarcely recognised the vibrant young woman who greeted her at Clarges Street as the same girl who had rushed off in tears at their last meeting. Hermione Digby-Lenton must be quite a woman if she could engineer so dramatic a change in a few months, thought Louise. She was unsurprised at the commission to make a duplicate of the oyster satin ball dress that had mysteriously disappeared, half finished. Perhaps she would learn one day what had happened to it, but on balance she suspected she would prefer not to know. In addition to the ball gown there was a whole range of frocks to be produced in a very short time and Louise was particularly exultant over the order for Diana's Court Dress – her first Royal

Drawing Room commission. The majority of debutantes had their costumes made by Reville & Rossiter and for a private dressmaker to receive such a commission from a client who could afford to patronise the leading supplier was the ultimate compliment to her skill. She had brought with her samples of that season's latest fabrics and they went through them to establish a colour theme around which to develop Diana's wardrobe. Eventually they settled on blues and greens for the livelier outfits and autumnal shades for the more subdued styles.

Louise was wildly excited about the Parisian trip. She had never been out of Britain before apart from her visit to Harold's grave, and for her destination to be the fashion capital of the world seemed a miracle.

Having taken measurements for the toile, she arranged the next appointment with Diana and said goodbye. In the morning room, Hermione welcomed her warmly and to Louise's astonishment offered her coffee. Tradeswomen were seldom treated to such small courtesies.

'What's your opinion of the suitability of a particular *couturier* for Diana?' Hermione asked. 'I've already suggested Patou, but since then I've begun to wonder whether Lelong or Chanel might be a better choice.'

Louise considered the matter carefully.

'I'd stay with Patou,' she said. 'Chanel is magnificent, but Miss Hartley is such a natural mannequin at the moment that I'm inclined to suggest she saves the Chanel magic until she needs it when she's older. As for Lelong, I'd practically kill for one of his ensembles, but they're very low-key and your niece is so striking that I think she could do full justice to Patou's sense of drama, even at seventeen.'

Her words were expert confirmation of what Hermione had been thinking when she suggested Patou. In one of his gowns and with her looks, Diana would have every man in the ballroom at her feet and every woman wanting to tear her to pieces. The two women agreed a convenient time to meet and discuss the chosen design from that season's collection. Hermione had already contacted the couture house and her special *vendeuse* had arranged to send sketches of her recommendations from the current styles. Normally the client visited the couture house in Paris and saw the clothes being modelled, but time was short and Hermione a sufficiently frequent visitor to Patou to request this unusual arrangement not to visit the *couturier* until it was time for the final fittings.

Before Louise left, Hermione offered an unexpected solution to her major personal problem. 'Mrs Kerslake, you seem to have a modern attitude without being giddy. Would you by any chance be able to recommend a young woman you trust who would be a good companion for my niece?'

The question was so relevant to Louise's private thoughts that she was temporarily speechless. Hermione, always considerate of others' feelings, misunderstood.

'I apologise. I had no intention of offending you by suggesting that you are some sort of appointments bureau,' she said. 'It was simply that you seem so well-informed and sensible that I would welcome a recommendation from you. My sister-in-law was called away before she could make the necessary arrangements. My niece's family circumstances have been a little unusual and I think a companion would be more suitable than a lady's maid.'

'Oh, I'm certainly not offended, Lady Stanmore. It just came as a surprise because I have someone very close to me who might be ideal, and it was almost as though you'd read my mind!'

She explained about Evangeline, tactfully editing out small matters like the baby. Hermione was delighted.

'When may I meet her? I'm sure that she would be perfect!'

Evangeline slid into the Clarges Street establishment as easily as if she had been born to it. Less than a year separated her from Diana in age and the instinctive compatibility they felt for each other eliminated any possible friction that this might have caused.

She took up her new post in mid-April, just in time to become acquainted with her employer before they travelled to Paris for the fittings on the Patou gown at the beginning of May. Hermione made everything blissfully easy for Diana, who had become agitated at the prospect of her mother's reaction to her acquisition of a companion.

'Of course I'm sure your mother will raise no objections, Diana. You have no personal maid; she can hardly expect you to manage with only Parker or Hoskyns to help you and we can't continue to share poor Irene unless I want a rebellion on my hands. Given your circumstances, I think a companion is more suitable anyway. Naturally Sarah will be a little concerned about the financial side, but I shall write to her this evening and make it clear that Evangeline's wages are a present from me. We'll make that my official Coming Out present, shall we?'

'Aunt, if anyone ever adds up all your unofficial Coming Out presents to me they'll have fits!'

'Just as long as your mother is not called upon to do so, I think we shall have little trouble on that score,' rejoined her aunt.

A suitably scatter-brained Hermione-type letter went off to Scotland that night and whatever Sarah's real feelings in the matter might have been, a stilted thank-you note appeared by return, in the same mail as a long sermon to Diana on control and direction of personal servants. Diana promptly crumpled this and flushed it down the lavatory, then went off to make up her own rules for dealing with Evangeline. She had never had an intimate friend of her own age. There were plenty of female acquaintances whom she had met at dancing classes, music lessons and children's parties over the years, but their mutual awareness of her father's unusual status as a very senior civil servant and a man without any personal fortune always added a note of wariness to her relations with such people. It had made her a natural target for the occasional bouts of malice in which all children indulge and she had learned early to be in the group but not part of it. Suddenly she had Evangeline's companionship and their mistress-servant relationship immediately eliminated many of the difficulties she had found in ordinary friendships. Here, at last, was a girl who was not competing with her for social pre-eminence, a girl whose whole function was to make her life run smoothly. On her part, Evangeline admired Diana's beauty and spirit and felt very warmly towards her as the reason for her escape from the dullness of Fulham to the world of fashion.

Within days Diana had admitted most of her romance with Ben Lassiter to the girl, although she fondly imagined that Evangeline remained ignorant of the intimacy of their relationship. The girl was not deceived. Little more than a year before, she had gone through a similar experience. Her burgeoning affection for Diana made her concerned that it must not end for Diana as it had for her, but she had no way yet of hinting that she was willing to hear more important confidences. Although the affair with Ben loomed large for Diana, the excitement of her new wardrobe and the Paris trip were temporarily crowding it out. At last the first week-end in May arrived and Hermione, Diana and Evangeline left for Paris on the Golden Arrow. Hermione smiled secretly as she watched the two young women strolling ahead of her aboard the ferry, and remembered James's reaction at first sight of Diana with Evangeline.

'Good God, old girl, you've made up a matching pair! They fit each other like bread and cheese,' he had exclaimed as he watched them talking together.

'Now why do you say that?' she had asked, intrigued. There was no obvious shared physical characteristic between the willowy redhead and the svelt brunette, except that both were of more than average height. Yet somehow she understood what he meant. They shared a certain spirit which really did make them appear to be halves of a single entity.

James will make a sensitive, thoughtful man one day if he's not very careful, she thought now with a chuckle. The ferry cast off, the gulls circled and she put thoughts of home and family out of her mind for the moment to enjoy her first visit to Paris that year.

The Golden Arrow introduced the English upper classes

to the comforts of the Pullman car and created yet another tier in the system of privilege which allocated a place to everyone. As well as conditions of unparalleled comfort in rail travel, the Golden Arrow boasted its own special first-class lounge on the cross Channel ferry. There the three women sat and talked about fashion, Paris and the Season. Hermione never ate luncheon during the journey, as the time scale was wrong unless one took it on the steamer. With Paris in prospect, she said, it was an insult to the palate to bother with what she called a 'packet-boat meal'. Evangeline was fascinated at the entire concept of Coming Out, almost, thought Hermione, in the manner one expected of an anthropologist observing the rites of a hitherto undiscovered primitive tribe. Diana was bursting with information, thrilled to have found someone who hung on her every word.

'The Season is a sort of carnival procession through a lot of social events that starts with the Royal Academy in May and finishes with Goodwood,' she told Evangeline.

'Goodwood – what's that?' asked her companion.

'It's a race meeting – quite the most attractive of all, in my opinion,' intervened Hermione, well aware that Diana knew nothing of it beyond the fact that her family had always attended.

'And what's an art exhibition got to do with a horse race, then?'

Hermione laughed. 'A very good question, Evangeline. Very little except that one sees all the same faces at both. As Diana said, the Season is a sort of carnival procession with people joining and leaving and rejoining as it goes from one celebration to another.'

'And do they put all that on just for a lot of seventeen-year-old girls to have a good time?' said the girl, looking perplexed.

'No,' said Diana, having the good sense not to sound patronising, 'it would happen whether we were there or not, but it's when Society and our Mamas decide that we're old enough to take off our pinafores and put on silk stockings and grown-up frocks and be seen – as if we were invisible before! The good thing about it is that once we've Come Out we can stop being carted around like babies and eating in the nursery and start dancing with young men and going to parties and theatres. My father always used to say it was the biggest marriage market in the Western world.'

Hermione decided it was time she gave the conversation a little gentle guidance.

'I think it must have started off as a way of ensuring that only the daughters of the aristocracy were acceptable in the best places,' she said. 'The theory was that one only became an adult and a lady after being presented to the ruling sovereign of the day, so at some time in the Season the debutante is introduced to the King and Queen at a royal Drawing Room by a woman who has been presented herself and who vouches for the bona fides of the debutante.'

Evangeline hoped it was not obvious that she had no idea what bona fides were.

'Once she is Out, it is necessary that the debutante makes as many friends and meets as many new acquaintances as possible, for these are the people with whom she will be mixing throughout her life. No one offers hospitality to someone who offers none in return, so the custom has gradually grown up of the debutante's parents holding a dance for her at some time in the Season. Then all the guests will invite her to their dances, and the whole social round builds up from that.'

It sounded to Evangeline to be a much more expensive version of the chapel outings, suppers and tea parties at which enterprising mothers directed the attention of the acceptable young men in her Welsh valley community to the charms of their daughters. She suspected that the motives were identical – matchmaking to a suitable partner in circumstances that attempted to guarantee that the man was capable of supporting the girl of his choice and that she was respectable and virtuous. Suppressing this thought, she listened to descriptions of visits to Eton on the Fourth of June, race meetings at Epsom and Ascot as well as Goodwood, the regatta at Henley and the right cricket matches at Lord's.

'It all sounds very healthy and out-of-doors,' she said eventually.

'Partly because the English take their sport so seriously and partly, I suspect, because it's always been much easier for young people to evade the older generation out of doors than at more formal gatherings,' Hermione told her. 'My maid, Irene, has been with me ever since I came Out, and when we get back I think we'll hand you over to her for a few days to talk about the things you will need to know to look after my niece properly this summer. You're going to be very busy, but I think you should find it interesting.'

Not half as interesting as if I were the one traipsing around to all these posh parties, thought Evangeline, then immediately tried to stifle her resentment and learn from the experience as her cousin Louise had urged her.

'Never make the mistake of thinking you're one of them,' Louise had said. 'Lady Stanmore is very kind and much nicer than any other Society woman I've met, but she *is* a Society woman. Whatever we may think, they believe they're better than us and it always shows just when you think you're all girls together. Let them build the bridges and come across to you, but mind you stay on your own side, otherwise they'll throw you into the river!'

Now, as the conversation bobbed back and forth, with Diana prattling enthusiastically and Hermione occasionally interposing an explanation so that Evangeline would not need to ask in order to understand something, it was hard not to forget what Louise had said, but she was determined to try. It was a calm Channel crossing and, by the time they had covered the forthcoming social calendar, the ferry was coming into port. Diana knew no more of the French railway system than Evangeline, as her foreign travel had not extended beyond Deauville and Boulogne, so they were both full of girlish pleasure at the novelty of the rest of the journey from Calais to Paris. Hermione caught much of their enthusiasm, and by the time the train chugged into the Gard du Nord soon after 6 pm, none of them felt the weariness that such a long journey might otherwise have caused.

As always, Hermione had reserved rooms at the Ritz – a suite comprising two bedrooms linked by a sitting room. She had arranged for Evangeline to have a bed set up in Diana's room, as she thought that the girl might feel too isolated tucked away in the servants' accommodation on her first trip abroad. She suggested that they should take a rest before dinner. She was so charged by the sense of excitement which Paris always created for her that immediately after having registered she decided on a short walk in the spring twilight before changing. The great city was at its best, positively humming with energy as Parisians and visitors slipped from café to bar and back again in the interlude they so charmingly called *l'heure bleue*.

Hermione was quietly enjoying an aperitif at her favourite pavement café when she received a jolt which was to make her wary for the rest of her visit. At the far end of the service area, a dispute had broken out between a waiter and two customers. It sounded as if the man felt they had been charged for too many drinks. The quarrel became louder and louder, the man bawling in good French but with a heavy English accent. The tone was familiar to Hermione but the foreign language prevented her from identifying it. Then the patron arrived, obviously concerned about the disruption the scene was causing, and ordered the couple out. Protesting furiously, they were hustled out into the street close to the railing which separated Hermione from the pavement. She gasped in horror as she realised the man's identity. It was Alexander Hartley. He was with a girl of no more than Diana's age, wearing a cheap dress of garish imitation silk and a great deal of make-up. She was supporting his dispute with the waiter with a stream of remarkably vivid abuse.

Hartley's formerly immaculate appearance was now decidedly seedy. His shirt appeared to have been worn for some days and the collar was slightly adrift above a loosened tie. His shoes were unpolished and his hair needed cutting. It was obvious that exile was doing him no good at all. Hermione started to turn away, hoping that he had not seen her, but she was too late.

'Holy Christ, they're even spying on me here! Is there no getting away from them?' he bawled.

His companion was bewildered. '*Qu'as-tu dit?*'

'Talk English, you silly bitch, or my poor stupid bloody sister-in-law won't be able to understand what you say and go blabbering it back to the Duchess and that mealy-mouthed brother of hers!'

Hermione feigned ignorance of the scene but Alexander was not to be put off. He lurched towards the rail which separated him from Hermione, dragging the French girl savagely by the arm.

'Here we are, me old Hermione – brought a nice little slice of French tart to meet you. Should keep the drawing rooms buzzing in Mayfair for a few days!'

She turned to him, reluctantly but firmly. 'Please Alexander, just go away. If you have any feelings left at all, you'll leave Paris altogether for a few days. I'm here with Diana.'

He gazed at her owlishly and for a moment she hoped that his daughter's name had restored him to sobriety. She was wrong. Instead he became tearful.

'My poor little Diana. Poor, poor baby! Separated from the only one who cared for her by the cruelty of the world! No one to love either of us . . . either of us. Russians sent me away. Sent me right away from my poor little girl . . .' He paused momentarily, then brightened. 'I know – I'll go an' see my little girl, go and cheer her up and tell her that her old father still hasn't forgotten her and that he still loves her . . . Take Marguerite, too. You'll like her, Marguerite – about your age, I should think. Old Hermione's a predictable little thing. Always stays at the Ritz. That's where my baby girl will be!'

Panic-stricken, Hermione reacted instinctively to save Diana from this horror. She turned towards Alexander and gave him her biggest, silliest smile. 'Oh no, Alexander, not the Ritz any more. We use the Plaza Athenée now. James decided the Ritz wasn't his style any more.'

'Pompous bastard – trust him to think the best isn't good enough and spend your money proving it. Right – I'll go straight over. Coming?'

'No, Alexander, I have an engagement. I have to stay here. Are you sure that you wouldn't prefer just to go home?'

He turned truculent. 'No home to go to. Lousy flea-pit of a room until ran into lovely little Marguerite. Now she's looking after me. Diana will help her. Diana wouldn't want to see her poor Mandarin down and out . . . She'd help me like a shot. Going to find her at the Plaza Athenée and don't think you can stop me!'

With that he lurched away, still holding the girl's arm in a vice-like grip. As soon as they had disappeared around the corner, Hermione rose, paid for her drink and hurried from the café to find a cab. She was back at the Ritz in moments, speaking urgently to the hall porter.

'There is likely to be a stranger asking for Miss Hartley. On no account is he to be permitted to know we are staying here. I should be most grateful if you and your colleagues will watch out for him and if he arrives at any time contact me to let me know he is here. But please make sure you are speaking to me before you pass on the information. I don't want my niece to be upset by this man.'

'Certainly, Lady Stanmore. We cannot let such a lovely young lady be distressed, can we?' The hall porter gave her a conspiratorial smile – probably thinks I'm protecting her from a middle-aged ex-lover, thought Hermione. Wait till he sees Alexander!

Back in her room she began to relax. She had every confidence in the Ritz's security against intruders, just as she was certain that Alexander Hartley would come there as soon as the Plaza Athenée denied all knowledge of their existence. Hermione wished she was as sure that the old Alexander, who could have prised information out of the most reluctant hall porter, had perished with the commencement of his disgrace.

The incident destroyed her pleasure in the trip. Throughout the next three days she was constantly glancing over her shoulder or reconnoitring ahead in case of a chance meeting. Hermione ensured that they stayed right away from the quarter where she had encountered him at the café and by the time they were due to depart for London she was half convinced that on sobering up he had decided to listen to her advice and leave Paris for a few days. She was wrong. The following Tuesday the girls had gone to the Jardin de Luxembourg to see the Punch and Judy show. Hermione had been attending a fitting at Patou on her own account. She returned to the Ritz and was on her way to the lift when the concierge called to her.

'Lady Stanmore – a moment, if you please! The gentleman you thought might enquire after your niece. He is here – in the small salon. But he asked for you, not for Miss Hartley. Do you wish to see him?'

Her first impulse was to refuse. Then she realised that in doing so she might risk his making contact with Diana. Steeling herself for the ordeal, Hermione told the concierge she would speak to Hartley. To her relief he looked quite different today than at their previous encounter. Apart from a defeated look, his physical appearance was as it had been during his Foreign Office days. He rose and came forward to greet her. Hermione sat down opposite him in a *bergère* armchair.

'I couldn't let you go home without apologising for that frightful scene the other evening, Hermione. I do hope you can forgive me.'

She smiled with a serenity she did not feel. 'Think no more of it, Alexander. I never saw you.'

'And you never sent me to the Plaza Athenée, either, I suppose! You're more of a tactician than I ever suspected, my dear. You react well under pressure.'

'Perhaps it's just as well. I'm encouraging your daughter in a friendship with a servant, just to try and undo some of the damage you and Sarah have done to her. Imagine, she's seventeen and I daren't let her loose on girls of her own class in case they tear her to pieces. You're responsible for that, Alexander, and the other day you proposed to compound your wickedness by introducing her to that little cocotte who appeared to have scraped you off the pavement. You should thank me instead of twitting me for my deception!'

His smile tried to patronise her and failed. 'I do, dear girl, I do! No one respects your adaptability more than I!'

'Please, let's stop pretending to each other, Alexander. Do you still want anything of Diana, and if so, what?'

'What I want she's probably not ready to give yet, so I'm not planning to burden her on this trip, if that's what you mean.'

'That's not an answer. What *do* you want of her?'

He gestured irritably. 'Nothing that would make sense to you – a gesture or a look, perhaps. Just the knowledge that there's at least one person who still sees me as the Mandarin.'

'And you'd complete the ruin you started in order to get that? I thought that in spite of everything else, at least you loved Diana.'

'Morale outrage is cheap when you're safe inside the magic circle! It's different out here among the wolves.'

'You put yourself there. Why should Diana pay the price of your greed and corruption?'

For a moment she thought he would hit her. 'One day you'll take that back! You and all your damned smug friends will know just what I did and be grateful!'

'Frankly, I doubt it. I'm not quite as simple as everyone thinks. I read the newspaper accounts of the enquiries and the court case and I heard all the gossip too. I think I've drawn some fairly accurate conclusions from the evidence.'

'And what might they be?'

'That you had an expensive line in mistresses who also happened to be more intelligent than you, Alexander, however highly you prize your intellect. I think you were manipulated and I think that now, too late, you know it. If you were a patriot bearing false disgrace for the good of your country, you wouldn't have been brawling drunkenly with a waiter and a tart the other night, nor would you have allowed your appearance to degenerate like that, even temporarily. That had nothing to do with having to keep some awful state secret – it was the apotheosis of a man who realises for the first time that he's been used and thrown away by people to whom he always felt effortlessly superior.'

His face was grey.

'Well, well! You're even brighter than I thought! Such intellectual gymnastics might eventually make you totally unsuited to that aristocratic bumpkin you married!'

'At the moment James stands out as a paragon of all the manly virtues in comparison to you, so I hardly think that your opinion of his capabilities is relevant. If you are determined to be the "parfait" gentil knight bent on cleaning the blemishes from his escutcheon, let's discuss that instead of my relationship with my husband. You say that we shall all be corrected in our cruel views of you when the truth is known. If that is the case, you will serve your daughter best by waiting until that happens and then trying to effect some sort of reunion. If it makes you feel any better, Diana is the one person whose faith in you has remained unshaken through this whole sorry business. She doesn't need you to arrive out of the blue and tell her that the world is condemning you unjustly; she believes that already, poor child. My fear is that if you do manage to confront her now you can only shake that faith.'

'Good heavens, Hermione, don't say that you're concerned to preserve my good name!'

'Not for your sake, I assure you. As long as Diana can go on believing in you as a hero, she stands a chance of making a future for herself. If she loses that, she loses everything. For once in your life, do something really chivalrous and preserve her illusions.'

'Who says that they are illusions?'

'If they are not, so much the better. When you are vindicated, you can sweep back into her life and give her the love and reassurance she deserves. Until then, all you can do by meeting her is to destroy her.'

They stared at each other in silence for some time. Hartley looked away first. His face twitched and he managed a travesty of a smile. Rising to leave, he struck a self-mocking attitude and said:

'And how can man die better
Than facing fearful odds,

125

For the ashes of his fathers
And the temples of his Gods?'

Hermione snorted in exasperation. 'If you really believed that, Alexander, neither of us would be here and Diana would have no problems.'

'You've got your way for now, Hermione, but don't rely on my co-operation for too long. It gets terribly cold outside the charmed circle.'

He left the hotel without looking back. The next day Hermione and the girls boarded the Golden Arrow to return to London. Having settled them in their seats, she went to lean from the open window for a last look at Paris. Well back on the platform, half concealed from view by a trolley piled with mail bags, stood Alexander Hartley. As the train began to move out, he caught Hermione's eye. He raised his right hand in a gesture which was half salute, half surrender, and smiled ironically. She had a chilling sensation that when they met again she might not score such an easy victory.

CHAPTER SEVEN

'Just a trifle passive, don't you think? Could have got in a bit of extra movement if he'd tried.'

Diana started violently and turned to look up at the face she loved best in the world. Then she remembered where they were and how closely observed. She turned back to the lack-lustre painting and muttered: 'Go away, idiot, they'll see!'

'Now is that any way to greet an about-to-be-acquaintance?' Ben grinned and looked very sure of himself.

At that moment Sir Joseph Mason, an old friend of her grandfather, bore down on them.

'Ah, there you are, Lassiter, next to the prettiest girl in the place!' He turned to Diana. 'Will you permit me to introduce a young friend, Diana?'

She was so impressed by Ben's ability effortlessly to arrange what he wanted that she became flustered, precisely the response expected of a gauche young woman just starting out on her social career. She blushed becomingly, glanced helplessly towards Hermione and looked suitably hesitant. Her aunt obligingly joined them in time to witness Ben Lassiter's formal introduction to the girl he had been making love to for a month. Hermione approved. Secretly she was also aware that this was not Diana's first meeting with the handsome young American. She was unconcerned about this but quietly made it her business to learn more about him by remaining in conversation with Sir Joseph while the young people went on looking at pictures and one another. Hermione was certain that any man who could so thoroughly command Diana's attention was unlikely to be a mere passer-by in her life.

She was impressed by what Sir Joseph said. Old family;

right schools; bit of a scandal due to high spirits, but all for the best, because it had enabled the boy to prove to his father that he could make his own money without family help. As a result, Lassiter senior was in process of a reconciliation with Ben and was asking English contacts to show his son something of London Society. Apparently the boy had been here under his own steam for some time. Now he was set to emerge officially in London as one of the most eligible young patricians of America's eastern seaboard.

Meanwhile, Diana was enjoying the satisfaction of introducing fellow debutantes to Ben.

'Venetia Greville? How do you do? Delighted to meet you . . . oh yes, I just met Miss Hartley . . . hope to be seeing *much* more of her soon . . .' Here his eyebrow twitched as he gave Diana a stage villain's smile dripping with innuendo. She hustled him away.

'Really, Ben, you must stop it! They'll all know what you mean . . .'

'And be unable to prove a thing and feel as jealous as hell about your adventures with a mysterious stranger. Come on, Lady D, you're thrilled at the stir you're causing!'

Her smug smile negated the heated denial which accompanied it. She could see Venetia Greville cross-examining a couple of other girls from her dancing class and looking furiously in her direction. Diana could guess the line the conversation was taking. Never had she felt more self-assured. Perhaps she would get some fun out of the Season after all!

Before they parted to progress to the next group of paintings, Hermione had invited Sir Joseph and his young companion to dinner later that week. True, these were very early days for Diana. She had not yet even been presented at court. But what if her grandfather's plan for a match with Roland Lenton failed to materialise? Even if it did happen, Hermione sensed a deep bond between Diana and Lassiter. Surely the girl would stand a much better chance of happiness if marriage whisked her out of the sphere of her dreadful mother and the squalid memory of her father's disgrace? And look what she would be going to! A substantial personal fortune, backed by family money that made Hermione's industrial wealth look positively middle class. How shocked the aristocratic Digby-Lentons would be if they read her thoughts! They were congenitally mercenary but somehow felt it more respectable if they contemplated it as seldom as possible. Hermione believed in planned materialism and was unmoved at the prospect of their disapproval. She had a sound grasp of practicalities and one of her favourite poetic saws was

> 'Love in a hut with water and a crust
> Is, Love forgive us, cinders, ashes, dust'.

The difference between her and the Digby-Lentons lay solely in their reluctance to face reality. Now here was Hermione's favourite kinswoman making all the right responses to a fabulously rich young man who clearly thought highly of her. Hermione surreptitiously crossed her kid-gloved fingers, assumed a sweet smile of stupefying simplicity and turned to rejoin her husband and father-in-law. James was watching the two men as they moved on together into the next room.

'Who was that with old Joe Mason?' he asked.

'A young American named Lassiter, dear. He seemed very pleasant. Sir Joseph obviously likes him. I thought he might make a useful partner for Diana some time if any little – awkwardness – arose about Alexander.'

'Hmm – good thinking, old girl. At times you surprise me!' James was already hypersensitive about the ambiguity of Diana's position thanks to her father's disgrace, but like the rest of the family he had not credited Hermione with the intelligence to help the girl. Now he looked at his wife with new respect.

'Interested, d'you think?'

'Oh, James, don't be so – so sudden! They've only just been introduced.'

'And?'

'. . . And I've invited him to dine the evening after she's presented at Court. Have I done the right thing?'

'Sometimes, Hermione, I suspect that you're brighter than the rest of us put together. And the best part of it is that you never let it show.'

She turned wide, mindless eyes on him.

'Really, darling, at times you do run on so – I hardly understand you! Just as long as you're happy about the dinner invitation. Oh – there's Marjorie Allingham. I must just have a few words.'

The Mall was jammed with expensive cars; the cars with expensive young women. King George and Queen Mary were holding their second Drawing Room of the 1928 Season. Diana sat, cool and graceful, at her aunt's side in the Daimler. This was the single event for which Hermione had been able to overcome the girl's antipathy to white. She could quite simply not have been presented wearing any other colour. Diana's glorious hair was flame-like in contrast to the colourless sweep of delicate silk. The obligatory three feathers that crowned the blazing cap nodded regally as she looked about her. Suddenly Hermione was swept with a burst of fury. With any father save Alexander Hartley, this girl would have wound up married to the greatest in the land, instead of scratching around for the attentions of a half-baked cousin, she thought exasperatedly. The mood softened only when she ruefully acknowledged that without that father, Diana would not have been Diana. Now her niece showed no trace of nervousness. She was faintly amused at the rapt attention of the crowds who watched the line of cars.

'If I were a clerk or a shopgirl, I shouldn't be standing out there gawping in admiration at silly stuffed dummies like us – I'd be working to pull the world down around their ears!' she declared.

'Really Diana!' It was Hermione's turn to be nervous. 'If your grandfather or Uncle James heard you talking like that, they'd be blaming me for letting you be influenced by the Bolshevik menace. Where did you get such ideas?'

'Oh, don't worry, Aunt H. I'm not out on the pavement, am I? I'm inside the Daimler. But if I ever do end up out there – look out, world!'

Good heavens, I believe she means it – and on the way to the Palace, too! Hermione thought inconsequentially. Eventually the crush of vehicles up ahead moved on and it was their turn to arrive at the portico of Buckingham Palace. The air was awash with expensive scents and sounds – Paris perfumes and Paris silks worn together, with mixed effect.

At the top of the great staircase, they were shown into an ante-room where attendants with long ivory poles straightened Diana's eight-foot silk train so that it would spread sinuously behind her as she entered the royal presence. Beneath the flimsy-looking gown was an intricately-constructed net corselet which held the train in position between shoulders and hips and prevented its weight from destroying the lines of the dress. Eventually their names were announced and Diana glided forward to execute the court curtsey she had been practising for weeks. There remained only the small matter of backing out of the royal presence without breaking her neck on her train, and she was safely back with Hermione.

'You looked ravishing, darling! The Prince of Wales was rivetted!'

'Aunt Hermione, I credited you with more sense! Every Mama in the room will be saying that today!' said the sophisticated young woman beside her. Moments later Diana's more childish side reasserted itself. 'D'you *really* think he noticed?'

Back at Clarges Street, Evangeline was in a lather of excitement. 'And did the Prince actually say anything to you, Miss Diana? How close were you? Is he very handsome in the flesh?'

'No he didn't; about nine feet and not really my type so I wouldn't know,' said Diana with a laugh. 'Come on, Evie, there were other people there apart from the Prince. After all, it was his mother and father I went to see!'

'Yes, but I had visions of 'im sweeping you off your feet

and inviting you to a grand ball tonight, you looked so gorgeous when you went.'

'Mmm, me and a hundred others. I rather think his taste runs to married American ladies if we're to believe those stories we read in the French magazines.'

On their recent trip to Paris they had been happily scandalised by the racy tales Diana had translated of the goings on at Fort Belvedere and of the American Thelma, Lady Furness, described as '*chère maîtresse du Prince de Galles*'. The British press was respectfully silent about such gossip, aware of the toughness of English libel law.

Diana regarded the presentation as one of the least interesting events of her Season and her attention was already wandering to coming engagements. She flicked at the skirt of her silk satin gown. 'Come on, let's get me out of this, I feel as if I'm wearing a shroud. Told you I should never wear white!'

'Miss Diana, you look like a fairy princess in it! Why do you hate white so?'

Diana glanced speculatively at her companion before replying with another question. 'How do you feel about your mother, Evie?'

'Seeing how we parted company, not much, I s'pose. She never did a lot for me, I know that.'

'Well, compared with the way I feel about mine, that's a declaration of undying love,' said Diana. 'Ever since I can remember she's been beastly to me, punishing me for things I didn't do, stopping me from having the friends I wanted, always going on and on about what a rotter Papa was . . . And she was determined that I should Come Out in a succession of horrid little-girl white party frocks. I would have been a laughing stock from Piccadilly to Goodwood and she knew it.

'I'm so glad she had to go away and that dear Aunt H is seeing me through it all. I hope Mama never comes back!' This was said with such vehemence that it drew a gasp of superstitious alarm from Evangeline.

'Oh, don't talk like that! You'll never forgive yourself if something happens to her now!'

'Don't bet on it, Evangeline. I've been punished in advance for the bad thoughts I have about my mother so I'm not afraid of any revenge that's waiting for me now. She's done most of it already.'

Diana was suddenly aware that she had voiced something of her true feelings about her mother to an outsider for the first time. Until today only her father and sister had shared any direct knowledge of Lady Sarah's tyranny.

'Somehow I can tell you about it, Evie, and it feels better. Will you mind listening if I complain about her from time to time?'

The other girl was round-eyed with suppressed curiosity. 'No, Miss, and I promise I'll never tell a soul . . .'

It was the beginning of forty-five years of shared confidences.

Diana's first grown-up dinner party at the family mansion in Brook Street was the realisation of her fantasies: a glamorous setting; an opportunity to wear beautiful clothes; introductions to new people; and the presence of Ben Lassiter, miraculously accepted by the Digby-Lentons as a worthy member of their circle. As Evangeline shook out the gorgeous new gown which had arrived at Clarges Street from the Kerslake workrooms only that morning, Diana sat at the dressing table brushing her hair. It had been cut by Douglas of Bond Street into a sleek burnished cap and Diana felt very adult with the new style. On the morning of her Court presentation, her Uncle James had handed over a small square leather case and mumbled something about his father not allowing Lady Sarah to keep them when she ran off with Diana's father. When the girl opened the box, she discovered a pair of diamond and aquamarine drop earrings, the perfect foil for her hair and tonight's frock.

'Louise must be going colour blind in her old age if she thinks this is "the delicate pastel tint of springtime to add a flush of elegance to the emerging debutante",' said Evangeline, parroting a purple passage from that month's *Vogue*. 'It's navy-bloody-blue!'

'No swearing, Evie,' said Diana, stifling a giggle, 'and it's not – that's *bleu de rève.*'

'Hmmm?'

'Dream blue, to you.'

'Exactly – navy. Still, she's right. You look nice in the pastel shades, Miss Diana, but in these dark colours you're really stunning. It certainly knocks almond pink a bit cock-eyed.'

'Ah, but that's because you haven't seen one of Lakie's designs in almond pink. She's making me a couple of pale frocks which look wonderful – lovely light greens.'

They chattered about clothes and cosmetics while Diana completed her toilette, then Evangeline helped her into the gown. As the maid stood back, both girls gasped involuntarily at the transformation it achieved. Diana had seen it only cluttered by basting threads and had last tried it on before hairdresser and beautician had turned her from a child into a young woman.

She could scarcely believe that the creature who gazed challengingly back at her through the looking glass was herself. The gown had severe straps and a deep square neckline. Extravagant chiffon panels floated away from the shoulders to trail dramatically on the ground. The chiffon in the gown itself was hand-tucked beneath vertical strips of deepest blue beads which formed the fluid tubular shape of the bodice and extended down to mid-thigh. There each strip was refined to an arrow shape and the chiffon poured through to form a softly-flounced skirt. The uneven handkerchief hem varied in length from mid-calf to ankle and swirled about Diana's long legs as she moved forward to look more closely in the cheval glass.

'Diawch, but she's really done it this time!' Evangeline was perceptibly Welsh only when very impressed or excited. 'You should be in *Vogue,* Miss Diana, you really should!'

The ensemble was completed with matching beaded Louis-heeled shoes and dark-blue silk stockings. Diana looked like a very expensive dream.

Before putting on her first grown-up evening dress,

Diana had been little more than a pretty child, made more noticeable by her bright hair. The social butterfly which now emerged was something different: a beautiful woman. She was unusually tall for the time – almost five foot eight inches. Her hair carried all the rich red tones of an Italian Renaissance painting. It was set off by creamy-golden skin, not the usual pale, freckled complexion of the English redhead. Her eyes were green. Always striking, now they had been emphasised further by skilfully-applied cosmetics. Diana's breasts were larger than current fashion dictated, but firm and shapely enough to permit her clothes to hang well. Her midriff and belly were flat, her hips boyish. Louise Kerslake's superb dark-blue gown played up all her numerous assets. Diana clipped on the diamond and aquamarine ear-droppers, took a final turn in front of the glass, blew Evangeline a kiss and headed for the door.

She achieved a salutary effect on the family and guests at Brook Street. Sir Joseph Mason had already arrived and was talking to the Earl as Diana entered the drawing room. There was an appreciative silence, then he murmured to his host 'Damme, George, you won't have that little filly on your hands for long when the Young Idea get a proper look at her!'

George Digby-Lenton was having similar thoughts and was already beginning to wonder whether he was being too unambitious for his granddaughter's future. Perhaps the Petrograd Communiqué fiasco wouldn't be as much of an obstacle as he had anticipated . . .

Hermione moved forward to greet her niece. 'My darling, you look magnificent,' she said quietly. 'Come and say hello to everyone. We're still waiting for a few people.'

So far the party comprised the Digby-Lentons – the Earl, James and Hermione; Sir Richard Grafton, a shooting companion of Lord Stanmore, with his wife Nancy and daughter Primrose, also making her debut that Season; Hilary Mounter, a widow and close friend of Hermione; and Sir Joseph Mason. Roland Lenton and his sister Catherine were expected, and Ben Lassiter arrived moments after Diana.

Hermione was ensuring that everyone had someone to converse with and making appropriate introductions. Eventually she brought Ben to Diana's side. '. . . And of course, you have already met my niece Diana' – she paused briefly but significantly – 'at the Academy the other day. Diana is fascinated by America. I'm sure you two will have plenty to talk about.' She moved on, playing the perfect hostess.

Oh thank you Aunt H, thank you for bringing us together so soon, thought Diana rapturously. They gazed vacantly at each other for a moment before realising they must generate some social chatter. Ben led the way, keeping up a bantering undertone of flirtation between the meant-to-be-overhead superfluities. Hermione was watching them and day-dreaming about what an attractive pair they made, when Roland and Catherine arrived. As they came in, Hermione was aware of an immediate change in the atmosphere. This evening might not turn out as well as she had been anticipating.

Catherine had never liked Diana. She was slightly older and considerably less attractive than her red-haired cousin. Both families were short of money. The girls had been thrown together because Catherine's mother held back her daughter's development as much as possible, and Catherine mostly mixed with girls of Diana's age. Roland was the centre of Catherine's world and she bitterly resented his obvious adoration of Diana, particularly as Diana took his attentions for granted. Catherine had Come Out the previous Season and had spent too many evenings standing alone and shunned in Mayfair ballrooms. There was some talk of a dusty, remote Yorkshire widower paying her intermittent attention, but nothing strong enough to raise her own self-esteem or make her envied by her contemporaries. As a result Diana had an enemy simply as a result of looking as she did and being loved by Roland. Her father's disgrace made her vulnerable to attack from Catherine and the older girl had no intention of missing her opportunity. She gradually moved across to join Primrose Grafton, who was looking at Diana's sumptuous appearance with the dismay of the eclipsed.

'Always rely on a Hartley if you want a vulgar display,' she murmured.

Primrose brightened. She had been making a miserable comparison between Diana's frock and her own subdued pale pink creation. Next to Diana she was all but invisible, a state of affairs which did not make her admire Diana.

'She'll need all the help she can get when she starts going to dances and people cut her,' said Primrose. 'I've heard lots of chaps saying they wouldn't be looking in her direction even if she had £10,000 a year behind her!'

None of which was strictly true. It was Primrose's mother who had expressed such a view, stung by the sight of Diana's long-legged figure cutting a dash at a tea party where Primrose had sunk without trace. Primrose was no intellectual but she knew intuitively that her mother wanted all the young men to think that way without being able to guarantee such a reaction. Unaware that she was acquiring two enemies more permanently with every smile and gesture, Diana charmed her way around the party. Primrose was becoming more waspish by the moment because she had her eye on Ben, who had not yet looked away from Diana for anything except a refill of his glass. Hermione had seated Ben and Diana together at the dinner table, but both Primrose and Catherine were within sniping distance. As soon as the older guests were directing their attention elsewhere, Catherine turned to her cousin with a look of intense concern.

'Your poor mother! I do hope that leaving London has done her some good. It must have been frightful for her to cope with all that gossip and knowing how impossible it would be – you know – when you started going out for your Season.'

Diana's stricken face rewarded her instantly. 'What are you saying? Mama is perfectly all right. Aunt Alice is very ill, that's all . . . Why should you think Mama is under a strain?'

Catherine smiled pityingly. 'Of course, Aunt Sarah would try to give that impression. She'd hardly want to let you see how upset she was. But if you're grown up enough to be Out, you should be aware of these things. Can't hide your head in the sand for ever, you know; it's not as if you won't have to get used to it soon.'

'Used to what? What are you talking about?'

Ben rescued her, apparently effortlessly. 'I think she's talking about a beautiful girl who's put every other female in the shade this evening, aren't you, Miss Lenton?' His smile was lazy but the tone was pure acid. Catherine flounced.

'I can't think what you mean!'

'Well, with Diana not knowing what you're talking about and you not knowing what I mean, we seem to have hit a rather unpromising conversation, so how about changing the subject?'

He turned to Hilary Mounter, sitting across the table from him.

'I keep meaning to take in a few night clubs to see how they compare with New York, but I haven't got around to it yet. Any recommendations about where I should start?'

'Oh, where else but the Embassy? The Prince of Wales and his set are often there and you can't be smarter than that. I confess I'd enjoy going again. It's ages since I was there.'

'Let's make up a party this evening, unless anyone has to rush off to bed when we finish dinner.'

'Splendid idea,' said Hilary. 'I'll ask Hermione when we leave you men to the port.'

Diana had withdrawn from the conversation. Catherine was watching her avidly, delighted that her first barb had found its target so surely. When she turned aside momentarily to talk to Primrose's father, Ben made full use of the momentary privacy.

'Come on, get back to being the Deb of the Year, you little goose! You're going to get a helluva lot more in that vein before this summer is over, and you have to remember it only happens because they're jealous. You won't find men doing it, I'll bet!'

It was hard to rally her shattered good spirits and he was surprised later when she agreed to go with them to the

Embassy. He had not been present in the drawing room when Catherine pushed her too far and she snapped back. Her cousin decided to give the family scandal a rest and attack Diana's originality instead. It was a mistake. Diana had no doubts about her appearance. Since the moment of seeing her reflection in the midnight blue gown, she had been sure of her own glamour. She was equally certain that Catherine was a frump.

'Don't you find dark blue a rather difficult colour, Diana?' Her persecutor was smiling sweetly.

'No, as long as one has the hair and eyes to show it off, it's quite easy. Of course, I can understand with your colouring it would be out of the question. So sensible to stick to beige!'

Catherine instantly felt relegated to wallflower status again. She was trying to recover her aplomb when Hermione came along with Hilary to discuss the nightclub proposal. Suddenly Diana felt equal to the whole thing. If only she could contrive to treat digs about her father with as much contempt as she did criticism of her appearance, she would have no problems. If only . . . if only it were that simple! This evening's dinner party was untypical. The generations tended not to mix so haphazardly and this occasion was engineered by Hermione and the Earl to launch Diana from a secure position in a small, controlled group. Now some of the older members of the party were ready to end their evening quietly while the younger guests were just starting to warm up.

The Embassy, in Bond Street, was the natural place for smart young people to meet. The clientele who made it chic were older – sophisticated women in their mid-thirties, married to complaisant men with interests elsewhere; and much-travelled men in their forties, notably the Prince of Wales and his intimates. There was usually a sprinkling of Americans, reflecting the Prince's preference for trans-atlantic fashions and women, but it would have been hard to imagine a more English pleasure dome. The Embassy managed to combine grandeur and intimacy in a long, lofty room with dark green and gold walls, broken up by deepest purple velvet curtains over the long windows. Ambrose's jazz orchestra played from a high balcony at one end of the room. The tables were arranged around the walls, where purple velvet banquette seating gave the drinkers and diners a view of the crowded dance floor.

The members of the Brook Street party who eventually moved on there were Sir Joseph Mason, Hilary Mounter, Roland, Ben, Primrose and Diana. Catherine had thrown a tantrum and gone home alone when it became clear that she could not dislodge either Diana or Primrose from the group and would therefore stand out yet again as a spare female. Although she knew she looked very attractive, Diana felt shy as they went in. It was her first visit to a nightclub and, in spite of Louise Kerslake's artistry, she felt gauche. Her nervousness was dispelled for ever within minutes of her arrival. Sir Joseph, who had gone to talk with a beefy looking man at the edge of a large, noisy group, came back and asked her to join him.

'Fella here wants to meet you, me dear. I think you may approve!' Before she had time to draw breath, Diana heard him say to the beefy man's companion: 'Your Highness, may I present Miss Diana Hartley?' and she was bobbing a curtsey to the Prince of Wales, then whisked on to the dance floor with him.

That part of the evening was a little blurred. He was considerably shorter than Diana, but danced well enough for it not to matter. He threw off a few banal remarks to which she responded and instantly forgot. Then she was back with Sir Joseph and Ben, who were talking to Thelma Furness. Lady Furness was watching Diana intently but clearly decided the girl was too young to constitute serious competition for the Prince's attention. They detached themselves from the royal party and joined Roland and Primrose at their table. Primrose was so impressed she could think of nothing derogatory to say. The men teased Diana kindly about her impact and she blossomed under the glow of attention she received from other tables. Perhaps being the Girl Who Danced With The Prince of Wales would stop people being beastly to her!

'Fairest lady, flee hence with me before the wicked prince carries you off for his own!' said Ben, striking a suitably melodramatic pose.

Diana noticed Roland's concerned look. He knows Ben isn't simply putting on an act, she thought. Momentary sympathy for Roland's feelings was swamped by her pleasure in the first experience of her power over men. Here she was, admired, sought after, glamorous. Who cared about old scandals?

Sadly for Diana's peace of mind, too many people did in fact care about old scandals. She was suffering from the dual disadvantages of family disgrace and comparative poverty. Society would have overlooked Alexander Hartley's infamy when it encountered his daughter, had he left her well provided financially. But to be penniless and disgraced in the *haut monde* of 1928 was one handicap too many. The invitations rolled in for all the best parties – after all, Diana was an earl's granddaughter and her own dance was to be held in the family mansion – but when she went to them she found herself received with some coolness. Hermione tried to treat the matter philosophically.

'It's pointless for us to pretend nothing has happened, Diana. Your father's conduct has made considerable impact on everyone in our circle, and of course the more thoughtless ones will make you suffer for it. They feel as if he has let us all down as a class.

'I'm going to say things now which you might regard as unnecessarily brutal, but believe me, my darling, I am saying them only because I love you and want the best for you. This Season you will have two suitors – Roland and Ben. I happen to think either of them would make an excellent husband, but you are very young and quite possibly you would prefer to wait a couple of years before marrying. If you *do* wait, I'm sure everyone will have put your father out of their minds by next year. Still, I'm not blind to the relationship between you and your mother, and she won't stay away for ever. If you become particularly fond of either Roland or Ben, I can't help thinking you will be happier with either of them than staying much longer under your mother's roof. That might sound like a cynical approach, but it's realistic and I'd like you to think it over very carefully when you come to consider your future. In the meantime, don't imagine I'm blind to the slights you are suffering. That little horror of a sister of Roland's doesn't help. Try to spend as much time as possible in male company. I think you'll be happier that way!'

Diana was taken aback by her aunt's openly materialistic attitude. There was no mention of love and romance, but attention to future security and permanent escape from her mother. She did not want her world to develop like this and turned angrily away from Hermione, but underneath it all a small voice told her that her aunt had only her best interests at heart. Hermione was absolutely correct about Diana's matrimonial opportunities. Ben repeated his proposal every time he and Diana were together. Roland screwed up his courage on one of their rare outings – a morning ride in Rotten Row.

Reining in his horse, he said abruptly: 'Look here, Diana, I can't wrap up what I feel in any sort of flowery talk; it embarrasses me like mad. But I think you're just about the best person I've ever met and I don't see how I could manage without you. Do you think there's the slightest chance that you might marry me?'

She burst out laughing. 'Oh, Roland – no kneeling with a bouquet? Shame on you! If I said no, would you seize my horse's bridle and gallop me off into the wild blue yonder?'

'Are you saying no?'

'Don't rush me. I need to think about it for a while. Did you know Ben had asked me too?'

'Well, I sort of guessed. What did you say to him?'

'Nothing. I really am awfully young, you know, and a lot has happened to me in the past few months. It's almost June now. Give me until July to think it over and I promise I shall give you my answer then. Is that acceptable?'

'I suppose it has to be. Will you come to Henley with me?'

'Yes, of course. But why the formal invitation now?'

'I don't know; I feel as if I have to pin you down somehow, make you remember I'm still here.'

She smiled at him with genuine affection. 'You'll always be here, Roland.'

'I didn't think you'd noticed. It's because I love you more than anything in the world. I'd die for you if I had to.'

'Let's hope it won't come to that! Wait and see what July brings.'

With that she spurred her horse unexpectedly and shot away, leaving him staring after her along the dirt road.

Edmund Dancey was Roland's only intimate friend. Superficially they were so unlike each other that acquaintances wondered what Dancey, flamboyant and very attractive, saw in the reticent, apparently dull Roland. Dancey had known the other man long enough to understand that appearances said little about character. Roland was important to him as one of the very few people he could rely on in any circumstances.

They had met, literally, on the playing fields of Eton. Roland, in his first half, a twelve-year-old bundle of silent misery, was making a fool of himself on the rugby pitch. Dancey, also in his first half and proving himself a natural athlete, came to the rescue of his puny companion. He covered Roland's worst errors and tactfully saw that the boy remained in the background for all but the most elementary play. When the session ended, Roland gave no indication that he had noticed any specially kind treatment from Edmund and the latter assumed the boy had failed to appreciate the effort expended on his behalf. He was proved wrong the next day in Latin Construe. Dancey's physical grace was useless when he was confronted with Tacitus and he began to make a thorough ass of himself in front of one of Eton's more supercilious Classics masters. Just as he was about to reveal his inadequacy in a barbaric swipe at translation, Roland smoothly interrupted with a question about possible alternative English phrases. The master's attention was re-directed and Dancey retired to obscurity with a huge sigh of relief.

Afterwards he confronted Roland. 'Damned decent of you to divert the Beak like that. What on earth made you do it? He might have been quite rough on you for cheek!'

Roland reddened, looked away and muttered: 'Least I could do after the pasting you saved me from at rugger yesterday. You'd only have left your dignity in the class-room. I might have left my front teeth on the field!'

He looked up and grinned. They were firm friends from then on. In due course they attended the same Oxford college and had rooms on the same staircase. Over the years they learned they were less dissimilar in important matters than seemed the case. Roland proved to be a talented oarsman and rowing was one of Dancey's favourite sports. Dancey developed a passion for Baroque music and obscure French literature, strong interests of Roland. Both were mad about theatre and went as often as possible. Dancey's prospects were no brighter than Roland's. There was a little family money, but not enough to support him as a man of leisure, and his talents suited him more to the life of a socialite or a country gentleman than a wage-earner. Dancey, however, was blessed with looks, charm and presence in abundance. In his early twenties he resembled the male dancers of the Ballet Russe – supple, agile, handsome, somewhat sinister-looking and with an air of sexual ambiguity which unsettled the older generation. He got by at a number of semi-cultural, semi-commercial pursuits on the fringe of the art world. His friendship with Roland remained as strong as ever.

While still at Oxford, Roland had rented a pleasantly ramshackle studio off the Fulham Road, part of a Victorian mews conversion designed for artists taking part in the Great Exhibition of 1851. Roland was no artist himself, but loved the bohemian atmosphere of the place and treated it as a semi-secret retreat. He was a very private young man and few people, apart from Edmund, Diana and Lettie, even knew of the apartment's existence, for he spent much of his time at his uncle's Mayfair house. Dancey had helped him find the place. Diana and Lettie had enjoyed the run of it ever since he took it in 1922 and they started dropping in on their way home from music lessons in Onslow Square. Dancey frequently borrowed it for purposes he discussed with no one. When Diana arrived without Lettie one wet afternoon he had sent her flying from the building, prickling with naive embarrassment at the suggestions she suspected he was making. At present he was installed there while Roland stayed in Mayfair with his uncle.

'When are you going to shake this girl out of your hair, old man? She's driving you mad and you seem unable or unwilling to resist her.'

Roland's troubled eyes reflected his doubts about discussing the matter, but he was clearly in need of advice.

'Dancey, I know she's head over heels with this American chap and I really don't care – I'm just terrified that he'll win the fight and take her off to America with him for good.'

'But aren't you jealous? You've always let her walk all over you and use you for her own little selfish schemes, but this time you must feel like withdrawing the permanent alibi you seem to give her.'

'I've never been jealous. What I love about Diana isn't within this man's reach – or anyone's I think. That's partly why I love her so much. Whatever he does to her, he can never own her; no one can. That's what's so splendid about her.'

'That, you old chump, is the largest load of twaddle I've heard for many a long day. Your Diana is a self-centred, spoiled brat. I know her parents are pretty foul but she's been allowed to get away with murder by the rest of you to make up for it. And don't forget, she *is* her parents' daughter. I sometimes suspect she's inherited incipient lunacy from her mother and I know she has her father's monumental ego. She's also breathtakingly beautiful, of course!'

'Dancey, if I were a stronger character, I'd horsewhip you for that!'

Edmund merely grinned at him. 'You've more character than I'll ever be able to muster, Roland. It's just not showy, that's all. It doesn't alter the fact that what you mistake for a free spirit is a trainee heart-breaker. God help us all when she's fully developed. I half hope this American does spirit her away. It might be better for all of us, particularly you. In the meantime, please stop this drivel about not being jealous. Any man who's involved with a girl who looks like Diana Hartley would be potty or perverted not to be jealous of Ben Lassiter.'

'Perhaps I expressed myself badly. I often do, you know. Things don't . . . er . . . come out the way I feel them. It's just that I know Diana doesn't care enough about me to put up with it if I try to hold her accountable for her behaviour, or to want me near her if I'm not useful – like providing an excuse for her to go out unchaperoned. If jealousy is wishing she was interested in me the way she is in Lassiter, and hoping he'll drive off Beachy Head in that bloody great monster of a motor of his, then I'm jealous. I just don't dare show it!'

'Bravo, my Roland! Who would have guessed such intensity beats beneath your cool exterior!'

'Now you're ribbing me. Please don't. You know I'm noted for my limited sense of humour.'

Both men laughed. Dancey went to get them another drink. When he returned, though, he refused to change the subject.

'So what are you going to do about your fatal woman?'

'Do? Just what I'm doing now; soldier on, secretly hope Lassiter drops dead or runs off with one of the Morgan sisters, and keep my fingers crossed that Diana will eventually need me enough to marry me.'

'You poor old sod! I'd almost prefer to enter a monastery than face that prospect. You're sure there's no alternative that will make you happier?'

'The Foreign Legion, perhaps – but you know I could never master handling a gun and marching in step at the same time, so it looks as though it's Diana or nothing.'

'Then God help you, Lenton. And I'm not sure whether I mean to help you to win or help you lose. I suspect you're damned either way.'

'Softly, softly, catchee monkey, Edmund!'

'Softly, softly, get trodden on by a deaf elephant, Roland!'

CHAPTER EIGHT

Hermione's elder son was in his first year at Eton, so the family went down for the Fourth. Ben was invited along when he expressed curiosity about this peculiarly English custom which occupied a prominent position in the social calender.

'Why the fourth of June – what's so significant about the date?' he asked James.

'George III's birthday old chap; very important day!'

'He founded the school, then?'

'Dear God, no! We were positively antique by the time he came to the throne. No, Eton was founded in the reign of Henry VI' – he became vague – 'Mmmm, hundreds of years before that. Ask Papa, my history's never been too strong. No, it seems the third George was very kind to us. Paid us a visit at a time when the middle classes were beginning to swamp the place a bit and reassured the right people about sending their sons off to school instead of keeping them at home with tutors. Bit like giving a grocer the Royal Warrant to stick on 'is jam labels. We started celebrating his birthday out of decent gratitude.

'Gradually it became a tradition and now it makes a good excuse for the parents to go down there once a year and hear what little oiks their sons have been. Adds a touch of the old marble halls to all those sporting events near the start of the Season, too.'

James rambled on about his own rather commonplace school memories for a while, then said: 'Do you good to come with us this year if you've time. One day you might have a son you want to send there.'

Having met a number of old Etonians in recent weeks and being aware that it had been Alexander Hartley's school, Ben doubted that, but he suspected that Diana would accompany her uncle and aunt and therefore accepted enthusiastically. James seemed to be taking quite a fancy to him and Ben wanted all the support he could get from Diana's family. The drive down was an odd echo of their outing the day he had first made love to Diana, but this time her trip in his Bentley was known and encouraged by Hermione and James and the Earl, who were taking the family limousine.

'Young George will be delighted to be seen with friends who have an open Bentley,' enthused Hermione. 'All he does is chatter about cars and how staid the Daimler is!'

'D'you think that one day we'll drive down here to see our son on the Fourth?' Ben asked Diana, pitching the question as light-heartedly as he could.

Her expression was unreadable and he wished he had not broached the subject. She was silent for so long he thought she was not going to respond, and he was beginning to cast about for another subject when she spoke.

'I can't imagine us ever having a son, Ben. There's so much . . . in the way.'

'Why should there be anything in the way? We're young, healthy and single and we love each other. Unless your mother decides I'm undesirable and makes us wait until you're twenty-one, I can see nothing at all in the way, and the sooner you let me close enough to get to work at charming her the better.'

Diana turned away and looked out at the passing hedge-rows. The silence lengthened.

'Dammit, Diana, there's nothing sensible in your attitude! Are you trying to find a way of saying you don't love me?'

'I love you more than anyone I've met and I can't imagine ever loving anyone else – but I'm afraid that won't be enough . . .'

'Enough for what, for pity's sake? I know it's a cliché, but I really can take you away from all this and make a wonderful life for us somewhere else. You'd love New York and New England and they'd love you right back.

With your looks and that cut-glass aristocratic English accent, plus my father's clout and both our money, you'll start right at the top of the heap and stay there. What could be wrong with that?'

'It's not England.'

'Gee, lady, wish I'd thought of that – that explains everything! What do I have to say to convince you that you belong where you're happy and that you'll have more chance of being happy in America with me than in England? Here you'll spend your life chained to an old scandal they'll never let you forget!'

'It's not just for me, Ben. Someone has to show them that at worst Papa was misguided. He may have been too trusting, but he would never have betrayed that trust.'

'My God, he's really indoctrinated you, hasn't he? He hung around long enough to stuff you full of those big ideas about England being top nation and an Englishman's word being his bond, then took a powder and left you and your sister to face the music. Your mother may be a monster, but in a way she's more of a hero than your father. At least she didn't fly the coop. She's digging in and daring anyone to say the wrong thing!'

'If you intend going on like this, you can put me out at Windsor and I'll take the train back to town. I don't have to listen to you!'

'Look around you, kid. These guys aren't going to forgive your old man for anything. In a sense it doesn't matter to them whether he betrayed them. To them his big mistake was getting caught. They wouldn't have minded how much of a villain he was if the whole mess hadn't gone off in his face.'

Diana stared at him, suddenly aware that there was much truth in what he said. And if there was, it made nonsense of her driving desire to prove Hartley's innocence. Why bother, if his accusers cared about the effect rather than the cause? She spoke no more about returning to London alone. In fact she said nothing for the rest of the journey, but stared gloomily out, blind to the beauties of the day, in mute contemplation of an apparently incorrigible world.

When they arrived at Eton the Digby-Lentons were already there. Hermione took one look at her niece, decided something was wrong and made an excuse to stroll away with her while James introduced Ben to other parents and to his son. The young American was only too willing to abandon Diana for the moment. He had heard enough of Alexander Hartley to last him a lifetime.

'What's happened, Diana?' Hermione asked. 'I thought you were looking forward to your little outing with Ben, but you seem quite miserable. Are you unwell?'

The girl's eyes filled with tears. 'He doesn't understand about the Mandarin. Every time I try to explain, he gets all impatient and acts as though Papa really were guilty of those terrible things people keep whispering about him. And it's just not true, is it, Aunt?'

Hermione stood still, wondering whether she should deliver one of her anodyne social butterfly remarks. A close look at Diana's face made her decide against it.

'Perhaps your father did do what people say, Diana. Have you any idea just what he was supposed to be guilty of?'

'Of course I have! At least, I – I think so; he stuck up for what he believed in and got blamed for letting the side down.'

'My dear child, I know that your education has been lamentably neglected, but for a seventeen-year-old just launching herself on the adult world, you sound singularly ill-informed. If you really want me to, I shall tell you what the papers said and what the Government said.'

'I – I suppose I should listen. I did read the papers when the enquiry was on but I couldn't really follow all they said about what had happened in the beginning, when the beastly letter was published. It would be better if you told me again exactly what happened, but I'm not going to like it, am I?'

'No, but it would be a very easy life if we all managed to avoid the things we didn't like indefinitely. I confess I'm somewhat concerned about whether this is the right time or place for the sort of thing I'm about to say. Are you sure you wouldn't prefer to put it off until we go back to town?'

'I'm wrecking everybody's day and I know I'm behaving like a spoiled child, but if I lose my nerve now I'll never be able to tackle it with you again. Would you mind awfully if we talked it out now?'

Yes, I would mind awfully, thought Hermione. This should be my day, with my son and husband; a happy few hours in the sun with nothing but strawberries to worry about. And instead I have to help this child to grow up gracefully!

To Diana she only said 'Of course not, as long as you promise to listen instead of rejecting everything out of hand. I'll set aside what the gutter press had to say. The serious newspapers which reported the court case and the enquiry said that the Labour Party lost a General Election because a letter had been circulated which purported to come from the Bolshevik Government to our trade union leaders, inciting the working class to rebellion against the State. The letter was a very crude forgery and did not stand up to close scrutiny, but by the time it was discredited, the Election had come and gone and the Conservatives were back in power by a landslide.

'The Labour Party pressed for an enquiry about how the Foreign Office had come into possession of the letter and, more importantly, how that letter got from Whitehall to the front pages of the newspapers. To its discredit, the Conservative Government refused to air the matter and it looked as if the whole thing would blow over. Unfortunately for your father, business interests are less eager to forget embarrassing incidents than politicians, particularly when their own pecuniary interests are at stake. A couple of years later a merchant bank sued one of its clients for failure to make full settlement of various international currency transactions. The client was a woman, but when the case came to trial it was obvious that she had acted with someone else in her dealings – your father.'

Diana looked as though she was about to faint. Hermione steered her gently to a wooden bench and sat down beside her.

'Forgive me if it's a little too much to take,' she said.

'You said you'd read about it and I thought there were just a few obscure things that you needed to have explained. Didn't you know any of this?'

'Y-yes, but reading about it is a lot different from having a member of your family telling you about it as though it were true.'

'Did you never wonder for a moment if the newspapers had got it right all along?'

'No, never! Grandpapa and Uncle James – and Papa himself for that matter – have always read the papers and snorted and said you can never believe what you read in the press, so I just thought they were telling their usual pack of lies!'

Oh, Lord, thought Hermione, she's still such a child, taking everything her elders say and swallowing it! Aloud, she said: 'I really think this is too much for you today, Diana. I'm beginning to think it's too much for me! Why don't we arrange for you to go home? I'll come with you if you like, but perhaps Roland would be better at the moment. We can always send you home in the Daimler and arrange for him to be around at Clarges Street by the time you get there. Put the entire business out of your head for a while, and then when you're a little calmer we'll talk it out in more appropriate surroundings. I had no wish to cause you so much pain today. I thought you just needed someone to help you accept the harsh realities of the situation.'

Now Diana was distraught. 'No, please, Aunt – I couldn't bear to leave it like this! There's no one much about at the moment. I must finish this and get it all straight, however much it hurts. Please go on.'

'Very well, if you think you'll be able to keep yourself under control. This is hardly the time or place for excessive displays of anguish.'

'No, I promise I shall try to behave properly, I don't want to let you down.'

'Well, the papers had another field day, as you know, and by the time they had finished even the Tory Party lacked the arrogance to refuse an enquiry. It found Alexander and one of his juniors at the Foreign Office guilty of gross misconduct, both men were dismissed from the Service and Alexander left England shortly afterwards. In private he hinted that he had been some sort of Government agent; that he had indeed been guilty of leaking the documents to the newspapers but at the secret instruction of some shadowy Government agency. He insisted that he was a patriot who had sacrificed his reputation to spare England from the danger of a Communist take-over. He has never changed his story and insists that some day he will be vindicated.'

Diana was listening with a look of passionate intensity.

'And he will be, won't he, one day? He told me he'd never been anything other than a patriot.'

Hermione said nothing.

'Aunt Hermione – surely you believe him?'

'I'm afraid I find it very difficult, Diana. No – please don't react as if I'm betraying you. I am trying to tell something of vital importance to the rest of your life. What did you make of the evidence when you weighed it against what your father told you?'

'It's obvious – they used him, then deserted him when he needed them!'

'Diana, this is something you will have to live with and you cannot go on behaving as if your father is automatically a wronged knight in shining armour. It is conceivable that he is a criminal and at best he has been unforgivably high-handed.'

'What on earth is that supposed to mean? You have no more proof that he was guilty than I have that he was a patriot! Admit it, it's just one person's interpretation against another's!'

'I wish I could regard it like that. But my reaction is unaffected by the two possible interpretations. I believe that he did something wicked for reasons that you might regard as insignificant. The most important one to me is that although I disagree with all the Socialists stand for, I am in favour of the electoral system which put them into power. At best, your father participated in a conspiracy to bring down his country's democratically-elected Government by undemocratic means. It doesn't really matter after that whether he did it because he thought Labour was unfit to rule or because he wanted to make a killing on the international currency market. Either way, his motives were dishonourable. At best they were the motives of a snob and a tyrant who thought he had more of a right to decide who should run this country than the people who elected the Government. I think that's dishonourable.'

'And I think you're a stupid, middle-class woman without the slightest idea of honour or anything else. What do you know about politics compared with a man who's spent a whole career at the top of the Foreign Office? How dare you say such things about my father?' Desperately hurt, Diana was lashing out at her aunt all too effectively.

Hermione's face darkened with real anger.

'Diana, you forget yourself. A sense of honour is not the sole prerogative of the aristocracy. If you think it is, I can only suggest you consider your mother's normal behaviour. Few women have a better pedigree or less real morality and you are in a better position to know that than anyone. As for your view of my political acumen compared with your father's, you might care to recall where he is and speculate how he is living today. The last time I saw him his grasp of international affairs was being utilised at a rather lower level than the one you normally associate him with!'

Her cold anger restored Diana to some sense of reality and for a moment both women sat in silence. With growing shame, Diana began to consider how well her aunt had treated her lately and how completely she had shielded her from the reality of her father's ruin until today, when her own behaviour had forced the whole affair to the surface.

Unable to meet Hermione's eyes, she said in a very small voice, 'I can't accept what you said about Papa, but I hope you can forgive me for saying such terrible untrue things about you. You've been my only real friend and I know you only want to help me. But I must believe in him, and if anyone says he's a rotter, even you, I have to defend him against them. Will you forgive me, please?'

Her aunt conquered an impulse to slap her rather than to forgive her and managed a smile.

'I have no reason to be ashamed of being middle class, my dear – and you must admit that my family's money has been most useful, to you as well as to the Digby-Lentons! Still, there's no profit in speaking of that now. All I want to do is to give you a chance of considering the possibilities for your own future with some detachment, not always in the light of some imaginary crusade on behalf of Alexander Hartley. If our talk enables you to do that, I can cope with the insults!'

'I think I need to do a lot of thinking. Will anyone be too cross if I go off by myself! I'll find my way back to you all eventually, but I must be alone for a while and I can hardly come to harm at Eton on the Fourth!'

'Never make the mistake of confusing my kindness with stupidity, Diana. I think some time on your own here might do you a lot of good. For a start it will give you a taste of being an outsider when everyone else is part of a group. It's less romantic than it might seem. When you're ready, we'll be waiting for you, and I promise that none of this will ever affect my attitude towards you after today.' With that she rose and moved away towards her family, leaving Diana alone on her bench.

The sunlit world around her seemed impossibly remote. Small knots of people passed her from time to time – boys in swallow-tailed coats and over-large silk hats and parents looking proud or bored or nostalgic. It was impossible to escape the festive occasion and the need to belong. Eventually she rejoined the family and tried not to be too put out that with the exception of Ben they seemed hardly to have missed her. It is a sad truth that significant absences are hard to maintain over a period of hours when one has nothing better to do than rejoin the group. The day passed in a haze of inattention. She had suffered a considerable emotional shock and it was taking its toll. Throughout the speeches in Upper School before lunch she was mentally remote. The day was practically over when she began to resume something approaching normal behaviour.

Ben had long given up trying to draw her out and was simply escorting her in silence. He clearly had no intention of getting involved in further squabbles about a man he had never met.

The traditional climax of the day finally hammered home to her that whatever truths Hermione wanted her to accept, whatever escape route Ben Lassiter wanted to offer, she was above all Alexander Hartley's daughter. She was committed to this society and this way of life and she was determined to gain the acclaim of her fellows, by winning, not running away. Deep down, Diana was too intelligent not to recognise that much of what she loved was window dressing and had no more objective importance than the scenery on a stage. Nevertheless it was her stage and she wanted to shine at its centre.

The Procession of Boats glided up the river, the crews clad in their distinctive costumes and white duck trousers. Right on cue, the sentimental strains of the Boating Song floated to the groups of spectators:

> Others will fill our places
> Dressed in the old light blue;
> We'll recollect our races,
> We'll to the flag be true,
> And youth will be still in our faces
> When we cheer for an Eton crew.
>
> Twenty years hence this weather
> May tempt us from office stools,
> We may be slow on the feather
> And seem to the boys old fools,
> But we'll still swing together
> And swear by the best of schools.

The last of the daylight faded and the fireworks began to explode at Fellows Eyot. As it was in the Beginning, is now and ever shall be; World without end . . . her brain ran on inconsequentially. The song insinuated itself again. That was Papa's trouble, he saw the world as an extention of Eton, a magic circle that would protect him for ever. He really had believed that they'd still swing together and swear by the best of schools. It was just a silly song but he thought his background would keep him safe. Silly song, silly Papa – he had thought he was a manipulator and really he was only a poor puppet. Diana decided there and then she was going to be a puppeteer. Only not in America. In England; centre-stage in the only puppet show that counted for her.

Her face luminous in the glow from the firework display, she turned to Ben. 'Take me back to Jermyn Street please and make love to me and then we'll talk about what happens at the end of summer.'

Ben was a man for fast effective solutions and thought the obvious answer to Diana's misery was withdrawal to a more welcoming social environment. He would never understand that for Diana such action spelled failure and disgrace and that she intended to triumph on this stage or perish in the attempt. Having failed to convince her that New York would be a happier setting for her future than London, he made the fatal mistake of trying to prove to her conclusively that her father was a villain – particularly when he knew Hartley's guilt or innocence were irrelevant to his peers and that they condemned him for having been discovered, not for having sinned. Hermione, with her infinite tact and patience, had managed to convey this to Diana at last. Although the girl was not able openly to acknowledge the point, she was close enough to accepting it to want the whole mess left undisturbed for the present. So Ben set out to arrange his love life as he would have solved a business problem, with predictable results. At first he did no more than make Diana vaguely uneasy. Driving back from Eton, he startled her out of her misery by announcing:

'Well, if nothing else will do, I'll just have to get to the bottom of this Petrograd business for myself. Presumably if I can prove to you whether he jumped or they pushed him, you'll be satisfied.'

'Don't meddle, Ben. It's best left alone.'

'But you're the one who's always so keen to prove the old man's innocence.'

'What if you can't?'

'Then he's guilty and your best bet is New York and me!'

'You never give up, do you?' Diana was not smiling.

'Sho' nuff don't, ma'am!'

'Think about it before you go any further, Ben. All this is quite unnecessary. Everyone keeps rushing me and I just want to slow down and get used to things. In a few months I may feel a lot different.'

'In a few months someone else may have pipped me to the post.'

'Carry on like this and it's a racing certainty they will!'

She meant it. Ben decided to keep his own counsel until he knew more about the scandal. But he was determined to win her by detective work and not to let the matter drop as she asked. A couple of days later he was having tea at the Clarges Street house, at Hermione's invitation. Roland was there, too. Diana seemed in better spirits and surprised them by announcing that both of them could escort her to Ascot for the royal race meeting.

'You wouldn't come to Epsom with me for the Derby,' said Ben. 'I thought you weren't interested in racing.'

'All Englishwomen are interested in racing,' said Roland. 'Anyway, if you think Ascot week has all that much to do with the racing, you're in for quite a shock. It has more to do with hats than horses.'

'Aunt Hermione warned me about the Derby,' Diana broke in. 'For the past few years it's rained solidly throughout the meeting. Some of the men said they hadn't seen so much mud since the Somme! And the traffic is so bad that you have to leave London by eleven o'clock to have any chance of seeing the race. I don't like horses enough to spend the day in a traffic jam in order to watch them running around in the rain.'

'Well, if the three of us are going down to Ascot, we can all travel in the Bentley,' said Ben.

'I don't recommend it, Lassiter,' For once Roland was able to keep Ben out of his depth. This was social territory he knew inside out.

'Why not? Will the rioting peasantry of Berkshire break up the car and hack us to pieces?'

'It's just that what Hermione told Diana about Epsom is almost as true for Ascot. There's a jolly good special train from Waterloo and it's far more comfortable than chugging along the road in all that traffic. The lunch tents provide a decent spread, so we can always eat there unless we want to join the party in Uncle Ralph's box. I've already arranged Royal Enclosure badges for Diana and me. Presumably your high-level contacts can fix you up with one.'

Christ, he's beginning to fight back, thought Ben. I'd better stake my claim fast. Ben had started out as he seemed doomed to continue at Ascot – on the wrong foot. His next gaffe occurred at Waterloo when the threesome met to travel down to Berkshire. He had taken great care over his clothes and was confident that his impeccable morning dress with pink carnation buttonhole was correct wear. Nevertheless, Roland greeted him with a slightly too tactful tapping of his own lapel, just at the point where Ben's Royal Enclosure badge was pinned.

'What's the matter? Surely I'm not wearing the wrong badge?'

'Er, not exactly. Your timing's a little premature, that's all. One doesn't put the thing on until just before going in. Rather ostentatious to travel all the way there announcing that you're in the Royal Enclosure.'

'How damned prehistoric!' Ben sounded scornful but his cheeks burned with humiliation. He was used to getting social matters right every time without even having to think about them. He disliked being an outsider, even a favoured one.

They arrived at noon, in time to see the royal party wheel into the courtyard in the landaus which had brought them from Windsor Castle. The Earl of Lonsdale had already completed his annual Ascot pilgrimage in the yellow carriage drawn by perfectly-matched chestnuts and driven by yellow-liveried servants. Ben, forgetting his earlier shame, began to enjoy himself.

'Hey, I could get used to coming here if there was a chance of doing it in a rig like that yellow job!'

'Apart from the royals, Lonsdale's the last horse-drawn survival,' said Roland. 'Before the war practically everyone arrived in that style. It was quite a sight. I remember my parents renting a house at Ascot for Race week when I was a child. I watched them setting off in this wonderful equipage and thought they were almost royalty, too. It was the only real way to travel!'

The royal family briefly acknowledged their subjects from the royal box before sitting down to a luncheon served by footmen in leather breeches. Ben began to feel hungry himself.

'I suppose we'll have to queue for food until mid-afternoon,' he said ruefully, looking at the crowds jostling outside the Luncheon Room.

'Good gracious, no! I'd die of hunger if we had to wait that long,' Diana told him. 'Come on, follow Roland.'

These people spend their lives raising barriers to keep others out, thought Ben wonderingly. It makes the New York Four Hundred look like a bunch of amateurs. The latest social divide comprised a scattering of marquees, all with obviously restricted entry, as Roland had fished out yet more badges which he distributed among them. The doorman at the Highland Brigade tent was a Scottish NCO in full Highland military rig. He glanced at their badges and ushered them inside, where uniformed mess staff served them lunch from regimental silver.

'Lots of regiments and the main London clubs have their own tents down here for members and their guests to have lunch,' Diana explained. 'Roland was in one of the Highland Regiments, so we come here. The Marlboro' Tent is considered to be at the top of the heap because it's the only one in the Paddock. You have to cross the track, as we did, for the others. Still, it's much better than lining up outside the Luncheon Room!'

It was a bright, sunny day and the temperature was

already climbing inside the tent. 'It's going to be a steamy afternoon,' said Ben.

Roland seemed pleased at the prospect. 'If you'd seen the opposite sort of Ascot weather, you'd appreciate this. I remember my first Ascot, in 1919, there was such a downpour on Gold Cup day that the women had to put straw champagne bottle covers over their shoes and make a dash for the stands. Those extravagant frocks look a bit sad under mackintoshes!'

After eating, they strolled to the Paddock to see the parades and place their bets.

'One of us does the honours for Diana,' said Roland. 'Not quite polite for ladies to place their own bets, y'know.'

Ben didn't know, and felt more than ever an outsider. Nevertheless, the horses were breath-taking. Ben came up the steps into the stand towards the starting line. All the colours looked as if they had been polished up specially for the occasion: the horseflesh was glossier, the jockeys' silks brighter, the turf greener than he had thought possible. Until then, Ben's interest in horses had stopped at polo and hacking. Later he was to attribute to this moment the birth of his life-long interest in owning and breeding racehorses.

Ascot enjoyed a unique glamour as Society's fashion parade ground. Roland was right about the hats. The sun shone on impossibly frothy headgear, topping equally frivolous gowns. Below the ranks of seats the privileged racegoers strolled in the green space between stands and track, some making no pretence of being there for the sport. But some races were more special than others, and Steve Donoghue rode four-year-old Brown Jack to victory in the Queen Alexandra Stakes to howls of wild enthusiasm from aristocrat and coster alike. Diana cheered as loudly as anyone, having placed her first-ever bet on the winner. She had chosen the Queen Alexandra Stakes because the name was a secret memento of her father. Her choice of horse and jockey was a simple matter of appreciation of physical grace and potential. Instinct paid off. The £30 she won would have covered the cost of three Louis Kerslake frocks, but as Diana did not pay for these the cash was a windfall to be spent as pocket money.

'I'm taking all three of us out to dinner tonight!' She was practically skipping at the prospect of being hostess for once instead of guest. 'How about the Savoy? The Duchess always felt it wasn't quite proper so I naturally longed to go!'

'Are you sure you want me along, Diana?' Roland was reluctant to abandon her to his rival, but his natural reticence gave him a horror of imposing himself on friends.

'Of course I do – I shouldn't have invited you otherwise!' She was still as entranced as ever with Ben, but now fear of what he might say about her father made her reluctant to be alone with him for long when they were not distracted by love-making. Roland's presence gave her an opportunity to flex the new self-confidence she was developing in the sunshine of male attentiveness and to hold off any unwanted revelations about Alexander Hartley's ambiguous behaviour.

They travelled back to town together in the Racing Special, now stuffy after a day in the sidings at Ascot. They took a cab from Waterloo and at the Hyde Park Corner end of Piccadilly Roland asked to be let out.

'I'll walk over to see Uncle Ralph and meet you at Clarges Street later if the Savoy's still on,' he said. 'The old boy usually likes to hear about the races if he hasn't been able to get there himself.'

As Roland's slender form melted into the afternoon crowds, Ben re-directed the taxi to Jermyn Street.

'Just time for a little bit of illicit nooky before dinner, oh fiery temptress,' he said, twirling an imaginary movie villain's moustache.

They tumbled into his little flat, high on champagne and victory, undressing each other almost before the door had closed behind them. In his most ecstatic moment with Diana, Ben was often conscious that the secret of her sensuality was its complete innocence. Instead of developing a trauma about sex because of repressive parental influence, she had been treated as though sexuality did not exist until she encountered him. As a result nothing was taboo, perverse or distasteful and she was always ready to match his passion with her own. It never occurred to him that she was as innocent of knowledge about pregnancy as about sex, although he was usually as cautious as his passion permitted. Unfortunately occasions like this afternoon, when they had drunk enough champagne for titillation, escaped his control. Diana, murmuring little words of excitement and endearment, was hastily unbuttoning his formal shirt. He still wore his morning coat.

'Christ, lady,' he said in atrocious mock cockney, 'another minute and you'd 'ave 'ad me wiv me topper on an' all!'

'Don't be vulgar, you wretch, and take me to bed at once!'

'As you're so eager, why not the hearth rug?'

He reached behind her and unbuttoned the high neck of her silk frock, then eased it from her shoulders and down her slender body. He dropped to his knees in front of her and began removing her garters and stockings. Diana pressed his head against her smooth, flat belly and her warm expensive scent swept over him. She kicked aside the extravagant clothing in a jumbled heap and crouched on the floor beside him, gently pressing him back and sideways until he sat on the floor with her straddling him. Ben managed to unfasten and remove his trousers but then gave up as she took delicious possession of his body from above. He stretched back on the rug, looking up at the beautiful, wildly excited figure above him and gave a little groan of pleasure.

'Oh, Lady D, don't ever change!'

Half an hour later, he set out to drop her back at Clarges Street to change for dinner. 'Ever come across a lady called Nina Chaliapin?' he asked.

She was at a loss for a moment then said: 'Oh, I vaguely remember when I was very small, she came to a party. Very Ballet Russe and exotic. Mama hated her on sight, of course. Stole too much of her thunder. She was never invited again.'

'I think for once your mother might have had a point. She was, shall we say, interested, in your father.'

Diana's face darkened. 'Am I going to want to hear this?'

'Depends on how much you value the truth. I've been doing a little digging . . .'

'And what if you've come up with dirt?'

'You said you had faith in your father and that if the world knew the truth it would be all sweetness and light. I've been trying to work out just how much straightening out the record needs.'

'And?'

'Well, I suppose one *could* class Ninotchka Chaliapin as the archetypal beautiful lady spy, sent out to tempt strong men to their doom; but that hardly puts what your dear Papa did in the category of King and country. More pleasure and pussy, I'd say.'

He had spoken flippantly, in an effort to remove some of the lethal potential from a situation which was getting out of hand. It was a fundamental mistake.

'You happen to be talking about my father, not some American gangster. I think you've said quite enough!'

Diana's eyes were blazing and the restraint with which she spoke was betrayed by her expression. Ben blundered on in a misguided attempt to repair the damage.

'Okay, so that was a bit cheap, but if you want to come to terms with the whole affair, as you say, you have to accept reality, and I think maybe it was just that – an affair that went terribly wrong.'

He mistook her silence for willingness to be convinced. 'After all, why should your father be any different from the rest of us? If you tried to lead me astray, I think I might betray all sorts of loyalties for you. I think she really was his *femme fatale.*'

'And I think you're a crass, vulgar foreigner without any idea of the way honourable English people behave. What you're suggesting is utterly outrageous and I have no intention of listening to it any longer!'

Her voice held a feverish intensity he had never heard before. The car slowed to walking speed behind a small queue of traffic outside the Ritz and Ben turned to answer her. As he did so, she opened the passenger door and jumped out, timing her departure so well that she did not even stumble as the big car idled along.

'Diana — wait — come back, you idiot! You can't just take off!'

Ben's protests were cut off by a cacophony of horns as the angry motorists behind pressed him to move on faster. He reached over and slammed the door, accelerating away and losing her in the early evening crowd along Piccadilly.

Back at Jermyn Street, he wondered what on earth to do. Another girl would have thrown her fit of temperament and then allowed herself to be coaxed back to contentment with treats, compliments and apologies. Not Diana. Ben was horribly aware, too late, that his attempted exorcism of her father's unholy past might also have wiped out his own future with the girl. Better to let sleeping fathers lie . . . and lie, he thought. It was 6.45 pm. They had been going to meet up at Clarges Street at 7.15. Ben decided that the worst she could do was to throw him out. And who knew? She might simply decide to ignore the whole thing.

He was wrong. When he arrived at the mansion, a parlour-maid showed him into the hall and went to announce his arrival. After a long pause she returned and ushered him in. Diana, looking exquisite and furious in her re-created dove-grey satin, was standing on the hearthrug. Roland turned towards him with an ambiguous expression which Ben would have recognised as pity had he known what was ahead of him.

'You Americans certainly aren't prepared to take no for an answer, are you?' she said, almost before the maid had departed.

He chose a light-hearted response. 'But you invited me to dine at the Savoy, remember? I make it a rule never to break engagements with beautiful women, however angry they might be.'

'All right, if that's the way you want it. Come on, we'll take a taxi.'

'But the Bentley's outside!'

'I'd no more set foot in that car again than travel in a costermonger's cart!'

Before he could respond to that, she was in the hall, shrugging on a velvet evening coat.

'You seem to have covered a lot of ground between half-past four and seven o'clock this evening, old chap,' Roland murmured. 'Too much, I fear!'

They went out into Piccadilly and he hailed a cab.

Diana attacked dinner like a starving refugee, albeit a refugee with perfect table manners. Ben had never seen so much food consumed so quickly. Hors d'oeuvres, soup, sole, roast lamb and Charlotte Russe (the last horribly appropriate, he thought) appeared and were dispatched in awesome quantity, accompanied successively by vintage white Burgundy and a superb claret. If I've lost, can Roland afford her? Ben wondered.

Throughout, Diana chattered pleasantly with Roland and insulted Ben's country and social origins. He attempted to handle it philosphically, treating the evening as punishment for his own insensitivity in trying to make her face the truth about her father. It became more difficult as the meal progressed. Finally, when Roland left them alone for a few minutes, he made an effort to deal with the rift and re-kindle their relationship on the old basis.

'I know you're hurt, Diana, but believe me, I was trying to create a future for us, not destroy everything,' he told her.

At first he thought she would pretend not to have heard, but eventually she responded.

'Well, you made a mess of it, and it's the sort of mess that won't be cleaned up in a hurry.' Her face was frigid with hostility and he could see no hope there.

'But why? This is so stupid. We love each other and it shouldn't matter what our elders did when it comes to our future. So why should we have to spend our time tip-toeing around a dead scandal?'

'Because it's not dead to me and because I find your persistent refusal to understand how I feel deeply offensive!'

'Baby, I know your education has been patchy, but I think it's time you started reading what Sigmund Freud says about you and me and your Papa. It's highly relevant to your behaviour now. It might come as a shock, but you're not *really* thinking of honour, England and the King when you come on so strong about him and his dishy little Russian. You're just plain old-fashioned jealous!'

Oh, Christ, he thought, I've done it again! I love the kid so much she can get me mad even when I'm trying to humour her, then I say appalling things and here we go again. There, indeed, they went again – this time beyond recall. Diana smiled at him. It was the snarl of a tigress.

'Please get up, say goodnight to Roland when he comes back, and go. After that, I'd appreciate it if you and your filthy little peeping Tom ideas would stay as far as possible from me and my family. If you don't, I'm tempted to ask my Uncle James to re-introduce the old English custom of horsewhipping cads!'

'Okay, Diana, you win. I think your only hope lay with me. On your own, you'll go on and on with this crazy daydream about your sainted father giving his all to save the nation, while the world laughs at you because they know he was just a middle-aged man who got so dick-simple that he sold his honour for a quick screw.'

Roland returned as Diana attempted to physically attack Ben. Luckily the table held her back, or the Savoy would have been treated to a scene which tested even its legendary sang-froid. He knew nothing of what had happened in his absence but Diana's immediate intentions were clear. He moved smartly in beside her, slipped an arm casually behind her and locked her into an unbreakable grip.

'I think perhaps you'd better call it a day, Lassiter. I'll telephone later if you like to let you know Diana got home safely.'

But now Ben, too, was beyond rationality.

'Frankly, I don't give a shit if she jumps in the Thames with you behind her!' He turned and left the restaurant, a number of openly interested diners watching him go.

CHAPTER NINE

That Royal Ascot night in the Savoy was fixed for ever afterwards in Roland's memory for a variety of reasons: first there was the strain of sitting in the restaurant for nearly an hour, chatting about superficialities in a pleasant monotone which became a monologue, as Diana failed to utter a single word after Ben's departure. It also turned out to be the night he made love to her for the first time and that she accepted his second, stumbling proposal of marriage. On balance, the monologue was the most clearly etched of these events.

To his relief she suddenly cut into his rambling account of last year's Henley Regatta and said 'Please let's go now.'

He paid the bill and they walked out across the courtyard, ignoring the audience spilling from the adjoining Savoy Theatre, and headed off through the fresh June evening towards the quiet of the Mall. She did not speak again until they were half-way up the wide road, approaching the bulk of Buckingham Palace.

'I don't want to go back to Clarges Street yet. Please let's go to the studio.'

After that she remained silent but apparently calm until they were inside the studio. As soon as he closed the door she gave way to huge, wracking sobs which he thought would never end. Unable to offer any comfort, Roland simply went off to make her some tea. When he returned with the cups, Diana had moved from the hall into the main studio and was sitting on an old chesterfield, still sniffling but more controlled than before. She saw the tea and managed a shaky laugh.

'Dear Roland! You understand me better than I ever give you credit for doing.' She took the cup and sipped gratefully at the fragrant Lapsang Souchong.

After a while, he said: 'You don't have to tell me, you know. I get the general idea of what's been going on. He asked me a bit about it a week or so back.'

'You know about all this?'

'No one knows it all, Diana, not even your father, I suspect, but one would have to be deaf and blind at the Foreign Office not to have picked up hints.'

'But why have you never told me anything?'

'There was nothing that would have given you any comfort. I told Lassiter as much and advised him to leave it alone, but some ass gave him a lead on this Russian woman, and after that there was no holding him.'

The ensuing silence lengthened to breaking point. Diana found the temptation irresistible.

'Wh-what do you know about her?'

'I told you, nothing that would give you any comfort. Do you trust me sufficiently to leave it at that?'

'For the moment. I can't guarantee I shall always feel like that, though.'

'Let's just say that if I ever think anything I know will help, I shall tell you. Now – will you marry me?'

'It isn't July yet.'

'I didn't think you'd even remember having said that to me. Were you really giving the matter serious consideration?'

'Yes, Roland. I've been doing at least some growing up recently and I've begun to realise that you and I have far more in common than I ever thought before. But I don't think I'm a very nice person.'

'What a dreadful wishy-washy little word that is! Of course you're not nice! God help you if you were – I certainly shouldn't be wasting my time in thankless pursuit of your affection!'

'You always turn out to be cleverer than I thought when I sit still and listen to you.'

'Then I wish you'd listen more often; perhaps we should both be a lot happier.'

She was starting to cry again. He joined her on the chesterfield, took the empty cup from her and then sat absently stroking her fingers. After a while he raised them to his lips and held them there, looking over the slim, strong hand into her eyes. The caress developed into a full-blown embrace. Hesitantly he touched her breasts outside the soft material of her frock. Diana, passive now, made no move to stop him. He eased the narrow straps off her shoulders and the garment slid down with a faint susurrus. He bent forward and kissed her breasts, almost reverently. She got up and let the gown fall, stepped out of it and moved it to a chair. He watched her unselfconscious grace as she walked back to him, naked save for stockings, garters and knickers. She stretched out a hand to him. He rose and followed her silently.

Later, lying on his bed in a patch of moonlight that bleached her hair to the colour of autumn leaves, she agreed to marry him.

'What made you say yes?'

'You didn't ask me whether Ben and I were lovers.'

He never told her that it had been unnecessary, for he had known the answer all along.

Ben did not call at Clarges Street again. When Roland left her outside her front door in the small hours, the Bentley was still parked nearby. In the morning when Diana looked down from the drawing room window, it was gone. She spent a nervous day half-expecting a telephone call or a note, but when nothing came she knew there would be no attempt at reconciliation. In spite of the huge unhealed wound inflicted by the loss, she did not regret his silence. After what had been said the previous evening, there could be no going back. Diana turned her mind to the future which she had once fought but now accepted as inevitable. She told Hermione over luncheon that she had accepted Roland's proposal. Her aunt was pleased, but it was clear that Diana was telling her only a fraction of what had happened suddenly to eliminate Ben Lassiter from the matrimonial stakes. It was agreed that her engagement would be announced on the evening of her dance, provided her mother and grandfather approved the match.

'Of course, my dear, that's almost a formality. I'm sure they will both be as delighted as I am. I think perhaps we should telephone your mother in Scotland with the news.'

Diana shrank from the thought. 'Please, Aunt H, I know I shouldn't be such a coward, but couldn't I just write to her? Perhaps Grandpapa could speak to her on the telephone.'

'I should find it rather hard to accept if one of my children did that. Why are you so anxious? You've done nothing wrong – you should be happy to break the news.'

'You know what she's like! I'm not afraid of Mama, but I am afraid that she'll say something to spoil it, something that will make it all pointless. Oh, please, Aunt, try to understand! Grandpapa won't – she's his daughter, after all.'

Hermione understood all too well. Incapable of finding loving words, Sarah was adept at souring the most pleasurable moments.

'Go and write your letter, Diana. I shall talk to the Earl.'

George Digby-Lenton was so pleased at the accomplishment of his mission that the small breach of etiquette was swept aside by his enthusiasm. 'No problem – the child always was a bit temperamental. I'll tell Sarah. Anyway, perhaps it's better this way. She can pour on the vitriol a bit overmuch when she's dealing with Diana, God knows why!'

He was heading for the telephone when he stopped and turned back. 'By the way, whatever happened to that American fella, Lassiter? Admit I had high hopes there. Rich as Croesus, they tell me. Now *that* would have knocked Sarah's nose a bit out of joint!' He snorted with mirth at the thought.

'Oh, I think it just petered out. You know how different their backgrounds were. I think it's all for the best . . .' At least, I *hope* it's all for the best, she added, silently.

Glentyrrel
June 30, 1928

Dear Diana
Your grandfather told me the news about your engagement
to Roland and I have now received your letter. What a pity

you did not think fit to telephone me yourself with the news!
Still, I suppose one must expect such behaviour in the light
of previous incidents.

I shall try to return to London, at least for a brief visit,
between now and the wedding; I hope to put in an appearance
for your dance and the engagement announcement. It would
never do for le tout Londres *to think your father had*
succeeded in driving me into hiding.

Please try not to encourage any further bursts of vulgar
display from Hermione. She may think she is being generous;
I find it difficult to approve the emergence of a young girl in
her first season in clothes which apparently pass as the pro-
ducts of a couture house. I received a letter from Primrose
Grafton's mama a few days ago which left me with the
gravest misgivings about the contents of your wardrobe.

Your loving mother
Sarah Hartley.

Only Mama would sign her full name in a letter to her
own daughter, thought Diana as the latest epistle followed
all her mother's other correspondence down the lavatory
pan.

There followed a period of mounting anguish for Diana
as she prepared for her dance and official engagement announcement with the nagging dread of her mother's
planned return for the double celebration. However reports
from the Highlands indicated that Aunt Alice's condition
continued to deteriorate. Something else was going on up
there, too, but Diana had no idea what it was. The adults
hastily started discussing trivia when she entered the room
and Hermione twice hurried off to Brook Street for a tête-à-
tête with James and the Earl after receiving letters from
the Scottish estate. Diana was unsure whether the letters
were from or about her mother. It was fairly clear that they
concerned something far more secret than the state of Aunt
Alice's health.

Finally, unbelievably, the day of her dance arrived, without the related arrival of her mother. Diana felt closer to a
prayer of thanks than ever before. She spent the morning

at the Bath Club, swimming and enjoying a massage. Then there was a light lunch before she and Hermione went to Bond Street to visit hairdresser and beautician. Louise Kerslake was waiting for her at Brook Street on her return. In Hermione's boudoir the Patou ball gown reposed on its padded hanger, resplendent with hand embroidery. It was so beautiful that Diana was almost afraid to put it on.

'You really must watch out for those big meals, Miss Hartley,' said Louise. 'I almost had a fit when I brought this back for you two weeks ago and it was too tight on the hips!'

The reaction at Patou had been positively scandalised. 'Madame Kerslake, if I were dealing with any other dressmaker I would say your measurements must be inaccurate,' said a censorious senior fitter. 'This arrangement is most irregular anyway, but for one of our gowns to be four centimetres out at the hips? Unthinkable! The client is either too fond of her food or she is *enceinte*!'

Louise considered what Evangeline had said during a recent afternoon visit to Fulham and prayed that it was just food. Somehow she had her doubts.

They were resolved as soon as she helped Diana into the finished gown. She had told the fitter to allow a little extra leeway even to the fuller fitting – just in case the client had been to a few more grand dinners, they were to understand. Just as well: it now fitted Diana perfectly and there was no question in Louise's mind that Diana was pregnant.

Not that anyone but her dressmaker would suspect, yet. The girl was naturally heavy-breasted with very flat stomach and boyish hips, so at this early stage the added abdominal weight did no more than balance her up. And Diana certainly exhibited none of the tell-tale signs of guilt and anxiety commonly visible in unmarried girls with such a secret.

'That's because the poor little devil doesn't know herself,' said Evangeline indignantly when Louise questioned her discreetly.

'If she's old enough to do it, she's old enough to know what happens next!' Louise was angry and protective on behalf of Hermione, whom she regarded as only slightly beneath the saints.

'Oh, for heaven's sake, Louise, who's going to tell 'er, I'd like to know? I'm not supposed to know myself – pure as the driven snow, I am, remember? How d'you think Lady Stanmore would take it if I suddenly started telling her niece she'd get in the pudding club if she was naughty?'

'Less of that, Evie! You weren't brought up in Tiger Bay, so don't talk as if you were!'

'Well it's true! Lady Stanmore thinks nice young ladies don't do it. Miss Diana doesn't even know what "it" is, but I'm pretty certain she's been doing something she enjoys for ages now without the faintest idea of what could happen. Lady Stanmore must think Miss Diana's mother told her all about it – after all, she's seventeen and her curse started four years ago – but I don't think Lady Sarah ever told the poor love anything.

'You've seen those daft debs she goes about with. Half of them still think it's all about storks and gooseberry bushes and the other half don't talk about what they're up to if they've got any sense. When the odd one does get caught out, she suddenly develops weak lungs like that Evadne Finch-Myles and has to go off to Switzerland for a long rest in a sanatorium. Her maid told me what sort of sanatorium that was!'

Louise was a practical soul and did not waste further time on recriminations.

'How far gone d'you think she is?'

'Hard to say. According to the nurses at the clinic I went to, with some girls it shows within weeks and with others they're half-way to the delivery room before anybody knows there's a baby on the way. From the way she's been behaving, though, it could be anything from a few weeks up to three months.'

'Good God – they're talking about a Christmas wedding!'

'Might as well wait a little in that case and do the christening while they're in church,' said Evangeline.

'Do stop being facetious. We can't just let it go on. It would break Lady Stanmore's heart if her niece got involved in a scandal of her own on top of that trouble over her father. After all her kindness, the least we can do is find some way of warning her so that she can get the wedding day moved forward before it's announced.'

'Your timing could be better, Louise. Haven't we got enough on our hands today, with Miss Diana's dance and the engagement announcement . . .' she tailed off in horror, realising the implications.

'Exactly, you silly girl! If we leave it until after today, Miss Hartley and Lady Stanmore will be telling everyone it's a Boxing Day wedding. Then there'll really be some red faces when Society starts asking why the sudden change to August or September! If Lady Stanmore, at least, knows before the announcement, she can tell people they want a short engagement and deal with the sudden little arrival when it comes along!'

'But if Miss Diana realises she's having a baby, she'll go to pieces about this evening. She'll never be able to go through with it.'

'She'll just have to, Evangeline. All I can say is she should thank her lucky stars her mother's not here. One look and that one would be on to her!'

Louise came to an abrupt decision. 'The best thing is for me to tell Lady Stanmore now, this afternoon. If she feels like talking to me about it, fine. If not, she'll work something out.'

Hermione was about to enjoy a glass of champagne. Her father had always said that one glass before a big evening gave a woman the zest she needed and she had never doubted the wisdom of such an excuse for a little self-indulgence. When her maid told her that Mrs Kerslake wanted to see her, she decided that just this once she might include the dressmaker in her private treat. After that day, she never regarded Veuve Clicquot in quite the same light again. She ascribed the dressmaker's apparent unease to the slight impropriety of her invitation. Tradespeople were, after all, freelance servants, and one normally did not invite them to stay for drinks, even privately. Moments later she was glad she had done so.

'I beg your pardon, Mrs Kerslake. I think I must have misheard you. My niece is *what*?'

Louise took a bracing gulp of the frothy wine and repeated what she had said. Hermione put down her glass and stood up.

'I don't think you and I have anything further to say to each other. Please leave.'

'Lady Stanmore, if there were any other way, I assure you that I would not be speaking to you in this manner, now or at any other time. But if I did not tell you now, the consequences would be unthinkable.'

'I find them quite unthinkable as it is. On what do you base this ludicrous suggestion?'

'The only one I know. She has outgrown her ball gown twice in a month, and before you suggest that she has been over-eating, it's all in one place.'

Taking advantage of Hermione's stunned silence, Louise speedily added her conviction that at the moment Diana was as ignorant of her condition as her aunt had been moments before. Hermione sat down again, beginning to realise why Louise had found it necessary to tell her now ... 'And you had to stop me letting everyone know they were to marry at Christmas. How can I ever thank you?'

'You already have, milady. You've treated me so well that I couldn't stand by and let this happen, even if it meant losing your custom. At least now there's the possibility of doing something about it, though apart from changing the wedding date I can't think of any immediate suggestions, because I really believe Miss Hartley is unaware of her condition. I'd better leave you now.'

'No – sit down and finish your drink. It will help me to talk it over with someone trustworthy. We have to find some way of broaching it with Diana that doesn't end in hysterics ...'

She poured more champagne and they began reviewing the possibilities.

In the end they decided that Diana could not be told before the dance.

'She is already under all sorts of pressure and I'm sure something went wrong between her and a young man she was seeing a while ago. She's borne up very well under the strain of her father's departure but I think that this would be the last straw if we told her today.'

'Is there no reason you could give her for putting forward the wedding date?'

Hermione became pensive. 'Yes, there is. Her aunt is very ill, as you know, and Diana's mother is with her in the Highlands. There are complications with which I shan't burden you, but as a result it's quite reasonable to tell my niece that family considerations make the change necessary. I can imply that it is solely her Aunt Alice's health and that should suffice. Yes . . . that makes a lot of sense.'

Relieved, Louise prepared to depart. Hermione delayed her again, this time momentarily.

'How much does Evangeline know of this, and how much do you trust her?'

Truth time, thought Louise. I hope my instincts are right about Lady Stanmore.

'Evangeline was the victim of identical circumstances two years ago, Milady, but with no possibility of marriage. My daughter Imogen is really her little girl. I trust her completely.'

To her immense relief, Hermione simply nodded. 'So there will be no problem about hints of this getting out?'

'She has never mentioned her own trouble outside my house. She knows about Miss Hartley because it was necessary for me to question her to know whether my guess was correct. I trust her absolutely, madam, as I said.'

'Good. Otherwise it would all be impossible. Diana is going to need someone close and thanks to her mother she has no friend from her own background.'

Talk about the colonel's lady and Judy O'Grady, thought Louise.

'Very well, Mrs Kerslake. You talk to Evangeline and I shall talk to my niece. Then tomorrow I shall have the

177

unattractive task of discussing the matter with her more fully.'

Louise went to see Evangeline. Hermione started to ring for a servant to remove the half-finished bottle and glasses, thought again about that evening, said 'The hell with Papa's advice!' and took another glass.

By the time she went to see Diana, the girl was ready for her big entrance, although it was still hours ahead and she must go through a dinner party before the dance. She wore a gown of eau-de-Nil silk chiffon completely covered from neckline to knees in beaded hand embroidery. The beads ranged in colour from milky turquoise to deep jade and when Diana moved the gown looked like flowing water touched by light. The pale-green fabric tumbled through in godets to ankle length. The outfit was completed by a smooth cap smothered in matching embroidery, with little pendant beads like water droplets around her face. Hermione's anger evaporated. No one will ever remain cross with Diana for long when she looks like this, she thought.

'My dear, you look lovely,' she said. 'I hope tonight will be a great success, and I'm sure it will be. Now, I have a favour to ask of you. Would it be possible for you and Roland to re-arrange the wedding date to early autumn this year rather than waiting until Christmas?'

'Why, Aunt Hermione? Is something wrong?'

'I'm hoping not, but there's very little question of your aunt Alice recovering, I'm afraid. I hesitate to raise such a melancholy matter now, but I'm afraid that if we postpone the marriage until Christmas . . .'

She began to feel guilty about the slight deception involved in the silent implication, but set it aside on the grounds that Diana was getting off fairly lightly for the moment.

The girl responded immediately. 'I'm sure there won't be a problem! Roland will probably be delighted to make it earlier – he's been muttering about what a long time it is till Christmas ever since I accepted his proposal! I'll ask him over dinner.'

'Thank you, darling. I shall talk to your uncle and grand-father.'

'Oh – didn't one of them suggest the change in the first place?'

Damn, thought Hermione, nearly gave the game away! 'Well, neither of them wanted to spoil your plans, so they left it to me to find out how set you were on a Christmas wedding. I shall just have to see that we've all got it straight now.'

And calm them down when they explode over her condition, she reflected forlornly. Explode they did. The Earl started to talk about thrashing Roland, and after James had voiced his astonishment that the young man had plucked up the courage he expressed similar views. Hermione calmed them by roundly condemning Sarah for neglect that amounted to a criminal act in allowing a girl as attractive as Diana to run around loose without the faintest idea of the consequences of sexual activity. The Earl was quite surprised at the range of his daughter-in-law's vocabulary. Overall, though, Hermione was pleasantly surprised at the way they took it. As soon as they knew the marriage was assured and that steps were being taken to hurry it along, they were satisfied.

'Happened before and it'll happen again, even in the best families,' growled the Earl. 'At least we know the Granby succession's guaranteed!'

They were particularly amenable to the need to keep the whole matter secret from Diana until after the dance.

'She could prove as unstable as Sarah and one at a time's more than enough,' said George Digby-Lenton.

This was the mysterious bit of family business from which Diana had been excluded in recent weeks. Her mother's capriciousness had toppled over into something more while she was in Scotland. At first they had assumed it was the stress of the scandal followed by the probably fatal illness of her favourite sister, but a further complication had shown up. It seemed that Sarah's affection for her brother-in-law, Alice's husband, was anything but sisterly. They had embarked upon some sort of affair in London around Easter time and her lightning decision to abandon Diana at the beginning of the Season had been influenced crucially by his impending departure for the Highlands, not by her sister's deteriorating condition. The affair had been stormy since then, as Alisdair had learned that having Sarah for passionate interludes was quite different from having Sarah twenty-four hours a day. His interest was replaced by hostility, Sarah's stability slipped further and now various people from the local doctor and a family servant to Alisdair himself were making regular appeals to the Earl and James to remove her – by force if need be. For once, Sarah Hartley's mental state made Diana's life easier. Without it she would never have escaped the wrath of her grandfather and uncle. They've probably decided that one dotty female in the woodshed is more than enough and won't risk Diana going the same way, thought Hermione, thankful that circumstances had eased her passage somewhat.

Two dozen family friends gathered at Brook Street for a dinner party before the dance that evening. The engagement had been an open secret for a few days, so the happy couple were placed together at the table and were already gracefully accepting the good wishes of those around them. At a point when the attention of both their neighbours was elsewhere, Diana told Roland of the proposed change of wedding date.

'I told Aunt H I hardly thought you'd object. I hope I wasn't saying the wrong thing on your behalf.'

Roland watched her silently for a few moments before answering.

'You know I'd marry you tomorrow morning, given the opportunity. But how odd of someone like Hermione to bring up a matter like Alice's illness at the last minute like this. She's usually far more considerate in her timing.'

Diana did not believe in wasting time speculating on others' motives. She preferred to act first and think later. The reasons for Hermione's apparent lapse interested her minimally.

'Oh, Roland, even Aunt H can't be perfect all the time! She probably let it slip with so much on her mind and then remembered today, when she had to sort out a date before the announcement. No great mystery.'

'Well, as far as I'm concerned, it's up to you and her to set the date. Just tell me when, my love, and I shall be there.'

She smiled at him and turned to talk with the neighbour who had just finished a lengthy discussion of the autumn's hunting prospects with a fellow field sportsman across the table.

The Earl claimed the privilege of the first dance with Diana. They looked very attractive together and he found it easy to put aside his irritation at the latest scrape created by his granddaughter's impetuous ignorance.

'We make a handsome couple, m'dear. Say what they will about your father, he came from good-lookin' stock and you do him credit!'

She was astonished. 'Grandpapa – I never expected to hear you refer to Papa so kindly. One could almost believe you liked him!'

'Couldn't stomach the bounder, but that has nothing to do with it! He's a bad lot, Diana, and I won't listen to any argument on that score, but that doesn't mean you should ever be ashamed of him. This lot of nonentities' – he made a grand gesture to include half the ballroom – 'aren't in his class. Born out of 'is time and never got used to it, that's all. Some of my forebears a century or so ago would have run 'im damn' close for villainy, foolhardiness and plain old-fashioned glamour. Can't get away with it these days, though. Then you could, with a little luck.

'Point I'm trying to make is this. Don't blame the old devil too much, but don't try to start a crusade for 'im, either. In his less self-indulgent moments, he'd be the first to tell you you're backing a loser. Start again as if you were an orphan. Now's the time – marriage, new life and all that. Don't waste yourself fighting lost battles.'

They danced on, Diana silently digesting the complex tangle that was her family. Eventually she found the courage to answer him.

'But what about loyalty, Grandpapa? After all, your family motto is "Unto Death". That must count for something.'

'Course it does, but in his view as well as the world's, Alexander's dead already. They just haven't buried 'im. Don't wait for the funeral!'

The conversation made Diana feel better. She began to see the first glimmer of a possibility that one day the Petrograd Communiqué would not be a byword for treachery but a half-forgotten memory. Even Grandpapa, the Mandarin's arch-enemy, was mellowing perceptibly. She enjoyed a perfect evening, satisfactorily observing the eclipse of such unfavoured souls as Primrose Grafton and Catherine Lenton as she danced by, the centre of attention, compliments and good wishes.

The following day came as a terrible shock. Hermione had assumed that no one would stir much before noon. She and Diana had stayed at Brook Street after the dance, and had not retired until 5 am. It was after luncheon, therefore, that she saw Diana in the library back at the Clarges Street house.

'Diana I have to talk to you about something very delicate. May I ask you how much you know about what a man and woman do, alone, after they're married?'

The girl reddened. 'Well – you know – they, er, go to bed together.'

'Yes, but have you any idea what they do in bed?'

'Sort of.'

'Do you know because you've been rehearsing?'

Her confusion was total.

'Oh, dear, Aunt H, do you have to ask? It's all frightfully embarrassing and I know it's not done . . .'

'But *have* you?'

'Well, yes, sort of.'

'One can't "sort of" do what I'm talking about, Diana. One either does or one doesn't.'

'Then yes; I have.'

'Do you know what happens after one does this?'

Her niece attempted to look sophisticated and failed dismally. 'I didn't think anything happened.'

'How do you think people have babies?'

Diana was not stupid. Innocence, not slowness, was to blame for her ignorance. In that moment she was no longer innocent or ignorant.

'Oh God. No.'

'Oh God, yes, I fear. Haven't you noticed you were putting on weight in front?'

'Well, you know how much I eat when I'm a bit worried. I thought I'd been overdoing it, that's all.'

As the significance of what Hermione was saying sank in, the blush drained from Diana's face. She turned white and began shaking.

'But everyone will know! No one will ever speak to me again!'

'I think we can avoid the worst, but really, my dear, you have been unbelievably foolish. You must have known what you were doing was wrong or you wouldn't have concealed it!'

'I didn't consider it at all, Aunt. I can't think why not. You must think me a most frightful fool, but at the time it seemed like the obvious thing to do!'

'Hmm . . . young men have been telling girls that since Adam was a boy!'

'Oh, please don't blame Roland. I'm sure he never intended it to happen!'

Hermione looked at her long and hard. 'Are you sure there's nothing else you wish to tell me, Diana? I'm aware that you were far more innocent than I realised, because your mother had neglected to instruct you in any way, and I'm quite prepared to listen if anything further is troubling you.'

Diana looked away hastily. 'No – nothing at all. But isn't this bad enough?'

'Well, it's not so bad, thanks to the change of wedding dates. We shall arrange everything for early September and after that just take matters as they come. Of course, it will be less than amusing to discuss the whole business with your mother.'

'Oh, God, I'd forgotten Mama!'

'In view of her share of guilt in this matter, I am prepared to deal with her on your behalf, so don't worry about that.

What I cannot do, however, is protect you from the inevitable gossip when you have a baby too soon after your marriage. There are limits to what people accept as premature, you know! That's something you'll have to come to terms with yourself. No one can help you there.

'To be practical for a moment, I think we must talk together, fully, about all this. It is quite unforgivable for anyone to have put you in such a vulnerable position, and from now on I intend to ensure that you understand precisely the functions of your own body. I suppose I had better take Lettie in hand, too, or they'll be re-naming the Digby-Lentons the Bunny-Rabbits!'

In spite of the grave circumstances, Diana giggled, and Hermione permitted herself an answering smile.

'Now, be off! I have to start organising your wedding and attempting to make your Mama behave like a human being for once! Oh, and Diana – it might help you to know that Evangeline is aware of your problem and has had similar troubles herself. That, of course, is a matter of the strictest confidence!'

Diana departed gratefully. Hermione gave Alexander Hartley's abandoned whisky decanter a longing look, pushed the thought aside and reached for her address book.

As if by pre-arrangement, Diana started being sick that evening. Disaster struck immediately afterwards. She emerged from the bathroom, feeling and looking deathly, and tottered into her room. As she sank into an armchair, the door swung open to reveal her mother. Sarah Hartley was at her awe-inspiring worst. Tall, ash blonde, immaculately dressed and furious, she was a Chanel-clad modernisation of the Furies of ancient Greek myth.

'Mama – what are you doing here?' Diana tried to marshal her defences against the inevitable attack.

'Arriving too late to salvage what remains of my family's reputation, it seems!'

She swept in and struck an attitude in front of her daughter.

'Leave us, Evangeline. This is not for servants' ears!'

Diana flung her a beseeching glance.

'Beg pardon, Ma'am, but I take my orders from Miss Diana and I think she wants me to stay!' Evangeline quailed but stood her ground.

Sarah turned on her savagely. 'You little Welsh slut – for that you're dismissed! I'm the mistress here and don't you forget it. Pack up and get out now – at once!' She turned back towards her daughter. Over her shoulder, Evangeline gestured reassuringly in an attempt to convey to Diana that she would find Lady Stanmore at once.

Now Diana caught the full brunt of Sarah Hartley's insane wrath.

'And as for you, you little whore, I might have known you'd go the same way as your father if I left that middle-class trollop Hermione to look after you for more than five minutes! Christ, Alexander would be proud of you now! He'd probably rent you out for ready cash given half a chance!'

Lady Sarah had travelled down from Edinburgh that day, having stormed out of Glentyrrel Castle early the previous evening after Alisdair had suggested that she needed a doctor as much as her sister Alice. Walking silently up the stairs at Clarges Street, she had seen the whey-faced Diana emerge from the bathroom and with the selective intuition of the mentally ill had immediately guessed the girl's condition. Now she had found a perfect target for her hatred of Alisdair, Alexander and the world in a defenceless girl. Diana was weeping in a mixture of outrage and fear. Evangeline had gone to find Hermione, her departure unnoticed by Sarah. Now she advanced on her daughter, teeth bared like a mad dog, flecks of foam appearing at the corners of her mouth. She spoke slowly and menacingly, the pitch rising relentlessly as her face bent closer to the cowering girl.

'You've been very . . . very naughty . . . and now you're going to be very . . . very . . . sorry! Naughty little girls are punished by their Mamas; punished very . . . very . . . severely!' She reached forward, seized Diana by the hair and dragged her bodily out of the chair on to the floor.

Involuntarily Diana reached up to protect herself. Refusing to relax her grip on the girl's hair, Sarah tumbled forward on to her and the two of them went down in a flailing mass of arms and legs. At this point Evangeline got back with Hermione, whom she had met in the hall, just returning from a cocktail party. It required their joint strength to drag Sarah off her daughter. When they succeeded, she turned on Hermione and started clawing at her sister-in-law's cocktail frock, shrieking abuse as she did so.

'Stop it, Madam!' Evangeline paid lip service to the mistress-servant relationship, but her tone was pure command. Sarah ignored her and renewed her attack on Hermione. Having delivered her warning, Evangeline struck – a sharp jab to Sarah's kidneys, followed by an open-handed slap across the face as the woman jerked around against the surprise attack. The slap stopped her in her tracks. She raised a limp hand to her already-flaming cheek, caressed it, then looked at her fingers as though expecting to see blood. Tears started from her eyes. 'Hurts . . .' she said, disjointedly. 'Hurts. Hurt myself . . .'

She left them and started wandering off down the corridor that led away from Diana's room, muttering vaguely to herself and clearly unaware of her surroundings.

'See to Miss Diana, Evangeline. I'll attend to Lady Sarah,' said Hermione.

Evangeline put Diana to bed. 'Come on, Miss Diana, it's all over now. We'll see that she leaves you alone. Don't you worry about a thing.'

But Diana was sobbing, almost beyond control herself.

'Evie, Evie, she's quite mad. What if that happens to me? I *am* her daughter; what if I go dotty? What about the baby? Roland's my cousin – you know what people say.'

'Yes, Miss – a damned sight too much, if you ask me! Now you lie quietly. I'm going to see if Lady Stanmore has sent for the doctor. I think he should see you too.'

'No Evie, don't leave me. She might come back!'

'Nonsense, Miss. If I know your aunt, your Mama's under lock and key by now! You rest there quiet and I'll be back in a minute.'

The doctor duly arrived and gave Diana a mild sleeping draught. Her mother received a hefty knock-out injection. Subsequently a specialist diagnosed extreme strain and anxiety and suggested that Lady Sarah would improve if she had plenty of rest and no excitement for a few weeks. A family council of war decided to ship her off to a kinswoman in Kent, where she could recuperate, it was hoped, in time to appear at the wedding early in September. In spite of Sarah's precarious mental health, her presence there was vital, even Hermione agreed.

'As Lady Bracknell said, to lose one parent is unfortunate; to lose two is positively careless!' she told James. 'She must be at the wedding and Diana will simply have to put up with the suspense.'

In the meantime, she thought, any chance the poor girl might have had of a respectable married life in London with a mad mother, a disgraced father and an embarrassingly early baby was minimal.

Roland preferred to take life as it came and avoid confrontations. But he was aware that Diana needed a defender against the mythical dragons which pursued her. He was deeply shocked by her pregnancy and half expected that James Digby-Lenton would attack him physically when he summoned Roland to break the news. His insistence that he was eager to marry Diana as soon as possible mollified Lord Stanmore somewhat. Roland withdrew to consider the changed circumstances. His first thought was that the latest crisis would crush Diana. It would be useless to tell a seventeen-year-old that even Society memories were short and that this year's scandalous young thing was next year's respectable matron. Even without the pregnancy he had already given up all thought of pursuing his Foreign Office career after marriage. No son-in-law of Alexander Hartley would get anywhere in Government service while the Petrograd Communiqué remained in people's minds. He dismissed it without regret. Diana was infinitely more important to him.

Nevertheless he had to earn a living somehow until he

inherited the family title and estates and he was increasingly persuaded that this must be done outside England. Already Uncle Ralph had offered to appoint him agent and manager of a small estate in Herefordshire – excellent preparation for his long term role – but Diana would suffer hell socially when the local grandes dames became aware of her condition and the inevitable rumours got out about her mother's mental instability. Best remove her from the scene of possible humiliation.

As he waited for his meeting with Buffy Exton, Roland wondered whether his latest plan would offer them the happiness he knew Diana desperately needed. Buffy was an old friend of his uncle, an ally in countless youthful escapades whose subsequent career had taken him to the Far East to open up a couple of Malayan rubber plantations as the developing market went through its first boom. He had returned to England with considerable reluctance in 1926, his health finally wrecked by malaria and hard drinking, and now peered at the world from the shabby grandeur of the Travellers' Club. Buffy had retained his two original estates, selling to Dunlop the handful of properties into which he had expanded in the fat years. In the couple of years since his return to England they had prospered, run as a unit by the man who had managed the smaller operation in Buffy's last days in the Peninsula.

Now, however, the manager had been offered a good job with Dunlop, and Exton was tempted to let him take it. The old man knew the rubber trade inside out and was aware that an enormous slump was about to descend. He thought the manager stood a far better chance of holding on to a decent job with a big company than continuing to make a living wage if the Exton plantations ceased to be viable. Nevertheles he was reluctant to sever all connections with the Far East. Its magic had never released him since the morning he had first gone ashore in Georgetown, Penang, at the turn of the century. He would have ended his days there had not illness destroyed the allure of the plan. Buffy's only son had died in the trenches during the

Great War, so there was no adult heir. His grandson, Jonathan, was just eleven years old and Exton wanted to hold on to the two remaining plantations until the boy was of an age to make his own decisions in the matter. It looked as though Roland Lenton might offer an ideal solution.

'Hmm – quite a handful y'know, taking on a job like this when you're not an old Far East hand,' he told Roland half an hour later. 'Most of the young men who manage plantations have had longish spells as assistants first, bit of responsibility without power, if you see what I mean . . .'

He awaited Roland's reaction.

'I know British estate management inside out, sir, and from the rough side, too. Managing little scraps for an older half-brother who's set to inherit the lot and doesn't care a button is no picnic.'

'Yes, man, but what about the natives, and the problem of the product and so on? Could you handle all that sort of thing?'

'However difficult the Tamils might be, they won't be harder to handle than a really stubborn Devon cottager. I'll manage – I have to; it's what I need to do. If you give me a chance I can assure you that you won't regret it.'

Exton thought over what young Lenton had said. In fact he had all but decided to give the boy a try even before seeing him. The adventurer in him liked the spirit of a young man who was willing to chuck everything and go off somewhere unknown with the woman he loved just to take her away from the pain of an old family scandal. Roland did not realise yet that the very scandal which necessitated their departure could also act in his favour. The two men ate luncheon together and by three o'clock Roland was setting out for Clarges Street to tell his fiancée that her first home would probably be in a stilt house among wild orchids and tropical rain forest. One look at Diana's woebegone countenance convinced him he was doing the right thing by taking her away from Europe. When he broke the news, she was transformed.

'You see, I'll have to drop the Foreign Office when I inherit from Uncle Ralph anyway, so I might as well chuck it now. Seemed a pity to pass up this opportunity while we're young and fancy free. And we can sail immediately after the wedding.'

He retreated behind his teacup to let her digest this, the best bit of information yet.

'So no one will have any idea . . .'

'Precisely. It will be years before we come back and such an old story won't even be of passing interest then, my darling. You know, we're very young and even if it's ten years or so, you'll still be in your twenties when we get back – and you'll be Lady Lenton then, mistress of a huge estate and unassailably respectable!'

She rose and positively danced towards him. 'Roland Lenton, that's the longest speech I've ever heard you make! Why weren't you ever this clever before? I think I should have been far nicer to you if you had been!'

Roland uttered an imperceptible sigh, then resolutely turned his attention to the future. It was useless to speculate on how different their lives would have been if Diana had found him interesting a year ago.

Hermione was sitting at her dressing table preparing for dinner when Diana slipped in to tell her the news. She glanced anxiously at her niece in the looking glass as she carefully replaced a hairbrush on the mahogany table-top.

'How are you feeling, my dear? A little better, I hope?'

Hermione's kind spirit reached out for comforting words to reassure the girl, but she found none. Then she realised that Diana was far from downcast. Hope flared momentarily before she accepted that a miscarriage at this stage would have produced a marked, if temporary, effect.

'Aunt, it's going to be all right! Roland's taken a post in the East and we're off to Malaya to be planters immediately after the wedding!'

The news aroused mixed feelings in Hermione – thankfulness that Roland was resourceful and caring enough to protect Diana at this most vulnerable time; misgivings about how long Diana's gratitude and joy would survive removal from the English Society niche for which she had paid such a high price. But Hermione was a realist. At this point, dignified escape was all; the rest was merest speculation.

'My darling, that's wonderful, but I shall miss you dreadfully! What shall I do without you?'

Diana embraced her with real emotion.

'I shall miss you, too, dear Aunt H. I'd be insulting you if I said you had taught me what a mother should be like, because you're really much too young and good for all that. But you're the only person who's really loved me, apart ... apart from Roland.'

The hesitation was not lost on Hermione. She realised the girl had another name in mind, hastily suppressed. Still, one never could tell. Roland shared all the right things with Diana to ensure a strong, life-long bond. And he seemed to care for her more than anything else, surely no bad thing. Hermione dismissed the doubts and swallowed the tears that Diana's impulsive declaration of affection had caused.

'I think perhaps we should lunch together tomorrow and make a few more plans, darling,' she said. 'If you really are going off immediately after the wedding the preparations will be fiendishly complicated.'

Then, before Diana went to change, Hermione said: 'I know it's usual for young wives to rely on native servants when they first go off on these junkets, but in view of the rather special circumstances in your case, I'd be far happier if someone went with you. Would you be prepared to accept Evangeline's wages and steamship ticket as an extra present from me to start you off on your new life?'

'Oh, Aunt, yes please, if you really can afford it! The second estate is unbelievably remote and I'm a little nervous at the thought of being there alone at the wrong time!'

Hermione made a secret decision to ensure that Roland saw she was not alone there at all during her pregnancy, but said nothing for fear of alarming Diana.

'That's settled, then. I've no doubt that a plucky young miss like Evangeline will jump at such an opportunity, so I'm not at all worried about her accepting the invitation.'

Hermione was right. Within ten minutes of hearing the

news, the Welsh girl had gone to raid the library at the Brook Street mansion for an atlas and was tracing their route with an eagerly shaking finger through the Suez Canal, past Ceylon to Penang.

As she told Hermione with a self-deprecating laugh, from that moment she was unable to rid herself of the memory of her Uncle Dafydd singing Kipling's 'Road to Mandalay' in the parlour every Boxing Day. Bet the old devil never thought I'd be the one of the family who got to see it, though, she reflected.

I know Diana will be safe with that one, Hermione told herself contentedly, watching Evangeline smile secretly at her thoughts.

CHAPTER TEN

Diana will go elegantly to her own funeral, Hermione reflected as she left her room where Irene and Evangeline were helping the bridesmaids to put the finishing touches on Diana's wedding preparations. Sarah was in the morning room with the Earl. Hermione could feel the ice seeping beneath the closed door and hesitated before knocking. After the melodramas of the past two months she felt she could live without more today. Finally she set aside the impulse to bolt and tapped the mahogany panel firmly before entering. Sarah turned sharply from the window, where she had been fighting for self-control. She was white-faced and clearly explosively angry but whatever Lord Ingleton had said seemed to be holding her in check.

'Ah, and how's our little match-maker? Still the most popular aunt in Mayfair?'

'That's quite enough, Sarah. The car is outside and you're leaving in a moment. Please confine your demonstration of ill-will to this room. Today will be enough of a strain without one of your tantrums.' The Earl turned his attention to Hermione. 'How is Diana? Is everything going smoothly?'

As usual, Hermione chose to look vacuous and well-meaning.

'She's quite lovely and almost ready. If you plan to be a little late, you'll probably have to wait a few minutes before starting out. Sarah, I think you and I should go now.'

Sarah made a visible effort to stay calm, stung by the serenity of a woman she had always considered to be her social inferior. They made an appropriate contrast. Hermione had chosen a delicate shade of old rose to enhance her black hair and pink-and-white complexion. She wore a picture hat whose lacy brim cast becoming dappled shadows across her face. The soft silk of the matching frock swept in bias-cut folds to ankle length. Sarah was the archetypal mature ice-maiden, her ash blonde hair almost hidden beneath a glossy little helmet of bronze straw, her minimalist coffee-coloured Chanel jersey suit cropped short at the knee. The green eyes which gave Diana warmth and sparkle were like shards of ice in her mother's leaner, paler face. She swept across to the table and drew on bronze kid gloves before picking up a large flat bag of glacé leather.

'Very well – if the fairy godmother is ready we'll go!'

Hermione turned back towards the Earl as Sarah headed for the street.

'Will it be all right?'

'I sincerely hope so. I've done everything short of thrashing her and I can hardly do that at her age! Perhaps I should have done it twenty years ago. I can only thank you for your patience and good sense, Hermione. You may choose to let the world see you as a well-meaning little fool, but I know differently and, I think, so does James. If it were not for you, heaven only knows how matters would have turned out. Better get off now, or Sarah will be back in playing the maenad again. Go along – we can talk later. I'll come out into the hall and wait for Diana.'

I seem to spend an unconscionable amount of time with my fingers crossed these days, thought Hermione with a sigh. The journey to the church with Sarah stretched ahead like the Gobi desert in winter.

As Walsh the butler closed the door behind Hermione, the Earl of Ingleton turned back towards the mansion's great staircase. Diana had just reached the half landing on her way down to him. Her beauty struck him like a blow and for a moment made him feel tearful, such was its intensity. Louise Kerslake's programme of self-education had recently introduced her to Tennyson, and when she read *The Lady of Shalott* she immediately visualised Diana as the virgin lady segregated from the world by a curse which permitted her only a mirror image of real life, with death the penalty for breaking the rules. The events leading up to the marriage had confirmed this fancy, and she had designed a wedding dress that echoed the look of the legend. In deference to Diana's hatred of white, she had used heavy satin in a rich shade of cream. It fell in a severe, straight line from shoulder to ground and tapered away behind in a six-foot train scattered with embroidered crystal flowers – the gown's only ornament. The long sleeves puffed high at the shoulder and widened to medieval trumpet shapes, their points trailing to the ground. Instead of the great mass of assorted blossoms which made that Season's brides look like walking municipal gardens, she carried a single arum lily. Only her headdress broke the severity of the ensemble. The tight little cap unconsciously echoed in silver her mother's bronze helmet. It was sewn all over with more of the tiny crystal flowers. A waterfall of fine cream tulle burst from the back and sides of the cap to cascade over her shoulders and overlay the train of her gown. The total effect was breath-taking.

Louise was a mistress of flattery and she had excelled herself with the bridesmaids' frocks. Lettie was no problem. She showed signs of being a less striking but still very comely version of Diana. But Roland's sister Catherine was the other attendant and her angular, colourless appearance was hard to enhance. In the end Louise had defied the usual conventions of blue, pink or mauve – all potential disaster areas for a girl with Catherine's sallow complexion and mid-brown hair – and had chosen soft gold. It performed a minor miracle on Catherine, and the style, too, made the best of her tall bony figure. Louise had used the same basic shape as in the wedding gown, but for the brides-maids she had taken the train from the shoulder line and had added a narrow belt with an ornate linked buckle at the waist of the frock. Each girl wore a small round cap of golden flowers instead of a veil or a hat. The complete set of gowns echoed each other's lines without excessive mimicry. Even Catherine was lovely; Lettie had become a beauty and Diana a goddess. Eventually Louise reaped an immensely profitable harvest of orders from the display of her talents which the wedding provided.

George Digby-Lenton extended his arm to his grand-

daughter. 'Hope young Roland has the good sense to appreciate what he's getting,' he said. 'If he doesn't, I might just
bring you back again!'

She smiled tremulously at him, grateful that he should
choose this moment to express pride in her and not to
touch on the haste of the marriage. They moved together
towards the front door, where the other servants had joined
Walsh to see them off. The butler glowed with satisfaction
that such a ravishing bride was departing from his establishment. Hermione and Sarah had gone to the church in the
Daimler. Lord Ingleton's Rolls-Royce Silver Phantom,
opulent in the September sunshine, awaited Diana and her
grandfather. Their progress through the streets of Mayfair
was watched with interest by the passers-by. In Hanover
Square a crowd of sightseers had gathered around the
portico of St George's and were making suitably appreciative comments on the bridesmaids' frocks. Diana's arrival
was greeted by a ragged cheer.

Inside the church, an organ arrangement of the Trumpet
Voluntary struck up. ('Never could stomach Wagner,' the
Earl had said. 'Have a good English send-off like your
Aunt Hermione' – so the Trumpet Voluntary replaced
Lohengrin.) The bridesmaids lifted Diana's train, Lord
Ingleton took her arm and they began their stately procession down the aisle. She was conscious of Hermione's
warm smile and of her mother's tight, furious face. A wave
of triumph washed over her and almost made her weep with
exaltation. Whatever happens now I'm free of her, she
thought. I can make my own way and decide later what to
do about Papa, but the Duchess can never touch me again!
The thought carried her away so thoroughly that she was
radiant by the time she reached Roland's side. He looked
into her face and decided that maybe, after all, he had a
chance of making her happy. It never entered his head that
her look of joy was only incidentally connected with him.

At the Ritz the guests were presented to the newly married
couple in the reception room to the left of the Arlington
Street entrance, where they drank champagne before

moving on to eat luncheon in the Marie Antoinette dining room. Hermione suffered agonies of suspense as she observed her sister-in-law's tight-lipped reaction to the luxurious provision the Earl had made for his granddaughter. It was painfully obvious that, surrounded by the green and gilt Louis XVI boiserie, Sarah was reliving her own elopement, wishing she had played by the rules and blaming Diana in some obscure way for her failure to have done so. In a sense it's a shame that the Earl chose to hold the reception here, thought Hermione. A quiet luncheon back at Brook Street might have proved less inflammatory to Sarah, and as Alice is so ill there was every excuse. Suddenly it occurred to her that Lord Ingleton had chosen the extravagant approach to avoid any risk that in later life Diana might victimise a daughter of her own for enjoying luxuries that she had missed. If he thinks that of her, he's failed totally to understand her temperament, thought Hermione. She's quite unlike Sarah.

Champagne, lobster, iced quails, crayfish mousse and chaudfroid of chicken were followed by fruit ices and wedding cake. Hermione pressed James into ensuring a constant stream of attention for Sarah, which succeeded in keeping her away from Diana. Unfortunately no one had thought to keep her away from too much champagne and by the time Diana went up to her suite to change, Sarah was becoming unmanageable.

'Can't you steer her back to Brook Street, dear?' Hermione murmured to James. 'I want to go up and help Diana but if Sarah sees me, she'll be up too and then I dread to think what might happen!'

'Don't think I haven't tried, old girl. Each time I mention it she says "Don't be stuffy!" and whips off back to the bubbly. Any minute now she's going to begin vamping the waiters, I think!'

'My dear James, if I thought there was a chance of that I should be far less worried. At least it would keep her occupied!' Hermione was too concerned for once to keep up her role of mindless social butterfly. 'At least try to keep her talking for ten minutes and perhaps I can contrive to get Diana and Roland back down, ready to leave, without Sarah realising that she's upstairs.'

James went off on his errand and Hermione slipped from the room to join her niece. Evangeline had come over from Brook Street to dress Diana in her going-away outfit. For this, Hermione had insisted on treating Diana to her first Chanel suit. She watched with approval as Diana shrugged on the dark blue cardigan jacket over a blue-and-jade matelot-striped blouse. An absurdly attractive cloche hat went with it, giving Diana the look of a sophisticated urchin.

'If you're ready, darling, I think the sooner you find Roland and go downstairs again, the better. Everything is ready in the car and Evangeline's trip is all arranged for next week. All you have to do is shout *au revoir* and go.'

'All I have to do is say thank-you for being more than a mother to me,' said the girl, tears in her eyes. 'I'm going to be all right, Aunt Hermione, and it's only because of your kindness. I shall never forget what you've done for me . . .'

'And neither will I, you dirty little bitch!'

Lady Sarah stood in the open doorway, very drunk and beside herself with fury. 'D'you think I'm too stupid to know what's going on, you slut? How many men have you been with altogether? Half London, I'll be bound! Are you sure your precious Roland's going to want you when he knows what you've been up to?'

'Get her inside, quickly,' Hermione automatically enlisted Evangeline as her accomplice, 'and lock the door behind her!'

'Mama, what are you talking about? Please, please don't disgrace me now!' Diana was on the edge of panic.

'Go to Roland, Diana. Goodbye, my love and good luck. I'll write to you soon. Don't look for me downstairs.' As she spoke she was corralling Sarah against the far wall, giving Diana an unobstructed path to the door.

'Oh no you don't. She's not getting away that easily!' Sarah's voice rose towards hysteria as she lurched forward around her sister-in-law. But she was not quick enough to dodge Evangeline.

'Sorry, Milady,' muttered the girl, as if excusing unavoidable *lèse-majesté*, then flung her arms around Sarah from behind and swung her away from Diana towards the bedroom.

Realising what Evie had in mind, Hermione threw open the door, bundled Sarah through it and disappeared inside with her, shouting 'Get Miss Diana downstairs now, Evie, then back to me!' The door slammed behind the two women and Evangeline obeyed orders in one poetic movement which swept up Diana's bag, gloves and dressing case.

'Out, Madam – you have a train to catch!' The Welsh girl was completely in control, even remembering to change to addressing Diana as a married woman for the first time.

'But we can't leave them like that – Mama has lost her mind again. Aunt Hermione can't cope with her alone!'

'Oh yes, she can, Madam, and the sooner you go off on your honeymoon, the sooner I can get back to help her, so off you go.'

As she spoke she was crowding Diana out of the suite and down the corridor towards the room where Roland had spent the previous night. She tapped the door. Roland, changed from his morning suit to travelling clothes, answered at once.

'Madam is ready to leave, Mr Lenton, and I think you should hurry. Lady Sarah is paying a visit to the suite.'

'Ah, umm, thank you, Evangeline, of course. You go back to Lady Stanmore – I take it she's with Lady Sarah?'

Evangeline smiled calmly for the benefit of two passing hotel guests. 'Yes, Sir, that's right. It would help if I could be there. I'll see you in Malaya in a few weeks. Have a safe journey.'

He began propelling a still-bemused Diana along the corridor away from the scene of potential disaster. 'Thank-you, Evie. Take care, and give Lady Stanmore my compliments.'

That, he thought, has to be the understatement of my life!

Back in the suite, all hell had broken loose. The fragile dam which retained Sarah's mental balance had ruptured, helped along by her massive intake of alcohol. She was in the grip of hysterics and was attacking Hermione with everything she could lay hands on, which included the

Ritz's heavyweight toilet articles from the dressing table.

For ever afterwards Evangeline associated the smell of eau de cologne with violence – Sarah had flung a bottle at Hermione and it had shattered pungently against the silk-covered wall.

The Earl's going to get one hell of a bill for extras, thought Evangeline, skipping sideways as a powder-bowl sped past her. Sarah struck Hermione a ringing blow to the side of the head which floored the younger woman. She advanced, teeth bared like a savage animal, ready to kick her adversary.

'Oh no you don't, you bloody cow!'

Evangeline had been brought up as a nice girl but she had a street-fighter's instincts. Deftly picking up a silky scarf which had been left over a chairback, she bent forward, grabbed the hem of Lady Sarah's frock and whipped it up over her head. Then, holding it closed like a sack, she secured it with the scarf, finishing the job by pushing Lady Sarah over on to the bed. It effectively ended the fight. Champagne and violence reacted together and Lady Sarah passed out inside her cloth prison. Hermione staggered to her feet and telephoned for the hotel physician in a voice that suggested a guest might be suffering some minor indisposition. Twenty minutes later a heavily sedated Sarah Hartley was removed via a side door and taken back to Brook Street, shortly after Mr and Mrs Roland Lenton had departed through the Arlington Street entrance for Victoria Station and the boat train to France.

In any other society, Roland would have been a wildly imaginative romantic. As an English aristocrat, he merely appeared quiet and reflective. He had, after all, been taught since birth that imagination and originality were at best highly questionable qualities. Nevertheless, his natural inclination occasionally broke through, with startling effect. His honeymoon with Diana was a case in point. Diana had gone to ground after the announcement of their engagement and the subsequent dilemma of dealing with her mother. Excuses had been made for her non-appearance at the endless stream of all-female luncheon parties which comprised the day-to-day activity of the Season between the set piece events. She had developed a passion for reading light fiction and Roland had responded to a plea from Hermione to provide more suitable material when her aunt discovered that Evangeline was supplying a steady stream of improbable novelettes. The result was a catholic selection of titles, taking in Evelyn Waugh, Christopher Isherwood, John Galsworthy, Edgar Wallace and Dorothy L. Sayers. Although her general education had been patchy, Diana's French was fluent and she also enjoyed Colette, Mauriac and Cocteau.

Generally, Roland pitched it correctly, offering a balance between light and heavyweight authors. The romantic gesture resulted from his one real mistake – T. E. Lawrence's *Seven Pillars of Wisdom*. Diana, like many of her generation, regarded Lawrence of Arabia as a glamorous hero. She threw herself into his convoluted autobiography with enthusiasm, and emerged dazed and bored.

'He may have been a whizz in Arabia, but I haven't the faintest idea what he's getting at as a writer,' she said. 'I've got mental indigestion!'

Feeling vaguely responsible for her boredom, Roland gave her a little nonsense novel which she would normally have been more likely to receive from Evangeline than from him – Dekobra's *The Madonna of the Sleeping Cars*. The book had virtually invented the popular image of the Orient Express when it was first published in 1924. Since then it had been translated into twenty-seven languages and had sold a million and a half copies in Europe alone. Diana devoured it, identifying totally with the heroine, Lady Winifred Grace Christabel Diana Wynham. For a few days she walked, lived and breathed Orient Express, collecting every scrap of information she could find on the great train and even getting hold of the latest timetable. A delightful idea began taking shape in Roland's mind. If they spent their wedding night in Paris, they could embark on the Express the following day and have a honeymoon en route to Istanbul. A few days in that most exotic of cities, then on by steamer to Port Said or Suez, where they could transship to a P & O vessel for Penang. Given Diana's new craze, no other trip could compete. Once the conceit had taken hold, there was no stopping Roland. Dekobra was most explicit in his description of the luxurious trappings of Lady Diana's gilded existence.

Roland's main wedding gift to Diana was a suite of opals ('I have a wayward streak which tells me that bad luck for other people means good fortune for us'), but in addition he equipped Diana to live out her fantasy. On her wedding morning, he telephoned to tell her a few et ceteras were on their way. These turned out to be a filled set of luggage identical to the baggage Lady Diana had taken along on her mysterious fictional journey. The star item was a mauve pigskin dressing case, fitted with silver-topped bottles and jars, including a bottle of Chypre and a platinum cigarette case full of Balkan Sobranies. One of the pair of matching grey leather suitcases that accompanied it was empty. The other was packed with diaphanous lingerie as worn by Diana's fictional namesake – raspberry-coloured pyjamas and a Nile green silk *peignoir*.

'Roland, you utter, utter darling! It's all too, too vulgar and I adore it! I'll love you for ever!' Diana rhapsodised on the telephone.

'I might hold you to that, make sure you mean it.'

She hung up and came back to re-examine her new treasures. The ticket folder with two first-class sleeper bookings was in the dressing case with the scent and cigarettes. Evangeline, starry-eyed, was stroking the filmy silks in the suitcase.

'Oh, Miss Diana, what a lovely beginning! Mr Lenton's going to be an absolutely perfect husband.'

At that moment, Diana agreed with her. After the unexpected drama of their wedding reception, Roland was relieved he had planned such an extravagant sequel. Something dramatic was necessary to relieve the tension her mother's performance had engendered. In the event, Diana was so excited by the journey which lay ahead that she had set aside the monstrous scene in the Ritz before they reached Dover. They were staying in the Plaza Athenée that first night and a late supper had been laid in their suite. By now, though, the events of the day and Diana's pregnancy were taking their toll. Although still determined to relish every moment, she was visibly weary.

'Don't you think you'd better rest a little before supper?' Roland was concerned at her paleness as she sat down beside the flower-decked table.

'Nonsense – you've arranged everything so perfectly I want to enjoy every last breath of it!'

She made a great display of tackling a tiny *foie gras* mousse. It was a brave effort, doomed to failure. She fainted gracefully over the entrée. Roland put her to bed and called the hotel physician, explaining the circumstances as the man moved from drawing room to bedroom. The doctor dismissed him kindly and spent a few minutes alone with Diana. He returned looking satisfied that all was as it should be.

'I regret it will be a chaste wedding night, M'sieur Lenton.'

Roland dismissed the point irritably. 'But will she be all right?'

'Perfectly. She simply needs to sleep peacefully and to wake up knowing there is no trouble coming tomorrow. She is in the best of health as far as I can see and a few days' holiday will do her much good. She is awake, if you wish to see her for a few moments.'

The doctor left and Roland went to Diana's bedside. She smiled up at him sheepishly.

'Hardly an ecstatic start to our married life, is it?'

'As long as you're all right, I'm happy. After all, we have the rest of our lives to make love.'

She took his hand and squeezed it gratefully. 'Get yourself some wine and come and talk to me while you drink it.'

When he came back and sat tentatively on the edge of the bed, she ordered him into it with some asperity.

'I was going to sleep out there on the chaise longue.'

'Don't be absurd – I shan't break! I want to go to sleep snuggled up to you!'

'Oh, all right, then . . . as long as I'm not disturbing you . . .' It was the closest they came to love-making for some time.

CHAPTER ELEVEN
Malaya, 1928

The Far East had been a bolt hole for Diana, a scarcely-considered place where she could hide until she had solved her problems. What she really wanted was to belong in London Society and live a life to which no scandal attached itself. Malaya was a poor second best and, although she had jumped at the chance to flee there, privately she dreaded it. The moment she set eyes on her new home, her perceptions shifted. She realised that this was a place to be valued for its own sake, to be savoured for the unique experiences it offered. The month-long journey East was pleasant and sociable. Deck games, sun-bathing, swimming and leisurely dinners were a delightful introduction to her new status as an independent adult. None of their fellow passengers aboard the P & O ship *Kashgar* was crass enough to ask when the couple had married; and it was still not obvious that Diana was pregnant. Consequently she felt no sense of awkwardness and settled down to enjoy her new freedom. Her day-to-day relationship with Roland developed as an easy friendship but perplexed her when they were alone at night. Diana's illness and exhaustion in Paris has passed quickly enough, but the Orient Express was not an ideal location for sexual athletics, so she was undisturbed that their contact remained platonic. When they arrived in Istanbul for a four-day hotel stop-over, and again when they joined the *Kashgar* at Port Said and occupied a comfortable first-class stateroom, she assumed that a romantic honeymoon would follow. It did not, nor was any explanation forthcoming. Roland simply left her while she prepared for bed and returned a little later each night, undressing, getting into bed, politely bidding her goodnight and apparently composing himself for dreamless sleep. Diana was troubled about his behaviour but she had nothing with which to compare it, so she put aside the whole matter and concentrated on enjoying the voyage.

Before the cool, velvety evenings had begun to pall, they were over. One morning Diana woke and went on deck early while the sky was still full of the delicate pearly colours of dawn. As the day brightened, ahead of the ship she saw a little cluster of trees appear over the horizon. It was Pulau Way, the islet at the top of Sumatra. The entire Indian Ocean seemed to be pounding upon its tiny beach, brilliant under the palm trees which dipped in a stiff morning breeze. Absorbed by the sight of land after so long, she stayed by the rail, watching fascinated as the land enlarged. The light strengthened and eventually Penang Island was ahead, a hump between the ship and the Malayan mainland. The strong breeze continued to whip the impossibly elegant palm trees. High mountains interspersed with tiny bays backed by cliffs and jungle completed the view.

By now her fellow-passengers were crowding the rails, newcomers and old China hands alike agog for a sight of this most exotic landfall. Roland joined Diana, assuring her that their luggage was ready for disembarkation, apart from her few personal things. All they had to do was wait for the gangplank to drop. It hardly counted as going ashore; they were leaving the *Kashgar* only to board one of the Straits Steamship Company vessels for Kuala Lumpur. The *Kedah* was the pride of the 'little white fleet', so called because of their white hulls and blue-and-white funnels. Fifty of these shallow-draught steamers plied the waters around the Peninsula. International liners called only at George Town and Singapore. They sailed at nightfall and reached Port Swettenham, where they disembarked for Kuala Lumpur, soon after dawn.

'I never thought I should get to like being up early, but it's all so fresh and beautiful here I could make it a lifetime habit,' said Diana as they stood at the rail watching another magical coastline.

'Lenton – over here. . . . Got a car waiting, old chap!' Ronnie Henshaw had been told to look out for a gorgeous redhead with a tall aristocratic type in tow. There were plenty of the latter around, but only one Diana Lenton. She glowed at Henshaw from afar and he thought with amused anguish of her effect on the largely male planting colony in the Peninsula. The sooner Lenton got her up country, the safer for everyone! He assisted Diana on to dry land and grinned as she wobbled on first prolonged contact with terra firma after weeks on a pitching deck.

'Takes you a while to get used to it, I know, Mrs Lenton. Some of the chaps who come into George Town from Ceylon on the little cargo vessels swear they actually feel landsick for a bit!'

Good God, he thought, when those eyes get to work on you it's worse, not better. Wonder how a tick like Lenton managed to land her. Aloud, he said: 'Thought we'd take you around the shops, go down to the Spotted Dog for a while to let you two recover your land legs, then we can go off up to High Trees in time for dinner tomorrow night. Hope you realise once you get there that you're in the home of the tinned pea and the stewed senile chicken – food's pretty dire if you stray away from curry.'

'In that case, we'll stick to curry. I've never had reason to believe I'd find tinned peas interesting and I certainly haven't travelled half-way around the world to check on whether I was right.'

Diana spoke with a friendly smile, but Henshaw was aware she meant every word she said. Here was one to put the other mems on their mettle, and no mistake! He hoped for her sake she would learn the unwritten rules fast and conform to them sufficiently not to bring out the hunting instincts of some of the vixens around Kuala Lumpur. He left that glum little prospect, suddenly aware that Diana had asked a question.

'The Spotted Dog? Oh, yes, sorry, it does sound a little peculiar to outsiders, I suppose. It's the Selangor Club –

friendliest club in KL and all the most congenial people go there. It's got heaps of out-of-town members, mainly planters and their mems from up country who use it the way the county gentry use their London clubs, as a base when they're up on a visit. It's a timber bungalow complex on the northern side of the *padang* – that's the big central parade ground and playing fields – with a couple of bars, tiffin rooms, card rooms, reading and billiard rooms. The Lake Club is a bit high-toned for us lesser forms of life; strictly for the *tuan besars*, I'm afraid' – Roland had been made a member of the Lake before he arrived, but Henshaw was unaware of it – 'but you get a good time at the Dog.

'There're all sorts of stories about the name, but I reckon Harry Kindersley got it right. According to him, his grandmother used to come up from her estate not far from KL quite often in the 1880s when they'd first planted it. She'd travel up by dog cart and picnic with her young friends under a tree on the *padang*. She had two dalmatians that used to go under the cart and the young bucks who got into the habit of trailing after this rather attractive mem would say "Are you going down to the spotted dogs this morning?" when they were arranging to go and shower her with attention. The Selangor Club was being built down there at the time and gradually the name was adopted for it, because the picnic escorts were the original club members, too, of course.'

The other version was less complimentary to European attitudes than the Kindersley story. 'Some people say the name is a snide reference to the fact that this is the one European club that lets in Eurasians, and even the occasional pure-bred Tamil. You don't see them in there very often but the mere fact that they're allowed to belong is startling here. It's not the sort of thing you'd find at the Lake.'

Henshaw escorted them to the car, then on to a morning of shopping for clothes and trinkets. Old China hands in London had told them to leave their 'local' clothes until they had arrived in the Far East.

'You'll get better fabric, better cut, almost instant delivery and exemplary service from a Chinese tailor in

Singapore or KL than anywhere in the West,' Sir Ralph had told Roland. 'Keep your money in your pocket or spend it on Diana's evening clothes for the outward voyage. Then get your kit the day you arrive before you go up country.'

A three- or four-hour delivery time for a batch of jackets and shirts for Roland and dresses, lightweight coats and skirts for Diana seemed impossible; but Henshaw's Chinese tailor smilingly dismissed their suggestion that some items could be left until their departure.

'Will be delivered at Selangor Club this evening. Lady want wear gown tonight?'

'Not if it's difficult.' Diana was enchanted by the idea but preferred to be considerate to such a helpful supplier. A few hours later she was able to lay the lot out on her bed to choose something appropriate. The something was a cloud of deep blue and searing pink silk. She had expressed doubts when the tailor recommended it, as brilliant pink for a woman of her colouring would have been anathema in Europe at the time. In the end the laughable price had persuaded her to experiment and now she was delighted.

'Some English skins no good for Malay colours,' the tailor had explained, 'but yours very good – golden, not white, sunshine, not fish belly! In one year you will be colour of beautiful Malay girls unless you stay out of sun all the time!'

Diana knew that Roland and Henshaw would have stalked out of the shop with her had they overheard, but she accepted the compliment for what it was: an accolade from a connoisseur who could see an alien beauty which also managed to satisfy his own criteria, and appreciate it as such. She also took pleasure in the Selangor Club, silently vowing as she sat in her cane recliner chair with a hole it its arm for a stengah or gin sling that she would never voluntarily return to Europe. Her determination redoubled when she was given a sliced mangosteen, which started her on an eternal addiction to tropical fruit. It was as well that the East was exercising such a positive influence, because even Diana's naivety could no longer protect her from recognition that hers was hardly a normal marriage. After a romantic evening they retired to their room and, as aboard ship, Roland started to turn away, having escorted her to the door. She put her hand over his and stopped him.

'Please come inside for a moment, darling, I want to talk to you.' He looks, she reflected, like a woodland animal afraid it's about to be shot.

Inside, with the door closed, she said: 'You know, it's quite safe to make love to me now. It won't hurt the baby. I went into it most thoroughly, having been so innocent to begin with, and it's what we should be doing just now, so why don't we?'

To her astonishment, he blushed deeply and turned away from her, walking agitatedly towards the window. Still not facing her, he said in a low voice, 'I – I don't think I can at the moment.'

'But Roland, why not? We're married, we're, uh, fond of each other; we're going to have a baby. Why not?'

'I just don't think I can, that's all. You know, I never was much for that sort of thing. After we, well, you know . . . I thought it would change, but it didn't . . .'

'Are you saying you don't *want* me?'

'No – I don't know – oh God, I wish I could sort out an answer for myself, let alone for you! I love you very much, my dear. I have ever since you were a wild little girl who adored her father so much she never noticed anyone else. You were so full of life and so anarchic in a world where everyone else seemed determined to die obeying the rules. But I never was terribly . . . physical . . . and it wasn't something that came into my mind much. Somehow I always thought it would just happen, and of course eventually it did, between you and me' – he said this last with a tone of wonder – 'So of course I thought it would go on just happening after we married.

'It didn't. I love you more each day, but I don't want to – to do that again yet. I found it wonderful when we did, but every time I even think about it now I get cold all over. I'm most frightfully sorry,' he finished lamely.

'Oh. That doesn't leave me with a lot to say, does it?'

'My dearest, I do realise how frightful this is for you,

believe me, and if I could change myself I would. I've started reading a bit about it but no one seems to have many sensible ideas apart from this Freud fella, and I don't much care for what *he* says. Can we go on as we've been going until the baby is born, just taking matters as they come? Maybe it will solve itself.'

'I don't really have any choice about that one, Roland.'

'No, er, quite. But please remember I'm not under-estimating the strain to which you're being subjected. I'm not one of those Victorian types who thinks nice women shouldn't want any truck with that sort of thing. Just bear with me a while.'

'All right, Roland, but please remember that taking matters as they come and letting it solve itself doesn't necessarily mean me turning into a dried-up little old woman waiting for you to discover your manhood. I may find that the solution is someone else.'

'I don't think I could bear that.'

'What makes you think I can bear the prospect of a lifetime without making love? I'm growing up a little more each day and what you are asking is the unnatural thing!' She was almost surprised to find tears splashing on to her cheeks, and, angry with herself for showing self-pity, she turned impatiently aside. He started forward to comfort her and refused to be shaken off.

'My lovely, lovely girl! I do promise I shall try. Please be patient a little longer!'

But when she had sobbed away her frustration, he tucked her into bed as though he were her older brother, then left the room as usual and went off for a solitary walk. Diana's new paradise was to be far from flawless.

Another glorious Malay dawn cheered her somewhat. Diana was beginning to realise, now that she was beyond the influence of both her parents, that she was a natural optimist. Roland might regard sex as other men did celibacy, but otherwise life was getting a lot better than she could have hoped a year ago. A year ago! Papa had just been disgraced, although she had still been ignorant of the fact, and about this time last year Mama had slashed her half-made oyster ball gown. And now she was not even without the gown; it was in her wardrobe trunk, although it would be too tight for her for about six months! She stood before the cheval glass in her room. Roland was still asleep and there was time to consider herself inch by inch in the glass and look for changes great and small. Diana saw for the first time that she really was a woman now. Although she was still short of her eighteenth birthday, her maturity was clear in the generously-curved lines of her magnificent body. Positively Wagnerian, my dear! she thought, a small giggle slipping out as she thought it. Oh, well, that would all tone down considerably after the baby made its entrance.

It wasn't simply the riper body, though. The face had lost its childish bloom and had benefited from the transformation. Diana knew that nowadays men found her riveting. That was something quite new — before they had thought her a cracklingly pretty girl, but no more — and it made up somewhat for Roland's coolness in that direction. It was the strange new combination of maturity and youth which captivated them, and she knew this instinctively without being able to define it. Now she realised that it was hardly surprising she looked changed after what had happened to her over those twelve months. Last time she had seen her mother, Lady Sarah looked far worse for the passage of the year than her daughter. One way and another, Diana was reasonably pleased with herself. After all, she was hardly passionately in love with Roland, so it wasn't a case of being all unrequited. It was just that the interlude with Ben had taught her to enjoy lovemaking . . . I won't think about Ben, won't-won't-won't! She shut out the rest of it. Time enough to dwell on Ben when she could handle it calmly.

She returned to stately contemplation of her new life. Now there was to be the adventure of the two new plantations, the development of a friendship with Roland, if nothing else (she was in no doubt that he meant it about being devoted to her and she was egotistical enough to appreciate that). Evie would arrive soon, and they would be able to gossip together about all the old hens of the Malayan Civil Service and Shell Oil wives. Then there were all the new tastes to learn. If Henshaw thought *she* was going to live like a mem with all this gorgeous produce around her, he had a shock coming! She was looking forward most of all to the baby. Diana knew she would never be a compulsively maternal soul, but she was ready for this child and anticipating it with considerable pleasure. Once Evie was there to reassure her against solitary childbirth, she would be more than content. Feeling buoyant, Diana dressed quietly and went out for a stroll in the freshness of the morning.

Ronnie Henshaw picked them up shortly after breakfast and they set off by car up the red laterite road to High Trees. It was a chokingly dusty journey and they needed frequent drinks and fruit to soothe parched throats. Diana and Roland were astonished at the totality of the jungle, so vast and monolithic that it gave the impression of being a seamless carpet through which settlements large and small had simply worn like holes.

'It's so – so green!' said Diana, then apologised, abashed, at the banality of her remark.

'No need, I know exactly what you mean,' Henshaw told her. 'It really does seem greener than anything you've ever seen before. When I go back to England on a home leave and hear people boring on about the greenness of Ireland, I think "you've never seen the rain forest, chum!" and make allowances for their insularity. Mind you, the light here is so intense that at times even the green goes. It somehow seems to tip over into blue. And at noon it's so bright that the colour in everything goes flat. But you'll really see colour when we stop for tiffin and lie-off at Dixie Smith's place in Pradash.'

He did not exaggerate. Pradash was a small settlement with a copra plantation and a police post. Dixie Smith was the District Officer there for the Malayan Civil Service – the MCS. It was within easy reach of Kuala Lumpur and had been developed long ago by local standards, so the settlement had attracted its own small permanent community. Vanilla, poinsettia and bougainvillea clamoured for precedence, filling the beds in front of the bungalows with riotous colour. The Malay women were equally vivid, moving with the grace of brilliant birds or butterflies among the houses, carrying hands of bananas, pots of water or babies.

'It's like the frock they made for me yesterday. The colours really should clash, but they don't. They blend into something quite beautiful,' Diana said. 'I can see what they mean, though, about the Malay skin colouring showing off the vivid shades, where an English pallor would just make them scream at you.'

She remembered that this had been the preamble to a most pointed compliment from the Chinese tailor and blushed, but neither man did anything more than agree with what she said. Dixie treated her as if she were the Mona Lisa incarnate and Henshaw wondered how long it would take the bush telegraph to spread the news of Diana's installation at High Trees. Thank God I shall be back down at KL with Dunlop by the time the bees start swarming around *that* honeypot, he thought. They drank gin slings – Diana very sparingly – and went through the ritual of a curry tiffin. She thoroughly enjoyed it, although it was fiery with chillis.

'I'm afraid you'll have scant choice over sampling the tinned peas tonight,' said Henshaw. 'No telephones up at High Trees and the boys will have done the standard stringy chicken with them.'

'After this splendid feast I may never eat again!' Indeed, Diana was much in need of the obligatory lie-off after they had eaten.

A silent but friendly amah showed her to a bedroom where she could rest. The chicks – cotton-lined split-bamboo blinds which served as combined window and curtain here – filtered the afternoon light to a cool blue in the spacious quarters, refreshingly emphasised by the large ceiling fan operated manually from somewhere outside the room where a small boy would be keeping it moving on a string attached to his toe. The amah came to awaken her a few hours later when it was cool enough for them to continue their journey. Diana was introduced to the glories of the up-country Malayan bathroom, particularly the Shanghai jar.

'Don't try to clamber inside it, my dear – not that you'd be the first, but that ain't the way!' Dixie had advised before she retired. 'Just because we call the place the bathroom. Europeans tend to think of it as a bath. Actually you're supposed to scoop the water out all over yourself. The jar's also pretty useful for cooling bottles of beer if you like to be wet inside as well as outside!'

Diana felt hot and sticky and was half wishing she had eaten less of the curry as she stepped into the bare, slat-floored apartment which was Dixie's bathroom. But as she stood scooping the wonderfully cold water from the Shanghai jar over her body with the generous Malayan ladle called a *gayong*, it refreshed her as physically as an ice drink – it was almost thirst-quenching. Dressed again in soft, plain cotton clothes, she joined Henshaw and Roland to complete the journey.

'... And this is your home for the next few years, Mr Exton and the rubber market willing!'

Ronnie Henshaw gestured ahead and at the end of a perfumed hibiscus avenue Diana saw High Trees. The name obviously came from the jungle giants which towered behind the bungalow. It was old, slightly shabby and very beautiful, surrounded by a verandah of heroic proportions where rattan chairs awaited their new occupants in the lilac-coloured twilight.

'What a journey's end!' was all Diana could find to say. Her expression made it clear to Henshaw that she meant it as a compliment.

Ronnie Henshaw liked this young woman and already felt her radiating an instinctive positive response to Malaya which was very like his own. 'I've a feeling that you'll find Terlengu even more appealing, but it's very primitive compared with High Trees,' he said quietly.

She turned and dazzled him with those unforgettable green

eyes. 'I think this must be the most perfect country on earth.'

Henshaw shook off her spell with great difficulty. 'Wait till one of you gets malaria!'

In the end it was the mems rather than the mosquitoes that put Diana off High Trees. As a farewell gesture, Henshaw had arranged a curry tiffin on the Sunday about ten days after his successors arrived there. By then Diana had explored around the estate, returning each day with armfuls of fruit and flowers, on one occasion even trailed by a tiny monkey lured by the perfect hand of bananas she was carrying. She had pleased the Chinese cook by going off to the kitchen to question him about what he and his family ate, and promptly saying she and Roland would be wanting similar meals. At first the man was merely bewildered.

'But tuans and mems not eat Chinese, Mem Lenton! Like much old chickens and peas-in-tins.'

'Not this mem, Lee To. My great uncle was at the British Legation in Peking in the 1890s and he told me about the Peking banquets and the wonderful meals they got in Canton when they went south. That's what I want to try.'

Lee To bowed and beamed in excited approval. 'No Peking – cannot do – but I come from Canton and you like Canton food!'

From then on, the peas and aged chickens disappeared. Char shui fan, sweet and sour pork, chicken with nuts and pineapple and all sorts of swiftly-cooked crisp local vegetables made a progression of infinite variety across the Lenton dinner table. Diana and Roland loved it. The local planters were not amused. At Henshaw's party, the mems got together to discuss shiftless servants, interminably delayed mail and the rubber slump – this last in the fuzziest terms – and convertly eyed Diana in the hope of finding a flaw. To their collective chagrin, most had heard immediately of the gorgeous young mem down at High Trees. To a woman, they were determined to find her dull and provincial. When they discovered she looked every bit as enticing as they had heard and furthermore that she had grown up in Mayfair and had an earl as her grandfather, they were far too incensed to sniff out Alexander Hartley and his scandal. But a couple of the more knowing matrons with an infallible eye for such matters recognised her pregnancy and started drawing conclusions based on her extreme youth. None had quite raised the courage to introduce the subject to their conversation, but Diana's innocence of their communal hatred of the extraordinary let her make a gaffe which tipped them into such open hostility.

Some of the worst wives were embroiled in non-stop complaints about the quality of poultry and the extortionate price of imported beef. Diana, trying to be helpful, burst out 'But why not eat Chinese style? We have wonderful meals all the time and they contain so little meat the price is nothing!'

The conversation stopped in mid-sentence. Then, frigidly, Maud Eldridge said: 'Are you suggesting that we should go native, Mrs Lenton?'

'Hardly – only that you give yourselves a chance to enjoy some of the food apart from the fruits. You don't have to embrace Islam or Buddhism to do that.'

Her flippancy, added to what they saw as arrogance in suggesting such changes as soon after her arrival, scandalised them. 'Here five minutes and you'd think she was an old China hand, conceited little bitch!' one of them murmured as she headed for the bathroom.

'More like an old China whore by the look of her,' said Maud Eldridge. 'In my day there was only one reason for a girl to marry as young as she has and then to look as she does so soon after. I intend to find out if things have changed!'

A few minutes later, smiling sweetly, Maud dropped her bombshell into a momentary silence over the cold drinks.

'A Spring wedding in London must have been quite wonderful, Mrs Lenton – I always think London is at its best in the Spring . . .' Diana was silent '. . . It *was* a Spring wedding, of course?'

The unexpectedness of the attack caught Diana unprepared.

'I – er – umm, well, no – it was the beginning of September.'

Maud evinced exaggerated surprise. 'Oh my dear, I *do* beg your pardon, how tactless of me! I thought what with you obviously expecting a happy event so soon, it must have been then.'

But Diana had caught up and overtaken her. Her smile was pure ice.

'What a quaint little expression! A happy event – what does it mean?'

It was Maud's turn to flounder, her suburban background exposed by the vulgar euphemism. 'Why, how dare you, you little chit! My family were planters when one of your ancestors was probably living in idleness off the backs of their tenants!'

'I sincerely doubt that, Mrs Eldridge. My father once told me that a certain type of woman goes out East to trap a husband who will keep her there in a manner to which she could never hope to become accustomed at home. I suspect you fit that category very neatly.

'Now I really must go and see that Ronnie's other guests have all they need. I hope you enjoy the rest of the party.'

She turned and strode off to join Roland and a group of men at the edge of the hibiscus avenue. Violet Unwin, a genuine member of the planter class to which Maud had claimed to belong, let out a squeal of glee.

'Good ol' Maudie – that put the brassy youngster in her place and no mistake!' Violet had been at the gin slings and they made her a little reckless. 'Didn't know your family was out here, Maud. Thought you stayed with some old uncle when you came over as a nurse. Where was the old family estate, then?'

Beetroot red with anger and humiliation, Maud was barely capable of replying. 'My uncle was the family I meant.' Her voice was almost inaudible.

Cynthia Cross, whose background was enough like Maud's to make her sympathetic, walked away from the derisive group of mems with her.

'Get Gerald to take you home. You can't be expected to stay after this.'

'Look at him! What chance d'you think I'd have?' Maud

gestured at the group of men by the hibiscus. Diana was managing a virtuoso performance of communal flirting and they were lapping it up.

'You're right, dear,' said Cynthia. 'Never mind, sooner or later you'll have a chance to get your own back, and I'll help.'

'I'll destroy her for that, if it's the last thing I do.' Maud's tone was quiet but she had stopped walking as she spoke and was staring across the grass at Diana. 'How I hate her!'

As she said this, Diana glanced up. Unable to hear the words, she was all too aware of the general meaning of what Maud Eldridge said and it made her shiver.

'Well, Mrs L, how did your first social function go?' Ronnie, Roland and Diana were sitting over a last gin sling in the darkness.

'Loved the men, hated the mems – oh, doesn't that sound fast?' Diana giggled.

'One could say it appeared to be a mutual reaction,' Roland said mildly, provoking a rueful chuckle of agreement from Ronnie.

'What sort of woman is Mrs Eldridge?' Diana's tone was deceptively casual.

'In my book, to be avoided at all costs,' Henshaw told her. 'She was a real cracker twelve years ago – one of the first European women to come out as nurses. She was as common as muck but there was one uncle by marriage with a down-at-heel estate and she used his name as if he were the Duke of Wellington. Of course, she was snapped up on the marriage market – even the plain ones were in those days – and Gerald Eldridge was considered quite a catch at the time. As soon as they were married she set out to impress people with her grand background and now she's convinced herself there's some truth in it. She has such a vicious tongue when she's crossed that the few people who remember her origins keep their mouths shut about it unless they're out of earshot of her.'

'What happens when someone *does* cross her?'

'Don't try to find out! She'll ferret away until she finds

out something unpleasant about them and spread it all over the ex-pat community. It's too small a world in which to be comfortable when everyone is pointing at you.'

Diana was pale. It was a moment before she spoke again, and when she did she seemed to be addressing herself: 'Just like London Society.'

Roland gave a slight start and turned to stare at his wife. 'Diana, what happened?'

'I think we shall be spending quite a lot of time at Terlengu, somehow, Ronnie. I *do* hope it's all you say it is!' She forced gaiety into her tone, but even Henshaw could sense her distress. Between them he and Roland kept the conversation moving. It was hard work, the relaxed mood that had prevailed before Maud Eldridge's name cropped up having vanished as though it had never been.

Later, in their bedroom, Diana turned tearfully to Roland. 'I don't care how backward and primitive and remote Terlengu is – I'm having my baby there and I'm staying there until it's old enough for no one to know the month it was born! And if that Eldridge creature is still here when I eventually return, I shall turn around and go back there. I didn't come all this way to have my life ruined a second time!'

Roland flinched at the pain in her voice.

'Diana, don't you think it's time you stopped running and turned to face them? It's no new thing for a baby to be conceived before its parents marry and you *are* respectably married to its father now. This woman doesn't matter, and even if she did, Malaya won't be our home for the rest of our lives. We shall be back in London within a few years en route to Granby, and no one will care a hang about when our child was born!'

'Don't you understand? Weren't you listening to what Ronnie said? The woman is relentless. She won't stop at the date of our wedding and match it with the baby's arrival. She'll find out about Papa and I shall never be able to hold my head up again! It was hard enough to bear with the whole of Mama's family behind me, but out here there's just us! It has to be Terlengu, Roland, it has to!'

Eventually he calmed her sufficiently for her to fall asleep, but he knew that acceding to her wishes was the only way of guaranteeing the protection she craved.

Mary Stamford represented a totally different part of Malayan planter society from the vindictive group who had come to Henshaw's curry tiffin. Diana found her waiting on the verandah when she returned from another of her solitary walks a day or two after her disastrous social debut at High Trees. She approached warily, ready for a re-run of the awful luncheon party.

'Mrs Lenton, at last! I thought I was never going to meet this ravishing young woman all the men are talking about!' There was no sting in her tone and her intentions seemed entirely friendly but Diana was still unsure of her ground.

'Come on, relax. You call me Mary and I'll call you Diana if I may. Once we're on first-name terms I can tell you why you had such a beastly time on Sunday.'

'Oh, so you already know. I wondered how long it would take for the whole thing to get about.'

'You'll soon learn that it's impossible to take a bath in these settlements without the neighbours knowing how much water you've used. If you want privacy you need to go up country and find your own clearing, strange though that may seem in a remote place like this.'

'That's precisely what I intend to do. As soon as we've sorted things out here, we're off to the other Exton estate in Terlengu and the way I feel now, I might stay there permanently.'

'Surely you're not prepared to give Maud Eldridge that much satisfaction?'

Diana was won over. 'What will you have to drink, Mary?'

They sat together for an hour, Mary Stamford filling in a few of the large gaps in Diana's education. She was refreshingly frank and completely devoid of malice. By the time she left, Diana felt she had made a valuable new friend.

'Ronnie Henshaw's all right, but he has his limitations,' Mary told her. 'Not the least of them is his sense of inferiority. He's excessively civil to people he regards as his social superiors and that puts him under a strain. So when he wants to relax, of course, he gravitates towards people he thinks of as being on his own level. In fact he does himself an injustice. Some of them are the absolute dregs, my dear, but he feels more comfortable with them.

'When he set up Sunday's little party, lots of us who were dying to meet you weren't even invited. Poor old Henshaw had obviously decided we might snub him and not come, so he saved himself the embarrassment by not asking us. As a result you had the pleasure of an afternoon with Maud, a pretty daunting experience for anyone. However, I gather you gave as good as you got!'

'Rather, but I know I've made an enemy and I can't face the thought of spending the next few years here being hounded by her.'

'I know she asked for it, but you rather led with your chin, too.'

'I don't understand you. All I wanted was to make friends with everyone.'

'My dear girl, surely you didn't believe that all of us live on tinned peas and imported meat?'

'Well, that's how they all made it sound.'

'My family have lived here since the 1880s. I spent my schooldays in England but apart from that I've always lived here. I may stand to attention when they play *God Save the King* but inside I regard myself as Malayan. Do you seriously think that I'd have spent my life ignoring the wonderful food that the Chinese produce in order to suffer a third-rate imitation of European cuisine?'

'Well – I – uh – just accepted what I was told. That's the way it seemed.'

'All I can say is that if you continue to act on that sort of principle, you'll be completely cut off before you're twenty-five. You have to let people speak for themselves, not decide their behaviour for them! Even the more reasonable women in Sunday's crop of guests were disposed to dislike you after you'd dashed in and dismissed them as a bunch of gastronomic philistines,' she giggled. 'Mind you – most of them are, but they don't think it shows!'

Mary promised to introduce her to the mems she had not yet met. 'You'll like some of them far better than the first lot,' she said, 'but remember that however insecure you might feel as the new girl around here, they all feel a little edgy in case the smart new wife from England looks down on them. You have to meet them half-way if you hope to fit in easily.'

They parted, Diana feeling a great deal better than before the older woman's visit. At least there was an alternative to Maud and social death!

But her obsession with her potential social acceptability was too intense to let her relax. In the days that followed, she developed a real friendship with Mary and a comfortable acquaintance with a number of the other mems, but she was still uneasy about the enemies she had made. In the end Roland decided he had to talk it out with her.

'I thought that meeting Mary had made it easier for you and that you'd feel differently about spending more time over here at High Trees,' he said.

'I began to think so too at one point. Then I got a mental picture of the satisfaction on that Eldridge woman's face as I gave birth too soon for it to be premature. It's pointless to pretend, Roland. I simply can't face it. When Evangeline gets here, we'll hang around for long enough for her to take a look at High Trees, then move over to Terlengu.'

'Henshaw's told me enough about its remoteness for me to have even more reservations than before about you having the baby there.'

'Let's go over and see for ourselves, shall we? I certainly shan't rest easy if you try to make me go through with it all over here.' And there the matter rested.

Ronnie Henshaw would have been delighted to have his views of Diana's probable reaction to Terlengu vindicated so absolutely. She fell in love with it at first sight of Kuala

Terlengu and at that stage felt she would never wish to live anywhere else. The master of the Straits Steam Navigation vessel *Lipis* unconsciously echoed Henshaw's comment on her ecstatic praise: 'Malaria tends to modify one's views somewhat!'

Nevertheless it was spectacular, especially with the cloud banks that heralded the onset of the Monsoon stacking melodramatically behind the steeply-sloping shore.

Evie was deeply impressed by the colours and contrasts. 'It's as if the gods who put those clouds up there knew how much you liked navy blue and laid it on especially for you, Madam!'

Roland teased her gently. 'Gods in the plural, Evangeline? I thought you Welsh were keen on just the one and tended to see him in rather Spartan terms!'

'Yes, well if I was that sort of Welsh I wouldn't be here now, would I?' Evie's tone conveyed the standing of such compatriots in her eyes. 'Our Dad was one of them. All hell and damnation every Sunday for the poor sinners and carve the last slice off them in the shop Monday to Saturday!'

'Mmm, I remember a chap once told me the Welsh pray on their knees on Sunday and on their neighbours the other six days of the week. You seem to agree.'

'I do, sir. At their best they're lovely – kind, generous, neighbourly. But break their rules and they won't rest till they have your blood. I'd trust these poor savages any day before some of those chapel-going hypocrites down Hebron Street in Fochrhiw!'

'They're hardly savages here, particularly the Chinese. They were civilised when we were still in caves.'

'So everyone keeps telling me. Well, you have your opinions and I'll have mine, sir. I'm sure that living out here will show us which one is right.'

She turned back to contemplating the coast and Roland withdrew, smiling ruefully. Game, set and match to you, Miss Owen, he thought. He could name a handful of planters who would have put Evangeline on the next boat back to England, or even discharged her, destitute, here in the East. The average Englishman in these parts was used to having his views deferred to by the lower orders, Asian and European alike. Mere disagreement was frowned on; outright rejection of the tuan's view amounted almost to blasphemy. Roland was as much of an original as Diana and despised his compatriots for such attitudes. He had great difficulty in regarding fellow planters as any different from the oil company men and civil servants, the native clerks, the Danish seamen, Malay peasants or even the Lascar deckhands who all combined to form this society, and in that time and place such an outlook was all but unique.

While he reflected on his foibles, Evangeline had approached Diana. 'Are you sure you can go through with this, Madam? It looks like pretty rough country to me. What if anything goes wrong?'

Diana laughed with a self-assurance she was far from feeling. 'Don't be silly, Evie, the days when women built like me had anything to fear from childbirth are long gone. I'll sail through it with your help and the doctor, and all those books I've been reading. It should be fine!'

'I still think the time has come to grit your teeth and accept that those old cats around KL can't do anything to you, Madam. Why should you of all people care if they do gossip? I know what your aunt would say: in a few years at most you'll be back in England as Lady Lenton of Granby and you'll never see or hear of any of them again.'

'I just don't want to give them the satisfaction of thinking they have *anything* over me!' said Diana with some ferocity.

'And for that you're prepared to risk your life having a baby in a hut up the jungle? If you weren't my mistress I'd have a couple of words for you!'

'And what would they be? You know me better now than to think I'd penalise you for speaking your mind.'

'Daft bugger – Madam!'

'How dare you, you impudent little . . .' Diana stopped, realising she had reacted just as she had promised not to. The two girls drew back and stared at each other for a long, significant moment. Then, simultaneously, they burst out laughing.

'Evangeline, what am I to do with you? You'll be un-employable if we ever go back to England and here I am supposedly the first woman on whom you pattern your future behaviour as a lady's companion!'

'The next one's going to get a shock, isn't she, Madam? Perhaps if you weren't such a cantankerous type yourself I wouldn't find so much of it rubbing off on me.'

'Nonsense! You're a born rebel and it's only because you are party to my terrible secret that you get away with so much!' At this point they both broke into uncontrollable giggles. Watching them from a distance, Roland was aware as he rarely had been before that neither was much more than a child.

Evangeline brought the conversation to a suitably un-explosive close. 'Perhaps I should just run off with one of these lovely Danish sea captains we've been hearing so much about, live a passion-filled life in my twenties and turn up back in Europe in my thirties a fully-fledged International Adventuress.'

'You would, too! What a shame this one is a sweaty old Brit without much hair – I might have got rid of you sooner than I'd hoped!' Companionably, they turned their attention towards the land.

The Terlengu coast was notorious for the shifting sand which closed and opened the river mouth every season in unpredictable fashion, frequently reducing the previous year's 200-yard-wide channel to 50 yards and subsequently restoring it after several vessels had gone aground. Now, in late October, conditions were still calm, although the rain clouds were building up.

As the *Lipis* approached the wharf in the short tropical twilight, they heard the ritual of a Malay sailor aboard *Will o' the Wisp* calling, loud and slow, the directions for a bedor to come alongside with its cargo of copra: 'tee-gah sting-ah . . . tee-gah bay-tul . . . doo-ah sting-ah . . . doo-ay bay-tul . . .'

As the sailor completed his directions the Master roared frm the bridge 'Laygo!' and the anchors went down so that the cargo could be winched aboard.

Their own steamship tied up after a gentle approach to the wharf.

'A splendidly calm trip and a happy arrival, Captain Smith. Thank you. We look forward to travelling with you again,' said Roland.

'Oh, you'd have had a more adventurous arrival with Mogey,' said Smith. 'Perhaps when you've met him you'll change your minds about my old tub.'

'Mogey?'

'Captain Mogensen – a Dane, Master of the *Asdang*. He's a bit of a Viking and likes to live dangerously. See him running the sandbar during the Monsoon and you'll be a landlubber for life. His Chief's a chap called Svendson and when they sail in those conditions he'll ring Full Ahead then call down the pipe to Svendson "And a half, Herr Svendson!". Puts the fear of God into you, I can tell you. Poor little Svendson and the engine room staff must have to sit on the valves down there! Mogey'll come to a violent end one day, but he has an exciting time, I'll say that!'

Captain Smith had the undivided attention of both Diana and Evangeline as well as Roland by now. 'There you are, Evie,' murmured Diana, 'that could be your grand passion!'

Or yours, thought Evangeline, covertly noting Diana's almost febrile interest.

CHAPTER TWELVE

Terlengu was heaven. In one sense the bungalow was more primitive than the one at High Trees. In another, it was far more sophisticated. Terlengu was a house in the old native style, with intricately-carved wooden trims outside. The airy rooms were minimally furnished with screens, mats, cushions, low seats and tables. Mosquito nets in the bedrooms were the only concessions to European taste. Henshaw had warned them that Buffy Exton had lived close to native style and that he himself had retained the tradition.

'If you want to spend much time there, Mrs Lenton, you'll be having to put in a few sticks of European furniture; but I imagine you'll take one look and then stay over at High Trees and let your husband nip over to Terlengu for short trips to see it's all right.'

Diana had been non-committal. The idea of Terlengu unaltered appealed to her intensely and she wanted to take a look before reaching a decision. Terlengu Plantation was all she had anticipated and more. It was visually ravishing, peaceful and abundant in native flora and fauna but lacked the female European presence that had made High Trees unsatisfactory. This last also held the key to Terlengu's drawback. There was no doctor within easy reach, the closest being at Kuala Terlengu, downriver. If something went wrong at the birth, Diana must rely on a native midwife and Evangeline to save her. Monsoon would still be in full swing when she produced, although she could not say so without disclosing the advanced state of her pregnancy. Therefore she would go through her confinement wherever she went into labour. The choice appeared to lie between Terlengu with no expert help, a chance of dashing to Kuala Terlengu and its doctor through unreliable weather conditions, or of going back to High Trees before the Monsoon and having her first child in hospital at KL. Diana felt fit enough at present to dismiss the last possibility out of hand.

Then she consulted Doctor MacIntyre at Kuala Terlengu within hours of their arrival and was honest about her condition.

'There's a possibility you'll not have considered,' he told her. 'Come down here and stay towards the end of your pregnancy. There's usually a few breaks in the Monsoon about the end of January, long enough for you to get down. We'll put you up and you can have your baby here, then there won't be too much risk. If anything looks like going wrong, Mogey can always provide an escape route.'

'Mogey? I thought he was some sort of glamorous Danish pirate captain! What connection could he possibly have with me and my baby?'

'My dear, he's the best seaman I've ever met, and the most courageous. If there's any trouble we'll have him standing by aboard *Asdang* to sail you down to Singapore Infirmary at the last moment. It's the extra safety valve you need.'

'From what I hear of the captain's attitude to safety valves that's not a reassuring remark!' But in spite of her ironic response, Diana was reassured. The doctor's suggestion offered her a combination of privacy and safety which had previously seemed unattainable.

'When do I meet this redoubtable Captain Mogensen? Everyone keeps talking about him but he's more elusive than the Scarlet Pimpernel!'

'Oh, you'll only see the master of this week's vessel at any given time. They're very busy men with tight sailing schedules and you see each man on average one week in four. You'll meet Mogey in due course. Everyone does.'

So Diana, Roland and Evangeline had departed for Terlengu, with the great banks of storm clouds building higher each day. Roland shared Diana's pleasure in the second estate. He was already proving adept at languages and few gestures smoothed relations with Malay, Chinese and Tamil alike than an effort to learn their respective tongues. Roland was born to be a successful planter in a remote province.

The wooden house hung like a jewel in its plantation setting against a green cloth of jungle-covered mountainside. A tributary of the Terlengu river skittered past, foaming eagerly to join the main stream a mile further down on the plain. As at High Trees, hibiscus pressed close around the domestic clearing, but the most spectacular slopes and watercourses around them transformed Terlengu into something altogether more exotic. The evening of their arrival at Terlengu, Roland walked out on to the verandah and discovered Evangeline watching a remarkable tropical thunderstorm which tore aside the purple-black clouds with triple blades of silver lightning. She wore a sphinx-like expression.

'Good evening, what's up? You don't look like a girl taking her first look at one of Mother Nature's great displays.'

'I was thinking about Mrs Lenton and the risk of her having the baby up here, sir. You know I'm in favour of her getting away from all those awful Perak mems for the confinement, but up here? What if she had a haemorrhage or something? It would kill her.'

Roland was as troubled as Evangeline. 'I've tried to point out that it's more remote here than any of us imagined when we were at High Trees, but she won't listen to reason. She's still insisting on being here, but of course she'll accept being in Kuala Terlengu for the last six weeks or so.

'I know, sir, but even if she's only determined to stay this side of the Peninsula, six weeks before the birth is cutting it too fine. I'd prefer her to go down for Christmas if that terrible river is still open, and stay down. Surely Dr MacIntyre wouldn't object?'

'Given his initial response to Diana – and to you, for that matter – I think he'd welcome it with open arms,' said Roland, 'but I could never leave the estate for up to three months at this time of year and she'd have to be down there by the first week of December to avoid the first real spate of the Monsoon. It's my job to run the plantations and the only place I can reasonably be when I'm not here is High Trees.'

Evangeline made no secret of her impatience with this response. 'Men have never been necessary when a woman is giving birth except when they happen to be doctors. She'll be happy to be in safe hands down there while you keep things in order up here. I think we should go three or four weeks before Christmas. You could come too and fight your way back up without too much trouble if it's possible for us to get there in the first place, so you could have Christmas Day together in Kuala Terlengu and come back here straight after.'

Roland was secretly relieved. He was brave when it came to personal safety, but the thought of having to be present while Diana endured unavoidable suffering which he had caused was already weighing on his spirits. The chance to be honourably absent while she gave birth was appealing.

When consulted, MacIntyre was enthusiastic. 'It'll have to be finely-timed, Lenton, because even when the floods calm down a bit, the river is unpredictable after the end of November. I'll gladly have your womenfolk down here earlier, any time y'like from now on. Shouldn't harm you any. Remember a lot of men are permanently alone on remote estates, so a couple of extra months solitude shouldn't do you much damage.'

'Well, if you mean that, there's plenty to do and my language studies will fill the evenings.'

'Delighted to have her, old chap. She can get to know the community, such as it is, and you can spend Christmas with her before the big separation.'

The more Roland thought about it, the more it appealed to him. Since their confrontation on arriving in Malaya about his indifference to love-making, he had made no move to remedy matters and it was beginning to embarrass him. Maybe separation from Diana would provide the necessary goad to his passion when they were reunited. So, as the river began to come into spate and Diana's condition grew physically obvious, she and Evangeline headed downstream to Kuala Terlengu, arriving, appropriately, in the middle of a tropical rainstorm.

Dr MacIntyre laughed at the sight of them. 'Always said it's the hallmark of a true beauty if she still looks good when she's wet through – and you look marvellous, my dear!' He turned to Evangeline. 'Come to that, Miss Owen, you look pretty enticing, too. I think I'm going to enjoy the next three months immensely.'

MacIntyre was far above the normal run of back country doctor in skill and breadth of ability. He was in Kuala Terlengu for two reasons: he adored rural Malaya; and he had married a beautiful Chinese girl ten years before, moving to the little port with her when the mems in the Straits region made their racist disapproval all too obvious. Concubinage and prostitution they tolerated and ignored; but for a tuan to marry one of the creatures! Really, it was too much!

Lin Lin had tried to dissuade her lover from the marriage. She was content to be with him and knew better than he what lay ahead if he insisted on legitimising their union. He would not hear of it, however. The marriage followed and when MacIntyre learned she would not be accepted by what passed for European society in the Peninsula, he solved the problem by removing himself from its sphere of influence. Lin Lin was drowned in a sudden storm five years later. There were no children of the marriage and superficially nothing prevented MacIntyre from returning to European society when the first wave of grief had ebbed. But his years of contentment with Lin Lin had excised any remnants of affection he might have felt for European ways and he chose to stay where he was. Here on the east coast the Europeans he did meet tended to be as much mavericks as he.

At thirty-five, MacIntyre was not yet middle-aged and he missed intimate female company. Lin Lin had been uniquely lovely and each time he met an attractive Chinese girl she suffered an inevitable comparison with his dead wife. On balance he preferred celibacy to a relationship which could be no more than a pale imitation of his marriage. From their first meeting, he was greatly taken with Evangeline. She exuded vitality and her fizzy, rebellious personality was a living rejection of the prejudices embodied in the stock middle-class reaction to socialising with servants. Diana treated her as a friend and MacIntyre came to regard her as a potential lover. Evangeline responded enthusiastically to his attention. Much as she loved Diana, she had tired quickly of her own effective invisibility in the shadow of this glamorous young employer. Brought up as the spoiled daughter of a prosperous small tradesman and later indulged by her cousin Louise, she had come unprepared to the servile role of a paid companion. After two years of sexual purdah, she grasped the opportunity to flirt.

In the days leading up to Christmas, Diana became tired and listless. 'Nothing to worry about,' said MacIntyre. 'The Monsoon tends to do that to mems when they're pregnant. Don't fight it. Rest a lot; indulge your little cravings for fruit and treats and you'll be through it in no time.'

Diana took his advice and spent a lot of time asleep. The rains exhilarated Evangeline and she used every opportunity to go out in a downpour or to watch a spectacular storm. MacIntyre usually went with her, grumbling good-naturedly about wet feet and the need for liberal doses of Glen Morangie to cheer him up. Late one afternoon they flung themselves into the shelter of the verandah just as the storm unleashed its full fury.

Evangeline collapsed dramatically into one of the rattan loungers. 'Drink, drink! All that rain makes me feel parched!' she cried.

He mixed her a Singapore Sling, got himself a whisky and bent across her to drop the glass into its hollow in the chair arm.

'Thank you Doctor.'

'Oh, Evie, don't be so proper. Neill is my name. Use it.'

She raised her glass and looked at him over it. 'Chin-chin . . . Neill.'

The slate grey eyes were made for drowning in. Instead

of straightening and turning to take his own seat, he remained bending over her. Raising his hand, he wound a tendril of her rain-moist dark hair around his finger.

'Evie, Guinevere must have looked just like you when Lancelot betrayed everything for her.'

She blushed and smiled, the childish dimples winking in and out of her rounded cheeks. 'Bet he thought it was worth it!'

'Oh, he did, he did. I wonder how you'd be as my "belle dame sans merci".'

'Now you've lost me.'

He grinned. 'Not surprising. I'm mixing my literary references hopelessly. That's a bit of Keats but I always equated his "belle dame sans merci" with Guinevere in my mind.'

'What does it mean?'

'Literally, beautiful lady without mercy, but it's more than that. Probably it translates better into English with another French phrase. She's a *femme fatale*. I think, perhaps, so are you. My fatal woman, anyway.'

He leaned closer. She caught the faint aroma of good whisky on his breath as their mouths closed gently on each other. The long, soft, exploratory kiss stirred her deeply. She shifted sideways in the chair and pulled him down beside her, trying to move so that he fitted into the chair with her. Suddenly she was aware that he was shaking with suppressed laughter.

'So it's funny, is it?' She began to thrust him away.

He went on laughing. 'No, you Welsh idiot, not the way you think. But it *is* funny that you're so reluctant to let go you're willing to sandwich us both in this glorified bread basket!'

She made a show of irritation but it was only a gesture. MacIntyre struggled out of the recliner and offered her his hand. 'Either come off somewhere more private with me now or let's sit respectably out here in our chairs and talk.'

He almost laughed again at her unashamed decisiveness. She rose immediately and kept hold of his hand. 'Lead on, Dr Neill!'

He took her in his arms again and kissed her, long and

deep, before they went off to his room. Later, held loosely in the crook of his arm as they lay beneath his mosquito net, she said 'You didn't waste any time trying to find out if I was a virgin, did you?'

He laughed, as before, with pleasure, not mockery. 'Oh, really, Evie! No untouched girl uses her eyes and hands and body every moment as you do to tell a man she likes him! You knew what you wanted and I'm delighted to say it was me. I hope it goes on being me, but I'll never be silly enough to think I was the first!'

'Oh, you are lovely, you rotten black Scot!'

'You're no so bad yoursel', wee Welsh hoyden!' He raised himself to his elbow and looked down at her body, which appeared slightly surreal in the blue-green light thrown by the drawn blinds.

She was perfect in this light, her snowy-white skin luminous in the dim daylight. The breasts were full, flattened slightly by her prone position, and her hips flared wide and generous beneath a long, neat waist. MacIntyre traced with his index finger the fine blue vein which ran from the base of her throat to her nipple. The slight pressure touched a nerve and her small, sleepy pink nipple expanded like a generous smile, swelling and hardening as his hand approached it. The sight stimulated him and he bent forward, pressing his mouth around it. Evie let out a sharp gasp and he felt the nipple swell and become rock hard against his tongue. He bit it lightly and she cried out, her pelvis arching demandingly against him, her fingers searching for him. She pulled at his hair and, when he raised his head, pressed his mouth down against her own, seeking out his tongue, moaning and pushing herself against him as she did so. Their mouths unlocked momentarily.

'You're making me throb all over, it's like coming alive for the first time,' she murmured. 'Give me your hand. Put it there . . . that's right, just like that . . . oh, cariad, you'll drive me crazy!'

Her lovely little body arched towards him again, mutely begging for fulfilment. He knew that if he entered her now

234

it would be all over in a moment and he wanted to prolong this most beautiful love-making as long as he could. His finger traced another, fainter vein, down between her breasts, over her rounded belly and down to her soft, cushiony pubes. Then he parted her thighs and gently stroked her as she became more and more ecstatic. Evangeline's small hands locked on MacIntyre's shoulders and her surprisingly strong fingers pressed hard beneath the collar bones as the tension in her mounted.

'Neill, Neill! I can't bear any more – finish it!' The fingers gouged at his back and in a single continuous movement he pressed her thighs apart and thrust into her. She was warm, moist and excited beyond reason.

As their bodies melted together she let out another cry and twined her legs around his waist, clinching them at the ankles and pressing him further inside her. MacIntyre felt as if he were being pushed through the girl and into another dimension. He heard another voice cry out – distantly, it seemed – and it took him a moment to realise it was his own. Evangeline's passion ended as explosively as it had mounted and in doing so brought his own to completion. It was as though he had become liquid and was being poured deliciously away.

After it was all over they looked at each other wonderingly. 'I'm not very experienced, Neill, but I don't think it can ever be like that again with anyone. Do women usually feel like that?'

He smiled sleepily at her. 'Can't speak for women, my love, but it certainly isn't always like that for men. I loved my wife more than I could ever say and the love-making was wonderful, but this – this was something that I think perhaps only the very luckiest lovers ever get.'

Evangeline ran her fingers gently down between his legs. He let out a groan of disbelief. 'I couldn't – marvellous though it was, I couldn't!'

She giggled. 'I know, you fool. Just felt like touching it. It's so funny the way it gets big and important and does all it should and then disappears until it's ready again. When it happened before I thought I was with a monster!'

'Perhaps you were, but it had nothing to do with that.' He was surprised that they could talk about her past without jealousy or self-consciousness on either side.

'Not really. He was a good-looking devil and the way he looked at me made my knees melt. I didn't realise that if you're young and healthy, all men should make you feel like that. I thought it was a thing you had to grab because it never came again and what a price I paid!'

He was half asleep but interested enough to pursue the point. 'Lots of women would think you should never feel like that, or at most once in a lifetime. And there you are, saying it happens with all men if you're young and healthy. You are a surprising girl. What brought you to that conclusion?'

'Stands to reason, doesn't it? All that fun wouldn't be wasted on one or two lucky people. It has to be for everybody. You don't need a university degree to work that out.'

'Some people don't ever manage to work it out, even *with* a degree,' he told her.

Cradled together, they slept for a while, waking in time to make themselves respectable for dinner.

Christmas passed quietly. Two days after Christmas Day the weather temporarily cleared and Roland took advantage of the calm spell to return to Terlengu. On New Year's Eve Diana met Captain Anders Mogensen.

'You'll finally have a chance to meet Mogey, as you've been fascinated by him for so long,' announced Neill MacIntyre the day after Roland's departure. 'I didn't say anything before Roland left, because there's nothing worse than being left out of a party when you have to be somewhere else, but Mogey invited me and any house guests I might have to dine aboard the *Asdang* and see New Year in with him.'

Privately he wondered whether he was wise to take her along. Diana was aware of his and Evie's relationship and approved, but that made her the odd one out with obvious implications for Captain Mogensen's role. MacIntyre dismissed the idea irritably. Diana Lenton was between six and seven months pregnant and hardly likely to want to start an affair or have the power to initiate one in her present condition.

And yet, and yet . . . he looked at her objectively. She was ravishing, one of those rare women who simply became more alluring as her pregnancy progressed. Her skin was translucent gold and the combination with red hair and green eyes might have been designed by a theatrical costumier. Although her abdomen was now very visibly rounded, her height and her large, firm breasts prevented her from adopting the classic pear shape of the pregnant woman. Mogey had never shown much interest in the Chinese or Malay girls in the area but MacIntyre knew him better than to think he was racially prejudiced. Looking at Diana, he had a premonition that the Dane simply preferred big, fair women. And oh, was this a big, fair woman? The doctor's privileged relationship with Evangeline had made him privy to Evie's conviction that Diana and Roland did not enjoy a normal sexual relationship, or any sexual relationship at all, come to that.

'I'm only surprised he ever got around to fathering anything on her in the first place,' she had muttered significantly.

If that's a cue for me to ask who else might have been responsible, I'm not encouraging her, thought MacIntryre. That's something for her and Diana and no one else. Nevertheless it led him to speculate on Diana's ripeness for the attention of a competitor to Roland. Mogey was all too eligible for that role. Neill MacIntyre was a fatalist and something of a spiritual anarchist, so when New Year's Eve arrived he simply gathered his little covey of womenfolk together and set off for the *Asdang*.

Anders Mogensen had other guests too, the Malayan District Commissioner and his wife and two Chinese merchants and their wives. All knew MacIntyre but not the two Englishwomen, so the usual polite small talk spread as introductions were made. Just as well, too, thought Evangeline. Perhaps they won't notice the immortal love scene that's being played out before our very eyes. Neill's vague apprehension had been well-founded. Mogensen took one look at Diana Lenton and knew there would never be another woman for him. She looked back and wanted him as she had wanted no one since Ben. They struck sparks off each other. An atmosphere of reckless risk seemed to enwrap them. After a few minutes of trance-like neglect of his other guests, the captain realised he must make an effort to conduct the evening as he had originally planned. These were his friends and he had no right to wreck the party they had looked forward to.

He took them on deck with their drinks. 'And now, a little touch of New Year entertainment,' he said. 'Not a patch on Chinese fireworks, but a gesture at least.'

One of the ship's rockets had been strapped to a post and Mogensen stepped forward ceremoniously to light the fuse. It zoomed up into the velvety sky with a whoosh of coloured sparks. The guests applauded happily, as much in appreciation of his thoughtfulness as anything else. Ashore, the villagers were wildly impressed. The muddy streets were well filled because most people had taken advantage of the unexpected dry interlude to enjoy a stroll. A young man dashed to the foot of the gangplank and yelled something in Malay. A crewman conveyed what he had said to the captain. Mogensen grinned, nodded and waved to the youth before giving the seaman an order.

'The neighbours loved it,' MacIntyre explained to Evangeline and Diana, 'but not all of them saw it and the youngster asked Mogey for an encore to show them. Being Mogey, he'll oblige, of course.'

He did, twice, Then, when there was one rocket left, a group of children gathered, jigging up and down and shrieking for more. Mogensen shrugged, still smiling, and gestured to the sailor to set up the last rocket.

None of the guests was sure what happened next, but the effects were spectacular. Perhaps the seaman was too excited by the jubilation on the jetty; perhaps Mogensen was too interested in playing the showman to give the little display his complete concentration. Anyway, instead of throwing a starry trail across the night sky, the last, largest rocket slewed over sideways, narrowly cleared the ship's rail and described a spectacular path at head height over the landing stage and straight on up the main street of Kuala Terlengu, scattering startled onlookers to left and right as it passed. As the little missile reached the crossroads a hundred yards away, a stray gust of sidewind knocked it off course and it veered through the open door of one of the settlement's three general stores — fortunately not owned by either of Mogensen's merchant guests. Inside the shop the rocket's path was blocked effectively by the stock of bottled Guinness. It hurtled into the pyramid-shaped display and ended its life with a spectacular explosion in which Irish stout was a major component.

The impressive silence which followed was punctured by a yell of uncontrollable laughter from Evangeline. Mogensen gave up the struggle to look repentant at the chaos he had caused and exploded into mirth also. Neill MacIntyre and Diana gave him a round of spontaneous applause.

'They'll either lynch him or love him all the more,' murmured MacIntyre to Diana.

They loved him. The ragged cheering guffaw that rose from the quay mingled with the crackle of the dying fire in the store; everything was too rain-sodden for a serious blaze to develop. Unable to suggest any more appropriate action, Mogensen shrugged and smiled sheepishly. 'I think we should go down to dinner now,' he said. They left the chaotic scene with some relief that the merchant still had not appeared.

'Well, what did you think of our Mogey?'

On the morning of January 1, Diana was on MacIntyre's verandah enjoying a breakfast of tropical fruit when he joined her. One look at her expression was enough to answer his question.

'Hmm, thought so. Wondered if I was doing the right thing introducing you to each other.'

This roused her to respond. 'Oh, really, Neill, you're worse for tea-leaf reading than Evie! I'm very, very pregnant and married. Apart from anything else, no man in his right mind would look at me in my present condition.'

'Point one: you are more ravishing than you've ever been and you know it; point two, Mogey is as mad as a hatter; and point three, you both looked as if you were devouring each other all evening. What about Roland?'

She shrugged and looked away, pretending a calm she was far from feeling. 'He's in no danger. I'm down here preparing to have our child, after which I shall rejoin him and we shall continue to be a young compatible married couple.'

'Try not to forget that, Diana. Watching you and Mogey together was like the duff rocket he let off – wonderful sight but hell-bent on destruction and not too fussy about how many people went with it. Don't take too many risks.'

She leaned over and touched his hand. 'I know you mean us all nothing but good, dear Neill. Try not to worry. I realise it may look a bit, well, intense, but I will try to behave, I promise.'

He smiled at her. 'Well said. I hope it works out all right, but if it doesn't, please talk to me. I'll always listen and I'll never condemn you, whatever you do. I'm not quite as emotionally impulsive as young Evangeline – God knows what she'd advise you to do if you turned to her for guidance!'

The picture he conjured up blunted the serious edge of their discussion and both laughed at the thought of Evangeline taking over such a crisis and turning it into a real life tragedy in three acts. They said no more about the matter, but both were aware that it had been postponed rather than permanently dealt with.

Anders Mogensen stayed away from Diana during his subsequent stops at Kuala Terlengu and with Neill's gently ironic encouragement, she managed to avoid pursuing him. With occasional respites, the Monsoon raged through January and February saw no improvement. Diana was vague about the stage her pregnancy had reached; too vague, even for a girl who had been so totally ignorant when she conceived, thought MacIntyre. Since she lost that innocence she's bound to have learned to count and she hasn't lost her memory, so why can't she give me a more definite date? Whatever the reason, the result was almost fatal to Diana. At the end of the first week in February, she went into labour, taking MacIntyre completely by surprise. He had become concerned about certain symptoms she was showing and had been working round to suggesting a hospital birth in Singapore after all. As Diana went through the first eight hours of an agonised labour, he cursed himself for not having insisted earlier.

'I've seen a couple of cases like this before with young Malay girls who weren't designed to become mothers at such an early age. It seems Diana is prone to similar problems,' he told Evangeline. 'I've no reason to think she'd have trouble in hospital, or that there would be any complications even with a home birth if she were five years or so older. But here and now she's in trouble. She has an unusual blood group and if she should have a haemorrhage there's no suitable donor.'

Evangeline was horried. 'But Neill, you've known her blood group for ages. Why haven't you made arrangements?'

'Because there was no sign of premature delivery and I thought I had a good three or four weeks to persuade her to go into hospital in Singapore.' MacIntyre's anger was caused as much by anxiety as anything else. 'I couldn't swear to it, but I'd guess she's lopped a month off her time.'

'So what do we do?'

'Only one thing we *can* do. Mogey's here, thank God. He's the only captain I'd dare trust with this little voyage. He's taking her to Singapore on the next tide and you're going with them.'

'Me? What about you?'

For a moment she thought he would hit her.

'Evangeline, I am the only European doctor between here and the Siamese border. I love Diana better than any woman except you, but I could never look myself in the eye again if I deserted my practice for forty-eight hours just because one Englishwoman was having a difficult labour. You'll have to stand in for me; it's only a short voyage.'

'A short voyage on which she could give birth and die. Come on, Neill, I don't give a tinker's damn about your people. She's my family and everything to me apart from you and I'll not have her dying because you want to play missionaries!'

This time he did hit her, a big, open-handed smack across the cheek. She recoiled in shock, then lunged at him. MacIntyre held her off without difficulty and as she struggled against his firm grip on her wrists, he watched implacably. 'Don't *ever* say anything like that to me again. Calm yourself before you cause a real disturbance here — remember your precious Diana is going crazy with pain next door and try to be a little more civilised.'

She slumped into passivity and MacIntyre continued: 'We'll save her, don't worry, but not at the expense of all the other people living in this region. Now I'll send a boy for Mogey and you get a few things together. When Diana has a rest between contractions, I'll go and see her.'

An hour later they were aboard the *Asdang*, with Diana ensconced in Mogensen's cabin, the only spacious accommodation aboard. It was a measure of MacIntyre's anxiety about Diana that he had sent one of his two Chinese midwives with Evangeline on the voyage. There was still a considerable gap between contractions, although Diana had been in labour for a long time, and at the moment she was resting, exhausted. Evangeline left her with the midwife and joined Mogensen on the bridge. He was white-lipped beneath his suntan, his passion for the woman below demonstrated in his disproportionate concern about her condition.

'How will the voyage be, Mogey?' asked Evangeline.

'Good for adventurers. Not good for mothers-to-be. The sort of run I do for devilment occasionally to see that Svendson is not going soft on me in middle age! I have some akvavit here. If you want to hold on to your stomach as we head south, maybe you should take some now.' Seeing her fear he became flippant. 'The caraway seeds are very good for the digestion!'

That restored her sense of proportion and she accepted a drink. They cast off. At that time of year, only the daring Danish masters of the SSN were prepared to risk the run at all and Evangeline rapidly realised why. Kuala Terlengu was sheltered from the open ocean by a long sand bar. Even inside it the water was boiling around the hull like an angry beast seeking prey.

'What will it be like out there?' She gestured beyond the bar.

'Hectic. Now, a little quiet, please, Fruken.'

He had the vessel brought about and appeared to run it directly at the sand bar. When they seemed about to go aground on the unrelieved sandy barrier, Evangeline saw a narrow passage off to the port side. But it was barely wider than the little ship and they hit the bar. Fortunately they did not go aground and after two further attempts they broke through. The open ocean took her breath away. Huge waves ran in, like the ones in Japanese prints that she had always dismissed as over-imaginative. What a time to learn she was wrong! The water hammered past, more like a mill race than open sea. The low-lying coast retreated to invisibility and Evangeline wondered whether they would ever stop heading east.

Eventually she found the courage to ask about it. 'I – I thought we were bound south, Mogey', she said hesitantly.

He managed a laugh. 'If I'd turned south outside the bar we'd have been washed straight on to it. The farther out I can get, the better. Even now, the minute I go south we'll be washed back quite a way but at least we stand a chance of getting through.'

For what seemed like hours they battled out to sea. Then Mogensen finally peeled off south, reached for the speaking tube and spoke his notorious order: 'Full ahead, Mr Svendson – and a half!'

Suddenly he remembered Evangeline's presence. 'Are

you all right, Fruken Owen? Most of my male passengers prefer to be below at this time of year and no woman has ventured up here at all after we leave port during Monsoon.'

'The only thing that would move me now is seeing how Mrs Lenton's doing,' Evangeline told him. 'I've never been anywhere so exciting in my life!'

He let out a shout of laughter. 'And to think I was worried you might get sick on my bridge! Mac had better watch out – I might just sail away with his woman!'

There was a momentary lull. 'Somehow I think you're already promised, Mogey,' she said quietly.

He smiled at her. 'I hope so. Please go below and make sure she gets through.' With that, Mogensen bent forward and kissed her gently on the mouth.

She touched his face. 'Try not to worry. She's a survivor if ever I saw one.' Praying she was right, Evangeline went below. She never forgot the voyage to Singapore. Much to her relief, Diana did not give birth aboard the *Asdang*, although it was a near run thing. An ambulance waited at the quayside in Singapore and Captain Mogensen waved them off, promising to see that the Chinese midwife was returned safely to Kuala Terlengu.

'I am back here in three days, Evangeline,' he said. 'I will come to the hospital. Please leave a message for me if you are not there – and see they take good care of her. I will make sure that Mac knows everything is going as well as can be expected.'

The labour lasted a gruesome forty-six hours from its commencement up at McIntyre's house in Kuala Terlengu. The obstetrician who eventually delivered Diana of a healthy son was surprised that mother and infant seemed unharmed.

'Unharmed, my eye!' Diana was not too weak to express indignation. 'At the moment I feel as unharmed as an earthquake victim. I don't think there's a single part of me that doesn't ache – one in particular!'

'Come along, Mrs Lenton, in a few months you'll be eager to have another baby.' The obstetrician was cheerfully sceptical.

'Don't bet on it; it's an experience which I prefer to treasure in my memory than to relive, thanks!' Secretly Diana felt relieved and grateful that her baby was alive and whole and that she had survived the experience intact apart from the aches and pains. She named her son Cosmo, after a dashing Lenton ancestor of the Regency period. She remained in hospital for two weeks, after which she was over-eager for discharge. Her consultant was determined that she was not yet strong enough for the return sea voyage and that convalescence at an hotel was inadvisable, a situation which solved the dilemma Evangeline had been contemplating for ten days. When he returned to Singapore, Anders Mogensen had contacted Evangeline at the Raffles Hotel.

'What will happen to Mrs Lenton when she is ready to leave the hospital? She will not be ready to go back to Terlengu and she certainly cannot come to an hotel with a new baby.'

'I don't know, Mogey. I suppose she'll have to stay in until she's fit to make the return voyage. But God knows how I'll persuade her. She's chafing about what a bore it all is already.'

'I have an idea, but I do not know how you or she will feel about it,' said Mogensen. 'I have a very comfortable small house here, which an old Chinese couple look after for me while I am away. There is plenty of room for both of you and the baby. I shall be away up the Siam coast for at least five weeks and you'll have the place to yourselves. May I put it at your disposal?'

To Evangeline it seemed a perfect answer, but her very romanticism warned her that it created a potentially explosive situation.

'What about when you come back? She'll be completely recovered by then and I'd have to be a baby not to see the way things are going to be between you. You can hardly not come to your own house.'

'Perhaps we can let that take care of itself, Evangeline. I promise I will not try to make her do anything she may regret.'

245

'My worry is that you won't need to force her – the way she looked at you on New Year's Eve she'll be counting the days.'

'Well, I leave it to you. Even if she decides not to see any more of me, I'd like her to take the house. She will need the rest before she goes back up to Terlengu. You're the one who will decide our fates, Evie.'

Now Evangeline was delighted to have the justification of the hospital consultant's opinion for her approval of a situation which satisfied her sense of melodrama. At the end of February, she collected Diana and Cosmo from the hospital and they moved into Captain Mogensen's bungalow. The elderly Chinese couple who looked after Captain Mogensen received their new guests with beaming pleasure. Clearly they were fond of their employer and wanted to ensure that his friends were as comfortable as possible. They also adored Cosmo on sight. So for the next few weeks the two young women were spoiled deliciously while they got to know city life in one of Asia's great bustling commercial centres. They both loved it – particularly the culinary delicacies that Mrs Lim produced for each meal. At first Diana simply sat among the flowers and shrubs in the spacious garden which surrounded the bungalow, while Cosmo progressively acquired a healthy glow under Evangeline's careful supervision. She had insisted on Cosmo sleeping in her room 'to give you a proper chance to rest and gain your strength, Madam', she said, avoiding any mention of the fact that it also left Diana alone in her bedroom should the handsome captain come courting on his return.

They were unsure of when he planned to come back, because he had been vague when he departed for the Siam run. But the Lims obviously knew. One day the girls got back from an exploration trip to find the bungalow in controlled uproar. Appetising smells wafted from he kitchen and Mr Lim bustled distractedly from room to room, tidying an already spotless house.

'Captain Mogey coming back today. Me and Mrs Lim make special feast of his favourite food for tonight,' he explained to Evangeline. She went to tell Diana the news, but she had clearly guessed already. She was in process of locking herself in the bathroom to prepare for his arrival. Evie could not resist teasing her. She stopped outside the bathroom door and said very quietly: 'Not thinking of doing anything silly, are we . . . Madam?'

A guilty giggle from within confirmed her suspicions and she went off to make her own preparations for Mogensen's first evening home. Diana had bought a dress especially for the occasion, although she had not admitted as much even to herself. It was a soft cloud of silk crêpe de Chine in the swirling marine blues and greens which suited her best. Since leaving hospital she had swum and walked a lot and had been careful about how much she ate. Now she was confident that she looked better than she ever had.

When he came, he took them by surprise. Diana swept breathlessly out on to the verandah and he was standing there, looking across the garden. She froze as she saw him but the noise of her arrival had alerted him to her presence. Mogensen turned very slowly towards her, as though savouring the prospect of what he was about to see. She watched him, mesmerised by his physical magnetism. The captain was unusually tall and well-muscled, with classic Scandinavian colouring – fair hair and brilliantly blue eyes. The hair was bleached silver by constant exposure to salt wind and sunshine. His skin was tanned mahogany brown and the blue eyes shone all the brighter for the contrast. These attributes alone would have made him striking enough, but he possessed an almost magical personal magnetism which increased his appeal tenfold. Diana was never able to decide whether this was merely an outward reflection of his anarchic, happy-go-lucky character or whether it was part of his chemistry.

Now his attractions jostled each other for her attention and her whole being responded to the irresistible appeal of the man in front of her. She felt as though he had been speaking to her, but all he said was her name – once and very quietly. After that they simply stood and gazed at each other.

Eventually Diana broke the silence. 'I can't call you Mogey. What should it be?'

'Anders. No one back in Europe has ever called me anything else.'

'Anders. How did we reach this stage without saying anything much to one another? I feel as though we had been exchanging confidences for years, but really this is only our second proper meeting.'

'I've always known you inside my heart,' he said. 'When I saw you it was as if you had slipped out of my imagination and become real by some miracle.'

'How old are you, Anders?'

'Almost thirty. Why?'

'I'm still only eighteen, but a little bit of me is saying that grown-ups shouldn't get involved as deeply as we appear to be on the strength of one chance meeting.'

He laughed. 'Don't try to be mature when you're about to abandon all your memsahib respectability and make a fool of yourself over a roving seaman!'

'That's just it – I can't understand *why* I'm so ready to risk everything. It's not just the way you look. I remember when Captain Smith mentioned you to me for the first time, I teased Evangeline about the possibility of her falling for you. I knew as I said that I was the one who would fall, not her, and when I eventually met you it was as though it had all been planned in advance.'

'You should be a Buddhist, then you could accept it as karma and let yourself be carried along by it without disputing the causes. For some reason the East makes Europeans behave in a manner they would never consider at home.' Their conversation faltered into silence and they started moving involuntarily towards each other. At that point, Evangeline arrived in a flurry of creamy-fresh cotton flounces.

'Mogey, you villain. You got started before you even had a chance to get back indoors!'

'Really, Evangeline, one day you'll go too far!' Diana was more irritated by the untimely interruption than by her companion's equally untimely familiarity.

The girl merely smiled. 'I came to say welcome home and to suggest that I poured everyone a drink,' she said. She dispensed stengahs and they all sat down together to enjoy the beautiful evening light. Having subdued his longing for Diana temporarily, at least, Mogensen set out to entertain the two women.

'While you're on the east side of the peninsula you should take the opportunity to go up to Siam and Indo-China; it's a wonderful place. Angkor Wat is one of the wonders of the world, and somehow it becomes more magical because you go there on a run-down old bus from Phnom Penh!'

'What is it?' asked Evangeline.

'A huge complex of Hindu temples and statuary about eight hundred years old. Its real glory is that it was lost for ages. The Khmer civilisation that built it moved on and there were no settlements around it that survived until modern times. So now it is deep in the jungle, this fabulous memorial to a lost people, quietly lying in its forest clearing.'

Both women were captivated by the picture he painted. Diana had read of the temple complex but had not realised how accessible it was from the east coast. She began weaving a private fantasy about travelling there some day with Mogensen.

He kept up the entertainment until dinner time with tales of the strange occult beliefs which the indigenous Malay population had no difficulty in reconciling with their allegiance to Islam. 'They are very flexible people and they don't like loose ends,' he explained, 'so they give Allah ultimate responsibility for the universe but accept that demons, elementals and ancestral spirits inhabit the everyday world with them.

'It's a frightening world, anyway, with wild beasts and cruel storms to contend with. I think those fears become more manageable if they are embodied. After all, if a demon exists, there also exists a formula for dealing with him. But what if the lightning bolt or the tiger attack were mere blind coincidence? I think they would find that prospect far more frightening because then they would have to admit that they had no control at all.'

Lim arrived to announce that the evening meal was ready. The couple had excelled themselves and mounted a feast of all Mogensen's favourite dishes. His guests exclaimed with pleasure at the huge display before them.

'We've been utterly spoiled since we got here,' said Diana. 'The Lims are wonderful cooks – but their food is quite different from what Lee To does for us up at Terlengu Estate and I thought that was classic Cantonese with a touch of Straits.'

'It probably is, but Lim's cuisine is the highest form of Straits Chinese and that's moved on considerably from the cooking of mainland China. When I bumped into him he was running one of the little mobile street kitchens in town. Have you tried them? Some of them serve the best food in the Peninsula.'

Mogensen went on to explain that Mrs Lim had been ill when he encountered them and that Lim's nomadic street life was not tailored to help her. The captain had needed a reliable couple to look after his new house and the Lims had needed a permanent home. They had moved in and had been with him ever since. The Englishwomen suspected that the Lims would have told it differently – they clearly held Mogensen in a position of esteem second only to Buddha – but he insisted that the arrangement was more to his advantage than theirs. The feast that followed commenced with tiny, pastie-shaped fried pastries, stuffed with pounded curried beef.

'It isn't strictly correct with the rest of the meal, but they know I have a great weakness for these,' explained Mogensen.

The puffs were followed by the true first course, Yong thou foo, a mixture of peppers, aubergines, little marrows and bean curd cakes, all stuffed with feather-light pork quenelles flavoured with onions, herbs and garlic and poached in an intensely savoury fish broth. After that the rest of the dinner was laid out simultaneously. The centrepiece was a duck, barbecued Malay-style wth coriander, fenugreek, cumin and turmeric and basted with coconut milk and lemon juice flavoured with a range of different spices. The huge variety of fish available in Singapore had figured in the girls' diet ever since their arrival but now they tried two new fish dishes – fried snapper with lemon grass, pineapple and shrimp paste; and prawns in chilli sauce. Fried rice with egg and cucumber accompanied the meat and fish. To freshen it all, there was a huge dish of rojak, the Malayan-Chinese salad of cucumber, mango, pineapple and red chillis, as well as a dish of bananas baked with orange and lemon juice. When the Lims bowed out, the last morsel had been consumed, accompanied by constant compliments as each new delicacy was tested.

Soon Evangeline, too, said goodnight. 'Little Master Cosmo needs some company and I expect you two have a lot of talking to do,' she said, managing not to giggle.

They moved indoors and sat sipping chilled mangosteen juice spiked with gin. Mogensen extended his hand and Diana moved across the room to join him. She slid into the encirclement of his bronzed arm with the pleasure of a child returning to a parent's secure embrace. 'I feel as if this had always been where I belonged,' she told him.

They kissed, long and serenely, then simply sat, letting the silence flow tranquil around them.

'How long do we have?' Diana asked after a while.

'I'm back for a week, then I'm due on the Kuala Terlengu run. I assume I shall be delivering you back there when I go.'

'I shall stay with Neill for a while.'

'Diana, I am not trying to raise difficulties so soon, but we have to make peace with *some* realities. The Monsoon is all but played out now. By the time we go north it will be gone. Your husband will want to see his son and to take him home – and home is Terlengu Plantation, not Kuala Terlengu.'

This silenced her and she retreated to private contemplation of the future. But he was not prepared to lose their earlier rapport.

'We have a week together. At this stage, it's more than we have any right to ask. Who knows what might happen after that? All I want you to remember now is that we must take time in moments, not plan in months and years. Then perhaps the months and years will look after themselves.'

He turned her to face him, tilting her face up towards his. Her memory threw her a fleeting glimpse of Ben Lassiter, centuries ago it seemed, telling her to live for the moment that day when they took a picnic to Runnymede and Bray. The image faded as Anders Mogensen kissed her long and deep and said 'Seven nights together. Isn't that enough for now?'

'Enough for ever, my dearest. At the moment it seems like eternity!'

He went with her to her room and stayed until dawn.

CHAPTER THIRTEEN

The bathroom at Terlengu appealed intensely to Roland's romanticism. Somehow it resembled a Roman bath house, he felt, in that it stood separate from the bungalow. Buffy Exton had installed a running water supply simply by having the small building constructed across the path of a stream immediately after it bubbled in a cascade from a spring set in high rocks. The area was well endowed with alternative sources of fresh water, so monopolising this one for domestic baths was practical. A bamboo pipe took the spring from the rock down into a cement-lined basin the size of an English suburban garden pond, whence it trickled back to its natural course through an outlet in the bath-house floor. The bather could also stand on a concrete slab and divert the bamboo pipe to splash a refreshing shower straight over himself. Both Roland and Diana loved the little building and had spent a lot of time there. While she was away, first at Kuala Terlengu and then in Singapore, Roland resorted there regularly to cool off, to think or merely to daydream about the idyllic life they would live for a few years in the East.

The nearest English planter, Edward Dare, lived about three miles along the river. He was unusual among the Europeans in this state at the time because he employed an all-Malay domestic staff. Most planters used Chinese workers in the house and Tamil plantation labourers. The Malays farmed their own lands and lived a parallel but separate existence alongside the rubber estates. During Diana's absence, Roland got to know Dare quite well. He was something of a recluse, an intellectual in the old classicist style who read Greek, Latin and Arabic more easily than the modern European languages. He had converted to

Islam a few years before and lived native fashion. After dinner he was apt to sit and discuss customs, tradition and myth with Dang, the Malay youth who ran his household, and his younger brother, Dhak. Roland often joined them and began to learn a great deal about the Malay culture.

One evening, having returned from a particularly relaxing session with Dare and the boys, he went straight to the bath-house and stood for a few minutes under the invigorating stream to wash away the sweat of his walk back. Refreshed but still wakeful, he slid into the basin and floated there for some time, his eyes half closed, dreaming. A sense of something disturbing the surface of the pool roused him. He opened his eyes and discovered it was a perfect hibiscus flower. As he watched, another bloom wafted down to join it. Roland glanced up and discovered Dhak standing behind him, casting the flowers into the water.

'Dhak! I say, old chap, you startled me. What's up?'

'Pardon, Tuan Roland. Not mean to frighten you. I did not wish you should walk alone through the forest so I followed. I have something to ask . . .' his soft small voice tailed off.

'Ask away.' Roland was aware of the Malays' superstitious dread of the jungle after dark and of the courtesy offered by this young man in escorting him back safely. The least he could do was listen to his request.

'I wish to be your boy – come here, work for you like Dang and Tuan Dare.'

'But Dhak, we already have a full staff. I don't need anyone else.'

'No, no, Tuan. You have servants for you and Mem Lenton together. Not have your own boy. Please let me come work for you.'

Before Roland could say anything further, the youth slid from his shadowy perch among the rocks and joined him in the water. Gently he began massaging the tired muscles across Roland's shoulders. Nothing could have persuaded him to stop the boy, although the action was an obvious prelude to more. Gradually the delicate brown hands eased down his body, manipulating the pectorals, pressing the vertebrae. Dhak was a natural masseur and by now Roland was floating in a state of dreamy pleasure where excitement seemed to have no place. Soon the hands were gently squeezing his buttocks and the boy began pressing the length of his sinuous torso against Roland's back.

It could not be called a surrender. Roland had put up no struggle, sliding as readily into the homosexual embrace as he had into the cool water. He turned to face Dhak, embracing him eagerly, kissing his eyelids and cheeks with a fervour he had never mustered with Diana. The boy moaned in pleasure as Roland's mouth covered his, tongue forcing between teeth, probing and caressing as it explored his new lover. Their bodies were locked tightly together and it seemed completely natural to Roland that he was experiencing a prodigious erection. The silky golden flesh, stretched taut over well-toned muscle, had nothing in common with a female body. It was lean and tough and, he finally acknowledged, more exciting than anything he had known until now. The boy guided him on, clearly enjoying a level of experience yet unknown to Roland. As his passion grew, Roland accepted his partner's curves and flatnesses as perfect. Dhak turned away from him, still managing to hold him close, and spread his buttocks to take the thrust of Roland's engorged penis. As the Englishman drove forward against him, he showered the boy's neck and shoulders with tiny, ecstatic kisses, further excited by the silky black hairs on his skin. He had clasped Dhak by the thighs as he turned, and was now pressing him rhythmically back and down towards himself. Suddenly he felt a warm gush against his hands under the cool water and Dhak relaxed fully against him. The complete surrender precipitated a thunderous orgasm in Roland and as his passion spent itself he drew his arms tightly around Dhak.

'Don't move yet. Just stay as you are. That was wonderful.'

Eventually Dhak eased him gently from the water and they moved together up to the house. The boy joined him in the big low bed and they made love with continuing intensity for hours. Roland drifted into a deep sleep shortly before dawn. When he woke it was full daylight, though still very early. There was no sign of Dhak. Later that day, the young Malay brought a few belongings over to the estate and moved in. When Roland explained the addition to the household staff, the Chinese houseman, who lived across the clearing with his family, made no comment beyond courteous acknowledgement. Dhak never gave the slightest hint of their relationship in public and managed to arrange his encounters with Roland when there was least likelihood of them being caught together. The estate settled back to its daily routine, its master fondly believing that only he and Dhak knew of their affair.

Diana stayed at Kuala Terlengu for a week before she was able to contemplate returning to Terlengu itself.

'Evie, how can I face him? I may be the mother of his son, but we no longer share anything else. I shall simply have to tell him we can't go on.'

Evangeline stared at her unbelievingly. 'Madam, I'll pretend the heat or the long journey have made you go funny and forget you ever said that. In fact when I think about it, perhaps you *have* gone a bit funny!'

'And what's that supposed to mean?'

'You gave up just about everything to marry Mr Lenton, whether you loved him or not. Forget about whether you owe him anything for a minute. Just think what it will mean to you if you confess everything now and leave him.'

'I have. It will mean I can go to Anders and share his life. We can be together always. I needn't be married to him – in his world we shan't need such conventional nonsense.'

'And what d'you think will happen to Master Cosmo? Surely you don't think Mr Lenton will just let you walk off with him – the next heir to Granby?'

'He won't need to. He can have Cosmo.'

'But you can't give up your son!'

'Why not?'

Evangeline thought of her own tigress reaction to

attempts to separate her from Imogen; of the sense of longing she still experienced to see her little daughter; of her regret that Imogen now belonged irrevocably to Louise. 'Because – well, it's just not natural, that's all!'

'Don't talk to me about natural. I wasn't leading anything approaching a natural life from the time I married Roland. If you only knew . . .' she stopped, reddened and bit her lip, obviously regretting the careless remark.

Evangeline was instantly solicitous. 'Has Mr Lenton been making you – that is, has he ever . . .'

'Forget I said anything, Evie. Just let's say I have nothing to hold me to a marriage I more or less fell into. Anyway, I've had enough of it and if the price is giving up Cosmo, I shall do so.'

And with precious few regrets, too, thought Evangeline. You certainly haven't wasted too much affection on the poor little blighter since you got out of hospital, and you weren't exactly the great earth mother just after he was born. Still, she reflected, everyone didn't find babies irresistible and Diana Lenton had faced the extra strain of falling madly in love virtually while she was giving birth.

Evangeline had been doing a lot of thinking about her own future. Neill had greeted her with a proposal of marriage which had stopped her in her tracks. At first she had dismissed the entire idea, refusing with the dogged inverted snobbery of a petty bourgeoise to contemplate the marriage of a paid companion and a professional man. She had soon got over that and had given the matter serious consideration. Neill was beginning to hope he had won her over and when she joined him on the verandah the evening after her return, he was positively beaming with anticipation.

'You're not going to like this, Neill – I can't say yes yet.'

'Why on earth not – surely you're not still on that ridiculous master-servant line?'

'No. It's far more serious than that.'

'I didn't think anything could be, the way you were mathering about it last night!'

'No, it's Mrs Lenton.'

'Oh come on, Evie – you can't reject me on account of some misplaced sense of obligation to Diana! She'd be the first person to understand how you feel.'

'You don't understand at all. It's not a matter of letting her down. It's more that seeing how she's making a fool of herself over a man has started me wondering what sort of judge I am of my own feelings. We're practically the same age and in spite of the fact that she's posh and I'm ordinary, we're a lot alike in all sorts of ways. I've just seen her convince herself that she's potty over a man she met five minutes ago. At the moment she's ready to destroy her whole world for him and hurt all the people closest to her; and I don't believe she loves him anything like as much as she thinks. What if I make the same sort of mistake?'

'For one thing, you are not a married woman with a newborn baby. For another, I have no doubts about your feelings or mine. And on top of that, who are you to doubt whether Diana's love for Mogey is as strong as she says?'

'That's the whole point; I'm very like her in lots of ways and I know I can be convinced by what I want to believe, although that may not be the way things really are at all. I think she loves Mogey so much because she *doesn't* love Mr Lenton and because she's not half as fond of the baby as she thought she would be. Rather than admit the truth and find some way of sorting out her marriage and at least acting like a good mother, she's going to blow up an exciting affair into the love of her life and try to run away from everything before she has a chance to fail at making the best of a bad job!'

'Even if you're right, that has nothing to do with us. You're not running away from anything, you're not involved with me as an escape, and you haven't any awful failure to cope with if you go on living your life as you did before we met. So where's the similarity?'

'You can be really daft at times, Neill! Of course I'd like to run away. I'm a servant. A very privileged servant, perhaps, but I still have to call Diana Lenton Madam even if she thinks of me as her best friend, and one day we'll go back to Europe and all this free-and-easy pals act will stop straight away. Then there's all this mess between her and Mr Lenton. That won't be sorted out in a month of Sundays and when we go back up to Terlengu, guess who'll be in the middle, literally holding the baby? My God, Neill, I'd have to be made of stone not to be tempted to run away from that lot!'

'Well, I have to admit you're beginning to make a bit more sense. But are you trying to tell me I don't mean anything to you?'

'God, you really *are* daft! Of course not – just that I'm afraid I may be blowing up the fun and excitement of being with you into something bigger because it makes things nicer for me, that's all. I'm not turning you down flat. But I need to know you a lot longer, love you for a while and see how we feel when we get used to each other and don't just want to tear off our clothes every time we meet. If I still feel like this about you in a few years time – three or four, perhaps – I'll marry you like a shot. That's if I'm not too old for you by then, of course!'

'You are some woman, Miss Evangeline Owen. I don't know where you learned your wisdom, but at times it scares me. I hate to admit this, because I want quite the opposite, but you're right. I'll wait for you and I promise I shan't even nag you about marriage, at least not when I'm sober! If and when you make up your mind either way, just tell me and I'll marry you or get out of your life. One thing I am sure of, and that's the fact that no one will ever replace you ... Now what are you crying about? You got what you wanted, didn't you?'

Eventually Roland solved the problem of Diana's homecoming – temporarily at least. He sent down a message with one of Edward Dare's estate workers to say he would be there himself within a week and would take Diana back up to Terlengu Estate after staying a few days with MacIntyre. The morning the message arrived, Diana was sitting listlessly on MacIntyre's verandah, looking down towards the harbour.

'Well, have you had a change of heart? You've been

pretty quiet about leaving Mr Lenton since we last talked about it.'

Evangeline's tone was sharp with anxiety. Diana seemed to weigh her words for a moment, then said: 'I shall be going back up with Roland. Anders doesn't think a shipboard life will suit me.'

Oh God, he's turned her down, thought Evangeline. That could be worse in the end than having her leave Mr Lenton. She waited for the inevitable display of emotional fireworks, but Diana stayed calm.

'I thought he'd throw away everything for me if I asked it, but he says it would be dishonourable. Why do I always love honourable men?'

'He is right, Madam. Once you'd had a chance for the novelty to wear off, you'd probably start feeling guilty too and it would poison everything, wouldn't it?'

'Oh, damn, I know he's making sense! I made a complete fool of myself and cried and shouted that he didn't love me and had only been using me. He just . . . just stood there holding on to me and let me rant until I was exhausted. Then he said that if it was only his honour, he'd give it up straight away without regrets. He didn't think I could stand up to it. That was why he wouldn't take me. And I didn't even have the consolation of thinking it was because he believed I had splendid moral principles. He said I'd be like a little girl on the boat for a while, playing with new toys. He said that after that, though, I'd have to get used to living with a seaman in a modest house in Singapore and that all those awful mems I look down on so much would be my social superiors and would take the greatest pleasure in snubbing me.

'At that point I started realising he knew what he was talking about, but I still wouldn't accept it. Then he said: "If you really want to know what it would be like, talk to Mac. He married his Chinese beauty and had to go up to Kuala Terlengu before he could find peace. If he'd stayed in Singapore he'd never have survived the pressure. Mac loves the solitude and he loves Malaya enough to stay. For you, this country is just a port of call. Make it anything else and it will destroy you."

'I went on being indignant but he's right. All my problems until now have been down to my wanting to be at the top. A life like the one he described would turn me into a sour old bitch in five years.'

Diana was not even weeping about it. She sat, staring dully ahead of her, perhaps seeing an image of her life in the foreseeable future. With or without Anders Mogensen, it was a bleak prospect. Diana continued to meet Mogensen during the following week. Now that their separation was decided, both of them took advantage of the temporary reprieve. They knew that nothing more than friendship could continue once Roland had taken her back to Terlengu. The night before her husband was to join her, she was curled up beside the Danish captain in MacIntyre's living room. Mac and Evangeline had tactfully left them alone together.

'If ever we have a chance to be with each other alone again, I want to take you to Angkor Wat,' Mogensen told her. 'It is my special place, the one place which never lost any of its magic from the day I first saw it. I should have known when I first set eyes on you why you were so familiar. You're a Western version of the goddesses sculpted on the sides of the temples – wide shoulders, big breasts and tiny waists, and faces that hold all the secrets of the world!'

'I don't know any secrets, Anders. I'm all on the surface.'

'Oh, but there you are wrong. Much of the time you behave like a spoiled child in a woman's body, and everyone should be angry with you. But they never are – only the ones who are jealous of you. Inside you somewhere is the secret of allure, the instinctive knowledge of how to draw people and hold them in spite of themselves. That's the greatest thing you share with my temple ladies.'

Next morning, Roland arrived. He spent a long time sitting beside Cosmo's crib, gazing down in dumb pride at the featureless sleeping bundle which was his son. At that moment he could have overcome his inhibitions with Diana and resumed their barely-started physical relationship, simply on the basis of the overwhelming feelings generated in him by fatherhood. Unfortunately Diana's tormented circumstances made her cool and unapproachable and the opportunity passed. Roland retreated inside his shell and the reconciliation was deferred. The evening before the Lentons' departure ended a day of perfect weather. Diana, emerging after her rest and bath, gasped at the sight of the green, pink and gold streaks which made the evening sky like a baroque painted ceiling. The air was soft and fragrant and a couple of lovely Malay girls in colourful clothing walked along the rough street outside MacIntyre's garden. Suddenly it was all too much for her to endure. She had been suppressing her misery successfully since Roland's arrival, aided by Mogensen's departure for the Gulf of Siam. But this evening was made for lovers and the thought of spending it with Roland overwhelmed her.

Diana strode through the garden and started towards the harbour. Why not really wallow in it and go down and be Madame Butterfly on the jetty? she thought, trying to laugh at her own folly. What she saw as the moorings came into full view made her break into a run. The *Asdang* was tying up at its usual berth. By the time she reached the landing stage, Mogensen was hurrying down the gangplank towards her. He grasped her, in full view of the passers-by, and treated her to an embrace that was anything but brotherly. Laughing and crying at once, she finally managed to speak.

'What are you doing here? It's as if I had a lovely dream and you made it come true! Are you really here?'

'It's no good – I got half-way up the coast and I couldn't bear it any longer. I can't do without you and if we destroy each other I just have to take the risk.'

He slipped an arm around her waist and they turned towards the gangplank, wrapped in a separate world. A group of children further along the jetty were watching them, fascinated. Europeans were not normally so demonstrative in public. As they gaped at this free show, one of them stepped a little too close to the edge, missed his footing and fell into the harbour. The Lascar seaman on deck gave a yell of alarm. The *Asdang* was not yet fully moored and was still in motion against the landing stage. Anyone in the water between vessel and shore was in grave danger of being crushed.

The commotion startled Mogensen out of his rosy dream. Turning, he took in what had happened and was on the move instantly. He ran along the landing stage, past the stern of the *Asdang*, and hit the water in a low flat dive, turning to swim back to the dark gap between ship and quay. Diana remained on the gangplank as if frozen there. Just beyond the vessel, the Dane started calling in Malay to the little boy. When the child bobbed to the surface, Mogensen told him how best to ease himself alongside the vessel, always working sternward towards safety. But he was a very young boy and terror gripped him before he could complete his perilous journey. Still speaking gently to him, Mogensen started to ease his own way alongside. Then he noticed an old iron ladder, hanging crookedly down from the jetty close to the little boy. It was rusty but might just hold the child if he could be raised to the bottom rung.

The *Asdang*'s bulk moved sluggishly towards him and Mogensen shut his eyes, waiting for the crunch as it destroyed the lower part of his body. He was lucky this time; the vessel swung ponderously away again without hitting the jetty and he resumed his progress towards the child. The boy was no trouble once Mogensen reached him. Numb with terror, he simply clung to the big Dane and begged for help. After soothing him for a moment, Mogensen showed him the ladder and explained what he planned. Two of his crew were already peering down at them and he shouted instructions, raising the boy as he finished. The presence of an adult reassured the little Malay and when Mogensen raised him aloft, he gripped the ladder, wriggling up swiftly to get his legs on to the lowest rung. In moments the two seamen had pulled him to safety and he collapsed in tears on the wooden landing stage.

The *Asdang*'s stern had now come right around to bump the jetty and Mogensen fancied still less his chances of covering the greater distance along the length of the vessel until he emerged forward. He preferred to risk the ladder, although it looked unsafe for a well-nourished adult. Mustering his full strength, he thrust himself up out of the sea to grip the ladder three rungs up. It creaked and shifted in protest, but held. Gaining purchase with his feet against the slippery woodwork of the jetty piles, Mogensen started forcing himself up towards safety.

At that point, Captain Smith's *Lipis* bustled around the sandbar into the harbour, creating a considerable wash as it manoeuvred to line up for docking. Mogensen was half-way up the ladder when it tore out of its fixtures, plunging him back into the water. Then the *Lipis*'s wash hit the *Asdang* and it swung back towards the landing stage with greater force than before. The Dane screamed once as the ship crushed him against the jetty, then disappeared beneath the sea.

He lived for nearly two days, his injuries so terrible that Evangeline prayed for him to die quickly. When they managed to get him out of the water, they rushed him to MacIntyre. The *Asdang* had hit him twice, the first impact crushing his ribs, perforating his left lung and rupturing a kidney. The second blow had taken him in the legs as his body toppled further into the water. His right leg was pulped and the ironwork of the old ladder had pierced his left calf and buttock.

All MacIntyre could do was to clean him up and keep him strongly dosed with morphine. 'If only the poor bastard didn't have such a survival instinct,' he told Evangeline. 'He's beyond all help now but another day of this will push Diana over the edge for good.'

Diana was inconsolable. She had not gone to the scene of disaster, staying rigid on the gangplank, knowing instinctively that the end had come and being unable to face it. After the initial panic of getting Mogensen up to Dr MacIntyre's surgery, it occurred to Evangeline to ask where she was. Her question was answered by the arrival of Captain Smith, leading Diana, who appeared to be sleep-walking.

'I dashed over after we tied up to see if there was any-thing I could do to help. She was just standing on the gangplank, clutching the rail and staring at the spot where he'd gone in,' Smith explained. 'One of the Lascars told me what had happened and I thought I'd better bring her to you.'

Diana allowed herself to be led into the sitting room, where she sat down and stared blankly at the wall. When he had a chance to leave Mogensen, Neill MacIntyre came to see her, then went back to the Dane, perplexed.

'I don't want to give her anything yet,' he told Evan-geline. 'I need to see what symptoms of shock she shows beyond this switching-off, or for that matter how long the switching-off lasts.'

He got his answer in two hours. Suddenly the air was rent by an animal shriek, then another, and another. They rushed to Diana. She had not moved but was sitting in the lamplit room, head back, screaming. MacIntyre slapped her sharply on both cheeks. It made no difference. Leaving Evangeline with her, he went for hypodermic and sedative. When he returned, he injected Diana and then went to see Roland Lenton. Roland was sitting in the darkness out on the verandah, as still as his wife had been inside. MacIntrye handed him a stiff gin sling and sat down beside him.

'Do I need to tell you or do you know?'

'I, er, know – well, I sort of guessed.'

'What are you going to do?'

'Do? Nothing. I love Diana. She's my wife.'

MacIntyre knew Roland well enough to understand that the man required no analysis of the situation. He knew in general terms what Diana had been doing and preferred not to have it spelled out. His continued presence was sufficient indication that he intended to stay and look after her.

'Good man. It's small enough consolation, I know, but Mogey'll never give you any more trouble. He's dead in all but name.'

'I wouldn't be too sure of that, Neill. I think he might give me more trouble dead than alive.'

Roland rose and went to Diana. He sat beside her all night. Evangeline occasionally topped up his drink, but otherwise left him alone while she took turns at watching over Mogensen. Diana came out of her sedation twice during the vigil and each time the eldritch screeching continued until MacIntyre administered another injection. At each awakening, Roland moved towards her and held her. She gave no indication she even knew he was there.

Mogensen died as dawn came two days later. He had never regained consciousness. His funeral came and went and still Diana remained in her catatonic state. By now they had moved her to the bedroom and undressed her. Roland maintained his watch, snatching catnaps and subsisting on fruit and alcohol. The first change came when Diana became restless. She started moving about in the big bed like someone in a natural sleep who was having a bad dream. Finally she snapped awake. She lay flat, staring at the ceiling and as still as during the sedation, but Roland sensed that she was fully aware again.

Suddenly she sat up, turned to him and said: 'I'd like a cup of tea, please, Roland.'

He made no comment, but went and prepared the drink himself. Returning, he sat beside her on the bed after handing over the cup. Diana drank it carefully, replaced the cup and saucer on the night table, then turned to face him.

'You're really the only man who never leaves me, aren't you, Roland?'

This first remark apparently burst the dam of her grief, because after that she sobbed uncontrollably for over an hour. Roland remembered the night they had sat together thus in his Fulham Road studio. It seemed like another time. He held her silently and made no comment. After the tears came more silence, but this time it was normal, not induced by shock or drugs.

'Forget I'm anything but your best friend,' he told her. 'Say whatever you wish; anything that will help you. I'm not going to leave you and I'm not going to torment you in the future with anything we discuss now. Do you want to talk?'

Stumblingly, she tried to explain the attractions of Mogensen, the inevitability of their affair, her need for reassurance in the absence of any sexual attention from Roland.

'I can't tell you I'm sorry about it, because I'm not. I'm just devastated that he's dead and I shall have to live the rest of my life knowing he only died because he came back for me. If he'd gone on the normal voyage he'd have been safe in Siam by now.'

'We all live out our time, Diana. No one kills anyone else in the sense you're talking about. At that level we all have free will and if he came back it was his own choice. Try not to feel guilty about it.'

The one thing Roland found impossible to cope with was his wife's apparent lack of concern at having embarked on an affair virtually before she had recovered from the birth of their son. His natural reticence and guilt about his own illicit relationship with Dhak – also initiated before his newborn son was even out of hospital – prevented him from pursuing the matter. Nor did he mention her apparent indifference to Cosmo, which he felt might be connected with her love affair. They did not discuss the possibility of separation. Before they went back to Terlengu, Diana went briefly to the little Christian burial ground outside the village and planted an orchid on Mogensen's grave.

Returning to MacIntyre's house, she gave Evangeline a lopsided smile. 'He would have said I was a sentimental idiot and demanded to be buried at sea,' she said.

'The orchids are for you, not him,' Evangeline told her. 'He'd understand that you need the comfort. He was a realist.'

'I don't want to give you any more sedatives or sleeping tablets,' said Neill MacIntyre just before she went home. 'Do you think you can manage without?'

'I have no trouble sleeping, Neill. I suffer when I'm awake, and I don't think you have any little pills for that.'

'It might be an idea if you stay down here a while longer. You're a long way from recovery yet.'

For the first time since the accident, she managed a proper smile. 'Stop worrying, Neill. I'm a horrid woman and all this misery is simply me coming to terms with my own awfulness. I've a great capacity for self-dramatisation and that's very close to the surface at the moment. Don't take my tragedy too seriously or you'll suffer more than I do in the end. And you'd better make the most of this bit of self-revelation, too. It's not really me, is it? Normally I prefer to live as if I were the heroine of a novelette. For the moment, though, I think I owe it to Anders to try and see things clearly.

'I'm going back up to Terlengu, where I shall turn into a model wife and mother, get to know Malaya properly and prepare to go back to England eventually as a seasoned planter. I might even spend a bit more time over at High Trees, attempting to see the mems as they really are and not as shadowy copies of the Society harpies I left in London. How about that for a self-improvement pro-gramme?'

'So sensible that it gives me further worries about your sanity.'

'Thanks, Doc – you're a big help! Seriously, amidst all the sorrow I've felt I have managed to take in the fact that Roland behaved beautifully. I, on the other hand, had been quite unspeakable up till then and I'm sure I shall be again. But at least I can try to be good. Take a look at Anders's orchids for me from time to time – and thank you for everything. See you soon.'

She turned and went out to the car, where Roland and Evangeline awaited her, the latter with Cosmo held firmly in her arms.

CHAPTER FOURTEEN

Inevitably, Diana and Krystyna Karpinska became friends. It was impossible to be European and in Kuala Lumpur in 1934 and not to notice Krystyna. She was almost six feet tall, with a thick mop of deep honey-coloured hair which contrasted oddly with her sooty black lashes. Her eyes were cornflower blue and opaque 'like broken shards in one of the really old restored windows in a church', mused Roland later. Her form was slim but big, with strong square shoulders and endless legs accentuating an almost masculine build. The voice, though, was a hundred per cent woman. A rich chuckle bubbled ahead of the introduction 'Krystyna Karpinska, unpronounceably Polish, of course!'. A long, strong, perfectly-manicured hand was proffered. 'D'you think I shall fit into the Ladies' Stand?'

They laughed, Diana delighted at the prospect of such an outrageous new companion among the pillars of social rectitude who surrounded her. The Ladies' Stand regularly reduced her to gales of mirth. It was a sort of enlarged decorator's step-up, just a double tier of plywood benches, enough to accommodate eight women crushed tightly together. Anyone who had been racing in England at Ascot or Goodwood would have dismissed it as a pretentious absurdity. It became less laughable and more touching when one realised that many of those who sat in it *had* been racing in England, and that their nostalgia enabled them to pretend that this little piece of plywood was a real stand on a major course.

'Are you disreputable enough for me?' Diana now asked in an undertone. 'If I meet just one more well-behaved little DO's wife I shall lose my mind!'

Krystyna struck the classic Marlene Dietrich pose from

Shanghai Express and said in creditable imitation of the star 'It took more than one man to name me Shanghai Lil!'

Both women shrieked with laughter, linked arms and went off to find a drink, looking out for Roland along the way. When they found him, he was unenthusiastic about Diana's new-found companion. Roland was incapable of anything less than exquisite good manners, but unease showed through as he made visible efforts to be courteous to Krystyna.

'Ah, um, yes – believe I met your – er . . . husband? – at the club last night. I say, Diana, shouldn't we be going off to see the Andersons now?'

Krystyna flushed and momentarily lost her composure. 'I see Karl-Erik has made all the necessary introductions and it remains only for me to steal away in shame' – she forced a smile that was a grimace – 'but I'm a fighter, so I stay and slug it out. No, we do not share similar views; yes, he does talk like von Ribbentrop; no, we do not often go out together; yes, he will return to Europe before I do. Does that clear the air a little?'

If anything, Roland was more alarmed than before. The wife of a sickeningly pro-Nazi Swede was enough of an unwelcome surprise as one's wife's newest social acquisition. When she began publicly disowning her husband in front of a couple of virtual strangers it became positively agonising. But, as he feared, Diana was intrigued. She was regarding the newcomer with even greater interest.

'All of which sounds irresistible, my dear. Tell me, do you always let complete strangers in on the interesting bits first, or save them till the end of Act One?'

It might have been the ultimate bitchery, but the two women instinctively understood each other and Krystyna recognised the underlying sympathy of a fellow outsider.

'Actually my married name is Lindqvist. It's just that I prefer to use my own good Polish name than anything so – so Aryan. I've had enough Strength through Joy to last two thousand years rather than just one! Just in case either of you harbours any deep-seated sympathy for the Fatherland, I have to announce that I'm not the daughter of an old Junker family. I come from nationalist Slav stock and' – in a stage whisper – 'Grandmama was a Jew!'

Roland flushed and failed to meet her eyes. Really, this woman was too much even for Diana's baroque tastes! After an anguished silence, he stammered out 'But, uh, that is, you and Lindqvist . . .'

'The best-laid plans even of the master race can go horribly wrong, Mr Lenton! He was the most beautiful specimen I'd ever seen, with wonderful Scandinavian manners, in contrast to all those damned hot-blooded impetuous Poles I'd spent my life with. My idiot family had sent me to stay with an aunt in Stockholm for the winter to brush away the provincial cobwebs of Poznan. Poor Karl-Erik! I must have been as much his dream of the Rhine maiden as he was mine of the Snow Knight – a big blonde countess from the Polish plains. Imagine the shock to wake up married and find that Brunnhilde was really an *untermaedchen* with a grandmother called Rebecca!

'Not that it happened that suddenly, of course. We didn't get around to discussing politics for some time. In fact I'd never done any serious thinking on the matter until he started introducing me to all these lunatics at the diplomatic parties he loved to attend. Then I began to hear things that had me wanting to join up with Rosa Luxemburg! At first I made scenes, insulted Nazis and generally tried to be as unpleasant as possible, in the hope that Karl-Erik would off-load me. Then I started realising that they weren't going away. They really meant all that stuff about a thousand-year Reich. So I started behaving well and going to the parties, circulating, listening and remaining friends with all of them. Some day, somebody on the other side is going to know what to do with all the contacts and information I've built up.

'In fact that's why I'm telling you two. I know people on their side, but I don't know who to tell on *your* side that I have something which could be useful. When things start getting worse, remember me and tell someone. I could be useful. Now – did someone say something about another drink?'

*

271

They filled the silence with inanities about the next race, curry tiffins and the Malayan character. Krystyna's astonishing frankness had finally worked, even on Roland. There was still a barrier between him and the Polish woman, but now it was one of reserve, not hostility. Diana was completely bewitched. Krystyna went back to High Trees with them that evening and stayed a month, broken only by a couple of token trips to Kuala Lumpur when social obligations demanded she should be seen with Lindqvist. After that her husband returned to Europe and she accepted an invitation to continue her stay in Terlengu and see the other, untouched Malaya.

The two women achieved the sort of friendship that Diana could never enjoy with Evangeline because of the unbridgeable class barrier. Diana and Krystyna were both from the privileged side of the fence and were therefore completely unselfconscious in each other's company. Pole and Englishwoman shared a common language of country house and private park which went back centuries. They were alike in their healthy contempt for conventions which they regarded as stuffy and were attracted to one another because each sensed an unorthodoxy in the other woman which echoed her own. Krystyna's Jewish grandmother and Diana's erring father had an unlikely quality in common: they were responsible for the two women's mutual tendency to regard themselves as outsiders in their own milieux, onlookers at parties in which they could never fully participate. Since the death of Mogensen five years ago, Diana had met no one with whom she shared such an affinity as she now discovered with Krystyna.

By spending five years at an English girls' school the young Krystyna missed much of the victimisation of Jews which flowed from Germany with the rise of National Socialism in the 1920s. As she grew older, back home during school holidays, she began to notice the contemptuous glances cast her way by the haughty children of Junker families who lived in Poland. Suddenly it was more fashionable than ever to claim German descent. Even the old Polish aristocrats were now slightly suspect. Krystyna's grandmother began to take on the characteristics of a skeleton in the family closet. The family protected her from painful contact with the realities of upper-class anti-semitism, but her two elder brothers experienced too much of it for their liking. When she was eighteen, they made an apparently ingenuous suggestion that she should winter in Stockholm with her Aunt Helga. It made sense. Swedish society was a little stuffy, perhaps, but certainly more sophisticated than what Poland offered at the time. And Sweden had enough of a liberal tradition for Krystyna's brothers and father to be confident that no boorish acquaintance would be likely to question her origins. She departed for Sweden full of excitement in time for the winter season.

Kark-Erik Lindqvist was big, handsome, rich and aristocratic. Had she been ten years older, Krystyna would have found his intellect far too limited but to a starry-eyed eighteen-year-old that seemed irrelevant. Their attraction was physical, mutual and irresistible. Their families were delighted at the match – in Karl-Erik's case there was only a doddering old grandfather anyway – and a suitably grand marriage ensued in the summer of 1929. Krystyna became aware of the nightmare that was developing around her in the spring of 1933 when they went to Berlin to help the new Reichschancellor celebrate his accession to supreme power in Germany. Until now she had given no more than the odd distasteful thought to the new German regime. According to her family's widely-expressed opinion, they were vulgar parvenues who brought the attitude of the thug to the legislative chamber.

Karl-Erik was dazzled by the glamour of his new heroes, and would have ignored objections to attending their parties had Krystyna voiced any. She looked the perfect fulfilment of an Aryan dream and had only to stand about being desirable to pass muster. As a result, she had weathered her initial reaction against the new acquaintances and worked out a way of dealing with them before any had even noticed a hint of hostility in her manner. They were hardly emotionally over-sensitive, anyway. Her husband though, could not fail to respond to her distaste, and they went through a few spectacular rows on the subject. Then, when she apparently became reconciled to the new order, relief quickly rubbed out any doubts about the sincerity of her conversion. The suggestion of a world tour in 1934 was something of a reward for a year's good behaviour. It must have been fairly clear, even to a man of his crude sensibilities, that her patience with the Nazi future was wearing a little thin. Karl-Erik was convinced that when she saw what he described as the mongrel races of Asia in close-up, she would fully appreciate the superiority of the Nordic ideal.

As she matured, Krystyna had come to loathe the very presence of the man she had married so optimistically. She regarded the trip as offering a hundred opportunities to conceal her growing distaste until she had worked out what to do about it. In Asia Karl-Erik became obsessive about the British imperialist past. His preoccupation was the result of a mixture of envy and admiration.

'How do they do it?' he said one evening, in Delhi. 'Here they sit, in a colony so vast it's almost a small continent, apparently whiling away their time on polo and club nights, and they have it all in their pockets without trying! The Germans put in consistent drudgery developing overseas interests and they are left with a few little rag-tag properties that were not good enough for the English, the French or the Dutch!'

'I always assumed that comprehensive historical know-ledge could not be a strong point in someone with your love of the National Socialist movement.' Krystyna failed to keep the contempt out of her voice but he did not notice.

'I don't understand. What has comprehensive historical knowledge to do with this?'

'Because, my dear man, the British and the Dutch and the French were from developed nation states which sent out their merchant adventurers to build new markets while Greater Germany was still a squabbling nest of petty princedoms. By the time the Junkers had stopped quarrel-ling long enough to fall in to some sort of order behind

Prussia, all the best options had been taken up. The British didn't go out to get an empire, but to make money. They realised later that they would need to maintain the empire to assure the money and the markets. By the time Queen Victoria came to the throne, the people who make the decisions had also decided to turn imperialism into a noble ideal on the principle that it sounded more respectable than commercial interest. Now they believe it themselves, but there's no reason why you should do so too.'

He regarded her owlishly. 'But if that was the case, why did Austria–Hungary fail to go out and do what the other great powers did? She was at least as important as any of them.'

'Quite simply because the Austrians never had the sense or the entrepreneurial skill, Karl-Erik – they saw money as dirty! You have to admire commercialism in order to embrace it enthusiastically enough to build a colonial empire, and the Austrians always thought trade was a disreputable thing you handed over to bourgeois and Jews!'

He winced and re-focused on modern India.

'But how do the British remain in control so effort-lessly?'

'If you believe it's effortless, you are even less observant than I thought! They're having to exert more effort every day, but it's proving less effective. India is slipping away from them – you can feel it. Africa is still half asleep and undeveloped, but this is an ancient land and its people have had enough of the British. The question now is whether the British will have the élan to let go gracefully when the time comes to leave.'

'Ancient? What are you saying?' He laughed scornfully. 'They're a bunch of savages with a mumbo-jumbo religion that actually believes in gods and demons! You can't put that up against a tradition like Europe's. I've little enough time for Christianity, but at least it's a sophisticated collection of ideas, not jungle hoodoo dressed up as philosophy!'

For once she was disposed to argue with him, but having

embarked on an explanation that Hinduism had adopted colourful images for its gods as an effective device for expressing complex concepts straightforwardly to a largely illiterate populace, she quickly realised he was not even listening. From them on she distanced herself from him as much as possible until by the time they reached Malaya they were virtually leading separate lives.

After the initial excitement of discovering a kindred spirit in Diana and getting to know her, Krystyna realised that she was developing a great liking for Roland, too. It surprised her because his English reticence and self-effacement were qualities which normally caused her to lose interest immediately. In him, however, they merely seemed part of the consideration he devoted to the interests of others. Years of close contact with Karl-Erik's unimaginative brutality had taught her to value such sympathy. A couple of months after Krystyna's arrival Diana had to travel to Penang, where a kinswoman of her Aunt Hermione was stopping over en route to Hong Kong.

'You're welcome to come along with me, Krystyna, but I can't help feeling you'd find Daphne Lethbridge intolerably dull,' Diana said. 'She sends me to sleep in ten seconds, even when I'm being kind to her for Aunt H's sake!'

'It's so wonderful up here that I'll happily stay, as long as Roland doesn't mind having me around?' Krystyna turned the end of the remark into a question, directed at her host.

'Good Lord, no! Delighted to look after you. You're a pleasure to have about the place, Krystyna.'

'Coming from Roland, that's a declaration of eternal devotion.' Diana was clearly surprised at the strength of her husband's reaction.

'In that case I shall stay and explore the enchanted forests. I think I shall have a better time than you, Diana!'

'So do I!'

Roland was gratified to hear a slight edge of jealousy in his wife's response. She had never reacted like this before and it was quite flattering. Evangeline took advantage of

Diana's planned absence to go down to Kuala Terlengu for a few days with Neill MacIntyre, taking Cosmo with her. She had been quite different during Krystyna's stay, sensing that her usual informal behaviour with Diana was out of place unless they were *en famille*. Diana departed by truck down the red laterite road, accompanied by Evangeline, Cosmo and a Malay driver.

'I wouldn't trust that one as far as I could throw a Welsh guardsman!' muttered Evangeline, looking back at the woman who waved to them from the verandah.

'Evie, you wouldn't trust your own mother if she was glamorous and under fifty!' Diana's tone was bantering but deep inside she shared her companion's misgivings. 'Anyhow, when have you known Roland pay a woman any attention beyond everyday courtesy?'

'How many women has he set eyes on since we've been spending so much time up here?'

'Take my word for it, Evie, that's unlikely ever to be a problem with Roland!' Diana's tone made it clear that she considered the discussion to be closed. They fell to talking about the good things Daphne Lethbridge might have brought from London and Paris.

Back at Terlengu Estate, Roland and Krystyna went their separate ways to rest through the afternoon heat. Roland came out on to the verandah in the cool of twilight in time to see Krystyna emerging from the little bath house. He watched appreciatively as she strode back towards the house, her loose-limbed stride accentuating her athletic shape beneath the heavy silk robe. Joining him, she flung herself down in one of the recliners, completely un-selfconscious about her scanty clothing.

'That bath house is heaven – I could spend half my life there!'

Memories momentarily silenced Roland and he hid his confusion by going to pour drinks. When he returned, she was disposed to chat about their life in Malaya.

'Which estate do you prefer, Roland – is it you or Diana who makes the choice to spend most time here?'

'At first it was Diana; she couldn't stand the mems over

on the developed side and ran away to hide up here. Eventually she met a number of people she liked over there – they're not all vulgar little women from the suburbs, after all – but by then she loved it so much here that she preferred Terlengu for its own sake. We both spend more time over there than we used to, but we're here more often than we're anywhere else. I've loved it from the moment I first set eyes on it. High Trees is all right, but this is the real Malaya.'

'Do you love it enough to spend the rest of your life here?'

'Heavens, I've never really thought in those terms – there's too much waiting for us in England one day. But there was a time when I suppose I used to daydream.'

'Love?'

'Krystyna, you're disconcertingly direct at times, you know!'

'Maybe, but you're not answering me, are you?'

'I don't see how I can. Surely you can see for yourself how unlikely it is that I should meet someone up here. I always assume that Diana and I are a fairly successful couple.'

'I'm not asking out of idle curiosity, dear Roland. I've grown fond of you both over the past weeks and it bothers me that there seems to be some barrier between you. The obvious thing that comes to mind is that an affair took place. I've guessed there's nothing going on now, but did one of you go off the rails a while ago and the other find out?'

'Both of us.'

'What – at the same time?'

'Part of it, yes. I think she started before and I went on after . . . Well, that is, I know that mine went on after. Forgive me; I never expected to have this conversation and I find it very difficult.'

'Please don't go on. I wanted to help, not cause you more misery. It's none of my business. Just tell me to shut up and go away. It's unforgivable of me to put you through this!'

'No, now that I've started to face it, I'd rather like to tell you. You're right. It had made a mess of things between Diana and me, and the way things are now I don't really see any end to it.'

'I must say, I can understand that there were any number of men around with whom Diana could have got involved, but there are no unattached European women out in this remote spot. Was it a Malay or Chinese girl?'

'No.' He was looking beyond her, out towards the forest.

'Then . . . oh, poor Roland. A boy?'

'I don't suppose you'll want to stay now.' His hand clenched tight around his drink and he moved self-consciously away from her, still not looking at her face.

Her laughter stopped him. This was the last reaction he had expected.

'Roland, you are an idiot! Why should that make me want to leave? You're my friend.'

'I can think of plenty of people who call me friend who would hound me from the country if they heard so much as a hint . . .'

'Hypocrites, the lot of them! Were you cruel to him? Did you mistreat him? Disgrace him? Did your relationship cause him pain?'

'No, on all counts. But that's hardly the point.'

'Of course it's the point. As long as you didn't force him or hurt him, it's your business what you do in private. Let the world go hang! I'm more interested in what Diana made of it.'

'Well, that's the trouble. It never really came out into the open. Both her affair and mine ended in tragedy. Her lover was killed in a waterfront accident. Mine was the victim of one of those terrible incidents out here when Malays occasionally run amok.'

'Oh, no! Was it jealousy or something?'

'Nothing at all to do with our relationship. The poor boy was with his family – he was a Malay – and his elder brother had just had a proposal of marriage turned down because the girl's father wanted someone more exalted. He ran amok and poor Dhak tried to get him under control. He was cut to pieces with a kris.'

Tears flowed, unheeded, down Roland's cheeks. He continued to speak in his normal tone. 'It was pretty well intolerable. You see, I couldn't tell anyone. Diana guessed, but she never alluded to any intimate relationship. So I had no one to tell. I rather think the brother had been having a similar affair with a planter friend of mine up the valley, but even if I'd been tempted to confide in the planter, the fact that his boy had killed mine and was now dead himself made that out of the question.'

'When did this happen?'

'During the Monsoon in twenty-nine.'

'But that was five years ago! Haven't you discussed it with anyone?'

'I started to tell Neill MacIntyre, but he's always been more Diana's friend than mine and he's involved with Evangeline. I have no reason to doubt his complete discretion, but somehow my nerve failed me and I kept it to myself.'

'What about your love-life with Diana?'

'There isn't any.'

'After five years? Roland, she *must* know!'

'She chooses to think it's because she had a lover. She's aware that I know there was an affair, because she was in such a state when he died that it had to be mentioned. But since then I think she's assumed I didn't want another man's mistress, which is the way she sees herself.'

'I don't quite understand why you married in the first place, unless it was simply to provide the obligatory heir for your family title.'

'Oh, I loved Diana – always have, still do. Look, having gone this far, I think I can tell you the rest. God knows I need to. The truth is that before Diana, apart from some awful failures with tarts, I'd never really tried anything. I think I was a bit of a cold fish, because I never had odd feelings for boys, either. Just never thought much about it and thought everyone else took it far too seriously. With Diana and me, it just sort of happened a couple of times.

But it was all on the same night, and that was when she got pregnant with Cosmo. It was before we were married. Later, I discovered I couldn't manage it again. She was very innocent and at first accepted it. Then she got hurt, then angry. Finally she was more or less driven into this affair and I couldn't really blame her for it.'

'So do you think you only like boys; that you'll never want Diana again?'

'It's beginning to look awfully like that. But when I made love to Diana that time, I really wanted to. She didn't provoke me or anything. I wish I understood it, because it's torturing me. I know it's just a matter of time before she finds another man and it will hardly be her fault then, either. But I love her so terribly that I'm scared I shall lose her.'

Krystyna said nothing, but got up to make them fresh drinks.

'What are you going to do?' he asked.

'Spend a relaxed evening with my friend Roland Lenton. Maybe get a little tight. Talk about people and places and things, and perhaps after a while come up with the odd helpful suggestion. But first of all I think we'll have another drink and then eat dinner.'

His relief was obvious. The mere act of confession had placed a huge strain on Roland and he could not have continued much longer under such intense emotional pressure. Recognising this, Krystyna had backed off and now awaited an opportunity to help him. Throughout dinner and for an hour or so afterwards, she alternated between telling him funny stories about her childhood and describing the more sinister aspects of her present life with Karl-Erik Lindqvist. The combination of merriment and meaty conversation turned Roland away from the introspection which had seemed an inevitable sequel to his earlier confession. Krystyna took charge of drinks throughout the evening, quietly ensuring that his contained very little alcohol – enough to relax him but not slow him down, she thought. Finally, she was ready for him. As he bent forward to light her cigarette, she drew his hand to her lips and kissed it gently. Instead of recoiling, as she had half expected, he repeated her gesture, taking her long fingers and pressing them lightly to his lips. Krystyna rose in one smooth, fluid motion, aware that any uncertain or jerky move now would destroy the fragile intimacy she had created so carefully.

She was as tall as he was, and stood facing him, willing him to kiss her. As his mouth closed over hers, she raised her hands and gently massaged the muscles along his shoulders and neck, an unconscious mimicry of Dhak. Their bodies gently touched, then moved closer, and she was relieved to feel his increasing hardness. At least there was hope! Krystyna stayed clasped in Roland's arms for some time, still reluctant to make any sudden moves. Finally it was he who pressed her gently back towards the door. They headed for her room, Roland instinctively avoiding the otherwise celibate marriage bed which had been the scene of his lovemaking with Dhak. In her room, she slipped out of her simple, long evening dress. Beneath it she wore only knickers, suspenders and silk stockings.

'Leave them on, they feel wonderful,' he said, stroking her thigh just above the stocking top.

He eased the panties down over her flat hips and they fell about her ankles with a swish. She stepped away from them, pressing against his growing hardness.

'Undress me, my darling. I love to feel your strong hands on me.'

Krystyna gently and slowly removed his clothes, taking a long, provocative time over his dress shirt. She slid to the ground and removed the silk socks, then squatted in front of him and slipped the underpants down his legs. She buried her face between his thighs, her lips working persistently and softly around his swelling penis. He gave a low cry and pressed her harder to him. She slid sinuously upward, pressing herself against him all the way, pulling his hand over her belly and breasts. Krystina was fairly flat-chested, with large nipples but smallish breasts and muscular shoulders.

'Just like a lovely young boy,' he murmured wonderingly.

'No, just like a different kind of woman to the one you're used to – we're all different. You probably prefer us like this.'

He bent forward to suck her nipples and they bloomed into excited rigidity against his tongue. His hands were stroking her back, sides and buttocks, enjoying every inch of muscular flesh. They were standing beside the bed, Roland with his back to it. Krystyna firmly pressed him back until he sat, then lay across it. He looked up at her lithe, athletic form poised over him and thrilled at the thought of being possessed by her. She got on to the bed and straddled him, reaching eagerly for his stiff penis, pressing herself down on it with an ecstatic wriggle. Roland gave a gasp of excitement and she exploded into passion over him, moaning a string of profanities, pulling his hands up to scrub at her breasts, then moving them down to clutch her small, tight backside. When he thought he had reached the highest pitch of arousal, somehow she managed to turn herself around without dislodging him, and pulling his arms tightly around her waist, drew him up behind her so that they were sitting upright with her in front, facing away. He pulled her back towards him, giving her the full thrust of his erection.

'Am I better than your boy?' she cried out.

'Better than anyone in the world – I want to stay in you for ever!'

His orgasm reared him up and over her, so that they collapsed on the bed with Krystyna pinned beneath him, face down. He felt her own climax rip through her as she convulsively clenched his hands against her thighs. After a while, with infinite gentleness, Roland turned her towards him. Krystyna smiled at him sleepily in the moonlight. 'Now you know what you've been missing. I told you I might come up with the odd helpful suggestion.'

'Which is?'

'Always make your women work for it – you'll both enjoy it more!'

One down, one to go, Krystyna thought as she awaited

Diana's return from KL. This one might be a little more difficult, though. How did you persuade a woman that her husband desired her again after years of abstinence? Finally she decided on a falsely direct approach. 'Roland's made a pretty desperate confession to me, Diana, and I haven't the faintest idea how to broach it to you.'

Her friend looked at her with barely-veiled suspicion. 'Are you going to tell me he's fallen in love with you?'

'Dear God, no! Quite the reverse. He's been seeking advice on how to engineer a reconciliation with you.'

The suspicion receded but was replaced by wariness. 'Has he told you how it came about in the first place?'

'Enough for me to think that you're no longer lovers because each of you is suffering under a different illusion. You think he doesn't want another man's cast-off and he's scared you might feel he's approaching you out of pity because you lost the man you really loved.'

Diana had been looking down at the floor. Now her head came up sharply. 'So he told you about Anders. What did he say?'

'Just that he thought his own difficulties had driven you to another man and that, when he felt he wanted to make love to you again, you were obviously in love with someone else; that because of the way you were separated from that man, anything he was likely to do to start a physical reconciliation might appear to you as nothing but pity. Isn't that a fairly accurate summary of the way you feel about it?'

'It would have been, except for one big thing you've missed. I was just beginning to think that perhaps I'd misunderstood his attitude when I ran smack into him hard at it with a native boy. Bet he didn't tell you that!'

Christ, she's a lot tougher than I thought! Krystyna was astonished that her friend expressed no shock at the homosexual act. It was simply offered as a complication in the matrimonial tangle. Krystyna feigned surprise at the entire matter.

'I confess I hadn't realised it was so complicated. How did you handle it?'

'Oh, it was quite a shock, I assure you. It's just that I've had years to get used to it and realise that it isn't such a great thing after all; certainly no worse than another woman. It caught me so unawares at the time that I just froze and watched. The strange thing was that I was more conscious before anything else that I was watching two people who were very much in love. They didn't notice me; they were far too busy with each other. I slipped away and sat on the bed back here as if I were frozen. There and then I decided that if Roland wanted to do that to Dhak he was hardly likely to want to do anything to me. So I assumed that although I'd got it wrong about him leaving me alone, the end result was the same. He just didn't want me.'

'Well he does – so much so that he took me aside and begged me to find some way of bringing the two of you together again. Can you imagine how important it must be to him for a man like Roland to confess all this to me? Obviously he wouldn't say anything about the boy. I shouldn't think he'll ever tell anyone about that.' She managed that deception without a tremor. Some lies were essential, and this was one.

'I did get round to reading a bit about it,' said Diana. 'That was when I realised for the first time that some men like both women and other men. Until then I always thought it was either one or the other. I might have tried a reconciliation at that point. But the boy was killed quite heroically in a terrible incident with his brother and I thought that would make such an impression on Roland that he'd never want to look at me again.'

'Do you believe now that he wants you?'

'Yes, because you're right about how hard he must have found it to talk to you about it, but I can't imagine any way that we can start again. After all, it's been years. How can we suddenly turn to each other from a standing start and pick up from that one night so very long ago?'

'Why not pretend your son has just been born and that you are both beginning to make love again for the first time? You may have to work on the illusion for a while, but perhaps it will do the trick.'

285

Eventually, it did, but it was no fairytale reconciliation. Diana's lush curves and female softness were not Krystyna's tough, boyish frame. Roland's willowy body bore no resemblance to the ultra-masculine attractions of Anders Mogensen. Nevertheless, both Roland and Diana desperately wanted a physical relationship. Roland's interlude with Krystyna had re-awakened his libido and he felt excited at the mere thought of sexual activity for the first time in his life. Diana was ripe for love-making after years of unexpected abstinence and responded aggressively enough for Roland to develop his passion with the help of a fantasy memory of the way Krystyna had taken him. Out of their often blundering but generally good-natured love-making, a second child was conceived.

When Diana told Krystyna she thought she was pregnant again, Krystyna decided it was time she left. Karl-Erik had been back in Europe for almost three months and had · written two letters, demanding with increasing anger why she was not at his side fostering his advance in the Third Reich.

'Why not chuck him? Stay here with us. He sounds too terrible to endure for five minutes.' Diana was indignant about the idea of her friend voluntarily going back to such a monster.

'I feel I have to go back,' said Krystyna. 'Europe needs all the people it can get who think of Nazism as a killer sickness that has to be cut out. I know I can be useful and I've a feeling it will be soon. Let's take one more trip together and then I'll go back and face the brute.'

'Where do you want to go?'

'Somewhere you've always meant to see. When you told me about Anders Mogensen's description of Angkor Wat, I watched the expression on your face. You need to go there. You need to see his dream with your own eyes. You need to see yourself as he saw you. Then maybe you'll really be free to love Roland properly.'

Neither woman believed this, but both realised that Angkor was a talisman for Diana. If it lived up to her dreams, it would serve as a refuge for the rest of her life.

Both of them were aware that she would never make the journey alone. It was now, with Krystyna, or never. There was a degree of self-interest in Krystyna's choice, too. In the early, awful days of her marriage she had taken refuge in literature from her husband's spiritual brutality. A happy discovery had been the French naturalist Pierre Loti. Loti had been bewitched since childhood by the vast Khmer ruins, then newly-discovered. As an adult he had visited them and had portrayed them for an avid public in a series of highly-coloured books. Krystyna had progressed from Loti's purple prose to more academic works on the Khmer Empire. Now she was within reach, she wanted to see the ruined splendour for herself.

They sailed from Kuala Terlengu aboard one of the little SSN steamers, calling leisurely at sleepy ports along the south-western coast of the Gulf of Siam. Just over the Siamese border they changed to a larger vessel which took them across the Gulf to the Cambodian coast. From Phnomh Penh a dilapidated bus trundled along a rutted main road through the eternal jungle. As they travelled, happily sandwiched between peasants with live chickens or baskets of fruit and vegetables, Krystyna told Diana what she had read of Angkor.

'The Khmers must have been a stupendous people. Now they begin to give you an idea of what a master race would really have been like. They couldn't manage a thousand years, but five hundred is pretty impressive. And they held a hundred and twenty kingdoms subject. Imagine, we're going to see a place that was at the height of its glory when Kublai Khan sent an ambassador there. It even impressed the ambassador, and Kublai's empire was nothing to sneeze at! He sent back a description of a golden city full of treasure, with concubines and dancing girls everywhere. They worshipped the phallus and they built great towers in celebration of it. Victorian ladies tended not to be shown the pictures in case they were embarrassed! There was nothing in the East to touch it.

'Imagine those lotus-crowned towers, the processions with elephants and dancers and jewelled palanquins . . . and then glory faded; they were attacked by the Siamese, who were far less civilised. It shouldn't have given them any trouble but somehow they just seemed to fade away. The great trade route was abandoned, the city and the temples fell into decay. Everyone forgot the Fu-nan Empire although it must once have been as great as Rome. The jungle surged quietly back across the Sim Reap Valley and covered it. There it stayed, untouched, until 1850 when it was rediscovered, and people have been coming to marvel ever since. The Khmers are still here, but they are about as much like their ancestors as the modern Italians are like Roman legionaries. They're not even curious about their past. It's barbarians like you and me who come to gape now.'

And gape they did. The ruins surged up majestically from the emerald forest which carpets Cambodia and the Mekong Valley. Huge carved towers rose through the rippling green like magnificent ships on some strange sea, their scale so grand that it was inconceivable until the traveller walked along the endless passageways with their carved ornamentation still fresh after centuries of neglect. The two women were bewitched by what they saw. Vast jungle trees had forced aside stone buildings and sculptures over the centuries, adding a further touch of perverse beauty to what was already strange enough.

'How Karl-Erik would hate all this!' said Krystyna. 'It's everything he loathes, cluttered, complex, no surface undecorated. About as far as you can get from the glory that was Greece and the grandeur that was Rome.'

Diana did not answer her. She was looking in delight at one of the nymphs carved in the stonework. These were the creatures to whom Mogensen had likened her and she was disarmed by the compliment. They were everywhere, an endlessly-repeated celebration of female sensuality. If he saw me like this, she thought, no wonder I was his obsession! The figures danced or worshipped, guarded temples or walked in processions. Their clothing and jewellery were different, but all seemed to share one face and one body. The faces were simultaneously serene and passionate, with broad, high cheekbones, lips and eyebrows curving like birds' wings, and delicately-pointed chins. All smiled with a secret knowledge which seemed to be promised to the onlooker in return for lifelong devotion. The bodies shared nothing of the classical Western obsession with male beauty. The shoulders were soft, rounded and pliable, but still managed to support breasts of surprising size and roundness. A long, slender waist flared into wide hips, with a flat belly and high navel. Most of the semi-divine creatures wore towering head-dresses, jewels on arms and necks, and filmy skirts hung loosely from rich girdles.

'He was right. The resemblance is startling,' Krystyna said quietly, coming up behind Diana as she gazed at a particularly lovely carving. 'Better to have had a love like that and lost it than never to know you look like that, even for just one man.'

Diana was crying, but with the exaltation of emotional release rather than in grief. 'It's quite a memento, isn't it?' she said through her tears.

They went on next day to Angkor Thom, the more recently discovered secular city, even more mysterious than Angkor Wat and breathtaking in the moonlight that bathed it as they turned from it for the last time. The two women said little as the bus trundled them back towards Phnomh Penh. It was not until they had re-embarked at Ream to cross back to the Siamese-Malay coast that they began talking about their trip. Even then, each had the good sense to leave Angkor's enchantment undisturbed by too much analysis of impressions.

'In my mind he'll always be there, not in the burial ground at Kuala Terlengu,' said Diana. 'No wonder he wanted me to see it. It's impossible to imagine unless you've been there.'

Evangeline was down at Kuala Terlengu when they arrived back. Roland planned to join them in a day or so, as Krystyna was going direct from the little port to Singapore and thence to meet her husband in Stockholm. The relationship between Diana and her companion had been strained since Krystyna's arrival. Diana was less conscious of it than Evangeline, for Krystyna's presence made the Welsh girl aware of the unbridgeable social gap between herself and her employer which she forgot when there were no outsider present. The morning after their return, Evangeline asked to see Diana alone.

'Madam, I've finally decided it's time for Neill and me to get married.'

'But Evangeline, how will I manage without you? I'm pregnant again and I can't think of coping without your help. Can't it wait a little longer? It's not as if you've just met and fallen in love, is it?'

'No, but there are other things. For a start I might want a family of my own and Neill is pushing forty now; hardly an old man, perhaps, but I want him to enjoy his family, not get grumpy because he's too old for crying babies. You know I'll be just down here and you'll either come to us for the confinement or go down to Singapore and then back here for a couple of weeks. It won't make that much difference, will it?'

'Well in that case, why change anything? You're happy the way you are with Neill. What's so great about having babies? Believe me, this one is as much of an accident as the first one. They certainly don't enrich my life! Oh, dammit, Evie, you're my best friend and sister as much as my companion and I depend on you.'

'Madam, I'm your servant. Unless I marry Neill that's all I'll ever be. I'm ever so fond of you but I don't want to think that each time one of your aristocratic friends shows up, I'm to be packed off to the servants' quarters. That's no way to live and I've no intention of doing it.'

Diana was shocked. 'But Evie, it needn't be like that! Surely Countess Karpinska hasn't said or done anything . . .'

'She doesn't have to, does she? Just listen to what you just said. "Countess Karpinska"! You call her Krystyna. I bet you'd die of shock if I ever called you Diana, but if you're my best friend it's the first time I've ever heard of one friend calling another Madam!'

Evangeline was in tears now and Diana silently cursed herself for her insensitivity. She moved across to the maid and embraced her. 'Come on, Evie, I'm so sorry I was too stupid to see how awful it was. Of course you're right. About the only way things will change is for you to marry Neill and then we can be friends properly. Come on, stop crying. We'll see the Countess off back to Europe and then we'll start afresh.'

Really? thought Evie, drying her eyes. Then how come you still refer to her as the Countess when you talk to me? Oh, well, some things never will change.

In the end, though, she deferred the marriage for almost another three years. Somehow, the importance of the unequal relationship diminished after Krystyna's departure. Something told Evangeline that a lot of bridge-building remained before Roland and Diana would truly regard themselves as husband and wife. Until then, Diana needed a friend close at hand and Evangeline was it, no matter what she thought of her subservient role. She also decided that, temporarily at least, Cosmo Lenton needed her more than Neill MacIntyre.

Diana's second son, Sebastian, was born with none of the alarms of her first confinement. She came down to Kuala Terlengu eight weeks before the birth was due but it proved an unnecessary precaution. The baby arrived with little difficulty, right on time. From the beginning, Diana adored him. Her coldness towards Cosmo, previously explicable as part of the way aristocratic women treated their children, was now doubly noticeable because of the attention she showered on Sebastian. Evangeline quietly dedicated herself to trying to compensate the elder child for his mother's indifference. To all intents and purposes, she became his foster mother. Her marriage date retreated into the future.

Neill MacIntyre was initially indulgent, agreeing with Evangeline about the need for a counterweight to Diana's favouritism for her younger child. As time passed, though, he grew impatient. His tolerance finally expired early in 1936, when Evangeline came down for a few days and spent considerable time fulminating about Diana's proposal to send Cosmo home to prep school in England at Easter.

'It's bloody disgusting, and I told her so! Poor little kid, he's barely out of nappies and she's packing him off to live with strangers. Well I'm just not having it. Keep him here another year or so, Madam, I said. It's bad enough that you never take any interest in him at all, but to send him away so young would be absolutely awful for him!'

She awaited MacIntyre's agreement. 'Let him go, Evie,' was all he said.

'What? You're the one who's so hot on Freud and all those other head doctors! You're usually the first to agree she's messing the poor kid up. Why the sudden change?'

'Because in your commitment to the child you seem to have forgotten completely that you and I have a little un-finished business. I should like to feel I had a chance of getting a wife and a family of my own before I reach re-tirement age!'

'But we agreed . . .'

'No, Evie, you told me what you were going to do and, because I admired your reasons, I went along with it. I thought, then that you would cosset Cosmo for a few months – a year, at most – and then you'd abandon yourself to my evil passions. Instead of that, you appear to be planning on ensuring that Diana's grandchildren grow up untroubled before you finally throw in your lot with me. Well, I'm sick of playing faithful old suitor and I'm about to assume the role of abductor. Either you tell Diana you're leaving her service or I shall do it for you. And before you start squealing about poor little Cosmo and his complexes, permit me to suggest that if he goes off to school in England, it might be the best thing for him. He won't have to watch his mother going gaga over his younger brother from morning till night and he'll find that lots of other little boys get sent away to school too. More to the point, it'll remove any excuse for you to put me off any longer!'

'But what about the holidays? He'll be all alone, thou-sands of miles from his family.'

'Oh, do come off it! You'd say black was white if you thought you'd get your own way. Diana Lenton has told me time and again that when the time comes to send Cosmo home to school, he'll have the whole Digby-Lenton tribe around his ears, with horses and parkland in the country and a London mansion when it gets dull. And from what you yourself have said about her Aunt Hermione he'll get enough motherly affection to make up for any lack to date. Stop piling on the agony!'

Evangeline grumbled but she knew he was right. Nothing within her power could change Diana's attitude to Cosmo, and in her heart of hearts Evie acknowledged the damage was already done. Cosmo would always feel second best with his mother. Perhaps Neill's view of the benefits of separation was the proper one. She went through a blazing row with Diana when it came to discussing the journey back to England with the little boy.

'You'll take him, won't you Evie? Be a real change for you and give you chance to see Lakie about your trousseau if you insist on marrying the good doctor!'

'Madam, if you insist on Master Cosmo going back to school, the least you can do is to take a home leave and spend a bit of time in England while the poor little devil is settling in. Perhaps he won't feel quite so cut off then.'

'I have no intention of setting foot back in England yet. When I go back it'll be as Lady Lenton, not before.'

'But Madam, you've been out here without a break for more than seven years. Practically everyone goes back for a while after five years. Why don't you?'

'When I go, it'll be as a winner, not as some little planter's wife from up in the boondocks. They've punished me enough in London for a lifetime. I'm not ready to give them a second chance yet.'

'So you'll abandon your kid just for the sake of your own importance. You selfish bitch!'

'What did you say?'

'You heard me. Perhaps you'd prefer me to say you selfish bitch, Madam!'

'Evangeline, I don't quite believe what I hear. If you'd

care to apologise for what you just said, I'll pretend you never said it.'

'But I did say it, didn't I? And what's more, I meant it. You're so completely eaten up with what you want, with what you prefer, with the way people feel about you, that it never crosses your mind how many people you hurt by all that selfishness. Well, it's about time someone told you and it looks as if it's got to be me. You certainly don't seem to listen to your husband when he tries.'

'That's it, you ungrateful wretch! I've no intention of standing for any more of this. You've been trading on your special status with me for too long now, Miss Owen, and it's about time I put a stop to it. You've been threatening for long enough that you'll decamp and marry Neill. Perhaps it's time you did. One day you might realise what an easy ride you've had compared with most ladys' companions!'

'Don't kid yourself. I was no impoverished little waif when Lady Stanmore engaged me. Louise was just trying to give me a chance to see a bit of life when she hitched me to you, and she trusted Lady Stanmore enough to think you'd treat me fairly. Obviously you never had any intention of doing that unless you needed me. Well, I certainly don't need you, and I'm off.'

She slammed out of the room and went for a long walk in an attempt to calm the storm of emotion that the quarrel had released. All the small resentments which had marred her affection for Diana over the years came to the surface. How could the stupid, blinkered woman have thought she was having such a good time? However well she was treated, she had always been a servant. Evangeline had appeared to accept the role assigned her, but only its basic unorthodoxy had made it even temporarily acceptable. Diana's callous indifference to her son's feelings had only been the flashpoint for their quarrel. The real reason was that Evangeline could no longer endure the injustice of her inferiority. When she returned to the bungalow more than an hour later, there was no sign of Diana.

She sat in a cane chair on the verandah to think over

what she should do next. Clearly there was no question of her remaining at Terlengu longer than tomorrow morning. It was already early evening; their row had occurred soon after the afternoon lie-off. Roland came on to the verandah and joined her. Embarrassed, Evangeline began to get up.

'No, don't go, Evie. I know what happened. I've been talking to Diana and she filled me in on it. It's most unfortunate and I think you've been close for too long to let such an unpleasant outburst end everything. I can't even offer any real solution. The way we run our world cries out for everyone to behave according to the rules. We three didn't do so because of all the special circumstances. You're hardly an ordinary lady's companion and Diana's not an ordinary lady, all of which means there was bound to be a crisis when your respective different ways of doing things collided head-on with what the world thinks is proper. It really is a mess, isn't it?'

'Yes, sir, but not one of my making. I don't want a quarrel. I love Mrs Lenton. But she has faults the same as I do and when she tries to pretend they're not there by coming the great lady, I can't put up with it.'

'No, I realise that. I'm also aware that your planned marriage to Neill MacIntyre gives us all an obvious way out. But I'm anxious that you and Diana should preserve the reality of the friendship which exists underneath all this mistress-servant nonsense and if we can stick the pieces together a bit now, perhaps that will be possible.'

In the end they managed an ungainly but workable compromise. Evangeline went down to stay with MacIntyre the following day and it was agreed that she should take Cosmo to England when the Lentons had completed their arrangements. She would take an extended holiday with Louise Kerslake in London and then decide whether she wished to return to work at Terlengu Plantation or to Kuala Terlengu and marriage with Neill MacIntyre.

When departure time arrived Roland, Diana and Dr MacIntyre all travelled to Penang with Evangeline and Cosmo to see them off on their long voyage. The breach between Evangeline and Diana had been healed, at least superficially, but Roland suspected that things could never be the same again between them. He watched his wife with mixed emotions and reflected that Diana would always have terrible problems because her heart pulled her in one direction and her mind and upbringing pulled her in the other. It was also the explanation for much of her charm.

CHAPTER FIFTEEN

Letter from Krystyna Karpinska Lindqvist to Diana Lenton.

Waldorf Astoria Hotel
NEW YORK
May 23, 1936

Oh, Diana, they tell us cruising is the only way to travel, and it is! Karl-Erik has this new scheme — journalism. Of course, 'The Future' is always the lynchpin of his plans and this is no exception. Svenska Dagbladet *have engaged him as a foreign correspondent. Clearly they see him as a sort of roving gossip columnist. He's happy to start off that way, with a view to making changes in the future, in an obvious direction! In any case, it gives him almost unlimited possibilities for popping up all over the place, charming the right people. I realise now that our world tour was a practice run at his own expense to show them what he could do. Apparently, when he went back to Sweden ahead of me, it was largely to write up his impressions of the trip as a series of feature articles.* Svenska Dagbladet *were already impressed by his name, but they wanted to be sure he was literate, too. There are just so many things even the most talented re-write man can do with rubbish!*

Our first adventure was the maiden voyage of the Queen Mary, *packed with British and American Society. There was a band at Southampton in preposterous black-and-gold uniform, playing* Britannia Rules the Waves *and we all filed aboard under a yellow canopy, obviously put up to protect us against English rain that never came. Droves of small boats saw us off along Southampton Water and, after we had left them all behind, we were taken off in parties to see the wonders the ship had in store for us — swimming pools, vast lounges, cocktail bars, smoke rooms, children's playgrounds, massage and writing rooms — even dog kennels! Of course, when we'd seen it we all settled down to spend our time much as we would on any ordinary Atlantic crossing. The women impersonate chorus boys dressed as sailors; the men swim and play deck tennis. Everyone eats and drinks far too much. There were various celebrities aboard, but I was quite surprised they had not managed to persuade someone like Dietrich or Gable to be on the first crossing. After all, Frances Day is just an English musical comedy star and Anita Louise is no Hollywood immortal, but they were the most famous show business faces aboard.*

In spite of all the luxury, I can't help feeling the French made a better job of designing a grand liner. We were on the maiden voyage of the Normandie *last year and if ever there was a woman's ship, that's it. You get the impression that* Normandie *was built for mistresses and* Queen Mary *for wives! The main colour theme aboard* Normandie *is black and gold. All the big names in French design were involved — a clear exercise in* La Gloire *— with Aubusson carpets, Dunand lacquers, Rodier fabrics and Colcomet curtains. Even the staircase to the Grill is golden! The* Queen Mary, *on the other hand, is a decidedly more sober, British affair. Nowhere is there a grand staircase where a* femme fatale *could make a dramatic entrance, and when one appears in public clad in full finery, there are no large mirrors where one can check one's impact. Definitely a man's boat, with sports facilities to beat the* Normandie *but fewer réveillon-style evenings* (quelle dommage!).

But my dear, nothing — nothing! — could ever compare with the approach to New York. I shall remember it as long as I live and one day perhaps I shall even become a New Yorker. Stewards started fussing about our luggage and people were going on deck long before we were due to dock. Small aeroplanes kept flitting past the portholes, hooters shrieked from the small craft that had come to escort us, and then we heard the first clash of bands and the rumble of the welcoming crowds. Fireboats in the harbour turned on their hoses and great arcs of white water plumed up in triumphal archways. Crowds lined the Battery, forty-deep according to the papers next day. When we finally disembarked we moved through cascades of confetti and tickertape. It must have been like this for Lindbergh! Now we're here among the sky-scrapers, mixing alternately with some of the most brilliant and the most brutally stupid people I've ever encountered, all of them rich.

The Cotton Club is all you've ever heard about it and more. So far I've been twice and have been lucky enough to see Duke Ellington (Mood Indigo *is now locked into my Polish soul*) and Cab Calloway. The audience was just as starry as the stage cast — it's still 'the' place to be seen in New York. Not, of course, that I ever go anywhere unsmart with Karl-Erik. He thinks the little people are there as decor, not to be known as individuals. In peacetime you exploit them; in wartime you use them as cannon fodder. Either way, no one in Society should waste time getting to know any of them. Trouble is that I tend to find them at least as interesting as the people in 21 and El Morocco, and far less dangerous. The other night, unable to take any more, I got away at dawn, leaving K-E deep in an anti-British plot with a rich Texan called Braun, and wound up eating sausage and buckwheat pancakes and drinking terrific coffee with a bunch of truck drivers. No, my dear, they did not present me with a trenchant analysis of the basis of worker-reconstruction of society. But they did not once refer to the master race and it is inconceivable that any of them will ever be responsible for an act more destructive than running down someone in his truck. If you still think that's a shocking crime, you should hear what the Nazis plan to do with people of my origins! The truck drivers told me I was a great broad even if I was a Polak, paid for my coffee and demanded that I came again. I just might!

Next week we go to London for two months of your celebrated Season. I'll give it your love. Watch this space for details!

Love from Krystyna

299

Letter from Violet Hartley to Diana Lenton.

Dear Diana

I know I'm a little beast for not keeping in touch, but I never was too good a correspondent. I do love your letters, though, and it would be rotten if they tailed off just because I'm such an idiot so please keep them coming. This is a bit of a special epistle. I am engaged to be married! Yes I know it's a bolt from the blue. Aunt H went quite funny round the edges but is super now. She will not let me break it to the Duchess who is off on one of her little bouts yet again, in Switzerland this time. Aunt Hermione says it was hard enough for herself to take and she's of sound mind. You know, she's getting much bolder than she used to be (Aunt H, I mean, the Duchess was always sure of herself, wasn't she?). When I told her that, she said the Hartley girls would make the Virgin Mary bold, which I thought a bit strong.

Anyway, more about my faithful swain. I wonder how long one has to be a swain to be a faithful one? If more than a couple of months, perhaps he isn't. My dear, he's a fully paid-up French count! Grandpapa found that one utterly impossible to swallow and spent hours gobbling over the Almanac de Gotha. Of course that got him absolutely nowhere because Raoul is in it unto the tenth generation or so! Terribly aristocratic but not very rich, I'm afraid. We're not doing too well as gold diggers, are we? Aunt Hermione said that at least I'd have a small assured income if the inevitable happened and he ran off with a cabaret singer when I was forty-one. D'you think she was trying to put me off or only teasing? It's just as well she brought the Carson Brewery money into the family, isn't it, or Grandpapa could never have made me a settlement, and although Raoul isn't interested in my money he certainly couldn't have afforded to keep me as well as himself. Still, he's got a lot of interesting business ventures and he'll soon be rich and we'll be all right.

It would be so wonderful if you could be here for the wedding but, as you don't seem to go in for home leaves, I suppose it's not on. We're getting married at Christmas. Grandpapa is being very uncooperative about me becoming

RC; says it's un-British. But Raoul's Mama is one of those ancient French aristos who never misses Mass and sends all her linen sheets to the convent to be embroidered on the cheap. I really can't see any way round it.

Louise Kerslake is making my wedding gown. Of course, who else could? Honestly, she's doing wonders, but she still can't quite manage that jump to a couture house of her own. Aunt Hermione is getting so interested in the fashion business that I wouldn't put it past her to set Mrs K up herself one of these fine days. That would really take Grandpapa's mind off my unsuitable marriage, wouldn't it? No sooner has he rubbed the tradesman's fingerprints off Aunt H's money than she reverts to type and opens a dress shop! Can't say I'd care to be in the room when that little firecracker goes off.

Oh, help, it's terribly late and I've hardly told you a thing about lovely Raoul. He's very handsome, all dark and smouldering and Latin, not the cool Norman French type at all. Makes me think of dark alleys around Marseille and Apache dancers and all that. The family have a whacking great château somewhere around Toulouse which would have disintegrated years ago in a harsher climate because they're too poor to put it back together again. They manage with a Paris apartment which is still in one piece and I suppose we shall have to live there with Madame la Comtesse. That might prove a little uncomfortable as, by marrying her seul fils, I shall be taking her title. Oops! And impoverished and a Protestant as well, I can't win, can I? She calls me ma chère a lot and looks straight through me.

Try to send me something exotic and Far Eastern as a wedding present. It will make la Comtesse think I have a sinful past and might even drive her off to live at the château!

Love love love Lettie (soon to be Countess of Montsegur)

Letter from Krystyna Karpinska Lindqvist to Diana Lenton.

Brown's Hotel

LONDON W1

October 31, 1936

Oh, lovely clean London – thank God we're back here! I've been silent apart from the silly postcards because I couldn't trust myself to write to you from Germany without betraying my bitter feelings. One can never be sure, there, just who reads one's outgoing mail. I have never felt before that I was being dirtied by my surroundings, but this summer in Germany I felt degraded by my mere presence there. If Karl-Erik had attempted to touch me I think I should have been physically sick. Fortunately the exaltation of all that nakedly-paraded brute force seemed to swallow his libido at one gulp, and all he required of me was my decorative presence alongside him at the public spectacles. It got worse in stages, beginning with the Olympics. I was not terribly bothered by all the Aryan propaganda at first. A girl doesn't tag along behind Karl-Erik for seven years without getting used to such cheap nonsense as Hitler's treatment of non-Nordic athletes. Their conspicuous victories were all the rebuttal that was needed. What did bother me was the all-pervading presence of those appalling Mitford girls, giving a gloss of spurious British approval to every event they attended. The fact that the daughter of a British peer happens not to mind standing next to that perverted monster Julius Streicher on public platforms gives him a degree of respectability which scares me.

The elder sister does her bit, too. She is a raving beauty who has always commanded attention in the expensive Society magazines and now she, too, is hanging around Hitler's coat tails. Both girls were house guests of Josef and Magda Goebbels during the Games. Karl-Erik practically worships them both, of course. He keeps burbling about the instinctive spiritual union of pure Aryan bloodstock that cuts across modern frontiers – anyone would think he was talking about horses! That admiration landed us at an event which I'd have given anything to miss. On October 5th, K-E came in,

302

simpering like a cat who'd stolen the cream. 'Pick out your smartest gown, my dear, we're going to a very important wedding tomorrow!' He refused to say who it was to be, but his manner made it obvious that it was someone of practically god-like status.

The following day, all was revealed. We attended the marriage of Diana Guinness and Sir Oswald Mosley! It's all incredibly hush-hush. Mosley became terribly pompous and said that one advantage of totalitarianism was that one could get married without the press hearing about it. He was right, too. There's no hint of it leaking out here in England and it seems that there isn't even any Society gossip about their affair, which turns out to have been the reason for her leaving her first husband back in 1932. For the past year, Mosley has had her tucked away in a country house somewhere in Staffordshire. The marriage took place in Goebbels's drawing room and Hitler himself attended. Mosley doesn't appear to share Diana's adulation for the Führer – probably feels overshadowed. Let's hope he stays that way!

That was a fitting end to our long stay in Germany. I couldn't wait to get away and was hard pressed not to thrust one of those awful cream-smothered cakes beloved by Hitler straight into his absurd little neurotic face, yelling 'Ich bin yiddisher!' as I did so. Well, we can all dream! What continues to bother me now that we're in England is that so many influential people seem to wish the Nazis well. If they're not out-and-out supporters, their attitude seems to be 'Better Nazi than Communist'. The Astors, Chips Channon, the Duke of Westminster – all are saying that we must not be beastly to the Germans. Hah.

To turn to something much more cheerful, you will see from my address that I remembered all you said about Brown's Hotel. It's divine! I'm making the most of it while I can, because Karl-Erik is unlikely to tolerate it for long. He keeps coming back from long lunches at the Ritz and name-dropping like mad. I only managed to get him in here when we arrived because a couple of his frightful pro-Nazi American contacts remembered staying in Brown's as children and thought it had been the tops. Now the Americans are out of sight, out of mind, and he wants to suck up to every right-wing Englishman in sight. I'd like to go to France for a while, but if I do I think it will be a solo trip. It has no place in Karl-Erik's Aryan tomorrow. I know that you'd think I'd be grateful to get away from him for a little while, but I want to stick close to him at present, in case I miss any useful information he might let slip.

Incidentally, your family has made my stay brighter. I followed up your suggestion and introduced myself to Lady Stanmore. Isn't she a delight? Perhaps because I'm not family, she didn't do the Mindless Butterfly routine on me but came across as what she obviously is, a charming, intelligent woman. I hope I have a chance to know her better. I had lunch with her and your sister Lettie three days ago. Diana, you never warned me! Having written that, I just realised, you have no way of knowing what she's like. She was just a child when you went away. In a sense, I suppose that's what she still is. But oh, boy, in other ways, she's as old as Lilith. She's no beauty but she doesn't need to be. She oozes sex appeal from every pore. And where Lady Stanmore might merely pretend to be empty-headed, Lettie really is. The impending French count may not be an unmixed blessing, but I'd guess that the Earl and your aunt have decided the sooner she's married to anyone vaguely acceptable, the safer they'll all feel! It's unexpected, because from what you've told me of your parents, both seemed very intelligent, whatever their other faults might have been. And you are hardly a dim-wit yourself. But poor, dear Lettie! Give her a pretty frock and a glamorous man, plus a big cocktail and a fashion magazine, and she'll play happily for hours. The soon-to-be-dowager Countess of Montsegur must be beating her head against the Louis XVI furniture at the thought of what she's getting!

Ah, I hear the measured tread of the master race outside. I'll stop now and write again when there's more news. Take care of yourself, dear friend. When you eventually come back here it's a frightening new world you'll be entering.

Love from Krystyna

Letter from Hermione, Lady Stanmore, to Diana Lenton

Brook Street
LONDON W 1
December 28, 1936

Dear Diana

I never thought I should feel more relief at the conclusion of a wedding than I did after yours, but your sister ran you fairly close. The happy couple are now skiing in St Moritz. I fully intended to write immediately after the ceremony, on Boxing Day, but what with pacifying your grandfather, assuring James that the world is not about to end because Lettie has embraced Rome, and negotiating a reception atmosphere as frigid as the weather thanks to the French contingent, this is my first chance. I really do not think we could have hoped for anything better. The Montsegurs are an ancient and very aristocratic family – as Madame la Comtesse insisted on telling everyone – and whatever Raoul's motives might have been, fortune-hunting cannot have been one of them. Both James and your grandfather spelled out to him her financial position and the non-existent chance of her ever getting her hands on money apart from her personal settlement.

The boy persisted, so I can only assume his intentions were honourable. It's just that men with honourable intentions so seldom look like Raoul de Montsegur! He is spectacularly handsome and has that French charm which depends as much on total ruthlessness as on the good looks which go with it. His mother behaved abominably until he appeared and then melted visibly. Naturally, she had assumed that he would marry a fortune. She didn't really care whether it was a French fortune but it had to be well-bred and Catholic. Instead of that, she got Lettie. Dearest Diana, what know they of flirts, who know not Lettie? I have refrained from discussing her with you in recent years, simply because I should not have known how to stop once I had started and I really don't think you would have believed me! After all, you last saw her as a pretty medieval damsel when she was your bridesmaid. She was like that until the winter after she Came Out and then she had a punctured romance with one of those old-fashioned cads who hunt the shires throughout the week and rich Society virgins during the week-end. He totally misunderstood Lettie's prospects, and by the time James disabused him – with much flourishing of horsewhips, naturally – Lettie was smitten beyond redemption.

I never enquired whether she had Given Her All: the answer was self-evident from her temporary misery at the time and her subsequent behaviour. Even her best friend would call that colourful! At various times since, I have more than half expected her to come home engaged to a South American polo player, an out-of-work actor and even a Negro nightclub singer (neither James nor your Grandpapa knows about that one and I pray nightly that they never will!). What really surprises me is that Madame la Comtesse has not succeeded in spying out our Lettie's raffish reputation. I suspect that she has failed only because she is so determinedly French that she ignores the existence of other nationalities and thereby missed Lettie's wilder excesses. I hardly know whether to be glad or sorry.

Somehow I think the elegant Raoul could be a very unpleasant man if he were thwarted. I hope matters turn out well for Lettie but my instinct tells me we shall be lucky to end the 1930s without a divorce in the family. Let us hope that he makes a lot of money out of what he mysteriously calls his 'little financial nonsenses' and that Lettie produces a lovely heir at their most prosperous moment.

I see with horror that I have not written to you since Evangeline brought Cosmo to stay with us en route to prep school. What a solemn little chap he is! James was very impressed at his self-sufficiency and said he had the makings of a 'fine tough fellow'. For myself I confess to having wondered whether seven was not altogether too young to separate him from his parents by such an immense distance. I know he could not have gone to school properly in Malaya, but was there no way of having him taught by a European tutor for just a couple of years before sending him home? He obviously missed you dreadfully, although he felt bound by his manhood not to discuss the matter! Try to cherish him a little, Diana, even if only by writing loving letters and maybe taking a home leave to come and see him next summer. You know we shall be delighted to look after him at Stanhope, but he is still so young. Oh, dear me! This is changing into the Children's Hour, what with Lettie and now Cosmo. I shall refrain from further middle-aged advice and turn my attention to you. Evangeline tells me you are in excellent health and heart and that she finally feels confident enough of your well-being to forsake you for her heroic doctor. I am glad. Evangeline was designed for love, not frustrated spinsterhood. From the little she said, I gather the good doctor might be just the man to provide it.

When she had delivered Cosmo safely to Somerset, Evangeline went to stay with Louise Kerslake. Louise makes more and more of my clothes every season. She is now so expert that only her originality distinguishes her from French couturières. She stamps a garment with as much individuality as they do. Unfortunately the severe financial climate here in recent years has prevented her from realising her ambition to set up a couture house of her own. She has done wonders as it is, but she still operates from Fulham and seems unable to raise quite enough capital to get started. Being a perfectionist, she is determined not to go half-way. It's Mayfair or nowhere for Louise! If it were not for the Earl, I should be sorely tempted to go into partnership with her. The business fascinates me; I can afford it; and Louise has earned the opportunity. Sadly, I cannot contemplate it in present circumstances. James might come round to the idea eventually, but his father, never! Needless to say I have not discussed it with Louise and, if I did, she might settle it once and for all by saying she would have no use for me as a partner. One never knows! Anyway, for now I shall go on being the perfectly-behaved Lady Stanmore, even if the boredom kills me! Write to me soon, my dear — and to little Cosmo.

My fondest thoughts, always, Hermione

Letter from Evangeline Owen to Diana Lenton

Fulham
January 3, 1937

Dear Madam

*The school said they would write and let you know Master
Cosmo was all right so I didn't then. I left it till I was
ready to start off back and then thought I should jog your
memory about his birthday. Please send him something special
and Malayan. It will make him feel big and important with
his little friends. I told you you shouldn't of sent him all the
way back here without any of the close family, you & Mr
Lenton, that is. Her Ladyship took to him straight off but
the poor little kid didn't know her from Adam and he just
wanted a good cry, not a clever chat. If it hadn't of been for
his Uncle James being all men together with him, I don't
think he could of stood it. I wish I was bringing him back
with me. I'm sure it would do the poor little mite more good
than being shouted at in a big old country mansion half the
year and trying to get to know a whole new family in another
mansion for the rest of the time.*

*I expect you will be angry when you read this as we had
all this out when I was still over there with him. But I still
feel the same and am sure Master Cosmo does. When I left
him I said, 'Shall I kiss your Mama for you?' And he said
'Why? She never kisses me unless she has to. Well she won't
have to now. Praps that's why she made you bring me all
this way.' Then he just turned round and walked back into
school all on his own. I was so choked I cried all the way to
Paddington in the train and it really wasn't till now that I
could face writing to you.*

*Please tell Neill there's a letter coming for him as well if
you get this and see him before his arrives. He's got some bee
in his bonnet about coming back over here to me if I don't
want to come back out East. That's just silly. I wouldn't
want to be anywhere else but Kuala Terlengu now, tell him.
Goodbye and I will see you in about one month.*

Evangeline Owen.

Letter from Krystyna Karpinska Lindqvist to Diana Lenton

Brown's Hotel
August 29, 1938

Diana – This letter is likely to get more and more disjointed as it goes on, but by the time you receive it you will probably know why. Those God-damned Nazis have got their eye on my country and the French and British might just let them get away with it. It seems obvious that they'll let Czecho-slovakia go under, anyway. If I hear one more appeaser say that England should keep her own house in order and tell the Czechs and Poles and Jews to mind their own business, I shall become violent.

I've been a bad correspondent this past year or so because I've been in Germany so much; and no one sane says anything controversial in Germany these days! Hence the cutesie-pie little cards and letters you've been getting that talk about the weather, the schnitzel and all things gemütlich. *One day I shall tell you all the gory details, but I don't have a year or so to spare right now.*

Down to important matters. First, I have finally parted company with Karl-Erik. Oh, Poland, will you ever be truly grateful for the interminable prison sentence I served with that man in your name? I doubt it. I used to have fantasies about my last show-down with Karl-Erik; how I'd sweep into a room, dressed in a perfect Dietrich-style outfit, and tell him what I thought of him and his gang of political thugs. When the moment came and I decided that I couldn't usefully learn any more from them, I thought about it and realised that I now hold him in too much contempt to waste a big scene on him. He really is a dreg of humanity and not worth the adrenalin. Finally I waited until we were in America a few weeks ago, booked a passage to England and just checked out of the hotel, leaving a two-sentence note telling him not to bother looking for me (I shan't tell you what the other sentence said, but it was not flattering).

So here I am, about to find some way of serving my country. Actually it's not that simple. I'm no more patriotic than anyone else. But I am a violent anti-Nazi. I've seen them too close and for too long to think civilisation can survive while they have any chance of power. I'm terrified about the prospect of them winning the war that's waiting for all of us. Now I'm off to see what I can do in the fight. There's no trouble involved in getting back inside Poland right now, at least if you're a Pole. This could be the last chance, though. If those pigs get away with Czechoslovakia they'll gobble up Poland too and I don't intend to be outside looking in when they do it. I'm trying not to take myself too seriously because I'm sure I enjoy some of it. But it's excitement I would gladly do without if they could all just disappear off the face of the earth. I may be a bit elusive in future. I plan to make this place my London base, but I've contacted your Aunt Hermione and she has promised to pass on my address to you if you ever want me and I'm not at Brown's. Of course, all this might be a lot of unnecessary nonsense, and by the time you get back to England I could be a lowly translation secretary in the War Office. Let's hope not, though! I've met a fascinating man called Edmund Dancey who apparently knows Roland and you quite well and says he might be able to give me some gainful employment. Somehow I don't think my income from the Polish estates will last much longer!

Be careful, darling. Watch out for the big bad wolf and come back to England soon. I think you'll be needed, along with every other sane citizen.

Love from Krystyna

Letter from Violet de Montsegur to Diana Lenton

Place de Perou
Paris
August 31, 1939

Dearest Diana
By the time you receive this I expect all sorts of ghastly things will have happened and heaven knows whether we shall still be here, in Château Segur or even in England, the way things are going. Aunt H says I should drop everything

except the baby and come dashing back to London for a very long visit. Although this sounds a bit melodramatic, I'm not all that sure Raoul would let me come if I wanted to bring Jean-Luc!

Oh dear, it's all such a terrible mix-up. At least his horrid old Mama is no longer with us. If she'd still been around we'd all have been shouting Heïl Hitler. Honestly, Diana, the old bat was obsessed with the man! She kept saying during her last few months that a French version of him was what la République needed to purge it of the filth flowing in its veins. It made me shudder just to listen to her. I'm afraid Raoul's a bit like that. He keeps swinging back and forth between saying the Poles are not worth a single French death and pledging himself to go out and die for la France and la Gloire. Quite frankly it's not at all what I had in mind when we were married.

If I complain he says we have a lot to thank the Germans for and, if it hadn't been for high-powered Nazis like Goering sending Party customers to his art and antiques business, we wouldn't be half as comfortable today as we are. I don't know anything about politics but when I see the newsreels of them screaming and shouting and strutting about I'd almost rather not be so comfortable. I do seem to be chattering on a bit but I'm a bit frantic to talk about it and it's harder than I thought it would be. I know what I think – I think! – but when I try to write it, it doesn't come out properly. I'm writing this just after the radio announcement on Europe 1 that we're now at war with the Germans. Raoul is out doing something for la France with a bunch of funny French aristos who would make Queen Victoria's outlook seem dangerously modern. You're the only one I can say this to, Diana. I almost wish he wouldn't come back and I do wish I could just be back in London with Jean-Luc and stay with Aunt Hermione. I can't cope with the way people are behaving here. They're either terrified or fierce.

I'd better stop in a minute and go to post this. If Raoul thought I was even thinking like this, let alone writing about it, he'd be terribly cross. Once or twice he's hit me a bit and it does scare me. The last time it left some marks and I *couldn't go out for a while and the maid kept staring at me. Oh, I'm sorry to get all silly. I haven't mentioned that bit to anybody else and when I wrote it down it looked so awful it made me cry to see it there. Somehow it was so rotten that all my family are so far off I have to tell them in writing when something nasty happens. Actually it was pretty beastly and really hurt. I fell over and he kicked me and I couldn't breathe very well for weeks afterwards. It's all right now but it did happen ages ago. Anyhow now you know why I want to get this letter off quickly, because if he comes back and makes me show it to him God knows what he will do.*

Before I stop I must tell you something really strange. I got a letter from Papa. Yes, after all these years, don't you think it's odd? He said did I think I might feel grown up enough now to want to see him and how did I think you would feel about seeing him. Apparently he knows where both of us are and he hasn't bothered us because he was afraid we would think he had disgraced us too much in the past. I can't think what to do about it. Raoul would never allow a meeting here. At first he thought Papa was terribly glamorous — patriotic upper-class spy and all that, keeping the horrid Bolshies at bay and willing to lose even his good name in the process. But then that bitch of a mother of his told him some of her friends on the Quai D'Orsay said it was gossip in diplomatic circles that he did it all for l'Amour, not la Patrie. That was it, of course. I've been treated as one up from a tuppeny tart ever since and Papa is mentioned jamais. *I really don't care what he's done, Diana. He'll always be Papa to me and nothing will stop me loving him. I don't honestly care if he had a torrid affair with a beautiful villainess and Gave It All Up for her. I just wish the poor old boy could have a little bit of happiness. Whatever he's done, he must have suffered enough by now. I know you're far away but can you think of some way to comfort him?*

I feel awful that I can't do much but Raoul does frighten me really. Maybe you can think of something I could do to help myself? I don't seem to be terribly good at it. Oh, my, this epistle does seem horribly gloomy, but perhaps you'll let me blame the war for that. People are allowed to be depressed when there's a war on, aren't they? Actually I'd have felt just as bad if we were still at peace, but at least it gives me an excuse to tell you a bit about how rotten things are just now.

I hope you will be coming back to Europe soon. I always feel better when you're about. Somehow you always seem to know what to do when I don't, like when Mama used to pull our hair when Nanny was on her day off.

Love from Lettie

Only you and Aunt H call me Lettie now. Keep it up!

Letter from Alexander Hartley to Diana Lenton

Place Lotti
Marseille
September 3, 1939

Dear Diana

I feel somewhat reticent about writing to you, even at such a dark time. I trust that your feelings for me remain unchanged, but recognise that, if they do, it must have required enormous courage for you to preserve them so. Given the circumstances of our parting so long ago, I thought it best not to approach you. I reasoned that if you ever felt the need to see me again, you would find me. It was a long time before I became aware that you were in the Far East; one no longer mixes in the same circles as in the past. When I eventually found out, I felt a little better. You could hardly have sought me out from the other side of the world and a letter would not have been an appropriate means of expressing the storm of emotion you must have felt.

The declaration of war has weakened my resolve. I am reconsidering my own position, having previously planned to end my days here in France. Now I am at a loss. England is unlikely to welcome me, although I would hardly be turned back at Calais. I lack the funds to move elsewhere and start again in any of the places which might be suitable. Switzerland would serve, but I cannot afford it. Spain or Portugal would be within my means, but can you see me living in either country? I fear that I must choose between danger here in France and renewed disgrace back in England. I think the danger will win. Disgrace was always harder to bear. I am writing to you now in case the coming conflict sweeps me away. I do not want to be swallowed up without saying goodbye. I should also like to know whether you will be returning to Europe soon. If you plan to do so and wish to see me, please write to me soon. It would make the difference between my staying here in France and moving back to England. I think that if you were prepared to accept me, England would be endurable after all. Should you feel that this is asking too much of you, your silence will be enough. Do not feel that I would condemn you. I realise that I have not been your greatest social asset over the years. You will always be my favoured daughter. I hope I shall always be your

Revered Mandarin

Letter from Hermione Digby-Lenton to Diana Lenton

Brook Street
LONDON W1
September 4, 1939

Dear Diana
I shall write at length about the awful events here when I have more time. At present I am in too much of a hurry. However I did promise Krystyna. If you're getting in touch with her, please do so through me from now on. I shall explain more fully later. Are you planning to have Cosmo back in Malaya or will you be leaving him at school? In my view he's as likely to be caught up in the war with you as he is here; it will merely be a little later, depending on how long the Japanese take over their decision to join in. My love to all of you. You are constantly in my thoughts.

Hermione

Letter from Cosmo Lenton to Diana Lenton

Glastonbury
Somerset
November 9, 1939

Dear Mama
They have just come and said that last post for the Far
East will be going off tomorrow and we all have to write our
Christmas letters now. I have also written to Papa. I hope
you and Papa and Sebastian are all right and that Evangeline
is too. I am going to Stanhope for Christmas and Great
Uncle James says I might get my own pony if I am very
lucky instead of just having to make do with one from the
stables. He said at half term that you had written to ask
them to buy one for me on your behalf, but I think really he
thought of it or Great Aunt Hermione did, because you are
often too busy for that sort of thing. I am sending your
Xmas presents with this letter and I am sorry if the snowman
on your calendar is a bit sideways but the glue slipped and I
had already put Papa's name on the one that came out
straight so you have to have that one. I didn't have time to do
anything for Sebastian and there wasn't anything in the tuck
shop I could see that he would have liked, so you'll just have
to say special Merry Xmas for him and I have put in a
specially bright card for him to make up for it.
It's ever such a long time since I have seen you and Papa.
When are you coming back? Won't the war mean you have to
come to England again? If not, you could think about me
coming back to Malaya because it could get jolly dangerous
here by myself.

Your Son Cosmo

CHAPTER SIXTEEN

By the start of the 1941 Monsoon, the more nervous planters had pushed the Asian war into the backs of their minds. All the news suggested that Singapore was an impregnable fortress with the whole of Malaya protected by its strength. The Japanese were smart enough in their way. They would know better than to challenge such might. Many of the planters submerged any doubts beneath extra interest in the mounting European conflict. Would their children be safer remaining at school in England, where war was already a reality, or back here, risking involvement in future hostilities but safe from the existing violence? Should they themselves go back to defend the land of their birth or stay to offer a united response to the invading Japanese? The Lentons' position was particularly equivocal. Sir Ralph was finally close to death, fading away after a long illness. Diana's grandfather had already written to her to say they had better return to oversee the estate during the old baronet's decline. But Roland was reluctant to let down Buffy Exton now, of all times. Buffy's grandson, the heir to his two Malayan estates, was doing some highly secret military training, and the war would clearly involve him fully for the foreseeable future. The estates would have to be sorted out well before the young man was in a position to take over. In the meantime, therefore, Roland postponed his return to Europe as long as possible in deference to Buffy's past kindness.

The Lentons were anxious enough to get back on their own account. Malaya would always have a place in their hearts, but after twelve years the pace there had become a little too leisurely for Diana's taste and even Roland experienced a growing desire to exchange the langour of the rain forest for the crisper air of rural England. In late November he went down to Kuala Terlengu as usual with Diana, intending to leave her there with Evangeline until the New Year. Neill MacIntyre gave a drinks party a few days after their arrival. Kuala Terlengu had grown considerably over the years since the Lentons' arrival on the east coast, but there were more Europeans at this party than either of them had ever seen in the area at one time. Over the gin slings the old China hands were dismissing as folly the recent heavy concentration of Japanese shipping off the north-east coast.

'Must be doo-lally to do it at the height of the Monsoon,' said the local DO. 'God knows what the silly blighters think they'll achieve in this weather. Perhaps they hope they'll frighten us away!'

Captain Smith, who knew the waters better, almost sneered. 'Have you forgotten there can be clear spells of a week or more during Monsoon, with flat calm and no rain? I bet the Nips haven't. If they feel like it, they'll be ashore the minute the present squall lets up, with no one to stop 'em because everyone knows the Monsoon is our best defence. Hah! How did we ever get ourselves an empire in the first place?'

Evangeline listened, believing Captain Smith more readily than the other man. 'Do you think they'll attack us, Captain?' she asked. 'Surely they'll be more interested in the Americans than us.'

'Oh, no, lovey, we shan't get off that lightly!' he told her. 'Of course the Americans will be the main target, but the Japs know they have to knock us out too because we provide safe haven for friendly shipping. In any case, the Americans are a military presence in the Pacific, not so much a colonial trading power. The Japanese need our raw materials if they're to win this war and I reckon they'll invade Malaya to get them as soon as the weather lets up.'

Evangeline's attention wandered to the military type who was chatting in a corner with Roland and Neill. What was so important that they needed to skulk off like that to discuss it? She joined them to find out. All three men fell silent. Then Neill forced a smile and gave her his glass. 'Well fielded, Evie! We were just thinking about another. I'll have a Singapore Sling this time.'

She gave him a look that was pure poison and went to get his drink. He must have been caught on the hop, she thought – I've never known him touch a cocktail before when there's good malt whisky in the house. The party seemed endless. When they had finally seen off the last guests and Roland and Diana had gone to their room, she turned on him.

'Right, you black Scot – tell me what that was all about. And no silly stories – I'll keep at you 'til you tell me!'

'What was what about? You do confuse me at times, Evie.'

'That cloak-and-dagger drama that kept you busy with Roland and the squaddie half the evening.'

'That "squaddie" was a lieutenant colonel!'

'That makes it worse. He should know better than to drag two middle-aged married men into his schemes. There are more young bachelors around than you can shake a stick at!'

'Not young bachelors who speak fluent Chinese and Malay, though. You're right, Evie, I'd better tell you. But no dramatics and no discussion outside this room – not even with Diana Lenton. Roland will quite likely tell her, but it's not to be discussed openly on any account. Things are a damned sight worse than the wireless and newspapers are making out. Colonel Johnstone has asked Roland to slip up to the Siamese border for a few days to do a recce. They know the Japs are close, but not exactly where they plan to come across or how well-organised they are. It's Roland's job to find out and report back.'

'And you?'

'Ah, well, that's a bit more depressing. They also want someone to go into the hinterland and set up groups of resistance fighters.'

'Then we're going to be beaten?'

'The military seem to think so.'

'But what about all that tough talk of Fortress Singapore?'

'Bunk. How can sea-directed defences protect the shore? They're pointing the wrong way. All the enemy has to do is invade by land instead of sea and he's got us. It seems that our only workable strategy will be to evacuate the women and children, then put up a bit of a fight while the specialists do as much as possible to nobble key installations. Then what happens? Well, we get out and re-invade when we're stronger, supported by the resistance groups I shall be helping to set up.'

'If you believe that, Neill MacIntyre, you'll believe any-thing. We'll be locked in like rats in a trap and everyone knows by now what the Japanese do to prisoners. I'm not having it. Either you leave with me when the time comes, or I'm staying with you.'

'Look, love, I think you're shouting before you're hurt. None of this has happened yet and there's a chance it never will.'

'You don't believe that any more than I do!'

'When I'm as tired as I am now, my gullibility knows no bounds. Roland goes tomorrow. I'm off in a few days. At this stage nothing is going to happen to either of us, so at least take it easy until I get back.'

He took her in his arms and firmly kissed away further objections. 'Thought you said you were tired, you lech-erous old devil!' she murmured, settling into his embrace.

'Nagging women do things to my libido – it's why you have such a hectic love life, you witch!'

'When are you off wherever it is?'

Diana approached Roland with a calm she did not feel.

'Oh . . . er . . . you realise I'm popping off for a while do you?'

'I had rather gathered something might be up.'

'Well, yes, I did say I'd take a look round up at the border for that Johnstone chappie. Shouldn't take more than a few days.'

'How dangerous is it?'

'Not very. Should make a bit of a break before Christmas. Just keep my fingers crossed I don't run into lots of Japs, that's all.'

'Isn't that why you're going – with the intention of running into as many as possible?'

'That's one way of looking at it. But I shall be all right, really. Even if they chopped me up, I dare say you'd manage all right.'

'Not as well as you might think. I can only bound about being the madcap Mrs Lenton because you're tucked away waiting for me, you know.'

'I wish you'd tell me that more often. Sometimes I feel pretty well unnecessary.'

She opened her arms and he came hesitantly to her, finally sitting beside her and allowing her to hold him like a child.

'Roland, what are we going to do? All my Hartley intuition is telling me we're in bad trouble and that nobody has any idea how to stop it. What happens if the Japanese invade?'

'Stop saying "if", old girl. From now on, it's a question of "when".'

He put out the light. They lay together in the darkness, silently considering their future. Next morning the wireless was fatuously dismissing as naval exercises the massive concentration of Japanese shipping in the Gulf of Siam. MacIntyre looked over the top of his coffee cup at Roland.

'Obviously it's time someone popped over to Siam and found out what they were really up to, eh Lenton? What are you going to say you're up to if they ask?'

Roland smiled shyly. 'I didn't think it was too likely that any of the more obscure sorts of religious bods would be up there, so I'm saying I'm a Seventh Day Adventist missionary. I've never encountered one at all out here. I don't think they can have penetrated into south-east Asia. Johnstone offered me a couple of Malay boys as protective covering – exploring potential new markets with my native helpers, you know the sort of line – but I don't want to involve locals. It's our fight against the Japanese, and if we lose, they're the ones who stay and suffer.'

'Be a bit of a scream if you ran into a real Seventh Day Adventist, eh?'

He did. Having registered in a modest hotel just over the border, Roland unpacked his overnight bag and was about to go out when someone tapped his bedroom door. Half expecting a fully-armed Samurai warrior, Roland opened up to discover a friendly elderly European on the landing outside.

'Mr Lenton, I believe?' The little man was positively skipping with excitement. 'I am Geoffrey Bridges. I run a Seventh Day Adventist mission in Sumatra and I'm here en route to meet some colleagues from China up at Phnom Penh. What luck running into you like this!'

'Yes, quite a coincidence.' Roland was bemused by it all.

'Oh, I see the hand of God in it, Mr Lenton. We must be the only two Seventh Day Adventists within eight hundred miles!' I'll drink to that, thought Roland, but perhaps Seventh Day Adventists don't?

He finally managed to fend off Bridges by saying he had withdrawn for a while to meditate. He wondered if they were given to meditation, but the missionary seemed content with his response and made his departure. The incident was the last bright patch Roland was to encounter for a long time. He hired an old truck and drifted around the border country for a few days, at home in what was essentially the same territory as his own patch over in Malaya. In the jungle he located several fresh air strips, driven roughly through secondary forest and obviously temporary, but potentially an effective launching point for an invasion force. They were so numerous that the Japanese had not even bothered to leave guards around them. They've obviously learned they needn't take us too seriously, Roland reflected.

He had gone into Siam in a truck driven by a couple of the DO's workers who were going over the border to visit their families. The only way back was to hire a Model T Ford and drive it along the beach which extended down the length of the east coast. Few traders were willing to part with cars in the little Siamese town, because the flurry of military activity assured them of plenty of local business. He started trying to arrange transport on the afternoon of

December 5, but no one wanted to know. He finally gave up after dark that evening and started again next day. Even then, it was late afternoon before he located a Chinese storekeeper whose business partner in Kota Bharu could use the car until he wanted it again. Roland could drop it off at the little Malay seaport within hours of returning to Kuala Terlengu. By the time he set off on the night of December 6, it was pitch dark. The calm of the past couple of days had broken and huge waves were crashing up the beach, so big that Roland had to stop several times for them to go out before he could drive on further. In spite of the inconvenience, he was relieved. If the sea was so rough, there was no question of seaborne invaders supporting the aerial attack which he now expected at any time. He got into Kota Bharu well after midnight and was passed through to see the brigadier in charge of the army unit there.

'They're coming the minute the weather clears,' he said. 'The airfields are ready and there's hardly a civilian vehicle to be had at any price. As soon as this weather lifts they'll be on us.'

'D'you think there's a chance they'll try tonight?' The brigadier was taking him seriously, thank God.

'I was sure of it when I set off, but they'll never get through that sea. Anything trying to land along the northeast coast tonight will be smashed to pulp. I never thought I'd be so glad to see the Monsoon blowing this hard.'

'Good man. You've done well. Hang on and I'll arrange some supper and a stiff drink, followed by a good night's sleep.'

'Thanks for the thought, Brigadier, but I've a wife and son down at Kuala Terlengu. I'm getting back there straight away if it takes me until dawn.'

Roland took some fruit to eat while he drove, and left. The Japanese invasion force came ashore through mountainous seas near Kota Bharu just after dawn. Later the same morning they bombed the American fleet at Pearl Harbour. Within hours of Roland's return to Kuala Terlengu, everyone was aware of the invasion and had packed ready to move off. Sebastian was jigging up and down with excitement. Diana was stunned at the suddenness of it all. Evangeline was preparing for a showdown with Neill should he show signs of intending to stay. That problem was solved by the arrival of Colonel Johnstone. He went into MacIntyre's office with the doctor and Roland.

'Good God, Lenton, how d'you think they managed it? I saw the sea down here last night and I wouldn't have believed a matchstick could come ashore through it in one piece. Apparently they're pouring in as if they knew how to walk on water! Anyway, MacIntyre, forget your little job until we've all moved down south a bit.'

'Down south?'

'Kuantan. The aerodrome there is an obvious prime target for attack and we want everyone we can get. That doesn't pre-empt your other assignment, Mac, but we want you based down there for now.'

'In the meantime, what about the locals? Who's going to look after them?'

'What makes you think they need looking after? They've always managed all right in the past.'

'They've never had hordes of Japs descending on them with blood in mind before, either. And the Japs are only coming because we're here, so we're responsible to some extent at least.'

'Nonsense, old chap. They'll just blend with the landscape and go on with their lives. One conqueror is much like another to them.'

Roland gripped MacIntyre's forearm and made a slight negative head movement. Mac kept silent with difficulty. Having handed out his decrees, Lieutenant-Colonel Johnstone prepared to depart.

'Mustn't get too tied up with trivia, Dr MacIntyre. Remember we're a bit of a remote corner up here. Singapore was bombed last night.'

'What?'

'Oh, it's not just those American johnnies at Pearl who've been getting it in the neck, you know!' Looking courageous and military, he left.

'Bumptious bastard! Bet he manages to stay out of the line of fire! Meanwhile, what about the poor bloody Chinese?' MacIntyre wanted to know. 'China's been at war with the Japanese for some time. I shouldn't think the Chinese community here can expect much mercy.'

'You'll have to let them get on with it for now, Neill, because we have our hands full with our own families. Let's get them safely out of the way and then I think we both have a look at the possibility of setting up those resistance support groups, using the Chinese as much as we can. It might give the poor sods a chance of setting up escape routes for their own people.'

The weather was the noisiest aspect of their journey south. There was little sign that an invading army was anywhere within a thousand miles. Either the other European families had beaten them to it or they were yet to start out. For a long time their shared truck was the only vehicle on the road. Then, gradually, they were joined by other European groups, until by the time they reached Kuantan they were part of a dust-coated motorcade. Makeshift arrangements were made to pass the women and children on south as soon as practicable. The men were to stay, either as part of the volunteer regiments which had been set up when the European war started, or to go off on specialised missions like those allocated to Roland and Neill. Diana was eager to be away. She abhorred dirt and overcrowding and had no intention of turning into a refugee hanging around the fringes of a provincial airfield. Having come to terms with the fact that Roland would be busy for a while, she directed her mind to the practicalities of accommodation and comfort as they moved south.

Evangeline was different. 'I'm not going on, Neill. I'm staying here and not budging until you finish what you're involved in, and that's final. Maybe I can make myself useful starting a canteen or something. They seem to have made precious few plans before dragging us all down here.'

'For once in your life, Evie, be reasonable! I don't know

where I shall be this time tomorrow or next week but I'm certain of one thing – it won't be here. They've already got far more men than they need; a bit of effective anti-aircraft support would be more appropriate than all these half-baked civilians pouring into the place. No, I've every intention of going off on the original jaunt Johnstone had lined up, and if I do you'll be more likely to see me down in Singapore now and then than up at Kuantan. Even if we hold on to this airfield, which I doubt, I intend to avoid it like the plague from now on, so kindly stay close to Diana and get down to Singapore!'

In the end, grumbling, she agreed that he was talking sense and arranged to move on with Diana and Sebastian. By the time their transport was fixed, their husbands had been assigned reconnaissance tasks and had left Kuantan. Both men departed during the night, without notice, leaving over-jolly notes looking forward to reunion in Singapore.

When they at last arrived in Singapore, Diana and Evangeline found it almost unrecognisable since their last visit. Its physical features had been altered by bombardment and the hasty erection of makeshift inshore defences. But the huge influx of planters from the Federated and Unfederated States were the main cause of transformation. Accommodation was at a premium and all three of them ended up sharing a room in one of the various clubs where Diana was a member. When Diana protested at the grudging offer of just one room, the harassed receptionist snapped that she was lucky to get anything; only members of at least ten years' duration were being accepted and she had been allocated the last but one room.

In the bars and on the streets, everyone was talking evacuation. The radio and newspapers continued to give the impression that Britannia ruled the waves and the Malay Peninsula and that any minute now the Japanese would be taught a sharp lesson. The inevitable follow-up announcements of still further 'strategic withdrawals' in the north lent a false note to their persistent optimism. Christmas and New Year came and went almost unnoticed. Refugees continued to flock in and they learned to be grateful that their room was small. It meant they kept it. In the large hotel suites families packed the rooms and overflowed into the corridors. By mid-January, after the evacuation of Kuala Lumpur, conditions were chaotic.

The two women wanted to be useful. At first both planned to offer their services to a hospital in shifts, one looking after the baby while the other worked. But Evangeline, trained by MacIntyre as his surgery nurse, was so obviously more useful than the eager but unskilled Diana that in the end Diana looked after Sebastian full time and Evie joined the staff at the Queen Alexandra Military Hospital. Neither Diana nor Evangeline had any noble ideals about staying to defend Singapore against the invaders. They simply had no intention of leaving without their husbands. At present the prospect of leaving with them seemed remote.

Roland had arrived briefly in the city between Christmas and New Year, staying long enough only to receive orders about setting up potential resistance groups. After that he and a couple of other Chinese-speaking planters spent their time ferrying lorry-loads of potential resistance fighters up to the frontier. All were young Chinese Communists trained in sabotage who at that point seemed to be the only people in Malaya with real practical skills to combat the Japanese. The time Roland spent away from Singapore got noticeably shorter on each trip, an uncomfortable reminder of how fast the front line was approaching the island. Neill MacIntyre was attached to an army unit, ironically not far from Kuantan airfield. Most of the time he was bewildered and incredulous at the level of incompetence displayed by those at the top who claimed to be masterminding the action.

'If I treated my patients the way they're treating this war, I'd be out of business in ten minutes,' he told a middle-aged sergeant after they had received yet another order to retreat without firing on the enemy.

'What d'you think's going to happen to this business, then?' said the sergeant morosely. 'I reckon it'll be bankrupt by January! It's like handing over the cash to the bank robbers instead of using the shotgun you've got under the counter.'

MacIntyre's unit were ambushed by the Japanese as they drove south-west from the coast. When the firing started the army driver confidently announced that their armoured car would withstand any small arms fire with ease. Next moment the inside of the vehicle was full of shrapnel as Japanese armour-piercing bullets tore through the inadequate armour plating, which itself then became part of the bombardment. Neill yelled in pain as a strip of the red-hot metal tore a furrow along his left arm. His companions were falling and crying out around him as they, too, were hit. Meanwhile the ambush party had departed as fast as it arrived; there were probably richer pickings back up the road was Neill's last thought as he lost consciousness. Miraculously their driver had suffered nothing worse than facial scratches. The remainder of the convoy limped into its next base that evening and MacIntyre was patched up after a fashion.

It was mid-January before the Singapore authorities agreed to the evacuation of woman and children. By then Roland was beside himself with anger at the attitude which was willing to sacrifice lives to maintain the myth that England could still triumph.

'You should have been sent out weeks ago,' he told Diana. 'Now that they're bombarding every vessel that moves, those Whitehall-trained idiots are handing them our next generation on a fleet of superannuated passenger liners and pleasure craft, just because they weren't prepared to face the prospect of defeat a month ago. I want you, Sebastian and Evie packed and ready to go by this evening.'

'Evie won't go anywhere without knowing what's happening to Neill; and I'm not budging without Evie. No one else will look after her. She says she's going on working at the hospital as long as they'll let her and I dread to think what she plans when they send the hospital staff out too.'

At that point Evangeline arrived back from her shift.

'I'm not having a child on my conscience, Madam, and if you think Master Sebastian can be just handed over to some stranger on a ship while you stay as my nanny, you're mistaken. You're going, I'm staying. I promise I'll leave the minute Neill shows up.'

Now Roland intervened. 'Evangeline, you have to face the possibility that Mac won't just show up. I don't mean I think he's been killed, but it's so chaotic back there that he might have been diverted by any number of things. He might not even still be on the Peninsula at all. Some units have been ordering vital personnel off in small boats. and I should imagine that doctors are high priority.'

'I'm not saying it's reasonable; I'm just saying it's the way things are. I stay till the last party gets off this God-forsaken island and that's that, but I'm not going to be responsible for Master Sebastian getting bumped off!'

Diana finally capitulated but refused to go until the last minute. She and Sebastian were among the two thousand women and children aboard the *Empress of Japan*, the last large passenger liner to leave Singapore in late January. Roland had gone back over to Johore. Evangeline was determined not to be upset about what lay ahead.

'See you in London, Madam,' she said. 'I always did say they were a lot of savages out here, and if this little lot doesn't prove me right nothing will!'

'Evie, please take care. I can't manage without you. Look now you've made me cry again. It used to be only Mama who could do that.'

Evangeline's own eyes were suspiciously moist. Her tone was extra brusque to make up for it. 'Nonsense, Madam. You're crying because you can't have your own way for once. Now get going or the bloody boat will go without you.'

'Don't swear, Evie. It's not ladylike.' They both managed a forced laugh. Evangeline said goodbye and went back to the hospital.

On January 31, Johore was abandoned and the causeway which connected the island of Singapore to the Peninsula was blown. Roland and a fellow civilian waited with army units to join in the anticipated fight for the bridgehead. It never came. Desultory engagements with the Japanese on the mainland were broken off and first the Australian army units, then the civilians of the Singapore Volunteers were ushered across the Causeway, along with a detachment of Argyll and Sutherland Highlanders who had fought their way down the whole of Malaya. Two of the less-hardened Volunteers broke and ran when a Japanese fighter plane buzzed them as they prepared to cross.

One of the Argylls turned on them. 'Dinna run, man, dinna run. There's been too much running in this fucking war already!' Roland was inclined to agree.

Singapore settled down to a siege, although all but the naive and the crazy knew it would be short-lived. On February 7, Evangeline ran into Roland. She had been living at the hospital since Diana's departure and Roland, who had been in action since the Causeway went, had hoped she too had left Singapore. 'Evie!' he cried. 'Still no news of Mac?'

'Course not! I wouldn't still be here if there was. But never mind that. Come to a wedding this afternoon.'

'You must be joking!'

'No, one of the VAD's fiancés has been wounded and he's here for treatment – nothing serious – so they're getting hitched before he goes back into action. You're invited as my escort.'

'I wouldn't miss it for anything.'

At two-thirty that afternoon, Peter Lucy married 'Tommy' Hawkins in Singapore Cathedral. The invitations had been issued in the newspapers, which were still publishing, apparently oblivious of the imminent conquest. Afterwards, at a reception attended by soldiers fresh from the front line, the guests ate traditional wedding cake which had been concocted in a baby's bath during an air raid. Exactly one week later, Singapore fell.

Cut off from his resistance groups – he hoped temporarily – Roland tagged along with the Singapore Volunteers. He spent most of his quieter moments wondering how the Japanese had failed to take Malaya weeks ago. On one occasion his group were withdrawn from patrolling the waterfront area to reinforce Australian troops who were under pressure on the island's north coast. Their platoon officer went on ahead and the Volunteers followed in trucks. At the rendezvous the officer flew into a frenzy because they had remained in the trucks under fire.

'You should have bally well got out of the trucks and advanced up the road in open order to avoid casualties,' he yelled.

'But we didn't suffer any casualties.' Roland strove to keep his tone reasonable in an effort to get on with things.

'Not the point, not the point! Trouble with you chaps is you don't think anything has to be done by the book. Well it does. There's a good reason for everything. Now back into the trucks, back down the road, and do it all over again – properly.'

'But they're fucking well firing at us down there and we're all safe, up here, where we want to be.'

'Are you disobeying an officer's order?'

To Roland's eternal regret, he did not disobey. He and the rest of the unit got into their trucks, drove back down the road, got out and started back in open order. Half-way up, a Japanese plane came over and started machine-gunning them. The survivors ended up huddled in the monsoon drain beside the road, soaked and demoralised. When they finally returned to the officer, he was oozing satisfaction.

'There you are, told you so. If you'd been in trucks, none of you would have got through!'

Neill MacIntyre had been patched up after the ambush and had spent the subsequent weeks participating in seemingly endless withdrawals down the Peninsula. Every time he prepared himself for a fight, there were last-minute orders to fall back. There were plenty of wounded men coming in and he kept busy looking after them. As they moved south, the natives watched incredulously. MacIntyre saw one old planter standing at the roadside explaining to a Malay: 'We'll be back, y'know. Strategic withdrawal, that's all. Letting 'em slip in then we'll box 'em up!' Mac hoped the

Malay's English was imperfect. It would be really embarrassing if the lad understood what the poor old devil was telling him. Finally they arrived at Johore and the various volunteer units were broken up. The Europeans were attached to one or other of the regular army units and MacIntyre found himself alongside a detachment of Argyll and Sutherlands. He crossed the Causeway only half an hour after Roland Lenton on January 31, without knowing it. Once on the island it never occurred to him to seek out Evangeline because he assumed she had been evacuated with the other women and children.

For the next ten days he was moved around wherever anyone needed a doctor. By February 13 he was based on the high ground of Buona Vista Lodge, overlooking the western perimeter of the city. The Malay Regiment was dug in there and at first MacIntryre was little more than a spectator. Then Australian and British stragglers started heading back through their section of the lines, the Japanese moved closer and they were suddenly at the heart of the action. He was one of a number of officers injured when the command post where they were meeting received a direct hit. The first-aid team sent him on to Alexandra Military Hospital, where he was hurried into the theatre for emergency surgery. Evangeline had been persuaded to leave just three hours earlier.

That morning the matron had called them in. 'I know that there is no such thing as race or colour any more to any of you working here,' she told them. 'Unfortunately, the European nurses stand out and we all know what the Japanese do to them when they take over. So far, no reprisals have been made against native nurses' (no mention was made of the possible fate of the Chinese girls) 'so we are evacuating the Europeans. All Asian personnel who no longer wish to remain are released from duty. From now on this is a strictly voluntary posting.'

One of her colleagues grabbed Evangeline's arm. 'Come on, girl, if there's a chance of seeing your husband again it won't be in Singapore. You'll do him no good staying around here to be raped and killed by a Jap!'

331

Evie was forced to admit the good sense of the argument. She went with them. The only barely adequate transport remaining in the harbour was an old tramp, the *Empire Star*. The nurses were driven straight down to the docks and sailed that day. There were no provisions aboard and no source of supplies. Crewmen combed the wharves and eventually located some crates of Guinness and cases of tinned asparagus. Otherwise they returned empty-handed. As the old tub left Singapore, Evangeline sat on deck singing *Rule Britannia* to show she was not beaten, occasionally taking a swig from a bottle of Guinness. Please, Neill, be free, be safe, she thought, as she watched the final bombardment of the supposedly impregnable city.

MacIntyre fully regained consciousness during the night. At first he was at a loss to recognise his whereabouts. He was in a hastily-converted store-room with other last-minute casualties who had been brought in after the main wards filled up. A couple of Chinese nurses were attending to the three post-operative cases.

'You'll be all right, Dr MacIntyre,' one of them told him. 'You caught a lot of shrapnel and you were a bit of a pincushion, but once the anaesthetic wears off you'll just be very sore for a few days.' She gave him some water and moved on to another patient.

A couple of hours later the Japanese attacked the hospital. Neill surfaced from a foggy dream to the sound of screams and cries. He was unable to grasp what was happening. Then a soldier in torn, blood-stained uniform said: 'I'm a pastor back in England. I think in view of what's obviously happening outside I'd better say a few prayers.'

It dawned on MacIntyre that the Japanese were killing every patient in the hospital. 'Bit late for prayers, don't you think?' he mumbled to the Chinese nurse.

'Perhaps not. I think they've passed by this room because it doesn't look like a ward.'

She was right. By the morning, discipline had been imposed on the victorious troops. The Chinese and Malayan staff were taken away but the European survivors of the massacre were allowed to live. Throughout the day on February 15, the more active patients helped the bedbound. By the evening, Neill's strength was beginning to return.

The band of Volunteers including Roland was close by. That evening they were told they were to make a bayonet counter-attack. The erstwhile civilians stood in groups, trying to meet each other's eyes and failing.

'I don't quite know whether I should be able to gut someone at close quarters, not even a Jap.' Roland was voicing the view of most of them. As it grew dark they were assembled again. Oh well, thought Roland, here's where I find out. But instead of an order to attack, they were given the news that Singapore had capitulated. Even the most reluctant warriors were stunned by the news.

'I say,' said one, 'I know we all feel the way Lenton does about bayonets, but I'm damned sure we'd prefer to fight than just give up. We can't just hand them the front door key.'

'I'm afraid we already have,' said the commanding officer. 'Now all we can do is wait. We are no longer our own masters.'

Maybe you're not, but I bloody well am, thought Roland. I'm not just going to stand around waiting for the Yellow Peril to arrive and run me in. As no one seemed to care what happened now, he slipped away. A couple of other temporary Volunteers joined him and they discussed the possibilities for escape.

'I reckon our one remaining chance is the yacht club,' said David Forster, a keen peacetime sailor. 'It's taken less heavy bombardment than the commercial shipping roads and there might be a few small craft still intact.'

They took his advice and picked their way through scenes of devastation to the yacht harbour. Many of the craft were damaged but eventually they found a fourteen-foot sailing boat, rigged it and got it into the water. 'It'll be a miracle if we get it through the minefields but it's better than just staying put,' said Forster.

They made it, sailing away from the city into the Straits, bound for Sumatra. 'What d'you intend doing now, Roland?' said Forster.

'First I want to find my wife and younger son, but that's going to be quite a job. After that, I think I'll try to get to India or Ceylon. When we were setting up Force 136, we talked over the possibility of India as an operating base. However successful they are, it'll take the Japanese years to invade India.'

'Careful, old man! That's what we said about Singapore a year ago.' Both men glanced back involuntarily at the pall of black smoke which gave the lie to that illusion.

At first Neill MacIntyre felt surprisingly fit when he stood up and tried walking about. Fellow patients urged caution. 'You're a mass of bandages,' said the peacetime pastor. 'If you move around you'll open something up.'

'If I don't move around, I have a feeling the Nips will soon open something up for me! They're not going to leave us undisturbed here for long and somehow I don't think they'll send an ambulance for me when they take us,' said MacIntyre.

He had until early the following week to toughen himself for what lay ahead. Then a squad of Japanese soldiers arrived and started pushing them roughly into loose marching formation. A couple of bedridden patients refused and were dragged away. The ensuing screams left few doubts about their fate. MacIntyre had grubbed around and found a cotton button-through shirt and pants which more or less fitted him. His own clothing appeared to have been cut away for surgery, and he had come round naked save for his surgical dressings. It took longer to find a pair of sandals in which he could walk comfortably, but he managed to get hold of some. Movement was still extremely painful but he knew there was no alternative except death. It got easier with every day that passed, in spite of discomfort from unchanged dressings. He was glad he had thought ahead. It was obvious that this was to be no ten-minute stroll. When they had formed up, a senior Japanese officer harangued them. Afterwards an interpreter explained that they were to be assembled with the rest of the civilian population and taken off somewhere to be confined.

On the eastern tip of the island, at Changi, stood the military barracks and a civilian jail. Days before their own long march began, the patients had heard the skirl of bagpipes as a battalion of Gordon Highlanders marched through with the thousands of other captured soldiers bound for the prison. Mac wished he could look forward to the help of the evocative music when they were moved out. When the sound of the Gordons faded, only the steady tramp of marching feet could be heard. Obviously no one felt much like singing. Now the remaining two-and-a-half thousand male civilians who remained in Singapore were marched out to Changi too, led by the Governor. It was rough going, particularly at the beginning. Their route lay through an area which had taken heavy bombardment. Severed telephone lines and tram cables hung drunkenly from their broken poles or snaked across streets. Damaged and burned-out cars created obstacles, and everywhere was the rich stench of decaying corpses. The cavalcade comprised schoolboys, grandfathers and men of all ages between. Some had come in the clothes they had worn when Singapore capitulated. Others had tried to bring possessions. In a very short while Mac realised that it would be all he could do to remain on his feet until they reached their destination. His determined exercising in the hospital had done him less good than he hoped. Beneath the dried-out bandages his festering wounds first started to itch, then to chafe. He wondered how long he would survive. It was not so much the march itself, as his state when he reached its end. He was all too aware that in his present condition, exhaustion was more likely than a Japanese soldier to kill him.

Along the way they passed hundreds of Malays, Tamils and Chinese. Many of them held tins of water and defied the angry Japanese guards to offer it to the tired marchers. MacIntyre drank sparingly from such a tin and gripped the hand that offered it in silent gratitude. Elsewhere along the route, the locals turned their backs on the defeated Europeans, not in contempt, but in rejection of the entire event. The going became a little easier when they got out into the coconut estates in the country districts. But by now any slight moderation in the rigours of the march was wasted on MacIntyre. A number of his wounds had broken open and he could feel the blood oozing into the stiff, dirty dressings. I'll be dogmeat by tonight, he thought.

Somehow he managed to make it to Changi. He sank to his knees inside the quarters assigned to his group, desperately trying to find a part of his body which did not hurt too much to rest on. He survived a couple of days before succumbing to blood poisoning. During one of his last spells of consciousness, they marched the civilian women in. The women did not come quietly as the men had. They practically stormed into the jail, defiantly singing *There'll Always Be an England*. MacIntyre prayed that Evangeline was not among them.

CHAPTER SEVENTEEN

London 1942

England came as an awful shock. Thirteen years had left Diana with an idealised memory of the climate as soft and gentle. Instead, in July it was cold, wet and bleak and appeared never to have been otherwise. Krystyna was in London and, within a day or two of her arrival, Diana arranged to meet her friend for lunch at the Ritz.

'Be prepared for something quite different from your memories of the twenties,' Krystyna warned her. 'It's packed with foreign royals in exile, English peers who are convinced it's safer than their London flats in air raids, and celebrities who think it's the chic place to be.'

Diana disapproved of the new ambience immediately. 'How have you been able to stand it for so long? It's positively unendurable! I never expected the Ritz to fall short of perfection, but it has, with a vengeance.'

Krystyna laughed. 'Darling, I am glad you said that to me, not to some of the parlour patriots around here. Repeat it too often and you might end up swinging by your neck from a lamppost!'

'But it's true. How do people stand it?'

'Because they have to, you goose! No one chooses to live like this. It's just better that all of us are uncomfortable but able to manage than that the rich go on as before while the poor starve.'

'I thought you hated the Bolsheviks. Lenin or Stalin could have said that!'

Krystyna began to lose patience. 'Diana, I know that you've risked shot and shell to come home and do your bit, but you won't help anyone, least of all yourself, by carrying on like that. We shall get a damned good lunch here because they are still allowed to sell some luxury items outside the five-shilling limit. Enjoy it, try to put yourself in other people's shoes for once, then spare a thought for what you can do to help win the war. It's a lot more constructive than snivelling about slipping standards.'

'So what have you been doing that's so damned hush-hush you couldn't discuss it on the phone?'

Krystyna was still smiling but her words were ice. 'Change the subject, Diana, or I shall get up and leave you here. One does not lightly ask questions like that anywhere, but *never* in public, understood?'

'Understood. Now stop being so disagreeable and tell me all the news.'

'Perhaps you'd better tell me all your news. Then I shall know where to begin. But do be careful what you say. Some things are best left until we're back at the flat.'

'Well, Roland's still Over There. I'll tell you later. Evie's with me. Aunt Hermione is based up in Leicestershire, farming the ancestral acres with the backing of armies of land girls, and down here she's involved somehow with Louise Kerslake in some sort of couture venture – I'm a bit hazy about that one.'

'I'm not – I started ordering clothes from Louise when I came over in thirty-six and I've become quite friendly with her. Tell you later – not for here.'

'Louise! My, aren't we democratic! Even I never got further than Lakie and that was more to enrage Mama than from any really egalitarian feelings.'

'Are you just practising to be a bitch or is this the real Diana Lenton?'

Surprisingly, Diana barely managed to stifle a sob. She looked round swiftly to ensure that no one had noticed her show of emotion, then touched Krystyna's hand. 'Please forgive me, Krystyna. I know I'm being impossible but I just can't stop. The last six months have been hellish, beyond anything I ever contemplated before. I used up every ounce of stamina I had getting us back over from Australia. They were determined we would sit out the war over there. Once poor old Evie rejoined us I thought she'd take charge as usual, but she seems to have had the stuffing knocked out of her for good. I've grown so used to having to be shrill and disagreeable in order to get anywhere at all, that I seem unable to stop now. The worst thing is the realisation of how much I depend on Roland. What a time to find out, not knowing when or even if I shall ever see him again. And as if that were not enough, Aunt Hermione has just told me that Papa has vanished in France without trace. What if they've rounded him up and sent him off to a prison camp?'

Krystyna forgave her immediately. 'Poor you! It is terrible, I know. You keep expecting something good to come along and make it a bit better and instead of that, everyone else is as worried as you, those bastard Germans are bombing us flat and there's not enough to eat! We're all used to it now, but being dropped into it like this when you've been sustaining yourself for so long with thoughts of home must be awful.'

Diana was rapidly returning to normal. 'Yes it is, but you were right. I am being a fool and the sooner I stop it the better I shall cope. It's even worse for a lot of people than it is for me, but you know what I'm like. I never think about other people's feelings if I can dramatise my own! Let's pretend we've only just met and start again, with the chirpy wartime Lady Lenton replacing Dreary Diana, the Displaced Person!'

'Good girl! I give you this; when you face up to your own egotism you're as ruthless with it as you are with other people's vices. Now, if you are prepared to have a virtually all game-and-seafood meal, you can eat like a princess!'

'How come?'

'The "luxury" category covers oysters, smoked salmon and game, among other things, and I happen to know that they have both the first two plus a limited amount of well-hung venison today. Interested?'

'Yes, yes and yes! Do we have to eat it behind screens in case any of the Other Half see us?'

'The secret is to look neither right nor left and to ignore the odd remark from gastronomic Puritans who think we're cheating on the entire principle of rationing.'

'No trouble there. After the practice I've had over the years in ignoring not-so-veiled references to my mad mother and criminal father, I'm an expert!'

They ordered a dozen oysters each, followed by smoked salmon ('On its own, please,' instructed Krystyna. 'I wouldn't insult it by eating brown bread with margarine as an accompaniment, and there's no butter today.') Roast saddle of venison followed.

They ended the meal with a pudding that tasted of wickedly pre-war ingredients, but they ate it gratefully without further comment. Their wine was superb – the Ritz's cellars were still well stocked. Conversation was minimal while they ate. Diana still followed her old crisis eating-behaviour pattern; Krystyna tasted this sort of food seldom enough now to want to appreciate it in silence when it came her way. Over coffee the talk picked up.

'So what have you done since you came back?' Krystyna asked.

'Well, someone had kindly got Aunt H along to meet me, otherwise I don't know what I should have done. Clarges Street has been taken over for some sort of offices, with just a flat left on what used to be the nursery floor. I was dreading the prospect of finding Mama there, but there's been quite a change in that direction.'

'You never did get around to telling me what happened to your Mama after she tried to mess up your wedding. Presumably she got over her little problem?'

'No such luck, at least not for a long time. The family kept her under lock and key for ages, first in a nice little country house with a live-in team of nurses, then in a very expensive series of psychiatric clinics, after Grandpapa decided there was no more chance of curing her that way. It worked, up to a point. By about 1937, she was supposedly fit to be let loose without going batty in public and assaulting anyone who resembled me or Papa. She finished off with a couple of years in Switzerland, which apparently did the trick. She came back to England and divided her time between Stanhope and London. Then Aunt Hermione noticed she was appearing less and less in Leicestershire and seemed to be slipping out of her old social circle in London, too. She started asking questions and discovered that Mama had "found God".'

'Oh, dear! Spiritualism or one of those terrible revivalist sects?'

'Neither, my dear. She discovered the Pope! She's now more Catholic than St Francis of Assissi. Aunt H eventually found her telling her beads in Brompton Oratory.'

'And it never wore off?'

'Not so far, anyway. When hostilities started, she said she'd have no part in any violence, whoever was to blame, and promptly went into Retreat for the duration as the guest of a closed order of nuns. It struck the medical men as a little incongruous that a previously violent schizophrenic was suddenly embracing pacifism so ardently. They gave her a complete physical going-over for a change – before, she'd seemed so physically healthy no one had bothered with that. And that was when they found Mama's trouble was physical, not mental.'

'I don't quite understand.'

'Nor did I, at first. This time they took a look at her head, instead of just asking about what went on inside it. They found a brain tumour which had been growing and causing pressure in all sorts of unfortunate places. At the beginning it caused violence and paranoia but by now it's so bad that it creates vast depression and inertia. It's too late to operate.'

'How do you feel about that?'

'As far as I'm concerned, Krystyna, she's permanently batty and anyway, sane or mad, mentally or physically ill, I hate her. She damaged me far too much for me to feel any compassion. As long as I don't have to see her, I don't care where she is. Apparently it's progressing quite fast now and she's unlikely to be alive more than a few months or so. At least her absence means I have somewhere to stay. I'm in the Clarges Street flat, with those busy little bees officeing away all day below me.'

'What about the boys?'

'Oh – I'm keeping Sebastian with me and of course Cosmo's already at Eton.'

'With Sebastian coming up to prep school age, doesn't Cosmo object to him staying at home when he had to go off to boarding school at about the age Sebastian is now?'

'Oh, of course he does! Cosmo objects to everything if he thinks he can thwart me or irritate me. I've explained that it's different for Sebastian, but he won't see it.'

'He is just a child, Diana. It must seem hard to understand why they are different.'

'I'm sick of telling him that when he was sent back to England to school, we were thousands of miles away and there could be no question of keeping him in Malaya. It would have set his education back years! Now I'm back, I think Sebastian will benefit more from living with me and being a day boy somewhere, or having a tutor. The way we got out of Malaya was enough of a shake-up for the child without sending him away as soon as we got back to England.'

'In that case, don't you think that in the interests of fairness you could have had Cosmo home too for a year or so? Eton would still have been there when you'd convinced him you were treating both of them fairly.'

'Nonsense! I'm not starting to pander to his notions at this stage, just because he thinks life isn't fair. The sooner he learns the truth of that, the better.'

The encounter with her elder son had taken place the previous day. Cosmo had been outraged. 'Why can't I come back to Granby with you and Sebastian? I haven't seen you for *years* and he's had you all the time!'

She was becoming bored. 'Because you're at Eton now. When Sebastian's time comes, he'll have to go to Eton too. In the meantime he can go somewhere as a day boy.'

As Cosmo continued to fume, she was struck by his resemblance to old photographs of her father at the same age. Strange, with such a strong likeness, that the boy had failed completely to capture her love. Sebastian was not the least like Alexander.

Krystyna's voice brought her back to the present. 'Come on, dreamer, let's go to Clarges Street. There are all sorts of things we can't discuss here. Or perhaps you'd prefer to come to my place if the boys are there?'

'No, it's all right. Aunt H is still in town and she's taken them off somewhere for a treat this afternoon. Seems to think Cosmo needs an extra dose of TLC, God knows why! Lakie has Evangeline down in Fulham. We're racking our brains for something she can do to pull round from this terrible black depression she's got into. Really, I'm trying to be patient but it's been months now and still she shows no sign of snapping back.

'There you go again, Diana! Evangeline doesn't know what happened to her husband and the only possibilities are that he's dead or in a Japanese camp. If it were the man I loved, I don't know which would seem worse. At least you know Roland got out and, even if you are separated by thousands of miles, you also know he's safe in Ceylon at present. It'll be years before Evangeline knows what happened to Neill MacIntyre. No wonder she can't handle it.'

Diana agreed Krystyna was talking sense. Her original complaint had not really been caused by a failure to understand Evie's feelings but by irritation that circumstances made her less attentive than usual to Diana's own needs. Now she set aside the topic. Other people's misery always bored her sooner rather than later. She started questioning Krystyna about her mysterious activities.

'Before we start, let me spell something out to you,' said her friend. 'I shouldn't really tell you a word of what follows; I'm breaching every security rule in the book. But I trust you more than anyone I know – God knows why, you old crab! – and I need an objective view of whether I'm really going to be doing anything useful. When you remember not to be self-indulgent you're a hard-eyed little realist, Milady!

'And incidentally, you really must start taking care what you say in public; anywhere outside your really intimate circle, in fact. All those years in the Far East have destroyed

343

whatever tact you might have started out with. This is London and you can't stand around broadcasting your innermost thoughts in that incredibly aristocratic accent on the assumption that half your audience can't understand a word you say and the rest are too unimportant to matter even if they can! On top of the downright offensiveness of your attitude, these days half the people in London will be doing something far too secret to be talked about. One no longer asks detailed questions about what people are doing!' She stopped for breath, half expecting Diana to order her out.

'No wonder Hitler wants to kill the bloody Poles and Jews. I'm beginning to agree with him.'

For a split second Krystyna was outraged. Then she let out a roar of laughter. 'Oh, Diana, I'll give you one thing. You're an original and you're not frightened of offending anybody! Now shut up and I'll give you a general idea of what I'm planning to do.'

Since the beginning of the war Krystyna had been inside Nazi-occupied Europe, helping to run escape routes for Jews, political dissidents and anyone else on the invaders' death list. The Secret Service had recruited her in 1938 and her departure for the family estate during the Munich crisis had been well timed. It enabled her to settle back into local society before the Germans invaded Poland in 1939. It was not in Krystyna's nature to be secretive and her striking appearance militated against such an approach. She special-ised in outrageous behaviour and relied on the conquerors' initial reluctance to persecute aristocrats to keep her ahead. At first she was so successful in running a ski-borne escape route across the south-eastern mountain range that many of her fellow resistance workers thought she was a Nazi col-laborator. Eventually she was forced out along her own escape route, but returned twice on secret missions.

On her second trip back she was almost caught. She got away but it was the end of her usefulness inside Poland. 'It was a laugh, really,' she told Diana. 'Everything went wrong from the beginning on that job. Finally I got on a train to Warsaw and, would you believe it, the resistance boys did their job so well that the rails had been sabotaged and we sat there for hours while they were repaired. Finally I got to Warsaw and of course the contact detailed to pick me up had moved on in case anyone got suspicious. I knew where my safe flat was for the night, so I thought, the hell with it, I'm walking there and if there's a problem I'll deal with it when I arrive.

'The flat was miles away and the weather was stinking hot. I was playing the part of the Polish lady of fashion and had on a Paris suit and steeple heels. By the time I got to the flat I could hardly walk. The Gestapo were closer to getting me than I thought. They had no pictures of Countess Karpinska, but a good description, and when I got off the train two of the vermin followed me from the station. I have the consolation that they must have got as hot and weary as me. Anyway, I eventually arrived at the flat, and to my relief the conniving old concierge there was one of ours. She checked me out and showed me upstairs. I was just making some tea when the Gestapo men arrived. They were so convinced they had me that they'd brought along a pair of my evening shoes which some bright boy had sent up from Sikorsk when the bastards began realising I was working for the Allies.

'Thank God the stupid Huns are so used to those bloody great strength-through-joy maidens with hairy legs and hiking boots that they've forgotten what fashion can do to a girl. The shoes they'd brought along were a delicate little pair of courts in rock-hard patent leather. They were fairly tight when I bought them and I'd worn them only twice, both times after a day with my feet up. That day I'd tramped about four miles in colossal heels. "I think I can guess who you are ... Countess Cinderella," said Goon Number One, obviously having watched too many Peter Lorré movies. "Just pop on your pretty shoes and then we'll be going to Headquarters for a talk." Whereupon he shoved the shoes at me. My dear, they were about three sizes too small because my feet had swollen so much during my walk. I have to admit even I hadn't realised how vain I was until I tried them!

'The Peter Lorré type was furious about being wrong and his sidekick was equally mad because he thought the boss had made them both look stupid with a cheap Hollywood detective stunt. I just stood there on one foot, laughing fit to bust. They weren't to know it was pure hysterics, of course. In the end I did a creditable imitation of a furious Society woman losing patience with nasty common little policemen and slung them out, saying if they thought I was dangerous they'd better come back next day with someone more important, because right now I wanted a cup of tea and a bath. The apparent mistake about the shoes threw them so utterly that they went like lambs. Once they were round the corner, I never waited to find out how long they remained fooled. The concierge tucked me away in a tenement somewhere and the escape route organisers got me out next day. Now I'm concentrating on France. I'm still not too familiar to anyone there, but give me time.'

'It all sounds terribly glamorous and cloak-and-dagger,' said Diana. 'Why do you have doubts about it?'

'Precisely *because* it's glamorous and cloak-and-dagger. I keep wondering whether I let the excitement fool me into thinking I'm useful when perhaps I'm no more of an irritant to the Nazis than a gnat is to a cart horse. I suppose that while I was in Poland, I was pretty sure I was useful. After all, I saw the people I was helping to escape from the country and they would have gone to their deaths without me or someone like me. Now, in France, I'm not so sure. The British secret organisations hate each other almost as much as they hate the Germans. And they hate the French Communist resistance so much it makes my dislike of Bolsheviks look like blood brotherhood. On top of that it's pure luck if an operative gets a good training and I have no faith in the strategic thinking of the men at the top. My training amounted to a week down in Hampshire in a country house, throwing a middle-aged commando around in unarmed combat sessions and being taught how to use pee as invisible ink. Hardly seemed worth the bother. If I have to chuck Germans over my shoulder and piddle on writing paper to win the war, we're lost already.

'I suppose I shall go on; it's the only way I have of actively fighting the Germans now I'm out of Poland. I just needed to spill it all out to someone close, and while I was doing it to look at the whole mess myself.'

'You seem to have supplied the answer yourself, too,' said Diana. 'It's quite clear that where you are, you have a chance of doing something, even by accident, of far greater benefit to the Allied cause than ever you could as a WAAF or a land girl. Admit it, Krystyna, you already have an answer. You're just depressed because the top brass are making such a balls-up.'

'How right you are! I don't suppose you're interested in having a go yourself? Someone you know quite well is running my little outfit.'

'So all this was just a recruitment exercise. Never trust a Pole!'

'Well, only partly. I really did need to talk. Why not come and have a drink with boss man and renew an old acquaintance?'

Reluctantly, Diana agreed, as much out of curiosity about the identity of Krystyna's commander than anything else. She was completely unprepared to meet Edmund Dancey.

'I might have known!' she said. 'You always were the type to revel in this sort of thing.'

'Somehow, Diana, it's hard to escape the impression that you don't mean that entirely as a compliment!'

'Quite right. No need to ask whether you're in this lot out of patriotism. It's purely the attraction of the chase, isn't it?'

'My dear, how did you guess? But one of the first lessons of successful intelligence work is never to trust a patriot. They're invariably prepared to charge into the abyss and take you with them. We schemers are much more reliable.'

'I wonder? Anyway, I don't think it will arise. I've been pondering the whole matter on my way over, and I'm simply not the type. If you want a bit of only semi-competent office help, I shall be delighted to oblige, but I'm not the stuff of which heroic resistance workers are made.'

'I suspect you do yourself an injustice, but think about it

for a while. In the meantime let's have a couple of drinks and talk about other things.'

Diana did not change her mind about working for Edmund Dancey. 'It's nothing to do with not wanting to do my bit and so on; I'm not joining you and Edmund and I'm not joining the ATS or the Land Army either,' she told Krystyna. 'Down in Devon there's a great white elephant of a house waiting for some officious ministerial man to requisition it and then we'll never get it back. Granby needs me more than England does.'

It certainly needed someone. Until the 1860s, Granby had been a prosperous but obscure estate set in the lush farmlands of North Devon. Then a nineteenth-century Lenton had married a rich woman and decided that the modest William and Mary manor house no longer fulfilled his social obligations. It was torn down and a lavishly hideous neo-Italian pile with sixty bedrooms replaced it, complete with a loggia very much after the Piazza dei Signoria and a Tudor revival stable block, built twenty years later when architectural fashions had changed. By the end of the First World War, Granby Hall was in an advanced state of decay. Roland's uncle had insufficient resources to keep it up and it was vastly too big for him anyway.

When the Second World War started the old baronet closed the Hall and moved into the hamstone Elizabethan dower house. He had died there early in 1942. Very little had happened to the estate since then. The land agent had managed to hold off inquisitive visitors from Whitehall and the War Office by asking them to wait until the new baronet emerged from the Malayan débâcle; otherwise the mansion would have become a billet for foreign troops or an army staff college long ago. Over my dead body, thought Diana, travelling down by train one morning in late July. I've waited too long for this moment to let some little bureaucrat take it away!

One way and another, things seemed to be sorting themselves out for her. She was bent on ensuring that the war would intrude as little as possible on her world. When she pointed this out to her aunt, Hermione stared at her in astonishment.

'But what on earth makes you want to hold the war at arm's length? It's swept up all of us – you, Roland, Krystyna, Evangeline and her husband, your father, even your sons are involved in the dislocation. I'd have thought the past six months were calculated to throw you in at the deep end, not to persuade you to avoid it all.' There was a note of disapproval in Hermione's voice.

'That's it entirely. You're all in there digging for victory and I'm not at all sure that there's any point to it all. Somehow I feel detached from it. I want to bring up my family and prepare some sort of permanent base from which Roland and I can live properly when this is all over and he comes back.'

'What if he doesn't come back? And anyway, don't you think it's just as much up to you as it is to the rest of us to ensure that there's a base from which everyone can live, not just Diana and Roland Lenton?'

'I'm sorry if it all sounds impossibly selfish to you, Aunt H, but then you always were a much better person than me. I'm not pretending to be a saint. I had my fill of people making grand gestures for the good of mankind when I was a girl. Papa did enough of that sort of thing to last us all a lifetime and look where it got him! No, I shall cultivate my garden!'

'Really, Diana, even someone at your level of political inertia must see that there is an essential difference between plotting against the Labour Government and fighting Adolf Hitler. If you don't, perhaps Devon is the best place for you!'

'That's exactly what I've been trying to tell you, Aunt.'

'No, it's not; you've been trying to make it sound as though your selfishness is more laudable because you recognise its existence. You're fond of me so you want me to give my blessing to your withdrawal from the biggest fight any of us will ever witness. I'm sorry, my dear, but I'm just not going to. Not that it will make any difference.'

Exasperated, Hermione left her niece to prepare her

departure and went about her own arrangements with Louise Kerslake before returning to Stanhope.

Diana enrolled Sebastian at Dartington Hall, a school whose advanced views of child psychology suited her better than the rigours of a traditional English prep school. It enjoyed the added advantage of being close enough to Granby to permit Sebastian to be a day boy. Before making her first trip down to Granby, she met Louise Kerslake to discuss what should be done about Evangeline.

'I don't know, Lady Lenton; she's a bit better now than when she first came back, but she's far from right. I've been through this sort of loss myself but after the first couple of weeks I knew I'd recover eventually. It's as if something inside Evie has broken and from now on she'll be a different woman. You know I'll be happy for her to stay here unless you want her back with you. She doesn't seem to care what she does.'

'Yes, I'd like her with me. I regard her more as a friend than as an employee and I want to do all I can to get her over this. But I need her, too – or at least, I need the old Evie. If she comes to Granby with me it will be as estate housekeeper, not as a paid companion, and that looks like being an enormous job over the next few years. If anything can make her get better, that should. There will be too much work for her to stay in her shell for long.'

'In that case, take her along and welcome, if she'll come. Staying with me will only remind her of the war every minute. I'm doing all sorts of things for the War Office and if she were helping to run the business she couldn't escape it. I don't think that would help at all.'

Evangeline agreed dully to the move to Devon. She decided to stay with Louise for a month while Diana was making her initial visit, then join her employer when she went down permanently in September.

Granby was a shambles. Diana silently thanked Great Uncle Ralph for having hung on to a couple of horses, because she was able to save precious petrol and ride around the estate. What she saw reduced her to gibbering rage.

Everywhere buildings were in disrepair, land had been half-used or abandoned; uncaring tenants had got away with agricultural murder. The slightly more conscientious had given up caring because the estate was no longer even fulfilling its obligations as landlord to repair and maintain. Only the best farmers had kept things the way they should have been, turning away from the estate office in exasperation and doing their own maintenance work. Overall, the picture was ghastly.

At the heart of the ruin was Lionel Phelps, the septuagenarian land agent. He would have been retired ten years before, or sacked for incompetence, had Roland been in charge. Sir Ralph, increasingly ill and lonely after the early 1930s, had simply ignored the advancing decay and spent more time in London to avoid confrontations with the tenantry. Now Diana was forced to wonder whether matters had gone too far for her to save anything. She telephoned Hermione for advice, but for once her aunt had no time for her.

'I told you what I thought of your Walden Pond notions when you were last in London, Diana. I haven't changed my mind and I don't feel at all sorry for you. Let them carry on to rustic ruin for a while longer; the war makes speculation about the future pretty futile anyway. I'm certainly not dropping the worthwhile work I'm doing up here just to come and tell you how to produce a better turnip.'

'But you yourself are turning Stanhope into a giant farm for the duration. What have you got against me doing something like it down here?'

'Because that's not at all what you have in mind. All you're interested in doing is creating a profitable empire for Lady Lenton. You're the sort who will never say "Dig for victory" without a patronising sneer. And in my small-minded way, I happen to believe in it! You sort things out yourself for once in your life, Diana. When you start showing you mean business instead of just cocking a snook at anyone with ideals, I'll be happy to help. Until then, I'm afraid you're on your own!'

She hung up, denying Diana even the small satisfaction of being the first to break the connection. Diana unearthed some pre-war bottles of gin and spent a maudlin evening drinking gimlets and listening to dirge-like classical music on the wireless. Ye gods, if this was the rural idyll, perhaps she should have accepted Edmund Dancey's offer!

Next morning she was ready for battle. Her first target was Phelps. At 10 am she swept into the dusty estate office in the stable block, startling the old man as he brewed a pot of tea.

'Ah, so that's why the estate is disintegrating. You're operating a tea room instead of a land management office!'

He blinked at her, too aged and dull to writhe under her sarcasm.

'Mr Phelps, you might think you are going to end your days tucked away down here with a sinecure job and all the black market farm produce you can eat; I have different ideas. I gather from my great uncle's will that he guaranteed a passable pension for you. Now is the time for you to take it. Please spend the rest of the week putting your business affairs in order, if that's possible, and then go. You can stay in the Agent's House until next month – that will give you a full six weeks to arrange accommodation elsewhere. If you've found nowhere by then, I shan't make you homeless. You can have one of the two gardeners' cottages which you allowed to get into such disrepair that the staff wouldn't stay there. Perhaps a few months in one of them will help you to understand the necessity of good maintenance.'

'But I've been here since 1910! You can't turn me out now, what will you do for someone to run the place? All the younger men are at the Front!'

'They don't call it the Front anymore, Phelps. That was the last time round. Or have you been asleep during the interim period? Quite frankly, if estate management is what's been happening at your hands for the past thirty years, I can do it myself and save a salary!' With that she left him pottering agitatedly among his dusty papers.

He may be a criminally incompetent old fool, but he's

got a point, she thought later. Who can I get to run the place? The only experienced men around here not in the forces are the working farmers, because they're in 'reserved occupations'. None of them is going to give up his own farm to run mine. At this point she spied Phelps's assistant, Roger Simpson, and vaguely remembered having been told that he was classified medically unfit for military service, due to a childhood ailment which had affected his heart. Diana was not optimistic about his usefulness. How could anyone who had worked under Phelps be even half-way competent?

For the first time since arriving at Granby, she got a pleasant surprise. He seemed a civilised, intelligent young man who was painfully aware of the level of mismanagement on the estate but had been browbeaten by his aged supervisor into letting well alone. When she had finished berating him for such inertia, he pointed out apologetically that in recent years Sir Ralph had made no funds available for improvements, so even a first-class agent could have done no more than mark time.

'Well you won't be marking time any longer, money or no money,' she told him. 'This place has to pay its way and it will never do that in its present state. Unless you anticipate the shortest land management career in history, you'd better get moving. Either you do Phelps's job a damned sight better than he knew how, or you're out too – and you don't qualify for a pension!'

She told him to draw up a full list of estate properties, the rents charged and the repairs contracted. Then she left him to it, having arranged to meet him for a tour of the mansion that afternoon. Diana had stayed in the old dower house since her arrival. It was fairly obvious that the main house required considerable work to be habitable at the moment. Even the dower house was bad. Some of the bedrooms had spreading damp patches; the old stone roof tiles came down like autumn leaves in every Atlantic gale; and the furniture and carpets displayed a shabbiness which could not be dismissed as interesting antiquity.

Preliminary inspection of Granby Hall revealed a far

worse state of decay. 'I don't know that there's much anyone can do,' said Simpson. 'Places in much better repair and with greater architectural merit have been demolished in peace time. Only the fact that resources to do it are unavailable in wartime has saved it so far.'

'I'm not bothered about it being pulled down; if it were only that, I'd kiss it goodbye with no regrets,' she told him. 'It bothers me though that someone from a ministry will decide we're close enough to the Channel and the Western Approaches to be a jolly good site for military use and then we get invaded by a bunch of outsiders. They'll push prices up, monopolise all the black market supplies of anything useful and mop up all the available labour. We'd never survive it. What we need, as we can't knock down the old monster, is some foolproof scheme for using it which won't bankrupt the estate in the process.'

'You might as well ask Hitler and Mussolini to admit they were only pretending and call off the war!'

'The trouble with you, Roger, is that you're a born pessimist. I'm not letting a bunch of Civil Servants or military brasshats get the better of me. I'll manage to come up with something. Now, having shown me what damp rot, dry rot and woodworm can do in the right environment, how would you like to join me for dinner and share the very unofficial hand of pork one of the farmers slipped me yesterday?'

'One of our tenants gave you a present?' He was incredulous.

'Of course; one must make a good impression on the new landlord, after all! Though between you and me, I think he has a weakness for redheads who tell him what a wonderful job he's been doing against impossible odds.'

Him and me both, thought Simpson, looking longingly at the gorgeous dynamo that was Diana Lenton. The fact that she's aware of her potency makes it even worse.

'Come along, Roger, stop mooning! We'll annihilate some of Great Uncle Ralph's claret, too. Roland always said it doesn't go well with pork but there's so much of it we might as well start on it. And then we can try to think up

354

some scheme to feed our white elephant. Black tie, please, even though it's just you and me. I've seen so many country boys the past few days that I need a little sophistication, even if it's illusory.'

They had a pleasant dinner but at first neither could come up with a notion that would hold Whitehall at bay without costing them anything. Having got nowhere, they dropped the subject of Granby for the moment and turned to more general conversation. Simpson had firm views about what had happened in the twenties and thirties to turn Europe into a war zone, and expounded them at length.

'It's all very well to condemn Hitler and Mussolini as odious; God, even the former appeasers are doing it now! But precious few people are bothering to look at why such thugs ever managed to get into power.'

'The self-styled experts keep telling me it's because the Germans are a sort of flock of militant sheep, always ready to line up behind the nearest brass band and march off a cliff; and that the Italians are a bunch of lazy degenerates prepared to follow a poser if he re-creates their historic glories. But I have to confess I find that all that national identity theory a bit glib.' Diana was politically uninformed but no fool.

'Quite. That sort of thinking might be a convenient line for Pathé Newsreel commentaries, but I'm being kind in calling it superficial. In my view, our whole society is dedicated to the ruthless suppression of weak people when economic hard times hit us, so that the privileged remain prosperous at the expense of the poor. These victims then become so oppressed that they look for someone even worse off or someone prosperous but vulnerable on whom they can vent their misery and frustration. We've tailor-made an audience for Hitler and Mussolini. I think our only hope of changing anything is to try to educate all classes from all countries to a level where they know that racial prejudice and authoritarianism are not answers but smokescreens.'

He went on for some time in this vein, increasingly flattered by his hostess's starry-eyed attentiveness. He had just delivered a neat summary of why Communism was too authoritarian an answer and Socialism too wishy-washy, when Diana silenced him.

'That's it, of course! Roger, you're a genius. You just saved Granby Hall from the bureaucrats!'

'What? But I was talking about the failure of international socialism!'

'Only in passing, dear boy! How about an international charitable foundation to bring together children of all nations and social backgrounds, say between the ages of fifteen and eighteen, to learn about a sort of non-denominational approach to government? Think of it – impeccable language teaching, to give everyone a couple of languages in addition to their own; good comparative analysis of political systems without pushing any single system as the right one; first-rate economics training as early as possible. How many schools have you heard of which teach economics to children? It's something they're supposed to get at university and it's dismissed for all but the specialists as a subject for long-haired intellectuals. Think of the publicity value at a time like this of setting up a place where the children of bombed-out East End families, of interned aliens, of Jewish refugees, could all mix together and be taught a non-political creed which equips them to distrust dictators and reject racial persecution. We couldn't lose!'

'But surely people would say we must leave that sort of thing until after the war is won?'

'Ah, that's just the point. Unless you have a scheme like this already functioning when the real need for it arises, you have no chance of setting it up properly. This will be promoted as the blueprint for all the others. And to emphasise its importance to Everyman, we stress that we're not training tomorrow's élite, but trying to give ordinary youngsters insights which will stop them trying to solve their social problems by beating up their foreign neighbour or taking protection money off a small shopkeeper.'

'You've already worked it all out, haven't you? You know, hearing you preach the doctrine like that, I believe you might pull it off!'

'Might? Might isn't enough. Will, you faint-hearted fighter! I *will* do it!'

And she did. Evangeline was dragged from her comfortable misery and bullied into supervising the day-to-day running of the residential facilities. 'But Madam, we haven't even got any facilities to run!' she protested, still nonplussed at the suddenness of the move.

'That's why I need you so desperately, Evie. From now on it will be work, work, work. No time to stop and wonder where everything is coming from. Mark my words, it will come.'

Diana turned out to have a natural flair for publicity and fund-raising. She seemed to know instinctively when they could hope to coax space in the restricted wartime newspapers. Her Society contacts were an excellent starting point for extracting money out of rich non-combatants in the name of a better tomorrow. Even her Aunt Hermione, initially dubious about the whole project, came around to it quickly. She discussed her change of heart while lunching one day with Louise Kerslake.

'I know it's just Diana manipulating the world to serve her own interests, but I have to admit that it's a marvellous idea,' she said. 'If we could create a sort of string of finishing schools for intelligent children of all backgrounds and mix them all up in a first-rate educational environment for a couple of years, it could be an enormous step forward. However much I suspect the motives behind her activities, I have to go along with the value of the probable results. In a sense, I suppose it's usually the self-centred who manage to achieve progress, almost as a side effect of their personal promotion.'

'Well it's working miracles with Evangeline and that alone cheers me up,' said Louise. 'She'll never really be her old self again, but she's getting closer to it than I would have thought possible three months ago.'

Evangeline was enjoying life again for the first time since leaving Singapore. Never one for abstracts, she was galvanised by Diana's obvious need for her help. There was no hint of Lady Bountiful patronising an injured old retainer. Diana needed what Evangeline could offer and was filling every waking moment of Evie's time with activity. Evangeline had long ago privately decided that Neill MacIntyre was dead. Now she even found herself beginning to take an interest in men again; well anyway, in a man.

Roger Simpson was young, handsome and courteous. For a couple of weeks, Evangeline began taking special trouble with her appearance when she knew she would be working alongside him. She managed to have urgent business in the estate office when he was about to come in for a cup of tea, or to be planning work at the Hall when he came up with a prospective contributor to demonstrate what needed to be done. Then she realised that, at least in this area, her efforts were wasted. She walked into the estate office one morning just as Diana was leaving it, and over her employer's shoulder she caught sight of Roger Simpson's face. His expression of dumb worship told her more than she needed to know. He was Diana's man and had room for no one else, although Evie sensed that the only encouragement Diana ever gave him was mild flirtation in the hope of achieving quick results from such behaviour.

It set back Evangeline's recovery for a while. Roger had never led her to believe he found her physically attractive and she did not think of it as rejection; but momentarily she had seen a way of living without Neill MacIntyre and, now that possibility was removed, she was once more forced to contemplate her emotional loneliness. She hoarded the sadness and returned to her work. God knew there was enough of it to keep her mind off romance, she thought.

Donations seemed to pour in from nowhere. Suddenly everyone wanted to be associated with this grand gesture towards peace in the midst of war, and with the beautiful Society woman who was responsible for it.

Only minimal structural work was possible on the Hall, not from lack of funds but because materials were unavailable. 'With our list of donors, we could probably rebuild from scratch on the black market, but somehow I don't think it would look good!' said Diana.

This skimpy work meant that the building was prepared for at least temporary occupation in less than a year. They were just applying the finishing touches before welcoming their first intake of students when Hermione contacted Diana at the beginning of August 1943.

'Don't say you're coming down to build for victory!' Diana was usually a generous spirit, particularly with Hermione, whom she owed so much, but she found occasional teasing irresistible.

'Please, Diana, no jokes today. I don't know whether I should come down or you should come up to London, but we have quite a task ahead of us and you have to get ready for some pretty dreadful news. It's Lettie . . .'

'Oh, for an awful moment I thought you were going to say it was Roland,' Diana interrupted.

'No, there's more. It's Lettie, her little boy, and – and your Papa. Lettie's in London.'

'And Papa and Jean-Luc?' The Devon scenery seemed cold and remote. Diana was practically certain of what was about to be said.

'No, Diana; just Lettie. Jean-Luc is dead. Your father has been deported to Buchenwald from France. He is quite probably dead too by now.'

The silence lengthened. Finally Diana managed to end it. 'Please tell me what happened.'

'Not now. Lettie needs you and you're going to need me. When can you come? Once you've seen her, I'll gladly come back to Devon with you both if you want me.'

'I'll come now, straight away. The noon train – oh damn this bloody war, there is no noon train any more. I'll catch the overnight mail train, Aunt H. Look after Lettie.'

CHAPTER EIGHTEEN

Violet de Montsegur never regarded herself as a great intellectual or a fascinating woman. She was the first to admit that crossword puzzles were her highest pinnacle of mental activity and that cocktails, colourful novels and fashionable clothes comprised her favourite pursuits. She had a profound love and understanding of jazz, but at the time it was still regarded as cheap, ephemeral music so her interest did not heighten her self-esteem. She had always been a timid girl: hardly surprising to anyone who knew her family. Lettie had been terrified of her mother and in awe of Diana, whom she adored. She regarded her father as God's greatest achievement.

When the Hartley world collapsed, it was her tragedy as much as anyone else's, but Diana received all the sympathy and no one save Hermione paid much attention to Lettie, who was dismissed as too young to understand. Temperamentally, she was quite different from Diana. When the smoke cleared after her elder sister's marriage, she settled down to prepare for her Coming Out and found her own methods of dealing with her complex background. Perhaps it was her pliability which made her so desirable; for Lettie quickly discovered that great beauty was unnecessary in the conquest of desirable young men. She was no more than pretty, with attractive reddish-blonde hair and blue eyes and a slender figure, but as soon as she was Out she attracted a stream of eager suitors.

Lettie herself would have been at a loss to explain why they failed to appeal. Almost immediately, she discovered she preferred men from a lower social class, or at least a completely different background from her own. A psychologist might have suggested that her father's example had made her flee men of her own class as potential destroyers. Lettie once told a mildly shocked Hermione that she just seemed to go for the rough stuff.

By the time she reached her mid-twenties, she had gone through a stream of exotic boyfriends. Only the contraceptive advice forcefully imparted by her aunt after Diana's disaster protected her from unwanted pregnancy. When Raoul de Montsegur fell in love with her, she was so relieved to have become involved with someone of whom her family would approve that she accepted him immediately. She spent the next seven years paying for her haste.

Raoul was an impoverished French aristocrat of impeccable ancestry and psychopathic inclinations. He eked out his inadequate income from the depleted family estates in south-western France by lending his name to various undertakings on the fringes of the Parisian luxury industries – leather, jewellery, fashion, antiques and fine art. He was the front man of an art-export company, which traded almost exclusively with Germany and had valuable contacts in the upper reaches of the Nazi Party. By 1938 he was supplying them with information about potential Nazi sympathisers in France as well as with pictures and porcelain. His information was invariably more valuable than the rather shoddy fine art he dispensed.

The very qualities which had attracted him to his English wife also made him ill-treat her. In a bad mood, he would occasionally hit her because it made him feel better. Then he found that her silent, fearful acceptance excited him. Here was a being completely in his power – how exhilarating to subdue it *completely*! By the late thirties, Lettie was taking frequent heavy beatings and feeling too ashamed to tell anyone that her handsome husband did it for fun. She did not dare to leave because the only thing they now shared was devotion to their son Jean-Luc, born on Christmas Day 1937. Raoul had convinced her that if she attempted to cut and run, taking Jean-Luc with her, he had enough high-level connections to have her stopped and to take the boy away. This thought was so unbearable that she preferred to stay and take her beatings. Lettie was stronger and more resilient than she thought.

When Lettie finally made a fearful half-confession about the violence in a letter to Diana, her sister was too far away to help, even had she found a method of doing so. Lettie only gave away even this much information because she felt the need to explain why she was unable to meet her beloved father when he proposed renewed contact. Having written to her sister she committed one of her bravest acts: she changed her mind and wrote to Alexander Hartley, arranging to meet him in Paris. She had been right in her hints to Diana of what Raoul would have done if he had discovered her. As it happened he was relieved to get rid of her because he wished to entertain some extremely dubious acquaintances at Château Segur in her absence. He knew that as long as she left Jean-Luc behind there was no doubt about her returning.

Alexander Hartley had worn reasonably well. He was still handsome, still distinguished. She was surprised at how French he seemed to have become. As children, she and Diana had always been permitted to tease him about his 'Milford' accent. He spoke perfect idiomatic French but his accent was execrable. Now that had changed. No one overhearing him placing his order at la Coupole would have thought him anything but a cultivated Frenchman.

'Papa! What on earth happened to your accent? It's wonderful, but so unexpected!'

'Hush, dear girl. When in Rome, y'know!' He refused to discuss it further.

He was angry and interested in her confession about some of Raoul's behaviour towards her and her description of her husband's increasingly extremist political involvement. Lettie had a good cry, for once without her father seeming to care about what people might think.

'I tell you what, Lettie. If you can come up with some way I might be able to see you more often, at least you'd have me to confide in; you know, just talk it out when he was really impossible, that sort of thing. I know it's rather feeble, but as long as he has young Jean-Luc to use as a threat, I can't offer anything better. I know what these damned Frogs are like when a foreign wife goes to law against her French lord and master. You wouldn't have a prayer. Let's try to meet and talk as often as we can, and perhaps later I can think of a better solution.'

'Where would we meet? Somehow I can't imagine being able to get to Paris too often on my own – anyway, he's here such a lot for the export business he might even see us together – and Marseille would be right out of the question. Wait a minute – how easy would it be for you to get to Lyons?'

'I've no great allegiance to Marseille. It's just somewhere to rest my head. As long as I could live fairly cheaply, I'd even move to the area if it helped. Why?'

'In that case, I think I've got it! Oh, goody, it'll be such a relief to see someone who really cares about me!'

'Come on, Lettie, do explain. You're not making sense. Why Lyons?'

'He's been getting a lot of things for the export business down there and to tell the truth he's not terribly interested in the stuff.' She giggled. 'You only have to see the quality of most of it to realise that! Recently he's found it more and more of a chore to do buying trips down there and he's fond of shouting at me about how I'd help him out by going instead, if I had any backbone at all.'

'Lettie, my girl, I think you've just developed a back-bone!'

It was even easier than she had hoped. They came to an arrangement whereby Lettie went off for four to five days once a month and bargained for the florid, over-stated provincial period pieces which seemed to please the German market so much. But by the time this was all arranged, Lettie was becoming increasingly disturbed at the thought that her father was risking his life to remain in touch with her.

At first it had appeared that the French would show the Germans they were still a first-class military nation. Some British citizens returned to Britain but there were still plenty of expatriate Englishmen and women scattered around France. Then came France's catastrophic fall in 1940 and the remaining British subjects were evacuated through Bordeaux or across the frontier into Spain.

'What are we going to do, Papa? I've got so used to you being here that it will be awful to manage without you!'

'Lettie, much as you love your son, I beg you to leave him with his father and come to England. I deserted you in 1927, I know, but I can't do it again. I'm not going back unless you come too.'

She looked at him, aghast. 'Oh please, Papa, don't leave it up to me! You know what a fool I am! I'll never be able to cope with the decision. How can I choose between you and Jean-Luc?'

'Don't be silly! There's no choice involved. De Montsegur may be a villain, but I've heard enough to be sure he'd die for his son. You're not abandoning the boy to any danger. When the Huns take over, Raoul will be treated like a king by the sound of things. You, my girl, are a different matter. You retain your English nationality, remember, although you're French by courtesy as his wife.'

'Yes, but they've not taken this bit of France. They're leaving well alone here, as long as we buckle down and accept the Vichy Government, and nobody seems to be refusing.'

'Dearest Lettie, you have a woefully inadequate grasp of what the Germans have in mind, I think. They won't stop at half of France. It's only a matter of time before they snatch the rest. And then your French title and husband won't protect you for more than five minutes. I want you out, now!'

'I really can't, Papa. I'm sure you're needlessly worried. But you're in far more danger than I would be. You're an Englishman abroad; no question of any French connections. They'll intern you immediately if ever they do what you think they will.'

'Ah, so now my uninformed little girl thinks they might just swallow the whole of France.'

She blushed and looked away. 'Well, umm, one does get to hear lots of things at the château from time to time . . .'

'Care to tell me?'

What she said over the next ten minutes increased his determination to get her out, but she was adamant that she would not leave without Jean-Luc. Fear for Hartley's own safety reduced her to tears as she tried ineffectually to persuade him to go back to London.

'Once and for all, Lettie, no! I will compromise, however. We'll stop meeting for the present and I shall just blend into the scenery, I think. I am not completely without friends and, remember, the Americans are still neutral. If I can persuade their legation to accredit me, I might be all right. Does that satisfy you?'

'No, Papa, but even I'm not stupid enough to think that will make any difference. Is there anything at all I can do to help before we part company?'

'Not really, my dear, except to take the greatest care of yourself. And try not to think too ill of my past misdeeds.'

'I never did, Papa. I didn't give a damn if you'd done it or not. I just loved you, rain or shine. Please don't get killed for my sake.'

'Now, now, it'll not come to that!'

'Won't it? I wonder.'

He managed to stay ahead of the chase until the summer of 1943, first posing as an American and later, after Pearl Harbor made that identity as worthless as British citizenship, as a Frenchman. Latterly he became a major link in one of the escape routes guiding fugitives down to the Spanish border.

Klaus Barbie's reign of terror around Lyons put a stop to his activities. He was co-operating with the combat resistance organisation when one of the group betrayed them. Hartley was picked up with three others – Frenchmen – when the SS raided the home of a captured member. As he was herded into a car to return to their headquarters, he wondered whether he would be able to resist much of what they were undoubtedly about to do to him. On balance, he thought not, so it was just as well that as an outsider working only temporarily with the group, he knew

365

virtually nothing of their activities. It might prove painful to him, but few others would be harmed by his revelations.

As the Germans bundled them up the steps of Montluc Prison, Hartley stumbled and lurched forward into the path of a civilian who was leaving the building. The man uttered a curse as they collided, presumably, thought Hartley, to dissociate himself publicly from suspect fellow countrymen. Steadying himself, he glanced into the man's face and had difficulty in concealing the astonishment of confronting Lettie's husband, familiar from the wedding picture she had shown her father. The Frenchman glared at him long and hard, then one of the soldiers behind them gave Hartley a shove that sent him sprawling and Raoul de Montsegur hurried away.

Inside the building, Hartley suffered nothing worse than the sort of roughing-up he had endured as a boy on the sports pitch. He knew better than to think it could last. When he was led away and locked up alone, he almost wished they had started on him immediately. He preferred not to have time to contemplate his future. When he was eventually pushed into an interrogation room, the first thing he noticed was the little pile of his personal documents in front of the man seated at the table. His forged identity card was on top.

Then his attention was diverted to the man. Francois André, a long-time member of the French Nazi Party, was perhaps the most infamous torturer in Lyons after Barbie. A traffic accident had hideously distorted his mouth to the shape of an open wound, earning him the nickname Gueule Tordue. He led Barbie's a hundred-and-twenty-strong personal army of aggressively pro-Nazi Frenchmen and was frequently turned loose on newly-arrested resistance suspects to soften them up. One look at his horribly distorted face was enough for Hartley.

He smiled timidly at his would-be tormentor and said: 'Monsieur, why am I here? I was sent to collect some old stamp albums for my friend's shop at the Aubrey house and the next thing I knew I was being dragged along here. There must surely have been a mistake; I'm a law-abiding citizen.'

Gueule Tordue did not move. 'We shall see about that. What's a colonial doing here in the first place, I'd like to know? Lyons isn't exactly a seaport!'

'Ah, Monsieur, I haven't been back to Martinique since I was a schoolboy. I came here to get an education and stayed with my father's parents. I wouldn't know my way round the island without a guide nowadays!' The monster's glare silenced him. Mustn't talk too much, old chap, sign of nervousness. They'll have you singing like Nellie Melba soon, anyway.

He watched almost objectively as the interrogator stood up and moved towards him. This is where I find out what pain really is . . . But there was a reprieve. As André drew level with Hartley, the door opened and a uniformed SS man came in, said something to André in an undertone, and both men walked out, completely ignoring their captive. The iron door crashed shut and he was left alone. The time dragged out into what seemed to be days but was less than an hour. Then someone else, a German, came in and took Gueule Tordue's place. He flipped through the pile of identity papers. Finally he looked up with a weary, sneering laugh.

'How long will SOE try to get away with all these lost island boys?' he asked, in English.

Hartley feigned incomprehension. 'Speak French, please Monsieur. I understand very little English.'

'And I believe in fairies, Lord Fauntleroy.' Hartley remained impassive. The German resumed in French. 'All right, Monsieur what d'you call? – ah, yes, le Farge; we'll skip the language lessons for now. Let's put it another way. In the past year I've had about a dozen stupid resistance men and British agents through here whose papers claimed they were born in Martinique before 1902. Now, le Farge, coming from that island, you undoubtedly know better than I that St Pierre on Martinique was buried by a volcanic eruption that year. Very conveniently, all the birth records were destroyed. Who can prove now whether you or any of the others were born there?'

Hartley contrived to look injured. 'Sir, both my parents

perished in that tragedy. It's the reason I never returned there from school. Am I to be blamed if traitors try to use my family misfortune to pretend they are true Frenchmen?'

His interrogator did not bother to reply, but merely spat on the floor in front of him, then resumed speaking in English. 'Come on, you old bastard, let's drop the pretence. Don't you like the name Hartley any more?'

Alexander was virtually paralysed. How had they done it? No one in Lyons knew his real name. If the resistance had betrayed him, all the Germans would have was his codename, Richelieu. His mind circled the possibilities. Raoul de Montsegur? But how? The man had never met him and from what Lettie said had refused to have his name mentioned once he knew the unpatriotic gossip about the Petrograd Communiqué. He was baffled. The SS man spoke again, partly in French, partly in English.

'Don't worry, "old chep"! I'm not going to beat you up. We've got a little treat in store for you, so I'll just leave you here to cool off for a while and think things over – like how much you plan to tell us and how soon – then I'll be back with the goods. Don't rush off anywhere. As you would say, ta-ta for now!' With a grotesque parody of a wave, he was gone.

Again, Hartley was unsure how long he waited alone. Eventually a guard opened the door and he was hustled back to his cell. There was a tiny barred window up close to the ceiling and daylight filtered thinly through the dirty panes. He was surprised that evening had not come. Today seemed to have lasted for ever. Gradually the weak light faded. The cell was furnished only with a broad wooden bench and a bucket. Some time after dark, a tin cup of water was thrust in to him, but no food was proffered. He did not sleep.

It was still pitch dark when they came for him. Two guards dragged him from the cell, along the corridor and back into the interrogation room. This time neither Gueule Tordue nor the German was there. Instead he was confronted by Lettie and a little auburn-haired boy whom he took to be Jean-Luc. Hartley forced his face to remain utterly unmoved. To his astonishment, his supposedly brainless daughter turned on the guards and started demanding to know, in outraged tones, why they had dragged her and her son half-way across France in the middle of the night to stare at some old Frenchman. She was in mid-rant when a middle-aged man arrived, clad in a smart grey suit and carrying, of all things, a long-haired Persian cat. He sat down beside the table, put the cat on his lap and stroked it until it purred like a miniature engine. The child stared at it, fascinated. Lettie turned on the man.

'I think you have a great deal of explaining to do, Monsieur! You are surely aware that my husband, the Comte de Montsegur, is a staunch supporter of your Führer and a loyal Frenchman. He will be outraged when he learns that you have imprisoned his wife and son. I hope you can produce some good reason for this insult!'

'A thousand pardons, Madame la Comtesse.' His French was heavily Germanic. 'It is regrettable that you had to be disturbed, but we had reason to believe that you knew this man and it is so important that we prevent sabotage, we felt you would understand the need to bring you here.'

'No, I do not understand! I've never seen him before in my life and I have no desire to do so again. My son is frightened, I haven't seen my husband since two days ago and I am very upset. Now kindly remove us from this dungeon and introduce this . . . gentleman to someone who might have a better notion of his identity!'

As she spoke, Jean-Luc had been moving closer to the cat, fascinated by its purring, its marvellous shaggy coat and its huge golden eyes. He was within inches of the animal when the grey-suited man half turned, smiled lazily at him and said 'You like cats, little boy?'

'Oh yes, sir! We have lots at home but they never come indoors because the dogs chase them out. He is very handsome; so smooth.'

'You are very handsome, too. I bet your auburn hair is as silky as his coat.' The man reached out, his pale, shapely hand casually rumpling the boy's longish curls. As his fingers touched the child's scalp, they twined viciously into the hair and he wrenched Jean-Luc feet into the air, throwing him down sideways like a bundle of washing.

The boy let out a scream of agony. Lettie lunged forward, crying out herself, but a guard grabbed her before she had moved a pace. Jean-Luc, still in pain and deeply shocked, started to scurry across the floor to his mother. The man with the cat watched him with a tolerant smile, then made an almost imperceptible signal to the guard, who loosened his grip on Lettie. She embraced Jean-Luc and showered him with caresses and comforting baby talk, her desire to attack the German wiped out in the need to look after her son. Hartley exercised every shred of will power not to over-react.

After a moment, in the most bewildered voice he could muster, he said: 'Please, sir, don't hurt this little boy any more. I really don't know what you expect the lady to say, but I don't think she can help you. If you think she knows me, surely you can see you must be wrong . . .' He was silenced by a blow across the face from one of the guards.

Suddenly the German seemed to lose patience with the whole business. 'Oh, for God's sake take them all away. I want some breakfast. I'll deal with them later.'

Alexander Hartley was man-handled down the corridor again a few hours later. To his relief, his daughter and grandson were absent this time. The cat man was back, without the animal. Instead he now carried a truncheon. He gestured at one of the two chairs beside the table. Hartley sat down, feeling sick.

'Hands on the table!' He obeyed, horribly certain of what would happen next. The truncheon crashed down across his fingers, smashing them. He was amazed that he managed to suppress any sound beyond a grunt. The pain was unbelievable. His tormentor moved away, almost casually, as though he had just patted a friend on the shoulder. Hartley concentrated on feeling relieved that so far only one hand had been attacked.

'That, *mister* Hartley, is a little foretaste of what is to come. But as we already know who you are, don't you think this is all a little pointless? I assure you that you will tell us all about your activities eventually. Why not save yourself and your family further pain and do it now?'

Hartley said nothing, partly because it was futile but mainly because he did not trust himself to speak without crying in pain. He had doubled up over the hand when the man attacked it. Now, with an immense effort of will, he placed it back, flat on the table. The fingers were smashed into a dreadful misshapen mass and were already swelling. The immediate trauma of the blow had prevented much blood loss yet, but he knew it would soon start, and that the pain would get much, much worse. At that point, feeling some gratitude to Providence, he fainted. When he recovered consciousness, he wished he would pass out again. Lettie was back, alone, and plainly terrified for her son. She took one look at Hartley's hand and let out a moan of horror. But she did not break.

Turning on the interrogator, she shouted: 'What a pointless bit of beastliness! Can't you see we don't know each other, you disgusting, stupid man? Leave him alone and bring me my son!'

The man turned on her and began slapping her face, systematically, back and forth, with a sound like a metronome, magnified a hundredfold. In seconds she was weeping, but apparently as much in anger as in pain. He stopped as abruptly as he had begun. 'All right, Madame. Since you value family togetherness so much, I'll bring you your son. Here he is.'

The door opened and the guard dragged in what appeared to be a pile of rags. It was Jean-Luc, unconscious, his face a mask of blood. The guard dropped the small body in front of Lettie and after a moment the child moved slightly and a tiny moan escaped the ruined lips. Lettie was incoherent. She fell to her knees beside the child and cradled him against her breast, sobbing brokenly. Her dress quickly became soaked with blood. No one moved or spoke. The child moaned again, then shuddered once. After that he was still.

The interrogator watched impassively a while longer, then said 'Come, enough of reunions, we have business to complete.' He moved across to Lettie and dragged her bodily back on to her feet, as unconcernedly as if he were helping her to board a bus. Then he reached out, seized the shoulder of her thin frock and ripped it away. Almost in a continuous motion, he started beating her about the back and ribs with the truncheon.

Hartley lurched forward, gasping at the fresh agony any movement unleashed in his smashed hand, and forced Lettie's body out of the way with his own, catching a glancing blow from the truncheon on his shoulder as he did so. He raised his uninjured hand to the German.

'That's enough! Christ, nothing is worth this. Get her away, now – and the boy. I'll tell you all I can, but it's precious little.'

He was faintly surprised that they were content with the information he gave them about the escape route and made no more than a half-hearted attempt to extract more from him – an attempt, nevertheless which left him minus most of his front teeth and with a burst eardrum. Next day, on the train which took him on the first leg of his journey to Buchenwald, he learned why. A fellow-prisoner told him that two of the three captured Frenchmen had broken. Their stories had confirmed that the Englishman knew nothing about their day-to-day activities and was only with them while opening up a new escape route. The Germans had desisted because they knew he had no more to tell them.

Lettie was taken away and bundled into a cell, where she suffered a mental collapse over the murder of her son. Eventually a woman in a white starched cotton overall arrived and took her away from the prison area. She was lightly tranquillised, given a bath and clean night clothes, then put to bed in a room that was like a hospital ward. When she awoke from a drugged sleep, she was escorted to an ordinary interview room of the type to be seen in any civilian police station.

Werner Knab was waiting there for her. He was the regional SD chief, physically the sort of German who was photographed for propaganda posters. Tall and muscular, he had the classic Aryan blond hair and blue eyes – the eyes a pale glacial shade like a lifeless mountain lake. He wore an expensive suit, his only political emblem a small Nazi Party lapel badge.

Knab was courteous and friendly to Lettie. He clicked his heels and bowed slightly. 'Good morning, Countess. I regret the unfortunate incidents here in the past twenty-four hours. Sometimes ugly acts are necessary and loyalty to the Fatherland forces on us actions which would be barbaric in other circumstances. I wish it had been possible to make things easier for you and I respect your loyalty to your father.'

'Wh-what have you done with him?'

'Unfortunately, as an enemy alien, we were forced to deport him to Germany for internment. Now that he has disclosed the information he was concealing, we shall not need to continue interrogating him, so when hostilities end we shall, of course, repatriate him. We shall also ensure that you are returned safely to your home.'

Lettie had managed to seal off anything more than the most superficial acknowledgement of what they had done to Jean-Luc. The dam would burst soon, but for the moment she was able to function only as long as she kept that one horror tightly locked away.

'Please, before I return to the château, tell me one thing. How did you know he was my father?'

'Yes, I don't think it will matter now if I do that. It was really a strange coincidence. It was a combination of your husband's good citizenship and accident.

'Raoul! I might have known he had something to do with it! But how . . .?'

'He had some information to report to Sturmbannführer Barbie which could not wait until their regular lunch date in Lyons, so he travelled here a couple of days ago. Monsieur le Comte had to come here to Montluc to make the report. As he left, one of a group of resistance men who had just been rounded up was pushed out of a van and bumped into your husband. He recognised your father from the framed photograph you keep in your bedroom at the château.'

She gazed at him in horror and disbelief. 'You're saying Raoul betrayed me? No, that's impossible. He'd throw me away without a thought, but never Jean-Luc!'

'All sacrifices are worthwhile for the Reich, even sons. Your husband would have been the first to agree with that.'

'Would have been?'

'I further regret to inform you, Madame la Comtesse, but your husband was killed in a resistance ambush on his way back to your home.'

'Liar! You killed him too, didn't you? What's wrong, were you afraid he'd turn on you for killing his son and give you some trouble? Did you kill him off just in case?'

'Really, Madame, you are clearly overwrought by your great loss. We all understand that. It is a time of dreadful grief for you. That is why we are sending you back home to the château.'

'You're freeing me? Why, d'you intend bumping me off on the way home, like Raoul?'

'Sturmbannführer Barbie does not forget his friends, Madame. He said the least he could do for a fallen comrade was to ensure the safety of his widow!' His smile chilled Lettie to the bone. She turned and let the white-overalled nurse guide her away.

In the ensuing days she went through several types of hell. Initially half the locals avoided her because they regarded her as a collaborator, while the others ostracised her on the assumption that, as an English widow in German-occupied France, she was a dangerous acquaintance. In the end good fortune intervened. Someone somewhere in the resistance decided she deserved some help and could be useful to them at the same time. They arrived out of the blue at the château with a couple of other fugitives on their way through to Spain. They offered to take Lettie along if she sheltered them for a few days until the other route guides were in position. She agreed, and a month later, demoralised and close to mental collapse, she was reunited with Diana and Hermione in London.

They held each other and sobbed for a long time over their father.

'Oh, God, Lettie, if only I'd been big enough to answer his letter when the European war was just starting and had held out some hope of reconciliation, he'd have come back here and nothing would have happened to you, Jean-Luc or Papa. It's all my fault!' As usual, Diana found a centre-stage role irresistible.

'It's no use looking back. He's gone now, and so's poor little Jean-Luc,' said Lettie. 'At least Papa had the chance to die bravely. He certainly made up for a lot with that. I wish there was some way we could remember him publicly. There'll be so many dead heroes in France when this lot ends that no one will notice the heroism of one more Englishman.'

'I've got it!' Diana was seized by love for her father and the desire to show how proud she was of him once more. 'The new school. We'll call it Alexander House! It shall be our homage to him for showing the world he was no traitor!'

Alexander House opened in September, to waves of publicity and praise for its unselfish aristocratic founder. By then, Lettie was having a nervous breakdown at Stanhope.

CHAPTER NINETEEN

Diana was at her worst when there were not plenty of eligible men around. At times during the early development of Alexander House, she privately cursed her own stupidity for managing to avoid the requisitioning of Granby Hall. At least there was a chance it would have been taken for officer training or something and she would have been surrounded by adoring males! Now she had a choice of Roger Simpson, the aged local GP, the vicar and a collection of monosyllabic farmers. Roland was still up to mysterious dirty tricks in the Far East and apart from occasional hints from home-coming comrades, she had no idea what he was doing. She was pretty certain that she was not going to see him again until the war was over.

After a listless start, Evangeline had taken over the administration of Alexander House as if born for the job. She served as mother substitute for the young new arrivals; tyrannical clerk of works to the jobbing builders; and confidante for half the area. Between tasks she also managed to run Diana's domestic establishment on oiled wheels, in spite of the shortages of both goods and money. She endured Diana's growing waspishness for a couple of months before losing patience.

'For God's sake, Milady, stop prowling about like a tigress and go on up to London for some hunting. I'm sick of you under foot when you're so bad-tempered!'

'Hunting, Evie? What do you mean?' The archness of Diana's question left Evangeline in no doubt that it was rhetorical.

'Your trouble is you're not being admired enough. It's no good expecting it from Roger Simpson; he's too much of a country bumpkin to get it right. As for the vicar and the doctor, neither of them looks like being long for this world! No, you need a few smouldering glances from a Free Frenchman across a crowded room.'

'Hmm, it'll be selections from Noel Coward next, by the sound of things. Well, if you think I'm that much of a pain, perhaps I had better take a break.'

'If you value my continued services at all, either here or down in Alexander House, you'll make it more than a break, Madam. You'll leave me to get on with it and you'll buzz off to London on a permanent basis, fund-raising or something – and come down here for a few days when you feel like it. Otherwise you'll get downright unbearable!'

'I thought you wanted me to help you pull through.'

'I don't know about helping me pull through; you're such a strain on my nerves at present that I think you're shortening my life. Come on, get away out of it. You know you'll be far happier. You only like the country when it's full of men to flirt with.'

So Diana returned to London, soon ending the pretence, even to herself, that she had enjoyed Granby once the novelty had worn off. If I'm to live happily in the country, she thought, it has to be in the lap of luxury. When it's all shortages and poverty, give me the city any day.

Hermione had been far more gentle with her since the news of Alexander Hartley's torture and deportation. Hermione still spent most of her time at Stanhope following the old Earl's death, particularly since Lettie was convalescing there. But she often came to London for short visits and now Diana became her friend in a way that had not been possible when she was a green girl and her aunt a mature married woman. At forty-seven, Hermione was still very attractive. Her hair retained its natural dark colour and as she took food rationing seriously she was slimmer than she had been for years. Her face was practically unlined and her steady, serene gaze as ageless as it had been sixteen years before. Her excellent education, wide reading and unfailing interest in other people ensured that she had friends everywhere. She gave regular parties where the most unlikely combinations of guests turned up.

One evening in the spring of 1944, Diana went to a drinks party which Hermione had arranged to make what she called a world-shattering announcement. Diana was surprised to see Louise Kerslake among the guests and suddenly realised what the news would be. Almost before the thought had formed itself, Hermione confirmed her suspicions. She called everyone to order by rapping on the marble chimneypiece with the handle of a paper knife.

'Ladies and gentlemen, now for my important announcement! You might have thought I was content to dig for victory and leave commerce to others. But my merchant blood will out and I've finally decided to take the plunge into trade. Starting in a small way thanks to cloth rationing, but, we hope, expanding rapidly when we've beaten the Germans, Louise Kerslake and I are going into partnership to open a British couture house! Louise – you'll be the designing talent – I'm only the Angel! Come and take a bow.'

Smiling, Louise moved forward. 'Hermione is doing herself less than justice. She has chosen premises, arranged the backing and set up some hard-headed financial projections. All we need is unlimited clothing coupons and peace.' She raised her glass, still half full of the Earl of Ingleton's pre-War Dom Perignon. 'To the Countess of Ingleton, England's most aristocratic *couturière*!'

Everyone joined in good-naturedly, Diana stifling her snobbish inclination to deny Hermione's aristocratic credentials. Shortly afterwards she found herself standing close to Louise. 'Congratulations, Lakie! A well-deserved boost. I still have that first gorgeous evening gown you made for me, carefully packed in tissue paper in the hope that handkerchief hems and flat chests come back. It was sensational, and I'm sure you will be a great success.'

'I do hope so, Lady Lenton.' Louise knew better than to address Diana by her first name, whatever her level of intimacy with the woman's aunt. 'Hermione has shown a great deal of faith in me. Now it's up to me to justify it.'

As if sensing the constraint between the two, Hermione moved across to join them. She was followed by a short, thickset man with the brightest blue eyes Diana had ever seen. 'Diana, this robber baron is Edward Rathbone. He won't leave me in peace until I've introduced him to you, so here we are. Eddie, my niece, Diana Lenton. Diana, Edward Rathbone.'

Hermione drew Louise away to warmer company and left Rathbone with Diana. He was the same height as she, and at close quarters the blue eyes were disconcertingly direct. After a moment's confrontation, he smiled broadly. 'Most people start glancing away after one of my board-room glares,' he said. 'By the look of you, you make it a point of honour not to.'

'Of course! Anyway, I've never seen such blue eyes and I was fascinated.'

'Oh, the colour makes up for the lack of it in my hair. I went white at thirty.'

She had been assessing his age as they talked and now estimated it as somewhere over fifty. 'I'm fifty-seven in a fortnight', he told her.

'Mind-reader! How did you know I was wondering?'

'Because when you looked at me, I got the distinct impression that you found me as attractive as I find you. I spent a good five minutes wondering about your age before Hermione introduced us. You've been doing the same about me for the past thirty seconds, haven't you?'

She smiled and nodded, then said: 'This is ridiculous! One doesn't run into strange men at parties and start speculating openly about their age or anything else so personal.'

'In this case, one does. I shall call you Diana if I may. At fifty-seven I have a lot of catching up to do and not much time to do it. I hope you'll permit me to skip the formalities with that as my excuse.'

'Have I a choice?'

'Not really, but occasionally I like to give a woman the illusion, at least. Incidentally, please call me Eddie. Edward makes me sound like a dead king. Still, given my age I'm probably lucky it's not Albert!'

'In that case, I shall call you Albert. No man deserves to get away with the overweening arrogance you're displaying!'

'You like it, though. I bet no one has ever told you what to do before.'

'No one since my mother went batty – Albert.'

'You have quite a capacity for party-stopping remarks.'

'So I've been told.'

'Well, then, let's stop this particular party and go and find some dinner. I have a feeling that you're not overwhelmed by the big announcement.'

'Oh, I'm quite glad for Louise Kerslake. She's so talented that she'll make her fortune now. But I can't quite see why Aunt Hermione needed to go back into trade. Her family have already made enough out of it to allow her to keep her hands clean for the rest of her days.'

Rathbone scowled, his good humour lost. 'And half the male members of your family, from what I hear. If you've decided you enjoy my company, I'll tell you now that I stay in a better humour with people who treat Hermione Digby-Lenton as the splendid creature she is and don't try to knock her down a few pegs because of cheap snobbery. From what I can gather, you're fairly beholden to her yourself.'

Diana flushed. 'You seem to know a lot about my intimate family history. Is Aunt Hermione in the habit of broadcasting it among her cocktail acquaintances?'

'I dare say you're far too self absorbed to realise it, but Hermione does not lightly divulge what you call intimate family history. I happen to be her closest friend, dating back to the days before she rescued you from a pretty grim girlhood. I was in love with her once, a very long time ago, and I still love her deeply in the passive sense. I've no intention of letting you insult a woman whom you owe so much, so I think perhaps I should withdraw the dinner invitation.'

Diana was deeply contrite. 'Please forgive me, Eddie. I shall offer my apologies to Aunt H, too, if you think I should. That was a thoroughly nasty little exchange and I regret it deeply. At this point I normally put it down to strain because my husband is overseas, but if I'm honest with you, it's because I'm a horrible bitch and I tend to behave like this once in a while.'

'Bravo for admitting it! That doesn't make the bitchery better, but at least you're not too far gone to recognise it for what it is. No, don't apologise to Hermione. It would be self-indulgent. Why let her know you think that way when it's unnecessary? Come on, savage, I shall give you that dinner and try to make you see the error of your ways!'

The relationship they started that evening introduced Diana to something previously beyond her experience: a man with the strength to dominate her and the desire to do so. Initially their physical intimacy stopped at clasping hands and fleeting social kisses, but they were both aware that this was just a prelude to more profound involvement.

'I don't know why I let you get away with it', said Diana one day after he had bullied her through a visit to Harrods. 'You're the exact opposite of everything I find acceptable in man or woman and yet I let you take over my life and set my standards. No one has ever got away with that before.'

He was unrepentant. 'Your trouble is that with all your apparent sophistication, you're as naive as a debutante in some things. You enjoy my bullying in the same way as your little sister enjoyed all those unsuitable affairs you told me about. I'm a fascinating bit of rough trade and you excuse your own behaviour by thinking you're just going along with it for the moment as a minor diversion. In fact it's what you've been looking for all your adult life and now you've found it you have no idea how to handle it.'

'Eddie, what makes you tick? One minute you're mingling with all the best people, with not a single give-away of your origins in your speech or behaviour; the next, you're deliberately being vulgar with me in order to shake me up a bit. What made you into the man you are?'

'Now that's a Lady Muck sort of question if ever I heard one – the sort of thing I always expect the Queen to ask when she picks her way around the bombsites the morning after a disaster!' He held up his hand to silence her indignant protest. 'And I know that like most of your ultra-snob set, you regard the Queen as too middle-class for words. Don't kid yourself, darling, she's playing at it. Her line is more ancient than yours and she could teach even you a thing or two about manipulation!

'Now, to get back to me. I'm amazed you've known me for three weeks and this is the first time you've raised the subject. You can hardly have thought I was qualified by birth to move in your exalted circles, so where did you think I came from?'

'I failed totally to place you anywhere. I asked Aunt H in the end and she smiled like the Sphinx and said either I'd have to ask you myself or remain ignorant; she had no intention of ruining such an intriguing puzzle for me.'

'I dislike many things about you, Diana, but I admire your honesty enough for little else to matter. Even on a small thing like that, it would have been so easy for you to give me some old fanny about the thought never having crossed your mind until now, rather than admit you'd been prying. But not you – as far as you're concerned it's truth or nothing and you have no more hesitation in hurting yourself by speaking it than you have in hurting others.'

'You may be the only person I'll ever be able to explain that to, Eddie, but not yet, even with you. I learned most things too old and too late, but I absorbed that particular lesson very early.'

'Now *you* intrigue *me*.'

'You'll have to remain intrigued. I simply can't say it. Perhaps I never will. Just put it out of your mind now and maybe I'll come back to it one day. Instead, you can tell me about the real Edward Rathbone, as we seem to be veering away from the subject at every opportunity!'

'So we do. Well, it's quite simple really. I started with absolutely nothing but a damned good mind, so in a sense I had the choice of what to be. You see, I have this disgusting belief in all that rubbish about people being able to do whatever they want if they try hard enough. I was born into the classic deprived slum home: newspapers on the floor, bread and dripping to eat from Monday to Wednesday and just bread from Wednesday to payday. No prospects, no hope; except for a tough old grandfather who regarded my Dad as no bloody good at all and was determined I wouldn't go the same way. Grandad hammered on and on and, as a result, when it came to me leaving school I went as an apprentice engineer in one of the shipyards, not as a steelworks labourer or a collier.

'That got me started, but wouldn't have taken me far if the game old devil hadn't kept on at me. Those were the best days of the workmen's institutes, where they'd built up superb libraries and took all the national newspapers, every day, for members to read. Grandad had me in there a couple of nights a week from the first shift I did at the shipyard. "A trade's all right as far as it goes, our Eddie," he used to say, "but for you it's not going far enough so tha'd best get a bit more book learning in your spare time to see where you're going next!" He was right, too. By the end of my apprenticeship I was the most discontented lad in the yard.

'My poor downtrodden little mother used to look at me in perplexity and wonder what was wrong with me that I wasn't satisfied to earn a princely wage, court a pretty local girl and then settle down for the hard graft of raising a family. Her view of the world was so different from mine that I couldn't even begin to explain to her. My Dad couldn't have cared less anyway. He said practically nothing to me or to her, called Grandad an interfering old bugger but never tried to stop him, and generally preferred his pigeons' company to ours. Looking back at it now, I think perhaps he'd suffered terrible disappointments in his life and he'd just opted out. He wasn't bitter or anything as positive as that; he just sunk into a permanent state of despair and tried to ignore the world.

'So there I was at eighteen, itching to make my mark and qualified as an engineer. In those days the Midlands was the place to be. What I'd learned in general engineering didn't tie me to the shipyard, although it would have done if I'd hung around a few years more. In Birmingham and Coventry they were screaming for anyone who knew how to handle a spanner and understood how an internal combustion engine worked. The motor industry was just beginning to get going. By 1910 I was earning top money as one of the most experienced senior motor engineers around, but I still wasn't my own boss. The company I worked for had the sense to take me off the shop floor and train me as a manager. I took to it like a duck to water. I understood boardroom politics better than I understood motor mechanics, and that was saying something.

'It was only a matter of time before a sharp. chap with a bit of capital noticed my skills and proposed a partnership deal. It was too good to miss; his money and contacts; my mechanical skill and organising ability. We couldn't lose, and we didn't. We got in a good three years making custom-built cars for rich foreigners before the First World War came along and made millionaires of us both.'

'From that I take it that you didn't drop everything to fight for King and Country.'

'Yes and no. At first I was too busy making money. I was also too cynical about the causes of the whole thing to believe it was worth being killed for. My grandfather had given me his views of the Boer War when I was just thirteen, and a lot of what he said made sense about any national hostilities. So I just sat tight and churned out military vehicles instead of luxury cars. But by 1917 there were an awful lot of interfering women shoving white feathers at men under forty with all their limbs intact and no visible scars. So I joined up – I still remember how tickled I was to be going in as a commissioned officer. None of my family had ever made NCO up until then. I experienced the usual horrors associated with that time and place, but miraculously stayed in one piece. When it all ended I was richer than ever; Willie, my partner, had been genuinely medically unfit and had looked after both our interests. He was anxious to expand into the mass car market with what we'd made, but I thought he was plunging too early. I thought there'd be an inevitable slump after the war and there wouldn't be enough mass market cash for cars.

'In the end we compromised. I stayed on in the luxury car company and took up a very small share-holding in the new venture. We agreed to operate them as separate businesses so that if one failed it wouldn't take the other down too; then I started looking around for a completely different field to invest in.'

'Knowing the bit I do about your business interests, that had to be department stores,' said Diana.

'Yes. I don't know whether you remember the original Hammond chain. The stores had done well in the late Victorian expansion of that type of retailing. They aimed at the very top end of the market, the sector immediately below the people who always had their clothes made by a personal dressmaker and did all their shopping at small exclusive emporia. Hammonds had done quite well in the nineties and in Edwardian days. But after that, they needed to come downmarket a bit and to do it with style. They missed out and instead tried to attract more of the real top people, who either resisted the whole idea or by then were no longer rich enough to spend on that sort of thing. They'd been shaky in 1914. By 1920 they'd had it. Wartime shortages had completed what bad market awareness had started, and they just ground to a halt. I bought them out at a laughable price; acquired a national chain for less than it would have cost me to buy the two London branches if the group had been properly managed.'

After that, his development of the re-christened Rathbone Group had been a classic example of intelligent commercial expansion. Rathbone had split the group into two types of shop: one of the London stores and the Edinburgh, Cheltenham and Manchester branches had become Rathbone's, catering for a similar market to Harrods or Fortnum and Mason. The other London shop and the eleven branches nationwide were still called Hammonds. They moved down to occupy the middle ground of retailing, what Rathbone described as Oxford Street rather than Knightsbridge.

'In a sense I couldn't go wrong by doing it that way. Hammonds took the cash away from the rising middle classes; Rathbone's nabbed the better class of shopper and flattered them with an atmosphere of exclusivity just slightly above the prices they were paying. It worked like magic.'

Having transformed the retailing group, he set about working an equally dramatic change on himself.

'At that stage I was still very much a successful working man,' he said. 'I can't say that you would have been in no doubt about my origins had you met me at a party then, because you wouldn't have met me. I just wouldn't have been invited anywhere that your type of people went, money or no money. So there I was, wallowing around in a social milieu I disliked, with no clear idea of how to change things.'

Rathbone had not made the classic mistake of many successful men in marrying the girl next door; but he had married well before reaching the top commercially, and the wife he ended up with was just as much of a handicap in the circles he was aiming at. Cynthia Wyfold was the pretty daughter of the solicitor who drew up Rathbone's articles of association when he and Willie Kerr set up their first company. She had been helping out at the office, showing off the secretarial training which her father had no intention of letting her use outside the family business. She was well dressed, reasonably amusing and genteel. Initially it was the gentility that did it. Rathbone was learning fast that manners maketh man, but had yet to acquire the means of distinguishing between the genuine article and the imitation. As a result he got the imitation.

Cynthia always crooked her little finger when she picked up a teacup. She was careful to say 'Pardon?' instead of 'What?', if she did not hear what someone said. She liked to see a pretty lace doily under the fairy cakes on her tea table. At first Rathbone was full of admiration for her social ease. Too late, married to her, he discovered that the people whose company he really wanted frequently said 'What?' when they didn't hear you; hated doilies, abhorred fairy cakes and tended to make crushing remarks about extended little fingers. Their women also swore like dragoons, particularly on the hunting field (Cynthia regarded both swearing and hunting as most unladylike). Matrimonially, he had made a bigger mistake than ever he had made in business. He was as ruthless in correcting it as he would have been in selling off an ailing subsidiary firm.

Cynthia would not hear of divorce ('Nice women just don't, Ted, even if they're the innocent parties'). He had no intention of going through life attached to such a social disaster, so he bought her an attractive house in Surbiton, where she had gone through the business of raising their two children and periodically bemoaning his appalling behaviour. Rathbone was not proud of his conduct, nor was he ashamed of it. He mentioned it to Diana purely to make sure she understood his marital status and as part of his life story.

'I'm skipping about a bit by going on about Cynthia,' he said. 'There I was in the early twenties, married to a woman I'd pensioned off, horribly ambitious socially but ignorant of how to start preparing myself for the circles I wanted to reach. In the end I tried approaching it as a business problem, because in a sense that's what it was. In business I'd succeeded by learning how to create the best, and doing it. That was clearly possible socially, because there's no question about money buying you into London Society. It's just that it has to be money backed by the intelligence to disguise your wolf's clothing in the right brand of sheepskin.

'I looked at some of the people who'd failed. A lot of them had tried to shed their lowly accents and had either wound up sounding like Cynthia or were so careful to construct their speech properly that they bored people to death with their slowness. All of them seemed to have gone to these titled types in reduced circumstances who claimed to be able to impart social polish at the drop of a fiver. The one thing that these social arbiters had in common was that they were not trained as teachers. They were decaying socialites with no qualifications in anything. In the end I realised that the right place to go would be a top-flight place for teaching rich foreigners to speak English. I was right. Those courses were run by first-rate academics who understood every nuance of the English language. I emerged at the other end with a vocabulary about three times as big as when I'd started, a thorough grounding in Received Pronunciation and no panics about dropping my aitches under stress. The ironic thing was that when I explained to the course tutor what I had in mind, he was so fascinated by the whole topic that he devised a sort of special course for me. Later on, I think he was involved with the BBC in training radio announcers.'

'I'm amazed you never thought of marketing it.'

'Of course I thought of it – and suppressed the idea immediately. The last thing I wanted was for other people to clamber aboard the bandwagon the way I had. The strange part was that the speech-training cracked the whole thing. The course organiser was the academically-minded son of a lord. He had all the social graces and I simply watched him and listened to him. He never noticed; just thought I was being especially attentive to the academic training. At the end of the whole exercise, he looked at me with a bewildered expression and said, "You know, Ted, there's something quite different about you from when we started this speech-training, although I can't make up my mind what it is." I just smiled at him gently and said "Eddie, please, or Edward. Somehow I don't feel like a Ted any longer"!'

'But surely Eddie's just as vulgar as Ted?'

'Yes, but for some reason Eddie has a vaguely buccaneering feel to it: you know, rich bookie or boxing promoter. Ted is just dull, definitely a payroll clerk or an insurance man.'

'You're a worse snob than I am!'

'Of course, my dear. Why do you think I find you so attractive? It was what stopped Hermione and me getting together in the end. She was far too intelligent to take such nonsense seriously and told me so. You know exactly why I behaved as I did, and in similar circumstances you'd do just the same thing. You and I share an awareness of the importance of appearances. Because we care about them, they matter more than anything else. In a way we're just as bad as poor old Cynthia.'

'How dare you suggest such an idea? Are you comparing me with some dreadful little hausfrau in Surbiton?'

He burst out laughing. 'This is time for the movie cliché "God you're beautiful when you're angry!" In this case it happens to be true, but what a mean little thing to be angry about.'

She glared at him for a moment, furious, then reluctantly began to smile. 'Okay, you're right. I am a dreadful snob, we are just the same as Cynthia, and Hermione Digby-Lenton is a plaster saint to be above such things. Now I suppose you'll get all snooty with me for criticising Aunt H again!'

'Not at all. I don't think Hermione is any happier for being free of these minor preoccupations. In fact I suspect it releases her considerable intellect to worry about peace, man's innate barbarism and similar great issues. I also suspect we have much more fun being sordid little go-getters. But don't let that precious honesty of yours stop short of something as important as this. See all your personal faults, not just those you find it easy to live with.'

'You are very good for me, Eddie. No one else dares to be such a bully. They're always afraid I'll up and leave them!'

'Not me! I know it will make you more interested in me. Added to which, much as I adore you, I'll never let any woman rule me to the extent that I shall tell her what she wants to know rather than the truth. If she does leave, there'll always be another along, eventually. I'm sure your life to date has already taught you that.'

'Indeed it has. A couple of times I've been convinced the world was about to end because the love of my life was gone. But how many times can a girl have a love of her life?'

'I don't know, Diana. I was rather hoping you'd make it one more time for me, though.'

'No wrapping it up with sweet music and low lights for you, eh?' It was 5 pm and they were sitting on the sofa in her Clarges Street drawing room.

'If it made your surrender more likely, I'd rebuild the Taj Mahal at Granby, brick by brick.'

'What I like most about you, Eddie, is that you don't know how to think small.'

'And what I love about you – and I mean love – is your inability to be frightened of anything or anybody. I'm ready to commit myself completely to you Diana, for good. Are you ready to accept that commitment?'

She was troubled. 'I don't know what to say. I have a husband who loves me very deeply. In my own way I love him too, although I make little pretence at total fidelity. What happens when he comes home? You have no intention of giving me up once you've got me, do you?'

'None whatever. But don't misunderstand me. When I ask if you are prepared for my commitment, I'm asking something different of you. I don't expect you to divorce your husband when he comes home. I shan't even be too unpleasant if you decide you cannot go on seeing me once he's back. What I ask is that you accept the permanence of my committment, respect it and go along with it at least while circumstances are as they are at present. I'm willing to take my chances when Roland comes back.'

She stared levelly at him for a long time before speaking again. 'What are you waiting for? You're arrogant, but you're not insensitive. Surely you know that sometimes too much talk can kill a love affair, when action could win your battle for you?'

He rose, obviously ready to leave. 'In that case, expect me to return, wordless, at eight o'clock this evening. No one can seduce a beautiful woman properly at five in the afternoon!' As he opened the front door he turned and said 'Don't eat before I arrive – I'll arrange a little something. *Au revoir!*'

The little something was a giant hamper which looked pre-war Fortnum's, but given the year had to be black market. He arrived with it promptly at eight, marching past her as she opened the front door and depositing it beside the tea table in the drawing room. Delivery complete, he gave her his attention. Diana looked ravishing. She had managed to choose an outfit which would have been acceptable for an evening at the theatre, but which, when worn for this private meeting, hinted at her complicity with his intentions. The floor-length loose gown of soft midnight-blue velvet was fastened from throat to hem with tiny pearl buttons which cried out for an attractive man to undo them.

'Come here, Diana.'

She crossed the room and stood in front of him. He embraced her fully for the first time as a lover. 'As you seem to have prepared yourself for this meeting rather more thoroughly than I, I suggest you open some wine from your refrigerator while this is chilling.' As he spoke he broke away from her momentarily, bent and opened the hamper. Bottles of champagne nestled invitingly at the top.

'You're hardly the impetuous lover, Eddie!' Nevertheless, she took the bottles.

'Oh no? Wait and see. I merely like to attend to our creature comforts first. Now, my lady, while you see to the drinks, I am going yonder to prepare myself for the fray.'

She gave a snort of mock exasperation and headed for the kitchen. Rathbone went into the bedroom and began to undress. He smiled to himself when he saw yet further evidence of her preparations. The bed was turned down and pink-shaded lamps cast a flattering, subdued glow across the room. A new towelling bath robe had been laid across the foot of the bed. He put it on and sat waiting for her to join him.

She arrived with the bottle he had suspected to be already chilling in the refrigerator, two champagne flutes and the *foie gras* which had been packed in the hamper next to his champagne.

'You greedy little beast. Do you never forget your stomach?'

'Not when there's a war on, dear man! Anyway, it seemed a pity not to show appreciation after you'd gone to so much trouble.' She sat down on the bed and spread some *foie gras* on slivers of Melba toast she had produced from somewhere. Handing him a piece, she took another for herself, swallowed it at one bite and raised her glass. 'To a long and mutually enjoyable relationship, Eddie. Thank you for brightening a very dark year.'

They drank, suddenly solemn, then he took her glass and put it with his beside the bed. Diana stood up and moved towards him, reaching out and untying the belt of the bath robe as she did so. She pushed back the edges of the robe and pressed her body against his, pausing as he kissed her, long and deep.

'All right, you've unveiled me. Let's get rid of your finery.' He unbuttoned the gown, caressing her breasts as he did so. When he had undone it to hip level, she shrugged off the sleeves and the garment fell with a gentle woosh to her ankles. Rathbone groaned with desire at the sight of her.

At thirty-four, Diana weighed the same as she had at eighteen, but her curves were deeper and firmer, with adult muscle replacing soft girlish flesh. Her breasts were heavy but firm, with large pink nipples that made the golden tone of her skin more pronounced. The hair on her head and body was the same flaming autumnal gold as ever, without a trace of early greyness. Her legs and arms were silky, slim and firm. There was no sign that she had given birth to two children.

'Great heaven, you look like some sea goddess standing there amid all that blue velvet. Let me touch you before you swim away!'

They were about the same height and as they kissed again she looked directly into his eyes. For some reason it heightened his excitement further. He pressed her down on to the bed and began kissing her face, throat and breasts, delighted by the way her nipples seemed to swell and take on a life of their own under the pressure of his tongue and teeth. But his lingering attention was short-lived. Diana's own mounting passion saw to that.

'Oh, darling, please make it quick! It's been such a long time and I've been waiting to do this ever since that evening at Hermione's. If you'd asked me then I would have, straight after we were introduced.'

'What, right there in her drawing room?'

'Well, out in the hallway, anyhow! Quick quick quick – we can play all night . . . I need you now.'

He seized her with an excitement bordering on violence. A woman as eager as this was something quite new for Rathbone and it inflamed him beyond reason. As he thrust into her she let out a cry of pleasure and shuddered convulsively, pushing him into an almost immediate orgasm. He collapsed against her momentarily but quickly freed himself and started caressing her face, shoulders and thighs.

'My darling, I'm so sorry! I really didn't mean it to be like that. It was just too much for me, having you so excited and so ready . . .'

'Stop apologising. I went right over the top as soon as you started and that set you off! I feel wonderful. Let's just relax and get to know each other a lot better now.'

It took them almost three days. Rathbone dressed briefly the following morning and went out to get essential supplies. Then they locked themselves in and enjoyed each other without a thought for anyone. The telephone was off the hook and the mail remained unopened. Eventually growing curiosity about what was happening in his business empire drove Rathbone back into the world. By then, Diana was addicted to their love-making and to the joy of his company. As she lay soaking in the bath soon after his eventual departure, she reflected that anyone else in her life, including Roland, would have to adjust to the permanent presence of Edward Rathbone.

It proved easier than she had anticipated. Their sexual compatibility was such that they soon settled into an almost marital relationship, the love-making underpinning but not dominating the rest of their contact. Until now the stores had been nothing to Diana but useful financial firewood to fuel the expensive aspects of their affair. Gradually, though, she began to take an interest and to realise that all was not well within the Rathbone empire.

'I'm seriously considering getting out and into something else when the fighting ends,' he told her. 'I don't know how much more mileage there is in my sort of store and I doubt whether I'm young enough to judge what will make a successful shop for the younger customers coming along in the next few years. We're holding our own now simply because anyone with any merchandise can sell it, given the existing shortages. Later on it will be a different matter.'

Diana said little at the time. Instead she spent a few days paying solitary visits to the Rathbone and Hammond stores within reach of London – which meant Rathbone's Knightsbridge and Hammond's Oxford Street and Brighton branches. What she saw depressed her, particularly when she looked at what similar stores with a younger image were doing. Rathbone's was much like Harrods, but there could never be more than one Harrods and, unless the junior store developed a more original individual identity, it would live in the shade for ever. The two Hammond shops appeared to have attempted to identify themselves totally with the Government Utility symbol. Furniture, clothes and everything else had a depressing uniformity. She emerged convinced that everything she had seen in them was either grey or beige. Where chain stores were trying to create a cheap and cheerful image and rival department stores were aiming for originality on a shoestring, Hammond's stayed cautious, safe and unenticing. Something definitely had to change.

Rathbone was away himself, visiting the Edinburgh and North of England shops for a week. After considering the problem at some length, Diana invited Louise Kerslake over for drinks at the flat. If Louise was surprised at such sudden intimacy, she did not show it. She spent an evening with Diana during which they went on from the drinks to discuss business over dinner, and by then she had forgotten any reservations she might have had. The prospects for commercial success were so enormous that they swamped anything else.

Diana's memory of the difficulty Louise had encountered in getting started as a *couturière* had led her to speculate how many others had similar problems. 'There must be so much talent in the rag trade, jewellery design, soft furnishings, furniture and just about anything else that we're sitting on a goldmine of innovators without giving them a chance,' she said.

'I've no doubts about that. Every time I go looking for specialised items for my collections, I run into people with wonderful ideas who are beavering away in sordid little back street workshops because their businesses need big city exposure and they can't afford to set themselves up.'

'So how about a group of top department stores setting up in-store shops for different young manufacturers? The high-price merchandise — couture clothes like yours, expensive jewellery and handmade shoes, say — would go out in the flagship branches, and the middle-market shops would have bright, stylish shops specialising in zippy children's clothes, smart maternity wear, costume jewellery — oh, you name it!'

With the image of the Rathbone Group shops firmly in mind, Louise took up the thought. 'It's brilliant; we could even have people like myself producing designer clothes for the expensive stores and ready-to-wear ranges for the high-street shops!'

By midnight, both women were slightly drunk, as much on ideas as wine. Diana had owned up to the identity of the store group; Louise undertook to broach the matter to Hermione. Diana was to take on Rathbone himself, possibly an insuperable obstacle.

He proved to be anything but that. 'I don't know why I failed to think of it, Diana. I really must be getting old. Of course we'll do it! My only reservation is that I doubt whether we shall be doing it alone. Like so many brilliant innovations, you won't be the only entrepreneur to come up with it, and post-war conditions being what they seem set to be, such development is inevitable. Still, we'll be among the first. Right, partner, when do you start?'

'I don't understand you. I'm no businesswoman."

'You are now. This is your idea. Develop it. I'll cut you in on the company to do it. Don't say you can't use the money!'

'Done!'

They went to bed to celebrate. It was only hours later that they realised they now had a perfect excuse to continue their relationship after Roland's return.

CHAPTER TWENTY

Secure as Eddie Rathbone's mistress, Diana finally began to enjoy the life she had envisaged as a love-starved girl. She was loved by a rich and powerful man; she had social prestige; she was châtelaine of an ancient estate; a social benefactress; a Society beauty; and now a partner in an expanding business enterprise. Her husband's imminent return from the Far East held no terrors. Evangeline ensured that Granby was a model estate and Alexander House a model endowment. Life was good. With the constant supply of black market treats which flowed from Eddie's bountiful coffers, it was sometimes almost possible to forget there was a war on.

Krystyna Karpinska abruptly shattered the illusion. She turned up at Hermione's flat one rainy evening shortly before the German surrender. Like Diana, Hermione had an apartment on the top floor of the family's London mansion, reserved when the rest of the building was requisitioned for official use earlier in the war. Hermione poured Krystyna a stiff gin and rang Diana.

'Please don't bother her, Hermione. I am sure she must be terribly busy, with the business and so on. Leave it. I'll be okay.'

'Don't be silly. You're too intelligent to expect me to believe such nonsense. I like to think of myself as your friend but you need someone closer than me now, and I have a feeling only Diana can help you.'

'I don't think anyone can help me any more. But I have to be with people I know, people who care about me, and all my blood family are gone.'

'Drink your gin. Whatever the doctors say, it does help. I'll get Diana.'

Her niece joined them within half an hour. She took one look at Krystyna then telephoned Edward Rathbone, who was dining with business associates at his club. 'I'm not available for a couple of days, Eddie. A friend of mine has troubles. I'm taking her to stay in Clarges Street until Friday at the very least.' She silenced Krystyna's half-hearted protest with a gesture. 'No, thanks all the same, but no one else can help. Aunt Hermione is on hand and she's more than capable if I need some back-up. Yes, she's a friend too. She'll probably explain. 'Bye. Take care.'

She turned back to Krystyna. 'Drink, talk, food, sleep, all or none?'

'At first, just flop, I think!' Krystyna managed a feeble laugh. 'I'm afraid I don't feel as if I'll ever storm an enemy citadel again.' She blinked rapidly several times and made much of draining her glass. Diana realised she had never seen her cry before. Then the tears burst through and she rushed to comfort Krystyna.

The Polish woman buried her face against Diana's shoulder and sobbed like a child. She was obviously trying to explain something, but it was still so fresh that it caused her too much grief to permit speech. Diana just held her, murmuring words of comfort, rocking Krystyna like a baby. Eventually she grew calmer. Hermione had re-filled her glass and she emptied it in two mouthfuls.

'I suppose I should watch it,' she said. 'I'll be blind drunk after another like that.'

'Whatever has upset you, perhaps it would be better if you did get drunk tonight.'

'No. I would still have to wake up tomorrow and it's best that I learn to handle this thing now. At least I've stopped crying.'

Between them they ensured that she did not try to tell them anything of was tormenting her that night. 'Just go home with Diana, have another big drink and then try to sleep,' Hermione told her. 'Diana, I have a couple of tablets which you can take back for her. They'll give her a dreadful head in the morning after all that gin, but they might be necessary.'

The two women went back to Clarges Street and Diana got Krystyna off to bed immediately. Her friend was so exhausted by now that the tablets appeared unnecessary. Wondering what could have happened to transform her so utterly, Diana herself went to bed. She was awakened just after 3 am by Krystyna, shaking with sobs and beyond calming herself. She switched on the bedside lamp and ordered Krystyna into bed with her.

'Come on in. You can't spend the rest of the night alone. You'll go dotty. Better be in here keeping me awake. With anything like luck you'll feel so guilty about it that you'll shut up and drop off!' That managed to provoke a small smile. Krystyna got into the big bed and cuddled down beside her, still shaking slightly with the intensity of her emotion. Diana embraced her gently and then said, 'Can you talk now?'

'I think maybe a little. But it will take a long time for the whole thing to come out. It hurts so much. I hardly know where to start.'

'Perhaps it will help if I ask you questions. The last time I saw you, you were on your way back to France. Was it anything to do with that?'

'Yes. It was a man. *The* man. He's gone, in a camp, killed by the Germans.'

'Oh, Christ, Krystyna, I'm sorry. However many times it happens to others, it's always new when it hits us, isn't it?'

'It's not just that. He was betrayed in the most terrible fashion, and when he learned what had happened he agreed to trade with the Germans. He would tell them about the network if they guaranteed the lives of all the members. Of course the Gestapo don't know the meaning of a bargain. He told them everything, then they loaded him and the others into a cattle truck for Buchenwald. He and the last of his men were murdered there immediately before it was liberated. I knew he was sent there and I've spent the past few months praying that when the camp surrendered he would be among the survivors. He wasn't.'

The mention of Buchenwald had set Diana crying too. Her father's death there was still an unhealed hurt.

'Was he betrayed by one of his own, or a collaborator?' she asked through her own tears.

Krystyna's fragile control broke again. 'That's the terrible thing. We betrayed him; the British. We sent the entire network to Hell because of some petty internal war between brasshats!'

Diana quickly realised that telling the full story would not help Krystyna in any way yet. That might come later. Tonight all she could do was cry and be inadequately comforted. Tomorrow Diana must devise some way of caring for her until the worst pain had diminished, then see if she could be healed. She resigned herself to a sleepless night.

It was mid-morning before she managed to contact Edmund Dancey. 'I don't care what your commitments are today, Edmund. You're lunching with me if you have to let down the Prime Minister to do so.'

'It's practically as bad as that, old girl, but from your tone I believe I know what's eating you, so as long as it's not before 1.30, I'll manage to make it.'

Diana left Krystyna finally deeply asleep, thanks to Hermione's two knock-out pills. She met Dancey at Au Jardin Des Gourmets, suggested by him because it seemed to manage to ignore rationing as long as one could pay piratical prices.

'Actually a workman's café would have been just as good today, because for once I don't feel like feeding myself.'

'Good God, the world must be at an end!'

'Not for me, but for someone else, I suspect. What have you done to Krystyna?'

'Diana, I haven't done anything to Krystyna. Why should you think I have? You know I hold her in the highest esteem and would take considerable risks on her behalf.'

'I'm using the collective you – you as British Intelligence, not Edmund Dancey.'

'Please, dear girl, not so loud. The war's not quite over yet, you know.'

'Bugger the bloody war! If you don't tell me what's

happened to her I shall start yelling all the snippets I do know at the top of my refined little voice!'

'I take it she's with you at Clarges Street? Good – I wasn't quite sure and, given her state when she left, . . . well, it's best she's with a friend.'

'And it seems she has precious few of them.'

'Hardly. It was just that she got caught in some strategic crossfire; or to be precise, her boyfriend did. Look, to put it briefly, she'd had a thing going with a terribly glamorous, brave Frenchman, leader of the resistance for a huge territory of France based round Paris and the whole area north-east towards the Belgian border. Jerry cracked their security and pulled the whole lot in. It was our biggest disaster since the Dutch networks were knocked over. The only reason Krystyna wasn't involved was that she didn't work with the chap; she operated down the Vichy end. They met when they were back in London between missions. They both dropped in and out of France like yo-yos. Until this mess they appeared to lead charmed lives, particularly Krystyna, judging by the number of brushes she had with the Germans. On the last occasion she saved the lives of two British agents by going down to military HQ on the morning of the execution and telling the Wehrmacht officer in charge that she was Eisenhower's niece. She said, if he had them shot, she'd make sure every German in the place would fry when the Yanks arrived. He swallowed it and she walked out with the two lads, promising to put in a good word for him with Ike when she was reunited with her uncle!'

'Stop trying to distract me, you bastard. That has nothing to do with what I want to know. She could handle his death; she's a tough girl and she knows better than you or I what war is about. The betrayal is what's unhinged her. Now you're going to tell me about the betrayal!'

'I wasn't trying to distract you. For that bit of bluff and a few other extremely brave actions, Krystyna has been recommended for the George Medal. Now if we'd betrayed her, would we be putting her up for this country's highest civilian honour?'

'Blah – you know how impressed I am by official re-cognition. She doesn't say you betrayed her directly; she says you betrayed this Marchand and his network. Did you?'

'I understand what she thinks happened. We asked a number of our people in France and their resistance men to volunteer to drop hints to the Germans about a planned Allied series of landings in the Pas de Calais. The arrange-ment was that if any of them were picked up, after they'd been knocked about a bit, they could reveal the 'plan' as if it were true. Then, as an attempt to save themselves, we told them they could appear to cave in completely in return for leniency from Jerry and tell all they knew. Unfortun-ately for Krystyna, her man and his back-up team drew the short straw. They were taken. Marchand made the deal with the Gestapo after they'd been given the false story, but it seemed they double-crossed him and sent the whole bunch off to Buchenwald. It was rotten luck but we didn't do it.'

'Are you sure that's the way it was? I get the impression that she thinks those men were deliberately fed lies by Brit-ish Intelligence and then betrayed to the Germans in the knowledge that they'd be bound to break eventually under interrogation. If that was the case, then you did betray them, didn't you?'

'Well, it's been said before – *c'est la guerre!* But Diana, I still don't agree that this is a true version of events.'

'Swear to me you don't believe it is.'

'What good will it do you or her to know I believe that version isn't true? She'll just think the Firm did it behind my back! Look, this is getting her nowhere. People are beginning to notice that she has some pretty hostile thoughts about what's happening. Can you do anything at all to help her?'

'Like what, bring her lover back out of the ovens at Buchenwald?'

'Diana, stop it. I feel rough enough about this already. No, take her down to Granby for a long recuperation. I'd rather she was not around London when some of the big intelligence battalions start massing here in a couple of weeks. Keep her out of harm's way. Let the soft Devon air work a little magic on her. Keep her safe. However she feels about me now, I admire and respect her tremendously.'

'At least that has a ring of truth. Tell me, Edmund, would your desire for her to disappear temporarily have anything to do with her belief that an internal war within the intelligence services was to blame for all this?'

Dancey put down his knife and fork and sat very still. 'She said that?'

'Yes, but nothing more; no details. I finally seem to have got through to you.'

'Take her to Granby, Diana, now – this afternoon if possible. Keep her there as long as you can and don't encourage her to speculate outside your drawing room.'

Next day, Diana recounted his words to a listless but calmer Krystyna. She smiled sadly. 'He's lying, Diana, or he's deceived by the same people who took in Marchand. I know the real story and I'll tell you when I can handle it without cracking up again. He's given you only part of the truth, and a distorted truth into the bargain. Anyway, what are you going to do with me? It'll play havoc with your plans to come to Devon now.'

'Nonsense. It's the least I can do.'

'I owe you a lot.'

'No you don't. About ten years ago you saved my marriage, remember? I'm the one who still owes you. Perhaps this will redress the balance a bit.'

She sent Krystyna on ahead to Granby in order to have a few days alone with Edward Rathbone. 'I admire what you're doing, my love, but how will I manage without you? And remember, the war in Asia is moving every day. Roland could be back with you by the next time I see you. What then?'

'For a start, you come down for as many week-ends as you can, as soon as possible, to establish a regular pattern which will continue after his return. I also want another good solid face around when Krystyna starts improving, so you can drag Aunt Hermione down as often as she'll come, partly as camouflage and partly because she'll do Krystyna the world of good. Now don't worry; we'll find a way of staying together.'

But on the train to Devon she was less sure. Roland had still been alive and unhurt a few weeks earlier, when two home-coming fellow officers had arrived from India with a letter from him. He was about to be dropped back into Malaya for a second stint helping to spearhead Force 136. The force, manned by Malays and Chinese-trained Communist partisans, was the only organised resistance to the Japanese in the Peninsula. Roland was one of the small force of Europeans who had helped to organise them from the time the Communists had started collaborating with the British against the Axis. A year or so before, he had gone in by boat and had spent several months setting up units in the jungle, managing to escape undetected at the end of the period. Now, with the Japanese in full retreat, there was still plenty of risk. They often fought to the last man and he was usually in the line of fire.

Diana was an admirer of Scarlett O'Hara's 'I'll think about it tomorrow' philosophy. Now she pushed the problem of Roland out of her head and concentrated on Granby, Krystyna and the rest. In Devon, a state of armed neutrality existed. Evangeline tried, but she could never feel anything except hostility towards Krystyna Karpinska. Whenever the woman appeared, her own servant status was established afresh. Matters were a little different now, because her directorship of Alexander House had altered her role. She was a manager rather than a domestic. Nevertheless she remained an employee, a fact which could be ignored in the Polish countess's absence. Strangely, the taut atmosphere had not depressed Krystyna further. It had put her on her mettle. She did not return Evangeline's hostility, but realised she must keep her wits about her to dodge it. The mental exercise did her good.

Diana talked alone with her on the first evening back. 'Have you thought what you're going to do now it's all over? You know as well as I do that it's only a matter of days before the end. It's all over now, bar the shouting.'

'I haven't a notion what I shall do. The estates have gone for good. There's probably a bunch of Commissars sitting in the salon at Sikorsk now. The Reds overran that part of Poland ages ago. Strange, I was always convinced I'd survive the war. I'm not one of those people who didn't bother to plan for tomorrow on the principle that a bullet or a grenade would get them long before then. During my activities against the Nazis it was obvious everyone liked the way I worked, and several senior people hinted that I'd never be without a job. With my languages and my field experience, I *was* lined up for a senior intelligence post for life.'

'I note you say "was". I take it the reason is still too painful for discussion.'

'Yes, but it's getting better every day. I'll be able to talk eventually. Shall we say I'm not expecting much from my former employers beyond the odd medal once hostilities cease.'

'But they can't just drop you. Your skills are hardly the sort of thing that will be snapped up by big business. You could starve as an unemployed spy!'

'Not me, Diana. I'll do anything to stay alive. Don't worry about that. I know now that I shall get over all this, largely thanks to you and Hermione, but by God, I'm avenging Marchand and his men if it's the last thing I do!'

'Take care. From Dancey's tone I gather it might be just that.'

'Oh, Edmund always did like a bit of melodrama with his intelligence work! That's why he's always been so fond of you and me. Says we're larger than life and when he contemplates us it takes his mind off reality.'

'That man always did know how to flannel. But I think in this case he's trying to give you a well-intentioned warning; and I don't think long-term unemployment is his major fear for you, either.'

'Take it easy. I can look after myself.'

Only a few days later, Roland arrived home, taking Diana completely by surprise. Eddie Rathbone had returned to London the previous day after a week-end at Granby. The first Diana knew of her husband's return was a call from the station master at Granby.

'Sir Roland's down 'ere, Milady. Says 'ave you enough petrol to drive down and pick 'im up because somebody else took the taxi.'

'Yes, yes! I'll be there in ten minutes. Thank you.'

Oh, Christ, she thought. Ten minutes to drag my thoughts away from Eddie and London and the business and back to a man I last saw more than three years ago on the other side of the world. Will I still even know him?

Diana had bargained without Roland's dog-like, unchanging devotion. There was no need to do anything but be herself. Whatever she did, however she responded, he would always love her. As they embraced at the station, she sensed that and for a moment was shaken by the realisation that he was actually a competitor to Eddie Rathbone. A day before she would have vowed he had no chance and that she would retain the superficial conventions only out of deference to their past relationship. Now she realised this was not so. In a different way, she loved Roland at least as much as she loved Eddie Rathbone.

He stood back and smiled at her. 'Sorry for the lack of warning. I think they decided I'd be corrupted by Marxism if they let me hang around with the Chinese any longer. One minute I was up to my elbows in jungle, the next I was being ferried out on the bumpiest old plane in the Far East. Anyway, Diana, here I am. I do hope this isn't all an embarrassment. Suppose I should have rung from London but for once I just wanted to surprise you.'

'No, darling, it's wonderful to see you like this,' she said, silently sighing with relief that he had arrived on Monday and not Sunday, when he might have surprised her in bed with Eddie. 'Now I've a surprise for you. Krystyna is here. She's had a bad time and Edmund Dancey and I agreed that Granby would be a good sanctuary for a while.'

She spoke with forced good cheer but Roland picked up her inadvertent use of the word sanctuary. 'Who's she hiding from, Diana?'

'I wish you could tell me that. She doesn't seem inclined to do so.'

In the end it was Roland who became Krystyna's confidant. Their special relationship rekindled immediately, and from the moment of his return Krystyna began to improve noticeably. 'Like a pair of lovers!' said Evangeline with a sniff.

'Evie, given my views on throwing stones from greenhouses, I think the less said on that topic, the better.' Evangeline glared at Diana and retreated to her office at Alexander House.

Diana spent VE Day in London with Edward Rathbone, returning to Granby some days later. Since Roland's return, she had felt free to move back to London and divide her time between Mayfair and Devon. Krystyna continued to be even more comfortable with Roland than she was with Diana. Diana in turn was still besotted enough by Rathbone to want to make love to him as often as possible. London therefore pulled her irresistibly.

At Granby, victory was marked by bonfires and a spirited recital by those members of the village silver band who had avoided being called up. Krystyna avoided the modest celebration. Roland returned from playing the lord of the manor to find her in the library, standing at the window looking down towards the sea and nursing a very big drink.

'Not even the smallest sense of relief at the peace?' he asked gently.

She turned, her expression implacable. 'I'm still at war, Roland. I still have scores to settle.'

'Don't think I'm not in sympathy with you, but what good d'you think it will do? I'm no believer in that "Vengeance is mine, saith the Lord" nonsense but, in this case, what can you hope to achieve?'

'I can talk to you without crying, Roland. I think I'm ready to tell at last. Perhaps tonight is an appropriate time, too. It's as well to question on Victory Night whether we really are at peace.'

'Tell on. Anything you say to me is between us two

unless you say you want me to pass it on. Diana has told me what Dancey said and your reaction. Pick it up from there.'

'I'll never know whether Dancey was in on it or not. I think not. He is a real friend, although I was too hurt to accept that when I stormed out and went to see Hermione. But his superiors are a different matter. They killed well over a hundred brave men because of a departmental wrangle and now they've covered it up by suggesting that bad communications within the network were to blame. What really happened was that the Special Operations Executive and the Secret Intelligence Service hated each other's guts. SIS determined to scupper SOE even if it endangered the British war effort.'

'But Krystyna, that's absurd. How can the two executive arms of one country's intelligence service go to war with each other when there is a real world conflict in progress?'

'Don't ask me, but they did. Bear with me and I'll spell out the evidence. It took me from when they captured Marchand in late summer 1943 until spring this year to piece the story together, but I've got it all now, and it stinks. SIS never did like the SOE. The top men were frequently heard saying SOE were a bunch of amateurs trying to play spies with a bigger budget than they deserved. When SOE made some bad mistakes due to inexperience early on, it looked for a while as if it would be closed down and lumped together with SIS. But it was reprieved and went on to do some really good work. Nevertheless it had earned the hatred of the Foreign Office, which instructed SIS to try to trip it up whenever possible.

'Soon after France fell, SOE was offered the services of a young French pilot called Gericault, apparently an ace flier who knew the territory around Paris and the eastern section of the Loire Valley like the back of his hand. Trouble was that he was shut up inside Vichy France and, as a non-combatant French national, hadn't a prayer of getting out legally. The first odd little incident was that he wound up coming out along an escape route which was reserved at the time for British airmen trying to get back to base and French resistance men who'd been caught and were facing certain torture or deportation. The only other occasional passengers were Jews who were in such immediate danger that their regular civilian escape routes couldn't handle them. Somehow, though, this French civilian, in no trouble with the Germans, was put out on this premium route simply because he had a burning ambition to make himself useful to Allied intelligence.

'When SIS had to give an explanation, they just said he was potentially so valuable that it was considered worthwhile. The awful truth is that he was a time bomb which they were planting on SOE.

'Gericault was trained in England for a senior job in the Vigneronne network around Paris. They had some splendid tacticians but until then their transport co-ordination had been so bad that they were losing supplies and key personnel to the Germans right, left and centre. Gericault's brief was to build up a safe chain of drop zones, secluded landing fields, the lot. He was parachuted back into France and almost immediately things showed an improvement. Marchand was delighted. For the first time his people were getting the sort of protection and safe supply lines they needed to carry out their work successfully.

'Gericault's good luck was uncanny from the first. No matter how noisy the plane, how patchy the cloud cover for a night landing, his drops seemed to be free from interception. Considering the record of his two immediate predecessors it was little short of miraculous. Some people began to wonder if it were not just a bit too good to be true. Then one day one of the girl couriers who had a good cover as a collaborator went to the Paris Ritz to see the Wehrmacht colonel who was her lover and unwitting informant. As she got out of the lift to visit his room, who should be getting in but Gericault. Luckily he was so deeply in conversation with a woman and two Germans that he didn't notice Gabrielle and she reported the incident.

'Needless to say, no one believed her, but Marchand observed the rules and put a watch on Gericault. They soon established that not only was he living at the Ritz, but so was his wife – the woman he'd been talking to. Remember, the Ritz was completely in Gestapo hands at that time. Marchand assumed that Gericault must have a secret secondary mission which was unknown to the Vigneronne group for security reasons, but he reported to London just in case. Nothing was done. No one even responded to the report. Eventually he waited until he was called back to London for de-briefing and told his briefing officer, a different man from his normal reporting agent. They panicked, said something was very wrong and promised an investigation. At that point, Marchand was told that the invasion was to be that autumn, in the Pas de Calais. Remember that; he was not told to pretend it was there and then, but that this was the real plan. Subsequently one of his lieutenants was given the same information and Marchand himself told his two closest comrades.

'Before Marchand returned to France, his briefing officer said they had a report that Gericault had been in touch with a senior Abwehr officer in Paris before the War started. Now the official line was that he had been pulled out of Syria early in the war, where he had been flying civil routes for a French airline. This conflicting report said he'd been involved in airborne drug-smuggling between Marseille and North Africa. It was agreed that Gericault should be brought back to answer the allegations now made against him. He came; Marchand and his boys were duly told that there was nothing in the treachery allegations; and Gericault returned to France.

'I'll come back to the main story in a moment, but let me tell you here that when I started digging after everything fell apart, I got hold of one of the pilots on the French run. According to him, Gericault made two trips, not one, to London during the investigation. On the first, he was picked up at the British end by an SIS car. I can only assume that he was an SIS plant. He was obviously reporting to them behind the backs of SOE. It's equally obvious that one of the senior directors at SOE was party to it, because he had kept quiet about Marchand's demands for an investigation.

'Anyway, shortly after Marchand got back from London, the whole circuit was taken in. The sheer scale of it was inconceivable – at least a hundred and twenty fully-trained under-cover operators and God knows how many French men and women working at grass roots level. Marchand and his lieutenants were convinced it was the big mopping-up before the Allied landings they expected that autumn on the Calais coast. They were ready to die under torture rather than confess. Then something terrible happened. Marchand had already been knocked about quite badly but they'd really not seriously started on him. He was taken into an interrogation room one morning and the last three sets of strategic plans sent over to his group from London were spread out across the desk in front of the Gestapo man. As soon as he saw them Marchand knew they'd been betrayed from inside, and that the Germans must already know about the autumn invasion. He took stock of the chances his group had of surviving the tortures that were in store for them and decided the price was too high – but only because the Germans already knew the basic plan anyway.

'So he did a deal. The entire Vigneronne network was now broken; after all 95 per cent of them were in jail. Therefore they could not become effective resisters again. He would give the Germans all the information he had on the autumn invasion if they guaranteed to intern all the Vigneronne group until hostilities ceased but to spare their lives. I admit I wouldn't have thought Marchand was so naive, but he had a streak of idealism that it seems not even the Germans could undermine. He accepted their word, told them what he knew, and they shipped the whole bunch off to Buchenwald and made sure they were killed before the liberation.'

'That's an utterly terribly story, Krystyna. Don't expect me to comment for a while. It's too much to take in immediately. But what interests me most as a first reaction is what happened to Gericault?'

'A good question. He managed to survive the sweep. Got out with his wife after the first groups were arrested. He arrived in London for one of the longest de-briefings ever, but I gather the officer in charge was the same man who had taken Marchand's reports and done nothing. They stood him down, put him on headquarters duty for the duration, and that was that. I'll get him if it's the last thing I do, but I want his employers even more.'

'Do you think you've fully worked out what they were playing at?'

'Oh, yes, finally. SIS knowingly recruited a German agent on behalf of SOE, who didn't know. The SIS chiefs hoped by doing so to create circumstances which discredited SOE and eventually destroyed it. In the end the war finished before their own bit of vengeance. But they've succeeded in ensuring that SOE doesn't go on after the war.

'I'll just add one nasty little postscript. Remember Moulin?'

'God, yes, the hero who might have saved France from post-war chaos if the Gestapo hadn't murdered him.'

'Well, I can't imagine anyone who could be described as less alarmist. Apparently towards the end of his life he was convinced that the level of bungling ascribed to British agents was too high and someone inside the service was working for an enemy agency. I think he was right.'

'Have you done anything yet about keeping tabs on Gericault for later?'

'Not really, Roland. When I think about it, the only friends I have on whom I'd lay this burden are you, Diana and Hermione. And I've told only you. So I have no way of knowing who I can turn to for help.'

'You've found him; me. But please don't ever mention this conversation to anybody. I don't care who else you tell – although I recommend discretion for your own safety – but if you ever say that I know anything about it, I shall play the archetypal silly ass. Understood?' She nodded.

'Right, now I shall keep an eye on Monsieur Gericault and wife. I'm interested anyway. We shall see what happens. As for you, young woman, I think it would be wise if you didn't actively seek vengeance until things have calmed down and got back on to a peace footing. There are all sorts of odd types around, willing to cut the King's throat for ninepence, and I don't want you suffering because you can't be discreet.'

'All right, Roland. Somehow, if you're looking out for everything, I shan't be so desperate.'

Roland spent some time on the telephone the following morning, then told Krystyna to forget all about it for the time being. 'Relax, get better, think about what you want to do. When Diana gets back I think we should all have a conference about Countess Karpinska's future, don't you?'

Diana had already given the matter some thought. At first she had discussed with Rathbone the possibility of finding room for Krystyna within the rejuvenated department store empire. Eddie thought it a splendid idea. 'Her title alone will give the whole enterprise some extra cachet. With a baronet's wife as managing director and a countess as a senior manager, we'd get coverage in every fashion paper in Europe!'

At first she agreed with him; then she talked to Dancey. He was horrified. 'Look, Diana, I'm holding some very nasty watchdogs on a short leash over our Polish friend. I've only managed it by telling them she's such a mental wreck after the Vigneronne collapse that she'll never be put back together again. How long d'you think they'll go on believing that if she's getting European press coverage as one of the brains behind a new fashion business?'

'Well, so what? The war is over now and it can't matter that much what they think of her. Their silence makes it fairly obvious they've no further use for her.'

Dancey blushed deeply at that and failed to meet her eyes. 'Actually, they've just decided to dispense with her services permanently.'

'Oh, then at least she'll have a bit of a pension to get by on until she decides for herself what she wants to do.'

'Er, no, I'm afraid not. They thought, what with her being a naturalised alien and promoting disaffection with HM Government forces and so forth. . . .'

'How much?'

'Four weeks pay and expenses. A little under £100.'

'Oh, shit, Dancey, not even you can dress that one up for them.'

'True, I can't. I've never been more deeply ashamed of my country. If I had any money of my own I'd add a couple of thousand to it and pretend it was an ex gratia payment.'

'Surely you must see she has to take a job, more than ever after that news. She won't want to hide down at Granby for ever.'

'I was wondering about that. Isn't there some sort of job down there? Something a little less front line than the store appointment?'

'Are you telling me she won't be safe in London, in the public eye?'

'Something like that, yes.'

'You prick! How can you go on working for them?'

'Unfortunately, darling, the one thing I share with the Marxists is the view that the end justifies the means. Although that sometimes leads to little individual horror stories like this, overall it makes sense.'

'I wish I believed that.'

Diana knew Krystyna would not be content to live off charity at Granby. If she were to remain there, a real job must be found for her. With the best of intentions, she committed an unforgivable blunder. On her return to Granby, without consulting Roland or anyone else, she sought out Evangeline.

'Evie, centuries ago I seem to remember your cousin Louise had ambitions for you to become the administrative director of her dressmaking business. How do you fancy finally taking it up as executive director of the fashion end of the stores development? With the organisational work you've handled at Alexander House, you could run rings around the London retail business in next to no time . . . why, what's wrong? Anyone would think I'd stolen your life savings!'

'I feel as if you have, Madam.' Evangeline was outraged. Alexander House and Granby Estate were practically her entire existence these days and now – Evie suspected she knew why – it was under threat. 'I've no experience whatever of retail management. I'm, what d'you call it – a first-rate institutional housekeeper at bottom. I also happen to be good at organising rotas and timetables and dunning people for contributions. That doesn't make me a potential business manager, or a potential anything in the retail trade.'

'But you're still under thirty-five. You can't vegetate down here in the country for the rest of your life.'

'Don't you mean the countess can't fit in up in town for the rest of *her* life – or at least for the next bit of it?'

Diana had the grace to blush. 'I was thinking of you, too, Evie.'

'No you weren't, except as a pawn. I may forget to speak properly from time to time but I'm not soft. The job you're thinking about screams out Krystyna Karpinska. You've got some reason for not being able to give it her, so you're planning to force me into it and give her my job. Well I can tell you, she'd be as bloody awful at this as I would be at that London job. If you want her to take over here, sack me. You certainly won't get away with it by just moving me.'

Incensed, Diana turned and left without further argument. Although she was furious at being thwarted, she knew Evie was right. She would be terrible in a London fashion store and Krystyna would be awful as a housekeeper, however grand the scale of the job. On the admin side she'd be all right, but the day-to-day overseeing of chores? Never.

Nevertheless she kept returning to the idea and finally came up with a solution she convinced herself was workable. She went back to Evangeline. 'Now look, Evie, the scope of this job is going to get far too big for one person over the next couple of years. It's not just your role which needs modification, but mine too. From now on, you'll be director of services at Alexander House and I'm offering Countess Karpinska the post of marketing and administrative manager. She'll take all the admin work off your shoulders and all the promotional work off mine. I've no more time for it now I'm managing director of Rathbone's.'

Evangeline's face assumed a closed, hostile expression. 'Would the countess report to me?' she asked.

'Well, hardly. Your jobs would not cross each other at all. You'd both report to me and we'd meet at regular intervals to sort out any snags that crop up.'

'Seems like a needlessly roundabout way of going on doing what you and I have divided between us without any problems in the past.'

'But will you at least give it a try?'

'I s'pose so,' said Evangeline grudgingly, 'but only because I know she's on her uppers!'

So commenced a somewhat uneasy relationship which was to last for just over a year. During that time it was not simply a case of Evangeline and Krystyna learning to rub along together. Roland had to meet Eddie Rathbone and absorb him as a frequent presence both in Granby and in London. He had also to adjust to a wife who was more businesswoman than lady of the manor; to get to know the two sons who seemed like strangers after such lengthy separation; and to try to minimise the alienation Cosmo had suffered thanks to Diana's indifference.

Through all the change and development, Granby began to prosper again. Rathbone insisted that Diana drew a salary from the company which she found quite astounding. She ploughed the bulk of it straight into bringing Granby up to scratch, and before long they were dealing with contented tenant farmers and overseeing an estate which at last looked as though someone cared.

They made a further killing when the War Office released the Clarges Street house and it became the joint property of Diana and Lettie. Office space in central London was at a premium due to the destruction of so much in the Blitz. Suddenly Mayfair was the place to do business, not merely London's most exclusive residential area. Eddie Rathbone assessed the value of the Clarges Street property with ruthless accuracy and bought it for the Group's head office for a figure that left Diana and Lettie gasping. Even after Diana had used part of her share to buy a neat little house in Chelsea to replace the top floor flat, there was a great deal left. She and Roland were no longer short of money.

Granby Manor rapidly lost the look of a beautiful but slightly dilapidated old lady and began to shine with care and attention. Lovely furniture, rugs and paintings were installed, as well as Lady Sarah's Bechstein piano from Clarges Street. 'She must be revolving in her grave because I'm getting pleasure from something that was hers,' said Diana.

The building was extended considerably, very much a luxury development in post-war England but made possible by the fact that labour and materials could all be produced on the estate. To accompany all this modification, Diana began entertaining, holding house parties most weekends. It served a number of purposes: providing cover for her affair with Rathbone; pampering new business contacts; giving Krystyna a chance to recover and get to know a new set of people. Above all it enabled Diana to queen it socially, a pastime of which she felt she would never tire.

Everything altered beyond recognition in the terrible winter of 1947. It started quite badly enough, when Diana received a call in the Chelsea house from her Uncle James. Never the most articulate of men, today he was virtually unintelligible.

'Could, er, that is, if you're not too busy . . . well, it's just that Hermione's a bit below par. D'you think you might pop over? The old girl, that is, well, do come.'

Fearing the worst, Diana went over to Brook Street. Like Clarges Street, the mansion had been turned to business use. It was now Maison Louise, Hermione's and Louise's couture house. Louise had the top floor flat. The Digby-Lentons had moved into the mews, where two adjoining cottages had been knocked into one to create a delightful modern house. The housekeeper, looking funereal, let Diana in. James bobbed to the top of the staircase.

'Ah, jolly good. Hoping you could make it, that is —'

'Uncle James, for God's sake calm down! What is it? I take it Aunt H is ill.'

'She had a massive coronary a couple of hours ago. They – they don't know if she'll get through the night.'

Diana was unable to absorb the idea. Hermione was a permanent part of her world, so close to Diana in age that the thought of disease and death never intruded into their relationship. She had been unsurprised when her mother faded away and eventually lost her grip on life altogether half-way through the war. But Hermione? No – she was going to live for ever!

Her uncle's sobs brought her back to reality. She looked at him in amazement. She had never seen him cry before and here he was, making great gulping noises, tears running unchecked down his face and marking his starched dress shirt.

'Oh, God, Diana, I never even told the old girl how I felt about her. Papa always made remarks about her money and all that and I went along with him, but I'd have wanted her without a penny! That night I first saw her at Rosy Logan's dance I just stood and gawped at her, didn't think she'd give a fellow like me a chance. But she did, and then when she turned out to be rich as well, Papa thought it was just that. But she was so beautiful, so – so soft. How can I manage without her?' He covered his face and sobbed even harder.

'Really, Uncle, she's not dead yet! People have survived heart attacks before. Come on, let's go in to her. If I know Aunt H she'll be lying in there wondering what all the fuss is about!' Much of this speech was bravado and when Diana saw Hermione, her brash facade almost cracked.

Her aunt was lying propped against a mound of pillows, eyes closed. The flesh of her face was blotched with bluish patches and her lips had the same tinge. Her hands were above the bedclothes, palms down, and the veins stood out on them like little vines, purple and angry. Sensing their entry, Hermione raised her eyelids, slowly as if conscious of their physical weight, and smiled.

'Diana. So happy to see you just once more.' That was

too much for James. He turned and left hurriedly. 'Come here, darling, sit on the bed. How are those two gorgeous men of yours?'

'Two? Aunt H, you're a wicked woman. Let's at least preserve some superficial decencies! After all, you did introduce us – if anything happened it was entirely your fault.'

'You mean it was entirely thanks to me! I could never have stood Eddie's drive, but you were made for him. It would have been a shame if he'd escaped us altogether!' A small spark of naughtiness survived behind the illness. 'He'll look after you, Diana. You need someone strong. Roland has a different type of strength . . .' She was weakening and Diana silenced her with a squeeze of the hand. Hermione made a great effort and began again. 'Do tell James to stop being miserable out there all on his own. It's natural that he should cry for me; I should be affronted if he didn't. Go on, bring him back.'

Diana fetched her uncle, who was vainly trying to mop up the signs of his misery with a large pocket handkerchief. Over his shoulder, Diana made a tiny wave and said, 'I'll be outside,' then left, hoping that James would nerve himself to tell Hermione how much he loved her just once before it was too late.

Hermione did not die that winter. Surprisingly, she rallied sufficiently to be moved to Stanhope when the long-delayed spring finally arrived. But she remained virtually bedridden and it was obvious that her future could be reckoned in months rather than years.

It was hard for Diana to handle the shock of Hermione's illness. She had always assumed she relied on the men in her life. Now she realised for the first time what a focal point Hermione Digby-Lenton had been. Diana retreated to Granby, weary of London in the iron cold of that most impoverished post-war winter. The snow sealed her in there before Christmas. It was the first one since the war when she had not been with Eddie Rathbone. He had returned to London from an early December house party in Devon when the first blizzards started. After that there was no question of his returning until the thaw.

The bad weather continued without a break until the beginning of February. Normally, Diana would have been in a spitting ill-humour by then but worry about Hermione had subdued her and she was merely quiet and withdrawn. A telephone call from Liz Radcliff, Eddie's personal assistant, changed her mood instantly.

'I know you're still snowed in, Lady Lenton, but d'you think you can get back to town? Mr Rathbone is ill.'

A vision of Hermione at their last meeting flashed into Diana's mind and she shivered. 'What is it? How serious?'

'No immediate worry, Madam. It sounds worse than it is. He's had a slight stroke – but it really is slight and the doctors are optimistic about his recovery. He's in the London Clinic.'

'Just how slight, Liz?'

'His left hand and the lower part of his left leg, but they're sure the leg will recover full use with exercise and the hand might improve. His speech and vision and so on are completely unaffected. He's making a lot of fuss because you're not there already!'

She closed her eyes. Thank heaven. 'I'll get there somehow, Liz, though God knows how long it will take.'

In the end the journey lasted almost twenty-four hours. They managed to reach the main Exeter road only thanks to an ancient horse-drawn sledge, stored for years at Home Farm as a curiosity. She and Roland tramped down the snowbound drive and Jack Drewett drove her from there. Roland stayed to look after Granby. It might be a long sojourn in London by the look of the snow drifts. A hire car met the sledge at the main road and took her in to Exeter, the closest station where trains were still running. From then on it took eighteen hours to reach Paddington, most of it spent shivering while the train stood beside frozen points. Diana went straight to the Chelsea house to get warm and clean herself up before seeing Eddie at the clinic. After her bath she rang Liz Radcliff for a report on his condition.

'Oh, I'm so glad you called! Are you in Chelsea? I'll come at once.'

'Why, what's wrong? He's not worse, is he?'

'I'll be over within half an hour. Wait for me, please!'

She arrived in less than twenty minutes. By then, Diana needed no further preparation for the news. 'He's dead, isn't he?' she said as she opened the door.

Liz nodded and started to cry. Diana took her inside. 'But what happened? You were so hopeful on the telephone. I thought he'd be demanding to come home immediately.'

'He would have been if it hadn't been for that bitch of a wife of his! She killed him as sure as if she'd pulled the trigger.'

'Cynthia? But how? I don't think he'd even seen her for two years or more.'

Liz was still crying. Somehow her tears enabled Diana to contain her own grief temporarily. 'It was the most horrible string of coincidences. You know he never liked the desk in the outer office to be unattended, how he had a junior sitting out there even if I was just with him for half an hour's dictation? Well it was the same when I went to lunch. They've always sent up someone from reception while I'm out. The day of his stroke, there were so many of the regular staff off with colds and flu that they had a number of temps in and one of them did the lunchtime session at my desk.

'She was very level-headed when Mr Rathbone had the stroke; got hold of Dr Lennon, sent for an ambulance, the works. But when the ambulancemen came, one of them said it was so cold outside that perhaps he should have a coat draped over the blankets in the wheelchair. Not knowing the place, she opened the coat cupboard in the outer office and found that big old British-Warm he hasn't worn for years. Off they went and when they got to the London Clinic, someone went through the pockets to find a next of kin. He'd left one of those flat notecases in the pocket and it had Cynthia's telephone number inside. It was probably fifteen years old, but of course she's never moved house and the number was up to date.

'By the time he'd come round and asked for you and me,

Mrs Rathbone was on her way there. She arrived after I'd left and started on him straight away about living too hard and fast and how the time had come for him to return to her and move into the Surbiton house, where she could look after him properly and he could have a nice quiet time pottering about with the roses. It would almost be funny if it weren't so tragic! He stood a couple of minutes of it, then ordered her out. She wouldn't go and he lost his temper. That was the end. He had another stroke, a massive one this time. The doctor told me he was dead before he hit the ground.'

Liz's outrage at Rathbone's unnecessary death had stopped her crying and now the two women sat staring at each other, taking in the full impact of his loss. 'She knows about you, Lady Lenton. She came marching into his office to make arrangements for everything and she said, "Well for one thing, I'll see That Woman doesn't come to my Ted's funeral. I'll make it family only, and in case she sends tons of flowers I'll make it charity donations instead." She means it, too. The announcement is in today's *Times*.'

Rathbone would have been proud of Diana's ruthlessness at that moment. The vision of Cynthia Rathbone in the Chairman's office at Rathbone House pushed all thought of grief out of Diana's head. 'Oh, Christ, that hadn't occurred to me – she'll get all the shops!'

Thunderstruck, they contemplated the possibilities that opened up. Diana had never been a major shareholder. Eddie had given her a token holding, but her money had been drawn as a large salary. She would not last ten minutes with his widow at the helm. That meant no income, and eventually no Granby, considering the way the managing directorship had shored up the estate until now. They sought solutions for hours, but came up with nothing. In the end Liz went home dejectedly, leaving Diana finally to come to terms with her grief.

But it was to be further delayed. Half an hour later the telephone rang. It was the store group solicitors. Could the senior partner come round this evening after the office closed? He had important details to discuss following Mr

Rathbone's death. The details turned out to be Eddie at his buccaneering best.

'Before I start, Lady Lenton, I must warn you that what I say is liable to be tested most stringently in a court of law. I can't see this going uncontested and I think a very strong case could be made against you. Mr Rathbone has left you the entire store group and his holding in Kerr's Performance Cars.'

'But he can't have done! That's – well, just how much is it?'

'At a conservative estimate, Madam, around £15 million. That is, of course, if you sold up. Potentially, with the economy getting back gradually to a peacetime footing, you could quadruple that in less than ten years.'

'But his wife and children? What happens to them?'

'Minor legatees, compared with you. He had a limited holding in the mass production car subsidiary that Willie Kerr started; a much smaller number of shares than in Performance Cars but of course, as it's the mass market, they've snowballed in value over the years. He's added the rest of his minor investments and the total is about another million, split up as a quarter of a million for each of the children and half a million for Mrs Rathbone.'

'But she'll never let me keep it! She'll break it on the ground that he'd lost his marbles!'

'Hmm, it seems Mr Rathbone shared your view. When he made this will just over a year ago, he first took the precaution of complete physical and mental screening by some of the best medical brains in the country. There are two psychiatric assessments swearing that he was saner than Sigmund Freud. No, she'll challenge the will on the ground that it made inadequate provision for her and their children. The way courts feel about deserted wives these days, she could well pull it off!'

But Diana was already smiling before he had finished. 'Don't worry, Mr Hardy. You'll have no problems with Mrs Rathbone. I think I can make her see reason without any trouble at all. Just leave her to me.'

The meeting with Cynthia Rathbone was short and

sweet, at least for Diana. It made up to some extent for her exclusion from Eddie's funeral. Mrs Rathbone came accompanied by her daughter, a tight-mouthed young hausfrau-type in her early thirties.

'I invited you over in case you had any silly ideas about challenging the will, Mrs Rathbone.'

'Silly? I don't understand you. It's hardly silly to object to your husband willing all the money elsewhere than to the family. Of course I intend to challenge it. And I shall win.'

'I don't dispute that, but I'm amazed that you're prepared to pay such a high price. I'd have thought that rather than have that sort of scandal you'd settle down on the income from your half-million and call it quits.'

'Scandal? What scandal?' All her genteel fears were aroused.

'D'you really think I shall keep quiet for five minutes? It will be all over the *News of the World* – Store Tycoon leaves it all to his Lady Love, or some equally appropriate headline in giant black type. I shall tell all, and claim it was a little thank you for warming his declining years.'

Cynthia Rathbone was white-faced and shaking. 'You wouldn't; you couldn't! What about your husband?'

'Roland knows all and understands all,' Diana said airily. 'We're far too secure with each other to care what the world says about us.' She thought she heard ghostly laughter from the Society gossips of her youth.

The conversation ended as abruptly as it began. Cynthia knew she was defeated but could not bring herself to concede. Finally her daughter broke the deadlock.

'Really, Mother! How long are you going to sit there and let yourself be humiliated like this? Of course we can't take it through the courts. I'd never hold my head up again at the tennis club and Tom has put the boys down for Harrow. How d'you think they'd like it?'

She hustled her mother towards the door, turning in the hallway to face Diana. 'There, you've got it all, and I hope it chokes you, you – you adventuress!' Her departure was accompanied by peals of laughter from Diana.

But pleased as she was with her easy victory, and with the size of her fortune, Diana felt vaguely guilty. She had expected to be far more deeply touched by Eddie's death. In fact she felt only nostalgia and a gentle sadness for him at having his life cut short. It was hard to admit the fact, even to herself, but had Cynthia won, Diana would have missed involvement with the business far more than she would have grieved for her lover.

She stayed in London for the rest of the winter. The weather gave her little say in the matter anyway, but there was no question that she needed every moment to take full control of the Rathbone Group. As she worked, she quickly recognised how intelligently Eddie had planned and rapidly came to terms with her own odd reaction to his death. She realised that while she had the business, so much of him lived on that he was practically still at her side. Since their involvement had embraced business as well as love, he had gradually pushed her into centre-stage. Retaining the title of chairman, he had handed over the role of managing director to Diana early on. When she protested, he said that as the ideas for the new group were hers, she should also have the responsibility for carrying them out. As a result, she had become thoroughly familiar with the group from top to bottom. The franchise negotiations, re-equipment, new merchandise decisions, promotional campaigns, all were Diana's. Eddie had handled the support adminis- tration, but it was easy enough to employ a good senior manager to carry on with that. A first-class managing director would have been irreplaceable.

Diana surprised Louise Kerslake by transferring a block of shares to her and appointing her to the board. She also asked Roland to take on a directorship.

'But Diana, d'you think I'll ever have the least idea what's going on there? Hardly my line, is it?'

'Well you'd better get used to it, dear idiot. This is our money, not just mine.'

'I say, isn't that a bit rash?'

'If you don't stop talking in questions, I shall scream! Of course it's not rash. I love the business but Granby is the centre of my world. This money is to bring it to its full glory. It wouldn't feel right if it was my giant pot of pin money and nothing else. We'll get the accountants to arrange the whole thing so that one hand washes the other and it takes care of the estate. If it makes you feel happier, I'll set aside my managing director's salary as separate income, just in case.'

'I wish you would. You're putting so much faith in our offspring! What if I died first and they decided to give you the old heave-ho, sell up Granby and live in the Caymans? They could, you know, it's not entailed. And they'd get the store group too.'

'Don't be absurd, Roland. Our sort just don't do such things!'

'Don't they? I wouldn't have felt very comfortable giving some of the Regency philanderer Lentons and Hartleys the opportunity.'

She dismissed the idea as preposterous, hung up the telephone and went to see her accountant about setting the project in motion.

Meanwhile, all was far from well at Granby. Evangeline had managed for a while to rub along with Krystyna, but the long confinement to the estate had worn out her patience. One of her major resentments came from the unthinking ease with which Krystyna merged into the above stairs life at the manor after working hours. Not for her the tactful retreat to solitude in her cottage in the grounds. While Evangeline spent the evenings alone in her flat at Alexander House, the countess dined at the manor and played backgammon afterwards with Roland.

They finally had an enormous row over a minor clash of duties, just as the weather was beginning to ease up. Evangeline slammed up to the manor and into the library where Roland was wrestling with some sheep breeding records. He started in alarm as she pushed the heavy door shut behind her and glared at him.

'Why, er, Evie. What on earth is the matter?'

'She's the bloody matter, that's what. I've had it up to

here. I'm not working another minute with her. All those continental airs and graces; "The Swedes have a way of doing it with caraway seeds" . . . "You should try it with more chicken giblets and a few tiny savoury dumplings" . . . "My mother always left just the merest sprinkling of crushed verbena in the linen cupboard to make the sheets wonderfully lemony". And we all know Evie MacIntyre is a slum kid from the valleys who drank her tea from a condensed milk tin until we educated her! Well I'm not taking it any longer. You can have a month's notice and stick it where the monkey stuck his nuts!'

'Please, Evangeline, don't dash off while you're so angry. I can't judge the rights and wrongs of such a situation; I only know it was very unwise to create it in the first place and if I'd been consulted it would never have happened. Having said that, here we all are having to cope with it. How about cooling off with a bit of a holiday?'

'Where would I go on holiday?'

'There's one obvious place; to Imogen and her husband. Have you no curiosity about your granddaughter?'

'Of course I have, but they're all in California. I'm hardly likely to traipse off there, am I?'

Imogen knew that Evangeline was her natural mother, although their years of separation had ensured that Louise had fulfilled the practical maternal role. She had grown up in a prosperous, loving home and was educated at the best schools.

Imogen had abandoned a brilliant undergraduate career at Cambridge to volunteer for the WAAF. She had fallen in love with an American airman within months, had married him and moved to California as soon as the war ended. Evangeline's few bright moments in recent months had been spent gazing at snapshots of their round, dimpled daughter lying on an airbed in their sun-soaked garden.

'I think it might be a good idea. Not permanently; we really do need you far too much here. Say, about three to four months?' He smiled conspiratorially and she understood.

'I see. Just long enough for Lady Lenton to notice I've

gone but not long enough for her to mess anything about too permanently.'

'I think we understand each other, Evangeline. Now I'm not taking any arguments. I'm paying for your ticket – first-class on one of the *Queen*s, I think – and I'm giving you some pocket money. Lord knows you've earned a bonus in the last year or so!'

She left, starry-eyed, to write to Imogen. Now for the hard bit, thought Roland. What on earth do I do with Krystyna, and how do I tell Diana? We'll end up with blood all over the floor and I suspect it's going to be mine.

Krystyna had already started taking her own steps to solve the problem. That evening when she joined Roland for a drink, she saved him considerable embarrassment by raising the subject of her bad relationship with Evangeline.

'I know the whole thing happened as a kind gesture to me on Diana's part, Roland, but I should have been strong enough then to refuse the favour. Evangeline is a competent woman who can run Alexander House single-handed. No wonder she hated me from the start. I haven't helped things either. I start off with the best intentions each day, then she makes me nervous because I've done something stupid and I hear my awful arrogant voice braying on about how it was done in the royal courts of old Europe and it makes me wince. God knows what it does to her. It's time for me to go and I only hope I've made the decision soon enough to have prevented too much damage to your relationship with Evie. She deserves better.'

'But where will you go? What will you do? All your considerable skills are in an area where no one will use you. Look, I've come to a sort of interim arrangement with Evie. She's off on a few months holiday. You have at least until she's due to return before you need come to any final decision. If only it weren't for that Polish pride of yours, we'd both be delighted to have you as a permanent house guest. I'm sure I could put you in line for enough business translation work to keep you in pocket money.'

'I love your kindness, Roland, but I can't exist on that for the rest of my days. That sort of treatment is one of the reasons Evangeline resents me so. She feels, quite rightly, that no one would save her if she were down on her luck. She'd have to fend for herself. Well, so must I. Anyway, I've been doing a little research and I think I've found something that uses my linguistic talents while financing a roof over my head. I shan't tell you more until it's firmly fixed – and not a word to Diana, either!'

'But where would you be based? I talked to Dancey the other day and he's by no means sure that London would be safe for you even now.'

'Oh pooh! He has an exaggerated idea of my continued importance. They'll all have forgotten me by now. In any case, you needn't worry on that score, either. I'll be worlds away from London.'

Krystyna refused to say any more about her prospective job. A couple of weeks later, soon after Evangeline's departure for North America, she went off somewhere mysterious for a final interview, having told Roland he need not worry because she was not visiting London. Diana had been home now for some time, had ranted at both Krystyna and Evie over their bad working relationship and had then admitted that it was not an ideal arrangement. Krystyna refused to tell her any more than she had said to Roland. She finally told all immediately after Diana had returned to London for a board meeting.

'I've known for a couple of days; I just couldn't bring myself to tell you while Diana was here because she would have exploded and tried to stop me doing it. Her heart's in the right place, but you're the one with all the good sense and in the end you might understand that any job is better that uselessness.'

'Good God, Krystyna! After that I half expect you to tell me you've signed up as a dustman. What is it you plan to do?'

'I sail on the SS *United States* from Southampton on Thursday. I've taken a job as a stewardess aboard ocean liners.'

'You, a floating waitress? Oh, come off it, Krystyna!'

'I have something in common with all the other floating

waitresses, Roland. I have no more money than they do. That's enough for me. They'll pay me well, give me comfortable quarters and I can see lovely New York again every couple of weeks. That's not too bad for a start. Oh, and I won't be visible to many unfriendly eyes there, either!'

He tried to put her off but deep down he knew she was right. Only snobbery told him the job was beneath her. It was ironical that Evangeline, who was ten times too highly qualified now for such work, could have taken the job tomorrow and he would not have protested. For Krystyna, unqualified as anything except an intelligence agent, he thought it was demeaning. He tried to keep the point firmly in mind.

'You mustn't breathe a word to Diana until I'm well on my way,' said Krystyna. 'Otherwise she'll be half-way down the Solent in a tug trying to drag me back! Tell her when I'm half-way there. Then she'll have time to reconcile herself to it.'

A few days later, Roland drove her to Southampton to begin her first crossing. As they said goodbye, she reminded him of Gericault. 'I've no intention of leaving my dirty work to you or anyone else,' she said, 'but in case the ship sinks under me or I get run over by a New York taxi, please try to see he gets what he deserves, however long you have to wait.' Roland promised, after heavy reassurances that nothing would go wrong for her now.

Krystyna had no objection to work and her duties aboard were not too exhausting, although she was glad to stretch out and relax each evening when she came off duty. No snob, she got on very well with her fellow staff. But she failed to take into account that the easy male–female camaraderie which had existed among Roland and Diana's set was foreign to the community she had just joined. To them, when a woman was as friendly as Krystyna, it meant she had something more than platonic comradeship in mind. As a result she discovered that one of the stewards had developed a serious crush on her by the third day out. She humoured him, teased him and was kind to him – all reactions which would have served as useful distancing tactics among her former acquaintances. Here it only made matters worse. His devotion grew more dog-like by the moment and by the time they reached New York he was becoming aggressive with any other men who showed interest in Krystyna.

She was relieved, therefore, to discover that Joe Blaydon was not making the return crossing. He had changed his usual work schedule to help out a friend on Krystyna's first voyage. Now he was to stay in New York for a rest period and resume his duties a couple of weeks later. She enjoyed the city which had impressed her so much a decade before, then settled down to a much less over-wrought return crossing. All seemed to be well with the job. Her supervisor gave her excellent reports and the management told her she could regard her position as permanent. They put her into a regular crossing schedule and asked her to re-join the liner ten days later.

Now she was at a loose end. Southampton was still in a bad way after the Blitz. The docks had been cleared and maritime traffic was back to normal, but shorebound re-construction was altogether a slower business. Beyond the acres of bombed-out former dockland warehouses were more bombed-out acres, this time of terraced houses. Further inland the suburbs were scarred by hideous temporary prefabricated bungalows and half-built estates being run up by the mile to re-house homeless families. Ten days in this? Heaven forbid, she thought. Sorry, me old Roland, it has to be London or Paris and I'm not strong enough for Paris's memories yet.

At that point Krystyna decided to risk renewed contact with Diana. She knew her friend would rant at her about the job, but she was lonely and longed for the company of an old companion. She telephoned the Chelsea house and Diana answered.

'You two-timing bloody Pole! Fancy walking out on a girl like that! You knew damned well you'd go for that job over my dead body, didn't you?'

'I rather thought you might have strong views, I confess. I'll bet poor old Roland is still in disgrace for aiding and abetting me.'

'Something like that, yes. I suppose it's too much to hope that you've rung to admit you were wrong and ask if you can come back? If so, the answer is yes, a thousand times!'

'Thank you for that, Diana. You've never let me down, have you? But you're right. The job is fine and I have no intention of quitting. I have a few days before taking up my permanent run and I wondered if we might get together.'

'Love to, darling, but I'm in London for the next two weeks. I suppose I could get down to Granby overnight this week-end but I'd be pushing it.'

'Oh, to hell with it, Diana! I'm coming to London. If I don't see some bright lights soon they won't have to bump me off; I shall die of boredom.'

'Would you come here? Oh, that's marvellous! We can have some fun together for a few days. I admit I think Roland and Edmund are rather overdoing the cloak-and-dagger bit. The war's been over for a couple of years now. All the same, are you sure you feel like risking it?'

'Try and stop me! I'm a bit long in the tooth to start avoiding risks now, anyway.'

'You'll stay with me in Chelsea, of course.' It was not a question.

'All right, you bully. I had an English nanny like you once. She made me a push-over for commands issued in that clipped British accent.'

'Are you suggesting I speak like a nanny?'

'Of course – a very aristocratic one, though. Strictly by royal appointment.'

'All right, so I'm a snob! Shut up and get on a train at once.'

'Your wish is my command, Lady Lenton!'

They spent a heady few days visiting theatres, shopping and eating. Diana insisted on giving Krystyna a dress from the latest collection for Rathbone's Designer Room. It was the spring of the New Look and Krystyna crowed delightedly over the yards of unnecessary fabric, the tiny waist and rounded curves of the new creation.

'There's so much work in it that it could walk about by itself,' she said. 'Wait till New York sees me in this!'

'It's a pity that more women aren't as tall as you,' Diana told her. 'It's going to make Mrs Average look like a bag of laundry.'

'She'll still be clamouring to get into it. After those skimpy little wartime skirts it's heaven to feel so feminine again.'

'Hmm, you're obviously *looking* feminine, too. A couple of smoothies over there haven't taken their eyes off you since we arrived.' They were dining at Gennaro's in Soho, Krystyna clad in the new dress by way of celebration. It was her last night in England.

'What smoothies? I could do with a little masculine attention right now.'

'There, down at the back. Don't look for a couple of minutes. They're practically *glued*, my dear!'

Moments later, Krystyna dropped her table napkin, bent to retrieve it and glanced at her unknown admirers. Her blood turned to ice.

'Diana, in a little while we're going to the Ladies! I hope there's an accessible rear window because we shall leave through it. Send the manager a cheque tomorrow for our dinner.'

'Krystyna, what are you talking about? Just because two personable men get a little attentive . . . oh, you know them.'

'All too well. One of them is senior SOE. The other is Max Gericault.'

'What are you going to do?'

'I just told you; make a break for it through the back window. It worked in occupied Dijon; no reason why it shouldn't work here.'

'Yes, yes, I heard you the first time! I didn't mean that. If the SOE man knows his stuff, he knows who I am and where to find me. What's the use of going through the window if they can just stroll round to the house and trail you from there? And incidentally, there's no window from the women's lavatory. You'll need to go on along the corridor past the kitchen. A door leads straight out into the delivery yard. There's a network of lanes outside it that takes you out behind Soho Square in one direction and Old Compton Street in the other.'

'Why are you telling me all this if there's no point in escaping?'

'Well, it occurred to me, if you go and I sit here toying with the odd drink and dish of zabaglione, it will be a while before it occurs to either of them that you're not coming back. You still have your key to the house. You could grab a taxi, nip back there, get your things, change into something less conspicuous than your present outfit and melt into the night. How about that? I have a fair bit of cash with me. You can have the lot in case of emergencies. I also have my chequebook so I can still pay the bill here.'

'My lovely Diana – I told you in 1942 that you should join Dancey's boys and girls. You just proved my point!'

'Just as well I didn't, or they'd probably be gunning for me as well as you by now. After Roland's account of what happened to Marchand, I wouldn't mind a crack at yonder Gericault.'

'You might yet. I made Roland promise that if anything happened to me, he'd settle my score with the sweet man. Right now I don't fancy my chances.'

'Nonsense, dear girl. You'll live to burn the bastard yet!'

'Don't be too sure. If he's survived until now with all the enemies he must have, he's not going to leave one non-essential Polish countess running around loose and dangerous.'

'Enough of this defeatist talk. You're wasting time. Off you go. The faster you're away the better.'

As her friend moved out towards the Ladies, Diana called a waiter and ordered two portions of zabaglione. Shame I can't eat them both, she thought with real regret.

She managed to keep the two men entertained for more

than half an hour. After that they clearly had a good idea of what had happened. The one Krystyna had identified as Gericault stayed. His companion left and did not return for more than a quarter of an hour. It was clear that he was discussing her with Gericault. The men rose, paid for their meal and left together. Diana gave them ten minutes before departing herself. Outside she was unaware of anyone following her, but even she knew enough about the expertise of professional shadows to assume they had put someone on her tail. She also assumed that when the SOE man originally left Gennaro's, he had gone to check her identity. They would know Krystyna was living at Granby, apparently still a mental wreck. Having seen her in London with a striking redhead in her mid-thirties, they would identify Diana quickly and get someone round to Chelsea within minutes. Diana prayed that Krystyna had not hung around in the house. Just in case they had not sent someone straight to the house, she decided to take them on a misguided tour. She took a taxi to Hammersmith to look in on Liz Radcliff, who was out. She strolled back to Hammersmith Broadway tube station, got on a train to Green Park, then walked through Mayfair to Maison Louise.

Louise was surprised to receive a social call from Diana, never a woman to mix business with pleasure. Diana sensed her bewilderment and hastily concocted a number of questions about the current collection. 'Forgive the intrusion, Lakie. I was out for a solitary evening stroll, realised where I was and thought I'd see if you were in. It really is rather rude of me to carry business over into your private life, I'd better go.' It never occurred to her to confide in Louise the real reason for her presence in Brook Street.

She finally took another taxi back to Chelsea not long before midnight. She had left herself with little cash when she handed over most of it to Krystyna and was forced to make the cabbie wait outside while she went in to get more money. There was no sign that Krystyna had ever been in the house, apart from an unsigned note, which simply said 'Thanks – wish me luck!'. The New Look dress was laid flat on Diana's bed.

Arriving back at Chelsea, Krystyna had changed into trousers and a nondescript sweater. She put on a pair of flat shoes and a woollen cap. Diana's jackets were all slightly too short in the arm, but she solved the problem by trying on one of Roland's, which was perfect. Tall but otherwise nondescript now, she emerged from the house and set off towards Victoria Station. There she took a train for the South Coast, spent the night in an obscure guest house in Brighton and travelled directly to Southampton the next morning. She felt uneasy until the liner had cast off and eased out into the main shipping lanes.

Morning brought no comfort to Diana. As usual, her daily housekeeper brought her coffee, toast and papers at 8 am. She stopped short at a down page story which reported the commital for trial at Surrey Assizes of 'French resistance hero Max Gericault' on a charge of gold and drugs smuggling. Surprisingly, given the seriousness of the charge, he had been granted bail. He was represented by Hilary Longton, KC, the most fashionable and expensive barrister in England. The story tried to say a great deal without transgressing Britain's stringent contempt of court laws. It implied that Gericault's defence depended largely on his superb war record. Otherwise his guilt was too blatant for denial. The implication was that he was still engaged in national security work, with a cover as a rogue, and that a badly-briefed or stupid police force had arrested him by mistake.

Diana read the story with mounting misgivings. If she were in Gericault's shoes, she would not want to have a woman running around loose and loose-lipped who would do all she could to prove his wartime treachery. If he still had friends in the Secret Service, that could lead to a quick end for Krystyna. Diana prayed for her friend's escape and telephoned Dancey to see if he knew anything.

He was beside himself, although trying to control himself. 'Diana, why now, of all times? What possessed the pair of you to start parading round the nightspots when our friend has so much to lose?'

'Don't be such an ass! We didn't know what was

happening in court, how could we have? Our friend spent so long in Devon that she was growing straw out of her ears by the end. She needed a breath of city air and neither of us had any idea this was happening. You certainly never said anything.'

'I was beginning to hope she'd settle down there permanently.'

'Dancey, she's thirty-seven. People do not retire at that age, whatever impressions to the contrary might be given within His Majesty's Civil Service.'

'Sorry, old girl, I went off half-cocked. I'm worried about her. I'm sure they know where she is. Can you check whether she's safe?'

'Not without leading them there. I'd advise you to let her be. She has a better chance if you do.'

They were due to dock at Cherbourg before starting the transatlantic voyage. Krystyna had come aboard as quietly as possible and had stayed in her cabin until they sailed. But she was on the first shift and had to work in the first-class lounge immediately after the ship left Southampton. Each time someone called her, she started like a frightened gazelle. Hell, she thought, I must have lost my nerve. I was less jumpy than this when I was in the field! But then you knew your enemy, her survival instinct told her. Now he could be anyone in this salon. She shook off the thought and went about her work as normally as she could.

When she came off duty an unpleasant surprise awaited her. She had been so preoccupied on embarkation that she had ignored the personnel list on the staff noticeboard. Joe Blaydon was one of the ship's company and he was waiting for her outside the first-class lounge.

'Hallo, gorgeous, surprise, surprise!'

She forced a smile to her lips but was less than enthusiastic about his presence. 'Hi, Joe. Look, you'll have to excuse me tonight if I seem unsociable. I'm terribly tired – tried to cram too much into my shore leave, I expect. See you tomorrow, okay?'

But he was in no mood for rejection. 'Crammed in too

much, did you? I suppose you had a string of fancy boy-friends all lining up to show you the sights when you got ashore?'

'Something like that, Joe.' She hoped her directness might achieve what gentle hints had failed to convey.

'You bloody teaser! What about me, that's what I'd like to know?' His voice was teetering on the edge of hysteria and two first-class passengers drew aside in distaste as they emerged from the lounge into the brawl.

'Joe, please! This is hardly the place . . .'

'This is as good as any. I thought you'd be pleased to see me. It looks as if I was wrong!'

She was becoming impatient. His petty jealousy seemed like a gnat bite compared with the trouble she was facing. 'Oh, this is ridiculous! Just because I like to be friendly with the people I work with, doesn't mean I'm madly in love with every man I meet. I like you, but I have no further interest in you and if you think differently, hard luck!'

'You bloody hard-hearted bitch! I suppose you make a career of stringing blokes along and then dropping them when they get too keen. Oh, yeah, I know your sort!'

Four more first-class passengers had emerged from the salon and were watching with distaste. 'Do you have to hold this conversation here?' said one of the men.

Krystyna tried to restrain Joe but he was beyond it. 'You just shut your fucking mouth, you stupid rich prat!' he shouted.

'Marion, Laura, go along to our staterooms. I'll deal with this. Now look here, my man, you've gone too damned far. I'm seeing the Purser about you first thing in the morning, then perhaps you'll wish you'd shown a little more respect!'

'Stuff the Purser – see the sodding Captain for all I care and tell him this tart would be better off cocking her leg ashore than making trouble on board ship!'

The man's companion persuaded him away. Krystyna had stalked off already, leaving Joe raging behind her. Her last impression was of other passengers cautiously avoiding him as if he were a dangerous animal.

437

She was alone in a staff cabin only because her room-
mate had reported sick at the start of the voyage, too late
for a replacement. Tonight she was thankful for her solitude. She locked her cabin door and lay down on her bunk.
Sleep proved impossible and by 3 am she decided she could
no longer endure the claustrophobic cabin. The com-
panionway outside was empty, so she put on a coat over
her pyjamas and went on deck. Once there, she realised
how silly the move had been. She was in precisely the place
where they would find it easiest to bump her off if they
had followed her; or, almost as bad, where the lovesick Joe
could find her. She turned to go below again.

It seemed an endless journey, punctuated by quick
glances over her shoulder. But by the time she got back to
her cabin, she had convinced herself she was over-reacting.
Krystyna reached out to unlock her door. As she did so it
swung open silently. She gasped and stepped back, half
turning to run. A strong hand grabbed her wrist and she
was yanked into the room.

'Joe? Joe, don't be silly, please!'

'Tut tut, Countess. Don't you know the difference between one suitor and another?'

The weighted cord knotted around her neck from
behind. She lashed out but clawed at thin air. She tried to
yell but only a thick gurgle emerged. Red patterns swirled
in front of her eyes as she slid down. The pressure of the
garotte prevented her from falling completely. Her
assailant kept her suspended there until her struggles
ceased, gave a last brutal twist and dropped her, pausing
momentarily to retrieve his cord.

Diana had returned to Granby the day after Krystyna's
flight. She told Roland everything. He rang Dancey.

'No good coming to me, old boy. Nobody's saying
anything to me. Lots of people have started making noises
about me having done my duty and isn't it time I returned
to Civvy Street. They seem to think two years service after
cessation of hostilities is quite enough and I'm beginning
to agree with them. I have several points of view which

the new regime would see as heresy. Honour to the brave is among them.' For this last he raised his voice, with the obvious intention of letting someone else overhear him.

Roland said goodbye and hung up.

Two days later the papers were full of the story. 'Resistance heroine strangled by jealous lover aboard transatlantic liner' yelled the tabloids. 'George Medal Countess found strangled aboard ship: steward sought' said the more restrained quality press.

The stories said much the same thing, at varying levels of sensationalism. The Countess Krystyna Karpinska, heroine of the Polish and French resistance, had fallen on hard times and taken a post-war job as a stewardess on the Atlantic crossing. Her attractions were too much for a fellow employee, who refused to take no for an answer. The morning after he had insulted first-class passengers when they interrupted a lovers' quarrel, he had been reported lost overboard. A fellow steward said that as he was coming off duty in the middle of the night, he had seen a figure resembling Błaydon jump from the stern of the ship. A cabin-to-cabin search of the staff quarters had revealed the recently-strangled body of Krystyna Karpinska in her cabin, one of her own nylon stockings knotted around her neck.

They sat in silence for a long time at the breakfast table in Granby, each remembering Krystyna as she had been in life. Finally, Roland said in a monotone: 'I'm told that Gericault is likely to get off this smuggling charge. HM Government is paying his legal costs, hence the pricey KC.'

'We can't just let her go unavenged.'

'I have no intention of doing so, but it will take time. With Edmund's help, in or out of the Firm, I'll keep tabs on this character. I promise you, Diana, as I promised Krystyna, that he won't go unpunished.'

Three weeks later, it was reported that the body of a youngish man had been washed ashore on the coast of Brittany. Dental records identified it as Joe Blaydon. The corpse was badly cut up, presumably by being trapped and battered against the ship's side, making it impossible to establish whether the man had died by drowning.

They did not discuss it further, then.

It took five years to catch up with Gericault. As Roland had been told to expect, he was duly acquitted of the Gatwick smuggling charges. After that he dropped out of sight for more than a year, to surface in France, on trial for war crimes. Again he was acquitted, largely because too few of the Vigneronne circuit had survived to testify comprehensively against him. The case was further obstructed by the British Foreign Office's refusal to open restricted files on their case before the expiry of the Fifty Year Rule. Once again Gericault, having been represented by the best lawyer in France, disappeared after his acquittal.

After the war Roland had retained many of his Far East contacts. He had developed sufficient expertise as an Asia Watcher immediately before the Japanese invasion of Malaya to be invited to advise several European companies which expanded in the region after 1945. By 1950 he held a couple of company directorships and served as a consultant for several other firms. He was one of the few old-fashioned Europeans who retained his links with the Communist partisans who had fought so bravely in Malaya. Now they were spread throughout the Peninsula and Indo-China, recruiting new members to win the peace for Marx and Uncle Ho. His friendship with them was based on mutual personal admiration that went beyond politics.

The passage of time had blurred the loss of Krystyna without softening it. Neither he nor Diana had forgotten his promise to the dead woman. Roland visited South-East Asia about once every eighteen months. Early in 1952 he told Diana he had to make an extra unscheduled trip.

'Why the rush?' she asked. 'I always thought they were fairly leisurely affairs.'

'This one has an unexpected bonus attached,' he told her. 'I can't say exactly how long I shall be gone; probably between three and four weeks. Keep an eye on the down page news in the papers while I'm away.'

He refused to say any more. After a fortnight of combing the minor stories about Ceylon and Taiwan in *The Times*, she was on the point of reverting to her normal superficial scan of the main headlines when a small headline caught her eye: 'French war hero victim in gang killing'. The story, datelined Vientiane, said that Max Gericault, a former French resistance fighter decorated by the French and British Governments, had been killed when the plane he was piloting had exploded in the air in up-country Laos. Only tiny fragments of wreckage were left, but police had reason to suppose that the crash was the result of sabotage. It was believed that Gericault had been carrying a cargo of smuggled drugs on a route which the Communist guerrillas had been trying to destroy for months.

'You never forget a friend, do you, Roland?' said Diana quietly to herself, 'or forgive an enemy.'

CHAPTER TWENTY-ONE

Marcus Gregg had been digging for background on the Petrograd Communiqué for a long time. It was 1952 and he wanted a good feature article for the twenty-fifth anniversary of the old scandal, now topical again with renewed public interest in Reds under beds. He had always been mildly obsessive about it and, although his popular daily paper wanted a big story, the cynic in him said their interest ended with tits and bums. Monday morning's editorial conference proved him right.

'Just remember our readers don't go in for too much highbrow political analysis, Marcus,' said the news editor. 'It's pointless to talk about Cabinet chicanery when our lot are screaming for crumpet. From what I recall of the Petrograd thing, our angle will be *cherchez la femme*. In which case, of course, the brief for you is to *trouvez la femme*!'

'Oh, very Continental,' said Gregg with a sneer. He was irritated by the fact that this case had a perfect central character for Bill Gibbings's scenario. It happened that Marcus preferred to pursue the political angle. Still, you couldn't have it all. Probably the official record would be so meagre that by Wednesday he'd be glad to go looking for the sex interest in the case. All the confidential Government broodings about it were protected for another twenty-five years, so Marcus knew he could rely on nothing more than old newspaper files and eye witness accounts to get him started. Then he struck gold in the most unlikely quarter.

He had been enjoying a relaxed love affair for nearly two years with an attractive middle-aged woman called Louise Kerslake. Louise was just the sort of woman he liked best: ultra-fashionable, financially and emotionally independent. She was about four years older than he, but so well-preserved that she appeared to be considerably younger. He knew she would never need to be grateful for the attentions of a younger man and it kept him on his toes. The piquancy of the situation was beginning to turn Marcus's thoughts towards marriage. Louise's apparent indifference to any change in her single status only intensified his interest. A frustrating day spent trying to make the Treasury and the Foreign Office disgorge records of the Petrograd episode made him preoccupied when he picked up Louise from a Berners Street dress warehouse. Driving back to her Mayfair flat, he mentioned the investigation.

'Good heavens, I haven't thought of Alexander Hartley for years!' she said.

'Hartley? I didn't know you took any interest in this sort of thing. How d'you know he was involved?'

'Oh, he was the father of one of my first Society clients. I've a lot to thank that family for. Her aunt ended up as my business partner. I'd still have been just a posh dressmaker if it hadn't been for the Countess of Ingleton.'

'Christ, yes of course! Hermione Digby-Lenton would have been Hartley's sister-in-law. I didn't make the connection before.'

'Well, it's not going to do you any good now, dear man. Poor Hermione's been dead for almost five years. I still miss her, too.'

'D'you stay in touch with the family at all?'

'Marcus, you really are so blinkered at times that it takes my breath away! Hermione's niece, Diana, is Hartley's elder daughter. She owns the Rathbone department stores where I'm developing the ready-to-wear boutiques!'

'And I've been sitting on the best contact of my career all this time without realising it! Lead me to her.'

Louise's tolerant amusement switched off abruptly. 'Diana Lenton has had enough problems over her father without you probing old wounds. You leave her in peace. I mean that, Marcus!'

'Okay, okay. On one condition. You sit down after

443

dinner tonight and tell me everything you know about the whole business, along with any contacts you can conjure up apart from the Lenton woman. As his daughter, she'd probably have been kept right out of what happened, anyway. If you were working for the family when the whole thing blew up, you must have taken more than passing interest in the scandal. You'll probably be able to come up with someone better than Lady Lenton if you really work at it.'

Louise wished she had kept her mouth shut. Although fond of Marcus, she knew he would sell his family for a good story, and once his curiosity was stirred he never let go. As soon as she had betrayed her connection with the Hartleys, she remembered another link with the scandal, potentially much richer for Marcus but possibly a greater hazard to Diana Lenton's peace of mind than even a meeting with Marcus.

Soon after the couture house opened, Louise had noticed a particularly free-spending client, a businesswoman called Naomi Chaplin. Initially Mrs Chaplin attracted Louise's attention because she always shopped alone. In this price bracket the bigger clients tended to be accompanied by husband or lover. Louise had seen enough prosperous traders go to the wall thanks to bad debt to be wary of customers who spent more than they possessed. She had fought too hard and waited too long for a couture house to let herself be ruined so easily, so her own credit vetting system was one of the toughest in the business. When Naomi Chaplin started placing really big orders, Louise had her investigated by credit assessment specialists before Mrs Chaplin had even asked to open an account. Louise's first concern was that the woman's prosperity might come from the black market. Around 1950 it was always wise to find out the source of a golden goose's fortune, in case it came from a commodity that was about to become freely available again.

Within a week the investigators were able to reassure her that what Mrs Chaplin was selling would never suffer a slump in demand. She was the madam of the most expensive brothel in London. Louise began to lose interest in the woman. Now she knew that payment was assured, Mrs Chaplin became just another client. But the investigators had added some extra information to their report. Puzzled that Naomi Chaplin had apparently leaped into existence from limbo in the closing days of the war, they had continued to investigate after establishing her profession. Twenty-five years ago, Mrs Chaplin had been Ninotchka Chaliapin, a.k.a. Nina Grant, and she had been the women in the Petrograd scandal.

When they had become more friends than business partners, Hermione had confided the general details of the affair to Louise. 'Something my niece will never accept is that her father's guilt is essentially irrelevant to her own feelings about him,' Hermione had said. 'In the end Diana felt betrayed because her father had been so involved with another woman that he was willing to destroy Diana's life. I never quite had the courage to confront her with that. Sometimes I think I was wrong. If I had, she might have managed to prevent it from colouring her entire future. That Russian woman wounded Diana more than anyone else could have. Heaven help her if Diana ever has a chance of revenge.'

Well, Lady Lenton's unlikely to get revenge, thought Louise, but at least she might be spared any more grief over this whole business, thanks to this Ninotchka. She turned to Marcus, pretending suddenly to have a bright idea. 'Forget Diana Lenton. I have a far more promising female for you to meet!'

Later, Louise considered the full implications of what was about to happen and realised that panic had flawed her reasoning. In attempting to protect Diana, she had turned Marcus loose on a woman with enough information about Alexander Hartley to smear Diana's family name afresh on the front page of every tabloid newspaper. By then, though, she had arranged the introduction between her lover and her client, with devastating effect.

She approached Naomi Chaplin two days after mentioning her to Marcus, when the woman came in for a fitting. 'Oh, Mrs Chaplin, seeing you has reminded me that I had something personal to ask you. I remember you once referred to having known a lot of foreign refugees in this country during the 1920s. A journalist friend of mine is doing a series about a big story that happened then involving the emigré community and I wondered if you might have known some of the people involved.' Louise stopped. It sounded highly improbable, which ever way you wrapped it up.

Naomi Chaplin had been studying her reflection in the cheval glass. Now she looked up, her speculative gaze meeting Louise's in the glass. She turned to face the couturière.

'This wouldn't have anything to do with the Francs Case, by any chance?' Her smile held no warmth.

'I have no idea, Mrs Chaplin. It was just that you were making quite a joke with one of my fitters a few months ago about your glamorous life in London when you came here from abroad in the twenties. It occurred to me that you might be interested to reminisce with this man, whatever he's writing about. What was the Francs Case, anyway?'

'Oh, come on, Mrs Kerslake! You're about my age. You must have read all about it. Your late partner certainly would have.'

'If you mean the Petrograd scandal, of course I remember. I wasn't aware it had been known as the Francs Case, that's all.' Louise was feeling deeply embarrassed. Clearly the woman was playing with her and now she had betrayed her knowledge of the affair she began to realise how ill-conceived had been her attempt to shield Diana. She made a belated attempt to withdraw.

'I seem to have made a *faux pas*, Mrs Chaplin. Please forgive me and think no more about it.' But the cat had the mouse under her paw now and was in no mood to release it. Ninotchka smiled again, radiantly this time.

'Nothing of the sort, Mrs Kerslake. You were right first time. It could be quite entertaining. Who knows what common acquaintances we might turn up, eh?' She began to change back into her street clothes. The fitting was over.

After giving Marcus Mrs Chaplin's telephone number, Louise went through a week of misery. She saw very little of him and when she did he behaved like a man in the grip of an obsession. Whatever Ninotchka Chaliapin was telling him must be rivetting stuff, tailor-made for a centre-page spread in the *Daily Post*. In the end she knew she must tell Diana Lenton what had happened. Perhaps it would be better to approach her through Evangeline. Louise telephoned Granby that evening.

'Evie, would there be any difficulty about you getting up to town to stay with me for a few days?'

'None at all. Lady Lenton's off with her sister and I'm being bored to tears by the yokels. Why, is anything the matter?'

'Not with me, but I need your advice and I'd rather not discuss it long-distance like this. It concerns Lady Lenton more than me or you, but you might have a better notion of what's to be done about it than I have. Has she ever said anything to you about what happened when her father was disgraced?'

'Only in roundabout ways. She used to go on a lot about how he was an innocent victim but I got the impression she was none too sure herself about exactly what he'd done. Then there was all that business during the war when he got mixed up with the Germans. One thing I was sure of then was that her attitude to him had changed a lot over the years. I don't think she'd ever heard anything to change her opinion. It was just that the whole rotten business put such a mark on her life that, when she'd lived with it for so long, she found it hard to think the same of him, even if she did still believe he was innocent. She just got fed up of having to live with what he'd done, I think. But he's dead and buried, Louise. What possible effect could it have on her now?'

'Oh, I seem to have opened up a cupboard and rattled the skeletons around by accident. Trouble is, they're not my skeletons and I'm afraid I might have hurt her without meaning to. Come on up to London, Evie. We must talk.'

Evangeline MacIntyre had aged harder than her cousin. She looked the older of the two, although Louise was the senior by some ten years. Evie had never really recovered from her husband's death in Changi jail and nowadays sometimes gave the impression of being a spectator in life rather than the spirited participant of pre-war days. Now all her interest was channelled into Diana Lenton's affairs, with Louise and her daughter Imogen completing her world. She arrived at the Mayfair flat the following evening, and over dinner Louise told her what had happened.

'So there it is, Evie,' she finished. 'Should I keep quiet in the hope that nothing is said to implicate Lady Lenton, or do I see her and warn her that the balloon's going up?'

'You can't pretend nothing's happening, Louise. That one's as smart as a barrel of monkeys and she knows so many people that she wouldn't be in the dark over it for five minutes. Anyhow it sounds to me as if this story will be good enough for all the other papers to jump on the bandwagon. With that bloody McCarthy business going on in the States, everybody is interested in Russian spies, and this old chestnut is tailor-made for the scaremongers. Lady Lenton is going to be fit to be tied over it whatever happens. It's better that she knows now that it's going to come up again, but above all that she should be told by you about your connection. It would be horrible if she thought you'd given her away. She'd never forgive you.'

'Yes, you're right. I'd better see her as soon as possible. It's hardly the sort of thing I can put to her on the phone, and if I try to say it in a letter it'll look even worse.'

'It'll be easy enough to get hold of her. She's coming to London with her sister straight from Stanhope. They might even be here already.'

Louise joined Diana Lenton for lunch at the Ritz next day. 'Might as well give her the best with what I'm about to drop on her,' she told Evangeline beforehand.

Diana was intrigued. Now that they were to be business associates, she saw more of Louise Kerslake than before, but their relationship had never been as informal as the friendship which had grown up between Louise and Diana's aunt. Previous luncheon engagements had been either at the couture house or at the London store, never on such 'social' territory as the Ritz.

'I always feel more as if I've arrived as a designer when I come here than anywhere else,' said Louise. 'It might be a bit staid these days, but I'm old-fashioned enough to regard it as the tops.'

'Mmm, Evangeline and I share rather more mixed memories of the place. As I recall, the last time your cousin was here she went three rounds with my mother and scored a knock-out, an act for which she has my eternal gratitude!'

Thank God for memories, thought Louise. At least she's set the scene for me. 'That must have been an extremely painful period for you, Lady Lenton.'

'It had its moments. Now I occasionally wonder why I was so overwrought about it all, but of course I've had more than twenty years to put it in proper perspective. Besides, however painful memories might be, they *are* just memories. One isn't required physically to relive the bad bits.'

'No, but what if someone starts digging up the past again?'

'I occasionally wonder about that, too. So far, it's been relatively plain sailing, but it's inevitable really. One just hopes to have died of old age by the time it happens, I suppose!'

'In your case, Lady Lenton, I'm afraid that's unlikely.' Before her courage failed, Louise recounted the events of the previous week. Diana sat opposite her as though frozen.

'I realise that I probably made a terrible mistake in introducing Marcus to this woman, but I honestly was trying to shield you from distress.' Louise stumbled to a halt, feeling like a traitor.

Diana spoke with obvious difficulty. 'There was nothing you could do. Some little rat would probably have got plenty of dirt from somewhere else; they might even have

449

found her for themselves. You can't be the only person in London who knows her background.' She sighed wearily. 'In a way it's almost a relief that it's happened now. I thought someone would be bound to do a "twenty-five years on" story in 1949, as the whole affair concerned the 1924 General Election. But witch-hunts weren't such big news then, so presumably it wouldn't have been so timely. How convenient that Papa was disgraced just twenty-five years before the Unamerican Activities hearings made Communist subversion such a fascinating topic! Well, at least both the boys are abroad, so its effect on them will be limited. Let's hope it will all be stale news by the time Sebastian comes home.'

'What about Sir Roland?'

'Oh, he's always been splendid about it. As far as he's concerned it only matters in so far as it upsets me. Unfortunately I'm still childish enough to be incapable of hiding how much it hurts.'

She ordered a large brandy with her coffee and drank it silently. Then her mood changed abruptly. 'Lakie, this is absurd. I'm not being plunged into despair by the threatened revelations of some old whore who's been dug up by an inquisitive journalist. She might as well pay for the privilege of re-opening this affair. I want to meet her. Perhaps your boyfriend could arrange it. If not, I shall do it myself.'

'Do you think that's wise?'

'No. Nor do I think it was wise to wish away so much of my youth in regrets about what my father may or may not have done. Now I think it's time for a little truth.'

'But Lady Lenton, what makes you so sure she'll tell the truth?'

Diana was puzzled. 'Why on earth shouldn't she? There's nothing in it for her any more if she lies. Whatever the facts are, they'll make a good story, so why lie now? If Papa was guilty of treason, it's news. If he was just a lecher in search of extra cash, even better.'

'You don't know this woman; I do, although not very well. I get the impression that she's a mass of resentments for all sorts of people and a born mischief-maker. I think she'd happily deceive you just for the satisfaction of feeling she'd put one over on you, and the same holds for Marcus, too. She looks to me like one of those people who always has to feel she's got something on the rest of the world. You'll never get the truth out of her, Milady!'

'Forgive me, but I must disagree. Are you going to arrange an introduction?'

'Very well, but I think she'll just try to hurt you as much as she can. I know instinctively that she's one of those people who thrive on the misery of others. She's going to tell you the very last thing you want to hear. I can virtually guarantee it.'

'I'm prepared to take the risk. I have no wish to go to my grave not knowing the truth about my father. However unpleasant it might prove, at least I shall no longer be confused.'

They met in a small consulting room at Louise's salon a few days later. The fashion house had three such rooms, designed for clients to meet the *couturière* or a senior *vendeuse* to plan a wardrobe or discuss a special order. Today the business in hand had little to do with fashion. Louise had banished Marcus Gregg at the front door. He was deeply disappointed.

'There's no room for you here, Marcus. Wait here if you wish, but I'd prefer you to go away. This is one of the most private meetings of Diana Lenton's life.'

'Precisely, and I want to earwig. Get the ripe emotional moments for my gentle readers. It'll be worth nine guineas a box!'

'Sometimes you disgust me. I've changed my mind about you waiting. If you want to hang around for the Queen of Tarts, do it outside. I don't want to see you at present.'

Grumbling, he went. He was so caught up in his story that Louise's growing disenchantment had escaped him completely. Marcus's matrimonial prospects were diminishing by the moment. A young trainee arrived with a tray of coffee. Louise took it from her and unobtrusively entered the room with it. Turning to leave, she hesitated momentarily beside Diana. 'If you want me to join you, Lady Lenton, just ring. I'll be outside. This room is completely private.'

When they were alone, Ninotchka unhurriedly studied Diana without bothering to ease their encounter with conversation. Eventually she said 'So this is the celebrated beautiful debutante. I shouldn't think our dear Alexei envisaged this scene in his most elaborate fantasies.'

'If you're about to try subduing me with bitchery, don't bother. You're a bit long in the tooth to play the beautiful adventuress patronising the gamine. Look at yourself some time. I'm a middle-aged woman and you're an old whore.'

'My, the gloves are really coming off, aren't they? Your father always said that an aristocratic Englishwoman had it in her to fight dirtier than anyone. We shall see. I am scarcely a beginner. Now, why was it suddenly so important to meet me? I've been around for years. Any time you wanted an introduction, you had only to ask half the men in your social circle. The other half are probably queer, so you'd know the right ones, I'm sure.'

'I never thought there was the slightest chance of prising the truth out of you while my father was alive; it's as simple as that. As long as he lived, it was a point of honour not to question his veracity by sneaking along to the other people involved and asking them to spill the beans on him. Once he was dead, I thought I should be allowed to let him rest in peace, with the secret as dead as himself. Now you seem determined to shout it to everyone who can hear, whether they want to or not. As you're out to disgrace me afresh, I might as well hear a little of what you plan to tell them about him.'

'I notice you don't say you want to hear the truth.'

'That's just because I'm not at all sure you intend to tell the truth. I'm interested in what you have to say. As to believing it, I shall decide that after I hear your story.'

'And what d'you suppose is in it for me? I don't stand to gain by discussing my past with you. I might as well not say anything at all.'

'Oh, no, there's an inducement to you to talk. If you agree to say in the *Post* only what you tell me, I shall agree not to sue for libel.'

'What if I refuse?'

'Then I shall ruin you – financially, of course. You ruined yourself years ago in every other way, I'm sure.'

'That's very amateurish blackmail. Everyone knows you can't libel the dead. They'd throw out any case brought by you on behalf of your father without a second glance.'

'If you don't agree my terms. I'll risk that. I suspect the temptation to take a sideswipe at me would be so great that you'd give me grounds to sue without needing to dwell on my father. Anyway, if I can prove that what you say about him holds me up to hatred, ridicule and contempt, then I have a case. You can only be interested in this whole exercise for two reasons: money and spite. I have to tolerate the fact that you'll make money out of my father's past indiscretions; I can try to ensure that you have to sacrifice the spite to assure the cash.'

'I might just prefer the spite as you call it to the money. Only I would call it truth, not malice. In that case you could find yourself having to sue me anyway, because I wouldn't care about not making money if I could have the satisfaction of making you uncomfortable.'

'I don't think so, Miss Chaliapin. I suspect you've been through enough bad times to value money rather more than emotional satisfaction, however strong the temptation. And newspapers are terrible snobs, you know, particularly the more vulgar publications. They might spout a lot about no fear or favour but, by the time my connections in the Old Boy network had got to work on the proprietor of the *Post*, you'd be last week's down-page bore. He's very keen on a peerage, and I know a couple of people who could either see he got it a year or two early or stop him getting one for ever. A story which would make him sacrifice that would need to be a great deal bigger than a spicy little "Where are they Now?" feature, don't you think?'

Diana was giving a virtuoso performance. Ninotchka, although furious, believed what she said. She had been the victim of too many such power struggles in the past to doubt their reality now.

'Very well, Lady Lenton, you win. I hope it gives you some satisfaction to know that your father was nothing more than a small-time crook and womaniser. How does it feel to know that the one possibility you always denied is the true story?'

A long silence followed. After twenty-five years of fanatical belief in Alexander Hartley, such a brutal confrontation with his shortcomings was unanswerable. Diana managed to retain her composure on the surface but she had nothing left to help her carry on her exchange with the Russian woman. She simply sat and listened.

Sensing her ascendancy, Ninotchka rubbed salt in the wound. 'He wasn't even strong enough to be an out-and-out rogue and admit he was crooked,' she said. 'I had to dress it all up in how he was helping to stave off the forces of evil.'

'But I've found out enough over the years to know there was certainly some sort of conspiracy to pass off an anti-Socialist document on the British public.'

'Yes, but that was nothing more than a smokescreen, you stupid woman! I had all sorts of unsuitable connections and some of them were the sort of White Russian exiles who get satirised in cartoons. They were cloak-and-dagger types and they believed in what they were doing, but it had no importance to real politics. They supplied the text of the Petrograd Communiqué – I never bothered to find out whether it was genuine or if one of their crazier people wrote it himself – and paid Alexei £5,000 to leak it to the papers. That was a handsome enough payment at the time, about five years' salary for him, and he was pretty well paid. But the whole point of it was what we were going to make in the currency speculation. I got the idea the minute this bunch of Russian half-wits approached me to talk to your father. Their £5,000 was small beer against what we planned to make on the currency, and we could use the £5,000 as a stake.'

'So what went wrong with this wonderful plan? If you

were so clever, why did a merchant bank end up suing you both for unpaid accounts and drawing so much attention to Papa's indiscretions that he was ruined?'

'Obviously you were too young to pay any attention to the international money markets at the time. Pure gambler's ill luck, my dear; the sort of thing you read about in novelettes and dismiss as unlikely. Europe's monetary system was in such a mess at the time that it was hard to decide which currency to buy low ready to sell high. It was no good getting Swiss francs. They were so high against all currencies, including sterling, that we'd have to pay too much in the first place. The German mark and the Italian lira were in such hopeless decline that even a big run on sterling wouldn't have made them a good bet. Spanish pesetas were no better. In the end it had to be the French franc. Alexander had avoided it at first because it looked quite strong and he wondered if it might be not much better than the Swiss currency. But it was a bargain against sterling when you knew what he knew. So he bought big, and so did I. We spent the Tsarists' £5,000 and a great deal more. Once we'd started buying it seemed a shame to stop short at a modest fortune when we could be set for life.

'Then we drew the Joker. The scandal broke; the pound nose-dived as he had planned. And at the same time there was a run on the franc! It had nothing to do with our little adventure. International confidence in the French economy suddenly took a tumble over some temporary setback and instead of going up, the franc went down overnight by more than sterling fell. In the chaos that resulted, we'd probably have been better off if the £5,000 bribe had just remained in sterling. As it was, we lost it, plus every penny of loose change your father could raise and a lot of credit that he couldn't hope to meet. If he hadn't been ruined by the political scandal, he'd have been bankrupt, so he might as well have gone one way as another!'

'What happened afterwards?'

Ninotchka assumed a look of innocence. 'I don't know the details. I did my best to protect your father from further embarrassment by staying away from him. I thought the best I could do was to fade into the background; even take the problem with the bank on my own shoulders if it helped. But they insisted on taking him to court too.'

'What about all that evidence your maid gave about you saying Papa would be all right because he'd ensured the defeat of the Labour Government and the Tories would be grateful enough to see he did well?'

'I was humouring him in saying those things. All my maid knew was what she heard me saying. But in fact I was just comforting him. Once he was ruined, he chose to say he had acted purely from patriotism. The new Government thought differently. They said they didn't believe the Petrograd Communiqué had any more than a passing influence on the voters and that there would have been a landslide to the Conservatives anyhow. So your father ended up financially bankrupt and politically friendless. Such a shame, but the world is hard.'

She sat back, stretching cat-like in her chair and visibly relishing the discomfiture of the woman opposite her. Diana remained silent for a time, assimilating what she had heard. She was sure something vital had been missed out, but she could not quite see what it was. Then a possibility occurred to her.

'I just don't believe that you were without political motives. I haven't managed to find out a great deal about you over the years but during the war someone who knew a bit about you told me you got out of Russia after being raped and mistreated as a teenager during the Revolution. I simply can't believe that an aristocratic girl who'd gone through something like that would be without sympathy for the people who wanted to defeat the revolutionaries. I think you were really working for the Whites all along and that you shielded them by betraying my father afterwards. He really did think he was acting as a patriot but you took the limelight off your Tsarist masters by setting up Papa as a cheap criminal!'

She was completely disconcerted at Ninotchka's burst of laughter.

'I find nothing remotely amusing in what I've just said.'

Ninotchka stopped laughing and turned on her. 'You really are a stupid bitch. What makes you think the Reds raped me? They'd been driven back into our section of St Petersburg after a couple of days occupying a bigger area. Our house was occupied by a funny little group of intellectuals who were less at home with firearms than my brothers. After the initial shouting of slogans and slapping of Tsarists' faces, they found they hadn't got too much killer instinct. They ended up talking politics with my father and playing chess with him while they held us hostages for a couple of days and the street battle went on outside. At the end of that time the Whites counter-attacked and a couple of the tougher Bolsheviks suggested getting out using us as shields. The leader wouldn't hear of it and said he wouldn't have our blood on his hands. He led them out and they fought their way through the garden. Most of them were killed out there.

'Then the Cossacks came. Don't think of the Hollywood version. They only looked like that when they were on parade. After three days of street-fighting all their piggish nomad savagery came out. Their uniforms were filthy and they smelled like their horses. Half of them were drunk. The front door had been smashed in the fight that dislodged the Reds. The Cossacks swaggered in and my father went forward to meet them, holding out his hand to thank them for driving away the revolutionaries. The officer shot him dead. My mother started screaming and two of his men grabbed her. When my youngest brother tried to free her, they shot him, too, but in the stomach, so he writhed around shrieking and it took him hours to die. The hall stank of blood and shit and they just laughed and slapped my mother. Then the officer informed my eldest brother that we were collaborators. Everyone knew that the Red scum killed all prisoners and if they'd spared us it was because we were secret Bolsheviki. Now we were going to suffer for it.

'What he really meant was that the women were pretty, the house was unlooted so far, and no one was likely to find out what they had done because Reds in the other houses had killed off our neighbours. So they had a holiday of killing and rape and theft on us. It wasn't the Reds who raped and orphaned me, you silly cow, it was the Whites! I'd run to hide upstairs in the confusion after they shot Grigory and I was watching them through the banisters. They ripped Mother's skirt off and the two of them held her while the whole squad of them took it in turns. I couldn't look away. They made my two surviving brothers watch. When Mother realised that they were there, she stopped screaming for their sakes and took it all in silence. Man after man, sweating and grunting like animals. I think she died before the last ones had been at her. She certainly wasn't conscious any longer. After a while they dropped her in a heap on the floor. They shot my two surviving brothers almost casually – quick bullets in the head as you'd dispose of a useless farm animal. Then they strolled off to the back of the house to see what they could steal.

'I just sat upstairs for ages, too terrified to move. After a while they started singing and shouting. They'd found the wine cellar and drunk it dry. I thought then it would be safe to go and see if anyone was still alive or if I could escape. Sometimes I wonder whether my life would have been better if I had just stayed up there until it was all over. But who knows? They'd probably have burned the place to the ground when they'd finished and I would have burned to death. What happened to me was better than that – just. I started to creep down from the attic floor and I got to the landing where the main bedrooms were. There was a sound somewhere, not the cellar, and I rushed into my mother's bedroom to find a new hiding place.

'It was a lovely room, all fresh blues and whites, with a huge four-poster bed draped with pink-and-white curtains. All the damage it had taken in the fighting was that the windows had shattered with the impact of some field gun fire a few streets away. I rushed to the bed and burrowed down into it. I still remember I was crying without realising it. When I saw the snot and tears running on to the lovely frilly pillows I hoped Mamuschka would not be cross with me for a second, then I remembered she was now a heap of bloody rags in the hallway. I must have cried out before I could stop myself, because it attracted the attention of the man who was coming up the stairs.

'It was the officer who'd shot Papa. His jacket was gone and he appeared just to be wearing his breeches and boots. There was a bottle in his hand and he was obviously drunk. Unfortunately he wasn't drunk enough. He was still capable of sex and he liked little girls, or so he kept telling me. He kept me there all night and through the next day. I thought I'd lose my mind, what with the things I'd seen and what he was making me do. Then two of his men came looking for him. They were such beasts they made him look like a gentleman and by now he was looking for novelty, so he handed me over to them.

'That was all I could take. I stopped thinking about what would happen to me or whether I even wanted to go on living. I was just determined to make them stop. One of them managed to get started. He lurched on to me and pinned me down, pawing at me. I lashed out but I was so small then I couldn't protect myself. The other one just started wandering around the room while he waited his turn, smashing what he didn't like and pocketing the things he thought he could sell. The officer was overcome by his efforts with me and he had rolled over and gone to sleep. He had slung his belt across the back of the bed above my head and as I struggled my hand brushed against it. There was a bayonet in a sheath there. I eased it out, drew my arm back and dashed the blade down into the Cossack's back.

'Of course I was so small and the angle was so bad that all I did was to enrage him by slashing him a little. He reared back over me and got his hands around my throat to strangle me. Instead of trying to shake him off I went on with the attack. I still had the bayonet and I whipped it down towards myself, then drove it straight up into the bastard's guts. I can still remember his inside emptying itself on to my mother's bed. Nothing I ever did all my life gave me so much satisfaction.'

Diana was staring at her, transfixed. There must be something she could say or do . . . looking at the hell that was still in the Russian woman's eyes after thirty-five years, she knew no one could ever say anything to change what had happened that October day. Whatever she might do to this woman after today, at this moment she understood her and sympathised so deeply that she almost loved the tough, vengeful figure who presented such a threat. Eventually, Diana managed to speak.

'But how did you manage to escape? Surely the other two were after you the moment you attacked him?'

'Another case of gambler's luck – but good that time, not bad. Almost before they had time to register what I had done, the whole house was shaken by a huge explosion. The heavy artillery had arrived and it was blasting the entire area to powder. I don't know whether the officer ever realised that I had killed the soldier in the bed. To someone half asleep, it must have looked as if the bombardment had got him. The ceiling came down on us all; heavy chunks of plaster and a damned great chandelier which made awful slashes in what was left of the dead Cossack.

'I rolled off the other side of the bed faster than I thought I knew how. I was stark naked and covered in the Cossack's blood and guts but I just ran. As I got to the door I tripped over my shoes and some sense of survival made me stop and shove my feet into them. The staircase was at a crazy drunken angle but I was light and I got myself down by pressing against the wall. Thank heaven the hall ceiling had come down too, along with a huge piece of staircase from the upper floors, and buried my poor mother and Grigory. I couldn't have gone past them. It would have been the only thing that could have stopped me.

'The street outside was almost as bad as the hallway. There were piles of fallen masonry, paving stones up everywhere, a broken gas pipe with the gas burning merrily. There was a shout behind me and I tried to run. I couldn't have survived another rape. But I tripped and started to fall. A big strong arm came round me from behind and I was swept up before I could hit the ground. I was turned over in the air to face him and found myself staring into a big strong face under a cap with red stars on it. Before I could scream or struggle, he'd managed to wrap part of his greatcoat around me while he shrugged himself out of it. To this day I can never work out how he did it without letting go of me.

'Somehow he got me into the coat. Then he just said "Is that your blood?" I shook my head. "No physical damage?" I shook my head again. "Good. Stay close to me and you might get through." I stayed with him for a year.'

'Who was he? How did you come to be in the West?' In spite of her antipathy for Ninotchka, Diana was absorbed by the story.

'He was a Bolshevik, very politically committed. In humanitarian terms he was the best, bravest, most honest man I ever met. Perhaps the only real man I ever met.' Her face had softened as she played with her memories. Then she resumed her story with a harder smile. 'Mere humanity inevitably intervened. I'm hardly a heroine of the Soviet Union, and I wasn't one then, either. I had no wish to pioneer the Siberian wastes or to make a Moscow a better place for the proletariat. Maxim was my only reason to be in Red Russia. I was swept along with him, back and forth across the war zone. He was off somewhere at a political meeting one night months later and the fighting broke through unexpectedly into the residential quarter where we were living temporarily.

'This time the Whites who attacked weren't drunken thieving Cossacks. They were people very like my family. One of the older men turned out to have been a friend of my father, who recognised me. It happened so soon after they burst into our building that I was never unfortunate enough to learn whether they would have committed any atrocities. They "rescued" me – remember I was still under sixteen years old, so they didn't ask whether I wanted rescuing – and took me off back to their headquarters. I never saw Maxim again. I suppose in a way I was relieved that someone else had taken away my problem of deciding whether to stay in this awful country with the man I loved or get out with the people who were heading back for the sort of comfortable existence I preferred.

461

'The group who adopted me were soon in full retreat and by my sixteenth birthday we had escaped to Paris. From there, I was on my own. There were relatively few ways for a well-educated young upper-class Russian girl without a family to earn a living in Paris in those days and I'm sure, *dear* Lady Lenton, you can guess what I chose as my career. I've been doing rather well ever since.'

A lengthening silence ensued. Ninotchka seemed no more inclined to break it than Diana. Finally, however, she resumed her monologue. 'My apologies for speaking at such great length. I thought I should let you know the full story to prevent you from harbouring further illusions about my commitment to the Tsarists. As far as I am concerned, politics makes beasts of men and I have no time for philosophies of the Left or Right. Since Paris in the early 1920s, I have been dedicated to the pursuit of comfort. Face the fact that my motive was money, and so was your father's. He was no wronged patriot.

'Anyway, who needed the Petrograd Communiqué to turn the country Conservative when there were so many bourgeois around convinced that revolution was just around the corner? Stanley Baldwin didn't need a gesture like that to return to power. Popular fear of the dictatorship of the proletariat would have ensured he romped home! If nothing else convinces you, surely that does? Above all it was a completely unnecessary act.'

Ninotchka's adversary sat silent and unresponsive, apparently thinking about what had been said. Eventually, smiling, the Russian woman rose to leave. 'Well, my dear, there you have it. I'm quite prepared to agree that you should see the story which comes from this discussion and to publish only material I have told you in the *Daily Post*. I can't help feeling you are wasting your time with the approval, though. Surely you agree that what you've heard is about as bad as it can be for Hartley's name?'

'Really, Miss Chaliapin, I credited you with more intelligence! You can't be under the impression now that I really care two hoots what you tell the yellow press?'

'I confess it surprises me.'

'I wanted some way of making sure I talked to you face to face. I knew my one chance of ever learning the truth lay in confrontation with you, not with your words filtered through some copy editor in a newspaper office.'

'Do you think you know now?'

'That, Miss Chaliapin, is something you will never be sure of.'

'I suspect that makes two of us. Goodbye "favoured daughter".'

Stunned by her enemy's knowledge of Hartley's private pet name for her, Diana watched in silence as Ninotchka departed.

Diana accepted Louise's invitation to stay for dinner. Evangeline was still with her cousin, and later the three women sat together in the luxury flat which occupied the top floor of the couture house.

'What I can't understand is why on earth you were so keen to see her when you were bound to be upset whatever she said.' Diana's action was incomprehensible to Louise, whose own character would have made her ignore the Russian woman's existence.

'I'm afraid confrontation has always been my way of tackling distasteful matters,' said Diana. 'God knows how much good it does; none at all, I imagine. She certainly hasn't given me peace of mind with what she said.'

'Did you believe her, Madam?' Evangeline was watching her mistress with deep concern.

'I don't really know. I certainly believed her account of what happened to her in Leningrad after the Revolution. That had an awful ring of reality to it. Reluctant though I am to accept what she said about Papa, there seems to be little choice. She made short work of my hopeful little attempt to suggest she was deceiving me for political reasons. I still feel there's something not quite right, but my good sense tells me that's no more than reluctance to accept an unpalatable truth.'

'How do you feel about the prospect of publication?' Louise took personal responsibility for Diana's current distress and was more anxious about this aspect of the affair than anything else.

'I'm not sure yet. I'm indifferent to it at the moment, but that's too good to last. I have an awful suspicion that I shall wake up at three o'clock tomorrow morning in a cold sweat at the thought of it all. Oh well, there's just one way to find out whether that will happen: to live through the night and then through the final act of this silly old scandal. Probably all I need to do is lay it to rest for good. If that's so, the publicity might be the best way of kissing it goodbye.' Her expression did not bear out what she was saying.

Eventually Diana said goodnight and went back to her Chelsea house. Evangeline arranged to join her there next day so that they could travel back to Devon together. After her departure, the two cousins sat moodily discussing Ninotchka Chaliapin and Marcus Gregg.

'What happened to him this evening? Did he hang around for that old Russian cat?'

'Evie, do you mind? That old Russian cat is about a year younger than me!'

'Sorry, love, but you look as though you could give her fifteen years. I keep forgetting what a crabby little old lady you really are under all that powder and paint! Anyway, did he wait for her?'

'Oh, yes, naturally. Marcus would die rather than miss following up on what happened tonight. He always pretends he does that sort of thing because he's a conscientious professional. In fact he's a nosey busybody!'

'My, my, we *have* gone off the old sod!'

'Well, what can he expect? No decent person carries on the way he did over this whole affair. Just imagine making your living by doing this sort of thing all the time! If it were me I'd feel dirty – I never realised before how offensive I find his whole line of work. I couldn't put up with it at close quarters. Oh, he must be wringing every detail out of her now! He waited out in the street because I refused to let him stay in the salon. He was jigging about on the pavement when I let her out and she got into his car. I saw them drive off before I locked the front door.'

'Oh well, maybe they deserve each other.'

'From what I can gather, Ninotchka Chaliapin is worth ten of poor Marcus, for all her sins!'

They had another drink together, turning the talk to deliberately lighthearted discussion of a new West End play, then bade each other goodnight. Louise was awakened by the telephone at 3 am. As she switched on the bedside lamp, her first sleepy thought was that it was she rather than Lady Lenton who would be lying awake sweating in the small hours.

'Mrs Kerslake? It's Bill – Bill Gibbings at the *Post*. Something's happened to Marcus. He always said to – to tell you if . . .'

'What happened, Mr Gibbings? Obviously nothing trivial by the tone of your voice.' She glanced up as Evangeline pushed open the bedroom door and came to join her.

'It seems they – that is, he – oh hell, there's no way of dressing it up. He seems to have taken this Russian bit off to a drunken party somewhere down Maidenhead way. Shouldn't have been driving at all in that condition, particularly the way he pushes that Jag of his. They went over the verge on a blind corner above a steep drop. Both killed outright. Police say the poor sod was full of whisky. Look, if there's anything I can do, just let me know, okay? Now will you be all right?'

'Yes, yes. I have my cousin with me. Don't worry. Thank you for your concern. Goodnight.'

Numb, Louise hung up. 'Evie, what do we tell Diana Lenton? Marcus has just been killed in a car crash up the Thames Valley, along with Ninotchka Chaliapin.'

Evangeline stared at her for a moment in silence, then said, 'I can't see why you're worrying what Lady Lenton will say.'

'No, you don't understand. The police say Marcus was drunk on whisky. But Marcus didn't drink whisky. He was allergic to it. It was his standing joke that it was the one spirit they'd have to tie him up and pour into him by force. Evie, someone murdered them.'

*

465

Evangeline and Diana stayed in London until after the inquest and Marcus's funeral, Evangeline to keep an eye on Louise, Diana to find out what was going to happen about the Petrograd story. The coroner's jury returned a verdict of accidental death on both Ninotchka and Marcus Gregg. An elaborate burial was planned for Gregg, with practically the entire press corps turning out to give him a good send-off. Ninotchka was cremated at Golders Green. Diana went along and peeped into the clinical-looking chapel at the end of the short private ceremony. It was quite empty save for a solitary male mourner in a sombre dark grey overcoat. She hung back as he emerged and started towards an anonymous green car. This was hardly the time or place to start asking him questions about the woman whose funeral he had just attended. She barely had time to glimpse a saturnine face, the left eye pulled down slightly by old scar tissue, and he was gone, into the car and out of her life.

Louise had said nothing about the whisky in the end. She and Evangeline decided that nothing could be achieved by stirring up something they felt they would never begin to understand. The important thing was that the death of the female lead in the story had effectively killed the Petrograd Communiqué feature. A couple of paragraphs appeared beneath a picture of the grim, twisted remains of Gregg's Jaguar, in which the passenger was referred to as the central figure in the celebrated 1920s scandal known as the Francs Case. Then Ninotchka Chaliapin was forgotten for good. This alone was enough to make Diana lose interest in the whole business. The woman had ceased to be a threat to her father's memory and hence to her own peace of mind. Why pursue the matter further?

Anyway, something else had happened which turned her in quite another direction. The day before she intended returning to Devon, feeling downcast she turned to her natural refuge at times of stress, Brown's. Some things changed over the years, but not her girlhood haven. It was still cosy and dark and English, still attracting discerning Americans and British families up from the counties, and still served the best teas in London. Diana had just consumed two large cream cakes and was starting to drink her cup of Assam when an American voice said, 'If my joints weren't creaking, I'd say I'd fallen through a hole in time! What the devil are you doing here, magic lady?'

She turned, hardly daring to believe what she knew she was about to see. At the next table sat Ben Lassiter, still all too recognisable twenty-five years after their spring love affair. 'Waiting for you to order me a Knickerbocker Glory, of course, what else? Don't say there's been a Florida revival and you're here to spend the second fortune!'

As she spoke he had moved across to join her. Now he beamed down at her. 'Hello, hello, hello, hello, hel-lo! The tooth fairy really came up with a bonus prize this time! No ice-cream sundaes. Just promise you'll have dinner with me tonight and let me look at you!'

'Done! I've gone off ice-cream a bit since the war, anyway.' They spent the next hour talking a little and gazing at each other a lot, rosy memories erasing the pain of their parting so many years before. By the time they parted to change for dinner, they were as much in love as ever.

He took her to Boulestin in Covent Garden for dinner. Throughout the meal she gazed at him, starry-eyed as a girl, listening to his life story and telling hers in bits and pieces. Diana had always assumed that their final row in the Savoy had made Ben abandon London for good. This was only partly true. He had been angry enough to give her up that night and for long enough to return to America within the week. After that he travelled all over the world for a couple of months, thinking over what had happened and coming to terms with his future. Eventually he had decided to return and contact her again.

'If I had to live in London to live with you, it was worth it,' he said. 'I still felt as hostile to your old man as I did that night in the restaurant, but I decided that with a little more tact on my part and a bit of tolerance on yours we could patch something up. I even managed to convince myself that, if you felt as strongly about me as I did about you, Lenton wouldn't have got past first base. You were very young, and with any luck your Aunt Hermione wouldn't have let you marry the first guy who asked you. How wrong could a man get?'

'When did you come back to London?'

'First week in October. I'd been down on the Riviera and I had an urge to go somewhere cool and fresh. A couple of people down there told me London was great in the fall. Not for me, baby! I breezed in and rang your Aunt Hermione to invite her for a cocktail. She sounded so flustered I thought maybe you were on the verge of announcing your engagement and thought I'd better get a move on. It wasn't until she came round to Jermyn Street that she spilled the beans. I can hear her now; that sweet little voice and that terribly sad smile – "Oh, you poor boy! You don't know, do you?". When she told me, I nearly dropped dead!'

'You mean Aunt Hermione actually saw you again in London? She never said a word!'

'You never learn, do you kid? Your Aunt H was a very bright lady. You were hitched and gone. What use would it have been to tell you that while you were marrying on the rebound, the guy you'd rebounded from was bouncing back himself? You could hardly have divorced Lenton a few weeks after you'd married him, dumped him in Malaya and come back for me!'

'How d'you know I married Roland on the rebound?'

'There you go again. Because I know you, Diana. After twenty-five years or more, I still know you better than you know yourself. You were crazy about me, just as much as I was about you. If we'd never had that blow-up at the Savoy, Lenton wouldn't have got a look-in. Your goddamned father was the only thing that I didn't understand about and we could have got round that once I'd learned to handle it.' He broke off, half afraid that even now she would re-start the old feud. But she merely nodded in silence and waited for him to continue.

'One way and another, Hermione was my salvation. She got rid of my other cocktail guests, fast, then cooked me some eggs which I ignored, poured me a huge whisky, which I drank, and saw me through the worst night of my life. Then she kept coming back to pick up the pieces. She was even responsible for what turned into my living. To take my mind off everything she dragged me off to the bloodstock sales, just because I said the one thing I'd loved in England had been the horses. I hate to say this, but it took my mind off my broken heart. One look at that horse flesh and I forgot everything else but the possibility of owning some of it!'

'You heartless beast – ten minutes with a four-legged friend and you'd forgotten my existence. So much for true love!'

'Come on, Diana, by that time it was four months since I'd seen you and here I was being told you'd got hitched only weeks before. I know I was obsessive about you but I'd been forced to live with the probability that you'd spit in my eye if I came within a mile of you ever again. Of course I let myself get distracted. Anyway, the upshot of it all was that I started writing huge cheques, encouraged by your glorious rogue of an aunt, and arranging to have all these beautiful beasts penned up at Stanhope while I dashed back to the States to buy somewhere to put them. Honestly, she saved my life!'

'And she never said a word about it to me! How typical of her. I don't think she ever did a rotten or a selfish thing in her life. You know she's dead, now?'

'Oh, yes. I read her obit in the paper. Heart attacks snatch heroes and villains alike, don't they?'

'So you didn't stay in touch over the years? Strange, you obviously got on so well I'd have thought it was a lifelong friendship.'

'In a sense it was. I'd have seen her every time I got within shouting distance. She put a stop to it because she said it would cause problems in the end for all five of us.'

'Five? Dear God, Ben, either you've got double vision or you've missed out a big piece of the story! Please spell out what you mean!'

'Look, you're not the only one around who's the

marrying kind. When I say five I mean you, Roland, Hermione, me – and Kathleen.'

'Kathleen being Kathleen Lassiter, I take it.'

'Now, yes. Then she was Kathleen O'Hara. She's from an old, rich, horse-breeding family in Virginia who actually raised stock from Diomed, that grey that won the Derby in England back in the eighteenth century.'

'Gosh, how quaint. I take it you married her for her horses!'

'Diana, you can't get away with being bitchy. Remember, you're the one who gave me marching orders. There never would have been a Kathleen if it hadn't been for that. I found a gorgeous spread in Virginia which wasn't going to leave me that much change out of my Florida millions, set myself up there, shipped out my horses and then began getting to know the neighbours. One of the neighbours just happened to have a lovely daughter who was different enough from you not to have to compete. Whammo. Propinquity did the rest.'

'And now, no doubt, you have a gleaming all-American home and 2.7 gleaming all-American children.'

'Bitch-bitch-bitch! Actually we have five, all pretty glamorous, and one of the most prosperous and best-known studs in the US.'

'It sound as if you *are* one of the most prosperous and well-known studs in the US!'

'She's Catholic. As I don't care either way, I was received into the Catholic Church.'

'Oh.' Diana subdued the desire to go on making hostile remarks about his wife and family. He was, after all, right about her having rejected him. 'I imagine, then, that you're rich, happy and successful. Lucky Ben. So why are you sitting here with me making very come-hither signals?'

'Because we both know this is something else. If you'd still been around, I'd never even have noticed Kath. I wouldn't expect her to understand this; I don't myself. I only know I've always adored you and I'll be unable to resist you even when we're both in our nineties. Let's not kid ourselves, though. The fact that I have a passion for

470

you doesn't devalue my love for her. We're very happy together and I imagine we'll go on being that way, although this is something I hadn't allowed for. Anyway, what about you? You don't appear to have spent the past twenty-five years pining.'

'One husband, two sons, one title, one country estate, eight department stores. Lots of money, thank heaven.'

'And happy?'

'It's not a word I apply to myself one way or the other.'

'People who say that usually mean they're as miserable as hell.'

'Don't say that, Ben. You're not in a position to do anything to change it.'

'What makes you think so?'

'You've as good as said so. You obviously love your wife and children and you have a wonderful life with your stud farm. There have been two men apart from you who might have been able to give me that happiness. Both of them are dead. What do you suggest I do, burn down your farm, murder your wife, sell your children as white slaves and then run off with you? Look at it another way. I may not be happy but I'm not actively unhappy. I have a very busy, successful life, friends and a husband who adores me. That's more than many women ever get a chance at.'

'And less than you intended having.'

'I'm beginning to think you're taking vengeance on me for what happened all those years ago, Ben. Will you treat me a little more gently if I say there were forces driving me then that made it impossible for us to be happy together?'

'Darling girl, forgive me. I've never stopped loving you for a minute and you're right, I was punishing you unjustly for ending it all those years ago. Come on, eat up your dinner and I'll take you home. I'm not going to make it even harder on you by starting it all over again. I couldn't leave Kath after half a lifetime of love and, if I go any further with you, that's what it will mean.'

Diana's usual drivingly acquisitive will was lacking for once. Passively she finished her dinner, allowed him to escort her from the restaurant and find a cab. They sat in an affectionate but mutually undemanding embrace in the taxi and when they arrived back in Chelsea she did not invite him in. He kissed her gently, understanding.

'You're being brave and altogether better than I'd have thought possible, Lady D. Bless you. I wouldn't have had strength for us both.'

He stood silent on the pavement as the shiny scarlet front door closed behind her, then turned and got back into the cab.

At 6.30 am the telephone shrilled out in his room at Brown's. 'Yeah – Lassiter,' he said, still half asleep.

'My, you haven't been staring at the ceiling in hopeless contemplation of your lost love, have you?'

The unforgettable velvet-on-broken-glass voice wakened him instantly.

'Diana. Anything wrong?'

'Not any more, but there was until you answered the telephone. Ben, I lost you before and I know I'm going to lose you again, but not like last night, I hope. How d'you feel about an early Chelsea breakfast?'

'I'll be right over.'

Half an hour later she opened her front door to him and, to his surprise, joined him outside. 'Come on, once round the block's good for the circulation!'

They held hands and walked along the Chelsea Embankment, still pearly in the morning light.

'You seem to fit in here, Diana. Somehow I can't see you buried in the country.'

'Oh, I love Devon. I spend far more time down there than here, but now and then I must get away. Chelsea suits me. Although it's becoming fashionable, it still has that slightly raffish air that you get from half-arrived painters and decadent literati. And of course, it has the lovely dirty river.'

After their walk they went back to the house for buck's fizz, smoked salmon, scrambled eggs, brioches and coffee. An open fire crackled in the breakfast room grate and it all looked like an extract from a Victorian novel. The champagne and their attraction for each other worked the inevitable magic and they were soon twined in each other's arms in front of the fire. Their loveplay had a gentle, unhurried air and between kisses Ben asked her questions about her family.

'They're very unobtrusive,' he said. 'If I were in our New York apartment I could guarantee a handful of them would be exploding on this little scene.'

'Oh, Sebastian is on a death-defying photographic jaunt up the Orinoco, believe it or not. He's been away for two months and doesn't expect to return for at least another three. I think he hopes it will turn him into the next Cartier-Bresson! Roland is out in the Far East for a month, looking up old wartime comrades.'

'What about your other son? I don't even know his name.'

'Mmm, he's in New York, learning a bit about Wall Street with some American friends he met at Oxford. Oh, no – what date is it?'

Ben did not reply. He had started unbuttoning her heavy satin blouse as she talked to him. When she began to ask the date, he was already stroking her breasts above the lace and satin of her half-cup brassière. Instantly she lost track of what she was saying, hungrily seeking out his mouth with her own.

Looking at her lying, half dressed, in the soft glow of the fire, Ben was swept by a passion he had almost forgotten. 'I want you so much I'm not going to make it out of these clothes,' he said.

'You'd better. I've waited twenty-five years for this!'

She stood up momentarily, unzipping her flared skirt in one long motion. She wore no slip, only a pair of lace-trimmed French knickers which matched the bra. In his excitement he had pressed the shallow bra cups down and one of her nipples peeped over the lace edging, with incredibly inflammatory effect. He slid to his knees, embracing her around her buttocks and burying his face in the satin panties. Then he reached up and slipped them down, pressing his face hungrily into the red-gold hair. Now he stood up himself and unfastened her bra.

473

'Just stand like that, pressed hard against me,' he said thickly, moving to unfasten his own trousers and pull off his crew-necked sweater.

A moment later, quite naked, they stood a hair's breadth apart. Diana's swollen nipples just brushed his chest and she could feel his penis, stiff with desire, throbbing forward against her belly. 'Take me now and don't stop all day, please, please!' She closed her eyes and leaned towards him. Lassiter hooked his hands under her thighs and lifted her slightly, moving her backwards to rest against the silk-covered wall. With one deft motion he had entered her, still supporting her with his arms beneath her thighs. She cried out twice in wild pleasure, but then said, 'Down, my love, please. Down on the floor. I want you feeling my breasts when you're in me.'

He loosened his grip and she slipped away from him. His fingers moved caressingly into her and she cried out again, 'You'll take me right over the edge! Oh please, please don't let it stop! I want it to go on always!' She wriggled convulsively against him and he groaned with the effort to stay in control. He wanted to come explosively into her again and again but dimly knew he was too keyed up for this to happen for a while.

They moved back to the hearth rug and she pulled him greedily down on to her. 'Now, now please! Kiss my nipples and take me all over, hard!'

As he did, she let out a wild animal cry and shuddered into fulfilment. He drew back slightly and said 'Jesus, you beautiful bitch, I want you for ever! I can't leave you.' She gazed dreamily up at him, crying with the satisfaction she was experiencing. He lunged forward into her and drowned in a kiss that seemed to go on for ever. As he felt his liberated spirit floating free he was sure that he wanted to stay here locked up with this woman for as long as they could remain undiscovered. No other excitement could touch this. She moved slightly and the beginnings of fresh excitement stirred almost immediately. She smiled and purred, taking his hands and pressing them against her breasts.

474

Then the telephone rang.

'Oh, Christ, no! I don't believe it! What time do people start calling you, Diana?'

'Damn!' she said, softly. 'That's what I started to say. The date ... my son's birthday. He always rings me just after midnight, wherever he is; I think he believes it will turn me into an ideal mother.' She kissed him again, clearly in anticipation. 'Get ready for me, darling, I'll be back in a couple of minutes ... after all, he is ringing from New York.'

Ben followed her over to the telephone and stood behind her, playing with her red hair, stroking the base of her neck, then gradually shifting his hands around her body to cup her big breasts. A moment before she raised the receiver she said 'Behave for a moment, Ben. I'll never be coherent with Cosmo like this!'

As she spoke he stopped abruptly in his love-making and moved away. She glanced at him, surprised, her lips forming a silent question. Then she was obviously listening to someone at the end of the line.

'Yes, Cosmo, happy birthday! I hope you're getting lots of exotic American presents? One in particular? What's that? You *what*? Oh, God, don't you ever think that there are more people to be considered when you act than just yourself? This could be for life and you ... yes, yes I know; but this isn't just another little adventure. Marriage should be the biggest step you can take. Look, we can't discuss it like this. I'll talk to you later. What d'you mean you won't be there? Oh, yes of course – honeymoon. Where? Virginia, why? Well if her parents are as surprised as me, I think it might be a rather frosty honeymoon. Maybe they wouldn't mind if I had their telephone number so that I could talk to you there over the next day or two. Yes? I'll get a pen. Wait a minute ...' She glanced up at Ben, but he had folded into an armchair and now sat with his face hidden in his hands. Bewildered but trying to hurry and therefore only half attentive, she went back to the telephone.

'Right Cosmo. Fire away. Yes, I have that. Oh, before

you go – what's their surname?' A silence followed. She sagged slightly. 'Oh. No, bad line, that's all. Yes, I've got that. Lassiter with two esses. Have a safe trip, Cosmo . . . and, er, good luck!'

Numb, she replaced the receiver. Lassiter's hands dropped to his lap and he looked at her in blank despair. 'How old is your son today, Diana? Twenty-four?'

'Yes.' Her answer was so quiet it was more just a lip movement.

'If you'd given the poor God-forsaken bastard just a few minutes of your precious time over the years, perhaps this would never have happened. For the past six months, my eldest daughter has been seeing a boy in New York and telling us she doesn't want to bring him home yet because he has problems over his own family and he doesn't want involvement with parents and brothers and sisters. She's pretty crazy about him but she didn't go into much detail. Only that his first name was Cosmo. It's hardly as common as Joe or Mike, which is why I fell apart when you first used your son's name on the phone. Erin's always been an independent kid and, if she thought he'd prefer it, she'd be quite capable of going off and getting hitched without telling me anything about it until afterwards. She was twenty-one three weeks ago, so she's old enough not to need my consent. It's her, isn't it?'

Diana nodded and eventually managed to say 'Three days ago. He saved the news until his birthday.'

'Well at least you and I weren't screwing each other silly when they were actually getting married.' As he spoke, he was dressing. He looked across at her in sudden disgust. 'Put your clothes on, you whore. You look indecent.'

She rushed at him, the shock and the mad coincidence of the past twelve hours overpowering her. 'How dare you? How bloody dare you? It takes two, and you were as keen on this as I was. I seem to remember someone a few minutes ago yelling out about never leaving and staying here for ever. You've changed your tune now, haven't you?'

As she set about him with flailing hands and arms, he caught her wrists and shook her furiously. 'You think I'm stupid or something? Thanks to you not caring enough ever to know what that boy's doing, he's married his own damned half-sister! You were pregnant when you married Lenton, weren't you?' She was silent, gasping for breath. This time he shook her so hard she was almost flung off her feet. 'Weren't you?' he yelled again.

'Yes, God damn it, I was.' Now she was as angry as he. 'And as I said before, it takes two. I didn't get like that on my own, you know!'

He let go of her, glaring murderously. 'You think I'm not as disgusted with myself as I am with you? It's almost as if some fucking cosmic practical joker set up this little reunion just to prepare us for the surprise package of the year. Your son and my daughter. My son and my daughter. Now folks, the family economy toast. Just one for both the bride's and the bridegroom's father. Gee, he's the same guy! How neat!'

He turned away abruptly and finished dressing. She still stood naked in front of him. 'If you don't cover yourself up in a minute, Diana, I swear I'll kill you! Now get out of my way. I don't know if I'll ever manage to tell my Erin what you and I have done to her, but whether I do or not you and I are finished. I never want to see or hear from you again. When I cool down a little, I may be less savage about you, but somehow I doubt it. You screwed up my life once a long time ago, and now you've done it again – but this time for keeps!'

Picking up his coat, he turned and walked out, leaving the door swinging wide. Still naked, she stood for a moment in the hall and watched his retreating figure, tears coursing unnoticed down her cheeks.

CHAPTER TWENTY-TWO

Alexander House prospered as Granby estate grew richer; the same legacy fed both. Diana frequently gave thanks to Edward Rathbone for leaving her the stores and to his self-effacing wife for failing to fight for her inheritance. The Alexander House Trust had first refusal of some of the best teachers in Europe and America thanks to hefty financial sponsorship from Rathbone Department Stores. All the outstanding young educationalists wanted to experience at first hand this dilettante's dream turned top flight international school. In the autumn term of 1971 a new teacher of animal and marine biology was recruited. Her name was Rhiannon Maxwell. She had a Cambridge Double First in zoology and geography and a Master's degree from Stanford. She looked much as Evangeline Owen had when she bewitched Neill MacIntyre in 1929 and she was Evangeline's grand-daughter.

Evangeline was still bursar and administrative director at Alexander House, a post she had created over the years as the institution grew from a fad of Diana's into a self-justifying operation. Without Evangeline it could never have sustained its unprecedented international standing. She sat on all staff appointment boards and her opinion was as good as a legal veto, however academically well qualified the candidate. She had a natural eye for both misfits and what she termed naturals. The smooth running of the whole establishment was a daily endorsement of her selective skill. She withdrew from the committee when Rhiannon was interviewed, identifying the young woman as her close kinswoman. 'Of course, none of them will dare turn her down now they know who she is, so my walk-out was just a little theatrical touch,' she told.

Diana. 'You learn corrupt politics at an early age in the Welsh Valleys!'

Diana was pleased to see Evangeline so animated again. In recent months she had slowed down noticeably, although her mind was as penetrating as ever and her wit as quick. But she was pale and much thinner and Diana had tried tactfully to introduce the subject of a full medical check-up. Evangeline would have none of it.

'Don't be daft. I'm as strong as a pit pony and these days sixty-two is no age at all.'

'That's precisely why I wish you'd see a doctor. If you're a bit run down you should sort it out now, or you'll make yourself really ill. Come on, Evie. I'll treat you to Harley Street as a hypochondriac's Christmas present, then we'll go and make pigs of ourselves over lunch at the Savoy. How about it?'

'Well, I'll have to think about it. I don't want you getting any ideas into your head about pensioning me off. This place saved my sanity after Neill went, and if I was cut off from it now I'd curl up and blow away.'

'Now you're being daft! This place couldn't function properly without you and well you know it. I just want to make sure you're fit to run it for another ten or fifteen years, you stubborn old mule!'

Rhiannon started working at Alexander House about then. She had a flat in the academic staff wing but spent a lot of time with her grandmother. When they met there, Diana was polite but cool. Rhiannon was puzzled and eventually asked Evie about Lady Lenton's reserve.

'Well, we're servants, aren't we? I get away with murder because I'm the quaint old character in the chimney corner who's been with Madam since the old Queen's day. You know, the one who's pointed out to little twerps as "that wonderful old girl, salt of the earth, no more like her when she's gorn" and all that shit!'

'Gran! You certainly use quaint old character language. Presumably that's from when you sailed around the Horn under canvas as a cabin boy!'

'Less of your lip, you cheeky little Madam! I'm quite

serious, love. That really is the way she thinks of us, when she thinks of us at all. She thinks all this Snow Queen nonsense is for the best because it saves the embarrassment which would arise if you were to expect to hob-nob with her socially.'

'What a load of outdated rubbish!'

'You know that, your friends know it. But Lady Lenton doesn't. That's the world she's always known and that's the world she expects to go on living in. After she's dead, she doesn't care what happens to it all. Does it bother you?'

'Not in the least. She's an interesting woman and I should like to know her better, but not if that's the way she feels. I think it's pretty rotten that you've had to live with that attitude all your adult life, though. Why have you put up with it? You could have gone into Great Aunt Louise's business or used the cash she left you to branch out on your own. What made you stay with her?'

'Inertia at first; then gratitude and finally, I suppose, love. I've got you and Imogen, but really I know Diana Lenton better than I know either of you and, for all her snobbery and selfishness, she's been pretty good to me.'

'Well, then, that's all that matters.'

Rhiannon soon changed her mind. In mid-October, Sebastian Lenton returned to Granby for a long break following his latest overseas photographic assignment. Sebastian had defied conventional wisdom and failed to turn into the over-indulged mother's boy that everyone said would result from the way Diana molly-coddled him. He had managed to avoid Eton permanently, staying on and completing his education at Dartington Hall. There they had ignored his temper tantrums until they vanished for ever and had encouraged the streak of originality which turned him into a good second-rate painter and a superb photographer.

Never in any doubt about what he wanted to do for a living, Sebastian avoided university and persuaded a top fashion photographer to take him on as a gopher. The gopher turned into an assistant, the assistant to a junior photographer. Eventually he took the plunge and started up alone. He learned fast that fashion would not hold his interest for ever, found limited satisfaction in news journalism and eventually made a lot of money as an advertising photographer while waiting for a permanent obsession to overtake him. Since the late 1960s he had been increasingly absorbed by wildlife and natural history photography. It did not pay well but it was fascinating. Gradually he built up a reasonably satisfying pattern of six months advertising work to pay the bills; three months wild life safari for pleasure and new experience; and three months playing or resting to prepare him for the next commercial foray.

Sebastian generally spent the final three months somewhere near Diana. He adored his mother, but with a cheerfully discourteous recognition of her faults which she found infuriating. They alternately fought and enjoyed each other's company, their relationship so close that Roland often felt excluded from it. This year Sebastian's visit to Granby began in the autumn and he had various wildlife problems to sort out before he went on another expedition. One evening he was deep in discussion with Roland about the problems of photographing marine mammals, when his father suggested he ask the advice of the new biology tutor at Alexander House.

'Really, Pa, how would a glorified schoolmarm be able to sort out this one? It's a teaser for an expert.'

'So is she,' said Roland quietly.

'What? Didn't quite catch that.'

'Mmm, nothing important. I think this schoolmarm might be a little different. Cambridge and Stanford science degrees; impeccable teaching qualifications; but above all a deep interest in practical marine biology. I gather that's why she was so interested in coming to Alexander House. She wanted somewhere with good sea access and a strong leaning towards practical work.'

'She chose Alex? I thought that with its reputation, it would expect to choose her!'

'Normally, yes. But really she's so well qualified that I think they'd have given her a top job in any of a dozen first-rate American universities or research foundations. She's half American, actually. Father married Evie's daughter at the end of the war. She even looks just the way Evie did when we were all out East in the thirties.'

'Pa, you sound positively nostalgic and the girl sounds intriguing. I'm off to investigate her. See you later!'

Sebastian, over six feet tall, lean and hard-limbed, with light brown hair and pale grey eyes, was a womaniser who had no difficulty in pursuing his hobby. Girls took one look at him and succumbed to the mixture of charm, talent, arrogance and animal sex appeal which he wore like a smart suit. At thirty-seven, he was a practised evader of matrimony. So far he had discovered no good reason to settle down to monogamy and what he assumed to be staid middle age. He looked nothing like his mother but shared a great deal of her personality. He lacked her capacity for melodrama and was more lovable for it. Rhiannon was lost the moment she set eyes on him.

He was no less taken with her. Her obvious physical attractions were backed by a first-rate mind which was largely devoted to the very area where his strongest interests lay. Sebastian was entranced and spent more and more time visiting her in the school labs or in her flat. Diana, usually voluble about his constantly-changing female companions, acted as if this one did not exist. Sebastian tried introducing Rhiannon to the manor once or twice, but she stopped him.

'It's no good, Sebastian, in your mother's eyes it's as if you're seducing the servant girl! Let's just leave it at you and me, and pretend the manor crowd don't exist. It's much more comfortable.'

'But they do and this is nonsense. It would be bad enough if you really were a servant here. This isn't the nineteenth century and, if I fancied and liked one of the maids, there's no reason why I shouldn't take her out. In your case, though, it's even nuttier. You're not employed by Mama and she has no possible grounds for treating you as if you are. The Trust is only her pet project. She doesn't own it and the staff are not answerable to her. In one sense, your grandmother is far more your employer than my mother.'

'She doesn't see it like that – and incidentally, neither does Gran. She has exactly the same sort of prejudices as your mother, except that in her they are preserved to prevent me getting hurt, not because she thinks they really count for anything. She believes I'll be treated to the classic maidservant seduction and casting-out.'

'I don't think one's allowed to do that sort of thing to a lady zoologist!'

'Oh, you silly sod, I do love you! At least you don't take it seriously.'

'Oh, but I do. I know Mama's petty obsessions of old and they can be hard things to crush. We could be in for a tough time with her.'

In the end they agreed to let the matter rest for the moment and see how things developed. They were still having enough fun inside a personal romantic bubble to be indifferent to the opinions of the world, or even of Diana Lenton.

When Evangeline attended the promised Harley Street consultation early in December, she already had a fair idea of what the specialist would say. She had gone to London a few days in advance of the main appointment and went along to his clinic's X-ray unit as well as giving blood samples. After he examined her and she had dressed again, he asked her to rejoin him in his consulting room.

'How much nursing did you do with your husband in Malaya, Mrs MacIntyre?'

'Enough. It's cancer, isn't it, Doctor?'

'Yes, I'm afraid there's no doubt about that. It might be worth opening you up to take a look. More and more cases respond to surgery and chemotherapy these days.'

'Not when you've got lumps where I've got them. How long?'

'If you did that much nursing, you know I can't answer that, Mrs MacIntyre. It depends on everything from the strength of your survival instinct to the balance of your diet. I wouldn't even hazard a guess, beyond saying you're unlikely to be here ten years from now.'

'Christ, if I'd only needed to be told that, I could have

stayed in Devon instead of traipsing up here on such a pointless trip! Come on – six month? Six years?'

'It's been a long time since I saw anyone at your stage last more than a year. It was a lot less with most of them. I seldom discuss it this frankly. I try to work out whether they really want to know and base what I tell them upon their attitudes. You're unusually direct about it.'

'It would be pretty damned stupid to wrap it up in cotton wool when I'll be having to cope with it face to face so soon, wouldn't it?'

'You're sensible – and very brave – to see it like that. Screaming and ranting sometimes help.'

'Not for me. What's the point? It's hardly likely to change God's mind. He tends to be a bit on the deaf side where I'm concerned!'

With a stiff smile she rose, thanked him and left. Outside she told Diana that the results of the consultation would be forthcoming within the week, then went off to join her for a large, expensive lunch. It tasted like sawdust.

Evie remained fairly strong and energetic until the New Year. Then she weakened abruptly and by the beginning of spring she was virtually bedridden. Diana was deeply distressed – far more so, she felt sure, than if the same thing were to happen to Lettie. With Evangeline, it was like watching a piece of herself dying. She went to see Evie every day, sitting on the edge of her bed to recount the latest gossip from the school or the estate. Her relations with Rhiannon remained polite but distant.

One raw March afternoon, they were talking about Lettie's notorious love life in the early 1930s. 'It's no good,' said Diana, laughing at one of Lettie's more dotty indiscretions, 'I'll never understand what made the girl tick.'

'No, you and I seemed to have more in common than you and your sister where men were concerned.'

'That almost goes without saying. We've been better than sisters. You've always said that, Evie.'

'You don't call your best friend Lady Lenton.'

Diana recoiled as though she had been slapped.

'Evangeline – that's for the world, not for us! You know it's meaningless convention.'

'Between you and me, yes. But don't you think I'd like to have been the girl who danced with the Prince of Wales? Don't you think I would have enjoyed sitting in the Ladies' Stand at KL Races, or being in the Members' Enclosure at Ascot? It means plenty to everyone *except* you and me!'

She's dying, thought Diana, and all this time she never told me. But she shouldn't have needed to, said her sense of justice. She's the best friend you ever had and you should have been sensitive enough to see it for yourself.

'Evie, what can I do now? It's too late . . .'

Evangeline's answer was unspoken. Her eyes strayed past Diana to the doorway. Rhiannon had just come in. Evie turned silently back to Diana.

'I understand. It's done. Can you ever forgive me?'

'Nothing to forgive, cariad. I needn't have stayed if it was so rotten. I had you. I had Granby. For a while I thought I had Roger.'

Diana's heart lurched again. Yes, there was much to make up for. At sixty-two she was learning for the first time that one was not always right simply in being true to oneself. Rhiannon broke the moment. Trying hard not to eavesdrop and failing, she bustled to the foot of the bed. Diana rose decisively, brushed a non-existent wrinkle for her skirt and moved towards the door.

'I must rush – see you later, Evangeline. Oh, Rhiannon, we have a couple of interesting guests of about your age for dinner on Thursday. I'm from the Planet Geriatrica as far as they're concerned. If you're not too busy, you might care to join us. About seven-thirty for eight? Perhaps you could let me know by this evening.'

She left, two thunderstruck gazes following her. After the door had closed, Rhiannon turned in amazement to her grandmother.

'What on earth brought that on, Gran?'

'Just my lady being Milady,' said Evangeline, relaxing contentedly.

*

Evangeline died at Easter. She was buried among the daffodils in the windy little churchyard overlooking the sea at Granby parish church. Sebastian and Rhiannon had become engaged three weeks earlier and she had lived to see their wedding date set. It was enough.

Roland walked back to the house with Rhiannon, Sebastian and Roger Simpson. Diana wanted to stay a while on her own. She sat on a bench, positioned to show off the spectacular view down across the sands of the estuary at the base of the low cliffs. Evie, dear Evie, she thought. It was bad enough when Krystyna went, but you were more. You were the other half of me; the realistic half. The better half.

She shed no easy tears. The grief ran too deep. All down the years she had taken for granted that they were bound together by friendship and not necessity. Yet when she tried to remember objectively, she realised that she had used Evangeline shamelessly to provide a background for the continuous variety show that was her life. It was no excuse to say that she had given Evangeline some good times. In the end she was excessively conscious that she had stood on her friend's shoulders to reach for the stars. Diana's thoughts turned towards Roland and she saw that she had used him in much the same way. There had always been someone more dazzling for company; always another social mountain to climb; but never hand in hand with him, always one step ahead.

Enough! cried her realistic streak. You're sitting here devising bad prose when there are living people around you who will feel better if you go and behave properly with them now, today, instead of promising miracles some time. Just this once, do it right, for Evie.

Much better, said a fading South Wales voice inside her head. You don't half overdo it sometimes, Milady!

Meanwhile the love match between Rhiannon and Sebastian also gave birth to a spectacularly successful business partnership. They pooled Rhiannon's scientific expertise with Sebastian's photographic talent, took an intensive course at a top film school, and started making wildlife documentaries. The intuitive understanding between them seemed to communicate itself to the subjects of their features, and the result was a whole series of award-winning films. Rhiannon's teaching career ended; so did Sebastian's bouts of advertising pack shots. Their work developed into a sequence of one major expedition each year and a long stint in the cutting room and sound studio. The results were magical. Between such exercises, Sebastian still returned to Granby, where Rhiannon too was now welcomed with open arms by Diana.

'I know Evangeline did something that changed Mama's attitude to Rhiannon,' Sebastian said to Roland months later, 'but Mama certainly acted on whatever it was. No half measures there!'

'No one could ever accuse your mother of being slow on the uptake,' Roland answered. 'She can be stubborn, opinionated to the point of bigotry and wildly wrong about almost anything at times. But now and then she sees the light so clearly that she'll stick to the truth it reveals through death and destruction. The best thing about Diana is that her virtues are as big as her faults. I wouldn't have her otherwise . . . well, not drastically so, anyhow!'

CHAPTER TWENTY-THREE
Devon, 1977

The drawing room was full of ghosts. Diana pressed back into the shadow beside the French window and there they all were in the damp September gloom.

Over by the Bechstein she could hear Krystyna Karpinska's throaty laugh as she leaned forward to turn the page for a desirable young man. Between the armchairs beside the empty hearth, a young and petulant Sebastian stamped and demanded to know why he could not go out with Mama. Evangeline glared at her from only a few feet away as though about to launch into one of her verbal tirades. Best-loved but most distant, Edward Rathbone and Roland stood talking together at the door, looking at her with fond concern on their faces.

Diana shrugged herself deeper into her trenchcoat, crushed out her half-smoked cigarette in a small Copenhagen bowl (Sacrilege! she heard a long-dead Evangeline cry) and turned away from the room to face her beloved garden.

Roland's dahlias were almost finished, dripping sadly in the late afternoon shower, matching her melancholy with their heavy, down-turned heads. And suddenly, unaccountably, her heart leapt exultantly. You're alive, you're back at Granby and you know how to fight a lot dirtier than Cosmo. Let him try to get rid of all this and see where it gets him!

A small voice told her that he already had it; that Granby's days as the Lenton family home were numbered, but she set it aside as pointless speculation. Something would happen. So much building and consolidation could not be brought down again within one generation – particularly when what she had rebuilt had started so many centuries ago. Car tyres crunched on the gravel drive as Green turned the big car towards the garage. She heard Lettie calling an anxious enquiry. Dear Lettie! Her stability was always so much more debatable than Diana's and here she was worrying that big sister had finally cracked. Diana turned back into the big room. The ghosts slipped away, banished for the moment by her sense of immediacy. But they would be back. This house had seen too much family history and drama not to hold traces of it in every timber.

The sudden rush of vivid memories had been brought on by the abandoned look of the dust-sheeted furniture after her month in France, following Roland's funeral. Diana had known at the time that retreat would not help her, even temporarily, but everyone else felt sure it was for the best, so off she had gone with Green and Lettie. And now, at her insistence, they were back much sooner than planned. She hoped her return was in time to prevent the loss of Granby.

By the time Diana had gone to her room, taken a bath and changed her clothes, Green had spread the word that Madam was home. Warmth was pulsing through the previously unoccupied rooms; the dust sheets had been miraculously whisked away from the elegant drawing room furniture. By the time she joined Lettie there for dinner, the place looked as if it had never been abandoned for more than five minutes. A generous log fire crackled in the great fireplace and the subtle glow of the lamps gleamed on the polished cut glass in the drinks cabinet. Diana poured stiff gins for both of them, then, while Lettie fluttered about worrying over tomorrow, she telephoned Roger Simpson. If he was surprised to learn she was back, he did not acknowledge it. Yes, he was free that evening and he would be delighted to come over for dinner. He would arrive in half an hour.

'Have you talked to Cosmo yet? Does he know that you're home?' he asked as she was about to ring off.

'Of course not. As far as I'm concerned, he's now the

enemy. I talk to him in front of a dozen witnesses or not at all from now on! You come over and we'll plan our campaign.'

'My dearest Diana – don't you ever give in? There will be no campaign. Cosmo has won. Please try to accept it and avoid even more misery. Make your choice of furniture and paintings, then pack up and get as far from the West Country as possible. The alternative is simply too painful to contemplate. I don't think you'd survive the dispersal of Alexander House.'

'Have we really known each other for over thirty years without you learning that I always get my own way? Come along over – we're wasting time with this silly conversation.'

And with that she disconnected, deeming a formal goodbye unnecessary.

Lettie found it impossible to contain her anxiety any longer. 'You know there's nothing you can do, Diana. None of us wants to see you lose. We all love Granby almost as much as you do and the last thing we want is for it to be turned into a grand hotel and Alexander House an ordinary boarding school. But Cosmo's holding all the cards, and this time you're not going to win. Isn't it better to retire gracefully instead of waiting to be stripped of everything?'

'He's not going to win, Lettie. That's the only thing I'm sure of.'

Apparently losing interest in the subject, Diana disdained to discuss it further. Instead she turned to another matter.

'Do you know tomorrow's date?'

Taken aback, Lettie paused for a moment. Then a flutter of new disquiet crossed her pretty face.

'Oh, my dear – the tenth. Your wedding anniversary!'

'Yes. I've never been apart from Roland on that date except during the war and I wasn't going to make this the first time. Somehow he seems to be here. I hadn't realised that Cosmo was moving so fast and I confess it was a desire to be close to poor Roland on our anniversary that brought me home rather than Cosmo's nonsense. Strange to think that this will be my first year without a card or some memento from Roland. He always sent me one, although he tried to laugh at his own banality in doing it.' Her voice trailed off. Lettie eyed her anxiously in the subdued lamplight, but her sister was dry-eyed.

When Roger greeted Diana he gave off the same sort of glow as the fine things in the drawing room. Neither Diana herself nor Lettie reacted. Both were used to men being in love with Diana, even in old age. It was a knack she had developed early and which had never deserted her – except for her elder son, who unfortunately found her entirely resistible. Everyone was pleased to see Simpson. He was an old enough friend to qualify as family, and very few secrets were held back from him now.

Roger had presided over the reconstruction of the estates ever since Diana had first set about it back in 1942. He had never married. There had been numerous superficial affairs, but since one summer afternoon so long ago an unattainable green-eyed redhead had held him in willing slavery, and no other woman could begin to compete. Now, grown old together, they were thoroughly at home in each other's company and each knew the other's probable reaction to a problem. He was all too aware that she would have to be dragged away from this struggle bound and gagged. The trouble was that, if she did not withdraw, he was afraid that it was the one event which could break her spirit.

While still at Eton, Cosmo had given up the pointless struggle to capture Diana's love. Since then he had devoted himself to proving that he could succeed without the featherbedding of the family estates. As a successful stockbroker he had never shown any interest in Granby, spending the minimum required time there.

That summer, the illness which had confined Roland to the estate for the past year had finally killed him. As soon as the funeral was over, Cosmo announced his intention as heir to sell up and divert the money to a Swiss investment company before going to live permanently abroad. He was deaf to the pleas of his four children to hold on to Granby. They loved it and shared their grandmother's almost tribal devotion to the place. It made no difference. Cosmo wished to sever all such links with the past. Alexander House still depended on Granby donations for its continued existence and therefore it was under sentence of death. Cosmo had always dismissed the principles behind its charter as high-minded pretentiousness, and it was probable that he would sell it off to anyone interested in making it into an expensive private school. That thought affected Diana even more than the possible dispersal of Granby.

Only after the family solicitors had convinced Diana that the new baronet had the right to carry out his threat did she bow to everyone's entreaties and leave England for a long holiday. Now she was back, the first hurt of bereavement firmly under control, and spoiling for a fight. It seemed unlikely that any of the people who loved her would be able to convince her that the fight was over before it began.

The trio sat down to a leisurely dinner: two handsome, apparently ageless women and a distinguished man all clearly enjoying each other's company. There was no sign that Diana's return had been unanticipated. Since her arrival, fresh bread had been baked and the big commercial freezer in the scullery had been raided for pre-prepared delicacies. No housekeeper in her right mind would have dared serve Diana a sub-standard dinner, particularly on the first night back from France. Soon after they had finished eating, Lettie decided to go to bed.

'I don't know how you keep going, darling,' she told Diana. 'I'm dead on my feet and I intend to sleep for twelve hours. You should do the same.'

'Yes, Lettie, I'm sure you're right.' Diana's absent tone made it quite clear she was not listening to her sister's patter. 'Sleep well and thank you for coming with me on such a doleful little trip.'

Lettie departed, suffused with warmth at the thought that for once she had been useful to Diana. Throughout their lives it had invariably been the other way round. Simpson watched his goddess appreciatively. He knew that Lettie's presence had been virtually an irrelevance. Diana was one of those people who retreated into herself in grief, bound her own wounds and then emerged apparently unscathed. She had simply been making sure that Lettie felt needed and cared for.

Over brandy and coffee, Diana reviewed her position. 'So what does he think I'm going to do – lie down and take it?' she demanded with some asperity.

'He would hardly confide in me, Diana. Ever since we met, Cosmo has resented the fact that I don't call you Lady Lenton in private as well as public, and he knows I'm firmly your man when it comes to war.'

'But you must know something!'

'He is painfully aware of your terrible temper and quite unreasonable tenacity of purpose, but he thinks that this time even you will recognise that you're beaten, take the best bits from the house and go elsewhere. He knows his children are likely to spend every possible moment with you and see very little of him for a long time, but he's stubborn and he thinks that money will bring them round in the end if nothing else does. Don't forget that his great need isn't to be loved. He wants to dominate. If he can control everyone around him he really doesn't care a damn whether they like him – let alone love him.

'Ideally I think he would like one of those terribly civilised family lunches or dinners when everyone gets together with you as the titular head of the table but everyone knowing that the real power lies with him. Then he'd kiss you on the cold cheek afterwards and take off for the Côte d'Azur, leaving you with your widow's mite. I'm damned if I'll stand by and see you subjected to that. I think I'd kidnap you first if you weren't prepared to absent yourself. If you lose, he's not going to humiliate you too.'

Diana was almost in tears. She reached out and gently touched his hand.

'My dearest Roger, I cannot tell you how grateful I am. You're the last faithful swain I have left and you're never less than wonderful to me.'

'I've loved you for so long that it comes as second nature,' he told her.

'Then will you do me a great favour tonight, without thinking I'm a crazy old woman?'

'Name it.'

'Please stay with me. Just come up to my room and hold me in your arms all night and protect me from the future. I can handle the past myself. Just hold me and try to pretend for us both I'm still a beautiful young woman and not an ugly old hag.'

Though close to tears himself, Simpson laughed.

'My dearest Diana, you must be the vainest woman in the world. I love you so much now that a proposition from you at a grand old age is just as tempting as it would have been in your prime, and you offer it to me with apologies about wrinkles and spare tyres!'

To his genuine amusement, she was furious. 'I'll have you know that I have a little cellulite and a few laughter lines – I do *not* have wrinkles and spare tyres! Now, are you coming with me or not?'

Still smiling, he followed her upstairs.

Roger was tactfully absent when Gillian brought Diana's tray next morning. It would have been unthinkable for her maid to find him in Diana's bed, although no reaction would have been obvious. Diana poured coffee from her favourite Copenhagen fluted blue pot and turned her attention to the neat stack of mail which accompanied her breakfast. As she casually flipped through the envelopes, the familiar handwriting on one stopped her with a terrible spiritual lurch.

Roland?

Momentarily a panicky grief clutched at her, making her incapable of opening the expensive parchment envelope with its decisive italic script address. Then her normal iron-hard courage returned, and with it, anger. Someone would pay for such a repellent practical joke and it would not be long before she decided on their identity.

But it was no joke. It was Roland, talking to her from beyond the grave with machinery set up before his departure.

Dearest Diana

I wish there had been a way to deliver this letter without the pain which I know you must have suffered when you saw the envelope. Sadly, there is no other way. I can only hope that this assurance of my continuing love for you from beyond oblivion will make up for it. I felt I might be forgiven the melodramatic gesture of arranging this letter for our wedding anniversary, as we have always exchanged gifts then and I felt that what this letter contains will be more necessary than any earlier presents.

It might never reach you and if it does not I have the infinite consolation of knowing that Cosmo will have behaved better than I feared. I am writing this some six years after we set up the legal machinery to save the estates from death duties. At the time I discussed with the lawyers the vulnerable position in which you would be placed by the necessity of trusting Cosmo with the spoils. I always chose to think the best of Cosmo but even so, by the end of our discussion, I was disturbed. Finally we achieved a compromise. If Cosmo behaved, no one would ever suspect that the heir to Granby had been distrusted. If he cheated, on the other hand . . .'

Diana's eyes widened incredulously, then triumphantly, as she read on. Oh Roland, Roland! How well you loved me; and how thoroughly, if reluctantly, you understood Cosmo.

She swung out of bed, ringing for Gillian as she did so. Roland's final touch, the obligatory wedding anniversary card, fluttered unnoticed from the envelope on to the silk quilt cover.

Happy anniversary, my darling, wherever you are, mused Diana. Strange, so many men had adopted a protective role towards her, as if fate were trying to compensate for her father's devastating betrayal. And yet it took this final act from her sometimes despised husband to make her feel she had truly recovered the loving armour of which he had deprived her by his death.

She could have handled the rest of her business over the bedside telephone, but this was a series of calls for which she felt the need to be fully dressed and made up. Executioners don't wear nightgowns on the scaffold, she thought gleefully.

Cosmo was still in London. He had an attractive house in Granby village where the family spent holidays and stayed for what he termed 'official tribal gatherings'. When Roland arranged the transfer of ownership he had hoped Cosmo would move in permanently and use his London house as no more than a base for visits. But Cosmo had never hidden his distaste for the rural empire which was so much his mother's creation. He found Alexander House particularly offensive, allegedly on the ground that its location destroyed the privacy of the best beach on the estate.

Diana rang him. Dammit, of course, he's such a Puritan he'll have been slaving in the City for hours by now, she thought. It was nine-thirty and she had dialled his home number. Erin answered. Even in a simple telephone greeting her voice exuded warmth. It faded when she realised she was speaking to her mother-in-law.

'Uh, he's not at the office as usual; he has some business elsewhere. I'll get him to call you in an hour when he's back.' She hung up before Diana could say anything else.

She curbed her impatience. Cosmo was nothing if not predictable. If Erin said an hour, that's what it would be. At ten-thirty Cosmo returned her call.

'Mama, you surprise me. I thought you intended staying in France until the end of the month.'

'Perhaps it's just as well I didn't, Cosmo. You might have advanced everything so far by then that it would have been too late for any reconsideration. Is that what you had in mind?'

'Oh, you mean the sale, I take it? No, why should I? There's nothing you can do to stop it. With the exception of the contents of the manor, I've owned everything else for almost seven years, you know that. There's no entail on the estate so I'm quite within my rights to sell. As long as I ensure that any buyer gives you adequate time to move out, I don't really see that I even had to tell you in advance that the sale was going ahead.'

'I'm amazed you didn't simply wait until I saw the property advertisement in *Country Life*.' He did not respond.

'What about Alexander House?'

'I should have thought the answer to that was obvious. You've always known I felt that was an ill-advised arrangement. Given your positively medieval way of setting the place up, I'm perfectly within my rights to dispose of the buildings and grounds as I see fit. The donations you've made from your Rathbone Stores income were to the charity itself, not the bricks and mortar. If you feel it's such a worthwhile enterprise, you can look elsewhere for premises and re-start the place. Not that I think that's feasible in any way. With property values standing as they do even you couldn't afford to do it.'

'Oh, but I shan't need to, Cosmo. The Trust isn't moving anywhere. I think that what I have to say might change your views considerably but even your razor-sharp mind might prefer to digest my information at a personal meeting rather than on the telephone. I'm travelling to London today.'

His mounting irritation was audible. 'This is quite unnecessary. You have nothing to say to me that could possibly change my mind and I certainly see no point in your dragging yourself all the way here the day after a tiring journey back from France. After all, you're no youngster, you know!' This last was delivered with a note of satisfaction.

'Forget any rubbish about a mother's sentimental plea, Cosmo. I can summarise my argument in one word. Blackmail. Now will you see me?'

'Where and when?'

'Lunch at Brown's, I think. The setting will be appropriate. Goodbye, Cosmo. Don't sign a contract on a house in Switzerland yet.'

'Landed the bastard!' she said as she hung up.

Lettie had drifted in during the conversation. 'Hardly an appropriate term for your son and heir, dear.'

'Oh, I wouldn't say that, Lettie. I wouldn't say that at all.' Smiling at some private joke, Diana went to find Roger.

497

He was in the estate office, running a final check that the files were in order. He knew his own job would be at an end when Granby changed hands. Diana showed him Roland's anniversary letter. As he read the final few paragraphs, Simpson's eyes snapped from the page to the face of his employer. 'You'd do this to your own son?'

'I'd do practically anything to practically anybody to preserve Granby and Alexander House. But if you look at it realistically, surely it's more a case of what he's prepared to do to himself?'

'I don't understand you, Diana.'

'I shall offer him alternative courses of action. The choice is his. I imagine his decision rests on how much he cares for his wife. I'm doing nothing to him beyond presenting alternatives.'

'I'm afraid you'll do it without my connivance!'

'Whatever makes you say that?'

'Because no piece of property is worth such cruelty. You shouldn't even contemplate it, Diana, least of all to your own son. Whatever he plans to do to you pales to insignificance compared with this.'

'I might have baulked at it if only Granby had been involved. But Roger, Alexander House has been my whole life's work. It's worthwhile; it achieves wonderful results. I might have gone quietly if he just sold off Granby and left the Trust as it was. But this? Never. I'll fight as dirty as I have to.'

'Well, this is just about as dirty as it's possible to get. I'll stay until you've settled everything. Then I think it's time I finally retired. The air around here isn't as fresh as it was a minute ago!'

She shrugged. 'Please yourself. Cosmo is about to learn that you have to be tough if you move into the big kids' playground! Perhaps you never learned that, either, Roger, but I've known it for a very long time.'

Diana caught the noon train to London, firmly refusing Lettie's offer to accompany her. 'I think you'd better stay and offer aid and comfort to Roger instead. He's wilting like a Victorian maiden. 'Bye Lettie. Expect a miracle.'

Diana was already studying her menu when Cosmo arrived at Brown's next day. She glanced up as he joined her. 'Hmm, I always knew food was no big attraction for you, but I thought that interest in our impending discussion might have got you here on time today.'

Cosmo feigned weariness and much-tried patience. 'Really, Mama, I'd have thought I was doing you enough of a favour by coming at all, given that hysterical nonsense you were muttering yesterday morning.'

'I have never been less hysterical in my life, Cosmo, and if you were as blasé as you're pretending, you wouldn't have started biting your nails again. Do try to stop. It's as off-putting now as it was when you were seven.'

Reddening, he snatched his hand from his mouth and tucked it out of sight under the table. He ordered a gin and tonic before attempting to resume his superior attitude.

'Right, so what on earth has given you an idea you can blackmail me? I must be the most squeaky-clean stockbroker in the City, my wife is equally blameless and at the last count none of our children was a junky, a drunk, a nympho or even a budding pop star. As far as my forebears are concerned, I think all the relevant dirt has been dished on them already. Anyway I'm content that there are no possible unrevealed skeletons there which would embarrass me.'

Diana ignored him until she had selected lunch, further infuriating him by ordering for both of them. 'Why must you do that?' he asked testily.

'Because you're so bloody ascetic when it comes to food that it would spoil my lunch to see you sitting there toying with soup and salad. Now you can shut up, eat what you're given and prepare yourself for confrontation.'

'Mama, I fail to understand how you can criticise others for sloppy speech when you give vent to such insulting utterances yourself.'

'You've always failed to understand that I live un-ashamedly by one rule for myself while imposing quite another upon the rest of the world. The silly thing is that no one need accept my judgements. It's just that they in-variably do, so stop behaving as if I'm a bully.'

499

'You always bullied me.'

'Not since you married. I gave up after that.'

'Yes, that always surprised me. One day swinging wildly between indifference and interference; the next, complete laissez-faire which has lasted from that day to this. You can't be afraid of Erin.'

'Not in any sense you understand yet.'

'Yet? That has an ominous ring.'

'It was meant to. I spy the arrival of our coquilles St Jacques, so I suggest we save the confrontation until we've eaten.'

Diana enjoyed every scrap of her lunch and noticed with quiet satisfaction that Cosmo hardly touched his. When the waiter had finally left them to their coffee, he sighed with relief.

'Now, please, Mama, get on with what you have to say and let me go. I've seen enough of you today for the next five years.'

'Don't worry, Cosmo. This will take moments. Though I hardly think you'll want to keep any business appointments after what I have to tell you. Now: one last chance to let the world remain safe and unchanging. Are you prepared to take your inheritance, run it as a family estate and let me go on administering the Alexander House Trust on its existing site? Say yes and you'll hear no further mutterings from me about blackmail.'

'Once and for all, no. I have no wish to live in Devon; I despise the Trust and its wishy-washy aims; I have no intention of pandering to my children's idiotic preoccupation with rolling family acres; and I fancy living in Switzerland. Does that answer your question?'

'Quite satisfactorily, thank you. How highly do you rate your chances of carrying through that plan successfully once your family and the world have been told that you are married to your half-sister and have fathered four children on her?'

He froze. Diana sat watching him, a pleasant smile on her face. The silence lengthened. 'Surely you have some views, Cosmo?'

'You filthy old bitch. You rotten, filthy, evil, hateful old bitch.' It was said in a dull monotone. He looked as if he were about to have a stroke.

'Poor Cosmo. You know what they say about sticks and stones – well it's true. Please try to remember that this conversation would never have occurred had you not tried to destroy everything I stand for.'

'So now you're destroying me and you're willing to cook up a stew of foul lies like that to do it. Christ, how on earth do you expect me to believe that?'

'I don't much care whether you believe it or not, Cosmo. The fact remains that Roland was not your father and he was so worried that you might try this sort of thing that he left a letter suggesting I proved it by pointing out that you and he had incompatible blood groups.'

'So what? If you don't care whether the world knows that you were a whore, it's no skin off my nose. As Papa handed over the estate to me while he was still alive and kicking with no mention in the legal documentation that the gift was conditional on my being his son, that's no threat anyhow.'

'Good God, Cosmo, I assume that the shock is pushing your mind on to that triviality and away from the main point of what I said, otherwise you'd stop messing about with the legal fal-lals and think about the realities of public disgrace. The year I Came Out I had two suitors: Roland Lenton and Ben Lassiter. Roland and I were married in September instead of Christmas as we planned because I was four months pregnant on our wedding day. I'm quite confident that if Erin asked to have her father's medical records opened, it would show Ben Lassiter had a blood group compatible with being your father.'

'That wouldn't prove he *was* my father!'

'No, but Roland's group proves that you were not his son, so unless Ben Lassiter can be posthumously proved not to have been either, we all know the obvious conclusion.'

'You'd never prove that in a court of law, never!'

'Silly, I shouldn't have to. I'd simply take it to court,

expecting to have it thrown out. The scandal sheets would take care of the rest. Now, Cosmo, which do you love best, Erin and your children or the thought of destroying me? The choice is yours.'

'I – I don't understand you.'

'No, I expect the shock has done awful things to your reasoning faculties. Well, if you love Erin enough, you'll die rather than let her know any of this. She's quite a woman, but I think she's rather too conventional to be able to live with the reality of incest. Given her Catholic background I could almost see her leaving you all and going into a closed order of nuns. Of course, she might even kill herself.'

'You bloody old hag. You really have no heart at all, do you? What about the children?'

'Ah, well, that really is a poser. I've always felt we create excessive taboos about the effects of incest on genetic heritage. After all, the youngest is coming up to thirteen now and they all look normal, healthy, strong and fairly talented. Obviously they got the best bits from everyone.'

'Mama, I shall go mad if you continue to chat in that cheerful, everyday tone while my world falls apart! I'm talking about the fact that this would destroy them all, as well as Erin and me.'

Her bantering tone vanished. She leaned across the table and almost hissed at him 'And I'm telling you that they'll only know if you persist with your insufferable plan to destroy *me*!'

That stopped him. He slumped back in his chair and stared dully at her.

'So you're pushing it back on me. My God, if I could kill you, I would, you terrible old monster.'

'Oh, I've no fears on that score, Cosmo. You'd never kill me; you haven't the guts. You might hire an assassin to do it for you, but you'd even stop short at that in case you were found out. No, if it's left to you I shall die in my bed. But I intend to see it's my bed at Granby, secure in the knowledge that Alexander House is flourishing. If you decide to see things my way, it almost goes without saying that I shall insist on an unbreakable legal covenant transferring the freehold to the trustees. Now, do you need time to think it over, or will you give me your answer immediately?'

'Just leave me alone, you old cow. Just leave me alone.'

'Very well, but not for too long, I'm afraid. I intend returning to Devon tomorrow morning. If I haven't heard from you one way or the other by midnight tomorrow, I shall start letting cats out of bags. Goodby, Cosmo. Please try to remember that the entire matter rests in your hands.'

She rose and left the restaurant without a backward glance.

Diana had no doubts about the outcome of her strategy. She was not a believer in love conquering all, particularly in connection with her elder son, so she assumed he would act from fear of scandal rather than desire to protect his wife and children. Whatever the reasons, he capitulated.

He telephoned shortly after nine o'clock on the evening of her return. Lettie was still clucking over Roger Simpson's abrupt departure. 'I just don't understand it, Diana. One minute there he was, promising support unto death, and the next he'd packed an overnight bag, said he'd got to chase up possible new houses for his retirement cottage, and left. He's coming back to sort out the bulk of his luggage and his furniture and things when he's settled somewhere to live.'

'No mystery, Lettie. I think he only stayed so long because he was worried I might not cope successfully. When he saw that I was going to beat Cosmo, he decided to get out before he fell under my spell again.'

A thin little tale, but good enough for Lettie, she thought. Her sister swallowed it without demur.

Cosmo was punctiliously polite when he telephoned. Diana assumed others were present. 'I thought over your arguments, Mama. I decided that on balance they made sense. Of course, I shall still be retaining my City business interests, so rather than have you move into the village house and us only using the manor every few weeks, I thought you might care to stay there for the moment. My solicitors are drawing up a deed of gift on Alexander House so that the Trust becomes landlord instead of Granby Estates Limited. That should be satisfactory, I think.'

'Perfectly, thank you, Cosmo. The matter we discussed yesterday will never be mentioned again, unless you choose to discuss it.'

'I hardly think that's likely. Goodnight, Mama.' He hung up.

'Game set and match to me!' Diana treated an astonished Lettie to a bear-hug. 'Some poor bastards will believe anything!'

'Diana, you're getting a bit near the bone again!'

'No, darling; still just talking literally.'

She settled into a tranquil, if solitary, life at Granby Manor. As always there was plenty of fund-raising and publicity activity to be done for the Trust and she could do as much or as little of it as she chose. Diana missed Roland more than she had expected. He had been too ill for a long time to be a real companion, but the fact that he was there when she needed someone to talk to or just sit with had made all the difference. The months passed without him and she began to realise all over again what a pivotal position he had occupied in her life. Lettie was eager to come visiting, but Diana had always been unable to endure her in extended doses.

She had invited Sebastian and Rhiannon for Christmas. Early in November she received a brief note from Erin, expressing formal regret that they would be unable to celebrate the usual family festival at Granby as they were spending the holiday with her mother in Virginia. Their eldest son Tristan was in India but the other three were going to America with their parents. Thank heaven for Sebastian and Rhiannon, thought Diana. I might have begun to feel just a little sorry for myself over Christmas dinner with Lettie. It would have been like being in an old ladies' home in Torquay!

A few days after writing to her, Erin paid Diana a surprise visit. She drove down from London alone and telephoned en route to ask her mother-in-law whether her arrival would pose any problems.

'Not at all, dear girl. I look forward to your arrival with intense curiosity. I find it difficult to believe that filial affection alone has drawn you down from London.' Her poker player's instincts prevented her from probing further. 'I hope you'll stay for a day or two – overnight anyway.'

'Oh. I was going to stay at our house. I thought perhaps it would be wiser.'

'What on earth for? It seems a bit much to switch on the central heating and all the rest of it for yourself when I'm rattling around up here with God knows how many empty bedrooms made up.'

'Well, if you're sure . . .'

'Of course I'm sure. Now get along and finish your journey.'

She wondered briefly whether Erin was just disturbed at Cosmo's inevitably peculiar behaviour since the September meeting with his mother, or if the girl had a more definite idea of what was going on. No point in speculating, she concluded. She would find out soon enough.

Erin had known for fifteen years. 'After I had Sarah, I went over to see Dad and Mother in Virginia. I left all the children here, either at school or with the nanny. It was the first time Dad had managed to get me alone over there since the mid 1950s. One evening he sat me down with a huge bourbon and told me about Cosmo.'

'You needn't explain. Even after all these years I know Ben's thinking well enough to understand the strategy. Separate her from distracting influences, give her a bullet to bite and then beat the girl around the head with the truth and see if she survives.'

'That's right! You obviously knew him well!'

'Not until too late, unfortunately. Had I understood him when I was seventeen, none of the rest need have happened. But I must admit I'm surprised at your calmness.'

'I've had a long time to think about it and come to terms with it. If you're basically a fairly calm person, it's hard to remain indignant for fifteen years without a break.'

'How did you react?'

'Depends on whether you mean short or long term. In the short term I went nuts for a while. Full-scale hysterics all over Dad's office. He'd had the sense to take me down to the den he had in the stable block for our tête-à-tête, so I could have smashed up the place without Mother having any idea. I swore and screamed and created and I think probably the worst thing was that I couldn't blame him for not telling me when it would still have done some good, because I'd had this silly idea about not telling him about Cosmo and me until we were married. Then, when I calmed down a bit, I realised it hadn't altered my feelings towards Cosmo at all. I'd always been a bit cool about you because you'd never been able to give him the love he needed. When Dad told me about what you went through that year, I became less keen to condemn you. Strange, isn't it? The minute I got some real reason to hate you, I started understanding you better, and I've always found it impossible to hate people I understand.

'Eventually I asked Dad why he'd told me at all, as it had gone on for so long. You probably knew him well enough to know he never did anything without having a good reason. He said that as we had three apparently normal kids, he thought it was tempting fate and the genetic pool to have any more. That was reason one. Reason two was pure opportunism. He felt he owed it to me to tell me some time and that when I went home for a visit alone for the first time, if it was all too much when he told me, I could just stay over there for good and sort of take refuge. We talked about it throughout my visit, every time we were alone. Mother has never known, you see. She'd never be able to handle it. In the end I decided that it made no difference at all to my love for Cosmo. It didn't even change the way I saw him.'

'Lucky Cosmo.'

'You come from a charismatic family, Diana. Once people fall under your spell, they're unlikely to shake it off. That's as true of Cosmo as it is of you, but you're too close to him and too hostile to recognise it. At the time, I drew a line on the child-bearing side. I tended towards Dad's view that three okay kids was pushing it some and I promised myself and him that I wouldn't risk another. I stuck to my decision for two years, then genuinely made a mistake. James was the result. Abortion never crossed my mind. By then I'd read everything I could lay hands on about genetics. I came to the conclusion that if no defects had shown up in the first three, there wasn't any great chance of it happening for the fourth. To tell the truth I was more concerned about the generations of first and second cousins who'd intermarried since the early nineteenth century to produce your and Roland's generation of Lentons. No wonder Roland had that dreadful inherited nervous disease. The shared Lassiter blood has probably done us more good than more inbred Lenton corpuscles would have! It looks as if I was right. Apart from an unbelievably strong family resemblance among them, our brood seem to be no different from any other family.'

'Will you believe me if I say I'm glad they are all right, and even more so that Cosmo didn't push me any further?'

'Yes; but I forgive you only because your action gave me stronger proof of my husband's love than I could ever have hoped for.'

'In what way?'

'I rather think you believed that if he gave in, he'd do it out of fear of what the world would do to him; that having surrendered, he would let you have your way and then isolate himself from me and the children, probably having told me why. You probably considered the possibility that he'd surrendered purely to protect me and decided it was unlikely. But that's precisely what he did. He's never told me a thing about that meeting with you. I guessed what had happened because I knew you felt so strongly about the Alexander House Trust and Granby itself that you would literally do anything to save them. And although Cosmo never told me what changed his mind, he was impotent for over a month. In the end his love for me broke down that taboo and now he's okay.'

'Did you consider telling him you knew all about it?'

'Yes, but I rejected the possibility for what you'll regard as a damn fool reason. I thought all along that he was giving you a lousy deal over Granby, just because he wanted to pay you back for not loving him. I didn't want his children to stop loving him too, because they blamed him for alienating you. So I've let him go on thinking I know nothing. At one stage I thought I might have to tell him just to cure his impotence, but that doesn't seem necessary now.'

Diana studied her in silence for a long time. Erin returned her gaze, clear-eyed, unembarrassed and relaxed. Eventually Diana spoke.

'You're an incredibly strong, well-balanced girl, Erin. I had something else I was considering telling you, but I don't think you need it.'

'If it makes any radical changes to what I've already come to terms with, don't. I'd rather not know, even if it would improve the situation. I *don't* need it. Whatever it is, let it go.'

Serenely, she took a long pull on her drink. 'Now, I'm off my diet for the week and the food here is always sensational. When do we eat?'

Erin stayed another three days and departed with the promise that she, too, would visit Diana when her children came to see their grandmother. 'If that changes and I let you down, it'll only be because Cosmo can't handle the thought,' she said. 'Of course, it goes without saying that I doubt whether he'll ever voluntarily occupy the same room as you again! Remember, my first loyalty is to him but, if I can manage both loads, I'd like to go on seeing you, too. Look after yourself, Diana.'

Diana cried for a long time after Erin's departure. Oh, Ben, she thought. What a man I missed! If you raised a daughter like that you were the man I thought you were and lots more.

December was well advanced and Diana had been in the Chelsea house for a week to finish her Christmas shopping. Just before she returned to Granby, Edmund Dancey telephoned her.

'I wasn't sure whether I'd catch you here or in Devon,' he said, 'but with Christmas hard on our heels I suspected you'd stay within easy reach of Harrods until the last minute, so I tried here first.'

'Edmund, only you would make contact again for the first time in – what? – twenty-five years and pick up the conversation as if we'd last met three weeks ago. I wasn't even sure you were still alive.'

'Oh, very much so, although I expect plenty wish I wasn't! I was thinking of inviting myself to share your Christmas, that is, if you've room for a solitary old bachelor!'

She was taken aback by his request. 'You're the last man on earth I'd describe as a solitary old bachelor. Of course I have room, and I'll be delighted to have you. My son and his wife will be with us. If you can bear their company, come on down.'

'Which son?' His tone was wary enough to make Diana think Erin's recent description of Cosmo as charismatic had been wishful thinking.

'Sebastian, of course. If it were the other one we'd have wall-to-wall grandchildren, too.'

'In that case, count me in. Cosmo was always a bit much for me. I invariably got the impression he was about to chastise me for not fitting into the appropriate social pigeon hole.'

'Mmm, well I'm afraid the poor chap has no intuition to guide him so he has to go by the book. Non-conformity worries him because he's unable to classify it. Anyway, enough of that. No one could be less conformist than Sebastian, thank God.'

Dancey arranged to arrive two days before Christmas Eve and rang off, leaving Diana still mystified about the purpose behind his impending visit.

The house party was highly successful. Sebastian had much of his mother's cheerful toughness and was not artificially tactful about mentioning his father. He spoke of him unselfconsciously, as he would have done if Roland were in the next room rather than the churchyard.

Rhiannon was her usual self, intelligent, bright and earthy. Every time Diana looked at her she was reminded of Evangeline – but Evangeline with a Cambridge First and no inferiority complex. Edmund Dancey was remarkably unchanged. His hair had turned silver, softening the somewhat Mephistophelean appearance of his youth; but he had aged gracefully and remained elegant and handsome. Diana wondered why she had ever found him daunting.

On Boxing Day Sebastian and Rhiannon went out with the local hunt. 'Come along, Mama, it will do you good to join us. Bet you haven't been out in two seasons!'

'Precisely why I've no intention of joining you today,' she told him. 'I shall start riding to hounds again eventually but I'm not foolish enough to risk it over the holidays and see the New Year in with every joint screaming for relief! You two go and enjoy it. Edmund and I will get drunk in front of a roaring fire. Far more civilised.'

In the end they went for a walk, down to the secluded beach below Alexander House. Dancey looked speculatively at the building as they passed it. 'I always wondered about your motives for that place, Diana. When you started it, I could have sworn it was no more than two fingers up to the men from the Ministry and that you'd pull it down or at least close it the day hositilities ceased.'

'That was my entire purpose at first. It was just a good way of keeping outsiders' hands off my home. I didn't want to live in the damned barn, after all, but nor did I want trainee commandos chucking each other about on the lawn or nubile WRENS learning semaphore there. Then the children started arriving. I think you're about the only person I'll ever tell how dreadful and how moving that was. Until then I'd kept the war at arm's length. Of course I knew that awful things were happening in Europe and elsewhere and that racialism and poverty and social division were the underlying causes. But it's quite easy to grasp such things intellectually without any emotional involvement.

'Most of the first youngsters were the children of alien internees. They were a bit bewildered, being as English as you or me but with parents who'd come from Naples or Vienna, and were therefore at a loss to understand why their fathers were locked up on the Isle of Man. But it was just confusion. Then the first group of Jewish refugees came in. They'd managed to get into England in the last days of the war. When we finally got them to talk about what had been happening to them in Austria and Germany, something started changing inside me, and I realised that however futile it was I had to try doing something to lessen the chances of it happening again. As a result Alexander House became permanent and I started meaning what I said in that stupid declaration of aims when it was first opened. Over the years I think the need for it has grown rather than lessened. The name I chose is self-explanatory; a little final public declaration of family solidarity!'

'Well, well, so the lady has a heart after all!'

'Ah, I wondered how long the attack would be in coming.'

'Attack, Diana? Why were you expecting an attack?'

'I've been puzzled about your reasons for wanting to come down here ever since you rang me in London. I didn't for one minute think that you were a poor lonely old buffer desperately looking up acquaintances to avoid a solo Christmas.'

'No, I must confess people do tend to notice I'm fairly self-reliant. What conclusion did you reach?'

'The only thing different this year from all the other Christmases is no Roland. Now that could mean you were finally able to declare your life-long passion for me, but I don't think that's any more likely than the loneliness story. So what else could there be? In the end I decided it was one of those ghastly "better out than in" confrontations that some people feel they must have when an old friend has died and they think that the surviving nearest and dearest can now be told a few home truths. So, you've come to administer the dressing down. QED.'

'Gracious, you do under-value yourself, darling! I've no intention of anything of the sort! It's connected with Roland, true, but I've come more in fulfilment of a promise to him than with any sort of vengeance in mind. You may have been quite fond of the poor old boy, but you never really knew a lot about him, did you, my dear?'

'What do you mean? There wasn't all that much to know, beyond the fact that he was a lot stronger and shrewder than outsiders gave him credit for.'

'I'm glad you noticed that, at least. He was also much more devious than they or you ever suspected. He was a man who knew how to keep secrets and you have only to look at things like Watergate to realise how rare that is. Some of those secrets undoubtedly died with him, but there was one story which he made me promise to tell you once he was out of the way. He had the answer to a huge puzzle which you never managed to solve and he died feeling dreadfully guilty that he could never tell you.'

'What is all this nonsense? Why couldn't he tell me? Tell me what?'

'One thing at a time, Diana. The reason he couldn't tell you is that I ordered him not to.'

'You? Oh, Christ, don't tell me you were his boyfriend too. I thought we'd got over all that before we left Malaya!'

'Not his boyfriend, Diana; his boss. Or perhaps you could say his commander-in-chief.'

'Philby, Burgess and MacLean style, you mean? Don't be absurd!'

'Yes, that would be absurd. We were much cleverer than them. For a start, no one ever caught us. For another thing, we were on the opposite side.'

'Well that's a relief, anyway. Look, Edmund, I have a feeling this is going to get very messy. Why don't we go back to the house and sit down with a lot of booze in front of a huge fire. Perhaps I'll be able to take it better there – or at least, take it seriously. Right now I don't know whether to laugh, hit you or burst into tears.'

They returned to the manor, silent in anticipation of what was to come. Diana found Gillian and left instructions that no callers were to be admitted. Then they adjourned to the library.

'Right. Fire away. And it had better be good after the build-up.'

'It is, Diana, it certainly is. To sum it up, your father was a spy for Britain almost until his last days; and your husband and I murdered Nina Chaliapin on behalf of British Intelligence in 1952.'

Her laugh was brittle. 'And when does your novel push Le Carré off the bestseller lists?'

'I'm telling you the truth, Diana. Longer ago than you might remember, Roland told you that if he ever found out anything about la Chaliapin that would do you any good, he'd tell you. This fulfils his promise. It's a long and complicated truth but I think it leaves you with a reality you will prefer to what you've had to put up with in the past. I'm not going to give you chapter and verse; we'd still be here next Christmas if I did. But I can tell you enough to give you a bit of peace and contentment at last.

'Alexander Hartley got himself mixed up with a very dubious bunch of people in the early 1920s. He picked up a devilishly attractive Russian piece on a trip to Paris and became so involved with her that he thought of importing her to England. Even with his weakness for incurring debt, he couldn't justify that, so he contented himself with frequent trips across the Channel to dally with her. Then, oh bliss, oh joy, she turned up in England, married to a conveniently invisible Englishman. Your father's cup was literally brimming over and he started seeing a great deal more of the young lady, by then known as Mrs Grant.

'He disapproved strongly of the Socialists and he was furious that they had been elected to govern England. Virtually took it as a personal insult. On top of that he was one of the multitude of upper-class people who really thought the Reds were going to take over. As a senior Foreign Office man he got a lot of Secret Service reports of Bolshevik activity in Britain and that was enough to make anyone paranoid. He was aware, though, that such material could not be put before the electorate without a public admission that our intelligence services spied on people going about their normal business. Obviously that was out of the question at a time when ordinary people regarded government as synonymous with honesty and high principles. So when the loonies who were cooking up the Petrograd Communiqué – it was a forgery, by the way – approached him through Ninotchka, he jumped at the chance of blackening the Communists and unseating the Socialists with one act, and planted the thing in the national press.

'At this stage he was still acting alone and for essentially honourable motives. After all, the intelligence information convinced him that the forged Communiqué was only a technical deceit and that what it said was just what the Bolsheviks were planning. Then, thanks to his personal financial problems, he got involved in some very un-patriotic business. Ninotchka told him the people who were so eager to place the Communiqué were aware it was an expensive business and therefore proposed to pay him £5,000. Remember, at the time that was more than five years' salary. After all, she said, he was going to place the document anyway, so it couldn't be regarded as real cor-ruption. He allowed himself to be convinced and took it.

'Unfortunately he was in such debt that the £5,000 would only have postponed his problems rather than solving them, and Madam Chaliapin-Grant knew it. So she came up with this fascinating little suggestion of a game of currency roulette. Cause yourself a run on the pound, hold plenty of foreign currency and sell it at the top of the market when sterling hits rock bottom. It looked foolproof. It all went wrong because the 1924 run on the French franc happened just as they were doing it and wrecked the whole thing.'

'Edmund, at the risk of being a bore, I must stop you. Ninotchka Chaliapin told me all this twenty-five years ago. She chose to lay the emphasis in different areas to belittle Papa, but essentially it's the same story. Why make such a fuss about it now? And why tag on a lot of rot about you and Roland bumping her off?'

'Don't be impatient. She told you exactly what she wanted to. The truth was very different. We'd been starting to wonder about la Chaliapin. There were some inexplicable aspects of her behaviour and personal history which refused to make sense.'

'We?'

'Come now, Diana, you must have realised it. The Secret Service recruited both Roland and me at Oxford in the early twenties.'

'Good God!'

'Heavens, I've finally managed to impress you! To continue: we were waffling around wondering how we could find out more about her, when your Papa came and turned himself in. He was at his Alexander Hartliest, all irony and sneers, this time largely directed at himself. Believe me, he spared himself nothing. Said he'd kidded himself for long enough that he was a patriot, when really he was a shabby crook trying to make a fast buck.'

'What did you do with him?'

'Told him never to do it again, then received him with open arms, of course. We recruited him too!'

'So my poor, self-deluding father was ruined for the sake of a pointless grown-up schoolboys' game. You sacrificed him for some tart who was willing to jump on any political bandwagon for personal gain!'

'When you're wrong, Diana, you're wrong in spades. Ninotchka Chaliapin was about as non-political as Stalin and she was a tart in the same way that a political assassin is a murderer.'

'Come on, Edmund, I sat and listened to her tell the story of the White Russians murdering her family and mass-raping her when she was barely fifteen. You could convince me of a lot of things, but never that she'd work for a regime that turned loose thugs like that.'

'Of course not. She wasn't working for them. She was a Red.'

'But she escaped from them when the Whites re-occupied the building where she was living, and they brought her out of Russia!'

'So that's what she told you. I did wonder. We nearly had fits when Louise Kerslake ordered poor old Marcus

Gregg out of Maison Louise that night when he was about to eavesdrop on your meeting.'

'Not Gregg as well!'

'Afraid so, old girl. I'm sorry that this is beginning to sound as though there were more spies around than ordinary people, but that particular night you were right in the middle of them. In fact I'd say that you, Louise Kerslake and Evangeline MacIntyre were the only three bystanders there.'

'Bystanders? I'd hardly call any of us that.'

'Now stop interrupting or I shall never finish. Marcus was a bona fide journalist; but then, of course, so was Kim Philby. It's a useful profession for a secret agent and you earn a decent living apart from what the Firm is paying you. The Chaliapin interview for the twenty-fifth anniversary of your father's dismissal was a good excuse for him to interrogate her without her realising it; except that she did realise it. God knows when it happened, but by the time she left you that evening, she'd rumbled him and was ready to give him a little surprise. Our Ninotchka still had gloriously pre-war ideas about sexy trysting places; she made eyes at Marcus and suggested they went down to Skindles at Maidenhead for supper. He went like a lamb. She murdered him on the way down; believe it or not, an eight-inch hatpin driven straight in under his heart.'

'As of about ten minutes ago, I'm prepared to believe practically anything. Go on.'

'We were following them. I'd been doing routine surveillance on Ninotchka for weeks with Roland as back-up and we joined forces that night because she'd never suddenly upped and left town like that before.'

'Hang on, if I recall correctly, Roland was abroad then. Yes, that's it. He was in the Far East. And I *know* he was there, because he really did do something cloak-and-dagger on that trip.'

'I know, Diana. I also know who arranged it for him. But he was only there for half the time you thought he was. For the first couple of weeks he was under cover back in England.'

'This is getting completely out of hand. You're now asking me to believe that two senior members of Her Majesty's Secret Service and one rather more junior operative were absorbed in tailing a middle-aged lady spy around the country because she'd perpetrated a Communist conspiracy in London a generation before the war. Not even we can have that many secret agents to spare!'

'If that was all she'd done, we should have had no interest in her at all by 1952. Didn't Louise Kerslake tell you what the lady did for a living?'

'Yes, she was a high-class madam, wasn't she? Someone told me years later that the house was quite near mine in Chelsea.'

'That's right. But she had very special clients and offered them very special services. Half the Commons and the Lords, plus a sprinkling of Admiralty and Air Force were in and out at regular intervals. Unless you were political or military you didn't get past Ninotchka's front door.'

'You mean she was still at it?'

'Up to her neck. She was in the process of doing us a vast amount of damage. She had more on those clients than the Profumo case ever put at risk; and remember this was ten years or more before Profumo, when the Cold War was at its coldest. We'd just learned that she was about to put the boot in with something so big that we had to stop her. That was why we took such a risk with Gregg over the whisky.'

'Whisky? I don't understand.'

'We'd taken a large bottle to use on Ninotchka if we needed to bump her off when we caught up with her. It never occurred to either of us that she'd do in Marcus. When we got hold of her she'd just spiked him. It was obvious that we couldn't let her walk away. She knew about Marcus and, as of that moment at least, she knew about Roland and me. So we sorted out a neat little drunk-driving accident which involved anointing Marcus liberally with the juice of the glens. Those were the days when our secret chaps were able to nobble coroners to some extent, so we didn't need to do a totally convincing job. It was just as well. Marcus was allergic to whisky. He never touched the stuff. We went through a few traumas over the next couple of weeks in case someone who knew him socially started poking around over it, but no one ever did. Ninotchka Chaliapin's career ended in solitude at Golders Green, with only Comrade Zharov to see her off.'

'So that's who he was! I often wondered.'

'He was the man who recruited her to the service which eventually became the KGB. He picked her up in Leningrad after the Whites did for her family. Apparently it was one of the great love stories. Neither of them ever really looked at anyone else again. But the Cause came first, so they spent most of their time apart. Presumably you were the woman at the crematorium. Roland had gone to the Far East by then to ensure his cover. I was away doing something else. I saw a report of a woman hanging around after they cremated her. You were noticed by the lad who was watching Zharov. The description was accurate enough for Roland and I to assume it was you, but we felt it was probably harmless given your interest in her connection with your father. We still didn't know how much she'd said to you that evening when you talked together, but we seem to have assumed rightly that there was nothing that really got you going.'

'Hmm, you've made me wish that I had followed through. Zharov sounds like an interesting man. How did he acquire the scar?'

'The war. He was at Stalingrad. I'm quite glad you didn't try playing girl detective with him. Indifference and ignorance are safer with the Zharovs of this world.'

'Perhaps I've missed something out. Let's go back to 1924 again. Why would it be in the interest of a Communist agent to set up a faked incident like the Petrograd Communiqué which could only injure the Bolshevik cause in this country? Surely Chaliapin would either have wanted to promote a real Petrograd Communiqué, and see it got to its intended recipients, not the front pages of the British newspapers; or she'd have had nothing to do with the plot to bring down a left-wing government which was likely to be sympathetic to Communist Russia.'

'You've not missed something out so much as misunderstood their political strategy. To a committed Russian-style Marxist of the time, it would have been a pathetic joke to define the British Labour Party as Socialist. The more ruthless Bolsheviks would have told you it's far better to have an oppressive right-wing government at the helm than pale-pink left-wingers if you want to encourage a revolution. The proletariat doesn't rise up and destroy the old order because of inadequate family allowance. But try them on no social security payments at all, unsafe factories run purely in the employers' interests, insecure rented accommodation and all the rest of it and you're halfway to persuading them they must kill the capitalists.'

'So Papa did exactly what they wanted when he unseated the Labour Government.'

'More or less, yes. We were pretty sure it would have happened anyway, if it's any consolation. There were too many worried shopkeepers convinced the workers were about to take over their businesses for there to have been any likelihood of Labour getting re-elected. Well, old girl, there you have it. Over all, does that show your Papa up in a better light?'

'There must be more, Edmund. Papa lived for sixteen years after the Petrograd Enquiry. You said he went on working for you. How? What possible use could he have been as an exile in France?'

'At first, just gathering general low-level intelligence. We had to go through with the dismissal thing so that Ninotchka remained unaware she'd been rumbled as a Communist agent. The value of that, which paid off in the 1950s, was a thousand times greater than any other effect of the Petrograd affair, although we weren't to know that in 1927. Having let him be disgraced, we sent him off to France and told him to play the ruined aristo to the hilt. To tell the truth he was a bit of an embarrassment until the French fascists and Communists really got going in the thirties and that son-in-law of his was right in the middle of the lunatic right. From then on Hartley was splendid. Of course, at the end he was acting purely as a father, and no one with an ounce of sensitivity could have expected otherwise in the circumstances . . . Diana, does it still affect you so much?'

She had been showing signs of distress since he started discussing Hartley's French exile. Now she was shaking with silent sobs. Eyes squeezed shut, jaw clenched to suppress her grief, she shook her head to silence him. It was some time before she had calmed herself sufficiently to speak.

'Sweet Christ, you will never realise, any of you, what you did to me! When you sent him off like that and asked him to do things he wasn't cut out to face, you signed my life sentence. Bastards, the lot of you, you, Roland, the whole fucking bunch of spies!'

He was completely nonplussed. 'What on earth have I said? I expected scepticism, maybe even a tantrum or two, but this? The whole story was meant to console you, not tear you to pieces!'

'Of course it tore me to pieces, because what you did to my father set me off on a crazy quest to be a top Society dog and so completely conditioned me into being lady of the manor that I even ended up blackmailing my son to continue the tradition. Many years ago, Louise Kerslake was talking with Roland at a party about romantic gestures. She said the most romantic thing that had ever happened to her was her wartime lover in 1917, writing to her posthumously to set her free and tell her he had provided for her. She said that although it was such a tragic thing to read, it gave her a wonderful feeling of being cared for still, after her lover had been taken away. I could see it impressed Roland, but I never realised then how much. On our wedding anniversary this autumn, I got a similar letter from him, written years before and left with his lawyer until the appropriate time. He had worked out that Cosmo might try to double-cross me. He had also worked out that he was not Cosmo's father. He loved me enough to write and suggest I stopped Cosmo by threatening to reveal he had married his half-sister as a result of my girlhood affair with Erin's father. In the letter he pointed out something that had completely escaped my attention over the years. His blood group was incompatible with Cosmo's. He'd known since very early on that Cosmo was not his son.

'I was prepared to do anything to beat Cosmo, but I'd never thought of that one until Roland wrote to me. But now that I've had time to think it over, I realise I was a monster to put poor Cosmo through all that simply to satisfy my dynastic urges. The discovery that you and Roland conspired in building up the cause of all my social climbing makes it worse. What an old phony I am!'

She sat back, drained by the strain of her confession. 'You see, if you hadn't driven the old fellow to France in pursuit of national cops-and-robbers schemes, I wouldn't have been so obsessive about his heroism – I wouldn't have needed to prove anything – and I'd probably have ended up in America, happily married to Ben. Thanks, old friend. I owe a great deal to you and my husband.'

Dancey broke in: 'But my big confession must make some difference. How do you feel about it?'

'About what, Edmund? About Ninotchka Chaliapin being a beautiful lady spy to my father's Jazz Age 007? About Roland conniving to exile my father as a crook instead of letting him be seen as a misguided patriot? Frankly, not a thing now that I've finally talked it all out. My real need to prove the Mandarin was honourable was a thing of my childhood. As the years passed, it faded. By the time the war came, I had come to terms with his probable villainy. You see, as I matured, I had really understood he was just another man, as capable of dishonour as anyone else. My periodic attempts to champion him really amounted to obstinacy as much as anything.'

'But you named Alexander House after him.'

'The one gesture I've ever made out of guilt. You see, he wrote to me from France when the war started, more or less saying that if I could forgive him, he would return to England. I ignored the letter, so he stayed in France. He watched his grandson tortured to death in the presence of his daughter, then he was deported to die in a concentration camp. I got quite a revenge for a little social disgrace, didn't

I? The naming was a tiny apology. And, of course, by then I knew about Buchenwald.

'What a family! Sometimes I wish we'd all been wiped out. Instead of that, I've schemed and worked to set up a dynastic seat down here, and after I've died the whole thing will go on. The thought makes me shudder!'

She stood up and moved across to the fireplace, staring down at the flames. Dancey joined her there, taking her gently by the shoulders and turning her to face him.

'Diana, there are survivors and there are casualties. You are a survivor. You've done some pretty awful things in your time, but you had some dire examples to follow. The only people who would turn from you with distaste are those you'd hold in contempt anyway. Think of the people you've cared about. Who among them would condemn you for what you did? One or two, perhaps, but on balance I think they would all understand exactly why you are as you are. Perhaps that will give you peace.'

She looked at him steadily. 'Do you understand?'

'I think you're a bloody miracle!'

'Coming from you, that's enough. As long as I can impress my immediate audience, it's always enough to be going on with.'